CELEBRITY

CELEBRITY

by
THOMAS THOMPSON

DOUBLEDAY & COMPANY, INC.
Garden City, New York

This book is for Betty Prashker and Robert Lantz.
And for my friend, K.R.

PROLOGUE

A
SILENT
PRINCE

Two lean men, weathered and intractable as bois d'arc fence posts, pretended to idle against the wall of the hospital corridor. They might have been taken for dutiful sons, resting, perhaps, from the ordeal of watching a stubborn father slip away. After ten days in place, they had become part of the landscape. They smoked ready-mades and rarely spoke and mainly squinted down at their boots, the prideful anchors of Texans, boots that gleamed like copperheads drowsing in the Big Bend sun.

When nurses or orderlies passed, or country women glued to the arms of farmers with turkey gobbler necks, the two men nodded politely and tipped their hats. Only when an enemy sashayed down the hall on some cleverly disguised errand did they tense—and betray their reason for propping up the wall. Thus far, their more exotic unmaskings included a counterfeit janitor whose mop bucket contained a camera, and a phony candy-striper whose towering wig concealed in its curls a tape recorder. Heave ho.

When such fraudulent journalism was suspected, the two men, who were plainclothes detectives for the Fort Worth Police Department, blocked the door of room 610 and became stone-carved lions. As is said in Texas, dawn could easier sneak past a rooster. Their orders were that no purveyor of news was to enter this room, and nobody had —even the sweet-talkers with blank checks and seductive arguments about the public's right to know. On the second day of the vigil, a photographer from *Paris-Match* offered $10,000 for two minutes inside. Tempting.

Their demeanor softened only at the end of each day, when the District Attorney of Tarrant County, accompanied by the doctor in charge of the hospital's most celebrated patient, made a regular visit. The prosecutor, whose name was Calvin Sledge and who intended to be governor of Texas by the time he turned forty-five, which was only four years off, was on this particular afternoon, as during the past fortnight, staggered by the easy riches of tribute. Within the sick man's suite, the hospital bed had become a steel sloop afloat on a sea of roses. Spikes of lemony gladioli, thick bouquets of asters and daisies, mums like emissaries from the sun brought warmth and cheer. Baskets of rainbow phlox and orchids in hand-painted china pots, even a dwarf banana tree whose branches had fingers of ripening fruit, these crowded every windowsill and dresser top. Telegrams and get-well cards tumbled to the floor with the slam of the door. If a king was dying or a princess betrothed, there could not have been more floral attention. But if the man for whom they were intended saw, or smelled, or felt the heady perfumes, he gave no sign.

Oh, he was alive; the machines to which he was bound so testified. But he was, otherwise, a void.

"Would you look at this," whispered Calvin Sledge, reading from one of the telegrams with an adolescent catch in his voice. "It's from the White House and it says, 'My wife and I and the nation pray for your speedy recovery.'"

The attending physician, Witt by name, shrugged. He was long ago sated by the tumult. "The Fords sent flowers, too. Sinatra sent a case of French wine. There's a telegram from Cary Grant. Elizabeth Taylor. John Connally. So far nothing from the Vatican, but Princess Grace's secretary called. Every room on the floor's filled up with posies. Some poor bastard three doors down got hay fever so bad from the pollen last night his heart went into arrhythmia."

Dr. Witt, a gangling farm boy of a man with jug ears, short cuffs, scuffed shoes, and a face that wore deep-plowed corn rows, was profoundly weary. He had not left the hospital since the patient was brought in. Gently now he took the withered, ivory-hued wrist, counted the pulse, scribbled numbers on a thick metal chart that was tied to the end of the bed and hidden by a fountain of erupting golden roses. Next he peeled back the corner of a thick bandage that swaddled the patient's throat. It was caked with blood but the physician nodded, apparently satisfied.

"Has he been conscious yet?" inquired Sledge.

"By strictest definition, no," answered Dr. Witt. He wrote something new on the chart. Sledge made a mental reminder to subpoena the records. Best he start the process immediately, realizing how cranky hospitals are with their documents.

"Has he said *anything?*"

"Nope."

"Nothing at all?"

The doctor shook his head mechanically. He added a new lyric to the dirge sung each afternoon. "And as a matter of fact, I don't much think he will."

"Ever?"

"That's my opinion."

"But sometimes you guys are wrong, right? I mean, cancers dissolve for no reason, don't they?"

"Yep," agreed Witt. "And the blind suddenly see. The deaf hear. The lame walk. The crazies write poetry. There's a Nobel Prize waiting for the fool who can define 'miracle.' What we're dealing with here is a fellow who's checked out—for reasons we'll probably never know."

"Okay to make a run at him?"

The doctor smiled and nodded, but his assent said: Why waste the time and energy? "You might as well teach those roses to sing 'The Eyes of Texas,'" he said, busy with the clamp on an IV tube.

Sledge leaned over the bed and tried to sound as routinely casual as a man visiting his tennis partner. "So, ole buddy, it's Cal. How you feelin' today?"

Nothing.

"Well, you're sure *lookin'* better. Gettin' a little color in those cheeks. . . . Seems like everybody's rootin' for you to get well. Did you hear me read that telegram from the President? I'd be mighty proud of that, if I was you. . . . By the way, I just saw some of your people down at the soda pop machine. They've got a prayer circle goin' for you. . . ." But reference to President and prayer brought the DA no response. He waited. Outside, an unemotional loudspeaker voice summoned cardiac resuscitation to a nearby room. Life and death dueling everywhere.

Dr. Witt gestured for Sledge to hurry. The DA's eyes telegraphed back silent frustration. What was the key to this jammed lock? There *had* to be one. Witt saw the impatience and motioned Sledge into a corner. "Listen," he hissed testily, "I've had patients who I thought were faking a coma. I grabbed their nuts and squeezed until they turned honest. But this guy is *out*. Can't you accept that?"

"No," said Sledge, shaking free and hurrying in rising anger to the bed. *"Talk* to me, boy," he commanded, the dictate causing no more stir than the clear fluids gliding silently into the patient's vein. Behind the sickbed, monitors of vital signs clicked and whirred, sensuous computerized lines leaping and falling, this series high, the next a tumble—peaks, valleys, metaphors for the course of men's lives. Now his time was gone and Sledge had failed—again. He wanted the subject to share his anxiety. "Goddamnit, fella, I'm gonna be real candid. For ten days I've walked into this room and tried to pound some sense into your celebrated skull. And you know what? I think you may be playin' a little possum. I think you hear just about every damn word I waste on you. I think you can open your eyes and look me man-to-man—and if you did that, you'd see I'm on your side. Gawd almighty, boy, I can't convict that sorry bastard lessen you gimme a break."

The doctor's patience snapped. He grabbed the DA's shoulder. But Sledge was not prepared to yield. He bent over the patient's face, smelled the sour exhaust of medicine. And he cried, "The numbers don't add up! Your EKG's okay. Your EEG's okay. Every damn ee-fuckin'-gee on the chart's okay. If you're really a carrot, then your next stop's a jar at UT Medical School. They'll be studyin' you for decades. Christ, fella, why don't you tell me what happened that night?"

"That's enough," ordered Dr. Witt.

"Please, Doc. Thirty seconds." Sledge was tired of tact. What he wanted to do was rage, threaten, spill all his confusion, disbelief, and endangered ambition onto the bed of roses. But he was being pushed toward the exit like a gurney with frozen wheels.

Something unexpected stopped them both.

Breath drawn, the prosecutor spun around and stared at the bed. From somewhere in the flowers had come a noise—faint, rattling, like a short hiss of steam from an old radiator. But it was human, not a machine.

"Did you hear *that?*" asked the DA with guarded excitement.

The physician shook his head. He would not admit to hearing anything.

"Dammit, well I did. I heard something," insisted Sledge. "It sounded like *rich . . . rich* something . . . I'll kiss your ass on Throckmorton Street if he didn't say . . ."

"He said nothing. Maybe he sighed. They do that. They sigh. They expel breath. Their guts rumble. He's got nothing much left to say anything with. . . ."

Outside, Sledge praised the two policemen for their vigilance. His darkest fantasies conjured emulators of Jack Ruby and Sirhan Sirhan, that new category of American celebrity—the assassinator. He told the guards he would return again tomorrow. "Not if you pull that crap again," interjected Dr. Witt. "One more scene like that—and I'll throw your butt out of the hospital. I'm the law here." Prosecutor and physician parted uneasily.

Engulfed by the roses, imprisoned by technology, the patient waited. Time passed; how much he neither knew nor cared. Later he opened his eyes a hairline crack, shut them quickly, content to be alone in the darkness. *"Which* night?" he mouthed again, silently, wandering through a door he had never quite managed to close, not in a quarter of a century.

Rain. He heard rain. How exquisitely appropriate. Soft spring rain was pelting the windows of what he reckoned was a long ago reserved chamber in hell.

BOOK ONE

THE
THREE
PRINCES

CHAPTER ONE

For seven straight days, rain tortured the heart of Texas. And when sun broke through the muck, clear and ripe on the third Friday of May 1950, it seemed both benediction and invocation. But it was only a tease, false hope. By midmorning the sun surrendered to fresh regiments of thunderheads and by noon the plains of north-central Texas were winter gray, sopping, and chilled. Beside the highways that fed Fort Worth, wildflowers fell, bluebonnets and Indian paintbrushes drooping like cheerleaders whose team had lost. The Trinity River surged out of its banks; the Brazos lowlands were becoming swamps of brown, sucking foam. The erupting hues of Texas spring washed away like makeup on a widow's face.

The rain was cussed by farmers, blessed by flu doctors and auto body shop owners, discussed by everybody, for there is nothing Texans relish talking about more. That the deluge was about to alter drastically the courses of several young and promising lives, no one knew this unpleasant Friday noon.

Kleber Cantrell took his anger out on his beast of burden, an elderly '38 De Soto, prewar hand-me-down from Father, a contraption uncanny in ability to reflect the owner's mood and world. Today the alternator was expiring, the last tire with tread was turning bald, assorted innards wheezing as it reached dry haven beneath the portico. There, nestled beside Kleber's home, the senile old tank gasped and died. The radio played on like fingernails growing on a cadaver and Kleber lingered a few moments, anxious to catch the noon news on WBAP. It soon became apparent that not much good was going on anywhere.

Harry Truman was whistle-stopping across the belly of America, leaping on and off cabooses, dedicating fruits from the pork barrel, draping Umatilla Indian blankets around his shoulders, scattering "hells" and "damns" like a farmer strewing rye, trying to convince a sorely unhappy electorate that under the sacred banner of the Democratic Party, the standard of living for 150 million Americans was sure to double—guaranteed *double*—within ten years. And as metaphoric companion to the storm clouds darkening the skies of Texas, a U.S. senator named Joe McCarthy was pissing on Harry's glory train, repeating a soon-to-be notorious accusation: "I have here in my hand a list of two hundred five names who are known to the Secretary of State as being members of the Communist Party and who nevertheless are still working and shaping the policy in our State Department." Joe was starting to worry folks, seeing as how Russia had just announced the detonation of the first red atomic bomb.

All of this Kleber heard and noted, but, uncharacteristically, with but half an ear. The news for which he risked a dead battery came last: "Well, fellow swimmers," drawled the announcer in a voice that commenced like butter and soured quickly to clabber, "like the feller says, if you don't like the weather in Texas, just wait a durn minute. Today we got somethin' for everybody. We got a norther due in, yes I said *norther,* and yes this is the end of May; we got more rain—maybe another inch and a half; we got hail, we got reports of tornadoes up around Wichita Falls and west of Weatherford. The only good thing I can pass on is that it's not supposed to freeze. No need to put the baby tomato plants under the tarp. But by ten o'clock tonight it should be colder'n a gravedigger's handshake."

So what else is new, fretted Kleber as he stormed into the house where he had lived every single day of eighteen years.

"Well, *shit,*" he swore, but not very loud. Even though no one else was in the house, his mother would somehow know if profanity was used. It was all too unfair. His epochal season—the final days of high school—was just about devastated by climatic caprice. Kleber aimed and threw imaginary darts against the kitchen wall. Class garden party? Rained out. *Wham!* Senior prom? At twenty prepaid bucks a couple? *Disaster.* Girls wading in with collapsed coiffures, gowns soaked to the calf, camellia corsages (three bucks a bloom and you *had* to buy two) dropping petals like molting turkeys. *Wham! Wham!* The way things were happening—or *not* happening—he would get about halfway through his valedictory address tomorrow night just as the roof of Will Rogers Auditorium collapsed. The best advice he could impart to the Class of '50 was how to build an ark.

Kleber peeled off his dripping red sweater and khaki trousers and threw them onto the mirror-waxed beige linoleum floor, an impulsive act that jarred the temper and tone of his mother's house. For a few edgy moments, he enjoyed the audacious feeling that came from standing in VeeJee Cantrell's kitchen clad only in his underwear. But he hurriedly found his bathrobe and regained the conformity of middle-class life in neutral gear.

He stared glumly out the window. The neighborhood hardly changed character under the assault of rain. Storm gray was as becoming as sunlight beige. This block of Cloverdale Avenue contained buff brick foursquare houses that were the aesthetic equals of orthopedic shoe boxes. Each had been constructed around 1928, the edge of the Depression. And each had waited obediently, like steadfast lovers, for the men to return from World War II. Here was the enclave of first-generation urban; most every parent on the block had been born on a farm somewhere and had come to the city in search of red silk and gold coins. Instead they found paycheck labor as insurance salesmen, vice-principals, gas station owners, civil servants, and plumbers. They married secretaries and shopgirls. They bred children, worshipped the Protestant God, paid taxes, and dared not ask for more. The residents of Cloverdale Avenue had reached their designated ceilings—one stories all—and settled for that. Kleber Cantrell could not wait to escape.

On the kitchen table, a basket of pale yellow apples contained a note for Kleber. His mother's orderly script gave a moment-by-moment itinerary:

Noon: Monnig's to buy graduation presents.

1 p.m. Harris Hospital—Visit Aunt Lula
(Worse, spreading they say)

2 p.m. Church—Alto Section Practice

3 p.m. Ike-for-President Petition Meeting
(I've got 114 signatures!)

4 p.m. Safeway (Hope 4 dzn. hot dogs enuf)

5 p.m. Latest—Home (Potato salad in icebox. Don't forget to hang up cap and gown on closet door to smooth wrinkles. Mack called twice. T.J. once.

Love, Your Mother)

One thing about Ma, thought Kleber, she never lets a body speculate about her march through the hours. Life With Mother was as itemized as a restaurant check. He wondered once if eighteen years and nine months prior, VeeJee jotted down: "9:20 p.m. Conceive Child, 9:30 p.m. Knit Booties." Presumably, thirty years hence, she would squeeze into her schedule: "3:35 p.m. Perish."

At least every other day, VeeJee sermonized on the gift of time, delivering a living legacy to her only child that robbed him of leisure. "Time is precious," the mother liked to cry. "Just before I say my prayers at night, I make a mental list of everything I accomplished that day. If there is one idle gap, I am ashamed. And if I have not learned something new, then I have wasted my brain and God's most blessed resource—time." Kleber would go through life unable to take a nap or a vacation without feeling guilty.

VeeJee's crowded agendas were eclectic. Already in less than half of 1950, she had mastered rose pruning, first aid with special honors in snakebite and cardiac resuscitation, and was well into the memorization of Proverbs. All of them. Moreover, she was eagerly learning about Communism, having discovered through the West Side Women's Current Affairs Circle that Joseph Stalin was not the rakish grandpa who linked hands with FDR and Churchill and promised not to munch any neighbor's boundaries. VeeJee was now persuaded that the Soviets were preparing to invade Texas. Two weeks earlier, she wrote a Hollywood studio in protestation of a planned film about Hiawatha. Conservative thought held that the Indian peacemaker was a Marxist hero. She even took down the framed print of two fluttering doves above gnarled hands in prayer. For years the picture had hung in the guest bedroom. "Doves are Red now, sad to say," she announced, with fervor that would rewrite Noah's Flood if permitted.

As per custom, VeeJee had prepared two perfect bologna sandwiches and chilled two Dr. Peppers for Kleber (nutrition had not yet caught her attention). Having once estimated for an arithmetic class that he had eaten enough bologna sandwiches to circle the globe,

Kleber was well into a second voyage. He ate hurriedly, knowing that the telephone would soon be ringing. On the third bite it did, but he waited until the seventh ring before answering. He did not want people to think he was eager for social summons. People in control were people who appeared busy. When he picked up the receiver, he breathed heavily, as if interrupted from something urgent.

"It's me, Mr. Wonderful," said Mack from across the street, his deep, gut-bucket voice gloomy as the hour. "What are we gonna do?"

"I dunno," replied Kleber. "Buy umbrella stock?"

"I just hung up with T.J. and he says the ball's in your court. You're the big deal class president, Eagle Scout, and sorriest football player who ever put a helmet on backward."

Kleber snorted something about Neanderthals. "Why do I take this abuse from people whose thinking process rarely rises above Doak Walker's rushing average? You're as funny as Martha Higby." Reference was made to the history teacher who, if not demented, dwelled in the neurotic vicinity. Higby was given to expressing agony at student ineptitude by yanking down the wall map of Texas and hiding behind San Antonio.

Kleber fell silent to think. At the other end of the line, fifty feet across Cloverdale, in another orthopedic shoe box, Mack Crawford waited, picturing his best friend chewing on the dilemma. No good to push. He well knew that Kleber might spend five minutes deciding to go left or right at the fork of a hiking trail. Such delays were irritating, but Mack tolerated them, as did T. J. Luther, the third member of the triad, as did anybody who sought commerce—social, business, or emotional—with Kleber Cantrell. The son of VeeJee rowed a steady boat.

Lightning rent the early afternoon with grimmest thunder as attendant. Ruefully, Kleber peered out the window at the day condemned. No glimmer of celestial pardon. "What's the consensus?" asked Kleber.

"That nobody's gonna turn up at the lake in this shit." Mack paused for mutual wallowing in the unfairness of it all. Then he quickly shifted gears, his wont, making it difficult to track his conversational path. "Hey, did you hear what Ted Williams did last night? He got PO'd at the fans in Boston and he stepped outta the batter's box and—now *get this*—he gave 'em quote an obscene gesture end quote. That means the finger! Ted Williams flipped off the whole world! The paper said they may fire him. Ted Williams!"

Without commitment, Kleber grunted. He had little interest in baseball, the closest major-league team being in faraway St. Louis, his own athletic talents confined to daydreaming in the seldom trafficked regions of sandlot right field. His favorite position was left out. What did intrigue him, modestly, about Ted Williams was the covetous feeling that a man could play a child's game, make a quarter of a million a year, and have every public utterance and gesture committed to type and ink.

Enough of Ted. The problem of the moment was more compelling. Kleber considered it from all sides. The evening's plan, long in the making, was for a dozen of the *couples that counted* to congregate on the shore of Fort Worth's major lake, cook hot dogs, consume large quantities of Pearl beer (provided the cantankerous old crank who ran the county-line liquor store went for T.J.'s doctored ID), listen to Nat (King) Cole records, and just . . . be together. It was not an official class function, only an assemblage of crowned heads, perverse in its snobbism—and delicious in adolescent torment. Tomorrow night *everybody* could come to the grad night blast at the Casino, the ramshackle old dance pavilion large enough for re-enactment of Civil War battles. Everyone would cheer over the unshackling of public school chains that had been in place a dozen years. Everyone would weep. Everyone would try and revel until dawn, as that was the expected rite of passage. But on this eve, only a few, the skimming of the cream, the fraction possessed of power or beauty or both, would be entitled to the memory of an elitist communion.

"Okay," decreed Kleber, "I say let's wait until five o'clock and watch the weather. If it's still raining then, maybe we can move it to Lisa's house."

Mack moaned. Lisa Ann Candleman, beloved of Kleber, was the daughter of a preacher. Social events in her home had all the gaiety of Mack's aunt's musicales. But he did not disagree: Kleber's word was always taken. "Yeah," he muttered. "But it won't be the same."

"It might be better," suggested Kleber. "I gotta hang up. That lady from the paper's coming over to do the interview."

"Oh, yeah," remembered Mack. "I still don't see why they're wastin' time on you." The tease was gentle. "Seems like they'd rather write up the Best All-Around Athlete or the Most Handsome Senior Boy, both of whom are one and the same."

"Quite wisely," said Kleber, "the reporter chose the Boy Most Likely to Succeed. A minor victory for intelligence."

"Time will tell," countered Mack, ringing off with envy not altogether hidden.

Her name was Laurie and she was such a pretty thing. She was too thin, and in sixteen years her body had not yet developed curves anywhere near generous, but her hair was uncut and gleamed blue black, and her eyes were the shade of dusk's last streak of violet. She was a night bird of a child—quick, nervous, hidden. Not many people valued Laurie's shadowy beauty because not many people knew she existed. Trouble was, Laurie never lived anywhere very long—a move a month was not uncommon—for Laurie's mother was always one jump ahead of a bounced check or an unpaid bill. Once the child boarded a Trailways bus to ride from Beaumont to Longview and informed her mother, "I *love* this house." Currently, mother and daughter resided in an abandoned trailer precariously balanced on cement blocks that squatted like jackrabbits on dirt ruts that wandered off a farm-to-market road that itself was a rarely traveled offshoot from the state highway linking Forth Worth and Weatherford.

Laurie had in fact only been to Weatherford once, a country town but five some odd miles from the trailer and noted for producing both watermelons that grow to a hundred pounds and the musical star Mary Martin. But isolation did not trouble Laurie, no more than the trailer's lack of electricity or plumbing, no more than the absence of her father. Whoever he was, he had been gone for years, God knew where, the crossbar hotel, more'n likely. All Laurie knew of him was a blurry snapshot, an unfocused man standing beside a pickup truck that was filled with chicken coops. He had heavy arm muscles and a pack of Luckies wrapped inside the sleeve of his tee shirt. He wore a straw cowboy hat and squinted somberly. His name was "sorry bastard," at least that was all Laurie's mother, SuBeth Killman, ever referred to him by. Hard times had fallen on SuBeth Killman. During the war, she prospered modestly, roaming Texas' many military bases and "entertaining our soldier boys." Now, five years later, her hair was bleached stiff as broom straw and her breasts were less like "Attention!" and more like "Parade Rest." Regularly SuBeth thrilled her daughter with plans for a new marriage, but the altar was elusive. In the spring of 1950, SuBeth found work uncapping beer for truckers at a roadhouse-grocery somewhere near the Tarrant County line and fed Laurie with pilfered cans of pork'n beans and box macaroni. Sometimes she brought home a customer—potentially a husband!—and on these important occasions, Laurie was expected to scoot. Her exit was not so much required because home was tiny and contained but one swaybacked daybed. The peril was that when Mama and beau began to party, the very real possibility existed that the home might rock off its cement blocks from overweight and sink into a sea of oozing red mud.

There was little for Laurie to do during the days when she was alone, save listen to "Helen Trent" on the battery radio every afternoon and "Let's Pretend" on Saturday mornings. She had dropped out of school long ago, the last formal lesson at the age of twelve, which was no great loss to education because Laurie had never managed big words, and numbers were hieroglyphics for all she comprehended addition and division. Mostly she passed the hours messing around with an old cat named Moses who enjoyed lapping Nehi Grape from a saucer, or tending black-eyed peas that Mama sold to roadside produce stands, if they stayed there long enough.

Each morning when SuBeth left for work, she turned around and yelled at Laurie, "Listen, missy, don't you wander off, hear?" Some days there were maternal warnings about what happened to foolish youngsters snatched by truant officers. Nonetheless, Laurie had a small streak of adventure and she defied Mama, making secret forays into the countryside. In less than six weeks of residence, Laurie had discovered many special places and things. Over this part of Texas hangs a certain gothic aura, which Laurie interpreted through her main frame of reference: fairy tales. The tiny graveyards of pioneers that popped up every mile or two were, by Laurie's reckoning, the sources of an imagined royal family, her ancestors. She found the grave of Davy Crockett's second wife and had to shoo away a herd of disrespectful mahogany-and-white Herefords that munched on the distinguished lady's grass coverlet. She knew of fields where bales of hay were stacked to resemble the stone castles of knights. There was one place where the bleached, sorrowful land was enlivened by a grove of willows that looked like chartreuse plumes on a royal lady's hat. When she saw old-timers on the roads, folks hunched over with stoops and creaking bones and bent joints, Laurie privately knew that the miseries were the penalties of evil magicians, not from the more likely source of mean animals and stubborn farm equipment. Once she pushed through a grove of mesquite and canebrake to discover the Brazos River. She stared almost hypnotized at the powerful, clear blue-green waters before she ran away yelping, afraid a curse or a spell was coming.

When Laurie was entranced by the fairy tales dramatized on "Let's Pretend," she recognized that princesses always had to endure a penance of unpleasant things—poisoned apples, a century of slumber —before getting life's reward, i.e., love and the prince. Thus did she establish a personal protocol. If she did something worthy, like wash the sheets in the creek without being told and hang them out to dry and put them back on the bed before Mama came home, then and only then did she grant herself a reward. By royal decree, the princess was permitted to open the treasure chest, that being a Whitman's Sampler Box containing most beloved possessions—the goddesses, carefully scissored pictures from movie magazines found in garbage cans or tossed away on the back roads of Laurie's life. Her current favorites were June Allyson, croaky-voiced and sweet as a church alto; Lana Turner, cold as Jack Frost but the kind of woman men whistled at; and the new one, the best one, the beauty beyond envy because nobody in the whole world came close: Elizabeth Taylor. Laurie's *most* precious icon was an old *Life* magazine with two articles she had committed to memory. The first was about a princess in India marrying a maharaja. The pictures were wonderful; drummers in leopard skins led the marital procession, trailed by elephants with blankets of rubies and emeralds on which sat the couple. They rode up a mountain where the top blazed with fireworks. But every time Laurie studied the pictures, she thought the bride looked scared, like a fox caught in a trap who would sooner or later have to chew her foot off to get free. And no wonder, considering as how the groom looked like the devil's first cousin. *That* marriage wouldn't last a year.

But on the very next page was the story of another marriage. Elizabeth Taylor became the bride of a handsome young man named Conrad (Nick) Hilton, and, by Laurie's estimation, they were the real prince and princess. Elizabeth was only eighteen (just two years more than Laurie) and the best picture was as she left the church in Beverly Hills, waving devotedly to the thousands of people who loved her. Laurie looked at this story so much that she was forced to ration herself for fear the ink would bleed from the pages onto her lips.

The only mirror in SuBeth's trailer had long ago turned the color of mustard and was veined like Grandma's thighs, but Laurie played like it was enchanted. Whenever she closed her eyes and held her breath and counted to ten and quickly popped them open, back came the reflection of Miss Laurel Killman marrying Mr. Conrad (Nick) Hilton. Laurie even had Elizabeth's shy smile down pat but was not yet able to accomplish the soft, tumbling hairdo.

On this May afternoon when the rains began again, and the winds stirred, and the farm animals got jittery, and the mesquite trees began to bend so hard that prickly limbs and bean pods flailed against the trailer like the arrows of Lancelot, Laurie put on a lot of her mama's cherry lipstick, made charcoal mush to serve as mascara, patted circles of red rock dust on her frail cheeks, and sat regally before the mirror declaring, "Yes, it's true, my name is Elizabeth." Mama spoiled it by turning up drunk with a shitkicker on her arm. "You just wash your face, missy, and take a walk! Hear!" ordered Mama, who already had one hand up the old boy's shirt ticklin' his chest while he mixed tomato juice and Grand Prize boilermakers.

So Laurie hurried out, putting a cantaloupe basket over her head so as not to let the rain wash away her mask.

Clara Eggleston was neither good reporter nor able writer, but she was dogged—and on this rainy afternoon fascinating to see. She appeared at Kleber Cantrell's door in a black wool skirt dog-damp from the storm, a white angora sweater whose fluff loosened each time she wrote on her steno pad and drifted about like droppings from a cottonwood tree, and on her fiercely hennaed hair sat a scarlet beret. She looked like a hot fudge sundae. She was forty-two years old, widowed from a Brooklyn soldier who brought her to Texas during the war and who suffered the maladroit fate of perishing beneath a slipped jeep jack at Fort Worth's air force base. Patriotic with grief, Clara remained, obtaining a temporary wartime job as obituary writer for the Fort Worth *Star-Telegram*.

Six years later she was still there—and professionally distressed over her beat: education. That meant spelling bees, a rare school board scandal, and profiles of outstanding students. Eccentric and lonely, she clung to a few imported shreds of liberal posture, as useless in Fort Worth as snow skis and rubles. At least Clara worked fast. Before the how-de-do's and weather talk were over, she had scribbled a competent portrait of Kleber: "Tall, about six feet, slim, honest wide-open face, Van Johnson type, sandy hair starting to thin (he'll be bald someday) . . . eyes that shift from innocent blue to calculating green . . . stares at you the way people do if they're smarter (or condescending) . . . a touch arrogant . . . this boy is on his toes . . ."

Clara, sitting in VeeJee Cantrell's best oatmeal velvet wing chair, then crossed her legs and revealed, to Kleber's astonishment, an apparent lack of underpants. Whereupon it became difficult for the subject either to look at or respond to his interrogator. Kleber began thinking about his dead grandmother in her coffin, a ploy frequently used to put down unwanted erections. Dimly he heard Mrs. Eggleston inquire as to the occupations of his parents.

"Well," he squeaked. "Dad's a wholesale grocer. Elder in the Presbyterian church. And Mom, she's real busy. She's a Republican—Dad says the only one in the history of our family and they cancel out each other's vote. She's in a lot of clubs . . . visits sick people in the hospital a lot . . . When she gets to heaven, she'll have stars in her crown."

Clara did not write the line down, disappointing Kleber, for he thought it was well phrased. Instead, the maddening woman shifted her legs again, encouraging the soggy black skirt to creep almost to the garter line. Now Kleber was prepared for a journey to genuine bush country. As often as he had bragged to Mack and T.J. about alleged trips to that forbidden territory, this was, truth tell, his first visual sighting. Desperately he wished for an algebra book to press against his crotch.

If Clara noticed, and surely she did, for the one factor of her assignment that made newspapering bearable was proximity to the young and the male, she betrayed no pleasure. Routinely she elicited the youth's remarkable dossier. Since junior high, Kleber had been president of everything, editor of the newspaper, no grade below A, laurel wreath permanently affixed to his brow. God obviously anointed this child leader of the maternity ward.

"Okay," said Clara briskly, "you mind if we get personal?"

"Personal?" echoed Kleber, unease renewing like the rains. He assumed give-and-take was over, having led the odd lady up to all the significant hilltops of his life.

"Just general stuff. For example, I read recently that unwed pregnancies among teenage girls are on the rise. Since you're the class leader and . . . ah . . . have your finger on the pulse of things, I'd like your comment."

"I don't have any," gulped Kleber. The only image that leaped into his head was recent, clandestine attendance at a notorious movie called

Mom and Dad. It had played at the neighborhood theater, to segregated audiences (boys at the 2 p.m. showing, girls at 4), with nurses roaming the aisles in case somebody fainted from the gruesome and graphic close-ups of sexual organs ravaged by VD. After this movie, Kleber had stopped masturbating for three difficult weeks.

Clara smiled. "Is there a steady girl in the picture?" she asked.

Finally a towline! Yes, oh yes. Lisa. Class beauty runner-up. Drum majorette. President of Methodist Youth Fellowship. From his wallet Kleber withdrew a photograph. Clara glimpsed yellow hair and blue eyes, cheese and milk, the poetry of Edgar A. Guest.

"Maybe I should talk to Lisa to find out what you're really like," jested Clara, watching Kleber swallow the lump she had perversely placed in his throat. "Is Lisa going to college this fall?"

"Yessum. Elementary education major."

"How interesting," said Clara in a voice that was obviously not. She flipped hurriedly through her pad, frowning at what appeared—from Kleber's viewpoint—enough material for a series. "Almost done," she said pleasantly. "Let's just turn philosophical for a minute." If the flustered youth on the head of her pen was the certified hope of tomorrow, then Clara figured her franchise extended beyond name, age, rank, and ribbons. "We sit here halfway through the twentieth century," she said. "Your Class of '50 gets a fresh start. A blank piece of paper. You want to be a newspaper reporter. So I ask you, what would you write on that piece of paper to make America a better place?"

Well, when a man gets a question like that, the best response is to blink many times, throwing up a shield for the panic therein. Kleber didn't know if a trap was set but he would tread carefully, cognizant that what next emerged from his mouth would leap into hot lead type and thence onto the breakfast tables of 200,000 Texans. The *Star-Telegram* was a powerful blanket that smothered a quarter of the state larger than New York, Pennsylvania, Ohio, Illinois, and all of New England put together. Best he not sound like Elmer Fudd.

Perhaps, in that mid-twentieth-century spring, there existed somewhere in America an eighteen-year-old gripped with *mal de pays*. But it wasn't Kleber Cantrell. Maybe the youth of discontent were infesting the stacks of the New York Public Library or squirming on the back row of freshman poly-sci at Harvard. But they were a rare species. Kleber's generation was both innocent and blank. Conceived in a

Depression and weaned in economic melancholy. Reared during world war when national purpose was unquestioned and joyous patriotism called for cheers when John Wayne waded onto bloodied beaches and mushroom clouds billowed over Japan. The American Way of Life was downright holy, sanctified by atomic majesty. There was no criticism. There was no question of leaving it, only loving it. Bumper stickers in Texas promoted rodeos, and tee shirts had nothing written on them other than BVD.

Thus, Kleber later reasoned, he could be forgiven that afternoon for failure to tear from the top of his contented head a recipe to alter the American diet. He was well nourished. All he could summon to agitate Clara Eggleston's pencil was a slice of eminently safe political weaponry that politicians would fire for years to come. Law and Order. In the recent months of 1950, Fort Worth, normally a gentle city, deceptively soft in western courtesy and antithetic to neighboring Dallas (a hard town of mercantile worship and pretensions of cousin-ship to New York if not Paris), had been plagued by criminal violence.

In Kleber's own neighborhood, where the only intrusive noises were jackhammers building a freeway and random assaults by red-bellied woodpeckers, a petty gambler entered his Cadillac one morning, stepped on the accelerator, and was promptly blown into an unsolvable jigsaw puzzle, along with wife and infant child. More followed. Mailboxes blew, garages exploded into flames, even priests began lifting the hoods of parish station wagons for perusal before ignition. Fort Worth, a city that liked being called "Cowtown," was becoming, warned a columnist, "Little Chicago."

"I suppose we should do something about all this crime," announced Kleber.

"Oh?" said Clara. "And what should we do?"

Kleber shrugged. "Maybe run every hood out of town for starters," he said, a sensible but, as life would instruct him, unconstitutional suggestion. "Or lock 'em up and throw away the key."

Clara put down her pencil in astonishment. She studied the face of the Boy Most Likely to Succeed. She saw there no hypocrisy, no rancor, no guilt, no sheets in the wardrobe. What she saw was Texas—acceptance of the way things were—and are—and, to the extent that a misplaced Yankee liberal could forecast—would ever be.

Blessedly for Kleber the telephone rang and the doorbell chimed in simultaneous interruptions. The call was for Clara, who returned with news that the photographer was en route. And at the front door were Mack and T.J., outwardly apologetic over intrusion, but at the same time delighted to crash the party. Besides, they stage-whispered, time was running out for Kleber's decree on what to do about the picnic. Kleber hushed them and made hurried introductions.

"This is Mack Crawford," he gestured, evoking a gallant if nervous nod, and a water-pump handshake from an athletic youth whose blond hair and fair countenance were like tapers lit in a cathedral of gloom. For many years Clara Eggleston had prowled the corridors and playgrounds of public schools and often she had glimpsed a youngster whose sexuality was difficult to ignore. But Mack Crawford was the most splendid male she had ever faced. Kidnapping-by-chloroform actually entered her mind. The lad's shoulders were broad and strong; both of her nigh trembling hands could not have circled his forearm. Had she thrown herself about his thighs, which was what she wanted to do, her hands would not have linked. And he moved and carried himself with a balletic grace that no person six feet four and weighing, she guessed, 210 pounds could possibly possess. Clara wondered: Does this boy know what he has for sale?

With real difficulty she was forced to turn away and meet the third boy in the room. "This is T. J. Luther," said Kleber. "Class Favorite, but really the Class Goof-Off." Crossing his eyes, T.J. bent forward to kiss the reporter's hand, tripping intentionally as he descended, sprawling on the carpet in an accomplished and amusing pratfall. This one, noted Clara, was thin and short and wiry, an imp whispering "psst" from the shadows.

"I'm ashamed to admit it," said Kleber, "but these clowns are my best friends. The three of us grew up together, on this block."

"The Three Musketeers," muttered Clara, transfixed only by Mack, behaving and sounding like an absurd coquette. The interview was forgotten. Sexual fantasies spilled like overturned ink, drowning any questions of purpose that remained for Kleber.

"No, ma'm," corrected T.J. "The Three Princes—with Pearl beer flowing in every vein."

"He's just kidding," interjected Kleber hurriedly. It would not please his mother, father, or any elder in his circle for the hometown paper to hint of hops.

"Three Princes?" asked Clara. "Is that a club?"

"Unofficial," answered Mack. "It's dumb, really. I'm sorry, Mrs. Eggleston. We didn't mean to butt in on the interview."

"No," insisted Clara. "Please go on." It mattered not what the athlete said, but only that he said it. Clara was grateful for any reason to look at him.

Instead Kleber seized the explanation. Once, long ago, in the first year of high school, a dramatic English teacher had used every trick in her pedagogic bag to interest the class in Will Shakespeare. A frustrated thespian who possessed the marquee-perfect name of Maude Silverlake, the determined lady was famous for balancing on the classroom windowsill to deliver Juliet's love for Romeo. On another day she leaped onto her desk wearing swirling rags sewn from Ralston Purina feed sacks and then enacted *all three* witches from *Macbeth,* clasping an uncorked thermos of hot broth as substitute for the steaming cauldron. Entertaining as such interludes were, Miss Silverlake sensed correctly that her students were not yet enamored of the glories of great drama. Thus did she hatch an assignment wherein the class would conceive an original play using the florid language of romantic melodrama.

"So the class wrote this thing called *The Three Princes,*" explained Kleber. "Actually, Miss Silverlake wrote most of it."

"I gather you three played the leading roles?" asked Clara.

"Natch," said T.J. "The girls voted for us unanimously."

"What was the plot?"

Kleber answered again. With the reluctance of a child forced to dance for spinster aunts, Kleber continued, worried now that this silly digression would intrude on his print. "Not much. There were Three Princes. The Prince of Power. The Prince of Charms. The Prince of Temptation. We were all chasing, I'm ashamed to admit it, the Princess of Eternal Bliss. Best I can remember, there were a lot of 'vouchsafes,' 'forsooths,' and 'alarums.' "

"Don't dump on it," said T.J. "The story was better than that. Each prince offered a token to the princess to win her hand. The Prince of Power offered to make her famous and important. The Prince of Charms offered endless nights of love. The Prince of Temptation gave her a gold cup with wine."

"Whom did she choose?"

"She couldn't decide," remembered T.J. "So she drank poison. Nobody wanted a happy ending."

"Let me guess," said Clara. She pointed at T.J. "You played the Prince of Charms."

"No, ma'm, I was the Prince of Temptation. I got people in trouble."

Clara nodded; she appreciated the casting.

T.J. continued. "And Kleber boy here was the Prince of Power, who put everybody to sleep with these stupid speeches about virtue and stuff. And Mack, believe it or not, was the Prince of Charms, which all of us agreed was the worst casting. I seriously suggested he play the Prince of Jocks and come out wearing . . . ah . . . shoulder pads."

The alluring imagery was shattered by the arrival of the photographer, a squat, malformed man named Bede whose specialty was standing between the goalposts during football games and firing flashbulbs into the faces of runners about to score, giving his subjects the look of cats streaking across a night highway with eyes glassified by sudden car lights. Impulsively, Clara decided it would be appropriate to photograph all three youths, though her words would deal principally with Kleber. She suggested Bede assemble the trio outside.

Bede shrugged. "It's raining again," he said. "You wanna pay two hundred dollars to get this Graflex cleaned, I'll shoot 'em in the Trinity River."

The front porch became compromise. Bede lined his subjects in a row against the Cantrell beige brick wall and raised his eye. "Wait," pleaded Clara. She loathed the ugly man who approached his art with the creativity of a tractor salesman. Her Three Princes were not condemned, awaiting a final bullet. Care must be taken. She choreographed a tight close-up on the faces, vertical in composition, one youth beneath the other. Flattering Bede's ego, she hinted that the picture might run big—page one, surely—and necessarily deep.

"You fix 'em, honey," said Bede. "I'll shoot 'em. Just hurry."

Being tallest and accustomed to standing at the rear of any photograph, Mack playfully pushed Kleber below his chest. T.J. obediently squatted on the damp cement floor.

Clara frowned. "No," she said. "Power first." She bade Kleber to stand upright. "Beauty next . . ."

"Beauty?" asked Mack.

"Sorry," said Clara, humiliation almost surfacing. *"Charm* under Power. And Temptation on the bottom—where it should be." Clara laughed hollowly and alone.

When the bulb fired, Kleber was smiling stiffly, obviously displeased to share the moment of celebrity with his friends. Mack was laughing in unknowing sexual generosity. And T.J. arched an eyebrow in perfect dead solid temptation.

CHAPTER TWO

The rain paused briefly near dusk, and Laurie crept cautiously back to the trailer in the mesquite grove, hoping that Mama's newest potential husband had departed. But his pickup truck was still there—sides caked with loam and a shotgun hanging in harness behind the driver's seat. Through the tiny portholes of the trailer struggled faint yellow light from a Coleman lantern. The music Mama loved best swam through the cracks, sad melodies from Nashville that sobbed of broken hearts and back-alley love. Laurie knew the matinee would now be extended into an evening performance.

She slumped down on a rusted old bed frame that Mama had dragged home the week before but, unable to squeeze it through the door, abandoned outside. Laurie was chilled, damp, and—to her surprise—mad. Seldom had she mused on the unfairness of life—she had no measuring stick—but at this soggy moment in her seventeenth year, she figured the scales did not balance. Nature agreed with her, for the order of day and night was capsized. Great horned owls were already out, as if it was midnight, spooky as goblins. Reluctantly, Laurie stood before the trailer door, fidgeted, decided she was in the right, knocked. No response. She rapped again. SuBeth opened the portal a crack. Her face was flushed and sweaty, hair tangled like a mop that had cleaned up molasses. She wore only bra and panties. The shitkicker danced around behind her. His body was all skinny and white, except for a burnt-red face and vee-neck, making him look like a color-book man some little kid had just started to turn into an Indian.

"Thought you was out walkin'," said SuBeth, displeased.

Laurie's answer was planned. "I was, Mama, but it's cold. I got the sniffles." The misery on her face was not total charade.

Some remote maternal chord was struck and Mama opened the door. But the shitkicker, having already invested three dollars in beer, two-fifty for a pint of Schenley's, and a yet-to-be-negotiated but probable ten-buck "tip" before his cannon could be fired, had a quick counter-notion. "You're sure a cute youngun," he told Laurie. "I was just tellin' yore mama that we might all go to the rodeo over at Decatur next Satidy night. Bet you'd like that?"

Laurie allowed as how she would.

"Well, then we got to make plans, hon . . . private-like . . . why don't you go back out yonder and sit in my pickup? It's real nice and warm. Okay, sweet thing?"

Without enthusiasm, Laurie agreed. Mama shot the shitkicker a glance that said sweeten the kitty; he found his overalls and tossed Laurie a quarter like it was a Friday-night paycheck. "Now you go on," said SuBeth. "It's cold standin' here in the draft." She whispered hotly in her daughter's ear. "This one's fixin' to propose. He's got eight hunnerd and forty dollars in the bank at Wichita Falls."

"That's real nice, Mama," said Laurie with unusual testiness. "Can I get a blanket?"

"Yeah. In fact, you can wear my coat," offered SuBeth. The trailer, layered with cigarette smoke, smelled of spilled beer. The shitkicker had the propane gas heater turned so high that the windows dribbled tears. Behind the curtained closet, Laurie found the soft blue coat, and, beside it, the pretty pink dress that Mama had bought last summer in incorrect belief she was to marry a cattle auctioneer. Alas, the gown had never been worn, hanging since like a wallflower with the $17.95 Sears, Roebuck catalogue tag still on the collar. Out of spite, or newfound courage, Laurie impulsively took the dress as well, smuggling it inside the coat, and hurrying out without a fare-thee-well.

For a while she sat in the pickup, enjoying the embrace of Mama's nice coat and playing with the dress, marveling over the lace appliqué at the bust line and the way the skirt billowed like an opened parachute. Once Laurie had secretly tried it on, pretending to be the bride of Prince Valiant, and it was a near fit save being too long and too loose in the middle.

She found other things to do. She looked at the shotgun a long time before she found the courage to touch it, then jerked back at the smooth, reptilian cold. In the glove box she discovered a flashlight whose beam bounced crazily against tree limbs and scared the evil owls from their roosts. On the radio she found nothing but faraway Mexican music and preacher screamings. Then she saw a muddy newspaper on the floorboard. Aided by the flashlight, she turned the pages. Nothing much interested her until the section with picture show ads. Laurie stopped and held her breath. At first she thought she had come across the very same treasured photograph of Elizabeth Taylor on her wedding day. Then, slowly making sense out of the big words above, the realization came that the reason Elizabeth was wearing a bridal gown here was that she was starring in a new movie called *Father of the Bride*. Best of all, it was playing in Weatherford, not five miles from where she sat! Maybe less, if she cut across the cattle fields.

"Well, I'm gonna see that show," she vowed. She had almost two dollars hidden under the daybed, secreted between the pages of a Jesus book somebody once gave her. First thing tomorrow morning, Laurie promised herself, the minute Mama was off to work, she was heading for Weatherford to worship her goddess.

Nourished by dreams, Laurie dozed. When she awoke, cold, startled, the trailer was dark. But music played on. Mama and the shitkicker were settling in for a long one. Laurie reckoned it was just after eight. Nothing to do but curl up and sleep. But when she put back the flashlight in the glove box, her hand brushed a wad of paper. Money. The ole boy had forty-two dollars. And next to it rested something small and cold and hard. Laurie shined the light and discovered a little gold ring, with a pale green cameo setting. It was a smiling old woman with a very long nose and a swan neck and her hair in a queenly French twist.

Not five minutes later, Laurie had wriggled into the pink dress that her mama failed to be married in, had torn out the picture of Elizabeth Taylor and secreted it beside her pounding heart, and was

walking barefoot toward Weatherford, shoes in hand. She wasn't quite
sure how to get there, but she would find the way. The princess *always*
found the castle. There was nothing to worry about. The shitkicker was
so drunk he wouldn't miss the five dollars Laurie borrowed. And she
would be back before he woke up to replace the ring.

Twenty some odd miles east, the Three Princes sat morose as exiles. They occupied T. J. Luther's jeep, parked beneath an awning of
the Toot 'n Tell 'Em Drive-in, known more familiarly to the clientele
as the Toot 'n *Smell* 'Em, attributable to the heady waves of perfume
and perspiration drifting fore and aft of the Venusian carhops.

Here was not where they had wanted to be. After the interview,
Kleber spent a frenetic hour in desperate attempt to salvage the picnic.
Lisa's mother set the tone, refusing to permit two dozen youngsters into
a home scrubbed clean as a copper-bottomed pot for Bible study class
the next morning. With every wile he possessed, and the number was
considerable, Kleber pleaded, but everybody said no, even VeeJee, who
would not tolerate an invasion of revelers along with the spirit of abandonment inherent in graduation eve.

About 6 p.m. Kleber decreed that the celebration of the celebrated
was, literally, a washout. His fallback plan—a movie followed by Mexican food—also collapsed. The girls elected instead to hold a farewell
slumber party at the home of Carralou King, daughter of a homicide
detective whose demeanor and dimensions approximated those of a
Brahma bull. A widower, gossip holding that his wife expired during
vigorous lovemaking, he guarded his child's breasts as if they were keys
to the slammer. T.J. bragged that he had once sipped from Carralou's
remarkable cones, but no one believed him. Whatever, once the girls
were in giggling assemblage hidden by the guard of Detective LeRoy
King, they were unmolestable.

Flattened by nature and circumstance, the Three Princes surveyed
a kingdom in disarray. Their chariot was a pocked and muddied jeep
whose speedometer had thrice spun past 100,000 miles. Their court
was a rain-slick parking lot, their royal banquet the Toot's Special
(burger, fries, root beer, 55 cents), the remains of which sat sadly in
an oily pond of spreading chili on a metal tray affixed to the window.
Nor did the most admired carhop, Ludeen of the strawberry hair and
lips, enhance the night. She told T.J. he was a "BORING LITTLE
PRICK" and had a "FILTHY MOUTH."

"You tell 'em, doughnut, you got a greasy hole," retorted T.J. He assured his companions that in truth Ludeen adored him. The evening was dying and T.J. considered it his due to revive the hour. "Hey," he said abruptly, "let's go catch the holy rollers." Mack and Kleber groaned. Twice in the past T.J. had announced the discovery of a snake-handling sect, but upon tiptoeing to the steamy windows of, respectively, the Worth Hills Blood of Lamb Tabernacle and the African Episcopal Redeemer Mission in niggertown, nothing more than feverish yelling and feet-washing was espied. Kleber felt modestly embarrassed by peeking in on an obviously heartfelt worship service, no matter how bizarre the theatrics. T.J. for some reason had been fascinated and hatched an unrealized scheme to volunteer as an usher and offering collector, having witnessed the promising sums of money dropped into milk buckets.

"You guys got no guts," announced T.J. He fell silent a few moments to consider alternatives. "Hey, how much money y'all got?"

"Maybe seven dollars," said Kleber guardedly, for suspicion was the most sensible posture in fiduciary encounter with T.J.

"By the way, you still owe me a dollar seventy-five for that tire I bought you," remembered Mack.

"What tire?"

"That night we had the flat in Forest Park."

"What night?"

"We were hecklin', remember? Those TCU guys were after us and you drove over that broken beer bottle." Heckling was the prank of last resort, something to do when a night was totally barren. It consisted of prowling around a lovers' lane in the park, spying on guys lucky enough to get a girl in the woods, usually concluding with the angered victim giving chase to the molesters.

"Oh, yeah," muttered T.J. in vague recollection. "Well, I ain't suggestin' we go hecklin'. And I don't wanna touch your precious bucks. But I just got one helluva idea."

"If it's another Dallas whorehouse, then I pass," said Kleber. Earlier in the spring, the three had motored to neighboring Dallas in response to T.J.'s exclusive tip that a spectacular new brothel had opened. Always the first to hear such bulletins, T.J. insisted that a live combo played, that the girls wore evening gowns and had pussies full of penicillin, that cocktails were served (a powerful lure in Baptist-parched Texas), and that during the "grand opening," a quickie could be negotiated for three bucks. Kleber and Mack doubted that such extravagant economy existed, but as T.J. had always been the pepper in their stew, they accepted. Trouble was, once in Dallas, the Hotel Queen could not be found. T.J. insisted it was smack in the heart of downtown, but endless circles resulted in nothing but the loss of a quarter tank of gasoline.

Then T.J. espied a nigger in a doorway. He wore a purple shirt and a jockey cap, clearly a dude who knew what was what. Boldly, T.J. rocketed over and asked directions. Then he brought the nigger to the car, invited him in, and said, "This here's Chigger. He's been there and he says it's paradise." Snapping his fingers, making quick sharp moans that approximated sexual rapture, Chigger guided Kleber's De Soto to a dark side street in a warehouse district. "The way it works, boys," said Chigger, "is I have to collect five dollahs each—up front. Then I goes inside and shows the boss lady the green and she'll know you gentlemums is trustworthy customers with *hard* money." Chigger paused for an unarriving laugh. He beckoned everybody close for a beery whisper. "I heah they gots a new gal in tonight only. From *Hollywood*. Usually sells her ass for ten dollahs—and that only buys a forget. But seein' as how Chigger's vouchin' for you, she just might come down to five." Chigger fanned his face like fire was near.

"Wow!" yelped T.J.

Ever inquisitive, Kleber asked, "What's a *forget?*"

Chigger grinned and showed gaps in his teeth that equaled the gold crowns. "Get on, Get off, Get dressed, Get out. Four *Gets.*" Uproarious fellowship.

Certifiably inflamed, T.J. thrust out his five dollars and coaxed similar contributions from his less passionate friends. The Three Princes watched as Chigger disappeared into the doorway of a gloomy, forbidding structure. And they waited, each confronting separate demons: Kleber's of getting caught, Mack's over inability to perform in copulatory debut, T.J.'s of popping off before even the first of the four gets could be realized. Five minutes became ten, twenty became forty, and T.J. was booted out of the car to see what happened. He went into the dark building and soon returned, sheepish anger writ large. "Well, we got screwed all right," he said. "That nigger took off." The building had long ago been abandoned. Chigger, fifteen naïve dollars in his pocket, had simply bolted up a stairway, slipped out an open window at the second-floor landing, and, presumably, danced across adjoining rooftops to windfall security in nearest niggertown.

Thereupon T.J. swore a vendetta that only began with murder, but by the time the Three Princes reached the city limits of Fort Worth, they were laughing tears unshed since childhood. It was to become a memory as hilarious as the time when, at twelve years of age, they attended a Boy Scout encampment at Lawton, Oklahoma, the purpose being to watch a regionally famous Passion Play of Easter Week. But on the night before Christ was nailed to the cross, T.J. led his comrades into a nearby off-limits wilderness where dwindling herds of buffalo lived under federal protection. Armed with slingshots, creeping on their bellies like Choctaw scouts, the boys searched in vain for the great beasts. They encountered numerous horned frogs, armadillos, slithery and squishy things, and prickly bushes that tore their hands and clothes—but nothing resembling the noble target of red men. Tired, spewing curses as forbidden as the territory, T.J. stood and fired his pebble at a nearby clump of cedar. Emitting a howl, it rose up and up and up to immense proportions. "I got one!" yelled the hunter at his hastily exiting buddies, Kleber and Mack fleeing in panic. "Wait up!" cried T.J. The others neither waited nor looked back, not until they heard a scream of authentic terror. The great beast was lumbering toward their fallen friend, who was sprawled on all fours and tangled in a bush. "He's gonna eat me!" squealed T.J. *"Do something!"* Paralyzed, all the others could do was bear witness as the buffalo knelt, extended an enormous snout toward the face of their obviously doomed best friend, and unrolled a fire-hose tongue.

For a full minute, which, by T.J.'s calculation and later telling of the tale, became at minimum the rest of the night, the buffalo calmly licked the little boy until, apparently content, it ambled away, squatted, and transformed once more into a slumbering clump of cedar. For years thereafter, T.J. would contend he reached sexual climax—his first—courtesy of a buffalo tongue. And though his currency was usually counterfeit when spent on veracity, T.J.'s rape-by-bison was too wonderful to disbelieve.

The thing about T.J. was that he led the parade. He was jester, always first, first to dump Brilliantine on his hair and slick it back into a duck tail (only outside prim Texas was the fashion called duck's ass), first to shave it all off save a Mohawk stripe down the middle of his bald head, first to paint the names of favored girls in white poster paint on his jean jacket (a fad that swept the city), first to steal the ornamental hood ring from a '48 Buick and drape it around the wrist of his then beloved.

By instinct, T.J. was enormously appealing. He was music and laughter, he was just over the fence of propriety where most everyone would secretly like to venture—if only for a look around. He was cocky, childish, usually in trouble but generally able to talk his way free, a good actor, funny, and *likable*. Kleber was smarter and Mack was stronger, but T.J. was the one about whom tales were told.

Thus did it come to pass on this empty night when T.J. floated an alternative to the gloom of stagnation, his friends listened. "Here's what we can do," said T.J. "We'll drive out the Weatherford Highway . . . and we'll buy a couple of pints . . . and we'll go to my uncle's old rent house. . . . It's deserted. . . . Nobody's been there for years. . . . May be haunted . . . !"

"And do what?" wondered Kleber. "Chase cows?"

"Well I dunno, *yet*," honestly answered the importuner. "Tell dirty jokes. Arm wrestle. Stand on our heads and jack off. Hell, the night is what a man makes out of it. At least we'll be together."

Mack began to demur; his aunt, with whom he lived, would not approve a late ramble without prior permission.

"Come on," scoffed T.J. "You're free, white, and eighteen. You graduate tomorrow. That old lady's not gonna whip your ass because you stayed out late on this night—of all nights." To the dare, Mack surrendered. On a football field he gave orders. But in the lifelong game of friendship with the other two, he was subservient. They were the only family he had. Kleber's first instinct was, similarly, to refuse. Feeling betrayed by the weather, by Lisa, by the grumpy gods who spoil the fates of young men, he shrugged. "Okay. Why the hell not."

When she reached the asphalt road, Laurie washed her feet in rain water, put on tennis shoes, and stepped briskly toward Weatherford. The night had gentled; a sprinkling of stars struggled through misty banks of clouds. That's a good sign, she told herself in encouragement. Then lights appeared at her back, faint as a candle's last pulse. Laurie put aside the impulse to hide. I'm not doin' anything wrong, she thought. It's a free country.

The lights came near and Laurie sidestepped to the shoulder, looking off toward a plowed field on her right as if inspecting the crop. Out of the corner of her eye she saw a baker's van pass on by. Her heart steadied. The night belonged to her again. But when Laurie reached the summit of a little hill down the road, the baker's van was waiting, lights on yellow park, motor idling smoothly with little puffs of blue smoke burping from the tailpipe.

She stopped.

"Hey," said a man's voice. The driver had the truck window rolled down and his head sticking out. "Need any help?"

Laurie shook her head.

"Car trouble?" inquired the man. He started backing his van toward her.

Without answering, Laurie crossed the road and continued along the other side, pretending she had no time for chitchat. But the van stayed even with her, moving forward, stopping like a hound dog. "Bad weather comin' in," said the man. "Where you headed this time o' night?" His voice was pleasant. He wasn't giving orders, just telling things. Laurie risked a side-glance peek and saw a friendly fellow, about thirty, with a ruddy face and a clean pressed white rodeo shirt with pearl buttons. He looked sort of like her daddy.

"Goin' to Weatherford," she finally said, not breaking stride.

"Well so am I. But you can't get through up yonder. Crick washed out the bridge. You got to double back and detour around that Assembly of God church." Trying to look grateful, Laurie nodded, forced to stop and reconsider. At this inopportune moment, the rains recommenced, fat drops splattering her mama's blue coat like heavy tears.

"You just get in this van and ride with me to Weatherford," insisted the man. "You're gonna catch pneumonia, otherwise." He opened the door and the seduction of warmth, music, and a kind-seeming host lured her within.

"What's your name?" said the man, whose words up close came wrapped in the smell of beer.

"Laurie, sir."

"That's a pretty name. I'm Butch. How old are you, Laurie?"

"Twenty-two," lied Laurie, holding her breath.

"That's real good. Least you ain't jail bait," laughed Butch, stepping on the gas pedal hard and fiddling with the radio dial until he found some music that pleased him. It was some old woman with a bad cold and she was warning, "Your cheatin' heart will tell on you . . ." Butch turned sharply off the asphalt road onto a dirt feeder, then another, and another, slipping and sliding in the mud while great sheets of worsening rain swept across the windshield like the sea crashing over rocks. For a time, Laurie kept her bearings, having wandered these melancholy parts by the light of many days. But soon she was lost, and Weatherford and Elizabeth Taylor did not seem one bit closer. She started to feel uncomfortable. Butch had a cooler of beer and he drank heavily, shrugging suit-yourself when Laurie declined, pouring suds down his throat, stacking empties neatly between his thighs until they fell on the floor, rolling with every turn and clanging like church bells. Soon his chin was wet with foam and he turned up the music to drown out the rain.

Suddenly Butch slammed the brakes and brought his van to a shuddering stop. "Well, damn," he swore, mashing the light switch and turning the world dark except for a weak, eerie green-yellow glow from the dashboard. "I can't see shit, honey bunch. We best just set a spell and wait this'n out." He swallowed two more beers, belched, and stuck the dead soldiers between his legs.

"Why hell, this ain't much, Laurie," said Butch, mushy with beer. He sent a caterpillar arm creeping across the seat back and it fastened on Laurie's shoulder. "Ever been in a tornado? Well, I was. One time over to Midlothian, me and this ole gal was havin' a party. We heard the rain and the wind commence to kick up, but we was so *busy,* if you know what I mean, we— Damn it's hot in this truck. I'm takin' my shirt off, Laurie, so's it won't sweat out the armpits. . . . Anyhoo, the next mornin' I says, 'Thanks for the merry-go-round ride, sweet thang,' and I walk outside, and I'll go to hell in a hand basket if half the roof of her neighbor's house ain't flat out *gone!* And just down the road, I see fence posts with straw stuck in 'em about half an inch deep. I mean, the winds was so strong the night before they blew straw into wood. *Imbedded it!* And there me and that ole gal had been the whole night, fuckin' up a storm so to speak."

At the memory, Butch laughed raucously. He tried to pull Laurie around by the shoulders to face him. She resisted.

"I'd better be gettin' on home," Laurie said tentatively. "I do believe it's slackin' up." Laurie touched the door handle, but Butch covered her hand quicker than a shell on a pea at the carnival.

"Some ole boy waitin' for you in Weatherford?" asked Butch.

"Nossir. I'm just goin' to the picture show."

"Well, I wouldn't lie, Laurie. That's the *biggest* sin. 'Fess up. Some kicker's waitin' for you, all steamed up . . . got his hand in his pocket right now. Feelin' some little ole pecker 'bout as big as my thumb. But you sure like it, don't you, Laurie?"

Laurie wondered what to do. Life had never placed her in a corner quite so imperiled. All she could summon was a remembered maternal order from SuBeth. Always be polite to elders. *Always*. "Well, I sure thank you," she said, her voice curtsying. "I just remembered Mama lives over there, so I'm gonna forget about the picture show and make a run for home."

Butch shook his head. He seized the girl's neck, yanked her head toward him, forced Laurie's face into the rough mat of chest hair, thence down into a patch of sweaty smooth belly flesh, burying her finally in the crotch of his jeans. Somehow he also managed to tear open the buttons and free his penis. Bereft of underwear, it rose swiftly, curving and throbbing like the tail of a mean dog. "Kiss me, Laurie," commanded Butch, with one hand squeezing the back of her neck and the other cupping his testicles and smothering her nose. "Just kiss me down there one time."

Laurie wriggled and yelled and flailed in despair, thinking one solution would be to bite Butch's pee-pee but that would be more revolting than kissing it. Then she saw the empty beer bottles on the floor. She clamped one in her hand and whopped the molester's elbow moderately hard. Lucky for her, she hit the funny bone. With a howl, Butch raised Laurie's head and started out to choke her. But she reached behind her back, located the door handle, and tumbled out backward, assisted by a slap on the mouth from Butch the Rejected. Landing in a pond of mud water, Laurie rolled and splashed, hearing Butch's farewell: "Piss on you and piss on all prick-teasers!" He slammed the van into gear and roared off, tires throwing mud like a gravedigger's spade.

Laurie ran, stumbling, sobbing, daring to look back over her shoulder only once for the reassuring sight of Butch's red taillights disappearing down the road. Then she sat down on a fallen limb and wept. The back of Mama's pink dress was ripped to the waist. The stolen money was gone. The old woman on the cameo ring looked like she couldn't wait to tell on her. Lifting her face to the night, Laurie let hard rain wash away the mud. But when she was clean she still felt dirty.

CHAPTER THREE

Not for many years had T.J. ventured to his uncle's abandoned farmhouse, and never by dark of night while half drunk in a rainstorm. But hazards did not hinder the night's intent. Gleefully he maneuvered his jeep through a maze of squishy country lanes, bellowing "Coming In on a Wing and a Prayer" in liquored tenor, triumphantly depositing his dazed friends beside a sagging barbed-wire gate that protected ten acres of scrubland. Set back about a hundred feet, seen poorly through sheets of rain, sat a squat two-room shanty built when Grover Cleveland was President and seemingly forgotten since.

Beside the house creaked a windmill whose slats had been abducted by the winds of the decades. What was left spun in clattery, gapped-tooth welcome. T.J. got out and shined a flashlight at the flotsam of unremembered lives—an overturned cotton wagon with wheels paralyzed by rust, a jumble of farm tools squeezed by wild grape vines, a child's tricycle stripped naked of paint and now the same sad cobweb color as the house.

He raced to the house and yanked the screen door handle. It thereupon shattered. T.J. sailed the crumbling frame toward a collapsed shed where, he remembered, once lived a sway-backed, ill-tempered mare named Cleopatra. "Daddy put me up on that horse when I was one year old," said T.J. "It's the first Kodak picture they ever took of me. I looked about ready to shit." He was stalling, not uttering but nonetheless wrestling with the apprehension shared by Kleber and Mack on the threshold of a long dead house. "Well," he said, finding bravado somewhere, "let's see what's what." Inside was the dank smell of newspapers mildewing in a garage but no discernible ghosts. Everybody got busy. Mack found candle stubs in a kitchen cupboard that coaxed the modest glow of buttered toast, and Kleber determined that the rusted tin-pipe chimney had enough draw to accommodate a fire of scrap boards. T.J. located an army blanket and a couple of shredded quilts. He prepared the party, setting out two fifths of cheap bourbon, three pints of gin, a few bottles of Dr. Pepper, a bag of corn chips, and several moon pies.

They shucked their wet clothes, spread jeans and polo shirts before the fire, wrapped themselves in scraps of quilt. T.J. uncapped the first fifth of bourbon, drank deeply with a grimace and a grin, cried "Yeow!" and passed it on. "Eat a Frito, then drink, and it'll be Communion," he said, proceeding to blaspheme further with a hoary reminiscence about alleged ravishing of a choir leader's daughter on Methodist retreat. Pretty soon clothes were dry, bodies warm, and gullets burning. When the bottle was drained, T.J. tossed it onto the fire, where flames ate away the label. The jug did a little dance and exploded into pieces like a stale store-bought pie. The sacrifice seemed enormously funny to the celebrants.

"Hey," said T.J., widening his role as social director, "I know what let's do. Let's each tell the best piece of ass we ever got." He jumped up, losing his quilt, grasping his pecker like it was a .45 ready to fire. Kleber envied the way T.J. handled nudity, which was to think nothing of it. He also wondered how T.J. maintained such a solid, compact physique, seeing as how he did no exercise more strenuous than beating off. No matter how many hernia-threatening weights Kleber lifted, the only muscles that flexed were in his head. "Well, that's easy for you," taunted Kleber. "Madame Thumb and her Four Daughters." He fell back laughing.

"How else do you get your heart started in the morning?" said T.J. He then demanded a response to an urgent matter, i.e., was it true that Sandra Locher blew the whole football team?

Mack shrugged, a gunfighter unwilling to deny or confirm his legend. But his face reddened and the source was not the fire. Seeing the discontent, Kleber delivered a diverting sermonette: "He who gets the most—tells the least. And vice versa."

"Bullshit," pronounced T.J. "Tellin' is more fun than doin'." He passed a fresh bottle around, sending Dr. Pepper as chaser.

"The *best*," began Mack haltingly, surprising everybody. "The *best* was in New Orleans. Last winter. When they invited me down to look at Tulane. I told you guys about it, didn't I?" The others shook their heads. Kleber was surprised, as Mack rarely talked about anything except game scores. The athlete told his story with difficulty but with an edge of pride. "Well, I went to the French Quarter that night and I found a place called the Monkey Bar. Real dark. Like a jungle. They didn't even ask for ID. So this girl comes up and sits on the next stool. Real pretty. Smelled like gardenias . . ."

"Wow," murmured T.J. "So what happened?"

"So we talked."

"About *what?*"

"Hush, T.J. Let Mack tell the story."

"Then she said excuse me. Said she'd be right back. Turned out they had a floor show; I didn't know that. Everything went dark red. There was a drum roll and this stripper came out. She had on a long sparkly evening gown. A parrot flew in from somewhere and unfastened her dress at the back of her neck."

"Jesus," breathed T.J. heavily. "Could you see her tits?"

"Yeah. And guess who it was? The *same* girl I was talkin' to. She was that stripper up there on the stage. She took off everything except a transparent G-string, they call it. . . . Then, when it was over, she came back to the bar and we talked some more, and—well, one thing led to another and I got up my courage and invited her to my hotel room. I was staying just down the street. She wanted cab fare, so I gave her ten dollars and my room key. . . . That's . . . that's about it . . ."

"Hold 'er, Newt," yelled T.J. "What the fuck happened?"

"She came on up about two a.m. and . . . well, you wanted to know the *best*." Mack smiled and only shook his head when T.J. demanded further details.

T.J. turned to Kleber and poked him on the arm. "Your turn." Kleber shook his head. "I couldn't possibly pick out the *best*," he lied. "Besides, I'm saving the choicest pieces for my memoirs. You'll have to pay someday to read my sex life." He stood up unsteadily, getting dressed and swallowing hard, trying to wash away the awful taste of whiskey and gin that was at war in his pipes. "Where the hell are we?" he asked.

"Pal, you're really bombed," said T.J. with delight. He wanted everybody to get drunk. He played like he was dialing an imaginary telephone. "Hello, Associated Press? Mr. Everything is drunk as a skunk."

"Where are we?" repeated Kleber.

"In T.J.'s castle," answered Mack, giggling.

" 'Tain't right," corrected T.J. "You're in my Uncle Bun's estate—which is for sale at the giveaway price of only one hunnerd bucks an acre. The palace here comes free . . . just like that whore I fucked in Nuevo Laredo last summer. Conchita sat there in my lap, with her tongue in my ear, and she says, 'Fuckee for love, honee. Free fuckee for love. Only ten dollars for room.' " As punctuation, T.J. attempted a Mexican hat dance around the remaining bottles, but his feet tangled and he fell, rolling like a log in a swift river.

"Uncle B-b-bun?" echoed Mack, stuttering on purpose, like he did for real until he was ten, that being the point in life when his body began to fill, when muscles gave social authority that growing up in custody of an eccentric old maid aunt had not. The day he pinned both Kleber and T.J. to the earth of Cloverdale Avenue was the day he stopped stammering.

"You got it," answered T.J. "Uncle Bun. Meanest sumbitch from here to El Paso. Looks like Roy Rogers and talks like Humphrey Bogart. He can cuss seventeen minutes without repeatin' himself. He thinks Gary Cooper's a little tooty-fruity. Been married 'bout eight times." T.J. was given to flamboyant portraits.

"*Eight* times?" asked Kleber, trying desperately not to throw up, trying to walk briskly about the room in search of intestinal order.

"Well, maybe only five or six. One of 'em was a beautician from Amarillo. Built like a brick shithouse. Uncle Bun came home one night unexpected and caught her and a goat roper in bed. Shot 'em both."

"*Dead?*" wondered Mack, who, like Kleber, bit on T.J.'s gold coins to determine their worth.

"Bun said they planted 'em, so I'd guess they was reasonably departed."

"What happened to Uncle Bun?" asked Kleber.

"Justifiable homicide," explained T.J. "Texas law gives a man the right to shoot his wife if he catches her fuckin' somebody else."

"Was there a trial?" inquired Kleber, standing now at the hole where the front door once hung and gratefully gulping moist night air.

Cracks of lightning were skittering across the prairie. The winds were reborn and howled like wolves.

"Course not," said T.J. "Uncle Bun said some people just need killin' and the jury bought it."

"Well, where's he now?" asked Kleber, feeling better and returning to the fire. He declined T.J.'s offer of more drink, being as how the world was still spinning severely.

"I dunno. Off rodeoin', probably," said T.J. "Or then again he could be in Hollywood shacked up with Linda Darnell. Him and Daddy said they'd give me ten percent commission if I sold this piece-of-shit land to some sucker. One thousand bucks. You want it?"

"I repeat," said Kleber. "Where are we? *Exactly.*"

"Jay-zuss, don't you hear anything, Mr. President? We're at Bun's."

"Listen, idiot, I know *whose* house. I wanna know *where* this property is. Exactly."

"Oh. Well, eighteen miles west of Forth Worth out Highway 80, turn left at the Burma Shave sign, the one that reads: 'Don't stick your arm or elbow out too far, it might go home in another car,' 'bout two miles south of that, more or less, then 'bout six jiggy-jag turns—and presto, here we are."

Nodding, Kleber assembled the information in his fogged cognition. Then he smiled in discovery. "Then I am pleased to inform Mr. and Mrs. America and all the ships at sea that we are sitting, standing, or, in Mack's case, lying flat on the very spot where Quanah Parker himself once walked. In fact, there was probably one helluva battle right here about a hundred years ago."

"Who's that?" asked T.J.

With concentrational difficulty and gaps of silence and burps—attributable to the mélange of evil spirits being assimilated by his unprepared liver—Kleber delivered a passionate eulogy for a personal hero. Quanah Parker, last war chief of the Comanches, was the half-breed son of a feared warrior named Nocone and his squaw, Cynthia Ann Parker, a white woman who had been kidnapped at the age of nine by the nomadic tribe.

"Quanah was a great man," said Kleber. "Greater than Geronimo or Cochise or Uncle Bun. The Comanches used to control all of this land, before there was an America, even, all the way from Mexico up into Texas and Oklahoma and Kansas and west clear over to Arizona.

They never stayed in one place very long. They were always moving, the best horsemen in history. And everybody was scared of them."

Disinterested, T.J. tried to end the solemn intonation. Kleber was peeing on the campfire. "Let's have a toast," he intruded. "Let's drink to us—the Three Princes—to Kleber and all the fuckin' stories he's gonna write, and to Mack and all the ass he's gonna stomp while makin' All America, and let's drink to me, Thomas Jeremiah Luther, to the million bucks he's gonna have in the sock before he's twenty-five." T.J. hoisted a pint of Schenley's.

"Wait, lemme finish," said Kleber doggedly. "There's more."

"What is this?" said T.J. "Kiss Your Favorite Indian Week? We're havin' a party. It ain't Texas history class."

"After the Civil War," continued Kleber, "the U.S. cavalry bottled Quanah up in this last little pocket of land." He hiccupped. "You see, the Comanches had dwindled down from tens of thousands of square miles of territory and were squeezed into this pissant piece of Texas. Quanah fought like hell. He got whipped and he lost most of his best men, but he regrouped and fought again. And again. And it finally came down to making a choice—either sacrifice his tribe, and they would have died for him, every last man, woman, and child—or make a deal with the government."

"So what'd he do?" demanded T.J.

"He surrendered."

"That figures," said T.J. "Fuckin' cowards, them Indians."

"No, listen," said Kleber. "He made peace by surrendering. And he negotiated about a million acres of land up in Oklahoma as a reservation for his people. And then, now here comes the good part, he leased back some of the land to the white men and they struck oil and ran cattle and made old Quanah rich. He was the only chief to go out in dignity. He became a pal of Teddy Roosevelt. He was the only Indian chief who ever slept in the White House."

"Bet they locked up the silverware," said T.J.

"Once Teddy went down to Oklahoma and went wolf hunting with Quanah. The old boy died a millionaire, with a big black jeweled coach and a mansion and about twenty wives."

"*Twenty wives!*" exclaimed T.J., finally locating a point of interest.

"Can't you get your mind off your dick for one minute?" said Kleber.

"No wonder the fucker sold out his people," shot back T.J.

"Why bother?" sighed Kleber. "I can't talk to Priapus."

"To what?"

"Priapus. A Greek god who had an eternal erection. There's a real disease called priapism."

"Well, how do you catch it?"

"You've already got it, pal."

T.J. snorted. "How come you told that boring story?"

"Because I wanted to, asshole. The point is that Quanah had to make a moral decision. He was at the crossroads. Every man gets there, sooner or later. Quanah could have got the shit shot outta him and his people. But he was wise. He died in glory. In bed. They named a town and a railroad after him. He's in the history books. He's famous for all time."

T.J. rolled that around in his head a minute. He nodded slowly. "I can buy that," he finally said. "I'm gonna be famous. I'm gonna ride down the street in a convertible and people are gonna wave at me. I intend to be so famous that when the newspapers print T.J., they won't even have to add the last name. I'm gonna have so much money that I won't even ask the price of the new Cadillacs."

Mack laughed. He applauded. "I like your story, Kleber," he said.

Kleber smiled gratefully. He threw an arm around the athlete's massive shoulders. It was like clasping a sequoia trunk. "Thanks. Okay, let's drink that toast. To the Three Princes. To muscles . . ." He pointed at Mack. "To brains . . ." He knocked on his own head. He looked quizzically at T.J.

"And to money and pussy," finished T.J. for him. "Of which yours truly will never get enough."

They drank with ceremony, passing the Old Crow with care, arms linked. It was then an enormous finger of lightning split the shed outside. A moment later they heard the cries. Somewhere in the storm, somewhere near, a woman in absolute terror was screaming.

The winds of fury had punished Laurie like an abusing parent. Her mama's pale blue coat snagged on a bramble bush, tore from her shoulders, whooshed into the skies. She ran after it, was beaten down by blinding rain and sprays of gravel and twigs that stung her face. The storm was awesome, the sky streaked by rips of jagged white and orange, gusts so powerful that Laurie had to hold her pink dress with both hands to keep it from being sucked into a whirlwind. Ahead a grove of pecan trees held out shelter, but as she approached, a new fork of lightning pierced a trunk not thirty feet away with acrid bursts of fire and steam. She ran this way and that, lost, hopelessly lost, prayers tumbling from her lips, oaths to Jesus and Elizabeth Taylor that never *ever* again would she take her mama's dress or any potential stepfather's five dollars. Shadowy, milling shapes loomed ahead, and, thinking them to be fellow refugees, she ran headlong into a herd of terrified Hereford cattle, forelegs bloodied from fences trampled in panic. She reversed direction and encountered a nearby creek that normally could have been skipped across. Tonight it was a churning river. For miles Laurie ran, throat raw, lungs burning, until, mercifully, in the far distance, materialized soft creamy light smiling in welcome through the jagged windows of a tumbledown shack.

When her screams were heard, Mack ran into the storm. Laurie saw him and fell against his body, sobbing and gasping. "It's okay," he said softly. "You're gonna be fine." He carried her inside, where Kleber washed the girl's face and legs. T.J. toweled her hair. Before long, Laurie was reasonably restored save for a few nicks on her fingers and a serpentine scratch on her shoulder. She arranged the ripped pink dress to cover her breasts but not before T.J. made note of their promise. Boldly he handed her the bottle of whiskey. She had never tasted any before, and though it made her gag, it delivered warmth. On the second swallow she smiled.

"I got lost," she said, still breathing in sharp gasps.

"So did we," said T.J. "What's your name, hon?"

"Laurie," she said. "What's yours?"

"Prince," lied T.J. easily, shooting the others a follow-me glance. Of all the aliases T.J. might have selected, none worked quicker magic. Laurie fairly glowed.

"Really?" she said. "Your name is really Prince?"

"Yes, ma'm." He bowed obediently.

"Prince *what?*" cried Laurie.

"Whatever prince you desire. At your service. Rescue from storms our specialty." When he wanted to, T.J. was as golden and gallant as Lancelot. And at this moment he sure wanted to.

Laurie turned to meet the others. "I'm T-t-tom," said Mack, uncomfortable player in T.J.'s charade.

"And I'm K-ken," stammered Kleber.

Speechless, Laurie stared in delight, equating rescue with the happy ending to an adventure in which Butch and the storm were the forces of evil. She was, moreover, right fuzzed by the bottle Prince kept shoving under her nose. Then they all sat down beside the fire, giving T.J. the opportunity to snuggle close and rest his knee against Laurie's. She did not stir, a signal interpreted by the Prince of Temptation as proof that all he had to do was walk past a tree and the ripest peach would fall automatically into his grasp.

Suddenly Laurie burst into tears. Reality intruded. "My mama's gonna skin me alive," she wailed. "The wind took her coat and look here, I tore her best dress."

"Well, it looks fine to me," insisted T.J. "Nothin' wrong that a little rinsin' out won't fix." He draped a cautious arm about her tremulous shoulders. "Just slip her off and Tom'll run outside and wash it— good as new. Right, Tom?" Mack nodded uneasily.

Laurie wouldn't have it. "I can't," she whispered.

"Course you can," encouraged T.J. "Us three came in here soppin' wet, and we stripped off and now our clothes are dry. . . ."

Laurie shook her head unbudgingly.

"Oh, I know," suggested T.J. "You're worried about us lookin'. . . . We'll go over there in the next room and turn our backs and close our eyes, and you can cover up with this blanket. Okay?"

Laurie said nosiree, and held out her hand before the fire, so that the purloined ring sparkled in the waltz of golden light. "That's real pretty," said T.J. But all his compliment did was infect the girl with fresh guilt and another gush of tears. T.J. threw a "do something, dammit" look at Kleber, who decided to help the seducer.

"It is beautiful," said Kleber. "Maybe it got you through the storm." He leaned over to peer at the cameo, at the pale green old woman with the long nose and neck. "Suppose it's charmed? Maybe it's got powers."

"You think so?" said Laurie, so enamored of the romantic suggestion that T.J. dispatched a fervent blessing to Kleber for thinking up dip-shit fairy-tale talk.

"Why not? I'd say it's at least a thousand years old. I'd say there's a charm passed down through the centuries that protects whoever wears it. Good Queen Proboscis here is powerful."

"Queen *what?*" muttered T.J.

"Queen Proboscis. Fancy for nose. Famous old Celt—royal house."

Laurie was thrilled at Kleber's gallantry. He made a courtier's sweeping bow and kissed the ring. But he stumbled and fell against T.J., causing the whiskey bottle to spill on the girl's bodice. Momentarily Laurie looked like she was going to bawl again but this time she only laughed. "Well, I guess this dress *is* due for a wash," she said. While the three boys faced the wall of the adjoining kitchen, Laurie disrobed and wrapped her slim body in the army blanket. Promptly T.J. hurried outside, swished the torn and smelly gown in a bucket of mineral-hard well water, and had it drying before the fire in three minutes flat.

"Life is perfect," he purred, feeding Laurie a moon pie and a Dr. Pepper, having cleverly enhanced the soda pop with three inches of gin. As she drank it down, T.J. winked at his friends. The night was once again under control. Not quite. Abruptly Laurie staggered up, swayed, looked goofy, and proclaimed, "I gotta get home."

"Whoa, hoss," disagreed T.J. "Just set a spell. Your dress ain't half dry. Besides, we'll all be movin' out before long and we'll drop you at the front door."

Laurie blinked her eyes like they were out of focus. "You boys live around here?" she asked.

"Naw. Dallas," answered T.J., lying so adroitly that Kleber whistled under his breath. "Where the girls aren't near as pretty as you, Laurie. We was on our way to Lubbock for the church meeting when the rains hit. Any port in a storm."

Laurie was radiant once more. "I'm pretty?" she said.

"Pretty as a princess," said the fraudulent prince with true-sounding tenderness.

Kleber noticed a torn scrap of newsprint on the floor. The picture show advertisement of Elizabeth Taylor had fallen out of Laurie's bodice. He glanced at it and produced another helpful compliment. "For a minute I thought it was you," he said, handing the treasure back. T.J. grabbed a look. "Well, it is you, ain't it, Laurie?" The Prince of Temptation was learning the lessons of flattery.

"Don't tease me," the girl said. "That's Miss Elizabeth Taylor."

"She's okay," agreed T.J. "But you beat her hands down in the beauty department." He floated a feathery arm about her waist and the blanket fell a little, enough to reveal custard-smooth shoulders. Kleber and Mack did not have to be told it was time to withdraw. Discreetly they tiptoed into the adjoining room, where it was cold and dank. They squatted on warped, rotting planks to wait out the latest notch on T.J.'s gun belt.

"You think he's gonna make out?" whispered Mack uneasily.

"Yeah. And then we'll have to hear about it fifteen hundred times."

Mack groaned and hugged his stomach. "I think . . . I'm sick. I think . . . I'm gonna throw up."

"Then go outside," hissed Kleber, scooting hurriedly along the floor on his butt. He leaned against the wall and his hands discovered a peephole. Let it be said that, under normal circumstance, Kleber Cantrell was not the sort of youth who would press a hungry eye to a knotted wallboard and spy on his buddy. Drink and darkness have tampered with many a good man's morality, however, and with but a minor lance of shame, the Prince of Power flopped on his stomach and grew transfixed. Which is to say he got an erection and the shudders simultaneously.

From somewhere in a remote corner, Mack intruded with a small voice. "I'm dizzy."

Kleber hushed him, witness to something more important, a tableau of living flesh that nothing in the dog-eared pages of Erskine Caldwell's prose had prepared him for. In fact, he hardly dared breathe for fear of shattering the spell. In the beginning, it was very beautiful. Silhouetted against the fire, indigo lovers knelt and faced one another. With care and tenderness, T.J. peeled the blanket away, murmuring honey words in Laurie's ear, making her laugh and toss her head back where it caught a splash of firelight. Her rain-washed hair gleamed and brushed the floor. Behind his peephole, Kleber felt envy. T.J. knew exactly what he was doing. The bastard hadn't been lying all these years. He cupped her face in his hands and gazed upon Laurie as if she were the woman for whom knights jousted and troubadours sang. And when they kissed, damned if a twist of wood didn't pop and shower sparks, just like T.J. was a wizard who evoked magic.

Only when he tried to ease her down onto the dirty blanket did Laurie begin to struggle. She tried to push him away, but T.J. met the challenge. It was like Problem 27 Solved in the handbook of seduction.

Grabbing the bottle, he gulped a mouthful of whiskey and passed it from his lips to hers, anticipating that she would cough and dribble. During the ensuing diversion, the Prince of Temptation turned whirlwind. In one astonishing fluid motion, he pulled off Laurie's panties, unclasped her bra, wriggled out of his own jeans, and kissed every square inch of flesh twixt forehead and belly button about forty-seven times.

Just when Kleber was thinking about unfastening his own trousers to relieve the pressure, Mack spoiled things. His nausea temporarily under control, the Prince of Charms chose the incredibly inopportune moment to plop down and plead, "I gotta get home."

"Shh," pleaded Kleber.

"Listen, I gotta tell you something."

"Save it."

"I'm scared."

"Then go outside. Don't fuck things up for T.J."

In the darkness, Mack squirmed and festered. "Kleber, please listen. That girl in New Orleans I told y'all about . . ."

"Can't it wait?"

"It didn't happen that way, K. Oh, I *did* wanna fuck her, and I *did* give her the key to my hotel room and ten dollars—but all I did was wait. I took six showers and brushed my teeth until sunrise. She never came. . . ."

"That's the saddest story I ever heard." Kleber sounded flip but he heard the anguish in his big friend's voice.

"Don't tell T.J."

"I promise. Your secret's safe. Now shhhhh." For a troublesome moment, Kleber wondered why Mack needed to make confession but, sin being relative, quickly returned to the knothole. This time the spectacle was marred by a clamp of guilt that had come to his neck, less from what he saw and more from the proximity of Mack, lying beside him now, breathing as heavily as the players in the other room. Voyeurism is best accomplished alone.

The fire blazed and T.J. hovered over Laurie, both in shimmering cloaks of gold. His sex brushed her flesh. She appeared not quite conquered. "No," she was saying. "Please, Prince."

"Oh, yes," murmured T.J. "You want to, Princess. . . . You have to. . . . You're so beautiful, Laurie. . . . I love you, Princess. . . ."

"Love?" said Laurie, twisting her face into a puzzle. She tried to sit up but T.J. pressed her back to the pallet.

"You'n me are gonna love each other, Laurie," he said. And with a thrust that startled the watchers as much as the intended, the Prince of Temptation plunged into darkness, tenderness abandoned, pumping until his face flushed scarlet and sweat popped out in crystal beads on his brow. Laurie cried out in pain but T.J. perceived her protest as passion. He fucked her ruthlessly, long past the moment when Laurie stopped screaming and went limp in his embrace. When he climaxed, T.J. yahooed and immediately took seconds, squeezing the girl's neck hard enough to leave fingerprints. Then he disengaged, ran to the wall and banged it with his fist. "Hey, you guys! She wants *more*. Come and get it!"

With studied casualness, like Sunday visitors who just happened to be in the neighborhood, Kleber and Mack drifted in. Both were struggling with the same private and grave concern: to screw or not to screw. And does the first time show? Kleber elected to glance at Laurie as if asked to buy shopworn merchandise. He pronounced the girl to be of no interest to him.

"Are you crazy?" taunted T.J. "You gotta dip yore bread in that gravy while it's still hot! I'm telling you, this one can go all night!"

Well, the way Kleber sized things up, here was a fork in life's highway. Not exactly a Major Moral Crisis, but a crossroads nonetheless. Down that way was possible rapture. Over yonder was failure, probably guilt and mortification. But what the hell, he reasoned. The lady from the paper said I had a blank sheet. Time to write a few lines. A man only regrets the things he *doesn't* do. So he dropped his pants and fell, rather clumsily, grateful that the fire was dying and that Laurie was little more than a shadowy pillow. He was, however, happy that his erection was present and accounted for, and admirable by his own reckoning, of measure more substantial than his predecessor's. He anticipated a cry of approval from the first female to receive it. Roadblock! Before the neophyte lover could ever locate an entrance to the cave of wonder, Kleber exploded, squirting thimblefuls of jism onto Laurie's legs, biting his lip to betray the horror of premature pop. He was forced to stay in the saddle several messy moments thereafter, fabricating moans of a man in the flood path of epic currents. He felt his performance was believable, excepting the curious way Laurie behaved. Or rather *didn't* behave. She did not move. Nor speak. Her flesh was chilled. He was very glad to leave her.

Then T.J. punched Mack's arm and cried, "Next!"

The athlete demurred. "It's gettin' late," he said.

"Course, she ain't the Parrot Girl, but she's got a few tricks up her puss." He tried to guide Mack toward the motionless girl. Kleber caught the panic in Mack's eyes and he understood. He was not the only virgin in the room. "Mack doesn't have to if he doesn't want to," said Kleber kindly.

"I want to," said Mack suddenly, carefully unbuttoning his fly and lowering his great strength onto the absurdly tiny child-woman. He felt for the first time the odd juxtaposition of texture—sweet skin and prickly roughness, the frame of sex. And, like new lovers and old lovers and scared lovers and jaded lovers, the Prince of Charms was forced to enact the charade of ecstasy. But his was not exactly the same embarrassment that smote Kleber. Worse. Mack could not even achieve erection. All he managed was a writhe and a whisper, and a begging at Laurie's ear, "I'm sorry . . . you're so beautiful . . ."

In the guilt of aftermath, Kleber seized his inherent role of leader. He commanded an end to the night. Devils rode him. "Laurie," he said sharply. "Let's be goin' on home, now. You get ready." But T.J. plopped back down on the girl, sprinkling her body with the final drops of whiskey. "Hell, she ain't ready to quit," he insisted. He squeezed her breasts. It was then that Mack grabbed Kleber's arm and implored him to follow. They went to a corner. "Something's wrong," the athlete said. He was deeply troubled. "I'm . . . I'm . . . Look," said Mack. He shined a beam of light on his penis. It was streaked with blood.

"My God," whispered Kleber, reminded that his own crotch was wet and sticky. He tore open his fly. He, too, was bloodied. Well, *of course,* Kleber began to explain. The girl's a cherry. Or *was.* Then T.J. started yelling again. "Hey, wake up, darlin'!" He slapped her face. "Don't pass out on us!"

Kleber grabbed the flashlight and poured light onto Laurie. She was a terrible sight. Her eyes, wide open, no longer violet, had turned ash. The beam crept to her flanks. The only color there was blood. Splotches of red-black stained her body and the blanket. Kleber knelt and put his ear close to her breast. He could not find a heartbeat. He grabbed her wrist. No pulse. He sat beside her a long while, knowing what was necessary to announce but unable to find the words. Finally he said it simply. "I think Laurie's dead."

Mack expelled a little laugh. "How could anybody die from . . . *that?*"

"You're crazy," said T.J. "She's playin' tricks. I oughta kick her ass."

Kleber screamed. "She's dead, *asshole!*"

"She's not!"

"Then you bring her back to life."

Mack ran for the door. "I gotta get some air," he said. But T.J. rocketed across the room and threw an armlock, squeezing until his friend's neck veins bulged. "Nobody's goin' nowhere," commanded T.J. "You listen to me. She's fine. She just blacked out or somethin'. . . . She was just fine when I finished. She was laughin'. . . . You remember that, don't you? If anybody hurt her, it had to be one of you guys."

Mack sagged against the wall. "I didn't do anything." It was true, but he dared not plead his case.

"You probably crushed her, you're so fuckin' big," said T.J.

"Stop it!" demanded Kleber. "Help me. We've got to get her to the hospital."

Mack started to whimper. "Just leave her," he said. "Let's get outta here."

"Are you nuts?" shrieked T.J. "This is my uncle's house. They'll find her. They'll trace us."

"Then *what?*" said Kleber. "Just what the hell do you suggest? It was *your* idea, T.J. *You* got her drunk. *You* fucked her first. She's virgin. You musta torn somethin'. . . ." He broke and backed away from the lifeless girl, smothered by revulsion. They stared at each other in mounting terror.

The Three Princes dressed Laurie in her pink dress and bore her to the jeep. They drove around and about until they finally came to a remote place where nobody seemed to have been, at least not on this tempestuous night. They placed her gently down on a bed of fresh wet oak and sumac leaves, concealed within a canebrake, directly beside a thunderous fork of the Brazos River. T.J. said just throw her in—but Kleber refused.

He placed a veil of weeping willow over her face and directed a moment of silent prayer. Centuries before, he recalled from history books, the great river had been discovered and named by Spanish explorers. Near death from thirst, they interpreted the waters as "Brazos de Dios"—the Arms of God. Kleber did not explain his reasoning to the others. But he felt it was proper to leave choice up to the river. The Arms of God could minister to Laurie—or pull her into a final embrace.

On the drive back to Fort Worth, T.J. buzzed like a fly nobody could swat. He seemed not to realize the enormity of their deed. "Oh, I think she'll wake up," he predicted rather cheerfully. "She just drank too much." Then, a little later, "You know, she probably had a heart attack. Just a little one. Sort of blacked out." And, later, certain destiny. "The river's got her now. Sucked clean under. Gars and gators havin' a little midnight snack. By the time ole Laurie Pie floats into the Gulf of Mexico, won't be enough left to feed a sea gull."

That did it. Kleber reached over and grabbed the wheel. "Can it!" he screamed. He mashed his foot on the brake and threw T.J. against the windshield. The Prince of Temptation spoke not again until his jeep turned onto safe and secure Cloverdale, waiting for her children as if nothing had happened. The block smelled sweet and washed. T.J. had an epitaph. "You gotta admit one thing," he said. "She was some piece of ass. Whoooee!"

"Listen to me," hissed Kleber. "Listen close. Do you know what we just did? Has it soaked in? Do you have one iota in your asshole head what happened tonight? I hope to God that girl is awake by now and home in bed. Let's pray she is. But she might be dead."

"I didn't kill nobody," whimpered T.J.

"Then let's go to the cops and confess and let them divvy up the blame."

"Don't tell anybody," pleaded Mack.

"Shut up, Crawford. Of course I'm not gonna tell anybody. We're all gonna erase the past six hours. If anybody ever asks, we drove over to Dallas and saw a show. We saw, mmmmm, *Sunset Boulevard*." Kleber quickly summarized the plot, finding it ruefully interesting that the film concerned a murdered writer. "Now we're goin' inside and act like nothin' happened. Tomorrow we'll all wake up. *Nothing happened.* Understand? If anybody breaks, then he pulls the switch on all three of us. Now *swear!*"

The Three Princes locked hands and pressed foreheads in a covenant of survival.

During the night, Kleber remembered that they had failed to remove Laurie's ring. The smiling green crone haunted him. But what the hell. She was gone.

Two days thereafter, on the front page of the Sunday paper, splashed joyously across four columns, glowed three faces of promise and ambition and desire. The forecast: PRINCES OF WESTERN HIGH FACE TOMORROW. Most of Clara Eggleston's attendant article had been severely edited. Oh, Clara was annoyed, but resigned by now to suffering flesh stripped from the bones of her journalism. Solace was to be had this Sunday morning not in words but in the beauty of photography. The picture was, she reminded herself, a personal creation. She lovingly cut out the photo and pasted it in her scrapbook. A few days later, realizing that newsprint quickly ages and yellows, vandalizing what by rights should remain forever young, Clara sneaked into the newspaper morgue, stole the original print and negative, and placed them under glass with a frame of silver from Neiman-Marcus.
On the back, impulsively, she wrote a fitting caption, borrowing an homage from T. S. Eliot:

> There will be time,
> There will be time to prepare a face to meet
> the faces that you meet . . .

Clara placed her icon in a dresser drawer, snuggled between soft sweaters and packets of sachet. For months thereafter she inspected the treasure twice daily, upon rising, before retiring, careful not to smudge the glass, always wiping away the kiss prints.
But as time passed, Clara came to look upon the fair countenances of charm, power, and temptation less often, having met a bald and pious widower who sold her an insurance policy, took her to duplicate bridge on Friday nights, bought her suppers at cafeterias, but never, alas, proposed marriage. The picture found its way into a cardboard box, thence to a forgotten corner of Clara's garage, where it rested unseen for almost a quarter century.
On a distant day of remembrance, Clara would hobble on swollen

arthritic ankles to search frantically for the princes under glass. And she would then sell her almost forgotten fantasy for $4,500, it having become the subject of unforeseen worldwide attention. Clara would weep a tear or two, for her juices were nearly dry. Then she would use the windfall profit to prepay a cemetery lot in Greenwood—where Fort Worth's best are planted.

At the rear of that memorable Sunday issue, there appeared minor mention *in re* the fate of another area youngster. Few people noticed it, for the one-paragraph brief saw print only in the early bulldog edition distributed to rural readers.

AREA GIRL REPORTED MISSING

WEATHERFORD, May 21, 1950. A 16-year-old girl, Laurel Jo Killman, has been reported missing by her mother, Mrs. SuBeth Killman. Parker County Deputy Paul Prikow said the youngster disappeared during the recent storms. He said foul play was "not suspected." Mrs. Killman also suffered a broken hip when the trailer in which she was living was blown off its foundation by high winds.

BOOK TWO

꩜꩜꩜꩜꩜꩜꩜꩜꩜꩜꩜꩜꩜꩜꩜꩜꩜꩜꩜꩜꩜꩜꩜꩜꩜꩜꩜꩜꩜꩜꩜꩜꩜꩜꩜꩜

THE
PRINCE
OF
CHARMS

*Remember that the most beautiful things
in the world are the most useless;
peacocks and lilies for instance.*

—John Ruskin

CHAPTER FOUR

Mack was an unwanted and unexpected issue, harvest of the seed from a farm boy out of Iowa planted into a country girl from Texas. His parents, who never married, met by pedestrian collision on the corner of Hollywood Boulevard and Gower Avenue, on an autumn noon in 1932, when both were hurrying to a casting office with hopes of obtaining bit roles in a motion picture entitled *Gold Diggers of 1933*.

Each had come to Los Angeles as members of the migration, the epic tide of hungry, poor, angry, ambitious Americans who washed West, toward the sun, to the edge. The Depression that settled across the land like a medieval plague turned its victims sour and bleak. If a man had a job, and thirty-four million Americans did not, the average weekly wage was seventeen dollars. Twenty thousand businesses went bankrupt in 1932 alone. Sixteen hundred banks collapsed. Oats sold for a dime a bushel, sugar three cents a pound. Just three years before, in 1929, Henry Ford sold 650,000 of his splendid automobiles. In 1932, sales dropped to 55,000—and a third of these were repossessed. Twenty thousand Americans committed suicide. The national mood was perfectly symbolized by murderess Winnie Ruth Judd. She slew two women, dismembered their bodies, and shipped the pieces to California in a rattletrap truck, blood dribbling all the way.

Clyde Blankenship was twenty years old when his modest but hitherto dependable world was ripped from his richly muscled arms. Here was not a youth who floated dreams, for he was born and reared on three score acres of permanence, fertile cornfields near Belle Plaine,

Iowa. The eldest of three brothers (and the fourth generation to till the heartland), he had the no-nonsense accommodation that life intended dominion to be a horse, a plow, a Model A, a Lutheran girl named Hilda, a Sears, Roebuck catalogue, and chicken every Sunday. Clyde was six feet six with hair colored like September corn silk, limbs as strong as cable wire, and was generally acclaimed the best-looking fellow from Cedar Rapids to Waterloo.

On a February dusk in 1932, he arrived home in fine humor, having paid court to Hilda and discussed marriage, only to discover his mother weeping and his brothers red-eyed with grief. The news was that their daddy had accidentally—and fatally—shot himself in the throat while hunting for quail. As there was two feet of snow on the ground, Clyde disbelieved the story. By midnight he learned the truth: the senior Blankenship killed himself in despair and disgrace over inability to meet a $250 bank loan for feed and tools.

After the funeral, Clyde and his brothers stood in line for two days and nights outside the Farmers Mercantile Bank, intending to beg the president for a merciful extension. But once inside, they learned in five minutes that foreclosure was irrevocable, the sum required having been swollen by legal fees, interest charges, and paper shuffling to an impossible $715. By summer, Clyde joined the Iowa Farmers' Union and linked hands with militant brothers to block produce trucks from reaching market. Theirs was a vain attempt to force prices upward. "Stay home! Don't sell!" they screamed, hurling bricks at headlights, wrapping pieces of chains around their arms and looking for faces to smash. The gentle farmland was awash in blood and milk purposely spilled.

Clyde's mother perished of heartbreak. His brothers, assault charges hanging above their leftist heads, took off for Mexico. Hilda married the bank loan officer. And in September 1932, Clyde surrendered, no longer believing Franklin D. Roosevelt's campaign exhortations that life on the farm was going to get better. He packed a Mason jar with Iowa loam and hitchhiked to California. On his first night in Los Angeles, having only thirty-five cents left in his pocket, he went home with a waitress from the bus depot. She was enthusiastic over his sexual possibilities—once he took a bath—but pessimistic over his chances of finding labor. More people were unemployed in the City of the Angels than in Iowa and Kansas combined.

"But the way *you* look, Clyde Blankenship," the waitress said, readying for round number four in a love match but two hours old, "you oughta be in pictures."

That very same year Lureen Adele Hofmeyer left Denton, Texas, possessing nine grades of public education, an unshakable down-home accent that made a two-syllable word out of "said" and "dead," mouse-colored hair dyed Harlow platinum, an envelope pinned to her brassiere containing eighty-five dollars willed by her recently deceased father, and the determination that if Ginger Rogers, a local girl whose ascent to world celebrity began with the winning of an amateur Charleston contest on the stage of the Majestic Theater in Fort Worth, could find beatification in Hollywood—then so could she. Everybody, *everybody* told Lureen Hofmeyer she was a better dancer than Ginger, prettier than Mary Pickford, and funnier than Kay Francis.

Her pilgrimage West took three months, almost aborting in Albuquerque, where a trucker robbed Lureen of her virginity and her purse, in that order, but she pushed on, thumbing to Phoenix, where she screwed selectively and profitably, enough to buy a Ford for fifty-five dollars that bore her just five miles short of downtown Los Angeles, where its spare tire blew and the engine ruptured in a geyser of steam. On foot Lureen ran toward Hollywood with more fervor than any Moslem ever sought Mecca.

On the autumn afternoon she met Clyde Blankenship, Lureen had been in Hollywood several months, had failed to obtain an agent, had stood in line (but was turned away) to audition for *Forty-second Street, Footlight Parade,* and *Flying Down to Rio.* The last rejection was particularly bitter, because Lureen had heard the film would have thirty-one production numbers with jobs for hundreds of girls, and because she told the guard at MGM's gate that she was Ginger Rogers' kid sister from Texas. She actually got ten feet inside the studio before the ruse was disbelieved.

The only man in her life was a married citrus farmer from San Bernardino whom she fucked every Sunday afternoon in the Wonderland Tourist Court of Van Nuys, earning $7.50 (and frequent sacks of lemons) for a slightly theatrical hour of moaning. He was sixty-eight years old. He never knew Lureen was faking. She was a capable actress.

The day did not pass when other men failed to note Lureen Hofmeyer, who by now had changed her name to Cassandra Astor. The

Texas émigrée was classically structured in the tradition of wenches and milkmaids. Her hips and breasts were earthy in an era when female stars were designed lean and sleek. But she acknowledged no fishing pole unless attached to it was the bait of an acting role. Aside from her Sunday matinee, she was disinclined to muss her marcelled coiffure—it cost, after all, six bucks, more than rent—for the sake of hedonism.

Yet Clyde Blankenship, who changed his name to McKenzie Crawford, was so remarkably formed that Lureen/Cassandra, morose over rejection as a "Gold Digger of 1933," permitted him to buy her a forty-five-cent plate of chow mein at a restaurant on Melrose Avenue. They dated infrequently thereafter, principally to swap carefully guarded secrets of casting calls. During Christmas week 1932, they went to Tijuana in a Packard touring car crammed with aspiring thespians, using an unexpected seventy-five dollars that Clyde/McKenzie earned for rolling down a rocky hill in Griffith Park in a week of stunt work on a Tom Mix Western. Then, on Valentine's Day 1933, Cassandra learned she was pregnant, due certainly to the great amount of tequila McKenzie poured down her throat on Christmas Eve in La Luna Roja Café. "If it's a girl, we'll call her Marguerita," said McKenzie, hugely pleased, promising marriage as soon as he banked a hundred dollars.

Cassandra did not construe his jest as humorous. As a matter of fact, she tossed McKenzie out the front door of the one-room pink stucco bungalow they were now sharing tenuously in West Hollywood, screaming that if it were not for the scandal certain to stain her career she would charge him with rape. After weeping three days, Cassandra drank two quarts of cod-liver oil, purchased but could not locate the courage to insert an eight-inch hatpin into her uterus, and on the appropriate morning of Labor Day 1933 was delivered of an eleven-pound baby boy in the charity ward of L.A. County Hospital. Denying her first impulse, which was to creep out and leave the bastard behind, she feloniously wrote on the birth certificate that her legal husband was McKenzie Crawford, an actor working in New York. She named her son McKenzie Crawford, Jr.

When the infant was three months old, Lureen/Cassandra met a woman about to travel by bus to Mobile, Alabama, and persuaded her, for thirty-five dollars, to deliver Mack, Jr., along the way into the arms of his aunt, Mable Hofmeyer. "Darling Sis, it's only for a few weeks," wrote Cassandra. "I have just been cast as star of the new Wallace Beery movie (and between you and me, he seems to like me very much!) and must go to Oregon to shoot forest scenes. When I'm back, I'll rush to Forth Worth and fetch my precious, precious baby boy."

Having dumped the kid, Cassandra never went back to Texas, never got a part in any motion picture, functioned successfully as a prostitute until her beauty narrowed and her body widened, and in 1939 became a hair colorist in the San Fernando Valley. Nor did she ever meet again the child's father, discounting a fleeting moment when she spotted McKenzie pumping gas in 1940 at a Texaco station on Ventura Boulevard. Still handsome, though heavier, he was losing his hair and his arms were tattooed. Later she heard that he enlisted on December 8, 1941, and, some years after that, was blown to death in a rain of bazooka fire on Guadalcanal.

The farm boy from Iowa died unknowing that in Forth Worth, Texas, lived his only son, unlawful bearer of his name, a child of almost twelve who was tall and fair and strong—spectacular progeny of the beautiful and the failed.

Considering the capricious winds that uprooted lives and blew them like dust through the Depression years, McKenzie Crawford, Jr., quickly known as Mack, was fortunate to have found refuge at the home of his aunt, Mable Lucille Hofmeyer, a dependable woman, hard worker, and devoted guardian despite a gothic quality that shrouded her life and home. Mable and her younger sister, Lureen, were the only survivors of a large East Texas timber-farming family destroyed by a pneumonia epidemic. After everybody was buried and debts paid, $1,100 each remained as legacy for the sisters. Lureen, soon to be Cassandra, danced through her dollars quickly, spending lavishly on acting lessons, cosmetics, and gowns, then using the last eighty-five dollars for her ill-fated thrust at California.

Conversely, Mable mourned fittingly, wearing raven dresses for one full year before moving to nearby Fort Worth and enrolling at Texas Christian University with intent of becoming a history teacher. Chance, however, directed her footsteps across the campus each morning beside a building where piano was taught, and where, in late afternoons, a chamber orchestra attempted Mozart and Bach. Mable recognized that she was continually tardy for courses and scoring poorly on examinations, due certainly to time robbed by eavesdropping on great music. Not an impulsive woman, she nonetheless altered the studied direction of her life. But as Mable happily began courses in piano and voice, becoming accomplished in both, a personal humiliation grew in concert.

Since birth she had been cursed with a vivid strawberry mark just beneath her left chin, tucked under her throat. As it was hardly bigger than a quarter, she had learned to live with it, softening the hue with creams, always careful not to look up at the sun, because as long as her head was level, or ducked girlishly, the defect was barely visible. In her early thirties, as she neared completion of a master's degree in music and entertained the fancy of moving to New York, the birthmark rudely enlarged, for no known dermatological reason. It crept resolutely onto her left cheek, tiny streaks of scarlet sprouting like rivulets of the Mississippi delta. Artfully positioned scarves and wisps of chiffon served for a time as reasonable camouflage, but when one beau, then another, then *each* suitor drew back in obvious revulsion to avoid a good-night kiss, Mable dropped out of college. She spent one year wrestling with suicide or descent into madness. Either seemed welcome. During these deliberations, she took a furnished room in the home of an almost blind, eighty-nine-year-old widow on Cloverdale Avenue. She rarely went out, seldom ate, spent almost every waking hour sitting at an out-of-tune upright piano from which she coaxed passionate, softpedaled Scriabin and Schumann. When the widow died and her estate was probated, Mable Hofmeyer was astonished to discover that she had been willed the house on Cloverdale, the furnishings, the piano, and $3,500. A note, the widow's last words, revealed: "You have made my final hours of life so happy with your music. I only pray the angels play their harps as beautifully."

When baby McKenzie arrived in December 1933 in the arms of a stranger, and stayed, and grew to manhood in the home of Aunt Mable, he became part of a house crowded with children each weekday afternoon and all day Saturdays. Little fists clutched dollar bills for an hour's assault on the keyboard or for vocal calisthenics that resembled, to Mack's ears, turkeys eluding the Thanksgiving hatchet. But Mack was not permitted social contact with young peers. During "business" hours, the child was ordered to stay quiet in his room, more specifically, *his side* of Mable's bedroom, for they slept in adjoining twin beds. The chamber was dark by architectural blunder—only one ill-placed window—and further shadowed by a never barbered elm outside. The only source of light was a forty-watt bulb between the beds, switched on at eight each night for a few moments of silent Bible reading and perusal of musical scores and unpaid bills. The entire house was dark, draped. Mable's explanation was that it cooled in summer and warmed in winter. Money saved. But as Mack grew older and wiser, he discerned that the real source of shadows was the curse of his aunt's birthmark. Always she sat or stood to the left of her pupils, her opposite profile as concealed as the dark of the moon. There was but one mirror in the entire house, on the medicine cabinet door. Mack had chicken pox for three days before Mable noticed the spots.

Yet there was never any doubt in Mack's mind that he was loved —and needed—by the lonely spinster. Many times each day, Mable told her nephew he was "precious" and she embraced him before school and after evening prayer. He was well provided. His library contained the masterworks of American literature (though nothing frivolous like Frank Baum or *Boy's Life* magazine). Food was abundant, even if Mable's cuisine was eccentric. A pioneer in health nutrition, Mable learned from a quack chiropractor that menus composed of greenery, carrots, and lemon honey would lighten her blemish. Mack did not taste meat until he entered the first grade and at lunch in the cafeteria stared with wonder (and revulsion) at hamburger patties swimming in brown gravy.

Questions about his parentage traditionally received vague response, accompanied by a whisk of Aunt Mable's heavily lotioned hand, as if warding off gnats. "Your mother lives in California and will come here one day soon" was a common answer, or "Your father, I understand, is also living in California working to make enough money to come and get you. Times are hard, McKenzie." One night, when he was six, the child chewed on a question and finally blurted it out. "Does my mama and daddy love me?"

"*Do* my mother and father love me?" corrected Mable. "Yes, I'm sure they do."

"What is Mother like? Is she pretty?"

"I haven't seen her for many years, McKenzie. But yes, she was attractive. She was very popular and gay and she could dance a whole day away."

"What about my father?"

"I never met the man. But I imagine he is tall and strong and well liked." Mable turned out the light and prepared for sleep.

"I'm going to California when I get big and see them," the child whispered. "Tomorrow I'm going to write Mama a letter."

Mack wrote the next day, and on many occasions thereafter, but Mable mailed none of the letters. She had no address for her lost sister. From time to time she telephoned Los Angeles information and tried in vain to obtain a number. She also wrote the L.A. Hall of Records and requested a copy of McKenzie Crawford, Jr.'s birth certificate, but the answer informed her that she was not entitled. A lawyer said it would take at least a thousand dollars to fight a bureaucratic battle for which she had neither funds nor, in truth, heart. Mack was the only thing she had in her life.

Pinpricks of guilt tested her conscience, and when her nephew was nine, Mable baked a chocolate birthday cake (a historic indulgence), gave him a biography of Puccini and a picture book about Salzburg, Austria. Wiping genuine tears from her eyes, she delivered a sorrowful and fraudulent message. "Your parents have been killed in an automobile accident near Los Angeles," she said. "They were delivering food baskets to poor people." Because her sister and whoever impregnated the foolish woman had not written, called, or made contact in almost a decade, Mable decided strings were better cut than left to dangle.

As she suspected, Mack's eyes did not mist. The child had scant frame of reference for parental mourning, not even a Christmas card, only a few snapshots of his mother once encountered during a prowl through Mable's closet. As the photos were dim as Mable's house, the tragedy of a mother never met and a father completely unknown caused no discernible cracks in the little boy's psyche.

What he did was eat three pieces of chocolate cake.

"I want you to know that I love you as much as any mother," said Mable brokenly, tucking her nephew in the adjoining bed and preparing to intone the 23rd Psalm in mock memorial. "And always remember this, McKenzie. Your blood mother is in heaven now, looking down at you. She will watch over you the rest of your life and see *everything* you do, so try and make her proud." That night Mack awoke often and stared at the cabbage rose wallpaper above his head. It was the first of about ten thousand nights when Lureen/Cassandra Hofmeyer/Astor/McKenzie would float on the ceiling of whatever bedroom in which Mack chanced uneasily to rest.

He was frail, shy, loath to speak out in class because his words came choked in stammers, so emotionally painful and, to the ears of his classmates, so cruelly funny that teachers rarely called on him. When asked his name, Mack screwed up his face and usually got stuck on the first syllable, "Ma . . . Ma . . . Ma . . ." It became a torturous appellation for a child who had none. By tradition, Ma-Ma was last to be chosen in the games of playgrounds. He was the final pickle in the barrel, a name called with exasperation by Kleber Cantrell or T. J. Luther, who were *always* team captains. Mack idolized these feudal lords, had watched them for years from the sanctuary of his front porch, had envied their soapboxes on roller-skate wheels, their tree houses, their kites, Cub Scout uniforms, allegiances, scraps over territorial rights, and access to teasable girls. Mable Hofmeyer disapproved of "rough children" and early on refused them entry to her house, explaining to Mack that she could not risk shattering the musical harmony within. The infrequent mother who telephoned to invite Mack to a birthday party was told by Mable that the boy suffered from a weak heart—rheumatic fever was hinted—and had to be shielded from robust activity.

In the fourth grade deliverance arrived—and from an unlikely savior. The new physical education teacher at elementary school, a lanky and buoyant woman named, wonderfully, Miss Joy, organized an informal track meet. Not privy to Mack's dependable disgrace, Miss Joy chose him to be the final runner in a 440-yard relay race, ignoring T.J. and Kleber's this-is-the-end-of-the-world groans. Panic flooded Mack's thin face. "I c-c-can't," he protested. "I'm n-n-n-not g-g-g-ood at r-running . . ."

The teacher knelt before the frightened child and forced him to look directly at her eyes. "I think you are," she said. "You're tall and you've got long legs. Besides, I'm not asking you to win. I'm only asking you to *try*." Mack made further protests, but Miss Joy countered each with encouragement. When no other excuse remained, Mack pointed down at his shoes, Thom McAn's, gleaming and unscuffed. Mable Hofmeyer's cardinal doctrine was that shoes remain, until outgrown, as pristine as the day of purchase. "I'm n-n-not supposed to g-g-g-et my sh-sh-shoes dirty," he pleaded. T.J. found this so funny that he leaped into a nearby sandpile and kicked up small geysers, causing the girls to squeal.

"Then take them off," said Miss Joy in sensible accommodation.

Granted, the act of removing a pair of polished shoes might not seem an act of liberation, and, indeed, the first time around the track in a practice run, Mack not only dropped the baton, he stumbled and sprawled flat on his face twenty feet shy of the tape. But clearly he was trying, and Miss Joy applauded, and Kleber commanded T.J. to cease the razzberries, for they were, like it or not, on the same team. And when the real race began, Kleber was the lead runner, staying even with a widely respected kid, passing the stick to an overweight dud named Paul who fell ten paces behind. In the third segment, T.J. churned and puffed but gained little ground and, thrusting the baton into Mack's trembling hand, taunted, "Take it, Ma-Ma. And *shove* it."

The distance Mack had to run was only 110 yards, but it loomed before him like the ascent to Everest. His competitor in the adjoining lane was not only far ahead, he was a year older, half Mexican, and a bully of such repute that even sixth-graders gave him the respect due a Joe Louis. Nonetheless, having no other choice, Mack ran, and in his ears were the exhortations of Miss Joy with her arms thrust out in encouragement. Somewhere, someplace, from some genetic storeroom whose doors and windows had long ago been sealed by Mable Hofmeyer, Mack located a source of power. His bare feet flew across the cinders as if life depended on them—and perhaps it did. In a riotous clamor of prepubescent shrieks and squeals, Mack (never again to be Ma-Ma) roared past Tony Garcia to break the string—and all the bonds that held him.

Miss Joy awarded Mack the victorious baton and he bore it home as Holy Grail, the first trophy in what would become a wall of gold and silver, tributes to his ability to run more fleetly, swing bats like a woodman's ax, throw or catch or dunk any ball of any size and any covering with a grace and good humor alien to brute power. The day after he won the race, Mack entered his aunt's home with shoes not only muddied but scratched. His knife-creased gabardine slacks, by dictum commanded to remain as clean as an admiral's dress trousers, proudly bore a rent from scaling a telephone pole in response to T.J.'s dare. Punishment was a swat and immediate bed. No reading. No supper. But Mack did not suffer. He had already dined at Kleber's house. VeeJee Cantrell sensed that here was a hungry child, and hers was a table that always contained enough fried chicken, mashed potatoes, and hot biscuits to feed a basketball team. For years thereafter, Mack ate around the neighborhood, rather like a welcome pup at the back door, his frame filling and swelling from the graces of a dozen surrogate mothers.

Sport became not only his identity but his passport to celebrity, a gift he was forced to enjoy outside his home. At the end of his junior year in high school, having set a new state record in football rushing yardage and owning a .402 batting average in baseball, he became a personal trophy sought after by many. Rare was the week when Mack did not dine out as guest of a college recruiter or an oil-enriched alumnus of a Southwest Conference university, sometimes at the Colonial Country Club, where Ben Hogan himself, Fort Worth's most famous athlete, would stroll in from the golf course and, on cue, second the motion. During such seductive feasts, Mack occasionally felt the press of a wifely knee against his—a beat too long. And though he did not respond to the action beneath the tablecloth, Mack early on learned that his flesh had value. He also came to realize that he did not like being touched.

Toward her nephew's acclaim, Mable Hofmeyer maintained a cool and rigid posture. Curfew remained at 9 p.m. school nights and 10 p.m. Saturdays. Mack's trophies and scrapbooks rested on the back porch, exiled to shelves above the wringer-washer. Though Mable's personal objets d'art (mostly bronze busts of Verdi, Rossini, et al.) received devotion and polish—a speck of tarnish was as unlikely to appear on them as leprosy—Mack's glittering bounty could have been empty milk bottles waiting to be collected.

On the memorable afternoon in 1949 when he hit three home runs and leaped an estimated ten feet into the air to destroy an opponent's line drive destined for a grand slam, Mack was borne up his sidewalk on the shoulders of Kleber and T.J. with half a dozen girls jiggling in delirious escort. Mable Hofmeyer appeared at her front door with the face of a candle snuffer. Later, Mack sat wordlessly before a supper of boiled celery, cucumber slices, and broccoli with lemon honey, paid courteous attention while his aunt rhapsodized over a student's honorable-mention award for playing "Träumerei" in the Euterpean Club's spring musicale, then endured a static-filled concert on the Philco box radio—Toscanini conducting the NBC orchestra from New York.

Disappointed that his aunt never attended one of his games, Mack finally stopped asking. The woman rarely left the house of shadows, and, more pertinently, he came to dread her traditional response. It went something like: "I'm working day and night to keep food on the table and clothes on your back, McKenzie." Once Mack dared inquire if his aunt really understood sport, almost reverting to his childhood stammer while trying to explain the exhilaration of competition, of events that were, to his thinking, as emotional and mathematical as great music. His huge blue eyes sparkled in the telling. He was ready for bed this night, wearing only pajama bottoms, his skin aglow from the heat of a shower. Mable did listen and Mable did recognize the eagerness of her nephew's rationale, but she found no charity in her heart. She simply shook her head and bade him good night.

She could not discuss the torment of envy that had grown over the years, grown to the point where Mable could barely look upon her unblemished ward. But she did talk to God about it. How, she asked Him, how could You damn me, a pious Christian daughter, curse me with the mark of Cain, while anointing the bastard son of a wanton mother and an unknown father with such perfect beauty that idolaters worship him like Baal?

Mack interrupted her meditation. "Please come to the game Friday night," he pleaded.

"Games are for children, nephew," she answered. "Have you read First Corinthians, Chapter 13, Verse 11? *'When I was a child, I spake as a child, I understood as a child, I thought as a child. But when I became a man, I put away childish things.'*"

"But I'm only seventeen," said Mack quietly.

"Closer to eighteen," corrected Mable. "You are a man." She went to the mantel and lifted a bust of Beethoven. "This *man* was short, ugly, unpopular, with a malformed head, and in later life, with ears that could not even hear a bird sing. Yet he wrote music that has endured for a century and a half. It will remain more precious than gold as long as human beings exist. I do not believe it is written that Mr. Beethoven played football." She made a gesture of dismissal. Past bedtime. Defeated, Mack felt anguish, along with the debt owed his aunt, a bill that could never be paid, at least not in currency Mable Hofmeyer deemed valuable. He went to the desk where she had begun tallying accounts, threw strong arms about her, and said shyly, "I love you, Aunt Mable. We're just different."

"I love you, too, McKenzie. You are my only blood kin." She tensed and drew away.

Mack risked another minute. "Can I know just one thing? It's important. Even though you don't *like* my games . . . are you proud of me?"

Mable did not look up from her paperwork. She scratched away with an old pen and she answered brusquely, "*'Pride goeth before destruction, and a haughty spirit before a fall.'* Proverbs 16:18. Good night, McKenzie."

They slept in the adjoining twin beds until Mack was well into an adolescence bereft of privacy. The most embarrassing moments came each dawn when Mack awoke with the erection that (T.J. always contended) gave cock its name. Yet he could not creep to the bathroom for fear that Mable would espy his manhood. It was necessary to stay securely under the covers and think pure thoughts, quote Bible verses, imagine Mother Lureen on her heavenly cloud, and wish—but rarely achieve—that the bone would wither. Not until Mable opened her eyes and bolted immediately for the bath did Mack dare to enter his closet, shut the door, jerk off hurriedly, promising, swearing to God, never, *never* to do that again. Until the next morning.

Two other bedrooms were unoccupied in Mable Hofmeyer's home, "guest rooms" they were called, though the only person ever to pass a night was a distant cousin named Alma who came to Forth Worth once from Abilene for periodontal work. Neither "guest room" was very appealing, one being dark as forest primeval with bedcovers and drapes to match, the other the hue of Mable's strawberry birthmark and having deepened over the years to wine. Yet Mack would have swapped half his trophies for the right of tenancy. Hints about the subject got nowhere. In his thirteenth year, Mack boldly came out and asked for a room of his own as his Christmas gift. Mable refused. "I've got enough house cleaning." Then, when a potpourri of odd jobs—lawn mowing, car washing, substitution on Kleber's paper route—endowed him with a modicum of financial security, he suggested that he pay rent, twenty dollars monthly, for which he would get a room of his own. "Blood kin does not pay rent in my home," answered Mable.

On lazy Saturday afternoons, as he listened to football games at T.J.'s house, six doors down on the same side of Cloverdale, Mack's eyes roamed covetously about the personalized chaos: pennants on the

walls, ticket stubs, pinups of Betty Grable and Rita Hayworth, a pile of
damp jeans and jockstraps odorous as fermenting grapes (by mutual
agreement, T.J.'s mother did not enter the room, finding more pleasure
in gin than Bon Ami cleanser), stacks of comics and detective magazines (some with innards replaced by sunbathing periodicals that fea-
tured photographs of lean Swedish nudes playing volleyball, and the
maddening thing was that the ball always seemed to be frozen by the
shutter in front of the Scandinavian clitorises). Most wondrous was a
private entrance through which T.J. could exit or enter without the attention of his elders.

Kleber's room, though private, was more orderly—as befitted an
Eagle Scout. Subject to daily inspections by VeeJee Cantrell, it was
necessarily void of any photo or word concerning sex (excluding certain pages of *God's Little Acre* that were hidden within a volume of the
Encyclopaedia Britannica). The other exception was Webster's Dictionary, frequently combed by the Three Princes in search of definitions
for "fuck," "shit," and "tit." Only the last was located, and after an ex-
tensive search, and under the spelling "teat." This caused T.J. to announce that the dictionary was flat-ass wrong.

"T-i-t is women. T-e-a-t is cows," he said.

Mack's predicament was well known to his friends, both of whom
shuddered at the penalty of sleeping beside Mable, a woman they considered since childhood to be the witch who entrapped Hansel and
Gretel. Nothing if not ingenious, T.J. devised a possible solution. Faking flu one school morning, he went to the nursing office, waited until
the RN turned her back to read his perfectly normal thermometer,
then snaked out a lightning hand to swipe a slip of paper with ℞ on it.
Next he persuaded a homely and adoring girl, hinting of carnal favor,
to type a letter for the attention of Miss Mabel Hofmeyer:

"During a physical examination recently prior to football practice,
it was discovered that your nephew, McKenzie Crawford, Jr., is suffering from what might become spinal curvature, due to the twin mattress
on which he sleeps. Further, as the boy is now six feet four and one
half inches tall, his feet hang over the end of the bed and circulation
problems might develop. It is my recommendation that he sleep on a
double mattress, preferably extra firm. Sincerely yrs., Roberta C.
Doyle, RN."

And it worked. Sort of. Scrutinizing the note with the attention of
a gem cutter, Mable granted her nephew occupancy of the forest room,

which contained a double bed. But she pointedly removed the door lock, explaining such was necessary in case of fire. Given an inch, Mack dared not take a mile. He moved cautiously, purchasing first a study lamp with a hundred-watt bulb, and, receiving no rebuke, bought next a secondhand radio from T.J. for $3.25, at last able to listen to sports instead of sonatas. He placed a few of his trophies on the windowsill, gratified to awake on sunny mornings and catch them sparkling in the sun. But that was the limit. He could no more hang a picture of Jane Russell's epic bosom on his closet door than he could prance naked into the kitchen for breakfast of bran and raw milk.

And at night, with nothing but an unlocked door as shield, he dared not explore the flagpole that rose inside his pajama bottoms— knowing that the instant his hand touched his dick, Lureen in heaven would send Mable across the hall a message—and his aunt would burst in with preachers, teachers, the FBI, and wart removers.

CHAPTER FIVE

Calvin Sledge, District Attorney of Tarrant County, Texas, prosecutor of those who molested life, limb, and property of 818,553 persons whose median age was 26.7 years of age, awoke with a start. His head was buried in a tangle of legal documents and police reports, where, sometime after midnight, he had slumped with the promise of shutting his eyes for no more than two minutes. Now it was dawn and the sun was already down to business, cooking his neck. His breath smelled like sour milk and his face was a hair shirt. Frantically he reached for a tin of aspirins to unloose the vise that squeezed his temples, and, in the search, knocked over a plastic cup of ice-cold coffee, which spread muddily across his work—metaphoric reminder of the condition of his case.

He blotted the stains and tore off yesterday's page from the calendar. June 26, 1975. "Lord, Lord," he muttered, "where's it all going?" A man spends a century to reach the age of forty, then every year after that spins by in two weeks. Time's race jarred Sledge fully if reluctantly awake. In less than a week he was expected to stroll confidently into the grand jury chamber, nod pleasantly at a panel of blue-ribbon citizens—good, decent, ordinary folks with neither entree nor frame of reference to the scenario of horror that duty required them to hear. If the drama played as Sledge intended, the grand jury would reward him with a true bill: indictment for first-degree murder. But if the presentation had holes (and the DA's headache renewed at this reminder, because if the case was a rubber life raft he would have drowned weeks ago), he would have to settle for assault with intent to murder. Maybe not even that. Grand juries usually dance to whatever tune the DA fiddles, but rare was the case as inflammatory as this one. So strong were the passions that these good people might turn around and indict the DA for malicious prosecution.

One option remained, tempting and almost irresistible. Sledge could sweep the coffee-soiled blizzard off his desk, close the file, extricate his present and his future from this tar baby. He could assemble the press, posture confidently before the thicket of microphones and arms that stabbed the air, put on the serviceable mask of civic dedication, and announce in a boyish drawl that would charm—and, with hope, convince—Walter Cronkite and Barbara Walters and *Time* magazine and the BBC that Lady Justice was duly served. "After exhaustive investigation," he could say, "the District Attorney has come to the conclusion that there is insufficient evidence to justify further . . ."

How sweet was the promise. He could get re-elected on that. Nobody would yell "whitewash." A few murmurs, maybe. But no screams. Nobody could accuse him of not *trying* to make a case. The bags beneath his eyes and the new gray in his sideburns would testify to that. Two years from now he could juggle the statistics and find some pissant numbers (like J. Edgar Hoover was so good at locating when it was budget time) warning everybody that crime was up 14 percent but lookee here, fellow taxpayers, my conviction record has jumped 22.4 percent. A famous South Texas sheriff got re-elected sixteen times on such sleight of hand. Just before election day, the celebrated lawman usually managed to arrest some nigger who promptly confessed to all unsolved rapes, burglaries, and armed robberies in the now peaceable realm.

Trouble was, Sledge had no interest in the lateral blessing of re-election. Another four years as DA was another four years in the same chair, another four years of trying to feed a wife and two kids and maintain appearances on $30,000 a year. After that, maybe a seat in the State Senate. And then he would be fifty. *Finito*. Step right in, elevator's going down. Maybe a little oil deal to grease the skids, enough to see the girls to college with something left to buy a Stratoliner for watching the Cowboys. Then an obituary on an inside column. Adding it all up, the sum was not dismal for a turkey farmer's kid from Yoakum who rouged corpses in an undertaking parlor to get through East Texas State Teachers College. Dammit, though, Calvin Sledge did not want to expire from Pike's Peak Syndrome. He had fought the disease since he was five years old.

Just before World War II, Willis C. Sledge took his wife, Rowena, his son, Calvin, and his daughter, Rose Sharon, on the only vacation of their lives, motoring in a 1936 La Salle to Colorado, where distant cousins operated a fishing camp. The grandeur of the Rocky Mountains stunned young Calvin, coming as he did from a piece of Texas where a ten-foot rise was called a hill. He begged his father to conclude the holiday with a drive clear to the top of Pike's Peak, unable to articulate but nonetheless fervent in his desire to reach a summit. Halfway up the coiling road, the La Salle wheezed and blew steam. Willis Sledge raised the hood, peered and drew back at the storm, announced it was time for descent to the bottom, surrender to the safe and sure. Calvin pleaded with his father; he had seen rest stops along the road where water for radiators was available. But father said to disappointed son, "We've seen enough, boy. The view from here's no different from what's up-a-yonder." Calvin continued to fret until Willis Sledge swatted him. "Just be glad we got this far," he said.

Halfway, mused the District Attorney of Tarrant County some four decades thereafter, is no way. Halfway is brick veneer, rhinestones, and kissing your sister. With that, he shaved, bathed with damp paper towels, and recommenced. His task was twofold: (1) to assemble fully fleshed profiles of the principals in an event of violence for which "sensational" was a bereft adjective and (2) to pray that as he did his homework he would find some scrap, some hunch, some *something* that would persuade a grand jury to indict and a trial jury to convict. He scribbled himself reminders to return overnight calls from the New York *Times* and *Newsweek*. And buy new scrapbooks. But task *numero uno* was to catch that hard-assed doctor and find out if there was any change.

The physician answered in the voice he presumably employed to tell terminal patients to get their affairs in order.

Sledge asked if there was anything new.

"He's better. We're moving him off the critical list. Bunch of new flowers. Natalie Wood sent a telegram and a case of Dom Perignon. And we threw some asshole out the door. Said he was Queen Elizabeth's throat doctor. His degree was from the *National Enquirer.*" Dr. Witt hung up.

The DA selected a bloated folder, shook out clippings and photographs, then, wasting more precious time, became once again a child staring in frustration at the top of a mountain and wondering just what in hell it took to get there. More pertinent, he admitted, what it was like to *live* there. Never mind die there.

"McKenzie (Mack) Crawford profile," he began dictating into the microphone, speaking slowly and distinctly in hopes that Darlene, his secretary and daughter of a major campaign contributor, might be able to transcribe his speech into something resembling English. "Mack graduated in 1950 and spent the ensuing summer working in Louisiana, putting up loran towers for offshore drilling rigs. In September that year, he enrolled at the University of Texas, Austin, on full football scholarship. . . . Lemme see here, according to *Sports Illustrated,* he worked out two weeks, hurt his knee, and red-shirted the season. Quote: 'I was mixed up that year. I couldn't handle the pressure. Everybody was grabbing me this way and that way and I felt like a steer being auctioned off at the Fort Worth Fat Stock Show. So I flaked out a year. I guess I wanted to see if there was anything *besides* football.' . . . End quote. . . . In the fall of '51, Mack didn't cut the mustard at Texas. Almost lost his scholarship. . . . But the next season, 'Man on Fire,' as the Houston *Chronicle* put it. . . . Hang on, Darlene, I'm lookin' for that *Life* story. Where the hell did you put it?"

A photographer for *Life* magazine spent two weeks in Austin during Mack's senior football season at the University of Texas. He used 96 rolls of film, which, at 36 exposures each, contained 3,456 images of a football player whose previous fame was parochial and confined to newspaper sports pages. Having shifted from end to fullback in his sophomore year, Mack broke conference records in rushing yard-age. As a junior he scored eighteen touchdowns; columnists began to murmur Heisman Trophy. Then came attention from the world's most pervasive photo journal.

Life's in-house motto, "Film is cheap," encouraged photographers to overshoot assignments. Thus was Mack captured during practice in which he plowed through would-be tacklers like a tank pelted with feathers. He was photographed in accounting class looking sleepy, in his room faking serious scholarship, dominant in a row of Sigma Nu fraternity brothers midnight-serenading a balcony of Pi Phi's wearing baby doll nightgowns and looking down on the athlete with the most urgent of need, at the wheel of an orange-and-white Chevrolet Bel-Air "earned" for summer work on the ranch of a South Texas alumnus, getting dressed in khaki pants and oxford-cloth button-down shirt and navy cashmere sweater (then taking them off), strolling across the lovely forty-acre campus of gnarled oaks and limestone buildings with terra-cotta Spanish-tile roofs. And, wherever he went or whatever he did, Mack radiated the power of sexuality. *Life*'s editorial intent had been only to include Mack in a survey of football madness across America. Photographers had been simultaneously dispatched to USC, Alabama, Nebraska, and Annapolis. But when enlargements were made of the Mack Crawford take, and when, at the Rockefeller Center headquarters of the magazine in New York City, women from the pub-lication's Fashion and Modern Living and ClipDesk and Religion de-partments began drifting into Sports on hoked-up errands, anxious to paw through the 11 × 14's that revealed Mack in the shower with a tease, through frosted glass, of taut buttock and silky blond pubic hair, USC et al. fell from grace.

It was Mack and Mack alone who made the cover and eight pages inside, became part of the New York Museum of Modern Art's library of photography-as-art, and conjured incalculable fantasies among thirty million readers. The cover, one of the first that *Life* ran in color, was blatantly sexual—candid, unposed, taken moments after Mack had completed a workout. He was wearing an old pair of orange gym shorts with rips to contain his massive flanks. His sweat shirt was cut off at the armpits and extended just below his pectoral muscles. His hair was damp and curly with sweat. The photographer had squatted and shot upward, framing his subject with a piercing blue Texas autumn sky that was the precise color of Mack's eyes.

The *Daily Texan* campus newspaper marked the event with a front-page headline: CAMPUS HERO BECOMES NATIONAL CELEBRITY, which prompted an erudite letter from a professor of semantics. "Our Mr. Crawford may well be a *hero*, seeing as how the word suggests a legendary figure endowed with great strength, courage, an illustrious warrior favored by the gods. But perhaps he should beware of *celebrity*, a word rather difficult for which to locate derivation. The prefix *cele* (or, more accurately, *coele*) means 'cavity.' The suffix *brit-y* probably comes from *brat*, defined widely as 'spoiled child.'" This correspondent then ponders: Is "celebrity" therefore "a trap for poorly behaved children"?

Celebrity's child basked briefly in the fallout before discovering a truism: statues of famous people get shit on by pigeons. Mack telephoned his aunt, who, not surprisingly, had failed to encounter *Life*. Her enthusiasm was minor-key. Mack's teammates reacted curiously. A pair of clowns sank instantly to their knees and salaamed when the cover boy strolled into the locker room, whereupon an assistant coach (a sour, unpopular man) chewed his ass from hell to breakfast for appearing five minutes late. On the practice field, custom began of wiping the football impeccably clean before handing it to Mack, which he found unamusing.

Vulgar gibes were made. It had always been Mack's habit to wait until the showers were empty before washing his body, he not being one to engage in locker-room horseplay—towel popping, pussy telling. The afternoon *Life* appeared, a six-pack of guards and tackles who *in toto* weighed three quarters of a ton tormented the star's embarrassed nude exit with the sort of whistles usually directed at maidens in bathing suits.

Friends drifted away. Strangers he had never met pretended to be confidants. An invisible shield was erected by the publicity. Mack was confused. He argued with himself that the source of the conflicting attitudes was, in the main, jealousy. But that did not make him feel better. He defended himself: "I didn't *ask Life* to take my picture." But he had willingly, in fact enthusiastically awarded the photographer two weeks of his time and 3,456 images of his face and figure.

Two games in the season remained; the press was calling them "Mack Crawford's last appearances" as if the sport required not eleven men, only one. On the Friday night before what was predicted to be a routine devastation of SMU, Mack found more than two hundred letters spilling out of his mailbox, including one from Kleber. He had not heard from his best friend in years. They had spoken on the telephone but a few times, and awkwardly, since the night that the Three Princes split into alien realms.

Dear Cover Boy:

My Lord, *Life* must be hard up—or fresh out of starlets. I saw you decorating my kiosk at 96th & Broadway. Bought 3 copies instead of dinner. Congratulations, I think. You're the only famous person I know excepting Dorothy Kilgallen whom I called up this week and asked for an interview. She told me she didn't grant them.

I'm working on my master's at Columbia in journalism—plus 30 hours a week at a candy store, employed to stop juvenile delinquents from shoplifting. They all look like T.J.—and by the way, have you heard from the Prince of Temptation? I lost track years ago. I'm glad nothing ever came of *that*.

How's your love life? Mine is definitely not a poem. More like a dirge. Good luck on the SMU game and then smear the Aggies. And write, if they teach that sort of thing in academic jockdom.

Your friend, Kleber.

P.S. Dammit, I miss Texas. Couldn't wait to get out of that cultural Sahara, and now it's like Mother Church pulling me back.

Mack was grateful for the letter, particularly the buried but key sentence, "I'm glad nothing ever came of *that*." *That* was the fear of a never quite forgotten night. *That* was the conscience-tormenting memory that had haunted Mack for five years. Kleber's matter-of-fact dismissal of *that* seemed to mean there was no more need for worry. Mack felt ropes slip from his body. On Sunday morning after the game, he promised himself, he would write Kleber a long catch-up letter and slip in some oblique mention about the death of *that*.

Intent, alas, was impaired by the unexpected. Hero got tackled by Celebrity. Mack played poorly. His head and his limbs were under disparate controls. Seven times in the first half he took the ball on routine handoff; four times it squirted from his hands in humiliating fumbles. In the second half, he did not fumble again, but he was thrown back like a boomerang each time he charged a notoriously weak SMU defensive line. Net yardage for the day: minus twelve. In the fourth quarter, momentarily returning to form, Mack located a hole to break through. Angrily did he defy everyone in his path, weaving, spinning, as determined as a nine-year-old child racing barefoot on a cinder track. And for a precious few moments he was in the clear, sweet and unmolested clear, nothing between him and the cymbals but November-browned grass in Austin's Memorial Stadium. The thundering roar of 40,000 partisans celebrated the star's renaissance. And then, only ten yards shy of personal triumph and team victory, he noticed an army of photographers lined between the goalposts waiting for him. Why he chose to gild his lily at this particular moment was an act he would never fully understand. But he did. He feinted unnecessarily to his left, thence to his right, razzle-dazzle on the Good Ship Showboat. And he fell, losing the game, limping from the turf in the fever of disgrace, complaining—falsely—as he reached the bench of a pulled groin muscle.

After the game, Mack sat dejectedly in a whirlpool bath, waiting until his teammates had drifted away. Then, with a wince of histrionic pain, he climbed out. If stragglers remained they would see his discomfort and pronounce it genuine. Dressing hurriedly, hating the lingering odors of ammonia and wintergreen, he limped through the steaming gauntlet of lockers. A slab of beef named Ramirez emerged from the acrid fog and blocked the way. Ramirez was ugly, his nose flat and thick, his body the door of a bank vault. He had begun his career at Texas as fullback, had been forced to shift to tackle when Mack was awarded the more glamorous position. "Need another copy of that magazine, honey?" asked Ramirez, making pucker noises. "I saved one for you." He threw Mack the *Life* cover. He had wiped his ass on it.

On autumn nights in Austin, when the team has won, the architectural oddity called the University of Texas Tower is bathed in shimmering orange light, glowing like the phallic centerpiece of a pagan festival. On the bleakest midnight of Mack's life, the tower was dark, the hour cold. Parked atop a hill overlooking Lake Austin, replaying the game in his head, he was inattentive to the coed named Barbara Lee who had been trying unsuccessfully to glue her body to his. She was wearing a pink sweater and had done everything short of seizing Mack's golden head and burying it in her pillowy tits. The only companions Mack desired were a bottle of Pearl and stony silence. What he wanted was to be alone. After the game and Ramirez's crude prank, Mack practically slunk out of the dressing room. Photographers and reporters hovered to pick the carcass; Barbara Lee was already ensconced, unevictable, from his Chevrolet. On the trunk someone had scratched "Fuckoff" with a beer opener.

Barbara Lee believed it her duty to make fire out of stone. What Mack needed, she reasoned, was a good woman. She had finagled her way into one of the *Life* photographs; the caption identified her as "girl friend." The truth was something else. They had dated but three times. Rumor held Mack's sexual appetite to be so voracious that he was systematically working his way through the choice sorority houses on campus. And indeed many of the fine young women who snared him for an evening later murmured to envious sisters that the athlete's prowess on the stadium floor was nothing compared to the trick plays he pulled on the leather cushions of his orange-and-white automobile. But had these witnesses been in a court of law, perjury would have been committed if a temporal liaison testified to anything more than a perfunctory, closed-mouth kiss of adieu. Mack knew they were his for the taking. The trouble was, he wasn't giving.

"Listen," butted Barbara Lee into the silence, jarring like an alarm clock ringing in error at 4 a.m. "You're about as much fun as a mud-pack. What's the big problem? It's just an old game."

That at least elicited a grunt. Barbara Lee found music on the radio, "Someone to Watch over Me," a melody designed to meld limbs. Mack turned it off. Undaunted, Barbara Lee chose to deliver items of social interest. "Did you hear that Claude and Mary Beth got pinned? Can you *believe* it? My dear, those two are so ugly they should give each other masks for wedding gifts. . . . Hey, do you like this color lipstick? Be honest. It's Tangee, 'Rhapsody in Pink.' Same color Jane Wyman wore in *Magnificent Obsession* with Rock Hudson. I saw that movie and cried six days. . . ."

Demanding a response, Barbara Lee positioned her head below Mack's chin and gazed up with sinuosity. She was blond and blue-eyed and could have been hatched from the same egg as he; both were perfect on the outside, both a glutinous mess within. Mack nodded. "It's nice," he agreed. She could have been wearing ashes and Crayolas for all he cared. "I started to wear 'Midnight Madness,' " she continued. "That's what Natalie Wood had on in *Rebel Without a Cause,* but it came out dark purple on me. Did you see that show? James Dean is to die. When he was lying on that floor of the police station, crying, tears all over his face, playing with that windup monkey. Well, what can I tell you? I saw it eight times. I'd still be in the Paramount Theater if I didn't have you. . . . Which I don't seem to have." Searching the face that had been on 6.5 million magazine covers, Barbara Lee was beginning to suffer—for the first time in her life—the angst of rejection. Boys had been looking up her dress since the nursery school slide. "Baby, what is it?" she fretted. "Tell me, honey, did I do something wrong?"

Mack shook his head. "I dunno," he said. "I just dunno. I guess I better get you home. . . . I've got this cramp in my leg."

"Well, I can fix *that,*" said Barbara Lee delightedly, reading in Mack's answer an invitation to a party that was not being held. She scooted across the seat and, not certain which limb had been strained, began massage of both. Mack tolerated the scurrying fingers briefly before clamping her wrists. "I don't feel up to . . . *that* tonight," he said.

"Sorreee," snapped Barbara Lee. "Do you *ever?* Look, Mr. Famous, let's not waste each other's time. Save both of us the trouble. Don't call when you get in the mood, *if* you ever do."

Mack drove Barbara Lee to the Kappa house without even remembering the trip, uncaring of her flinty face, grappling with problems more demanding than her seldom vacant vagina.

Later that night, he tried to write Kleber an answer. "Great to hear from you . . . I'm fine, just fine . . . Can't think of much to tell you . . ." He crumpled the paper and threw it into a corner, where it landed beside a stack of *Life*s, stopping short, respectful of idols. He tried to sleep—but replayed the humiliating game instead. How he wished for somebody to talk to, but the most famous athlete in America lacked a single friend whose ears were trustworthy enough to listen—and understand. He recalled Kleber's definition of friendship, "Somebody you can call at 3 a.m. to bail you out of jail." Who do I call? wondered Mack. Associated Press?

About an hour before dawn, he pretended there was a telephone on his bed and he placed an imaginary call to New York City. In the fantasy, Mack played like Kleber promptly answered, torn away from a party with music and laughter. Kleber seemed to be surrounded by people who liked him because he was smart and witty and *not* because his picture was on a magazine cover. And Kleber was delighted to be disturbed by a call from the Prince of Charms.

Mack imagined himself saying to his friend, "Listen to me, Kleber, just *listen*. I need somebody to listen to me. It's Mack. And I'm scared. Yeah, it's true, Mack Crawford is scared. I did a really shitty thing this afternoon. . . . I ruined the SMU game. . . . And I made up a phony leg injury as an excuse. And you know what? It doesn't matter a helluva lot. Not the game, not the lie. . . . You saw that 'famous person' on the cover of *Life?* Well, here's a little scoop. Cover Boy can't get close to any girl without thinking about *that* . . . *that* night and *that* storm and *that* girl. (Hell, I can't even forget her name no matter how hard I try. It's *Laurie,* remember?) I'm glad it doesn't seem to bother you anymore. . . . Me, it's like one of those damn pimples on your chin that festers up and breaks and finally goes away—only it keeps coming back. . . . Still listening, K.? I just decided I know the answer to one thing. . . . Ted Williams had the answer. . . . Remember that time when he gave everybody the finger at Fenway Park? Well, he was right. . . . Fuck 'em. . . . Fuck everybody in the world who wanted to touch me yesterday and right now it's almost dawn and I'm the Saturday-night leper. . . . Nobody comes near me, and that's just the way I like it. . . . Truth of the matter is, it doesn't feel much different. I miss you, though, Kleber. Why do things get complicated? If you find out, lemme know. . . ."

The door to his room burst open. Trying mightily to stand tall without succumbing to the tumbler of pink grain alcohol punch clasped in a bear's paw appeared Mack's down-the-hall neighbor, a freshman quarterback from Sweetwater, Zeke Mahaffey. A bucolic youth with a face so reddened by past-curfew spirits that his freckles were lost in fire, Zeke was embarrassed. "Oops," he apologized, bouncing from one side of the door facing to the other, "wrong room . . ." He giggled. "I'm drunk as a damn skunk."

"That's not a bad place to be," said Mack. The room was dark and Zeke was silhouetted by hall light.

"How come you're still up?" blurted Zeke. "Everything okay?"

"Okay."

"How's the leg?"

"Better. Thanks for asking."

"I mean really, truly, cross your heart and hope to die okay?"

Mack laughed and nodded. Given a choice, he would not have admitted Zeke Mahaffey to his chamber on this difficult night. But no one else had come, even in error, to offer fellowship. "Can I ask you something, Zeke?"

"Sure. Wanna drink?" Zeke thrust forth his glass.

"Yeah," said Mack, sipping the sweet, potent punch. "How come I fell on my ass just ten yards from the goal line?"

Zeke pondered and smiled in unknowing tenderness. " 'Cause your head went one way and your feet t'other. Don't mean shit. Man can't help it sometimes. Last year in high school, I threw four interceptions in the Plainview game. Next week I connected nine out of thirteen. Same arm. Same stadium. Some days, you *have* to fall. But there's always gonna be another game, Mack. Hell, next week you'll whip Aggie ass from here to Amarillo. . . . Right?"

"Hope so, Zeke." He made as much sense as anybody.

Zeke backed out of the room. He felt he had overstayed his welcome. The caste system in Hill Hall seldom allowed meaningful moments between senior stars and freshmen scrubs. "You want a couple of C's for your leg?" offered Zeke. He took two codeine pills out of the pocket of his cowboy shirt.

"They'd help," said Mack, praying they would seal his sleep until noon. "Can I ask one more favor, Zeke?"

"Shoot," nodded Zeke, obeying the *droit du seigneur*.

"Would you just sit here a minute until I go to sleep?"

"Howcum?"

"You need a reason?"

"Why hell no. I'll sit wherever you say, Mack." Zeke positioned himself on the edge of the famous bed—it, too, had been in *Life*—and attended Mack like he would a sick animal on his daddy's farm. Pretty soon, when Mack's breathing was deep and regular, Zeke decided it was okay to leave. Which he did, with the clumsy caution of someone very bombed but determined not to make a sound, paying no heed atall when Mack reached out for his hand, holding it tightly. Zeke accepted the overlong grasp as friendship and nothing more. He did not know that Mack wanted at this moment to be the toucher and not the touchee.

In the morning, Mack found a Houston newspaper shoved under

his door. The banner on the sports page must have gotten laughs around the composing room. It read: GOLDEN BOY FALLS ON HIS BRASS. Mack busied himself for hours, sitting on the floor, carefully ripping seventeen covers of *Life* magazine into precise little confetti ribbons, then studying in fascination as pieces of himself circled round and round before disappearing in the commode.

CHAPTER SIX

Kleber sat chilled before his typewriter, suffering from the late-November cold that two sweaters would not banish, frozen similarly in his attempt to write cogent prose for a term paper on "The Press and the Presidency." Having chosen to defend the gentlemen's agreement between journalism and Franklin Delano Roosevelt, Kleber had commenced by arguing that both compassion and the national health were served by neither describing nor photographing the crippled President when lashed to a lectern or pushed in a wheelchair to joust with Winston Churchill. "Metaphorically, a lame President would have symbolized a sick country," he wrote, content with the premise yet unable to make transition into why the public's right to know was best unserved.

Thus marooned, he drifted for hours, staring out a fourth-story window on West 110th Street, far more interested in the current events going on in New York City and seen through unwashed glass. Below, on the ribbon of dying park beside the gray, menacing Hudson River, Puerto Rican kids threw stones at faraway garbage scows. Kleber became fascinated by the texture of the tableau—the melancholy shades of autumn, the scuffed leather jackets, the ribbons of scarlet cloth tied around sweating foreheads, the posturings, swaggers, the leader, the goats, the tensions, the arrogant eruptions of power. He could have written ten pages on this without stopping for thought. His forte was reportage. What he loathed was "think pieces" on matters over and done with. One more semester, Kleber promised himself, then never again the smell and rust of library stacks.

Two flights down the pay telephone rang—and rang. Kleber wondered why some student didn't answer, remembering that anyone who was not a displaced prisoner of academe was away for Thanksgiving holiday. His own feast the preceding afternoon had been $1.19 worth of cardboard-tasting turkey at a Greek coffee shop. A pounding at the door broke his self-pity. "Hey, Texas, fo' chou," yelled Bananas, the black thick-bellied Cuban super who was traditionally too occupied arranging cockfights in the basement to attend mundane tenant needs of heat and warm water.

"Kleber? It's your mother," said VeeJee Cantrell, surprising her son with uncharacteristically extravagant use of long-distance, the second call in two days. On Thanksgiving afternoon, she rang and described in punishing detail the hometown feast he was missing, the prayers being said for him, a summary of the warm and benevolent Texas autumn, and an urgent Q. and A. inquiring of Kleber's health, financial condition, and standing in Columbia University graduate school. All of it was accomplished before the operator could cut in and announce termination of the maximum three minutes frugal VeeJee intended to purchase.

"Hi, Mom. I *still* wish I was there to eat leftovers."

VeeJee bore directly to her reason. "Son, did you see the papers this morning?"

"No, ma'm. Did the Communists come ashore at Galveston?"

"Kleber, don't be fresh. Have you read those Red Alert pamphlets I sent you?"

"No, ma'm. But I heard Adlai Stevenson speak last week. He's the greatest man in America. I'd give all the money I've got—which is about three dollars—to get him elected President."

"Kleber, liberalism is just a virus. I knew you'd get infected when you went to New York. Don't provoke me. I'm calling about Mack. Your best friend, remember?"

"Cover Boy? I wrote him last week."

"Listen to me, son. This is long-distance. Mack got hurt yesterday in the Aggie game."

"Hurt? How? Bad?"

"I don't know. The *Star-Telegram* said he was carried off the field unconscious. If you want to send him a get-well card, it's Memorial Hospital, Austin. . . . Now study hard . . . we've got a big investment." The line went dead, VeeJee having delivered the morning news, on and off, unknowingly an excellent journalist. Immediately Kleber rang Austin but learned only that "Mr. Crawford is in serious but stable condition." He tried a little reportorial end run, pretending to be a reporter from the New York *Times*. But the ice-toned nurse wasn't buying.

Mack did not even start the final game of his college career, benched not for the inept performance of Saturday last, nor because of the suspicious "pulled groin muscle" that healed by Monday practice as if brushed by divine hand. Clearly a sliver of animosity had been driven between the prince and his courtiers, festering under the rays of national publicity. Until quite late in the fourth quarter, Mack graced the sidelines, head bowed, helmet in hands, orange-and-white uniform as unsullied as the beribboned chrysanthemums on the breasts of Texas women.

With three minutes remaining, the score tied 14–14, Texas was only twenty yards shy of the A&M goal line, yet as powerless as a shadowboxer in attempts to score one last time. Then Mack was sent in as courier of a secret play. His entrance evoked the roar of celebrity recognition, and a few boos. The Aggie team sneered collectively at the clean and graceful giant, this symbol of aristocracy, at all the men in white buck shoes who married women with charge accounts at Neiman-Marcus. It loomed as a showdown between one Cadillac and eleven John Deere tractors. Rawest envy filled the farmers' faces and Mack smiled back in haughty condescension. For the first two plays, his presence seemed without major purpose, a star on stage with no lines to speak. The Texas quarterback, Wendall Collin, simply faked a handoff to Mack and then rammed the ball into the gut of a halfback for minor yardage. Twice Mack was nonetheless swarmed, and twice the most publicized athlete in America arose from the mud pile empty-handed, a magician whose rabbit had disappeared.

Then, on third down, Collin took the snap, danced six paces back, feinted to his right and apparently intended to shovel a lateral to a wingback dancing attendance. Mack, having drifted to the far left opposite side, looked like nothing but a transparent decoy. Just as an exultant horde of Aggies crashed forth to destroy Collin, the quarterback slammed his brakes. Without even looking, he rifled a hugely risksome bullet pass twenty yards sideways, cross-field, expecting Mack Crawford to be in the neighborhood. And he was—catching the pass with the ease of a handshake, having only a dozen yards to traverse, and ten seconds to do it. Screaming, the crowd leaped up, feet stamping the tiers with the power of an earth tremor. Drums pounded. Smokey, the Texas victory cannon positioned just behind the goalposts, prepared to fire. The gods smiled on Texas. Photographers ran puffing. Mack churned his legs, lifting them like pistons to his chest, bound for a glory corner empty as all West Texas. No one could intercept him. Three Aggies thrust toward the runner in desperate fury, attempting the impossible, trying to slice him out of bounds.

What happened next provided a tale to be told for decades. But no one knew or guessed the heart of the matter. In a splinter of a second on this Thanksgiving afternoon, Mack confronted both necessity and challenge. His manhood was on trial. Validation could come only by supreme testing of his strength. Thus did he spin and change direction, offering his body to the enemies, feeling his flesh seized high, middle, and low, dragging Aggie tacklers like chains across the white stripe, but at a terrible price. As he scored, he crashed into the Texas cannon, careened into a goalpost, flying through a forest of tripods, smashing into the fender of a radio equipment truck. Helmet ripped from his head, blood staining the gold hair in the last light of autumn, his bones snapped and he fell—a sun eclipsed—into darkness.

A team of medical disciplines collected before the moonglow light of the X rays. Among them were a neurologist, an internist, a dental surgeon, two orthopedists, and, briefly, a plastic surgeon who inspected the jagged tear that began below Mack's left eye and slithered south to the earlobe. It did not require urgent artistry. "How the hell did his helmet come off?" the plastic surgeon asked.

The neurologist answered. "From where I sat, it looked like the crazy SOB yanked the sucker off himself. Like he wanted everybody to *see* him." He went on to opine that the skull fracture was serious but not likely to impair Mack's mental faculties. "Lord God," murmured Dr. Samuel Voker, for two decades chief repairer of thousands of bones broken by athletes at Texas. These X rays taxed not only his expertise but his credulity. "Short of some tomfool lying down on a track and inviting the Southern Pacific to run over him, I've never seen bones busted like these," he said. Destruction of the patella, fibula, and the peroneal nerve was indicated.

"One of the sportswriters says he was home free," commented a second orthopod. "But the kid ran head on into the Aggies. *On purpose.*"

"Yeah," grunted Sam Voker. "I saw it. Either Mr. Crawford was showing off, which is possible, considering that stunt he pulled last week against SMU . . . or he committed the damnedest act of self-destruction I ever encountered."

In excruciating pain, blurred but still conscious despite the mercy of Demerol, Mack lay nude, his perfect body slashed with red streaks and crusts, like a painting ripped by vandals. The nurses who washed him pretended to pay nothing but professional attention but later they spoke of his sexuality. His penis, half erect from some involuntary command, sloped heavily across the crease that divided his trunk and thighs. His pubic hair was matted with blood. A homosexual orderly sneaked a photograph, processed it at home, and sold prints for ten dollars.

"I'm Sam Voker," said the orthopod. "You're gonna be okay, son. But we need to do a little patchwork on your legs. Can you hear me okay?" Mack nodded. Voker continued, being the rare doctor who explains clearly what he intends to do. "The left leg's a problem. There's a little fracture across the tibia—what you call your shin. The right leg, and when I use the word 'leg' I'm referring to the knee on down, that's messed up pretty good, too. Now I want you to do something for me. When I touch your big toe on the right foot, I want you to wiggle it for me."

Doctor touched; patient strained. The toe did not move. "That's fine, son," lied Voker. "Try it again." Nothing. Voker turned away, saddened that the peroneal nerve was apparently crushed. In the worst of these cases, a victim suffers a dropped foot and drags it to the grave. "All right, son, we're going into surgery soon. I'll be fixing up the patella—that's your kneecap—and working on the tibial plateau, the top part of your big leg bone just below the knee. The X rays indicate a little break." The truth was that it was totally shattered. "When you wake up, you'll be in a cast. In fact, two of 'em."

Mack managed one question. "How . . . long?"

"The cast'll start at the top of your thigh and go on down to the big toe. On both legs. They'll have to stay on eight weeks minimum."

"Did we win?" asked Mack.

Voker shrugged. "Depends on how you look at it."

The house on Cloverdale Avenue waited like a mausoleum with Mable Hofmeyer perfectly cast as caretaker. Mack returned home just before Christmas, borne like a milk can in the back of Zeke Mahaffey's truck, carried into Mable's indigo bedroom delirious and weak. Zeke stood around trying to be cheerful and helpful, but Mable showed him the door.

Reluctantly, Dr. Voker had granted Mack permission to spend Christmas at home in Fort Worth, issuing a stern dictate that the patient must return to Austin by New Year's Day. Mable, however, had a different course of treatment, to which her nephew agreed. "There's no need to go back to Austin," she said. "There are plenty of competent physicians in Fort Worth." On Christmas Day, Mack awoke only long enough to open his present from Mable, a gray flannel robe. The Demerol cadged from an orderly in the Austin hospital provided holiday warmth.

He hated Voker. The surgeon had lied to him. Now Mack fully understood the magnitude of his injuries. He found no cause for optimism in the guarded prognosis that, with intensive therapy, he "should" be able to walk, perhaps in a year. "I'd say you'll be eighty percent of normal," Voker predicted. In Austin, the surgeon had come to Mack's bed twice a day, happy as a carpenter whose fence did not warp in the rain. He gave interviews to the press. The doctor got his name in the paper often. One afternoon during grand rounds, when Voker turned up in Mack's room with fourteen doctors and medical students, lecturing as dispassionately as a museum guide, the athlete yelled, "Will you get the fuck outta here?" He did not want any more medical talk. He knew all he wanted to know. His right kneecap was totally gone—bits and fragments of bone stored in a jar, probably in Voker's bookcase. A stainless-steel bolt was the replacement, strengthened by a piece of bone stolen from the hip. Pain was beyond description. His right foot was as useless as a sparrow without wings.

But Mack was home now, and each night Mable Hofmeyer fell to her knees in prayer. She did *not* ask that God heal her nephew's legs. She thanked God for delivering the boy once again into his rightful custody. She had little else to be thankful for. Just past sixty, Mable looked half again as old, and frail as a porcelain shepherdess. Nothing in the house had changed, save piano keys more yellow and shrubs outside the windows that had grown like the beards of uncaring old men. Few pupils came for lessons anymore, Mable having become the neighborhood curiosity, the crazy lady in the haunted house. She had little money, less life. But she had Mack, and the two of them clung as cripples, physical and emotional. Over the holidays, Kleber, home from graduate studies in New York, ventured across the street and tried to visit. He was turned away by Mable. On the morning he left, he slipped a note under the door:

Mack — I tried to bring Christmas cheer, but you seem to be sleeping all the time. Listen, pal, just because you've got a couple of broken wheels doesn't mean the car's been totaled. I know you're hurting bad, and I won't intrude. But I want you to know I'm with you all the way. And be warned: Next September I start on the Houston *Call-Bulletin*—a master's in journalism and I get $58.50 a week! And if you're not up and around and able to beat me at any given sport, including 3-legged sack races, then I may break your arms as well. I miss you, friend. Any night you need somebody to talk to, call me up. Don't worry if it's late. I'll probably be needing to talk to somebody, too. — K.

Mack read the letter and tore it up.

The University of Texas athletic department sent Mack Crawford a registered letter to begin the New Year 1956. It announced: (1) his athletic scholarship was canceled, (2) his room and board revoked, and (3) his Chevrolet had been stolen from the dorm parking lot. His academic transcript was enclosed, revealing that his total credits placed him far short of a diploma. Mack wrote in response, saying, in effect, fuck-you-I'm-not-coming-back-anyway. His medical insurance was then canceled. He was twenty-two years old with two broken legs and $115 to his name, which he gave to Mable. A dark house was perfect. To ensure their peace, Mable disconnected the telephone.

On a wintry late-January morning, when the elms and pecans of Cloverdale Avenue were beaded with ice and a bitter norther blew its wrath across the plains, Mable Hofmeyer answered her seldom rung doorbell to discover a young woman on the porch. She had two large suitcases in her hands, a dusting of snow on her shoulders, and the cheery aura of a fireplace in the kitchen. "My name is Susan French," she said, offering her business card in reaction to Mable's persimmon face. "I'm from Dr. Dudley Morgan's office. I'm his physical therapist." Even as Mable made vigorous protest, Susan French was across her threshold, locating Mack's room, chirping "Good morning!" opening drapes, cracking windows, and sniffing at the offensive odor of an unwashed man in a foul room.

"Who the hell are you?" grumped Mack. He looked awful. A scraggly blond beard dribbled around his chin and his skin was yellow paste. Beside the bed were vials of medication; Susan snatched one up to read the label. Mack grabbed it from her hand and shoved it into a drawer.

She introduced herself, began setting up a strange-looking box with wires that snaked out and connected to small round paddles at the ends. Mack said, "I don't know any Dr. Morgan. There must be a mistake." He strained to raise up on his pillows.

"Relax," said Susan. "Here's the deal. Voker got worried when you didn't go back to Austin like you promised. So he called his friend Morgan in town here and said—quoting him accurately—'I busted my ass putting that youngster's legs back together. And unless somebody forces *him* to do a little work, then I might just as well have sawed off the goddamn things and bought Mr. Crawford a tin cup, some dark glasses, and pencils.' I like Voker. Salty old son of a bitch." Susan yanked away the musty coverlet to peer and poke. The larger cast on the right leg had a small square previously cut out by Voker. A window in an igloo. She pinched the exposed flesh in the window and got a yowl.

"That's just what I wanted to hear," said Susan. She slapped goo on the window and positioned the two paddles on exposed skin. "You're about to feel a tiny little buzz," she said. "And if you don't, there's plenty of time to buy the cup and pencils." Before Mack could protest, the therapist flipped a switch and sent 150 volts of electric current into the paddle heads. Mack's leg convulsed. "Great!" she exclaimed, studying her watch. "Now we wait thirty seconds and do an encore."

"That hurts," complained Mack.

"Wrong," corrected Susan. "It tingles." She prepared to shock him again. "What hurts is if that leg atrophies and you spend the rest of your life with traumatic arthritis. That's *pain,* buddy. Okay. Let's go." Whap! Mack's body jerked up from its elevated pillows like a marionette getting its strings pulled. "That's wonderful," said Susan. "We'll be doing this two or three times a week. Dr. Morgan will get the casts off in a month. We'll have you on crutches by spring. Little whirlpool, some isometrics, lots of swimming, and a good hour every day of weights and pulley work . . ."

"Wait a minute, lady," said Mack, surly once more. "I don't know what the hell you're talking about. Nobody asked you to come. I haven't got the money to pay you. And I sure as hell ain't gonna let you barge in here three times a week to shock the shit out of me."

"Haven't electrocuted anybody yet," said Susan, busy writing on a clipboard.

"Maybe you don't hear good," said Mack. "This is *my* life. I don't care if the muscles atrophy. I don't care if I get traumatic arthritis. I don't care about anything except getting you out of my room. *Now!* And close the window. It's cold. Pull the drapes. The light hurts my eyes."

"Finished?" asked Susan. "Now give *me* the courtesy of listening. If you want to stay in this bed the rest of your life, that is your decision. Just like the decision you made to play football. You took that risk. That's what life is all about. Options. Choices. Decisions. But I'd like to help you out of this . . ."

"Why?" asked Mack. "Why waste your time?"

"Because I'm good," she answered. "Damn good. And because . . ." Susan stopped, about to laugh.

"What's funny?"

"Because . . . because I'll kick your ass if you don't," she finished. "Admittedly, it's not the most tactful phrase I could have chosen."

But Mack smiled. "I'll think about it," he said. Behind his grouchiness was interest in this purposeful woman who worked efficiently and with humor.

"Fine. Now, *diet.* I'm leaving these menus with your aunt. High protein, low fat, skimmed milk—quart a day if you like. Fresh vegetables. You're a jock. You know what I'm talking about. Training camp food." With that, Susan French packed her cases, dropped two pamphlets about physical therapy on her patient's chest, and touched his cheek gently. "You're my first celebrity patient," she said. "I couldn't possibly screw this up."

For the next visit, Mack had combed his hair, and the one after that, he had shaved, splashed on lotion, and was impatiently drumming his watch, reminding the therapist that she was ten minutes late. Susan produced a bunch of sunny daffodils and a pile of *Sports Illustrated* magazines that she dumped onto his bed. "Bribes," she said. "It's quadriceps time." Mack's task this day was to concentrate on his right leg, contract it with all the strength he could summon, and hold it for a count of ten.

". . . four, five, six . . ." Susan tolled, pleased even though Mack could sustain no more. "We'll be up to ten by next week, and twenty the week after that. When you get to one hundred, we'll dance."

"Dance for me now," teased Mack.

"Rule Number One. Don't socialize with the patients," said Susan, a little flustered.

On her way out, she was stopped by Mable at the door. The old woman wore a purple scarf on her head, pulled down to cover her cheeks. She looked like a Russian babushka. "I have very little means," she whispered. "I hear that Dr. Morgan is a carriage-trade physician. I don't think we can afford you anymore."

"Please don't worry about money," said Susan, trying to take Mable's hand reassuringly. It jerked back as if endangered by acid. "The only thing that's important is to get that beautiful ox back on his feet. You can help, Miss Hofmeyer. His attitude alone is worth half a miracle."

Mable ushered the young woman out her door and stood behind the screen, veiled. "Only God can bring miracles."

"I can't argue with that," said Susan. "So if you have a connection, give Him a ring." She waved and hurried down the slippery steps. Something came to mind and she stopped, turning back. Mable was still behind the screen, watching, suspicious.

"I've been meaning to ask you, ma'm. How many pain pills is Mack taking a day?"

"I don't know," answered Mable. "He suffers a great deal."

"It's very important that your nephew not get too dependent on medication," urged Susan. "Would you mind speaking with Dr. Morgan?"

"I don't need any doctor to tell me what's best for my blood kin."

Susan's face, usually sunny, clouded. "Be careful, Miss Hofmeyer. *Please.*"

The door was locked on the following day, and though Susan could hear classical music thundering from a piano within, no one answered her repeated knocks. She rapped until her knuckles hurt. Two days later she tried again. The house was quiet. No answer. Susan walked around back to Mack's bedroom and tried to peer in the window. It was draped and locked. She called Mack's name and scratched on the pane, fretting that someone would take her for a burglar. Later in the afternoon she returned and slipped a note under the front door. It begged that somebody admit her, but no one did.

A week of mounting worry. Then Susan assaulted the house on Cloverdale by arriving in the pre-dawn chill of 6 a.m. She pounded the door and slipped in a new note: "I am going to stand out here and rap all day and all night and tomorrow and the day after tomorrow. Please let me attend my patient." She placed a leather glove on her hand and commenced to pound away.

Promptly Mable opened the door. As nice as nice could be, the old woman had dolled up her face with clown circles of rouge and lopsided smears of lipstick. She smelled of too much Woolworth's perfume. "Why, good morning," she said. "I was just about to write you a letter, Miss French. Mack has a fine new doctor. He's doing very well and we won't be needing you anymore. Both of us are grateful for your Christian concern."

"Who?" demanded Susan. "What doctor?" She knew every orthopod in town.

"I don't believe that is your business." Slam.

In the alley behind Mable's house, a grocery truck stopped. It was late February, almost three months from the Thanksgiving afternoon when Mack was injured. By custom the delivery boy honked, summoning Mable to accept her greenery. She came out, a heavy shawl shrouding her head like a slipcover. Quickly a middle-aged man in a business suit darted out from behind the truck and raced for the back door, left ajar. Susan French materialized as well. Both were inside the house before Mable could figure out what had happened and rush screaming about them.

"Mack is resting," she cried.

Sam Voker was already in, following Susan toward the bedroom. He threw his name brusquely at Mable.

"You have no right!" she cried.

"Madame, I have every right in the world. My patient needs me. . . . Good Lord!" Voker stared in horror and threw his hand to his nose. The stench of unwashed bed linens, urine, decaying flesh rolled out in waves. Beside the filthy pallet were candle stubs, encircling bronze busts of Beethoven and Mozart and a polychrome picture of Christ in His agony. Scattered among them like toy soldiers were a dozen small medicine vials. Unconscious, drenched in sweat, his body wasted by forty pounds, Mack slept heavily, his eyes ringed in dark shadows. The surgeon seized his arm and took an alarming pulse. He slapped his patient's face. Hard. Again! "Son!" he yelled.

Voker whirled and looked at Mable with disgust. "What in the name of God have you done to this boy, woman?" He raised Mack's head and cradled it. More slaps. "Mack! Wake up!" Seeing the pills beside the bed, Voker quickly identified the contents, swept them to the floor in anger. "Call an ambulance. Fast!" he directed Susan. Later it would be calculated that in the weeks since Christmas, Mack took—or was given—more than four hundred Demerol tablets, enough to slay a man less young, less strong. Susan noticed one other grotesquery; Mable Hofmeyer had been sleeping in Mack's bed. Her perfume practically drenched the sheets with its odor.

Six months later, his casts removed, bones knitting, weight regained, countenance once more fair and handsome, McKenzie (Mack) Crawford, Jr., leaned on crutches before a justice of the peace and married Susan Martha French. Sam Voker was best man. The groom was twenty-three and wore a newly purchased pair of trousers from Montgomery Ward and a UT letterman's jacket. The bride was twenty-seven and wore a soft pink dress with daisies embroidered at the bust line. She failed to notice that Mack immediately shut his eyes at seeing the gown for which she paid a hard-earned $29.95. After the ceremony, he requested carefully that she not wear pink again, explaining that it was his least favorite color.

As neither bride nor groom possessed credentials of interest to a society editor, the wedding went unreported. *Sic transit gloria.*

Mable Hofmeyer did not attend. In the immediate weeks after the extrication of her nephew from the house, neighbors heard music. Unusually, the windows were thrown wide. The melodies were mainly gospel, Mable's shrill, piercing soprano soaring above the foursquare chords. But at night, from within a house that bore no light, the music seemed at war—one precise phrase of Mozart followed by atonal shrieks—rather like a rebellious child banging fists on a hated keyboard.

One late May afternoon, during that gentle hour before supper when youngsters ride bicycles and play tag and revel in the joy of being new, a small child skipping rope saw something strange. She stopped and stared and giggled. "Look at her," she called to friends.

Mable Hofmeyer was stumbling down the front steps, weaving as if intoxicated through the maze of overgrowth that was the front yard. Except for a strip of dirty bed sheeting wound about her head, she was naked. Thrusting out her arms toward heaven, she lifted her mask to the setting sun. She collapsed. Six hours later she died at Harris Hospital. Autopsy revealed the pathetic old woman had been suffering a series of cerebral strokes. Her brain was pocked with dead cells, a piano with dark keys that made no sound. In her stomach was the residue of forty-five Demerol tablets.

The coroner thought her face so interesting that he took a picture of it. Mable would one day be celebrated in a dermatology magazine. The entire left half of her face, from neck to hairline, like an over-ripened berry, was violent, ghastly crusted red.

CHAPTER SEVEN

Twenty years later, Calvin Sledge rang the bell of this very same house on Cloverdale Avenue. A cascade of soft melody chimed. While he waited, the DA observed the neighborhood. Defiant of time, the old block was young again. Architects had created façades of diagonally sawed redwood strips and Moorish latticework to mask the beige brick dowagers. Half-moon carriageways curved gracefully into sculptured lawns where St. Augustine grass grew dense and lush as carpets. Italian cypress stood as geometric sentries on territory once the claim of dandelions and woebegone crape myrtle. New families were moving in, willing to pay $90,000 for houses first sold a half century ago for $3,000, breeding children named Jason and Christopher and Dawn, heirs to the ancient kingdom of Kleber and Mack and T.J.

In the 1960's, Fort Worth swept to the west, pursuing the lure of newness, settling into subdivisions that sprouted like Johnson grass on the dusty plains twenty miles from city core. But the elixir of suburban life turned sour when freeways became clogged corridors of lost time and noxious smoke, when gasoline rose to sixty cents a gallon—scandalous where oil once squished beneath farmers' plows. It was then that the old neighborhoods, those blights to the eye and to fashion, those blocks as shunned as the old people who continued to live on them, became once again desired. Like old chests discovered in attics, the houses required only a peel, paint, and new brass fittings to regain the allure of youth. They offered a sense of permanence in a time when social foundations were crumbling.

Calvin Sledge well knew that the woman he had come to question had never moved away from Cloverdale, even though her purse would have permitted an ascension to Westover Hills, the tony enclave across the red cobblestones of Camp Bowie Boulevard. There existed estates that approximated Tudor England, and villas seemingly transplanted from the cliffs of the Côte d'Azur, and museum-sized homes as marbled as the hotels of Miami Beach. For many days now, Sledge had been rejected at the entrances of these opulent homesteads, informed by condescending maids and butlers that their employers were "resting" or "unavailable," which translated into get-the-hell-off-the-grass. No Croesus or Midas—and there were many in Westover Hills— seemed *vital* to his case, but the DA was nonetheless bent on touching every base, suspecting there was a scrap of information hidden *someplace*. During a week of personal humiliation, Sledge had not even dared to flex his legal muscles. He had instead heeled like a subservient hound and backed off through courtyards of Italian tiles, past Henry Moore sculptures sitting next to pots of riotous homegrown orchids. He got into a dusty tan county-issue Plymouth sulking beside Mercedes

450 SLC's, as out of place as fried catfish on a platter of caviar. It should be said that Calvin Sledge was not a man to forfeit any match, but ambition required that respect be paid to Westover Hills. Should he one day seek the governor's chair, then here was the fount, along with River Oaks in Houston and Highland Park in Dallas, from which political blessings, i.e. money, flowed. It would not be politic to bang on doors copied from the Medicis and strong-arm cooperation for a yet-to-be-proved murder case, and then return two years thereafter with a chaw of humble pie in cheek—and hat in hand.

But Cloverdale Avenue, even with a face-lift, required no such tact. He rang the bell again, and when no answer came, banged on the creamy grill screen. Inside he could hear a stereo playing harp music. Obviously the dame was hiding. He was mad enough to start throwing subpoenas around Cowtown like poisoned darts. "Dammit, lady," he grumbled, "open the goddamn door."

The woman who presently did was in middle age but her beauty and bearing made perjury out of time. She was the classic paradox that is Texas Woman, steel coated in cream. Her hair, honey streaked with untouched silver, was yanked back impatiently and tied with a piece of home-woven blue macramé. Her jeans were straight-legged Levi's, but her feet stuck out bare and clean and tender. Her blouse was fragile peach blossoms but the arms it sheltered were strong, arms to rock a baby or fire a rifle. The lady was sexy and tough, capable of quoting the Bible in one breath and telling a dirty joke in the next. And get away with both. "Damn, I'm sorry to keep you waiting," she said. Her slender, angular face was flushed damp with the color of hard work. "I was out back trying to shoo those damn squirrels outta the pecan trees. Got stuck on a limb."

"I wish I was the fire department rescue squad," said Sledge approvingly, looking over her shoulder into a living room where once Mable Hofmeyer coveted shadows. Now the walls were bleached hot white, setting off chrome-and-glass etageres, black leather sling chairs, lime-and-orange Mexican rugs, framed posters from Hollywood movies, snake charmer baskets from which reared spindly dracaena trees that brushed a skylight ceiling. Here was a room for a woman proud of her looks and secure in her taste.

"Well," she asked impatiently. "What are you selling?"

"Oh, sorry, ma'm. You're Mrs. Crawford?"

She tensed. "No. Susan French."

"But you *were* Mrs. Mack Crawford."

"A thousand years ago. I don't use Mack's name anymore. . . . Just who the hell are you, mister?"

Sledge produced both his calling card and his badge. "One of my assistants spoke to you," he informed.

"I remember. Didn't he tell you I hung up on him?"

"Yes, ma'm. That's why I'm here. Thought maybe I could bell the cat. Two minutes?"

"You bastard, you trapped me. *Two minutes.*" But she smiled, rather graciously. Figuratively, Sledge crossed his fingers. Susan brought him iced tea with fresh-picked mint, and corn chips, and listened attentively to his pitch. What he needed was information about Mack, what he had been doing in Fort Worth, *anything,* whatever she might contribute to the lunatic mess.

Susan French nodded and—Sledge prayed—prepared to tell a tale. But what she did was draw drapes quick as long departed Aunt Mable. "I'd help you if I could, Sledge," she said. "But Mack and I were divorced a long time ago." Sledge damn well knew that. He had a clipping from Liz Smith's New York gossip column that told of the broken marriage, the uncontested divorce in Juárez, the property settlement for the child that supposedly included one million dollars in trust.

"But you stayed in touch. You spoke. He called you when he got in town." Sledge was lying, but ten years as a prosecutor teaches any man to play bluff poker.

Susan shrugged. "Hell yes. We talked now and then. He used to get sauced about two a.m. and call long-distance . . ." She jumped up. "I don't know anything. Leave me out of it."

Sledge held on to his seat, unwilling to capitulate. If he had been bent on seduction, had he found Susan French on the next bar stool at some saloon, he would not have quit until she slapped his face and kneed his nuts. "Mrs. French," he began again.

"*Ms.* French," she corrected, feisty as hell.

"Ms. French, I put it to you that you have a moral and legal responsibility to cooperate. I could subpoena you. And if you ignored me, I have it in my power to send marshals over here and physically carry your trim little behind to the grand jury."

Susan clapped her hands. She seemed amused. "Then do it! That'd damn sure liven up the six o'clock news. I teach a class in self-defense at the Women's Club. We just got in this little spray can called Rapel.

You squirt it at a rapist and he drowns in skunk juice. Try me, Mr. DA. Send in the troops." To which Sledge found a ten-cent laugh, the approximate worth of his threat.

But as he laughed, an idea slammed home. He assessed it. *Cruel?* Yes. *Perverse?* Probably. But *worth* it? He shelved the scheme, becoming diverted by a photograph encased in Plexiglas and positioned prominently beside Susan's chair. The face was of a lad in middle teens, blond like Mack, intriguing like Susan, but curiously solemn. He appeared to be a child who had played hide-and-seek all his life.

"Where's your son now?" risked Sledge.

Susan froze. The tea glass shook in her hand. "In school. Europe . . ."

"Maybe I should find him . . ." tested Sledge.

"And I'll call a press conference and accuse you of persecuting an innocent youngster. Jesus, Sledge. Let's not get in a pissin' contest. Your two minutes are up."

The prosecutor nodded, picked up his briefcase, let his fingers dance across the cowhide. He persuaded himself: this may be the most base act I've ever committed. But—no pain, no gain. Here goes. The dame's gonna heave me on the sidewalk anyway. "I'm leaving," he promised. "Just one thing. Answer me one thing—and I'll disappear."

"Shoot." If for an instant the woman's composure had deserted her on mention of the boy, now it was back. And that was precisely what Sledge intended to detonate. First he hemmed and hawed, inflating the suspense, toying with his case as if it contained the master key to the secrets of life. He made his voice a brew of gallantry and frustration. "It's like this . . . I just don't understand how you can treat this mess like . . . like *nothin'* happened . . . I mean, when I knocked on your door you were out back chasin' squirrels outta trees, and now you're sittin' here like a diamond necklace embedded in a cake of ice. I gotta be honest with you, lady; my office is an ongoing earthquake. . . . And your eyes aren't even moist. . . . Makes a man wonder if you're holding anything back. . . ."

From the moment she opened her front door Susan French had faced Sledge smack in the eye—man to man. But now her lashes fell like surrender to unfightable exhaustion. She stared at the briefcase and answered softly. "You want to see tears? I can show you buckets full. What else? Anger? Screams? Tantrums? Come around some midnight. You might hear me throw another empty bottle of scotch against the wall. . . . What else do you want out of me, Sledge? A confession? Well, okay. Here's a confession. I did it. Now go indict me."

Sledge raised his hands. Enough. He pulled a sealed manila folder from his briefcase. "I say you're playing with fantasies," he said. "I wonder if you've got the guts to look at the truth."

Susan stared at the folder. "It was an *accident,* Sledge. The papers say so. An *accident.*"

He tossed the folder onto the glass coffee table. "If you decide to open it, the first two pictures are in black and white. The rest are living color. Look at them and then show me where the accident part is. . . ."

After a time, Susan opened the folder—casually, like it was a Christmas gift catalogue from Neiman's—and glanced perfunctorily at the first picture. Slowly she turned it over, looked at the next, betraying no emotion, a woman playing solitaire with images of unspeakable horror. The first time Sledge studied them he ran to the sink and plunged his face in cold water. The DA had seen a thousand dead men but none was precedent for these.

She looked at hell's nightmare and she broke, of course, as Sledge knew she would. But it was not sudden, not like the snap of a limb in a storm. Her face just changed—changed like a blank sheet of photo paper dropped into a pan of developing fluid. Nothing at first—then faint traces—detail emerging—features forming—eyes widening—terror coming into clear focus—mouth tightening—tears forming—tears spilling—tears ruining the image—beauty contorted—blurred—gone. A picture to reject.

"I'm sorry," said Sledge honestly. "I shouldn't have put you through that."

Susan hugged her body, rocking back and forth, keening. "I hate you," she said. "I hate you so much that I know now why people kill. . . . Get the fuck outta here. . . . But come back tonight. . . . Late. . . . You want to be famous, don't you, Sledge? You want to be a celebrity. . . . Come back and I'll tell you what it's like. . . . Then you tell me if you really want it that much . . ."

That night, fully composed, Susan French affixed one price tag for which there would be no haggling. "You leave my son out of this," she said.

Sledge agreed.

"I mean, you promise not to call him as a witness—or even interview him?"

Sledge nodded.

"Where do you want me to start?" she then asked.

"At the beginning," directed Sledge.

"The beginning? Christ, what is the beginning of anything? With Mack, you begin with his beauty. . . . I know that beauty's not the word we use to describe men. But handsome won't do it. Sexy, desirable, masculine—yes but no. *Beauty* is the beginning and the reason . . ." She smiled and let it flow. She was a talker. Sledge settled back expectantly.

"I never told Mack this," she went on. "You see, I was a liar from the day we met. I came on with false credentials. I said I worked for an orthopedic surgeon named Morgan here in Fort Worth. The truth is that I was on the county payroll. Charity cases. Black men with legs lost to cancer. Mexicans with arms crushed in car wrecks. Welfare stuff —though we didn't use the term then. *Relief.* That's what it was. A kinder euphemism. One morning in 1956 this call came in from Austin. Old Dr. Sam Voker down there was mad as a cut bull because Mack's aunt kept hanging up on him. He wanted Tarrant County to send somebody out and check on his patient. . . ."

Sledge began to make discreet notes on a yellow pad but Susan covered his hand firmly. Nothing could be written down.

"Soooo, when I saw that name . . . McKenzie Crawford, Jr., . . . on the work sheet, I grabbed it quicker than a dollar bill on the sidewalk. . . . I knew Mack, you see. Well, that's not the truth, either. I didn't actually *know* him, never shook hands with him . . . never *touched* him. . . . But I sure as hell knew what he looked like. I was in Austin studying physical therapy at the same time he was down there playing football. I even got a job at the athletic dorm—serving scrambled eggs on the breakfast line—just so I could look at him. . . . I went to every football game and I didn't then and don't now know a goddamn thing about football. . . . I cut out his pictures from the newspaper. . . . I slept with a scrapbook full of *him*. . . . When *Life* magazine put him on the cover—that first time—I bought ten copies and made a collage on the wall above my bed. . . . I was so crazy I used to hide on the campus behind a statue of Sam Houston and wait every afternoon for him to pass by. . . . I may still have a clump of dried grass somewhere that he actually *stepped* on. . . . I know what you're thinking, Sledge. School Girl Crush. It was beyond that. I was crazy, *seriously crazy*. Mack was all the Prince Charmings a little country girl like me ever dreamed about. . . . Mack was a sex object, and that was pretty avant-garde in the fifties. Women weren't supposed to cream in their underpants over the Mack Crawfords of our world. But we did. At least I did. . . ."

Sledge smiled but he felt a twinge of embarrassment. He was not yet comfortable in the community of liberated women. And never would be. He steered his subject onto more traditional ground. "So the therapist married the patient?"

"Yes," answered Susan pleasantly. She fell silent. Her thoughts moved to some intensely private place. Then a great sob burst from her throat. Tremors of emotional aftershock rattled her body. The afternoon's photographs had somehow resurrected in her memory. Sledge's mind raced. He had to get her off the manila envelope with its awful pictures. "I could use a cup of instant coffee," he said hurriedly.

She nodded, everything suddenly smoothed back in place. "I might even do better than that."

They sat at a butcher-block table in the kitchen until 2 a.m. They drank two pots of thick black chicory coffee and finished a plate of chicken salad and a wedge of Brie. When the DA left, weary but anxious to drive immediately to the courthouse and dictate the worth of the night, he felt reasonably nourished. Susan struck him as candid and useful. She seemed truthful. He did not even notice the nondescript car parked a hundred yards away at the corner of Cloverdale and Camp Bowie Boulevard, nor did he glimpse the thin and solemn young man sitting at the wheel.

But the young man saw Sledge. And five minutes after the prosecutor had cleared the neighborhood, the young man was sitting in his place at the very same butcher-block table. And once again Susan French was sobbing.

Their first year of marriage was smooth and easy, at least from Mack's point of view, he having taken—or been given, or settled for—a wife who functioned as nurse, therapist, cheerleader, homemaker, psychologist, provider, and faith healer. Each morning Susan got up before the sun did, usually tired but determined to transform Mable Hofmeyer's dungeon into a honeymoon cottage. She ripped down the thick, musty drapes, hired neighborhood kids to help tote the threadbare furniture into the garage, splashed white and yellow and spring green paint on walls and windowsills. She threw out death and summoned life. Each morning at seven, her face carefully made, breakfast started, Susan woke Mack and put him through exercises. For several months after his casts were removed, the simple act of bending the knee brought enormous pain—but Susan dictated a hundred before she would bring fresh-squeezed orange juice, hot coffee, bacon and eggs to her husband's bed, along with the sports page. After breakfast, she affixed ten-pound weights to his feet and counted encouragingly as he lifted his limbs three hundred times. By 8 a.m., she was squealing out the driveway in a '48 Studebaker, earning $52.17 a week from tending other broken bodies in her care, but always calling home at least twice a day to ensure that Mack was all right and filling his regime.

Their lives were frugal and simple, like tuna fish casseroles. Rarely did they even go out, Mack not wanting to be seen on crutches. Friends were as few as leftover dollars. The enemy within was silence, Mack feeling sorry for himself and stiff-arming the world. Susan fought this battle by finding a few extra minutes in her race through the hours for studying the sports page—alien territory. This enabled her to pop out with rehearsed remarks such as "I can't believe Don Larsen pitched that perfect game in the World Series yesterday" or "Sad about Archie Moore. He should have hung 'em up instead of getting knocked out by a bum like Floyd Patterson." Sometimes these ploys worked; more often than not Mack played deaf and mute, sitting on the edge of his bed while his wife chattered, raising and lowering his legs like a machine with no purpose. Then there were the nights when Susan found her husband in one of Mable's "guest rooms," since turned into a storehouse of trophies. Mack liked to lean on his crutches and brush his fingers against the glittering treasure, pridefully placed on shelves that his wife had carpentered out of plans in *Popular Mechanics*.

Mack permitted a decorous embrace before lights out, but if Susan held on to *her* trophy too long, he threw the penalty flag. Off sides. Time for the bride to move three feet back, into Mable's bed. Usually she stretched a lonely hand across the chasm, and some nights Mack accepted it, his huge rough fingers touching hers in what Susan interpreted as some kind of awkward love. But in her heart she knew it was a tip to the porter who carried luggage. And exhausted as she always was by nightly chimes at ten, she never found easy sleep.

A year after marriage, the sorrowful fact was that love was but a word and not a deed.

The catalyst of their first real fight, if blame can ever be properly fixed in marital war, was Kleber. Without appointment, he appeared at the door, a bottle of California burgundy in one hand, yellow roses in the other, and acting as exuberant as a terrier pup demanding adoption. "If you're Susan," he said with a low, approving whistle, "don't bother to wake up the gimp." Mack hobbled from the bedroom on crutches, a trifle theatrical to his wife's perception, wincing as he turned twenty paces into a journey of two miles. The men eyed one another tentatively, like newcomers to the sandbox. Then Kleber threw a bear hug, holding tightly for the moment that males are allowed in social commerce.

Kleber raised his dukes playfully. "You wanna go a couple of rounds? I finally got this bully where I can handle him."

Mack melted into good humor. He said he was glad to see Kleber.

"Now don't get nervous, Susan," said Kleber, "but I actually love this big ox. And how he ever caught somebody as fine as you is a mystery for the ages." Kleber uncorked his wine. They toasted to "old times" and "good times." For six months, Kleber had been working in Houston as a cub reporter. He looked the part, thought Susan. Rumpled sports jacket with pockets stretched to accommodate note pads. Sandy, thinning hair in need of trim. Horn-rimmed glasses enlarging green-blue eyes that always seemed to be darting about, catching every detail. He was glib and quick, master of ceremonies for the evening, dredging up childhood memories from Cloverdale, deprecating his years in New York and his inability to find a single girl who could comprehend his Texas accent.

With every punch line he stopped and waited for Mack to catch the conversational ball and run with it. But when each time it fell in uncomfortable silence, Kleber threw again. And though his talk was anecdotal, set pieces honed by previous tellings, it entertained. Kleber was a performer, making Susan wonder if he always took center stage, or was in mere duty on nights when his audience was dull and drab. She was quietly miffed at Mack, at his squirming in the chair and holding on to his crutches like the end was near.

Mack did not say two dozen words in the first hour. He was yawning by seven forty-five.

"Another toast," proposed Kleber, raising a glass that on the morning would contain Mack's orange juice. "To friendship, happiness, to getting what we all want—and cross-our-hearts-and-hope-to-die we'll never let seven years go by again without seeing each other." Mack pretended to drink. Trying to save the night, Kleber proposed an impulsive drive to the north side for an enchilada fix at Joe T. Garcia's famous restaurant, but Mack declined, pleading he was too tired, too weak for a crosstown journey.

"Well, pal, I think you'd feel better if you got out more," said Kleber. "You look fine. When are you going to throw away those things?" He gestured at the crutches.

"Pretty soon."

"Then what?"

"Whatta you mean?"

"I'm talking about plans. Life plans. You used to talk about coaching."

Mack shook his head. "I'm not interested in sports anymore," he said. "I've been taking this accounting course by correspondence . . ." Susan bit back the impulse to reveal that Mack quit after the first lesson, that she finished the six that followed and got her husband a proxy B. He could not even balance the checkbook.

At the curb, on familiar turf, the Prince of Power made awkward goodbye to the Prince of Charms. Reunion over. Mack leaned on his crutches, fidgeting like a child with a poor report card. He had not wanted Kleber to visit. That was obvious. And now he did not want him to leave. Kleber picked up on it. "What's the matter?" he said quietly.

"Oh, nothing," said Mack. "Thanks for coming."

"Nothing? You can't fool a fooler. That pain on your face all night doesn't come from busted bones."

"I dunno. It didn't turn out the way we thought it would."

Kleber tried to sound cheerful. "We're not exactly over the hill. It's still the salad course. . . . Feel up to a walk? To the corner and back?"

Mack grinned and dropped his crutches, but on second thought he picked them up. At the boulevard, bulldozers slept, alien monsters whose mission was to obliterate the past. Already devastated were the drugstore that sold the vital youth merchandise of prophylactics and pinball games, the mom-and-pop bakery whose ovens created the sensory delights of sweet rolls crammed with apricot jam, the five-and-dime where kites and Scout knives were once found. Everything was now being replaced by a monstrous Do It Ur-Self Home Fix-Up Center, larger than an airplane hangar. Mack interrupted Kleber's reverie with a question thrown into the night. "Do you ever think about . . . *her?*"

There she was. Out in the open. Tangible as ropes, Kleber saw the bindings that wrapped his friend. He nodded. "I figured *that's* what the trouble was," he said. "And I'd like to tell you the answer is not only no but *hell* no. Never give her a moment of my time. . . . But the truth is, I think about that night just as often as you do. . . . Once in New York I got so crazy I actually wrote it all down . . . the storm . . . the booze . . . T.J.'s hot pants . . . Laurie . . . the river . . ." Kleber fell silent. He could not complete his sentence. After a time he went on, "And you know what? It was the best thing I ever wrote! Oh, I wasn't in it, of course. Neither were you. I changed all the names. I moved the setting to Louisiana. The Brazos became the Mississippi. But the fucker flat out sang! I mean, it had more passion than Madame Bovary. I titled it *The Three Princes.* I even thought seriously about trying to sell it . . ."

Panic flashed across Mack's face. Kleber hastened to reassure him. "Don't worry. Nobody's ever going to read it. After I finished, I told myself, Laurie, my poor dear, you are over and done with, your night is from this moment on forever and finally exorcised. Gone, skeedaddle. Lights out."

"*The Three Princes* . . . I wish I could have read it," said Mack.

"Well, guess how long the exorcism worked? The next morning there she was again, Laurie sitting on my typewriter, swinging her legs, draping that pink dress over my keyboard. . . . Then time went on, a week, a month. I don't guess I felt the old stomach churn for a good three months, not until I walked in your door tonight. Not until Laurie's ghost squeezed smack in between you and me."

Mack nodded. "I know. I saw her, too."

"Listen, Mack. We've punished ourselves long enough. Seven years is an adequate penance. It's time for a new covenant. No more guilt. Deal?" They grasped hands and promised to forget that night, and to seal the oath they found clods of hard clay and threw them against the bulldozers—another vague but satisfying expulsion of demons.

On the stroll back, Kleber urged Mack to rev up his life. "Get busy," he suggested. "They can't hit a moving target. That's my motto." Kleber complimented Mack once again on Susan. He said she appeared to be an exceptionally fine woman. He did not say how much he envied his lame friend for being able to commit—no matter how tenuously—to an intimate relationship. Kleber usually spent about five minutes with somebody before moving on fast. It was not emotionally satisfying, but it was new, always new, and it was safe, or so he told himself.

Later, preparing for bed, Susan asked carefully what the two men had talked about on their stroll.

"Not much. Wouldn't interest you." Mack swung on his crutches toward the bathroom, where he would change into his pajamas. He always undressed in privacy, an unnecessary bit of modesty, seeing as how Susan had nursed him for months and bathed him in bed. This time she beat him to the door and blocked his way. Her dander was up. "How do you know *what* might interest me, Mr. Zipper Mouth? You made me feel like some sofa on loan tonight. . . . Kleber probably thought you send me back to the store in the morning. . . ."

"Please, hon, I'm tired."

"You're tired. You don't know what the word means. And would you like to know what interests me? *Anything* would interest me. I'd be interested in knowing how many goddamn leaves fall off the cottonwood tree, seeing as how you spend all day staring out the window."

"Don't cuss." Mack planted his crutches and attempted to detour around the obstacle in his path.

"Why the hell not?" Her wrath was a demon genie rearing from a long-corked bottle.

"Women shouldn't cuss, that's why not."

"Well is that so? Well piss on that. Shit on that. *Fuck* that. Oh, excuse me, maybe I shouldn't cuss in a foreign language."

Mack refused the quarrel and the crude truth, retreating to the bed. He got but a few steps before Susan lashed out and kicked one of the crutches from beneath his armpit. He sprawled on the floor. "You don't need those anymore," she yelled. "They've become a crutch." At that she laughed, pleased by her irony. And while she laughed, Mack rolled over and over like a lumpy ball, hands flung forward for help. He was in trouble.

"Oh God," Susan cried. "I'm sorry, baby." She rushed to him and lay prone beside the giant man. "Are you okay? Let me help you."

"Just let me alone."

Later, in the dark, in their separate places, Susan spoke softly. She was not even sure if Mack was awake. "I didn't mean any of that. . . . I love you, Mack. . . . I don't know words strong enough to tell you how much I love you. I need you, too. I need you and love you . . ."

After a time, Mack said, "I know you do."

"Am I doing anything wrong?"

"No. You're perfect."

She was crying to herself. She reached out for his hand, but Mack did not take hers.

Something unexpected happened.

A reporter from the *Star-Telegram* telephoned Mack a few days thereafter. Kleber had planted the idea, suspecting that a new ray of the old limelight might solder both limbs and disposition. The *Star-Telegram* published a poignant account of Mack's two-year struggle to mend his legs and it came wrapped around a striking photograph. Mack was pictured leaning on a cane and happily tossing a football to neighborhood children, something he had not done before and which was the idea of the newspaper's cameraman.

Mail soon overflowed his box—letters of praise for his grit, requests for his autograph, religious tracts offering inspiration. The picture was transmitted on the AP wire and mention was made on the CBS evening TV news. Job offers followed. A sporting goods chain in Houston telegraphed an opportunity to manage a new suburban branch. Fort Worth's Parks and Recreation Department proposed that Mack become a roving counselor and playground coach. A Dallas clothes manufacturer asked if Mack wanted to model bathing suits for a mail-order catalogue.

One afternoon, Susan hurried home from work and found her husband gone. It was the first time. Worried, she set out to scour the neighborhood. Mack had thrown away his crutches and was dependent now only on a cane, but he had not seemed strong enough for a venture beyond the perimeter of the block. After a fruitless half-hour search, Susan had her hand on the telephone, dialing the police. Then a pale blue Cadillac paused outside.

At the wheel was an attractive older woman obviously in high spirits. Diamonds glinted from her hand. Beside her, similarly aglow, sat Mack. He got out of the car, waved a cheery goodbye, and walked with steady strength into the house. The setting sun was at his back and Susan marveled at his beauty. He looked about eighteen. Two years of casts and crutches had swelled his arm muscles, even as his legs had dwindled. For a long time he was misshapen, a barrel on cane stalks. But now through exercise his legs were equal to the powerful torso they supported. He was not even using his cane. He was mended.

"I was about to call out the Marines," said Susan, reaching for Mack's elbow. He shook her off. He required no help.

"I was going to surprise you," he said. "I've been working out over at the high school track. . . . Whew, out of breath." He sat down on the steps and rested. "About a week ago, I tried walking around once, without the cane, and it felt good. The next day I walked two laps. Today I walked a hundred yards and ran ten. Sort of. Next week, I'll run a hundred and walk ten."

Not until after dinner did Susan inquire, with oh-by-the-way curiosity, after the identity of the woman in the Cadillac. Mack answered openly. "She's Mrs. Bowman. She was at the school hitting tennis balls against the wall."

"Oh?" Susan wanted more. Mack provided nothing.

"Who's Mrs. Bowman?" she asked later.

Mack shrugged. "Some rich lady. Her husband's a big Texas alum. They took me out to dinner once at Rivercrest when I was in high school."

"How come she drove you home?"

"I don't know. She was leaving when I was leaving and she asked if I wanted a ride."

Susan would probably have harped a little more had not Mack surprised her by wrapping his arms about her shoulders. He kissed her nicely. "Love you, hon," he said. Then he fell into bed and was immediately asleep.

Neither coincidence nor a passion for tennis had brought Catalina Bowman to the high school athletic field. Had she wished to practice her mediocre game, she could have patronized any of the three country clubs to which she belonged in Fort Worth and Dallas, or she could have asked her husband, Barron (Bear) Bowman, to build her a court, their Westover Hills estate spreading over six acres with numerous 60-by-110-foot rectangles available.

The photograph of Mack in the *Star-Telegram* had brought purpose to a tedious morning for Cat. Drinking breakfast, midway through a second bloody mary, perusing the fashion advertisements and considering a drive to Dallas for a prowl through Neiman's, or, alternatively, returning to bed with *Forever Amber,* Catalina Bowman glanced at the sports page. She looked at it for a long time. "Yes," she murmured, excising Mack's image with a long, flame-colored nail on her right index finger. "Yes, indeedy."

Fort Worth society knew this about Cat Bowman:

She was on the shady side of forty, though by candlelight, or glimpsed through a martini glass, charity might reduce the count by half a decade. She was rich, vastly rich, her personal fortune exceeding her husband's uncountable millions. Cat was the only child of a dead daddy pirate who accumulated twenty full sections of East Texas land whose oil beneath the earth approximated in value the pine forests above. She was civic-minded, or so the newspapers said, a fund raiser for causes as diverse as a home for unwed mothers and the preservation of pioneer artifacts, and a churchgoer—Episcopal, of course. She knew art, once snagged Gregory Peck and Jennifer Jones for the centerpiece of a memorable dinner, and had a widely admired ass which nobody knew had been trimmed and tucked by a plastic surgeon in Rio de Janeiro.

Fort Worth society also suspected, hinted, and whispered that Cat played around, but in a manner of great discretion. Nobody ever caught her at it. During parties, which she loved, her eyes did not roam, and her arm did not unlock from the hearty embrace of Bear Bowman, the boisterous, 260-pound husband to whom she had been married for eighteen childless years.

Fort Worth society certainly did not know that what Cat Bowman cherished more than community stature, family legacy, and the Church of England was a clandestine fuck—but only under conditions of unusual drama. She stalked certain sexual game with expertise. Her prime requirement, unbreakable, the sacrament of sex, was that the target in her sights had to project *celebrity*. He had to be a male coveted by multitudes.

It began early in her marriage, a revelation of such power that denial became impossible. Attending the Fort Worth Fat Stock Show & Rodeo, midway through the saddle bronc competition, Cat realized that unless she obtained carnal access to a lean and courageous cowboy named Bart, her life could not continue. Three months were required to learn that Bart lived in Gallup, New Mexico, with a plump wife and four children. Eight thousand dollars had to be spent on private investigators, on books to educate her on the breeding of quarter horses (Bart's avocation), a wardrobe to enhance her figure and establish her as a fellow breeder, and hasty invention of a sorority sister from long ago who needed solace after the sudden expiration of a cancerous husband. Money and time were well spent. Cat sat on the cowboy's cock for ninety rewarding minutes at the Navajo Motel near Albuquerque, obtained his autographed photo, placed it in her safety-deposit box, and often thereafter paid onanistic homage in the privacy of a bank booth.

More challenging was the male model she encountered in the pages of the Montgomery Ward catalogue while ordering paving stones. He was posed in underwear briefs that bulged with extraordinary promise. To get inside this forty-nine-cent article of clothing, Cat traced the man to Chicago, purchased cameras and took instruction on their use, convinced Bear that her presence was required in Illinois for the board meeting of a charity, rented a studio near the Ambassador East Hotel, and at 4 p.m. on a stormy afternoon, paid the glorious fellow $500 cash to (1) pose for her cameras in his underwear, (2) pose without his underwear, and (3) place his disappointingly modest member into Cat's nonetheless excited lips.

There were others. A fundamentalist preacher from Atlanta. An Italian count met in Rome and cornered in Houston. A tenor trapped in San Antonio proved, alas, homosexual, but for $1,000 he sang "Celeste Aida" in the nude. Given her druthers, Cat would have preferred that Mack Crawford lived in, say, Oregon, and was, ideally, a congressman glimpsed in *Time* magazine and thrusting for the vice-presidency rather than a gimpy washed-up jock living but twenty blocks away. But what the hell; fame was her game, and the most magnificent-looking man in recent visual memory would soon discover a determined surprise on an unplanned mattress. The only challenge to Cat was to make it, well, *challenging*.

It should be said that Catalina never considered herself unfaithful to Barron (Bear) Bowman. Indeed she loved the huge man greatly, copulated with him happily, and intended to stay his wife forever. Bear was her yacht; the others were dinghies. And by Cat's reckoning, she was a virgin with each new moon.

CHAPTER EIGHT

The curtain rose on a splendid Texas night. A harvest moon, heavy and yellow, hung as if engaged for the occasion smack above the brick terrace of the Bowman estate. Showers of stars seemed close enough to touch and became brilliants sewn on ebony velvet. The air was warm and sweet, enhanced by the redolence of palmyra and jasmine and vanda orchids flown on Bowman charter from Hawaii, then tossed artfully into the pool to float through flaming torches. The vulgarity quotient in Texas is low; money is spent in reflection of the owner's purse.

The buffet table stretched forty giant steps, and at that was barely long enough to accommodate roasts of bloody Texas beef, quails toasted maple brown, a witches' caldron of Bear's own chili (whose recipe, requiring both venison meat and an armadillo heart, had won an international cookout and which needed a side saucer of yoghurt to temper the fires certain to ravage novice throats). Colored servants who didn't seem to know the Civil War had been fought on their behalf padded about starched and stiff, so obedient they appeared ready to sing "My Old Kentucky Home" if Massa snapped his fingers. A mariachi band airlifted from Guadalajara assembled in the forecourt to serenade sixty shrewdly mixed guests, two of whom were Mack Crawford and his jittery church mouse, Susan.

Catalina Bowman had anticipated apprehension and thus swept forward to welcome the young couple. "We're *so* flattered you could come," she gushed, sweet as peach pie, effusive in fraudulent praise for

Susan's home-sewn frock. The hostess herself was gowned in meringue chiffon from French couture, cabochon emeralds at her ears and throat. Beside her sweated Bear in white dinner jacket and ruffled dress shirt whose collar strained to cover eighteen and one half inches of redneck. He pumped the arrivals' hands like an oil rig. "Mighty proud to have you and this pretty lady," he said genuinely. "Y'all come right in this house and make yourselves to home."

On the patio were certified delegates from the Planet of Celebrity: A U.S. senator, a granddaughter of Franklin Roosevelt, a niece of Lord Ismay, the actor James Stewart, a Houston multimillionaire presently wooing Hedy Lamarr. But as word worked its way through the glitterati of Mack Crawford's identity, he and his exceptional looks became an object of principal attention. Conversation softened from concern over the Supreme Court's school integration ruling (certain, it was believed, to cause further violence such as the riots current in Little Rock) and segued into memories of Mack Crawford's legend on the playing fields of Fort Worth and Austin. Men slapped his back, recalling scores as indelible in Texas minds as the fall of the Alamo. His autograph was scribbled on more cocktail napkins than Jimmy Stewart's. Susan noticed many lush women eyeing her husband with interest, but as often as she looked, never once did she catch Cat Bowman in covert inspection. By evening's end, Susan was chiding herself for having imagined that this gracious and beautifully mannered woman had offered more to Mack than a ride home.

In sodden farewell, Bear hugged them both. "Now that you young-uns know where we live, let's be seein' more of each other, heah? Latch string's *always* out."

"That'd be real nice," said Mack, winner of the first game he had played in two years.

Clever in business, Catalina Bowman remarked to Bear soon thereafter that one of the family enterprises, a Ford dealership, had grown fiscally anemic. Privy to ledger sheets, Cat observed that the Bear Bowman Ford Co. sold 315 fewer units in 1957 than the year before. Moreover, the present sales and profit curves were in descendancy.

Bear growled. "Times is bad, hon. Ah cain't put dollars into a feller's pocket."

"True," remarked Cat. "But we *can* prime the pump." They were taking breakfast beside the pool, Bear drinking coffee and frowning over the *Wall Street Journal*. Like many rich Texans, he was a lifelong Democrat who nonetheless voted for Eisenhower—and was now ruing his support. Under the nation's first Republican since Hoover, America was mired in what the bureaucrats called a "recession" but which smelled like breadlines. "It sez here," lectured Bear, "that 5.1 million people are unemployed—and suckin' on the public tit. It sez here gasoline is up to 30.4 cents a gallon, but nobody's makin' any money outta it 'cause the goddamn Ayrabs are undercuttin' the shit outta me. It sez steak's up by 31 cents a pound. It sez it takes $1,250 to send a boy to Harvard for one full year compared to $455 ten years ago. What it don't say is that Ike better get off the golf course and pay some attention to the folks who put his khaki ass into office."

Having pre-read the *Wall Street Journal* as homework, Cat quoted from memory. "It also says that the average family income is $5,200—that's up 70 percent from ten years ago. And has it come to your attention yet that General Motors' profits are expected to be a right tolerable $1 *billion* this year?"

Bear put down his paper, not to exclaim over GM's good fortune, but to threaten dismemberment of a Mexican gardener clomping across the putting green.

"Hon," pestered Cat, "did you hear me?"

"I did. What's GM got to do with the price of potatoes?"

"It means that people *do* have money. It means that our chief competitor's gettin' it. It means we either goose those ole boys who are *not* selling our Fords. Or it means we sell the goddamn dealership and raise turnips." Cat worked her way to this dire forecast with caution; she knew how much Bear adored the company that bore his name in scarlet neon, an ego massage that could be seen from miles away.

"Honey bunch, don't bother your sweet little punkin' head with bidness. Why don't you just get your hair done, play some bridge, and let me keep the cookie jar full." Bear ordered his chauffeur to ready the Cadillac. He was leaving for Austin to squeeze a couple of legislators. His construction company coveted a state contract to build unneeded roads that would lead, coincidentally, to undeveloped property owned secretly by Bear Bowman.

Catalina sighed and kissed her husband on both of his red-veined cheeks. "I'll do that, hon," she said. "And hurry home safe. We'll talk about things . . . in bed . . . tonight." Her perfumed hand feather-dusted Bear's thickening crotch and, hinting of temptations that might well stop a man's heart, sent her mate on his way.

A fortnight later, Mack Crawford joined Bear Bowman Ford Co. as salesman and drawing card. His salary: $300 a month with the promise of twice that in commissions. The bonus: a cherry-red '57 convertible that he was instructed to drive liberally on the boulevards of Fort Worth, its top down. His costume was designed personally by the boss's wife. All of the salesmen dressed in the ensemble, but it suited Mack particularly: tight blue jeans, alligator boots, snowy white golf shirt with a laughing bear at the breast, and a baseball cap with stitching across the brim: BEARS LOVE YOU. From the car radio blared country music, from Mack's face radiated a happy grin, and, while Catalina watched and congratulated herself and bided her time, the new salesman became, as planned, a star. In his second month of work, Mack broke sales records (many of his customers having been secretly sent by Cat in collection of personal due bills). The dealership's over-all sales rose 17 percent.

One afternoon, a television commercial was scheduled to be filmed on the sales lot, using, as per custom, the sales manager as spokesman. This fellow, Luke Lester by name, a Baptist deacon, had once won a fiddle contest. Bowman's thirty-second spots on location television tra-ditionally opened with Luke sitting atop his desk, Bible in view, framed by American and Texas flags, sawing furiously at the opening bars of "Friendship," then drawling, in earnest emulation of John Wayne, "Down here at Bear Bowman Ford, we don't fiddle around, folks." When the commercial appeared, viewers were known to bolt to the set and switch it off, hurrying to responsibilities in kitchen or toilet.

Unaware that his star was about to set, Luke readied this day for a new appearance. Catalina Bowman then arrived with an altered sce-nario. She instructed the production crew to film Mack Crawford driving into the lot at the wheel of his red convertible, preparing to step out, only to be engulfed by a squealing posse of eight beautiful young women attired in cheerleading costumes from Southwest Conference universities. The denouement was a tight freeze-frame close-up of Mack's lipstick-smeared face and a slow pan up past his blue eyes to the embroidery on his cap, BEARS LOVE YOU.

Seeing what was happening and angered at the theft of his celeb-rity, Luke Lester immediately telephoned the boss at his offices in the

Fort Worth Club Building. "Bear," he cried, "yore wife's over t'here changin' things. She's gonna bring ever' preacher in town down on our heads. We got a damn stag movie goin' on."

That very evening Bear prepared to scold his enterprising spouse but she countered by placing soft fingers that smelled of lilac against his lips. A plea. "Just wait, hon." Veins humming with Wild Turkey, Bear sat a week later before a television monitor and viewed Cat's labor. His eyes widened when long-legged girls in short-tailed skirts leaped into view, and his foot tapped enthusiastically with "The Eyes of Texas." At the freeze, Bear hugged Cat and said, "That's the best damn show I ever saw. Play 'er again."

The television budget was tripled. And Bear approved Cat's suggestion that Mack's photograph be used in all print ads. Luke Lester was summarily fired, though he wreaked biblical vengeance some weeks hence by sneaking onto the lot and breaking seven windshields. The commercial, which played forty-eight times each week on Fort Worth and Dallas stations, not only sold the hell out of Bear's Fords, it solidified and painted in gilt what Cat had so diligently sought. Mack became an object of intense feminine attention. Women streamed into the dealership for glimpses and test rides. They followed Mack, honking horns, on the streets. They drove onto Cloverdale and past his home, hoping to espy him shirtless. His mail was not only abundant but lewd.

Mack was packing a suitcase with resort clothes appropriate for a week in Acapulco. "Sure wish you could go, hon," he told his wife. Ford dealers were congregating for a regional pep talk and unveiling of the new model on which the company had lavished $250 million in design and tooling. Talk was it would chase Impala off the road. "Bear says the wives aren't invited this time. But next spring there's a wingding in Vegas and he promised we could go together."

"It's okay," sighed Susan. "I couldn't get off from work, anyway." A curious inversion had occurred in the marriage, as if wife had lent husband three pints of blood and had gotten back tap water in return. She was pale and tired; he was vigorous and fresh, spinning like a newly wound top. Her emotional ledger was out of balance, and though she recognized the primal source of discontent, the reason eluded explanation. Saluting the hypocrisy of it all, she even wished she had not put the pieces of beauty back together again. Like an old maid aunt with a strawberry birthmark, Susan had liked caretaking better when Mack leaned on her in every way.

When the first rays of spotlight spilled over to warm her by osmosis, Susan had enjoyed the glow. In the red convertible, riding beside her prospering and famous husband, Susan saw the waves from other women and recognized them as blue ribbons to wear on her breast. Teenage girls who rapped at the door in search of Mack's signature settled for *her* autograph, and in their eyes were the fantasies of what went on *chez* Crawford when the lights went out. "Oh, we make love seven times a day usually," Susan imagined herself confiding, sister-to-sister. "The man is a satyr. *Insatiable!* Twice in the morning, a quickie in the afternoon at a motel, on the sofa between cocktails and dinner. My Lord, the brute chases me from room to room all night long." And there were times when she wanted to spill the truth: "He kisses me on Wednesday and hugs me on Saturday."

Twice, perhaps thrice, Mack had made what charitably could be termed an advance. Returning home from a sales meeting with Bear and the boys, well laced with bourbon, stumbling, goofy, sloppy, he fell into her arms, whispered of love, turned out the bedside light—darkness remained an imperative—and together they rolled about like chicken crates in the back of a pickup on a country road. A few articles of clothing got shed, ears nibbled, lips brushed. But zippers stayed locked. And if Susan ever took the initiative and clutched her husband's belt buckle, the laughing bear commenced, with arguable conviction, to snore.

What was the reason for this unnatural problem? Susan did not know. Jealousy had come and gone. She did not believe that other women were the barrier between them. Nor did she doubt Mack's often professed need for her. She had even banished the feeling that the crime of no appeal was hers. Other men—doctors, patients, delivery boys, Bear even—transmitted messages which did not require a decoder. Briefly she had even wondered if Mack was queer, but *that,* considering his stature, his strength, his allure to other women, was clearly absurd.

She bought a marriage manual and placed it pointedly on the bedside table, where it remained unread. With delicacy on the far side of tact, she raised the issue over wine and music, suggesting that professional counseling might enrich their union. And always Mack swore oaths of eternal love, promising to think about the "problem," making excuses, slipping away. If he saw her tears, he made no effort to dry them.

When his suitcase was packed, Mack began the nightly ritual that prepared him for bed—a half hour of grueling calisthenics that flushed his body, filmed him in sweat, and made Susan jealous of the energies being spent on muscles. Usually she joined in, determined to keep the lines firm as she neared thirty. But on this night she only watched and brushed her hair slowly, contemplating an exercise that would require the wiles of Lorelei and the courage of Columbus. When Mack began his shower, Susan waited until steam began crawling out beneath the closed door. She meditated a moment more, stepped out of her white nylon baby doll, dabbed liberal splashes of Jungle Gardenia at her temples and nipples, and set forth to share the vapors.

"Hey!" cried Mack, more or less what Susan anticipated in this first communal shower. "What the hell are you doin', hon?" He revolved hastily to face the wall.

"Remember how I used to rub your back?" she said, groping through the hot steam and feeling wonderfully mischievous.

"I'm already finished," said Mack, which was a lie. His body was still luxuriant and slippery with lather but was blocked from rinse by a naked intruder. "Honey, *don't,*" pleaded Mack as Susan ran her tongue down his spine. Well, perhaps the clouds of humidity cloaked the difficult moment. Perhaps the guilt of an Acapulco holiday by himself settled in. Perhaps it was the good humor and fun with which Susan approached the project. Whatever, Mack allowed himself to be slowly peeled from the wall, and when he faced his wife, she had to back off for a second. Something wonderful had come between them.

Excited by the presentation, Susan didn't know exactly what to do next. Instinct suggested, however, that she best act fast. In a blur she fell into her husband's embrace and though not yet *ready*—as the marriage manual euphemized—guided Mack toward the score of his life. Alas, as happens to most men, the runner stumbled. The phone rang and intruded on Mack's concentration, perversely summoning the mental intrusions of dead aunts, mothers, and girls in pink dresses. Mack got scared, stepped on the soap, and fell, Susan still locked to his body. As the lovers hit the water, Mack climaxed and Susan joined in with a cry of great passion. The least she could give him was pride in accomplishment. Urgently Mack then scrambled from the tub, seizing a towel and racing squish-squish for the telephone. It stopped ringing as he picked it up.

Susan emerged from the steam and sat on the edge of her husband's bed. "Well," she said, "the fellow was wrong. Anticipation is nowhere near realization." Mack smiled proudly, but, reclaimed by modesty, he reached for the lamp. Susan dotted his arm and forehead with the kisses due a victor.

"Was it . . . okay?" he asked.

Susan nodded enthusiastically. "It was *Olympian,*" she said. Then the phone rang again. "I'll get it," said Susan. "You deserve a rest."

She went into the hall and spoke for several minutes.

"Who was that?" asked Mack when she returned with a smile on her face.

"Bear. He says be ready at seven-fifteen. The car'll pick you up."

Mack nodded and reset the alarm. "Did he say anything else?"

Susan shook her head. It was a lie, but a white lie at worst. She slipped into her husband's bed. Not only did he permit the trespass, he fell asleep cradled in her arms like a baby. They kissed often during the happy night.

Impatience barely concealed, Catalina waited for Bear to stuff a lacy Mexican wedding shirt into his belly. Day's end. From the Bay of Acapulco came gentle breezes delivering the sharp smell of brine, intercut with ripples of night-blooming jasmine and lemon blossoms. Their bungalow had been carved into a cliff as if home to wealthy troglodytes and had been personally selected by Cat, located many twisting paths and cascading steps from the main portion of the El Mirador Hotel. To find this chamber almost required a compass, a guide, and the most sober of diligence—which was as Cat desired it.

In fine fettle, Bear enthused over his new eminence as a monumental purveyor of Ford products. He reverberated as well from the wall-to-wall bounce that Cat had put him through the night before. A hickey on his throat and scratches on his back were testimony to high passion, and he remembered standing on the balcony buck-ass naked (surf slapping the rocks below like the applause of spectators) and watching native boys fly off the cliffs like brown birds in search of grub only to plunge as if shot by a .30/.06 into the floodlit sea. And all of this was going on while Bear squeezed fresh lime juice onto Cat's fine jugs, then licking driblets off until the fool got heartburn. Their fiesta had continued until well past 2 a.m., Bear blissfully unaware that anything beyond tropical abandon occupied Cat's mind. Truth was she enjoyed every minute, her pleasure being heightened by the knowledge that, since she had wrung Bear inside and out, he would now require at least two days' rest before the sap rose again.

On this, the third evening of a seven-day conference, the agenda offered a yacht cruise with dinner and a slide-show presentation of Ford's truck line. Everybody was supposed to get on board by seven with homecoming at midnight. Cat had begged off, giving as an acceptable excuse that her time would be better spent rehearsing Mack on the speech he was to deliver the next morning (followed by a showing of the now famous sixty-second TV commercial). Bear did not argue. He knew his wife was a perfectionist. That she insisted on testing the sound and lighting systems with the boy seemed appropriate.

"How do I look, hon?" demanded Bear, feeling on the far side of silly in white duck pants lashed with rope, and huaraches that stopped well short of his size 14 feet.

"Like a hot tamale," purred Cat, who looked pretty torrid herself, wrapped in a long silk peasant gown whose fabric was screened in hibiscus blossoms. She wore a real one behind her ear.

"Keep a light burnin' in the window," said Bear. "I'll be back a little after midnight."

"Oh, *I'll* be up," promised Cat. "If *you* are . . ." She winked lewdly, bestowed a brisk toodle-oo kiss, and settled into a chair with clipboard and business papers.

Mack arrived at the bungalow, as bidden, at seven sharp. Catalina welcomed him with a double margarita, frosted counterpoint to the fever of recorded guitar and the diorama of the tropical sun melting across the sea below. She said their "rehearsal" would be delayed an hour, something about the hotel meeting hall not yet cleared from a cocktail party. They sat on the terrace, faces washed by becoming gold light. Never adroit in purposeless talk, Mack stared at his drink. When it was gone, Cat refilled the glass and stood directly before him, in arm's reach.

"Bear and I are so happy with your work," she said.

"Thank you, ma'm," said Mack. "I'm truly grateful for the chance."

Time passed. Night arrived. Torches on the rocks below leaped into flame. And along with this back lighting, like the surprise of life bleeding through a theatrical scrim, came the reality that Catalina Bowman's gown was transparent. Moreover, she wore nothing beneath the diaphanous cloth.

Mack, beginning his third double margarita, found a scurrying lizard on the wall to study. "The way things are going," continued Cat, "well . . . we just may have to open a new branch out west of town. Of course we'll need a capable manager."

"Yessum," stammered Mack. "That'd be good. Lots of folks movin' out that way."

"How old are you, Mack?" she asked.

"Ah, just about twenty-five, ma'm," he answered, giggling. The tequila was cooking.

"Well, I think you have a little time left," said Cat. "But after thirty, watch out. God only grants you three erections a year. Spend them wisely."

"Ma'm?" Mack assumed a laugh was required but his attempt was feeble. He was very uncomfortable.

"You're some famous person, Mack," she said. "Our own little celebrity."

Mack had no response.

"How does it feel to be famous?"

"It's okay. I'm just a medium fish in a small pond."

"But people *know* you, Mack. You're popular with women."

Mack disliked the line of conversation. He looked at his watch. Quarter to eight. "Shouldn't we be gettin' over to the rehearsal hall?" he asked.

Catalina nodded. Now came the only tricky piece of business, but she knew her lines and she had her props. "Yes," she agreed. "Just one thing, though. Excuse me a sec." From the bathroom, Cat fetched a burlap shopping bag. "Mack, honey," she said. "Before we start work on your speech, I need to tell you about this new promotion idea."

Unsteadily but obedient, Mack rose. "Yessum," he replied, words thick as porridge, vision so unfocused that he saw about three of everything.

"So, figuring as how we're all down here in this unbelievable beautiful place . . . it *is* magical, isn't it, Mack?"

"Yessum."

"Mack, you must stop calling me 'ma'm.' You may call me

Catalina or Cat or 'sweet thing.' I'm only a very few years older than you. Agreed?"

"Yessum . . . er, Mrs. Bowman."

"So, we've got access to the new model . . . and tomorrow afternoon, after your speech, we'll borrow the car and take some publicity pictures. We'll start with you driving it along the beach, sort of showing it off. . . . How does that sound?"

"Fine," said Mack. "Whatever Bear wants . . ."

"It's *my* idea, Mack. Give credit where credit's due. It was my say-so that got you hired in the first place. Did you know that?"

Mack shook his head. The bungalow was dark now. Vaguely he saw Catalina lighting tapers that smelled like lemon drops. She tossed him the burlap bag. "Try these on," she ordered. *"Everything.* . . . The pictures will start out with you all dressed up inside the car, then stripping down to a bathing suit and running into the waves."

Later.

"They don't fit too good," complained Mack. An understatement. The clamdiggers that Cat had purposely purchased two sizes small were in grave peril of shredding from waist to thigh. His shirt was similarly constrictive, being an emulation of a French marine jersey, sliced low to reveal a tangle of glistening chest hair. The horizontal blue and white stripes rippled like the muscles of his wide gap of flat tanned belly that were left uncovered.

"Hmmmm," said Cat. "Come over here by the light." Quite carefully Mack slunk to the fireplace and accepted a fourth margarita, enriched in his absence by ten milligrams of Miltown. "Perhaps the chambermaid can let these britches out a little," she said, wedging two fingers into Mack's rump and creeping like a tightrope walker around to the front, where a major button popped. "Otherwise, you look marvelous," pronounced Cat. "Now . . . let's see the rest."

From the moist well of embarrassment, Mack stalled. "The rest? There isn't any . . . *rest.*"

"You found the bathing trunks, didn't you?"

"I think . . ." said Mack. "I think you *forgot* something."

"I never forget anything," said Cat. "Now get busy. We've got work to do." As Mack struggled to get out of the shirt, Cat knelt and helpfully peeled down the clamdiggers. While she worked, she closed her eyes. Her fantasy demanded darkness before the ultimate revelation. Then Mack stumbled over his trousers, lurching forward. His body touched Cat and the moment for which she had endured three devious and dangerous months was here.

"Oh my!" she cried in gratitude, staring dead ahead at Mack's privates, hanging from a thin waist string like grapes on a tendril. With no hesitation, Cat severed the string with her fingernail, simultaneously opening a clasp at the neck of her gown that sent it floating to the polished red tile floor. She was naked and so was he.

"Oh, ma'm," said Mack fearfully. "Wait." He wanted to back up but his ass would be literally in the fire. "We shouldn't do this . . . I've got too much respect for Bear . . ."

"Respect, my ass," said Cat, rising fast and gluing her body to his. "You've been tossing those buns around since the day we met. I bought and paid for 'em. Now let's see if I got my money's worth." She shoved Mack onto the bed, slipping as he tumbled neatly beneath his body. She pulled her purchase onto her chest, where the Prince of Charms sat like an oversized and underexperienced jockey astride a long-in-the-tooth filly from which he wanted desperately to be thrown.

At that precise moment, a series of unscripted events occurred to spoil Catalina Bowman's finale. To the sudden eruption of "Guadalajara," the bungalow door burst open. Standing there, smiles fast fading, half circled by a mariachi band whose players commenced to hoot and scream with laughter, appeared Bear Bowman and Susan French Crawford. Secretly, Mack's wife had been flown to Acapulco on Bear's private plane as a surprise reward.

As might be expected from a fine actress, Catalina improvised brilliantly. With horrendous shrieks she pummeled Mack's chest, almost convincing one and all that divine providence had spared her from rape. The trouble was, Mack grinned like the village idiot, closed his eyes, and passed out cold.

At noon the next day, Mack awoke on the floor—abandoned and alone, like a child who had fallen asleep in a theater seat. Marriage and career shattered, he flew back to Fort Worth, missing the unveiling of Ford's highly anticipated new automobile. The $250 million model, metaphoric companion of the disgraced salesman, featured a gull-winged tail, several hundred pounds of unnecessary chrome, and a nose that resembled both toilet seat and horse laugh. It was called the Edsel and Mack never got to drive it along the beach at Acapulco.

Bear and Cat Bowman prepared to cross-file for divorce, but after consultation with attorneys decided that division of their empire would be as difficult as slicing off the boot tip of Texas. For twenty-seven years thereafter they lived in financial détente, but never again came physically closer than the three feet that separated their eventual crypts.

Susan denied Mack entrance to his own house. She did not, however, seek immediate divorce. Her menstrual period failed to arrive, and eight months, twenty-three days post-Acapulco she was delivered of a fine, strong, perfect infant son: Jeffrey McKenzie Crawford.

Mack was unable to attend the birth, for he was by then a resident of New York City. Fate had dispatched an unexpected samaritan to lift the falsely accused womanizer from the gutter of life's highway. The BEARS LOVE YOU commercial had continued to run on Fort Worth–Dallas stations long after the unpleasant incident in Mexico. During this lame-duck period, a would-be theatrical producer named Arnie Beckman missed a plane connection in Dallas and was forced to endure a beery night at a motel near Love Field. He was terribly out of sorts, having wasted several fruitless days searching America's middle for angels willing to invest in a Broadway play.

The first time Arnie saw Mack Crawford aswarm with coeds in a red Ford convertible, his gaze locked briefly on the cheerleader skirts. But when the commercial played twice again on his screen, Arnie murmured, "Jesus! *Oy gevalt.*" Had he been kneeling in a creek bed one hundred years before, straining pebbles through a screen in search of gold at Sutter's Mill, Arnie Beckman might have cried, *"Eureka!"*

BOOK THREE

༒༒༒༒༒༒༒༒༒༒༒༒༒༒༒༒༒༒༒༒༒༒༒༒༒༒༒༒༒༒༒༒༒༒༒

THE
PRINCE
OF
POWER

You shall have joy
or you shall have power, said God.
You cannot have both.

—Ralph Waldo Emerson

CHAPTER NINE

Calvin Sledge slipped out of his office and crept down the back stairs of the Tarrant County courthouse, avoiding the infestation of reporters and photographers that trailed him like ants following watermelon juice. In the parking lot down the street, the flatbed truck was still there, infuriating to the prosecutor and symbolic of the maniacal carnival the case had become. He glanced at his watch. Ten minutes to five.

At 5 p.m. sharp the old rugged cross, which was twelve feet high and embedded in blood-red carpet and blanketed with calla lilies, would blaze with 640 light bulbs; the organ would burst into jackhammer gospel; the tambourines would rattle like a menaced den of sidewinders; and The Chosen's flock—last night police estimated at least a thousand—would commence to sing, shake, hallelujah, and collapse to the pavement in spasms and gibberish.

The only twinge of satisfaction was that no television crews waited to cover the show. Sledge hoped the networks had wearied of holy rollers in nightly celebration of church's mini-victory over state. On the morning after the arrest, the truck arrived at high noon, parking directly at the courthouse front door, creating an immediate and monumental traffic jam. Thousands of workers on lunch hour gathered to gawk at the spectacle of sixty-six young women—one for each book of the Bible—clad in virgin pure white raiments with plastic thorns about their foreheads, holding placards with biblical allusions to vengeance, justice, and persecution.

A delegation of The Chosen's elders had materialized in Sledge's outer office, but the furious District Attorney sent word that he would

not receive Christ Himself without prior appointment. Immediately
Sledge called the chief of police and demanded that cops be sent to
force the truck from the street. But even as he spoke, a squad of lawyers from the City of Miracles was filing motions in federal court, seeking to enjoin the DA from suppressing religious freedom and right of
lawful assembly. Sledge counterfired with a low-key but common-sense
plea that the Bill of Rights had not intended mob scenes before the hall
of justice. An accommodation was reached in judicial chambers: the
truck would move off the public street and onto a private parking lot.
"Services" would be permitted only after 5 p.m., when the business of
the courthouse was done, and "amens" had to be pronounced by 10
p.m. so as to give other prisoners in the upper reaches of the building
an opportunity for sleep.

And to the delegation of elders, Sledge delivered a terse handwrit-
ten statement: "I appreciate your interest in this case, but an investigation is ongoing, and in fairness to all concerned, it is not appropriate
for the District Attorney to meet with special interest groups." Had he
not been politic, Sledge would have appended: "Especially when they
are fanatics."

At Harris Hospital, Dr. Witt was cranky. He presented the DA
with an itemized bill, $3,295.14 for private security guards to beef up
city cops on duty. Now every entrance, exit, and elevator was guarded,
and the two plainclothesmen outside the patient's suite had become six.
"What am I supposed to do with this?" asked Sledge. He had no funds
to pay for private guards.

"This is your circus, Calvin," snapped the doctor. "You pay the
clowns." He refused to permit Sledge even the tiniest peek at the patient. "He's stabilized," said Dr. Witt.

"What does that mean?" asked Sledge.

"He's conscious. His eyes are open. He's not gonna die. And if he
stays the same another seventy-two hours, I'm going to recommend
moving him to a sanitarium. Hell, Calvin, I cannot permit this institution to be under siege."

"Can he talk?"

"He hasn't."

"Lemme just ask one thing," said the DA. "If I was to call you
into the grand jury room next week and ask you if your patient is able
to speak—*if he wanted to*—or is he playacting, how would you respond?"

Dr. Witt stared hotly at the prosecutor, then softened, finally stabbed his intercom. "See if Sam Reiker can join us," he told his secretary.

Presently a very lovely woman arrived. She was in middle age with a face of encompassing tenderness. Her shoulder was where a man would wish to put down a weary head. "This is Samantha Reiker," introduced Dr. Witt. "The best ENT man in Texas."

Dr. Reiker smiled graciously at the confusing introduction. At her heels was an intern named Clyde Watkins, caught up in the front-page drama and carrying a thick envelope of X rays and medical records.

"Now, then," began Dr. Reiker. "What do you know about vocal cords?"

"Zip," answered Sledge.

"Okay. Say something."

"Say *what?*"

"Anything."

Sledge blurted out, "Murder." And he added, "Ma'm." Then, "Doctor."

"Sam's fine. I'm getting used to it." She was a Yankee; Sledge caught her accent. Quickly the woman specialist went to the blackboard and drew an outline of a man's head in profile, with throat and chest cavity beneath.

"Now, Mr. District Attorney, when you chose to speak the word 'murder,'" she began, "and I'm going to oversimplify this and avoid using technical language, a signal originated in this area of your brain." She chalk-pointed to the cortex, about an inch above the temple. "An impulse that we do not fully understand raced down via cranial nerves and the spinal cord to the lungs. Involuntarily, you drew in a breath of air and expelled it in order to get the word out. If you had wanted to whisper 'murder,' your brain would have ordered just a tiny dose of air. If you had screamed it, or sung it for eight beats, the prescription would have been for a great big batch of air. With me so far?"

Sledge nodded. Samantha Reiker was a good teacher. She drew another diagram, of the larynx and vocal cords. "The larynx is just a valve whose primary function is to prevent the aspiration of fluids or solids into the lungs. Most animals—dogs, monkeys, whatever—have one. And most animals have these little pieces of mucous membrane we call vocal cords. There are two of them—see—kind of like the two upright sides of a triangle. . . ."

Sledge interrupted. "Then why can't animals talk?"

"Good question," answered Dr. Reiker. "Man—or *woman*—didn't talk at first." At the feminist nuance, Sledge frowned. The doctor continued. "Our earliest ancestor used the mouth and teeth and oral cavity as a tool and a weapon—for fighting, for gathering food. Not until mother nature, or God, or evolution—you fill in the blank— taught him to use a club to kill his enemies and his dinner, only then did that free the mouth and teeth and oral cavity for other functions. Such as articulating sounds in a special way so that they had meaning. That was about a million years ago, give or take a few millennia. A bit of time had to pass before we got to Demosthenes."

"I made you digress," said Sledge. "Back to vocal cords."

"Yes. Okay, you produced air to set these two pieces of membrane vibrating—thousands of vibrations in a fraction of a second. When you were a kid, did you ever place two blades of grass between your fingers and blow on them and make a whistle?"

Sledge nodded.

"Same thing. So you've formed a tone now. But it's blank. It's got no character. This sound moves up to a resonator in the pharynx. Here various factors shape it into your own particular voice—tenor, so- prano, twang, etc. It's now as unique as your fingerprint. Nobody in the world has precisely that sound. Then the brain steps in again, sending additional impulses to a speech-forming articulator in your mouth. And, *voilà,* out comes 'murder.' "

Sledge absorbed the lecture and the teacher. He wondered whether Samantha Reiker would make a good witness. Certainly she was direct and credible, but she came on a mite too polished, too eastern, too lib- erated, too condescending for down-home jurors. If the box was filled with blue-collar men, they might not take kindly to a Yankee doctor woman. "Go back to my original question," ordered Sledge brusquely.

Dr. Reiker seemed slightly annoyed at the prosecutor's dictate. "You mean, can the patient talk?" she said. She shrugged. It meant, flip a coin.

"But surely, lady, you can tell whether somebody's lying or not," said Sledge with a snap in his voice.

The doctor turned to her assistant. "Clyde, can I borrow your throat for a minute?" The young intern obediently threw his head back and opened his mouth wide. Samantha Reiker found a crooked mirror with a built-in light from the recesses of her crisp smock. She bade

Sledge to peer down into Watkins' moist, glistening red passage that ended in blackness.

"*If* I took you in that patient's room and let you look down his throat—which I'm not about to do, by the way—it'd appear about the same as Clyde's here. As far as I can tell from visual examination—and X rays—and from some slightly more sophisticated tests, there is some damage to the cricoid cartilage at the base of the larynx. *Some.* Not a lot. The bullet nicked it, apparently. There's also some calcification, which is not unusual in a man that age. You know how some people's voices get deeper and huskier in middle age? That's one reason. Calcification."

Sledge's impatience veered out of control. The lady doctor was dodging the issue that brought them together in the room. "Then, dammit, what's your opinion? With all due respect, lady, you may be facing me in a witness box not very long from now."

Dr. Witt interjected quietly as a pacifier, "Sam, maybe you should tell him about hysterical aphonia."

Dr. Reiker drew a long breath and nodded. "Aphonia meaning the inability to speak. It can be as ordinary as a singer who suddenly loses his or her voice—or as complex as somebody who sees something or does something so psychologically traumatic that it becomes impossible to speak. I don't know much about it. It's shrink territory."

"*Cannot? Ever?*" pushed Sledge.

The doctor regarded the prosecutor coolly. "I didn't say that. Your boy may sit up an hour from now and deliver Mark Antony's funeral oration for Caesar. On the other hand, he may go to his grave without ever making a squeak. We'll just have to wait and see. I think that's all I have to tell you, Mr. Sledge. Good afternoon."

If the DA had been looking at her face instead of at the fist he was slamming into his palm, he might have noticed that he had not charmed the woman specialist.

The Cantrell house on Cloverdale Avenue remained the dowager on the block, the old lady without a face-lift. It befitted the enduring occupant. VeeJee Cantrell had further reason for resisting the fashion of architectural gussiment. In her last will and testament, unlikely to be ready for many years because she remained at seventy-two a foursquare woman of strength and energy, she directed that the house be donated to the Fort Worth Public Library so that "future generations can visit the home where Kleber Cantrell was reared and where his early papers are on file." She recognized this as an act of substantial conceit, but she loved her son and was proud of him, and by her estimation, his immortality—and thus her own—would be preserved.

Already VeeJee had received Calvin Sledge several times during the course of his investigation, being a woman who respected the law in deed and bumper sticker. She greeted him politely on this pleasant late-June evening. For a time they sat on the front porch, the scent of VeeJee's gardenia hedge in ripest bloom washing away the odors of courthouse and hospital. They drank sourish lemonade, made small talk, watched fireflies dance across the lawn like ideas forming and dying, listening to youngsters down the block coaxing one more inning from a softball game. Sledge reveled in the interlude, envying the security and serenity of VeeJee's world—four decades in this very same place in these very same chairs.

"When did they stop building front porches?" mused the District Attorney, considering for the first time the fact that new houses placed patios in the back yards, secluded by fences, sealing families from view and neighborly contact. It seemed a curious reflection of American selfishness.

"About the same time they stopped putting running boards on automobiles," answered VeeJee. "Somewhere along the line somebody said, 'Whatever is sensible and practical and useful, let's get rid of it.'"

"It's nice out here," said Sledge. "It reminds me of the time when people didn't have to lock their doors."

VeeJee nodded. "There was a time when everybody on the block would sit outside after dinner on summer nights—talking, visiting, strolling around. Everybody knew everybody. Now nobody knows nobody. It might as well be one of those apartment buildings in New York. Kleber told me he lived in one of those for ten years and never even shook hands with the people across the hall. . . . Shall we go inside? I assume you'll be taking notes."

"I kinda like it out here, ma'm," said Sledge. "First breath I've caught all day."

"Kleber liked to sit out here. Home base, he called it. After my husband passed away in '68, Kleber and I sat out here the night of the funeral. He'd flown in from London. He was working on one of his books. He sat right there, where you're sitting, and he said, 'Mama, whatever you do, don't sell this house. If it's a burden financially, then let me buy it and you can live forever rent free.' I told him I'd sell my arms and legs first. People don't have roots anymore. That's what's wrong with this country. We're a nation of drifters."

Sledge intruded gently. The old woman was garrulous and if she got started on right-of-center politics, the night would tilt and waste. "Mrs. Cantrell," he said, "I really need your advice. . . ."

"Well, come in," she ordered, ruminating along the way. "Those three youngsters, Kleber, Mack, T.J. . . ." She pronounced the names without rancor. "Grasshoppers they were; they used my front porch as a 'command post' during the war. I can't tell you how many dead Japs and Germans littered the yard. . . . The strange thing about those boys, they were always together. Never two against one. And the whole neighborhood knew they were special. . . . A woman up yonder at the end of the block, Mrs. Foster, she's gone now, stroke, she used to be the church secretary, and she said once, 'The Lord Himself smiled on these boys . . .' "

It was dark in the Cantrell living room, and when VeeJee stopped talking and found a light, her eyes were newly red and wet. Sledge could think of nothing to gentle her. He fell back on cautious flattery. "Mrs. Cantrell, I'm up that proverbial creek. . . . I've spent almost a month trying to build a case. And the truth is, I don't know much more'n what you've read in the papers."

"I've given you leads," she pointed out.

"Yes, ma'm, and I thank you. I value your counsel, ma'm. I think you're a wise woman. And I know you're honest. But a lot of people are telling me to quit. The pressure's heavy. They think a trial will give the town a bad name."

"Who's *they?*" she demanded.

"Old Judge Carmichael, for one. He's retired and he's eighty-five; he called and he said, 'Calvin, I wouldn't touch this with a ten-foot pole.' I'm not a quitter by nature, Mrs. Cantrell. I guess what I need to ask you is, do you know something I don't?"

"Quit?" VeeJee's voice cracked the night.

"You know the defense posture," said the DA. "They're claiming it was an accident . . . and hell, I dunno. Maybe it was."

"Nothing's an accident, Mr. Prosecutor. Every human act has purpose. Your responsibility is to find it. Find the truth."

Sledge made his move. He had her now. "Then I've got to ask you again. Will you let me go through Kleber's personal papers? I promise to take good care of them."

The old woman frowned. "I've told you ten times," she said. "There's nothing new in them. There's nothing relating to this matter. I have nothing Kleber wrote that's more recent than a good year ago."

"If there was an answer in those papers, you'd never forgive yourself if I lost the case. Now would you, Mrs. Cantrell?"

She fretted and wept a little and finally gave him two large boxes —only a fraction of the total accumulation. But enough to keep him busy. He had to sign for them like checking out a book from the library, on official stationery.

At his office, almost midnight, Sledge remembered to call his wife. Marge was annoyed, but not overly so. He could judge the gradations of her impatience the way a parent identifies the character of a child's tears. "It's just as well," she said. "I already drank all the gin and burned the satin sheets. The kids are fine, too, now that you didn't ask. They're watching 'Dirty Harry' and smoking marijuana."

"I must tell you someday about Caesar's wife," said Sledge, bantering, but irked at his mate's injudicious tease in an era of electronic ears.

"That'll be real nice," said Marge. "And maybe we can also talk about Caesar's ambition. Write when you hang somebody." Click.

Half past one in the morning. Through the unwashed courthouse windows, Sledge stared down at the flatbed truck. The cross was dark and ominous, The Chosen's followers asleep and sprawled at its base like exhausted revelers. Two new signs framed the cross like crucified thieves: VENGEANCE IS MINE, SAITH THE LORD. And GOD IS THE ONLY JUDGE. Sledge held in his hand a note that Darlene had taped to the office door. "Billy Graham called from the airport. He's praying for you and everybody. Don't feed the fish. Love, Darlene."

Sledge tore old Billy into pieces and tossed him out the window. Indestructible, the fragments caught wind and soared across the city. He stared next at the fish tank. Two of the expensive little suckers were belly up. Nobody was on his side anymore.

In a corner of the office were the two cartons VeeJee had loaned him. They joined the other fragments he had collected of Kleber Cantrell's life—*lives*—a garage sale of words written and spoken—books by him, magazine articles, folders thick with newspaper clippings, video and audio cassettes. The enormity of this man's work brought envy to Sledge. He ran his fingers across the spine of a book, touched the raised letters that spelled out the author's name, turned it over to covet the picture on the back, the celebrity that comes for writing something that people will buy and read and keep.

Books had never been close friends of Calvin Sledge: they were the labors of Hercules, necessary evils to wrestle on his odyssey to the bar. Nor was he adept at putting words together; his legal briefs were thorough and competent but parched. These shortcomings were not of undue concern to the DA. Voters did not check his name on a ballot because he served up intellectual pies, piping hot from the ovens of a widely admired brain, with allusions to Santayana and Aristotle like wisps of meringue. Sledge's café served chicken-fried steak and potatoes. He was, by personal assessment, a determined hound who would find and fetch the stick no matter in what thicket it landed.

But however reliable these merits, no matter that he was honest, moral, and worthy, if the ceiling fell fatally on his head, the forty-one years he had occupied earth and air would vanish. His wife would remarry; his daughters would take the names of other men; some other lawyer would occupy his chair. Life's cruelest truth: he would be forgotten, as most men are.

But Kleber Cantrell would survive—because he knew how to slam adjectives against nouns and make verbs shimmer and dance at his command. So would the other two men in the folders before him, those whose notoriety had backed Sledge into a bleak and introspective corner of loneliness. "None of them is any different from me," he assured himself. "They put on their britches one leg at a time." But it didn't wash. Sledge played by the rules; the others ran out of bounds. And damn it it all to hell and back, *they* were the ones for whom the bells rang and the bulbs popped.

In the nippy pre-dawn of Monday morning, December 8, 1941, Kleber waited on his front porch. He was eight years old, sleepy, yet consumed with excitement, having passed the night in restless twisting of the radio dial, pursuing news—more news, *new* news—concerning the Japanese attack on Pearl Harbor. Huddled within two blankets, the child looked up and down Cloverdale, watching lights blink wearily on, disappointed that no one seemed as interested in the beginning of war as he. When Chuck, the TCU student who threw the morning paper route, rode by on a noisy Cushman motor scooter, Kleber ran excitedly to the curb. "You're late," he cried, catching the paper. Chuck gave him the middle finger. Obviously *he* didn't care too much that the Japanese had snuck across the Pacific Ocean in warships and dispatched 360 planes to bomb and sink the U.S. ship *Arizona* and capsize the *Oklahoma*. That was all the radio had said during the night.

Kleber ran into the house and devoured the thick black headlines: JAPAN BOMBS PEARL HARBOR—FDR TO ASK DECLARATION OF WAR. But the edition was disappointingly slim, Monday never being a day of allure to advertisers. Nor did the paper contain any photographs. Kleber's passion for visual confirmation would not be fully satisfied until the December 29, 1941, issue of *Life* magazine came, trumpeting from the cover: FIRST PICTURES OF JAP ONSLAUGHT SHOW DEATH AND DESTRUCTION AT AMERICAN BASE.

Nor had the outbreak of war altered the rigorous discipline that was VeeJee's routine. Already she had breakfast going in the kitchen, bacon sizzling, oatmeal boiling. She kneaded white oleomargarine and dropped in a packet of orange dye powder to fool people (but not Kleber) into thinking it was butter. By six-fifteen, her hair was twisted into a thick steely bun, her face scrubbed and her lips coated with a pale pink lipstick, her note pad open on the counter and containing an agenda that never had room for sloth, naps, or idle thought. Personal illness was simply not tolerated. Kleber could not remember a single hour when his mother was ill. Her strength was astonishing. Nor was sleep indulged. Often VeeJee exclaimed, "If only a body didn't have to sleep. Just think what a person could do if she didn't spend a third of life in bed." VeeJee was not an emotional woman, at least not for others to observe. Kleber never even saw tears in his mother's eyes until an April afternoon in 1945 when he arrived home from school. VeeJee was shaking with sobs. "President Roosevelt just dropped dead," she told him, as if announcing Armageddon.

On the morning after Pearl Harbor when Kleber appeared in the kitchen, newspaper in hand, eager to discuss war, VeeJee said sternly, "Get cracking, son."

"Mama, *please,* Mama, can I stay home from school? The President's going to talk about the war on the radio." Kleber knew his chances were next to nothing, but he made the pitch with passion.

"Of course not," answered VeeJee. "Education is more important than war. Besides, whatever Mr. Roosevelt says on the radio will be in the paper tonight." She poured lumpy oatmeal into a bowl and set it before her son. Glumly, Kleber stared at the mess, orange oleo spreading across it like melting lava. "When I was your age," she recalled, "World War I had been going on for two months before we even knew it. Word didn't get around so quick. Come to think of it, maybe it was better that way. We learn things too fast nowadays."

Kleber addressed his cereal and his paper. He hoped VeeJee would not dip into the near-dry bucket of memoirs. She had been to this well so often that Kleber knew her stories by heart, i.e. how she had left a dust bowl farm in Arkansas at the age of sixteen, had come to Fort Worth to find work as a department store clerk selling sheets, how she had intended to complete her high school education (needing two more years) but accepted instead the gallant, down-on-the-knees proposal of the first beau who asked her out—a dashing, high-humored cattle speculator named Kleber Cantrell, Jr. Though she never said so, VeeJee assumed she was marrying money, the Cantrell name carrying pioneer luster in Fort Worth with several shoots from the family tree enriched by land and fatted calves. But VeeJee chose the one branch that did not bear fruit, her husband going broke but a few months into their marriage in 1926. He treaded water a couple of years thereafter in ill-fated schemes until the spigot was turned off by brothers and sisters. Financial disaster was a prelude to personal tragedy. The couple's firstborn child, a daughter, perished from tuberculosis at the age of three. Cantrell then disappeared into a speakeasy called Sudie's, located in a notoriously sinful district of Fort Worth once called Hell's Half Acre. He stayed stone drunk for a year, despite tearful promises to his wife, who on one occasion brought their second infant, Kleber III, and stood outside the honky-tonk with eyes blazing and luggage packed.

Salvation and sobriety were delivered by a Baptist preacher named J. Frank Norris, who considered it his mission to cleanse Fort Worth of satanic temptation. In a flamboyant career, Norris had (1) turned monkeys loose in the sanctuary of his church and introduced them as Charles Darwin's cousins, (2) shot and killed a political enemy in the pastoral study but won easy acquittal, and (3) considered himself adjacent to the Pope as the most important man of God not only on planet Earth but in the entire universe. The Reverend Norris burst into

Sudie's one midday and discovered Cantrell holding up the bar. Seizing a bottle of moonshine, the preacher smashed it, pushed the drunkard's pathetic features perilously close to the tragic puddle of spirit and shards, and, while camera fired, exhorted repentance and return to the flock.

It worked. Cantrell located tedious sales work in the wholesale grocery business, rose to a managerial position, became a devout Presbyterian, and left the running of his home and the rearing of his heir to VeeJee. The father, in fact, had little commerce with his son, finding rapport instead in the Bible, which he read for an hour each morning in solitude and again each night before retiring at nine. There was little else in his life. Rarely did the elder Cantrell break out of this pious isolation, but these were the moments his son treasured. When he wanted to, Cantrell could knit a yarn as well as Will Rogers, possessing, as did most Texas men, a wondrous love of the land and its legends. But his commitment to religion had robbed Cantrell of his zest for then and now. He was gambling on the hereafter.

When Kleber became a man and looked back at these formative years, he awarded his father one deserved medal: the old man's religion was a solo act. He did not smother wife and son with enforced dedication to the word of God. True, the family attended church on Sunday and fellowship suppers on Friday (these a welcome relief from VeeJee's shoe-leather roasts and dead gray mush vegetables), but if on the other days of the week wife burst out with "dammit" or son skipped dinner in favor of William Faulkner, father did not thunder the approach of hellfire.

And there was another family fact that took years to become evident, if indeed Kleber ever sorted it out in his mind. Wedged between a mother who concealed emotions and a father who spoke mainly to God, Kleber found a calling that would allow him to intrude on other, more accessible lives—if only for an instant.

When his father took a seat at the breakfast table on the morning of new war, Cantrell glanced but briefly at the headlines. He intoned a lengthy prayer for Roosevelt, the United States, and the warriors of God.

"Daddy, can I stay home from school and listen to the President on the radio?" blurted Kleber in rare contradiction of his mother's position.

"Kleber!" VeeJee's voice was sharp.

"Mama said I couldn't, but, Daddy, *please*. It's a day of history."

The father, thin, pale, paused in methodical intake of oatmeal. He always ate neatly to avoid stains on the white dress shirt from which his wife expected three days' use before a new wash and iron. He looked at his eager son with patience. "I expect school's more important than war—in the long run," he said. "I don't see how war can be of concern to children."

"Well, I don't know about that, Daddy," said Kleber a little sassily. "I'd like to be in Pearl Harbor right this minute lookin' around."

"What on earth for?" asked the father.

"Well, I don't know if you can understand it, but whenever I *read* something interesting in the paper, I want to go see it for myself."

"By the time you get my age, son, you'll have seen things you'll wish you hadn't. Life becomes things to forget."

"Eat," ordered VeeJee. "You're both spinning your wheels. Time is golden." Man and boy obeyed.

On Christmas morning, two weeks into World War II, Kleber unwrapped a gift from his parents and discovered a toy that would change his life. It was a miniature printing set with rubber stamps for each letter of the alphabet, caps and lowercase, plus commas, periods, and—perhaps from mispackaging—twelve exclamation points! Immediately Kleber pressed stamps against the ink pad, and onto the wrapping paper he spelled out: "ThanX!! I LOvE ThIS!!! PrESxensT!" Later that morning, Kleber's best friend, T. J. Luther, appeared to strut around on his new Schwinn bicycle, and both boys disappeared into the bedroom. Enchanted with the printing set, T.J. stamped out "PUsSy" on his left arm and "I FuXCk GirLLs!!" on a slice of homework paper.

"Hey, this is great," exclaimed T.J. "We can write dirty stories and sell 'em. I'll draw pictures." Immediately T.J. began dictating a promising saga of the neighborhood girl named Macushla who was renowned for very major "teiats," but having little patience and less spelling ability, he abandoned the epic. That was fine with Kleber, for he was not remotely at ease in matters sexual. He was not even sure if he believed what T.J. had told him three months before, namely, that men put their peters inside women and made babies. The stork made better sense. He could not imagine his parents in such root-hoggery. He had never even seen them naked. They did not kiss, at least in front of their son.

"Well, they did *once,*" T.J. assured him. "Else you wouldn't be here actin' like a stupid shit-ass."

"You're lying!" cried Kleber.

"Bet you a dollar," shot back the informer. "Just ask 'em. I dare you. I double dog dare you."

"I *will,*" vowed Kleber, but, of course, he never did. Nor did he ever receive a syllable of sexual counseling from his parents, a puritanical shortcoming not uncommon in Kleber's generation.

Stuffed and sated with food and toys, Kleber sprawled on the floor beside the twinkling Christmas tree and studied once again the December 22, 1941, issue of *Life,* with the somber black-and-white cover of "Old Glory," wrinkled but billowing proudly in the wind.

As Kleber read *Life,* as his father read Deuteronomy, as his mother read *Reader's Digest,* war bulletins interrupted Christmas music on the Philco radio, a contraption so bulky that it took all three family members to move it during VeeJee's twice-yearly furniture dance. General Douglas MacArthur had "repulsed" two attempted Jap landings on the Philippines, but he needed more men, more equipment. A garrison of "gallant U.S. Marines" was standing off attacks at Wake Island— Kleber raced to the Rand McNally atlas to find the remote place—and, when queried by radio if they needed supplies, fired back, "No, just send more Japs." Everything he heard Kleber absorbed with evangelistic patriotism. He shuddered at cartoons picturing Japan as a treacherous serpent which was about to be decapitated by the united forces of American soldiers and the home front. He sneered at Germany, whose troops, according to *Life,* were infested with bugs and were led by General Louse and Field Marshal Typhus. These could be exterminated only if "every man, woman, and child in America joins hands and fights." The child fell asleep on the floor, beside the tree, war in his ears, and was carried unknowingly to his bed. He awoke on December 26 determined to do his part.

In the week between Christmas and New Year's, Kleber roamed energetically about his neighborhood, stopping women in the A&P, men at the Gulf station, kids on the school playground. He knocked on doors, even Mable Hofmeyer's, who declined him admission but from behind the dark screen stated that she would play "God Bless America" at war bond rallies, if asked. On New Year's Eve, VeeJee granted him permission to stay up until midnight in his room to hear the radio celebration from Times Square. The next morning, when the child did not appear for breakfast, VeeJee found him asleep on the floor, hands, face, and clothes lavishly stained with ink. Beside him, neatly stacked and clipped together with straight pins, were six 11 × 14 sheets of drawing paper that formed the first edition of CLOVER-DALE NEWS!! WAR XXXXTRA! Her impulse was to yank the boy up for a scolding, but she began to read the laborious, hand-stamped endeavor and by mid-page was absorbed. Soon after that she was misty-eyed with pride, both over the content and from appreciation of the remarkable industry of an eight-year-old. Forgiving misspellings and grammatical blunders, VeeJee learned a great deal. The next-door neighbor, George Sorrel, was enlisting in the Navy on January 1 and entrusting his wife, Evelyn, to run the Gulf station at the corner. A couple down the block were becoming air-raid wardens. Winnona Celler was losing all three of her sons to the Marines (and two would not come home, a lead item in a far-distant edition of Kleber's newspaper). T.J. was training his nuisance mongrel Rufus to "sniff out spies." Someone was digging a bomb shelter; someone else was hoarding sugar and coffee, "just in case." And the very last item, which the elder Cantrell confirmed was an accurate quote, brought alarm. It was news to VeeJee. "My daddy says HE LoVes HIs counTRy and wil FIte for IT. He maybe to OLD. But my DAd is inlixstxxing anYWay. PLeaSE COme HOme SoOn.!!!"

On her personal list of abhorrent behavior, right up there beside wasting time and a malnourished mind, VeeJee positioned bragging. She raised her son with nails hammered into his cognition—family business stays within the family (there wasn't much to tell, anyway), money is not discussed with outsiders (no worry there, either), trumpets shall not be blown to call attention to achievement. If deeds are worthy, heralds will sound on their own. But VeeJee was so proud of her son's newspaper that she typed carbons and distributed them to neighbors. People began to call for copies, along with items contributed to the next edition (which, due to Kleber's school work, did not appear until February 1942, and which contained this headline scoop: My FATher FLUNKs ARMIe EXam!! with a bulletin revealing that Mr. Cantrell would instead labor at the "bomber plant" in Fort Worth constructing B-24's). A copy found its way to the *Star-Telegram,* and Kleber's picture was taken to illustrate a feature article with excerpts of his primitive but interesting reporting. The city editor was heard to remark, "This is damn good journalism. An eight-year-old kid found a local angle for the biggest story of the century."

The CLOVERDALE NEWS ceased publication some three-plus years later, in September 1945, due to the disintegration of the rubber stamps and the ascendancy of its editor to a higher station in life. The last front page bore twin headlines: "JAPS QUIT—WE DROP A-BOMB ON THEM," along with "Kleber CANtreLL Enters JR. HIgh School (GuLP)!!!!" The three boys from Cloverdale went off to junior high together and promptly split in search of doors that would open to them. T.J.'s immediate attention was directed at girls, noting that the buds on the chests of sixth-graders had somehow ripened over the summer into fuller blossoms. Mack found the athletic fields that he would soon dominate. And Kleber observed, alarmingly, the delineation of power. At this early milestone of life, already he discovered it was money. Dollars were the social cleaver. Camp Bowie Boulevard, the avenue of red bricks which as a child he thought led to Oz, split the west side of town like an aorta. His side, the south side, was home to men who punched time clocks. Across the boulevard were the men who owned them. And now all of their children were ingredients in a sudden salad, tossed with Mexican youngsters from the Trinity River bottom, and farm kids from the vegetable baskets west of town, even orphans from Lena Pope Home, whose blood was rumoredly mixed and who, if tales were to be believed, were dull and strange and perhaps even dangerous. The progeny of the middle to lower class walked to school or rode bicycles. The delegates from Across the Boulevard arrived in chauffeured limousines, or Cadillacs driven by sleek, sweet-smelling mothers on their way to Dallas to shop. Some even had chariots of their own, their fathers having pulled courthouse strings to obtain licenses for children not yet fourteen. Money meant popularity, Kleber came to understand. Money was buying lunch in the cafeteria every day instead of consuming sandwiches brought from home. He grew to hate egg salad—warm and sulphurous and messy by noon. He was ashamed of bologna, whose garlic odor swam out of lockers and stained paper bags and identified its consumers like tattoos. Money was the right of passage in the center lane of school corridors. Those without it (Kleber got twenty-five cents a week allowance) were condemned for the nonce to creeping unnoticed on the soft shoulders.

Recognition came first to Mack, who ascended from the pack in recess games to a third-string position on the football team. While Kleber burned in envy, the monster sprouted six inches and added forty pounds in his thirteenth year, earning by spring semester the favor of coaches and moneyed young women who lingered to drive him home. His body and his face were commodities. This market always had customers.

A social niche of dubious character opened for T.J. when, not quite thirteen, and barely past five feet in height, he ascended the mountainous flanks of a ninth-grade girl from the orphanage whose breasts were of such proportions that merely to brush against them in the lunch line was a merit badge. If T.J. was to be believed, and he was, for soon thereafter he gained school-wide repute as the "nookie bookie," the definitive source for which girl was willing and which girl was not, he lured the motherless child, Ruby by name, into a scraggly clump of cedar and on a wintry afternoon when the sun was gone by four-thirty, inserted his hairless tallywhacker into her wonderland.

Kleber, cursed by lack of romantic energy and athletic inability, treaded water much longer. In a three-paragraph essay for seventh-grade English he described himself:

"I am an ordinary kid with light brown hair and freckles. I like to play football but I'm not good at it. I like to tell jokes but I can't remember them. What I like best is to read. My favorite authors are Albert Payson Terhune and Richard Halliburton.

"My best friends are two boys from my block, Mack Crawford, who *is* good at sports, and T. J. Luther, whose whole life is a joke.

"My ambition is to become a newspaper reporter and go to the next war. I want to be famous. And I probably will be."

His words merited an approving comment from the teacher but did not serve as a lightning rod to collect the currents of popularity. Plodding through the critical year as miserable as a farmer whose seeds would not germinate, Kleber despaired in the threatened loss of his best friends. Usually he walked home alone, Mack being busy on the playing fields, T.J. presiding in the bushes behind the chemistry lab where clandestine cigarettes were smoked and poontang analyzed.

But in the eighth grade Kleber located a passport for admission and power in this alien new world. Again, it was the seductive strength of ink on paper. The school newspaper, a frail four-page sheet that appeared monthly and contained wan pleas for better school spirit and moldy recapitulation of athletic events, went largely unread, serving better purpose as spitballs, paper airplanes, and liners for the cages of small mammals in biology class. On an autumn Saturday afternoon, Kleber roamed about the Fort Worth Public Library, his weekly custom to check out the maximum six books allowed per visit. He chanced into a reading room where out-of-town newspapers hung on racks like shirts drying on a line. When the closing bell clanged at six, he was absorbed, traveling in a land of glamour, encountering fascinating names and places. Gossip columns written by men named Walter Winchell and Leonard Lyons told him why Frank Sinatra was unhappy with Ava Gardner, that Ethel Merman appearing in *Annie Get Your Gun* was the "hottest ticket" on Broadway, that the bikini bathing suit shocked Paris fashion not only for its daring but due to the fact it was named for and introduced but five days after the United States began nuclear testing on a South Pacific island of the same name.

As Kleber left the library, he said to the dour woman who stamped the due date on books, "Did you know that Bernard Baruch had lunch at '21' restaurant last week in New York and coined the phrase 'We are in the midst of a cold war?' "

"No," said the librarian. "But it's very interesting." She smiled and seemed grateful for the information and looked at Kleber in a new light.

For several weeks thereafter, Kleber listened. He could be found at the edge of conversational circles in the lunchroom, eavesdropping on the mating dances performed by his society's most celebrated members. He pumped Mack for the "inside poop" on the school stars in sport. From T.J., he pried, with no effort, salacious tidbits, including rumored affairs of certain teachers. Then, obtaining permission from the typing teacher to spend an extra hour after school, he hunted and pecked out two tightly composed pages of gossip. He titled it "Tiger Tales" and dropped the work casually on the desk of Hazel Busher, journalism teacher. Across the top he wrote in bold hand, "I want to be a columnist in every issue. This is a sample of what I can do."

Hazel Busher, an ebullient spinster whose only brush with reporting had come thirty years earlier when she edited a state teachers' college yearbook, summoned the boy. Her reputation was that of an eccentric who sipped through the day from a thermos bottle that allegedly contained fruit juice. But because her eyes glistened and her manner grew more exuberant as the jug was visited, a theory grew that she was partaking of gin. Never in three decades of teaching had Hazel Busher encountered a child with a spark of journalistic potential. Now standing before her was a solemn youngster who was clearly on fire. Kleber's work was captivating. The teacher had even found confirmation in his column of a rumor that the school's most desirable bachelor, an assistant coach, was dating the principal's secretary, an item that delivered both disappointment and envy.

"Why did you write this?" she asked Kleber.

"Is it good?" he countered.

"That wasn't the question. Of course it's good. I asked you *why?*"

"The main reason is because I wanted to. And it satisfied a certain nosiness. I suppose a nicer word is curiosity."

"Do you know *why* it works?" asked Hazel, sucking Sen-Sen. "Because it has *names* in it. Lots of them. People like to read their names in print."

"I know. That's why I put so many in. I think we should run the names in boldface . . . so they'll stand out."

Hazel smiled at the youngster's use of jargon. "Some of this is a little . . . do you know the word 'risqué'?"

"Does it mean risky?"

Hazel smiled again. The boy was cocky. "Yes and no," she answered. "Look it up. Can you write this once a month?"

"Sure."

"Don't start something you can't finish."

"I won't be finished until people get tired of talking about themselves—and I get tired of listening."

Three decades after his debut as a gossip columnist, Kleber was secreted in the heart of France, self-exiled to a gamekeeper's cottage on the grounds of a fourteenth-century château near Tours. The seclusion was to finish a book—working title, *Bellyaches*—a compendium of personal angst that began with the assassination of John F. Kennedy and concluded with the resignation of Richard Nixon, news of which he had translated laboriously (but joyously) from *Le Monde* the week before. On this middle August afternoon in 1974 when Ceil Shannon arrived in a rented Citroën, she found her lover in insufferable humor. By design Kleber had no telephone, had leased the cottage under a pseudonym, had sought out isolation but now found it almost unbearable. He was cut off from the world events that he had spent a lifetime reporting and now he felt like a junkie kicking cold turkey. The Paris *Herald Tribune* arrived two days late; Kleber wasted hours each day driving to the nearest village and telephoning an AP buddy in Paris to have the ticker read to him.

He was unshaven, grumpy, and judging from the assemblage of empty wine bottles stacked in a corner like votive candles at the shrine of a martyr, was bent on finishing last year's crop of Beaujolais before the new grapes were pressed. "One gathers," said Ceil in greeting, "you are rewriting *Down and Out in Paris and London.*"

"In comparison of my mood today," answered Kleber, "Agrippina was Mrs. Wiggins." He kissed Ceil with need and gratefulness, sweeping a pile of rejected pages off a milking stool for her to sit.

"I can see," answered Ceil. "Are you being your basic scold, or has some new global calamity brought purpose to your life?"

"Nothing much new," said Kleber. "Just the mundane ticks of time. India, which cannot feed, clothe, or house its people, just set off its first atomic bomb, a wondrous expenditure of funds. Solzhenitsyn, exiled from Mother Russia, has turned up in America to replace J. Edgar Hoover as the sweetheart of the right. Patty Hearst is kidnapped. Allende is killed, presumably by our own meddlers. And Nixon, who should be in jail, has found cloister in California. See, nothing worth remarking over. . . ."

"I thought you'd sworn off the front page," said Ceil. She looked about the room and shuddered. "I couldn't write a sympathy note in a dump like this. I rather pictured something like Jimmy Jones's apartment on the Quai d'Orléans. . . . Come on, I'll buy you dinner. There's a two-star restaurant down the road which I'm certain has escaped your custom."

They dined elaborately: two dozen *belons,* the oysters of France whose flavor would be desecrated by cocktail sauce, a great pile of steaming white asparagus from the Black Forest of Germany, *loup de mer* grilled in butter and fennel, wild strawberries drowned in *crème fraîche.* "How can you write about the end of the world after a meal like this?" wondered Ceil.

"When you learn how to make chicken-fried steak, I'll not only propose, I'll proclaim gourmet parity."

"I brought you a clipping," remembered Ceil. "Gene McCarthy has already written your book for you—in one paragraph." She read out loud some wry observations by the intelligent senator who made a quixotic stab at the presidency in 1968: "From the founding of our government in 1789 to 1972, roughly, we went from George Washington to Richard Nixon, from John Adams to Spiro Agnew, from Alexander Hamilton to John Connally, from John Jay to John Mitchell. . . . One must wonder just how much of that kind of progress a nation can stand."

Kleber laughed and applauded. "I shall steal it," he said. "A little thievery is research; a major heist is plagiarism."

Just then a vacationing correspondent from *Newsweek* spotted the couple in their secluded alcove and sent over a bottle of wine. Under the cloak of fellowship, he coaxed an interview from Kleber, who, whether he wrote words or spoke them, was usually quotable.

"This may sound like a naïve question," began the correspondent, who was young, not yet thirty, and ambitious, and somewhat awed in the presence of a writer whose name was a household word and a woman playwright whose works had been performed in a score of languages.

"Remember Edmund Wilson," said Kleber. " 'There are no naïve questions, only naïve answers.' "

The correspondent relaxed. "Okay then, *why?* Why do you write? What got you going at such an early age?"

"Haven't a glimmer," answered Kleber. "I am certainly not Presbyterian and emphatically not Buddhist, thus ruling out the old predestination script. I doubt if genetic legacy was much involved because my parents believed literature began with Genesis and concluded with Norman Vincent Peale. All I can remember from my personal dark ages was an insatiable curiosity to find out about other people. And the carrot on my stick was the reward of deference. A kind of inexplicable power. Recognition from people whose names I rubber-stamped into print. Everybody needs validation."

"Then you're saying . . ." interrupted the correspondent, attempting to shape a vague answer.

"I'm saying," went on Kleber, feeling Ceil's fingers tickle his palm under the table like a demented gypsy, "that very early on, I discovered people like you and me have access to hidden rooms, entree to private lives."

"You make journalism sound like breaking and entering," said Ceil.

"That's as good a definition as I could dream up," said Kleber approvingly. "In fact, I shall steal that, too." He tapped on the correspondent's pad. "Write down that I said it. I promise she won't sue. She owes me too many due bills."

CHAPTER TEN

Guilt in a hangman's cape and a skeleton mask danced above his head. Chills and fever took turns in assault of his body. On the morning after his graduation from high school, on the Sunday dawn when his photograph radiated from the front page with the promise of purpose and opportunity, Kleber struggled in nauseated contemplation of the English language's shortest and most maddening conditional: *If.*

If it had not rained for two weeks straight. *If* the girls, particularly Lisa, had not selfishly gathered for a slumber party and left the Three Princes to fend for themselves. *If* T.J. had not hatched an impulsive idea. *If* he had only paid heed to his dependable better judgment. *If* the stupid hillbilly girl in the pink dress hadn't gotten caught in the storm. If. If. *If!* Every man has an hour of his life that he would like to take again, from the top, but no bargain with God has ever turned back the clock. Now each time the phone rang—and it cried incessantly—Kleber braced for his appointment with destruction.

Each time the door to his room opened, he expected to see his mother's face turned chalk white or his father's lips trembling in bewildered pain. Their bodies would sag in betrayal, mortification. Get dressed, they would tell him. The police are on the way over to arrest you for gang rape and murder.

He fantasized the trial.

In the very same suit he wore to deliver the school valedictory, he would take the stand and swear with hand on Holy Bible that his virgin organ did not even penetrate Laurie's quite willing (and obviously experienced) privates. He would transfer the crown of guilt to the seductress. She asked for it. But what, he wondered in his torment, *what* if his semen had been found caked in her pubic hair? That alone might send him to the electric chair. But he reassured himself: surely the swollen rapids of the Brazos River would have washed away his deposit. But what if the girl hadn't died, hadn't drowned? What if she had only passed out, like T.J. speculated, had only fainted from the enthusiasm of her passion? The brief solace contained in this scenario did not last long. If the girl was alive, logic dictated, then surely she was sitting at this very minute in the Weatherford police station, bruised, bleeding, helping the law weave a rope strong enough to snap three princely necks.

During the night, after his address, after the tassels were turned and the flashbulbs popped, after the embraces and tears from parents and teachers, after the party and a tiff with Lisa over his inexplicable "moodiness," after avoiding Mack and T.J. (which was not difficult because each of the trio was anxious to dance clear of the others), Kleber crept into his home.

It was 4:15 a.m. VeeJee had left him a note on the kitchen counter. "Dear Son: Nowhere on earth is there a mother's heart that beats so proudly tonight. Your speech was wonderful. I almost cried. Your father extends his congratulations, too. Sleep late. I'll make French toast. Your Mother."

Kleber read the praise and his stomach churned. He was unworthy of life. Suicide seemed the only possible rag to wipe up this mess. VeeJee's medicine cabinet contained nothing of mortal threat, unless a person could overdose terminally on cold cream, mouthwash, denture powder, and an old bottle of Hadacol. There were not even aspirins, VeeJee refusing to tolerate headaches. Beneath the kitchen sink, Kleber poked around and found bug killer, Clorox bleach, and drain-opening powder. He poured a dab of each into a coffee cup and, fascinated by the smoke that rose like the fumes of a deranged scientist's vial, summoned courage to sip. But as the final draught approached his nose, he coughed, feeling simultaneously a burning sensation on the lacy cuff of his rented tuxedo shirt. Damn! A drop of the home-brewed hemlock had splashed onto the fabric, had eaten quickly to the skin. Well, suicide was seductive but suffering was not. Hurriedly Kleber dumped the gunk into the sink, flushed it with water, raced to his own bathroom to find shaving lotion to overcome the odor. The next morning, VeeJee's kitchen smelled like a Mennen Skin Bracer factory.

Somehow he got through the night and the morning and by late afternoon his reputation was still intact. He began to feel better. Lisa telephoned, sympathizing over his sudden "flu." She apologized for their quarrel at the grad night dance, accepting all the blame. The fires of hell licked at his feet for another week, but as June began they at least turned down to simmer.

He continued to devour every word of each day's newspapers, searching for some word of the girl and the storm. It puzzled him. Then, when nothing turned up, it occurred to Kleber that rural news was printed in an early edition that did not land on his front porch. He went to the *Star-Telegram* morgue (what a perfect name, he thought) and found the bulldog edition of the Sunday paper. At the back were a few lines of type that sent his heart into panic. The small headline read: AREA GIRL REPORTED MISSING.

He had to find out more. He was good at asking questions and now he would use that talent. He drove to the far north side of Fort Worth, found a heavily patronized pay telephone within the grounds of the cattle exchange. No chance of the call being traced. He rang up the sheriff's office in Weatherford. A dull voice answered. "Sergeant Maynard." It was not the name in the newspaper but he could not afford to be put on hold.

"Ah, Sergeant, this is William R. Pattinaux of the Dallas *News* . . ." He had deepened his voice and put a handkerchief over the mouthpiece to further cloud the tone. He slurred the fake name.

The officer's voice snapped to attention. "Yessir. What can I do for you?"

"Well, the city editor asked me to check out some little ole pissant item in the Fort Worth paper about a missing girl. Laurel somebody. From that big storm. He thinks it might make a human-interest story. Anything come of it? Did she turn up?"

"Naw. She just took off."

Worried that the bawling of calves being herded into pens might betray his position, Kleber pulled the telephone booth door and held it tightly closed. His hand trembled. "There was some notion of her possibly being drowned. What d'you think?"

"Well, it's *possible*. That was some storm. We had a twister or two. But more'n likely she just ran away. Her mama's kind of your undependable type. Didn't provide too good. The little girl—well, she wasn't *that* little—she knew these parts right good. Personally I don't think she got lost. Just got fed up."

Kleber was beginning to feel relieved. But he glanced nervously at cowmen strolling to and from the auction barns, men with faces as wrinkled as their jeans. None of them looked like plainclothes cops. But you never knew. He wound up the conversation hurriedly.

"Then there's no reason to suspect . . . foul play?"

"Naw. There's no story. Nothin' unusual about some little ole gal who gets pissed off at her mama and runs. She'll come home 'fore long."

"Thanks, Sergeant." Kleber slammed down the phone and wiped the receiver clean of fingerprints. He felt his blood race but he was proud of his enterprise, a curious juxtaposition. Then Kleber took an extra step. He drove to Dallas and found another pay telephone. He called Parkland Hospital, located a resident in gynecology, identified himself as a drama major at SMU writing a play, and asked straight out, "Is it medically feasible for a woman to die from . . . ah . . . sexual intercourse?"

"Are you putting me on?" asked the young doctor, laughing.

"No. *Really.* I have this scene I want to write. A guy forcibly . . . *takes* a young woman . . ."

"How young?"

"Sixteen or so. But she's built good. It's her first time. Just tell me, could she die while . . . doing it?"

The doctor grew serious. "Not likely," he said. "Not unless your protagonist has a twelve-inch whacker or uses a Coke bottle. In that case, he could tear the uterine tissue and cause hemorrhaging."

"I see. If the girl was . . . taken by force . . ."

"You mean, raped?"

"Yes. Could she die of fright? Maybe a heart attack?"

"I've never heard of such a thing. But I'm a doctor. I deal in facts. Your job is playactin'. . . . If you write it good enough, it doesn't have to be all that true."

Kleber murmured another hurried thanks and hung up. He drove back to Fort Worth with his eyes on the road but his mind reclaimed by the awful night in Uncle Bun's shack. He remembered all the textures—the sounds of the storm, the touch of flesh, the glow of fire, the feel of rotting wallboard, the sweat masks of men in passion and woman in terror. *But Kleber was not a participant in the drama.* He had somehow removed himself from the stage and was now sitting in the audience—watching, recollecting, dictating an account as if he had only been a witness. A shield had fallen to divorce him from personal reality. It would not soon go away.

This is something to believe: no one ever chose journalism for the money. With seventeen years of education crammed into his head, with a master's from Columbia framed under glass and snuggled inside a carton of personal icons—Steinbeck, Faulkner, Hemingway—Kleber Cantrell began work on the Houston *Call-Bulletin.* He would earn $58.50 a week. After taxes it came to barely $40—a dollar an hour. The federal government's phrase makers had not yet come up with "poverty level," but had there been one, Kleber would have fallen below it.

His career began so auspiciously that it seemed the croupiers of chance had been waiting for him to take a seat at the table. Having been informed by letter to report for work at 6 a.m. sharp on a September Monday, and being the child of VeeJee Cantrell, Schedule Queen, Kleber carefully rehearsed his processional. Arriving in Houston on the day before, a ferociously humid Sabbath when shirts stuck to backs and people struggled like mosquitoes unable to fly away from the honeypot, he leased a furnished room. It was clean and old, rather like the landlady who rented little pieces of her oxblood brick house on the decaying inner edge of exploding Houston. For ten dollars a week, Kleber was entitled to occupy a twelve-foot-square converted back porch with opaque plastic sheets tacked against window screens to keep out the wind. He would sleep on an imitation maple bed, single size, bathe in a stall shower that smelled of Lysol, dry his body with gray towels thin enough to read newsprint through, and comb his hair before a cracked mirror in which his face looked like a surrealist painting. He would also slumber in the bosom of Jesus, because no matter how often he took down from the wall a polychrome picture of Christ in Ascension and stored it in his tiny closet, the Son of God always reappeared miraculously over his head.

The landlady, Mrs. Edith Saller, a childless widow of seventy-four, mothered her tenants, who, counting Kleber, numbered seven. The other six were dead-eyed bachelors, bowlers, and beer drinkers. Kleber was the first roomer in Saller House history to have work more interesting than lubricating automobiles. Thus did the good lady introduce her catch to the others with pride, a hostess whose salon was newly graced by celebrity. Though he feigned modest indifference, Kleber sort of relished the nods of envy and respect that appeared on the faces of men who had lost.

Twice that Sunday afternoon, Kleber drove the route from the rooming house to the newspaper office—eighteen minutes portal to portal. But on Monday morning, despite arising at four and setting out in the fogged hothouse darkness, he got lost, became ensnarled in a maze of newly altered one-way downtown streets that seemed the chaos of a child unable to assemble an Erector set. Kleber stopped beside a streetlamp to study the city map when, suddenly, his attention and a glass storefront window nearby were simultaneously shattered. Next, like an animal caught in a trap, came the piercing wail of an alarm. Two shadowy figures broke into view. They were dragging a burlap sack and racing across an intersection just ahead. His first instinct, though Kleber never admitted it, was to stick his head out the window and ask directions from the fleeing men. But neighborliness was scuttled when a black-and-white police car, siren screaming, red and white lights spinning on the roof in wrath, burst like a rocket fired across the same avenue down which the two men had run. It squealed around a corner where, out of sight, there came the sounds of conflict. A crash, metal against glass. Shots. Cries. Explosion. Whooshing noises. Screams. The crackle and afterglow of fire. When Kleber finally summoned the gumption to attend his franchise, he beheld one dead burglar, one dying policeman, one overturned and thoroughly demolished cop car—blazing. And blood from good and evil were literally on fire, comingled in a hellish pool of gasoline.

Twenty minutes late for work, but exuberant over the insurance policy in his pocket—notes scribbled on the back of a city map— Kleber bounded up the sagging steps of the Houston *Call-Bulletin,* found the city room on the second floor, stopped the first person in view—a white-haired lady who looked like Norman Rockwell's favorite model. Where could he locate one Mr. Clifford Casey, city editor?

"That prick over there," gestured the sweet old woman. "And if I were you, kid, I'd sit a spell and wait. He's doing his shit-ass act this morning."

For the first moment of his life, Kleber questioned the wisdom of his career calling. The toy printing press of Pearl Harbor Christmas had led to *this?* Before him was the city room. It resembled a factory condemned, a ship lurched, a tenement beyond salvage by the cosmetics of urban renewal. Spanish-arch windows twelve feet high were as yellowed as the newspapers stacked on their sills. The floor was a warped, rippling carpet of carbon papers. If a cleaning woman had lately been present, then she was surely dead and buried in one of the waist-high metal mesh baskets that overflowed like Etna. The air was so thick and foul that if one held out a hand and stared at one's fingernails, they would visibly blacken like time-stop photography. When Kleber later on saw the film *Snake Pit,* set in an insane asylum, he remarked that Hollywood could have saved some bucks on scenery by using the city room of his newspaper.

At the heart of this darkness was a croquet-wicket-shaped assemblage of odd-lot desks, a thick and misshapen playpen for the man who lived and ruled within. At half past six on the first morning of a young reporter's life, Clifford Casey was, no other word comes close, terrifying. Four years later, Kleber was well tempered by devotion and love but the feeling held. Clifford Casey was a runaway train. He was the bully of every child's schoolground. He was a grenade with the pin pulled. He was both gladiator and emperor. He was one of those men who would make a liar out of the measuring stick that said he was only five feet eight. Clearly he was twice that, with a belly that stored at any given moment ten gallons of beer. Kleber had no more desire to approach him than to sleep on the Gulf Freeway.

Telephones grew on Casey like leech mutations, one cradled under his neck, another glued to an ear, a third waited in his hand, and he managed at the same time to bark into a squawk box on his desk that connected his rage to a photographic darkroom somewhere in the building. Swirling around was the cacophony of fifty clacking typewriters, more phones ringing, whoops of reporters triumphant in prose or the moans of those imprisoned by blocks, and—above all—the passion of Clifford Casey, Othello drowning out full chorus and symphony. Every few moments, the man would abruptly halt whatever he was doing, throw powerful arms about his waist and embrace himself in surrender to the pain of ulcers. Then, as purge, perhaps as encore, he cursed himself, his staff, his job, his day, his world.

Kleber fidgeted to the edge of idiocy, then found courage to speak his name. "I'm Kleber Cantrell," he said lumpily. "I'm supposed to start work this morning." He held out his letter of acceptance.

Casey glowered back with the affection people give car repossessors. "I'm real happy for you, son," he said. "Just sit there." The city editor gestured to a cobbler's bench beside the desk, the type where prisoners await interrogation.

"Yessir, but I saw . . ." Kleber began eagerly to tell his tale.

"Son, *set*. We got a city edition to get out." Casey yelled into the squawk box. "When? Oh Lord, *when?*" Muffled sounds came back, like from somebody lost in a mine cave-in. Casey's brow knitted into corduroy and he cried, "Then bring the motherfucker out here wet! If I don't get some art in thirty seconds . . ." He left the ultimatum incomplete, turning to Kleber for a fraction and muttering, "They're killing me, son." Imprecating photographic sloth, the city editor rose and commenced to shepherd his flock, bustling around the ancient desks, threatening one writer's ear, sweet-talking the next, keeping in his head a running score of half a hundred breaking events . . . a lost child was found, a tanker had run aground in the Houston Ship Channel, a civic leader was dying, triplets were born, a group of Hungarian émigrés intended a potentially violent demonstration at noon in a Houston park protesting Russian control of their mother country (an event more interesting to the newspaper than riots and valiance in Budapest). All of this was captivating to Kleber, but none of it compared, on his Libran balance of news value, to the story in his pocket. He squirmed. He knew the answer but the teacher wouldn't call on him. "Sir . . ." he started, daring to intrude on Casey's ear.

"Yeah?"

"Sir, on the way down here this morning, I . . ."

"Son, I know you're eager. I know you've got a goddamn master of journalism from the goddamn Columbia University, which, if you've got a dime, will get you on the bus. But if I don't get this edition out by eight-ten, then there ain't gonna be no cocksucker paper for you to lavish your goddamn brilliance on. Okay? Now just set quiet and play with yourself." Casey spent what seemed his final breath on the squawk box. "Louie! Will you get your spaghetti ass out here with that art?"

A photographer with the dark leathery face of Sicily ran puffing, holding a dripping Graflex negative in his hands. Casey leaped up and seized it and stared. "Jesus," he mourned. "What the fuck is this? Midnight in Nairobi?" Kleber peeked at the poorly lit image of an overturned police car. "Hell, Case," said Louie, not the least bit chastised, "when I got there nobody was left but the wrecker driver. Pete's at the hospital trying to get the shot cop before he goes into surgery." The photographer shrugged; he had labored thirty years at this paper. His viewfinder was not going to be ripped from his hands because he produced a dull and dark picture of an event that loomed major on Monday but which would be as forgotten as gum wrappers on Wednesday. Besides, on his assignment nail waited a bride at nine, a Rotary Club speaker at eleven-fifteen, a golden wedding at two, and a basket of eight springer spaniels at two forty-five. The paper loved puppies and enduring marriage.

Casey tossed white tablets into his mouth and chewed furiously, holding his stomach. "Go dry the fucker," he told the photographer, then leaning across his desk, almost prone, exhorted speed from an elderly, gleamingly bald-headed rewrite man named Art. Earphones clamped to his head, Art was taking dictation from a police reporter somewhere in the field, trying to assemble disjointed information into cohesive copy. Rewrite men are valued resources and Art was a good one but Casey was treating him on this morning like a goldbricker. He ripped paper out of Art's typewriter while a copy boy, hovering like a surgical attendant, inserted a fresh sheet. The city editor read aloud: "A policeman and a hijacker shot each other dead just before six a.m. today in downtown Houston. A second officer was critically wounded in the violent gun battle at the intersection of Chenevert . . ." Toward heaven looked Casey, hands in prayer. He begged, *"Please,* Artie, we're gonna *play* this fucker. It reads like a Baptist sprinkling. Get the fuck into the story and stop clearing your throat."

Art shrugged and took off his earphones. "I'm not exactly dealing with E. B. White here, Casey. Scotty's hung over. He's trying to pull somethin' together out of the police reports."

"Why do you do this to me?" asked Casey. "I'm gonna have to go over to the scene myself and find out what happened so I can put some news in this fucking story. Where are the fucking quotes?"

Louie reappeared with a damp print and Casey loped toward the engraving room, cropping with a red grease pencil on the run. Kleber seized the moment, suspecting his career was in peril of ending before it began, but calculating the risk outweighed the punishment. In pursuit of the city editor he hurdled a wastebasket, collided with the fashion editor as she emerged from the toilet, and caught Casey on the threshold of the engraving room. With acid fumes watering his eyes, he blurted, "Sir, Mr. Casey, sir. I know you told me to wait, and I know how busy you are, and you're probably going to can me, but I *saw* it."

"Saw *what?*"

"I *saw* the shoot-out. I was parked on the street trying to read a map. I was lost. I heard glass break and then I saw two guys run across the intersection, and then this police car came tearing after 'em, and . . ."

"Well, kiss my royal Irish ass," said Casey. "Why didn't you tell me, son?"

"Sir, I tried . . ."

"This ain't no debating society, son. You got to speak up." Half carrying the cub back to the city room, he gave the foundling a home. "Write it, son," he said, gently, tenderly. "Take a deep breath and let it come out. You got seven minutes."

Words, thousands of words, had flowed from Kleber's brain to his fingers to his paper since the first edition of the CLOVERDALE XXXXTRA!! Normally they had come as dependably as tap water. But now, hands poised over the keyboard of a battered Underwood whose case was stained with burns, coffee, sweat and blood, *paralysis*. He watched the second hand on the city room clock revolve twice. Five minutes left. His page was blank. Beside him, the sweet-faced lady with white hair, whose name was Millie, and who covered criminal courts like a hanging judge, was actually gnashing her teeth—Kleber heard them grind—while she twisted her hair into Medusan serpents. The "e" key on her machine had jammed, causing Millie to bawl in profane but unheeded irritation for repair. Kleber tried to concentrate. He finally wrote, "I saw death this morning . . ." He paused and he added, facetiously, ". . . my own." He crumpled the paper and began anew. On the other side of him sat an ashen-faced city hall reporter named Horace who had three lighted cigarettes burning—one in his mouth, one in his fingers, one on the edge of the desk. A butt fell, ignited a wastebasket. Horace threw coffee over the flames. Nobody even looked. It appeared as routine an occurrence as the great belch that Horace emitted after each sentence completion.

Meantime, Millie, enraged because no one had come to oil her "e," rose, lifted the machine high above her head, and dropped it, witch-cackling as pieces shattered. This time people looked but no one commented. The copy boy brought a substitute typewriter and Millie began to pound out the report of a double murderer freed by some judge on a technicality. He envied her speed and purpose. He tried again. "I saw death this morning," Kleber wrote. "One man was of the law, the other outside it . . ." He rather liked the beginning and was trying to keep it going when Louie the photographer interfered. He appeared with a Graflex and said, "Case wants a mug shot for the home edition." Kleber stood against the wall, blinked, lost another minute. Distractions smothered him: hunger, thirst, kidneys, the wish he had taken a different route to work. He hated this job. Everybody around him was at least two-thirds demented. He was frightened. He was about to fail.

"How's it comin', son?" intruded Casey. Quickly Kleber covered his humiliation with his elbows.

"Okay," he lied.

Casey saw the meager product. He placed arms of compassion on the young man's shoulders; no mother ever wrapped her child in so soft a blanket.

"Imagine, if you will," he began, "that Kleber Cantrell is on the way to a party. En route he sees a terrible tragedy on the street. He goes on to the party and, of course, he wants to tell about it. Right? So *tell* me, son. In your own words. Just tell me. Tell me what you saw this morning."

"You mean . . . here? Out loud?"

"That's right. Nobody's listening. Just you and me." Somehow Casey blocked out the hurly-burly around and about them.

"Well," started Kleber, astonished at how the roadblocks were falling. "It was my first morning as a reporter, and I wanted to be here on time. I'm never late. It's a compulsion of mine. But the streets of downtown Houston are confusing. They're flat. No hills. No landmarks. Besides it was dark and foggy and eerie. I got lost. I stopped under a streetlight to read a map—and somewhere nearby glass broke. Hundreds of pieces sounded like they were falling. Then, through my windshield, about fifty feet ahead, I saw two men run across the street. They were like shadows in a cemetery. They were dragging something, a feed sack, I think. . . . They must have been wearing tennis shoes, because at that moment it was quiet. But then an alarm went off; it started softly like a singer controlling her breath and it got louder and louder . . ."

Casey held out his hands. Red light. "Stop, son," he whispered. "Write it just the way you told it . . ."

Kleber protested. "That's not writing. That's talking."

"Listen to me, son. Forget journalism school. Forget the biography of Horace Greeley and Joseph Fucking Pulitzer. Forget your ethics class and how to count headlines and the technique of interviewing. There is only one thing to know. We're in the business of communicating information. Now, you just *told* me a story, in your own words, that grabbed my attention. I was fascinated by every goddamn pearly syllable. You can just as easily *write* that story on paper and it will hold my interest. In fact, it will thrill my ass. That's *power,* son. The man who has something to say—and a talent for making people listen to him—is possessed of power as valuable as alchemy. Okay?"

"I just want it to be good."

"Climb down off the mountain of art," ordered the city editor. "This ain't gonna be the best story you'll ever write. Nor the worst. Only the first. There'll be three more today before I'll let you go home. And six tomorrow. If your fingers aren't bleeding by Friday, it won't be because I didn't jump on 'em. Now turn 'er loose, son."

He bolted away, blood pressure rising over some new impediment. He yelled over his shoulder at Kleber, "Don't write it good. Just write it fast. Short takes!"

Exactly thirty-two minutes later, after Clifford Casey tore the last paragraph out of Kleber's typewriter and raced it by hand to the composing room, the copy boy dropped a proof of page one on the city desk. "Com'ere, son," growled Casey at Kleber, thrusting out an ink-wet sheet for his wrung-out scribe.

EXCLUSIVE!

CALL-BULLETIN REPORTER WITNESSES
DUEL OF DEATH AT DAWN

Rookie Cop and Hijacker Slain
On Downtown Houston Street

By Kleber Cantrell

They fell, the two men, arms outstretched for one another, their blood spilling and mingling. When the fire began, their clothes

burned away and it became impossible to tell who was the policeman and who was the thief—only that two young men were suddenly dead . . .

Kleber was both pleased and a little startled. In the historic tradition of street commerce, the front page was a siren designed to lure.
The city editor was a master of paint and perfume. He had lifted a
paragraph toward the end of Kleber's account, set it in boldface at the
beginning, moved paragraphs around, inserted quotes from a police
spokesman, creating a provocative package. "We'll have your picture in
the home edition," said Casey. "If you're proud of yourself, you little
punk, you should be. Now gimme a three-by-thirty-three cutline on this
goddamn baby hippo." He threw a glossy at Kleber, and with it, a
wink, well done.

This was easier. Kleber called the zoo, dashed out a silly poem
that absurdly rhymed "hippo" and "tiptoe" and "slippo." The city editor stuck a stubby finger down his throat in mock gagging, initialed approval, and sent Kleber to Jefferson Davis Hospital, where the wife of
the critically injured second policeman from the morning shoot-out was
keeping death watch. Assignment: tears and color.

He found her sitting in the waiting room, a young, nineteen-year-
old woman, heavily pregnant, hair in pink plastic curlers, holding her
husband's photograph in an antique frame, attended by cops and
brothers-in-law. To intrude on her agony seemed impossibly cruel, but
Kleber did not even hesitate. He had the power. Dressing his face in
sadness, introducing himself as an eyewitness, he murmured, "I'm very
sorry, ma'm. I saw it all. Your husband was a brave man."

The wife, who would be a widow by lunch, clasped the reporter's
hand and sobbed, but in the rain she delivered the mail. Out poured
Mel's biography, the record cabinets he was building, the Little League
team he was coaching, his lifetime dream to be a policeman, the pre-
monition she had from the night before that the shadows of danger
were hovering. Long after Kleber had filled his pad, she kept talking,
flattered by the reporter's favor, awarding him—a total stranger—the
scrapings of her soul. All of which made the night final edition, and
eight months later won local and state prizes for writing under deadline
pressure. By that time Kleber could barely remember the tears and
blood of his first day.

Journalism, Kleber came to perceive, is not the stuff of reflection.

Every day is new; every morning contains new lives to examine, to probe briefly, to sketch with a few lines, then move hurriedly to the next. Kleber loved his profession. The real power, he grew to understand, was never having to stop long enough to deal with himself. It kept a man's house secure from ghosts and their secrets.

The ten dollars a week that Kleber paid Edith Saller also gave him admission to the widow's living room, where the other "gentlemen" congregated nightly, their stomachs rumbling with chili dogs and Grand Prize beer. They smoked Luckies and Chesterfields, waited for the wrestling matches on TV, accepted and promised to read the Jehovah's Witness pamphlets distributed by Edith like a farmwife strewing grain. Kleber passed an occasional quarter hour in the "communal room" but quickly determined that his co-roomers were men with whom he had scant desire for social congress. One of them, Howard the Bragger, wanted it known that he had personally won a substantial portion of World War II in Europe, had slept with Rita Hayworth, and had owned three Packards and one Fleetwood Cadillac. Since Howard currently worked for a hardware store and earned, generously, fifty dollars a week, his anecdotes seemed to lack 24-carat credibility. Another, Clarence the Tub (these being private nicknames endowed by the writer-in-residence), was retired from "custodial engineering." That meant janitor, but Kleber never called him on it. Clarence's greatest pleasure was in the appearance of Gorgeous George on television, giving him occasion to remark that the platinum-curled grappler was, and here Clarence pitched his voice falsetto, "rooty tooty fruity." His mission in life seemed the ferreting out of homosexuals; Clarence insisted they swooped down on him like bats in the night. But Clarence, who weighed 280 pounds and had not seen his own privates since his third belly flap covered them, betrayed himself when he asked Kleber to obtain free tickets for a wrestling match. Clarence emphasized his request with a playful armlock that stayed around the reporter's neck a sexual beat too long. Kleber was getting adroit at staring through masks. There was also Augie the Prune, whose recalcitrant bowels defied all laxatives. Leo the Lothario was neglectful in retirement and often forgot to wear his toupee when he set forth each evening to seduce maidens at a nearby tavern.

Kleber had been in residence more than a month before he even noticed the one old owl in the pen of bantam roosters, a curio named

Daniel Titus who always sat in the corner and rarely spoke. He looked eighty, admitted to sixty-five, was somewhere in between. His house slippers were smooth and creaseless because he shuffled, unable anymore to lift legs that had taken baby steps when Texans were still fighting Indians. The other roomers ignored Daniel, the general feeling being that the wheezing old man neither heard nor saw much and was too senile to keep track.

But one night after Kleber paused to catch the evening news on television, the old man raised a frail hand like a flag of surrender. He bade Kleber to listen. "I've been reading your articles, Mr. Cantrell," said Daniel Titus. The voice was firm. Its owner was polite and courtly. "It's quite excellent. I can even tell when you write something and they don't give you a by-line."

Kleber paid thanks and noticed that in the old man's black serge lap was the graceful prose of Walter Prescott Webb. They exchanged admiration over the great Texas historian. Then Daniel was seized by a terrible spasm of coughing. Thereafter, Kleber chatted with the old man infrequently. He enjoyed Daniel's wisdom and scholarship, but he was unwilling to adopt an old dog (no matter how friendly) that came to his back porch.

On another night, the roomers were quarreling over politics. Clarence the Tub asked Kleber for whom he had voted in the 1956 presidential election.

"Adlai Stevenson, of course," he answered.

"Adlai's tooty fruity," said Clarence.

"How can anybody be against Ike?" demanded Howard the Bragger. "I know Ike Eisenhower personally and I can tell you he's as honest as they come."

Kleber arched an eyebrow. "You *know* the President?"

"Why hell yes. Shook hands with him twice. He's a farm boy. Family man. Next time you run into him, big shot, just ask. He'll remember Howard."

Clarence jumped in again. "Adlai's for the niggers. If he'd a got in, we'd have to call it the Black House." He thought it was the funniest remark ever made.

Sighing, Kleber retreated. Then, uncharacteristically, from his corner, Daniel Titus spoke out. "I can understand why a fine young man like Mr. Cantrell would favor Mr. Stevenson," he said. "Mr. Cantrell's business is language. He must use it properly. Mr. Stevenson speaks with eloquence. There are very few defenders of the King's English."

"You mean the *Queen's* English," howled Clarence, ending the moment.

The next morning, when Kleber dressed for work, he found a manuscript and a note slipped under his door. They were from Daniel Titus. "Dear Mr. Cantrell, I apologize for the boors in our midst. Don't let their ignorance get you down. They cry the sad cries of everyman: *Look at me. Pay attention!* You enrich this house. Respectfully. P.S. Attached is a little something I wrote. I would value your comment."

When Kleber got around to glancing at the old man's work, he was taken by the elegance and style. Daniel had written of the Coushatta Indian tribe, a melancholy remnant in Texas history, eking out a barren life in the great forest that encompasses much of East Texas. Because the forest wilderness was being threatened by greedy timber speculators, Titus warned that it could soon become as denuded and sorrowful as the Indians. Well, it so happened that the newspaper loved the Big Thicket, as the forest was called, championing its preservation along with whooping cranes. Intending a gracious surprise, Kleber submitted the old man's piece to Casey, who said he might, with judicious trimming, run it on the Saturday feature page someday.

Brusquely the city editor snipped the tail of Kleber's soaring kite at least once a week and brought him back to earth—usually for a valuable lesson. In his third month of work, Kleber took his seat at the city desk, prepared for fire, flood, scandal, or even the nuts who called on deadline with fillings in their teeth that picked up CIA radio signals. Instead, Casey sentenced him to exile.

"Helen's on the rag," said the city editor. He referred to the obituary writer, a quiet heavy woman who sat in a distant corner and composed beautifully typed death notices. "Gimme four obits for the home."

"What do I *do?*" asked Kleber, wanting counsel.

"Just write the goddamn obits, son. Every day ain't page one."

Kleber asked Millie for guidance. Gnashing teeth and cursing him for mashing her muse, she said, "Call up the goddamn funeral homes and find out who croaked. They'll tell you the ones worth putting in the paper." Unhappy with the dunce cap he felt was on his head,

Kleber rummaged through the fresh inventory of Houston's newly deceased and found five kicked buckets of stature sufficient to merit newsprint. He dropped his due on Casey's desk twenty minutes in advance of the noon deadline. For the rest of the day he took dictation from reporters in the field—where he wanted to be—and at 3 p.m. prepared to go home. "Stick around," suggested Casey. The city room thinned quickly until only Casey and the cub remained, the editor cropping pictures and trimming overnight features. He ignored Kleber squirming uncomfortably on the cobbler's bench. Just past five he looked up. "Those obits ain't worth shit, son. I'm disappointed in you."

"Sir?" Kleber was not accustomed to criticism.

"Oh, I put 'em in the paper. Didn't have time to fix 'em. But if you *ever* hand me copy like this again, my earnest advice is for you to seek work selling shoes at Monkey Wards."

"Sir?"

"Will you cut that subservient 'sir' shit. Case will do."

"I did my best, Case. I called the funeral homes and got the names and talked to the families. Are there mistakes? Did I spell somebody's name wrong?"

"Hell, I wish there were mistakes. Here. Read this motherfucker out loud." He tossed Kleber a carbon of his work, giving it the appeal of a cow chip scraped from the bottom of a boot. Kleber read:

Robert P. Maltz, 72, a pediatrician and lifelong Houston resident, died last night in St. Joseph's Hospital of cancer.

He was a member of the Harris County Medical Society, on the resident staff of several local hospitals, and was active in Jewish charities. He is survived by his widow, Marian, three children, and six grandchildren.

Funeral services will be held Thursday at 2 p.m. at the Settegast-Kopf Chapel. The family requests that no flowers be sent. If desired, memorial contributions should be made to the Harris County Cancer Society.

Casey grimaced. "You'll notice I'm still awake, although my passionate desire was to take a nap. First, a few rules of the house. We don't say 'cancer,' we say 'he died after a long illness.' The editor doesn't like cancer, just like the editor forbids pictures of snakes because he thinks they frighten pregnant women. And we don't say Jew.

The editor believes that Jews don't like to be called Jews. We say so-and-so was 'a member of the Jewish faith.' And we don't say 'don't send flowers.' Florists jump our ass. Florists advertise. Got all that?"

Kleber did, but he wished he didn't.

"None of this, however, is the reason why this work is unacceptable, son. Would you agree with me that what you just read was *boring??*"

Best that he nod, reasoned Kleber.

"Then, *if* it bores you, God knows it's going to bore the reader. And do you know *why* it's boring? Because nobody lives on this page."

"The man's dead, Case," said Kleber, risking smart-aleckness.

"He sure is. Now this old fart, Maltz. Maybe he delivered five thousand babies in his lifetime. Did you ask his widow?"

Kleber shook his head.

"You should have. Maybe one of 'em turned out to be Deanna Fuckin' Durbin. Maybe Maltz grew the world's best Scarlett O'Hara rose. Maybe he carved the Torah on pinheads. Maybe he killed eighty-five Germans in World War I. Maybe he played two-handicap golf. Maybe he once caught an eighteen-pound widemouth bass. My point, son, and I'm only gonna make it once, is that every single person who ever walked on this miserable planet Earth did *something* interesting. *One thing!* I'm not sure I agree with Balzac or whoever the fuck claimed there was a book in every life ever lived. But I do believe there's at least a paragraph. And if you can't find it, then go be a flack for the telephone company. You'll make more money."

Stricken with a new malaise, the fever of shame, Kleber stared at the floor.

Casey was not done. "I wouldn't be floggin' your ass if I didn't think you were worth it, son. Lemme ask you something. What do you wanna be. Good? Or famous?"

"Both," said Kleber without hesitation.

The city editor smiled. "That's illegal. It's bigamy. And it's hardly possible. Come on, I'll buy your worthless ass a beer." The two men walked across the street to a Chinese restaurant. Several glasses later, Casey made fleeting mention of a wife, Judy, and two daughters who were stashed in a suburb. The marriage, Casey's third, was imperiled.

"I'm sorry," said Kleber, privately surprised that his mentor had any personal life at all beyond the city room. Casey was always there, the first to arrive, the last to leave. Often he slept on a macerated leather sofa in the sports department. The man existed only in the grip of news.

"Well don't be," said Casey. "I built the trap and I baited it and I stepped into it all by myself. My advice to you is get ready. I don't know any poor bastard in this racket who has an enduring personal relationship with anybody. There's not enough time." He drank two more beers. "I used to dream about a great love affair. Epic! Head-on-collision time. It don't happen, son. The best us poor SOB's can hope for is an emotional sideswipe."

Kleber bounced into Daniel Titus' room and sailed the slim Saturday afternoon edition of his newspaper onto the old man's lap. Drowsing, listening to *Tosca* on the Metropolitan Opera radio broadcast, Daniel was startled. His rheumy eyes beat rapidly and he seemed annoyed, as if pestered by children throwing pebbles at his window. "Look at page eleven," commanded Kleber, finding Daniel's bifocals and affixing them to his pale and fragile ears. The old man stared for a long time at the eight-column headline that heralded his composition about the Coushatta Indians in the Big Thicket. "Oh dear," he finally said.

"Isn't it terrific!" said Kleber. "They loved it. You should hear the staff talking. Everybody said it was beautiful writing."

"Oh my," said the old man in dismay. "I didn't intend for you to publish my little scribbling. I just wanted you to read it." Kleber misread the concern on Daniel's parchment face as modesty. He had two more rewards: a check for twenty-five dollars and an invitation to dine the next night with some press people. Daniel was grateful for the money but insisted he could not take dinner. Kleber refused the refusal. And, sadly, Kleber got his way.

Millie of the gnashing teeth and serpentine curls could feed twenty people with a spaghetti casserole whose ingredients cost about four dollars and did so every Sunday night, attracting the orphans and strays of Houston journalism to her little brick house near the Shamrock Hotel. Kleber always attended, not only because of free food. He had grown to love the old bat. Behind her profane eccentricities, Millie was one magnificent newspaperwoman. Her late husband had been a legendary managing editor who was crushed to death under the wheels of a drunk hit-and-run truck driver. Through political contacts at the courthouse, the killer escaped punishment. Millie, a young society reporter at the time earning twelve dollars a week, was so outraged at the miscarriage of justice that she demanded to be transferred from weddings to criminal courts. She was still there four decades later and woe unto any judge who turned a murderer back onto the streets. She was far past retirement age but nobody was going to bell that cat.

"Millie thinks she is the last bulwark against fools, liars, and hijackers taking over the city of Houston," once remarked Casey, "and hell, she may be right."

Spiffed up in a shirt borrowed from Howard the Bragger and a hula-girl tie loaned by Clarence the Tub, Daniel Titus received a warm welcome from the crowd in Millie's living room. Casey pumped his hand and said, "Damn good writing, Mr. Titus. Let's do it again." The old man was installed in the most prominent chair and people gathered around with cheap red wine and compliments. His cheeks soon began to glow and his eyes sparkled with new life. A modest ray of celebrity was warming him. People were paying attention to somebody whom the parade had passed by. Millie personally served Daniel a heaping plate of her spaghetti. But Kleber noticed that she then stepped back, stared at the old man, and got the kind of look on her face that said: *Where have I seen this guy before?* It didn't last more than a couple of eye blinks.

Kleber forgot about it immediately because he got into a verbal shooting match with Horace, the city hall reporter and igniter of wastebaskets.

"I'm scared," said Kleber. "We've got a golfer in the White House. And while Ike's practicing putts in the Oval Office, the world is about to blow."

"Well, if it does," said Millie, "you won't read about it in our paper. Give Casey a local murder any day."

Horace, who would die in six months of a cerebral hemorrhage and who would be buried in a coffin paid for by a collection taken up among the staff, fired back. "If you wanna worry about something, kid, worry about the niggers. It's the biggest story of our town." As Horace pronounced the word, "nigger" contained no undue slur. Liberals said "knee-grow" and hypocrites said "nigra." The Houston *Call-Bulletin* style was to print "negro" with no capital letter. Nor did "negroes" receive the courtesy of "Mr." or "Mrs." That was the way it was.

"Every federal court decision since *Brown* v. *Board of Education* in 1954 has been on the side of the niggers," said Horace. "And the first day in Houston some redneck daughter comes home and tells her pipe-fitter daddy that she's sittin' next to a boy in school who has a *very* dark suntan, there won't be a white sheet left for sale from here to hell."

Casey stirred and snorted. "With little respect, Horace, and Kleber, you bastards are gloomier and doomier than H. V. Fuckin' Kaltenborn. I'd rather hear Millie describe the Ten Greatest Autopsies she ever attended." He patted the sofa seat beside him. "Com'ere, you old hussy."

Millie shook her head and poured jug wine all around. "I wouldn't sit next to you in the celestial choir."

"Happily, that is a decision neither of us will ever get to make," retorted Casey.

Kleber laughed. He loved the way they talked. Tough, funny, newspaper people used deprecations as camouflage to protect soft and bleeding hearts.

"Tell Kleber your dream murder, Case," ordered Millie.

"Sure. It would be finding you dead and buried under all the god-damn typewriters you've wrecked."

"Come on, tell him."

"Well," said Casey, "I have this fantasy, see. One morning I'll get to work and the police reporter will call on the hot line." He glanced at Kleber as if to say: Be Ready. "His voice will be hushed. He'll tell me to send Louie to the Shamrock Hotel. The cops just found a body. It'll sound so goddamn intriguing that I'll go out there myself. It'll be just before the sun rises, in that purple velvet moment. She'll be floating in the pool . . ."

"The victim?" wondered Kleber intrusively.

Casey nodded, frowning because his reverie was disturbed. "She'll be on her back, with her hands drifting beside her like water lilies."

"Wouldn't she be at the bottom of the pool if she's dead?" insisted Kleber.

"A good tale cannot be interrupted, my young friend," cautioned Daniel.

"Thank you, sir," said Casey. And to Kleber, "Will you stop being a goddamn literal shit and just listen. Have you no romance?" Kleber zipped his mouth.

"She'll have long thick hair, dark as midnight, streaming behind her like Dracula's cape. And she's naked—a body to make a man's heart skip three beats. Around her exquisite neck is a thin and perfect chain of diamonds. She's vaguely foreign-looking, South American maybe, with skin soft and sweet like honey. Her eyes are wide open. Even in death she's still staring at the son of a bitch who slew her— and she's smiling. Mona Lisa should have such a smile. There hasn't been a body in a pond as beautiful as her since Ophelia. . . . And, just beside her left breast, so small, so neat it might be mistaken for a beauty mark—a .22 bullet hole."

"Write it just the way you told it," murmured Kleber in praise.

"And, of course there'll be no ID," said Casey. "The hotel won't be able to identify her. She's not registered. Her fingerprints aren't in any police file. Aw shit, son, we could play that motherfucker two months. Street sales would be up sixty-five percent the second day."

"Who did it?" asked Kleber.

Daniel Titus smiled and put a wrinkled finger to his lips. "Solving it would kill the story," he said. "The mystery has just begun."

"Mes compliments, Monsieur Poirot," said Casey in an atrocious French accent. He bowed at the old man and scowled theatrically at Kleber. "We don't know who did it. The way I figure things, there's a convention of goddamn congressmen or ex-FBI agents meeting at the hotel, and every one of the cocksuckers is a suspect. We'll turn a lot of lives inside out. Maybe a year—hopefully *two* years—will go by. Then, one morning, just before the city edition deadline, some poor bastard will walk into the city room, ask for me, clear his throat, and make confession. His conscience is malignant, you see. Louie will take his picture. And then the confessor, his soul rinsed, will pull out the same .22 pistol and fire it into his ear. He'll fall mortally wounded onto the city desk. But he won't die for another two weeks. A little death watch won't hurt street sales. And, of course, we'll pick up his hospital bills and fuck the *Post* and *Chronicle*."

"And *that,*" said Horace the city hall reporter, "is all ye need to know about journalism. One lady in the lily pads is better than twenty million Chinks chopped into parsley."

Every newspaperman is an armoire of anecdotes and the room soon hummed with tales pulled from the drawers of memory. But the hour was late, the eyelids of Daniel Titus were drooping, and Kleber had to be at the police station by 5 a.m. prepared to sort through the horrors and humors of the night. On the way out he stopped Casey and complimented his yarn. "I hope it happens," he said. "And I hope I get to write it for you."

Casey shook his head sadly. "It can't happen, son," he said. "If it did, I'd lose my dream. We make a living out of facts. But we make a life out of dreams."

At the front door, during the good-nights and thank-you's, Millie invited Daniel back. But Kleber saw that, as her mouth did one thing, her eyes were taking his picture. On the drive home, the old man fell asleep. And Kleber forgot once more about the way Millie had scrutinized his old friend. The reporter found a new and unwanted passenger in the car—the ghost of another girl murdered and drowned. Laurie was sitting on his dashboard pert and pretty, swinging her legs, blocking his view. I've got a better story than yours, Casey, thought Kleber. But the trouble is, I can't tell it.

Edith Saller had a gallbladder operation, and when she returned to her rooming house, things went to hell. She painted the place in bile. She raised everybody's rent. She jerked the TV set out of the living room because the noise disturbed her recuperation. The tenants had nothing much to do except drink more beer and smoke more Luckies and quarrel even louder. Leo the Lothario's heart stopped during an arm-wrestling match with Clarence the Tub and the poor man fell dead, his toupee disconnected. Leo expired half scalped. A search of his room and his accounts turned up seventeen dollars, and when no relatives could be located, Leo was buried in a pauper's grave. Kleber had to drive the gang to the cemetery and afterward he bought them oysters and beer, recognizing that each of the others faced the same cruel and poignant exit. Daniel Titus was unable to attend Leo's planting. He, too, was leaving, having been evicted for non-payment of six weeks' rent. Kleber pleaded with Edith to let the old man stay until an anticipated relief check arrived. The reporter even paid half the overdue sum himself. "I owe $813.72 to Methodist Hospital," said the landlady. "And if I don't pay my bills, they'll send the sheriff."

Everything Daniel owned fitted into one large laundry bag—a few books, two changes of underwear, a string tie, an alarm clock, a hot-water bag, a sheaf of Kleber's articles, and five copies of the issue that contained his Coushatta Indian article. Packing wore him out and he sat on the stripped bed puffing. Kleber noticed that he had on one black shoe and one brown one. "Then that means there's another, identical pair in my duffel bag," said Daniel, too tired to change. The next stop on his journey, probably the last, would be a county home where the ancient and unwanted were dumped. "Oh, it won't be so bad," insisted Daniel. "Mr. Gorky once said, 'To an old man, any place that's warm is motherland.'"

Kleber was emotional but the old man was not. He gave his young friend an alarm clock. "The bell is a harridan and I don't want her around anymore." And from the innards of his musty black jacket, dust erupting as he pulled it out, Daniel presented Kleber with a fine gold railroad pocket watch. "It's about a hundred years old," said Daniel. "I was told that Robert E. Lee's adjutant carried it at Appomattox."

"I couldn't possibly take that," said Kleber. He would sooner steal coppers from the eyes of a dead man.

"But you must," said Daniel. "Our mutual friend, Mr. Adlai Stevenson, said the worst thief is the man who robs another of the only true precious gem: time. You have filled my hours. So I want you to have this little memory of our time together."

At the end of the week, Kleber gave notice to Edith and moved into a one-bedroom apartment nearby. It meant scraping and building furniture out of orange crates. His salary was now up to sixty-five dollars a week. But it was worth the sacrifice. He was moving too fast to get snagged by rusty old nails.

The journalist lives a paradox, being both the prisoner and the squanderer of time. Kleber counted each hour, deadlines roping him like the rings of a sequoia. But the days and the weeks flipped past like the pages of a book left open in the wind. He reminded himself one Monday to visit Daniel Titus but then it was suddenly Friday and no longer September but November. Casey pushed him; the young reporter's productivity was remarkable. In one remembered week alone he wrote fifty-eight stories, among them:

• An interview with Eleanor Roosevelt, who, sensing that her magisterial presence terrified the youth whose pencil shook against his pad, poured him tea and said, "Houston is *such* a beautiful city. Last night, while the plane circled around waiting to land, I looked down and the lights of your city sparkled like jewels." Kleber committed the gracious quote to paper and said, "That's such a lovely sentence."

Eleanor Roosevelt laughed and patted his arm and whispered conspiratorially, "I know. I use that line in every town I visit."

• An account of a suburban bank opening.

• A tragic paragraph about a housewife who, having worked in a hotel laundry all day, entered her home and discovered her husband in bed with a lady friend. She sliced off the head of the mistress with a machete, rammed the bleeding weapon into the heart of her husband, and fired a shotgun into her own mouth. Kleber wrote four violent pages, but Casey chopped his prose to seven lines. The victims were poor and black and died on page 27.

• Stories on the lagging United Fund drive, a couple married for seventy-three years whose recipe for enduring relationships was "benign apathy," a four-car collision that killed nine children, and a profile on Leopold Stokowski which caused the conductor to write a letter of complaint because Kleber said his hair and teeth were the same color: greenish yellow.

• An exposé of a faith healer who had pitched a circus tent south of town, just beyond the city limits and the scrutiny of Houston police. Kleber attended a service, watched "The Reverend Jerry Job" send his milk buckets on endless journeys through the two thousand worshippers, many of whom were lame or blind or suffering from hideous disease. They made "love offerings" when they could not pay their rent. Later that night, Kleber slipped into a small, private tent behind the big top and watched Jerry Job coerce $1,200 from an illiterate colored woman, proclaiming that her stomach cancer was then and there dissolved. The woman was carried off in a stretcher. She was smiling. She died two days later. Kleber's ensuing article, which revealed that the evangelist (1) had once been arrested for drunken driving, (2) had been sued for divorce on grounds of adultery and now enjoyed the companionship of a seventeen-year-old female assistant, (3) was being investigated by the IRS, took up the bottom half of the *Call-Bulletin* front page. It won him several prizes and was reprinted in journalism textbooks as a classic example of feature writing. But on the night it appeared, when Kleber confidently expected Jerry Job to fold his tent and silently steal away, the preacher's audience swelled to four thousand, and the next night was six thousand. Jerry Job extended his engagement another seven weeks and each evening he read Kleber's article from the pulpit, delightedly waving it about as "testimony from the devil, a challenge from Hell." Kleber thereupon learned that power has a reverse gear.

Then along came a plum. Casey dispatched Kleber to Austin as substitute for a reporter who had fallen ill while covering the legislature. He was to stay a week. On the third day, a page pried him out of the press gallery. His office wanted him immediately on the telephone. When he connected with Casey, the city editor said, "Where's that old fart you brought to Millie's house that time? Daniel what's-his-name?"

"Daniel Titus. How come?"

"Millie wants to talk to him."

"Why? What about?"

"Son, I don't ask Millie what she's up to. No more'n I'd ask a hurricane to turn right and miss Texas to hit Louisiana. Just tell me where the old geezer lives now."

The red flag of trouble rose and Kleber pretended he didn't know. Casey hung up, seemingly unconcerned. At the end of a week that became unexpectedly overlong, Kleber hurried back to Houston, dashed into the city room, and found Millie working late, canary feathers stuck to her sharp teeth. Ravaging her typewriter, she looked up and bawled triumphantly across the empty room, "Daniel Titus! *Daniel* and *Titus!* Two books from the Bible. I never forget a name."

Kleber asked what she was writing but Millie shooed him away. When she finished the twelfth and last page of her story, she thrust the proud package for him to read. He absorbed it on many levels, notably the pile-driving power of her narrative and the diligence of her research (she had interviewed Edith Saller and Clarence the Tub and Howard the Bragger and, heartbreakingly, old Daniel himself from a sickbed in the poorhouse). But mostly he read with the wrenching pain of loss. Dimly he listened to Millie prattling on. "Subconsciously his name stuck in my head when I read that piece on the Coushatta Indians. And when you brought him to my spaghetti party, I tore my brains out all night trying to remember. How do you like it?"

Kleber mumbled something unintelligible.

"Case loves it," said Millie. "He's running it page one Monday."

Forty-one years ago, it turned out, Daniel Titus robbed three Houston area banks, stole a total of ninety-four dollars, shot and slightly wounded a deputy sheriff, and was tried and convicted. Sentenced to life imprisonment, he escaped from a horse-drawn paddy wagon on the way to Huntsville Prison and disappeared in a pine forest. It was 1915. The *Lusitania* sank the same week off the coast of Ireland, killing 1,195 people. The Ku Klux Klan had just revived after sleeping since Reconstruction. Woodrow Wilson was President. Rogers Hornsby, a Texas lad, swung his first major-league bat. Millie was a girl reporter, the only one in town. In a Gibson blouse and a dress enriched by four petticoats, she had covered the trial of Daniel, his escape, and the unsuccessful manhunt. From his own lips she had learned—while Kleber was in Austin—that the old man's four lost decades were richly spent. He had found gold in Alaska, had taught American history in Oregon, had loved four women and married two, had once deposited $50,000 in a Georgia bank that collapsed during the Depression. He had come back home to Houston to die, believing that his footprints had been blown away by the sands of time.

Kleber tried to defend him. He pleaded with Millie, then Casey, begging them to destroy the story and spare an old man's last hours from disgrace.

"I can't do that, son," said Casey.

"Then maybe I should quit," threatened Kleber mildly.

"That would be vainglorious, son, because I'd still run the fucker."

He turned to Millie. "Why dig up an old grave? Nobody cares."

"You're wrong, son," answered Casey. "I do. Millie does. And I suspect you do, too. What if that goddamn faith healer of yours had turned out to be Horace's brother-in-law? What if he had begged you to kill it? Would you have wanted your story tossed in the bucket?"

Kleber protested that the analogy was unfair. But it wasn't. They had him. "Write your story in past tense," he warned Millie. "The old man's obit. That's what you're putting in the paper."

"I didn't write the story," said Millie with tender common sense. "Daniel Titus did. He lived his life. All I did was come along and find it."

"He'll die," prophesied Kleber. "You're going to execute a nice old man. I hope you both sleep well." He stormed out of the city room but on the drive home realized that a principal reason for his passion was the simple fact that Millie, not he, had located a terrific story. He was jealous.

The story ran. Daniel Titus was arrested. Louie took a photograph that appeared in newspapers all over America, a tiny bag of gray bones yanked out of the poorhouse and toted into city jail by two cops larger than Goliath and Colossus. The public was aroused. Mail flooded Houston, its newspapers, its civic leaders, its conscience. Daniel Titus was hastily tried, convicted, and given a suspended sentence. He further received some $8,500 in contributions from readers and sold his life story to 20th Century-Fox for $50,000. When Kleber last heard, the old man was living very comfortably in Santa Monica on a bluff overlooking the Pacific.

"There's a wonderful postscript," Kleber told Ceil Shannon many years later. "I was reading a book published by the University of Texas Press, some collection of obscure folk poetry and essays on cowboys and Indians. Guess what turned up? The article old Daniel 'wrote' on the Coushatta Indians, the one that I managed to get published in the paper. Turned out it had been stolen lock, stock, and semicolon from the real author, one Chief Yellow Cloud."

Ceil wondered if Kleber still had the pocket watch.

He brightened. "Oh yes, the watch. The wonderful gold timepiece that Robert E. Lee's adjutant carried to Appomattox? I treasured it so much that I had it appraised for an insurance policy floater. They told me it had been made in 1951, was a not very good copy, and was worth, at that time, a generous six dollars."

CHAPTER ELEVEN

Calvin Sledge dipped into the cartons he had borrowed from VeeJee for the better part of two days and nights. He was looking for names, for people to interview who might contribute something valuable concerning the character of Kleber Cantrell. He read around in hundreds of newspaper clippings, magazine articles, bits of books, and personal letters written by his subject to many of the most famous names in the

Western world. But he finally came to an unexpected judgment: there was not much to discover about Kleber Cantrell from his own words.

The man had spent a quarter of a century intimately bound up in the celebrated lives of others, but he had concealed himself. Kleber did not even use the first-person pronoun. He never wrote how *he* thought and felt, only how *others* did. Sledge summoned a pair of investigators and gave them an embarrassingly slim list of leads—a girl or two Cantrell used to date, an ex-wife, some old newspaper cronies. And the prosecutor somehow knew that his snoops would come back more or less empty-handed. "We're dealing with a fuckin' phantom," swore Sledge. "Everybody knows his name; everybody knows his work. But nobody knows *him*."

The DA's men struck out first with Lisa Ann Candleman, who would not answer her door or come to the telephone. Sledge angrily drew up a subpoena but he cooled off and put it aside, suspecting she was too far back in the picture to contribute much. Which was more or less correct.

It had been Kleber's intention to marry his childhood sweetheart, Lisa of the dairy-poster looks. Each of their high school yearbooks had been signed by classmates with forecasts and cupidic doodles about love, marriage, oodles of children, and golden anniversaries. An alleged gypsy fortune-teller at the State Fair in Dallas peered into a crystal ball in 1949 and predicted: "You will have six children, five of whom will be sons and all of whom will bring you great honor." Kleber was less interested in the prophecy than in the gypsy's credentials. She insisted she was an authentic émigré from Rumania but weaseled when Kleber questioned her about the twang that seemed indigenous to eastern Texas.

Nonetheless, upon leaving the tent and strolling the midway in search of the Chamber of Horrors, Lisa threw her arms around Kleber, kissed him on the mouth as ardently as if they were on the Champs-Élysées in April, and said, "I don't care if she's phony. I hope Madame Fortuna is right because I love you." For Lisa, shy, decorous Lisa, preacher's daughter Lisa, to embrace in a throng of 50,000 people was an act approaching copulation in the window of Leonard's Department Store. Kleber would remember being embarrassed and failing to respond and hurrying to the freak show, where he disbelieved the authenticity of a hermaphrodite and demanded but was not granted an interview with the unfortunate creature.

Six years disappeared. While Kleber went away to study journalism, Lisa remained in Fort Worth and obtained a degree in elementary education. She stayed in her parents' home, waiting—for the mail, for the rare long-distance call, for Christmas, for him. She served as bridesmaid for two sisters and seven friends, sewing and wearing nine taffeta gowns with matching dyed pumps in peacock blue, dusty rose, and apple green. Her beauty ripened and was appreciated by many men, none of whom received more than a gracious refusal and a demur that she was "engaged to be engaged."

At the age of twenty-three, she had become a capable teacher of second-grade children, soloist in the church choir, excellent golfer, and frequent browser at department stores, where she chose and rechose patterns of china, crystal, and silver in anticipation of the day when they would be registered in *their* names.

Kleber whizzed through town en route to Houston and his first job, causing Lisa to take a posture that was, for its time, aggressive. Properly reared Texas women did not play offense. On a night when her parents were away attending a church retreat, Lisa invited her elusive suitor to dinner. She planned the evening with care. She filled the living room with flowers—summer's last brilliant yellow roses. On the phonograph rested Mantovani's newest album, *Music for Lovers.* Her dress, on which she spent six weeks sewing from a *McCall's* pattern, was old ivory lace, a sheath that clung to her body and revealed a daring and tanned décolletage. In contradiction to fashion's dictate, the hem stopped just above her knee. She looked at herself in the mirror and thought she looked as wholesomely beautiful as Doris Day. By candlelight, she served shrimp cocktail, filet mignon, and non-alcoholic cider splashed into two crystal goblets that Lisa had just purchased, mentioning by the by an intention of completing the set with wedding gifts.

And the evening collapsed. The subject was him, not them. Kleber was a lecturer and not a lover. He spoke of journalism, of Adlai Stevenson, of liberal politics, of movies called *La Strada* and directors named Fellini and Renoir, of the Rosenbergs, of philosophers Camus and Sartre, of his belief in "existentialism," which he defined for her as meaning living *for* and seizing *of* the moment (but not *this* moment).

And Lisa found herself trespassing in alien soil, pretending to be interested, able to offer in return only tidbits of local news—Carralou had married, Wendy had divorced, Roger and Maggie Mae had twins, Miss Bellson died while teaching algebra—a menu as unappealing as the French-cut green beans that dried and withered on her plate.

Only once did talk take a turn that she construed as a possible chance to reach the destination she intended this night. Abruptly Kleber mentioned money. "I'll only be making $58.50 a week in Houston," he said while paying compliment for the lavish meal. "So it's gonna be pork-and-beans time in the old town tonight."

"But you'll get raises," she encouraged him. She chose her words cautiously. "And I hear the Houston schools pay better than Fort Worth. I can probably make $350, maybe $400 a month. Together, we'll . . ."

Smoothly he stepped sideways. "That's great," he said. "Just give me some time to get settled." He asked if she had read *The Stranger* by Camus. She had not and never would. She did not need a Frenchman to define loneliness and pain.

They ate peach ice cream, homemade, and sat briefly, awkwardly, on the sofa. Lisa put on Mantovani but the needle stuck and music for lovers had a crack. At a quarter to ten, he put his arms around her sagging shoulders and the kiss was melancholy. He was at the door and almost out before Lisa blurted out what she had wanted to speak all evening. "What's wrong?"

"Wrong?"

"Yes. Between us." She was trying not to cry.

"*Us* is perfect," reassured Kleber. "*Us* is just like us has always been."

She was not pacified. "There's nobody else, is there?" Lisa knew the question was etched in a loser's despair. But it came out that way.

"Well of course not. I'm too poor. Besides, you put blinders on this horse about ten years ago." And he was gone, leaving Lisa to wash the crystal goblets, to place them carefully in the box with the red velvet lining, to carry a vase of melting yellow roses to her bed table, and to weep softly and bewilderedly until she fell asleep.

Perhaps it would have assuaged the pain of rejection—and there is no more critical wound—if Lisa could have known that Kleber's intentions were honorable. There were no other women in his life; none that counted. He had fucked a few but had forgotten them all. He did plan to marry the girl who had sat—literally and figuratively—in the chair beside him since they were sixteen going on seventeen. But some men, particularly those who find romance in language, cannot speak the words of their own heart. What Kleber wanted was to put Lisa on hold. He would get back to her. She was definitely on his list of things to do, tucked neatly into a personal agenda that VeeJee wrote for her son: college, work, marriage, success, children, civic responsibility, church. A narrow path, but he was a dutiful son and would stay in bounds.

With certain exceptions, Kleber ran the course. He slacked on civic responsibility, mainly because he was never in one place long enough to feel kinship and because he felt reporters should not march in picket lines, only cover them. But he did quietly, and anonymously, establish journalism scholarships at several universities. He never set foot in a church again once he left his father's house, exception being when in France and then only to make aesthetic pilgrimage to the cathedral at Chartres, where he savored the glacial beauty of medieval stained glass.

And he did marry, but not Lisa Ann Candleman. He sired one son and one daughter, with whom he maintained a distant, almost anonymous relationship. But he brought such honor to his family house that an elementary school in Fort Worth was given his name.

Yet on the occasion of his fortieth birthday, a night of devastation to any candid man, Kleber was alone, in San Francisco, in a suite at the Stanford Court Hotel. Flowers, fruit, wine, telegrams, and a stack of thirty-four telephone messages from callers as diverse as Lillian Hellman and Nancy Reagan attested to the fact that he was desired. An hour earlier, an auditorium at Berkeley full of students, book buyers, and star fuckers had listened, questioned, applauded, sought his autograph, and requested that he pose for pictures with his arm slung around strange shoulders as if somebody's best friend. But now he was chilled by the years and fearful of the night and there was no one to hear confession. Ceil Shannon was in Canada, unavailable, watching a script she wrote being filmed, some romantic tragedy about a married aide to Trudeau falling in love with a French girl with morality and separatism getting in their way. She had sent a telegram that, though clever, did not substitute for her absence on this dismaying midnight: "JE T'ADORE. POURQUOI? JE NE SAIS PAS. MAIS TU EST MAG-

NIFIQUE ET FORMIDABLE. FELICITATIONS. TU COMMENCES ENCORE. ATTENDS-MOI. CEIL." Kleber tried to call but got bogged down by a provincially testy and Gallic operator north of Quebec.

He took a Seconal and ten milligrams of Valium. He got into bed and grew bathetic. For reasons he did not explore, he called Fort Worth. When a woman's voice, brusque, sleepy, answered, he said hesitantly, "Lisa?"

"Who is this?" The tone was not felicitous.

"It's Kleber, Lisa. It's my birthday . . ."

"Oh. Just a minute." The voice took on new respect. There was muffled talk. Hidden sounds. Another voice came on the line.

"Kleber? Is it really you?"

"Lisa? Who answered the phone?" Kleber often asked questions for which he did not really want answers.

"Sandra." Pause. "My roommate. Where *are* you, Kleber? In Fort Worth?"

"No. I don't know. It doesn't really matter. I just wanted to hear your voice. I shouldn't have called this late."

"Well, what a nice surprise. We're all so proud of you. I read your name in the columns all the time. You looked great on Johnny Carson last week. When are you coming home?"

"Home? Oh, soon. Someday. Soon . . ." It was past midnight in San Francisco. Past 2 a.m. in Texas. Kleber had nothing more to say. This was a bitter caprice. The thought came of simply hanging up, of blaming the lousy telephone company should the need for apology ever arise. Apologize for what?

"I'd love for you to visit my class someday. I've told my students about you so many times they groan when I mention your name."

"Still teaching, eh?" Why, Kleber wondered, *why* was he still on the line?

"Twenty years next September." She sounded proud.

"It goes by fast, doesn't it?"

"It does."

Silence. The gap of miles. The wilderness of decades. Two strangers were on the brink of forgotten tears.

"Lisa? . . ."

"Yes . . ."

"Lisa . . . I . . . Sometimes I wish I could start over . . . Maybe I took the wrong turn somewhere . . ."

"No, you didn't, Kleber. We all do exactly what we're supposed to do." Her voice was stronger than his and clear and unregretful.

"I believe that, Lisa. Sorry to wake you up . . ."

"Have you seen Mack lately?"

"Who? Oh, Mack. Yeah. I saw him somewhere the other day . . ." His words were beginning to slur. The sedatives and wine had hit. "New York, I think . . . Palm Springs, maybe . . . He's fine. Real fine."

"Can you *believe* what happened to T.J.? Never in a million years would I have dreamed it . . ."

"Maybe you did, Lisa . . . It's all a dream. Go back to sleep." He hung up and opened a bottle of Laurent-Perrier with the lovely white flowers painted on the bottle. That the cork crumbled and the wine was flat, that his Maalox-lined stomach was churning, that tears kept coming long after he had commanded them to stop—all of these were part of the sum.

Calvin Sledge had no trouble tracking down Kleber's first wife. In fact, Wife Number One rang him up early in the investigation. She expressed her grief over the tragedy, inquired as to the progress, and offered her assistance in any way that might be helpful. The prosecutor dispatched an assistant to Houston who interviewed the good lady for three hours, then returned to Fort Worth with a bag of hot air.

"She ain't even talked with the guy for five years," the assistant DA reported. "She gets a child-support check every January 1 for ten thousand dollars from some lawyer in New York. She says Cantrell was always dependable and a kind man. She's been married three times since him—but she took his name back. I think she dines out on being Kleber's first wife."

The fact of the matter was, Wife Number One lasted, in Kleber's recollection, approximately ten minutes, about as long as it took to read that day in 1958 an eighteen-page letter from VeeJee which included medical bulletins on various tumors, aneurisms, and gallstones discovered in kinfolk; hints on economical casseroles and how to make ends meet in the Eisenhower recession; the sorrowful news that Mack Crawford was separated from his "sweet, lovely" bride and had moved to New York, where he was in a Broadway play; and, stapled to a wad of clippings from the *Reader's Digest* that warned against smoking cigarettes and thinking left-wing thoughts, an appended paragraph:

"Kleber, I'd like for you to look up the daughter of an old friend, Sarah Maynard, whom I knew years ago in Fort Worth. She moved to Houston during the war and is married to a prominent lawyer. They have a lovely girl named Adelle. She is about your age and I understand she sings, collects antiques, and is well traveled. Please do this for your mother. Love. P.S. Don't forget. Love again."

Intended or not, Mama made a match. Letters crisscrossed Texas. Soon Kleber received a cheery invitation to dine at the River Oaks home of Randolph and Sarah Maynard, whose rung on the social ladder was several slats up from Edith Saller's back porch. Set back in the piney woods like a dowager concealed by her fan, the house was antebellum white and ablaze with the crimson fire of azaleas. Everything gleamed and smelled of lemon oil, even the Negro who took Kleber's '49 Chevy and hid it behind a grove of eucalyptus as if it were the mule of a poor relation. The lawyer and his wife shared red hair, ample frames, hearty laughs, and a belief that the Democratic Party was as undesirable as lepers.

Kleber was presented to and seated beside their eligible daughter, Adelle. She was comely and fine. VeeJee's assessment was understated. Adelle was twenty-three, well appointed, quiet and attentive. She looked vaguely foreign, thin and dark, like a Venetian *contessa*. Kleber wanted to know more about her but the evening was squandered instead on Randy Maynard's two favorite topics, the University of Texas football team (that Kleber had grown up with Mack was a major plus) and the necessity of electing Richard Nixon to the presidency in 1960. The guest was encouraged to reveal some racy and ominous tales of murder from the police press room, which he did, entertainingly.

He was invited back, this time for a barbecue. While Randy grilled steaks and filled his guests' eyes with smoke, Kleber spoke more privately with Adelle. She was wearing western riding pants and a tennis sweater from Ole Miss. He found out that she lived at home, sang in the chorus of a little theater, had no political tilt whatsoever, and went to Europe once a year, coming back with geegaws and doodads that she intended one day to sell in her own shop. Randy overheard this and laughed, as if his little girl proclaimed intention of performing heart surgery with her coloring book scissors. And when Adelle walked him to his car, unless Kleber misinterpreted, she looked urgently at him with frightened brown eyes that said: Get me out of this.

They dated for a few weeks, economical outings necessary due to

Kleber's meager salary. When he took Adelle to Millie's for spaghetti supper, Casey was expansive in his approval. In fact he ogled her the whole night, making Kleber feel he had done something praiseworthy.

"If you're looking for an old man's blessing," said Casey in benediction, "then I sure as hell give it, son."

That night, parked in front of Randy Maynard's estate, Kleber was in the middle of an anecdote about Jerry Job, the faith healer, when he suddenly stopped. He saw that Adelle wasn't paying much attention. She was looking at him but she wasn't listening. He was a man who made a living out of putting words together and he spoke one of life's most important sentences with total lack of grace. "Do you think we should get married?" asked Kleber.

"I'd love to," said Adelle.

"Really? You mean it?"

"Sure."

"Do you love me?"

"If you love me."

With neither making more declaration than that, they were wed, eloping to Nuevo Laredo and angering both sets of parents. Nine months and twenty minutes thereafter, they became the parents of a fat and merry son who was named Randall Houston Cantrell, delighting both sets of grandparents. And eighty-six days after that, they were divorced, in Juárez, a severance of such catastrophic and unprecedented grief in two families that Sarah Maynard was hospitalized for chest pain and VeeJee Cantrell suffered headaches that no power of positive thinking diminished. The dissolution of marriage was obtained by Kleber, who, along with seventy-seven other marital wounded, jammed into an ocher stucco chamber where a Mexican judge called off each name—with linguistic difficulty—from a clipboard. Everyone who wanted to be divorced raised his/her hand, signed documents in Spanish, and watched chameleons skitter about the sweating walls as witnesses. Immediately after the ceremony, each severee was urged to purchase souvenirs at the curio shop that adjoined the court, rumoredly owned by the magistrate's brother-in-law. Kleber, feeling a curio was necessary to complete the day's business, bought a stuffed *toro* for his infant son, paid his lawyer $1,100 (a sum borrowed from his newspaper's credit union at 6.5 percent interest), and dropped everything off to Adelle, who shook his hands and said she was sorry it all happened and assured him that he would have unlimited access to the baby. She was far more excited over the shop she was opening to sell geegaws. It would be called Quelle Surprise.

The whole experience—from dinner to marriage to birth to divorce—lasted less than eighteen months. For a time there was pain, but not the kind associated with soul-tearing loss. Kleber's chief emotion was embarrassment at having failed. He worried what his press colleagues would think of him. What further bothered Kleber, but not very long, was his total inability to shape the story. Everything he *wrote* was by now well constructed. But this sad chunk of his life was bad journalism. The lead paragraph was soft, the middle fuzzy, no end at all. The marriage just quit. Casey would have thrown such a tale across the city room. Had the marriage been a corpse—and it was—the coroner would have found a few lacerations but no bullet hole through a vital organ. While waiting on divorce day in the clammy little Juárez courtroom, glancing about and indulging reportorial speculation over what terrible words and deeds had caused seventy-seven other anxious men and women to assemble in this humiliating *cantina,* Kleber regretted that there would be no airing of the issues. This was assembly-line divorce and in a foreign language. In his fantasy, he conducted a private trial. It helped him get through a very long afternoon and it reconvinced him of the worth of what he was about to do:

EL JUEZ DEL JUZGADO: Señor, why did you marry this woman? Was there love?

KLEBER: Because she was pretty and interesting and she came from a good family and my mother recommended her and Casey liked her. And she needed me. And it was time to get married.

EL JUEZ: *Love,* señor?

KLEBER: I think so, I thought so. It was mentioned between us. I can't really define the word.

EL JUEZ: What were the problems? Money?

KLEBER: No. I had gotten two raises. I'm making $92.50 a week. They say my future has no limits in journalism. I'm really good at what I do. And Adelle worked part-time in an antique store. We lived rent free in one of her father's tract houses. It was really something—kind of mini-

Colonial with pillars and a patio and family room, central air conditioning, and a brand-new washer-dryer from Sears.

EL JUEZ: Sex?

KLEBER: Can we go off the record here?

EL JUEZ: This is definitely *in camera.*

KLEBER: Fair to middling. Okay at first. Neither of us had much experience. On the wedding night, she, ah, well, she sort of bled.

EL JUEZ: Ah, a *virgen!*

KLEBER: I suppose.

EL JUEZ: You seem disturbed. Did this sex and blood disturb you?

KLEBER: Maybe. Is that relevant?

EL JUEZ: That is between you and your señora.

KLEBER: The sex, it sort of petered out, excuse the expression, when she got pregnant. Neither of us knew what we were doing, you see, and she conceived right off the bat.

EL JUEZ: Women are beautiful when they are pregnant.

KLEBER: I didn't find big bellies to be beautiful. And I was afraid that I would hurt her—or harm the kid. We stopped having sex.

EL JUEZ: Was there jealousy? Other women?

KLEBER: Absolutely not. I was faithful. Oh, I did *meet* this lady named Ceil Shannon in the course of my journalistic duties. But as God is my witness . . .

EL JUEZ: This court does not require extraneous oaths, señor. Did you communicate with your wife? Share experiences? Listen to one another?

KLEBER: Well, I certainly tried. I can't tell you how many nights I came home from work ready, in fact *eager* to tell my wife all the fascinating people I interviewed—Jack Benny, Margaret Chase Smith. Why, once I walked with Harry Truman all over downtown Houston at six-thirty in the morning. Just me and a former President out for a stroll. That night I wanted to tell Adelle all the details and she said, "The plumber didn't come and the baby has croup."

EL JUEZ: Did you fight?

KLEBER: Not by my definition. There was only one little flare-up. She was refinishing this old chest and I knew she liked that kind of stuff, so I asked her a lot of questions. Like, how old was the piece of junk, and what country it came from, and wouldn't it be cheaper to buy a new one, and why wasn't my dinner ready? And she got hot and snapped at me. She said, "Why is it I always feel you are interviewing me?" I told her she was childish. And she said, quoting her exactly, "I don't need *another* father, thank you."

EL JUEZ: The divorce petition before this court charges Kleber Cantrell with "mental cruelty" and "incompatibility." How plead you?

KLEBER: Not guilty. But I still want the divorce. I can't stand being tied down to one person.

EL JUEZ: Then you shall have your wish. Better luck next time.

KLEBER: There won't be any next time.

"Do you remember when we met?" asked Ceil Shannon, oiled and cooking in the blistering June sun of Palm Springs. She lay on her stomach, floating on an orange rubber raft in the actor Robert Wagner's pool. Kleber had borrowed the house, an elderly, thick-walled adobe hacienda, for a few weeks while his friend was in Europe shooting a war series for the BBC.

"Yes. The Boer War, I believe." Kleber was sitting under an umbrella, typing revisions on a film script that was an adaptation of his Broadway play about Daniel Titus. On the stage, *Star Boarder* had been set solely in the living room of Edith Saller's rooming house and now it was Kleber's challenge to "open up the play."

"I remember the *exact* moment," said Ceil.

"You should. You broke up my marriage."

"Oh, I hope so. Which one?"

"Both. History will record you on the same home-wrecker list as Circe and Delilah. . . . Hon, give me a break. Either embrace hedonism fully—or go write Bella Abzug a letter." His work was two weeks overdue and on the morrow Kleber faced an invasion of studio executives who wished to read what their $500,000 package had wrought. He hated screenwriting, considered it the literary equivalent to painting-by-the-numbers, had never before adapted his own material. But the U.S. government was desirous of $178,000 in back taxes and the interest meter was running.

Climbing out of the pool, Ceil shook her hair like a wet dog, spray flying and misting Kleber's pages. She apologized for the damage and offered to rush the manuscript into the microwave. "That's okay, honey," he said. "Maybe the drops'll be taken for tears." They sat for a while in a double chaise. He was forty-two years old, she somewhat older. Together their years totaled almost a century but they snuggled like kids, holding tight to watch the sun disappear behind the San Jacinto Mountains. In Palm Springs the day leaves fast, like a stage prop falling in summer stock. On the far side of the raw and desolate ridge, to the west, another two hours of light illumines California. But here nature penalizes the resort city, which, to Ceil's thinking, was justified. She disliked the arrogant indolence of a place that welcomed Spiro Agnew with one hand still smarting red from getting caught in the cookie jar, that named boulevards after Bob Hope and Frank Sinatra. Kleber, however, awarded Palm Springs no character save that of refuge. He needed a place to hide from the telephone—his life had become a series of caves. And when he called Ceil in New York and begged for company, she came running. She promised not to molest Kleber's concentration with rude remarks and prophecies of brain rot. But when the bats came out, Ceil went in. She leaped out of the chaise and fled. "They're fruit bats," he called after her. "Totally harmless. They're only after dates." He enjoyed watching the tiny slivers of black fly in at dusk from the mountains, darting and swooping with nearly invisible grace around the ancient palms. But Ceil was certain these hideous squadrons were thirstful of alien liberals who found fault with Republican Xanadu.

Kleber hollered that he was mixing drinks but instead he found a cape in Natalie Wood Wagner's closet, tied it around his shoulders, dolled up his mouth with red lipstick to resemble Dracula after a mid-night snack, and chased Ceil lustfully around the bedroom until both collapsed howling onto the bed. Then they made love, slowly, easily, the best kind, quitting after Kleber's knee cracked, as it often did, sounding like the orthopedic complaint of an old-timer. Without or-gasm they melted into the velvet wrap that only time and trust can give two people. "Would you mind if I said 'I love you' ten times," whis-pered Kleber. "I'd like to make a few extra deposits in the bank."

"I would love it," said Ceil. After eight he drifted off and she finished the count. An hour later, when he awoke, it was dark. Ceil had lit candles and she was sitting at the end of the bed, chin on knees, watching intently. He felt embarrassed and reached out for her. But she shook him off. "Do you know how I would write you?" she asked. "I would put down, 'My lover is long and lean and soft.'"

"I hope you're not describing my equipment."

"My lover is the most beautiful when he is asleep, when nobody is looking at him except me. No poses necessary. When his hair isn't art-fully combed and the bald spot shows. And the mustache droops. And the hair on his chest looks like a trampled patch of silver and gold weeds."

"Who is this decrepit person you're talking about?" jested Kleber. "Com'ere." Ceil obeyed, slipping under his arm.

"Do you know what you looked like when we first met?" she asked.

"I'm afraid to ask."

"Li'l Abner." Ceil giggled, ducked Kleber's mock swat, and sprang out of bed naked. She picked up the telephone. Kleber watched her and thought that he would have put on a towel. But Ceil did not carry the cross of Protestant Texas modesty. Besides, her body was better than his. There was not a wrinkle on her face and her cheekbones could still cut glass. She maintained the frame of a runner and could probably beat him at any given sport. In fact it was difficult to keep clothes on her. The first two days and nights in Palm Springs, Ceil had stayed naked, getting dressed (and complaining about it) only to dine at a nearby Mexican restaurant, where Truman Capote joined their meal without invitation and made appetites disappear with a nonstop, ghoulishly generous description of capital punishment.

Ceil dialed a number and waited.

"Who are you calling?" asked Kleber.

"My husband," she answered. "Haven't checked in lately. He worries about me."

Fourteen years earlier, neither was prepared for momentous encounter. Both were, in truth, peevish and surly. Kleber was annoyed at getting yanked off a breaking page one story, the search for a kidnapped child that had provided him six tense days of journalistic melodrama. On the seventh, when nothing much new was happening and the police seemed stalled, Casey ordered Kleber to substitute for the paper's drama editor, who had called in sick. That meant drunk. A long-standing commitment had to be filled, interviewing a young woman playwright from New York who was in Houston directing the world premiere of her new play.

During the two bleak hours while Kleber stewed in the foyer of the Alley Theater, waiting for a backstage script conference to be completed, the kidnapped child was found. Kleber missed the payoff. It turned out she had been locked in a closet of her own home the whole seven days. She was the prisoner of her mother. The kidnapping was a grotesque charade by a desperate woman trying to get her estranged husband back. "If I had known *that* while I was waiting for you," Kleber told Ceil years later, "I would have strangled you then and there."

He did not feel qualified to question a maker of drama. Kleber's theatrical expertise was limited to seeing a touring company perform *A Streetcar Named Desire* once in Fort Worth with Judith Evelyn playing Blanche DuBois so bitchy and batty that he rooted all the way for Stanley Kowalski to lay her out. In New York he had seen a couple of musicals from the vertigo of third balconies, and, more recently in Houston, he had endured *Krapp's Last Tape,* whose title, he felt upon leaving gratefully, should be reversed. He vowed never to venture within a quarter mile of any marquee bearing the name of the playwright Samuel Beckett. Life *is* absurd, but Kleber did not require an old man peeling a banana and going mad in front of his tape recorder to demonstrate the theory.

Ceil Shannon wrote her master's thesis on Samuel Beckett. At the Sorbonne. In French. At nineteen. A biography from the Alley Theater's flack informed Kleber that his subject was the daughter of Sean Michael Shannon, a Manhattan banker who endowed entire productions for the Metropolitan Opera, and Rachel Kraus, a poet and professor at Vassar. "Miss Shannon, 28, has had six plays produced off-Broadway, including the acclaimed *Woman Lost, Woman Found,* her study of George Sand and Frederick Chopin, which won the Obie Award and has been performed in eleven languages. The Alley Theater is proud to present the world premiere of *A New Life,* a drama of three pioneer Texas women. The year is 1845 and all have been widowed by an Indian raiding party. One of them gives birth during the play." Kleber braced for the worst. He planned to clap for the redskins.

The theater was square—a converted fan factory—whose playing floor was surrounded by four sets of bleacher seats. When Kleber was permitted inside, he discovered lighting technicians setting gels, spilling pools of off-kilter color. Out of the darkness, a commanding figure emerged, striding toward Kleber with slices of her face and body daubed with eerie shafts of amber and pink. Ceil Shannon was almost six feet tall and her gait was that of a colonel inspecting the troops. Her hair was hidden inside a N. Y. Yankee baseball cap. She was sweating and angry over a backstage fight just ended in a draw with a temperamental actress. Of one thousand things on her mind, 999 were more urgent than a date with a local reporter. The press agent led her to Kleber and she sized him up and said curtly, "You've got ten minutes. Shoot."

Unaware that he would be interviewing the Pope, Kleber said, "I've been waiting for you two hours and now you've only got ten minutes?"

"Nine. I'll take your questions."

"I don't work that way. I like to hang around and watch and then talk."

"That's splendid. Watch all you want. But what you see is not for review, okay?"

Kleber nodded and took a seat in the bleachers. A technical rehearsal commenced immediately and he began to scribble furiously. The first words on his pad were "rude" and "cunt." Casey would get three grafs which he could stick under the obit column. He started to leave, but he decided to wait and watch five minutes of the play, knowing it would be terrible. By quoting a couple of lines of rancid dialogue, he would shore up his pan.

Four hours later, Kleber was still in the theater, having forgotten pregnant wife and reportorial responsibility. He was transfixed by a stage piece whose scholarship in Indian culture was commendable, and

by a woman who upset his personal chart of organization for the opposite sex. Kleber had all women defined and categorized: Mothers (Vee-
Jee), Wives (Adelle), Teachers (Hazel Busher), Whores (Laurie and
Sisters), Working Women (Millie), and Misc. (Edith Saller). Each
had certain value and each dwelled in a compartment. Cross-switching
was not allowed.

Then along came Ceil Shannon to step in and out of the chicken
coops, shattering his stereotypes. She was a self-actualized woman who
fascinated him and scared him. Dissatisfied with the lighting, she
climbed to the ceiling like a steeplejack and rewired two entire banks.
She mothered her actors, psychoanalyzing them, teaching them, quoting from Shakespeare and Lynn Fontanne and W. H. Auden. She
seized hammer and saw and rebuilt the set. She hemmed costumes. She
redid makeup. And no matter what her function of the moment, she
was in control, sexy, desirable. Kleber slipped out of the theater without saying goodbye because he did not want to break the spell.

The next day he fretted over an inadequate story. Nothing he
wrote came close to capturing this remarkable woman. Then the phone
rang. Ceil was calling to apologize for her boorish behavior. It was a
clean and forthright admission of bad manners. She asked if he had
any more questions, and though he had several, he asked but one. "It
didn't say if you were married. Are you?"

"I am indeed," she answered. "Are you?"

"Sort of," said Kleber.

"I'll appreciate whatever you can do for the play," she went on.
"Maybe we'll see each other again sometime."

"I'd like that," said Kleber, feeling fourteen.

"Call me if you ever get to New York."

"I will."

Casey read his piece later that day and said, "Did you fuck this
dame?" Kleber took offense and asked how the city editor got such an
idea. "I never read such an ass-kissing paean, son." Kleber did not see
Ceil Shannon again during her stay in Houston, not formally. But he
did wait outside the Alley Theater three midnights in a row, just to see
her leave.

Calvin Sledge had a slim dossier for Ceil Shannon. He had tried to
reach her by telephone in New York and London but she did not re-

turn his calls. He had a clipping from the Milestones section of *Time,* from 1972:

"DIVORCED: Kleber Cantrell, 39, prize-winning journalist, author, playwright, and panel-show creature; from actress Noel North, 32, his second, her first, after fourteen months of marriage. In the Dominican Republic. Though uncontested and grounds for the action undisclosed, Cantrell has long enjoyed the companionship of feminist-playwright Ceil Shannon, 40, who is married to producer Saul Greene."

On the night before the grand jury was to meet and hear his case, Sledge was awakened at 4:15 a.m. by a telephone call. What sounded like a youth trying to disguise his voice by using a poorly accented falsetto said, "The Shannon woman is in Fort Worth. Cantrell's whore slipped into town yesterday."

He woke up fast and put three investigators on her tail.

BOOK FOUR

THE
PRINCE
OF
TEMPTATION

*There is a charm about the forbidden
that makes it unspeakably desirable . . .*

—Mark Twain

CHAPTER TWELVE

Thomas Jeremiah Luther was arrested before he was even born. His mother, believing erroneously that she was only seven months pregnant, grew homicidally angry one still, fetid spring afternoon in 1933 and decided to kill the penurious philanderer who was her husband. Magdalena Gomez Luther had, she reasoned, casting herself as judge and jury, excusable grounds for murder. Her womb contained the fourth issue of Victor (Peavine) Luther, the man she married at the age of seventeen. On that long ago day her legs were as lean as a filly's, and her waist so slim that Peavine could and did cup it with his hands.

During the hour that murderous fantasy grew from thought to deed, Magda believed her cause was just. In her bedroom mirror, an intricately hand-carved heirloom that her grandmother had imported from Mexico City in 1884 with the legend that the Empress Carlotta preened before this very pier glass, Magda beheld a fat woman. Herself. From the front, sideways, or rear, Magda was a brood sow. Her breasts were as large as gourd squash in November and her ass would not squeeze into a picture show seat, which was an academic plight because there was not a spare dime in the house on Cloverdale. Her head ached. Her three extant sons, two, four, and seven, yelled for supper despite their having devoured two pounds of paternally indulged peanut brittle and refusing to share a crumb with their mother. The unborn and unwanted imp within her mountainous stomach was performing a non-stop Saturday-night kick-and-stomp dance.

Victor (Peavine) Luther was due the blame for all of this, believed Magda. Though she was seven-eighths native Texan, the remaining fraction was noble Spanish blood, aboil with the passion for Latin revenge. Her husband had not been home for three days and three nights. Each time Magda had telephoned the Luther Land & Minerals Co., the new secretary, sounding like Magnolia Mushmouth with a singsong voice that concluded every sentence in a melodic ascent trill, repeated: "He's *still* not heah, Miz Luther. Like ah bin'a'tellin' yew, Mistah Luther's over to Longview on that new oil play. Ah'll tell him yew called. Ah hope yew ain't sufferin' in this heat. Bye-bye." Magda decided her eyes would provide more reliable information.

She went to her closet and found nothing among the size 8 dresses that would cover her now size 18 and growing-daily body. Sobbing, she yanked down one of Peavine's creamy linen shirts and a pair of sea-blue yachting trousers in the pocket of which was the last straw, the nail in his coffin, the verification if not *sanctification* of her desperate act. She found a lilac-scented note—men tend to keep their death warrants—that cooed like a lovebird in a cage: "Dearest Peevie: Thank you for the beautiful silk hanky from Paris, France. This is the best job I ever had. You shouldn't spend money on me but I love it. Sincerely, Jewel."

Jewel was Magnolia Mushmouth.

Swaddled in the betrayer's clothes, Magda gathered her three sons, kissed them with an emotion mid-distance between devotion and good riddance, left them in the care of a neighbor, and took a taxi to Peavine's office in the Flatiron Building. There she dredged out of the colored elevator operator the information that Mr. Luther and his secretary had left for a "meeting" at the Arlington Downs Race Track between Fort Worth and Dallas. Persuading the cabbie to transport her COD and emphasizing her request by cleaning fingernails with a butcher knife, Magda was delivered to the track. Arlington Downs had been open since 1929, the creation of an immensely wealthy Fort Worth oilman named W. T. Waggoner. He claimed the reason for the track was to encourage the raising of thoroughbred horses, since betting was definitely illegal in the State of Texas. Waggoner even hired a small army of plainclothes bouncers to evict anybody who bet on a horse. In this year of 1933, however, the Texas legislature surprisingly voted to permit pari-mutuel betting (an indulgence that only lasted four years before the Baptists closed the windows). Magda immediately spotted Victor (Peavine) Luther in the forecourt amid a throng of touts, dapper as Valentino, standing out like a vanilla cone in a cotton suit and a matching hat carefully tilted over one eye like a rakish window awning. His arm embraced a young, thin, and adoring cookie in chinoise crepe whose name had to be Jewel. A band in red, white, and blue uniforms played "Life Is Just a Bowl of Cherries" but to Magda's ear it was "Valse Triste."

Muttering Spanish curses, debating whether to stab her husband or his play toy first, Magda waddled through the festive crowd with the butcher knife gleaming in the sun. She provoked stares and titters. Jewel saw her, screamed like a cat about to be dropped off a bridge, and swooned. The sight caused Peavine to abandon his intended wager and race off alone, in denial of his mistress, to his 1931 Ford, into which he leaped and sped away with urgency and prudence. Unwilling to relocate her taxi, Magda chose to steal a forest-green Packard whose keys had been left in the ignition. A good driver, alas, Magda was not.

On the first right-hand turn required to pursue her about-to-be-slain husband, Magda was unable to rotate the steering wheel, it being wedged by the breadth and width of her fetus-swollen torso. The Packard ran off the road, knocked down a barbed-wire fence, smashed a 20 Mule Team Borax billboard into kindling, dismissed several milk cows, and concluded a vivid journey with the front end squeezed like an accordion, the radiator a geyser of steam, and halted by the enduring strength of an oak that had grown in hitherto unmolested peace for a hundred years.

Immediately police arrived and arrested what they mistook for a dazed and dumpy fat man on charges of felony car theft, reckless driving, and operating a motor vehicle without a license. But when the fat man moaned, screamed sharply, and slithered from the grip of the law onto the moist green Texas earth, breaking water and delivering then and there a 9 lb. 3 oz. son under the shade of the insulted oak, two cops had a tale to tell the rest of their lives.

Ever resourceful, particularly when the need arose to save his skin and protect his name, Peavine arranged through family connections for charges to be dropped. An editor friend at the newspaper was persuaded to block publication of an amusing account of the burlesque, buying Peavine's story that Magda was "feeling poorly" and "under mental strain." And Peavine swore such impassioned repentance that Magda took him back, after he signed a notarized promise to pay her $200 a month for the rest of her days (money she could use to buy silk hankies or peanut brittle or throw into the Trinity River—no strings attached) and $160 a month to feed and clothe his sons. If the fool was so much as one hour late with the money due—the document spelled this out clearly—Magda would inherit a legacy of $50,000 due Peavine on his fortieth birthday, frozen in trust by his recently deceased father's will.

They lived together another thirty years, although Peavine continued to womanize. After being caught, he established the wise policy of trysting only well out of town and never with the same girl twice.

Their financial course was like the drive of a Sunday golfer—occasionally straight, more often a slice to the rough. The only hope of security collapsed when Magda reluctantly agreed to let Peavine invest his legacy in the drilling of three wildcat wells that produced nothing but foul mud water that smelled of sulphur. Of course Magda suspected other women, but she kept her wagon hitched to the sad old horse for two very good reasons: (1) Somehow Peavine always managed to pay the money due her, on time, and (2) she realized, with the ache of truth, that too many years and too many pregnancies had eroded her sexual allure to a condition nearer Marie Dressler than Claudette Colbert. She remained fat, with four kids, in a Depression. Her chances of finding another husband were as remote as discovering a pearl in a can of sardines. Besides, on Mother's Day, Christmas, and sometimes in between, the sorry bastard said he loved her, throwing both arms about a waist that would require a third to circle.

There is, Magda grew to understand, no explaining genes and environment and what youngsters make out of their lives. Her first three sons grew from being pesky children into the most banal of men—taxpayers, faithful husbands, fathers, church collection takers, uncomplaining of labor in plumbing and bookkeeping and undertaking—mule work unlikely to enrich wallet or soul. Her fourth, Thomas Jeremiah (called T.J. in the crib and forever after), did not know that his natal hour became fodder for one of the most hilarious documents contained in the files of the Fort Worth Police Department.

But on his twenty-fifth birthday, when police telephoned Magda to report that her youngest son was once again in the slammer, drunk and disorderly and needful of $140 bail, T.J.'s life seemed irrevocably on course to the same kind of collision that hastened his birth. At the crossbar hotel, Magda appeared with fire in her eyes and smoke in her nostrils. She slapped seven twenty-dollar bills on the counter, preparing to seize her son by his left ear, twist it counterclockwise, and drag him to the nearest priest, having relocated the Catholicism of her Spanish heritage. But at reunion with her tedious child (and, at the age of twenty-five, with a war behind him, T.J. still carried the adolescent innocence of a choirboy) Magda capitulated again, as she always did, to his charm, guile, and, in no small due, to her own guilt.

She knew what he would say and she could have recited his penance in unison: "Oh, Mama, it was a mistake. I didn't do *anything*. They got the wrong man. I promise, Mama." Two other guys in the café on Mansfield Highway started fighting over the waitress. Somebody else pushed the owner onto his pinball machine and broke the glass and rang up 412 free games and short-circuited the air conditioning and the neon sign. And Magda *believed* it. By the time she reached Cloverdale Avenue, Mama was ready to sue the police for false arrest. She fed her boy, tucked him into bed, and gave him the last twenty-five dollars in her pocketbook to buy a new suit from Robert Hall's so he could apply for a "fantastic" job.

As did Kleber and Mack, T.J. suffered tormented hours and difficult days in the aftermath of Laurie's seduction and disposal beside the flooded Brazos River. But it was not of the same character. Being the only battle-tested swordsman among the Three Princes, T.J. was not tormented by the guilt that paralyzed his best friends. Many bucolic maids had pressed willing and not-so-willing bellies against his, and not a single one ever told on him. He immediately convinced himself that Laurie was a girl practically begging for what she got, who probably passed out from hearty intake of strong spirits, who was back home weeding bean hills and wishing for another taste of T.J.'s cock-a-doodle-doo.

The lance that pierced the Prince of Temptation was one for which he had neither defense nor frame of reference—the rude shock of passage. On the day that high school was over, T. J. Luther's power base dissolved. Its foundation had been the alliance with Kleber and Mack. Now the kingdom of the Three Princes was no more. One moment he had been the Most Popular Boy, the next he was outside the fairground with no ink stamp on his wrist to get back in. Nor did he possess credentials useful to negotiate a future. That his grade point average hovered closer to D than C, that he had never felt the need to read a book when the girls sitting beside him permitted peeks at test papers, that he was master of no trade and servant of no ambition had always seemed irrelevant. How could a young man worry about what he would "be" when he "grew up" when life, by his definition, was a laugh—and being *liked* was its coronation?

On the morning after high school graduation, T.J.'s total worth was $11.15. But he spent the entire day caressing the yearbook, two pages of which were devoted solely to him. That attested to value incalculable in dollars. An enterprising girl editor had, with Magda's cooperation, assembled a picture biography. Not a single photograph suggested a thought in T.J.'s head more serious than "Where's the bottle opener?" In his baby chair, he grinned like a circus clown with oatmeal and jam smeared across his face. At the zoo, six years of age, he and a chimp shared secrets, both winking. When girls appeared beside him, giggling, pubescent, they attended his pranks like the handmaidens of Bacchus. The year T.J. was head cheerleader, according to the caption, "School spirit was never higher." And his official senior photograph presented the Prince of Temptation in cap and gown, only his eyes were crossed as if examining a ladybug on his nose. Beneath, an inscription in his own writ: "The party begins when T.J. arrives; the party ends when T.J. dies."

His best friends put him on ice. Neither Kleber nor Mack would answer the door or return a phone call because they were "sick" or "resting." When he saw Kleber at the corner filling station putting air in his tires, T.J. tried to pick up like nothing had happened, suggesting parties and pleasures. Kleber shook his head and said coldly, "I don't think we should be seen together. Not for a while."

"Why the fuck not?"

"If you've already forgotten, then you're sicker than I thought." Kleber drove away hurriedly as if under orders to leave a contaminated area. A few weeks later, returning from an enforced family trip to San Antonio for a summer reunion of Magda's clan, T.J. discovered that he was alone against the world. Mack had suddenly left for Louisiana to work in the oilfields; Kleber had gone off to college early. Both departed without a fare-thee-well to the friend they had spent more time with over the past eighteen years than their own families. Briefly T.J. nursed the perverse notion of anonymously calling Weatherford police and squealing on the shit-asses, but common sense dictated that the net of vindictiveness might pull him in as well. Finally he convinced himself that two defections were hardly a threat to his popularity. Fuck 'em and forget 'em. He called around for new troops. Across the boulevard, the Rivercrest and Westover Hills kids were busy buying flannel pants and white buck shoes and button-down shirts to wear to college and fraternity rush parties. They told T.J. hello and goodbye faster than Magda said "fat chance" to his request for a ten-buck touch. The firm earth on which he had always walked was suddenly fissured.

So he slept late. He rose at midday and passed afternoons at Burger's Lake, tanning his fine body and swimming furious circles around the cold spring-fed pond until he was weary enough to nap on a towel until dark. At night he sat alone in his jeep at the Toot 'n Tell 'Em Drive-in, depressed because nobody was in congregation there, nobody but the dregs, those who, unlike he, possessed no social luster.

Magda watched her son mired in gloom for several weeks. Though she did not like to cook (only to eat), she prepared a special dinner that began with homemade tacos, went on to chili pie, and concluded with pecan surprise. She gained four pounds in the cooking but T.J. partook listlessly.

"Are you sick, honey?" she asked, pressing her hand against his forehead.

"Don't think so."

"But you don't feel good, do you?"

"Don't know how I feel, Mama."

Magda spoke cautiously. Her scheme was to fire him with enthusiasm for work. "Will you listen to your mama *once* in your life?" T.J. shrugged. "I think," she said, "that it's time you decided what to make of yourself. What do you want to be?"

"Rich," answered T.J.

"Be serious," pleaded Magda.

"I *am* serious, Mama. I wanna be rich. And famous. I wanna walk into a restaurant and get the best table, automatically. I want people to point at my car when I drive down the boulevard. I wanna live in Westover Hills. I want people in China to know my name. I wanna buy you a mink coat every Christmas. I wanna get so much mail they have to send a truck every damn day. And I want Kleber Cantrell and Mack Crawford to kiss my ass."

"Thomas Jeremiah!" Magda looked shocked.

"You asked me what I wanted, Mama."

"Everybody wants to be rich and famous," said Magda wistfully.

"But Mr. Aesop told us about the squirrels who ate well in the winter because of their hard work while the grasshoppers starved." She fetched the newspaper and shoved the classified ads before his nose. Several job opportunities were circled. T.J. glanced at them and snorted. "Sixty cents an hour. That's . . ." He hesitated, his grasp of multiplication being minimally dependable. "That's twenty-four dollars a week. Less taxes. I'll be able to live just as well as any nigger in Lake Como."

T.J. bolted from the table. He locked his bedroom door and spent the night drinking blended whiskey and looking at himself in the yearbook. His mother ate all of the pecan surprise, deciding not to save a single slice for an ungrateful son.

The next morning, June 25, 1950, Communist troops from North Korea swept across the 38th parallel of an Asian country not one Texan in ten thousand could position on a map and quickly seized Seoul, capital of the south. Within hours, Harry Truman, who only five years before had dropped two atomic bombs on Japan and presumably blinded any more slanty-eyed visions of territorial tampering, commanded U.S. air and sea forces to "give the South Korean government cover and support."

Less enthusiastically, the scar tissue of world war barely healed, America raised her flags again.

When the news broke, T.J. was in downtown Fort Worth, intending to offer his talents to an employment agency that advertised for "junior executives." At a red light he heard businessmen in seersucker suits cussing the new gooks. And in the next block, in the window of a U. S. Army recruiting office, something stopped him cold. It was a poster that asked: ARE YOU THE BEST? The portrait below the challenge served up a perfect hero, saluting as crisply as his uniform, chin taut, eyes alert, fruit salad festooning his blouse like roses on the homecoming float. And damned if he didn't look just like Audie Murphy! Every schoolboy in Texas knew Audie all right, the handsome, mean little sumbitch who practically won World War II single-handed. Audie's name was right up there beside Doak Walker and Sam Rayburn and the Alamo martyrs. He was the most decorated hero in the history of America. The victor's spoils were Hollywood contracts and his own biography. Then, just like an omen, the sun slipped behind a nearby building, shadowing the recruitment office window and making Audie's face disappear. Its replacement was T. J. Luther.

On July the Fourth, 1950, T.J. was in Fort Hood, Texas, his duck-tail shorn, sleeping on a cot the YMCA would have rejected, but convinced sure as farts follow the morning after chili beans that by Christmas he would be a poster boy himself. Besides, in the remote possibility that somebody might falsely accuse him of being somehow connected with the unlikely disappearance of that ole Weatherford whore, the medals soon to crowd his left breast would dissuade the world of *his* guilt. Heroes served their country, after all, while Mack the Shit-ass played football and Kleber the Turd wrote fairy tales.

Perhaps General Sherman anticipated Fort Hood when he uttered his famous malediction, "If I owned Texas and Hell, I would rent out Texas and live in Hell." The nearest town, Killeen, is as beautiful as a boxcar on a desert siding, and the earth on which basic trainees crawl is favored by serpents, lizards, and vegetation that God decreed had to have prickles and needles. The summer sun would make a camel faint, and in winter, northers snatch the coat from a man's back and blow it to the Gulf of Mexico. The normal stay for an inductee is eight weeks, at the conclusion of which most men consider transferal to the combat zone a blessing. T. J. Luther resided at Fort Hood for two whole years, including eighty-six days in the brig, a prison not radically more punishing than the conditions outside. He never did anything severe enough to merit disgrace and discharge, but he always did something troubling enough to impede his quest for heroism. When not serving time for bookmaking, bootlegging, or brawling, T.J. was a competent soldier. Trained as a medic, he learned first aid, cardiac resuscitation, and how to fake influenza. And he was good at his work, unless he overslept or overdrank. Sergeants yelled at him all day with threats to grind his gluteus maximus into steak tartare, but at night, in the cafés of Killeen, the same tyrants asked for strategic advice on how to advance and conquer farmers' daughters who were holding out for second lieutenants.

T.J. made corporal for two weeks before his stripes got ripped for AWOL. The closest he got to actual war was Japan, where, after several weeks of "orientation," the gooks quit on him. An armistice was signed at Panmunjom, affording the opportunity to return home. Which

T.J. did, turning up on Cloverdale in full uniform one August night in 1953. No bands were playing. No banners flapped from the front porch. He waited five minutes before Peavine even answered the door. Magda apologized. They had been playing canasta and watching Perry Como on the TV singing "Don't Let the Stars Get in Your Eyes." They said they were glad to see him, but not a whole lot.

There are, roughly categorized, two kinds of work. Men with talent and intelligence and drive can run governments, or create art, mend limbs, teach and reach for wisdom. Men whose hands are stronger than their dreams settle for hammers and calluses. But between attention and accommodation is a high wire in the wind. Here is where men with dreams but no talent must balance, men of schemes and overdrawn bank accounts, men whose days are more difficult to endure than their nights. In this sad and sorry club, the Prince of Temptation found membership. Quite a spell down the road, things would pick up, but not the way T.J. expected, and not until he was off the track, over the edge, and at rock bottom.

"I'm afraid, Mr. Luther," said the woman with purple-rinsed hair at the Texas Employment Commission, "your work experience is unlikely to qualify you for an 'executive position.' Your résumé is not impressive. High school graduate, *barely*." She was a blunt old bag.

T.J. set her straight. "I was elected the most popular boy in a class of three hundred and fifty students. That's something likely to impress any employer."

"Yes. Being liked is nice. But personnel directors tend to view a college degree as a more valuable indicator. Have you considered college?"

"Oh, yes, ma'm," answered T.J. "I'm sure plannin' on that. Night courses. Weekends. I won't be satisfied until I get my master's, probably my Ph.D. But in the meantime, let's face it, I need a job. Coat and tie work. I look real fine in a coat and tie."

The job lady glanced over his eager shoulders and grimaced. A herd of impatient men milled like cattle, waiting to reach her desk. Black and brown faces, white-trash faces, blue-collar men, despairing wreckage of the Korean War, the Eisenhower recession, the rural migration to the cities, united by the common denominator of nothing to do. T.J. would have been insulted by inclusion, but the purple-haired woman smelled the same sweat on his shirt and saw the same panic in his eyes.

She closed his folder. "I'm really sorry, Mr. Luther," she said. "But without some college . . ."

T.J. refused to get lost. "Look, lady, I'm gonna level with you. I coulda gone to college like all my friends. I coulda drunk the same beer, pledged Kappa Sig, got a degree in goof-off, chased women, come home to Daddy and to a job in his oil business. But I saw things a little different. I chose to serve my country. *Somebody* had to. I fought the Communists. I wasn't lookin' for medals and fame, that's for sure. But now it turns out I musta gone through the wrong door. Nobody gives a damn what I did. This ain't the America I was taught to love." He stood up and, glory be, T.J. finally looked just like a recruiting poster. Purple Hair's eyes misted. She heard Douglas MacArthur fading away. Her own son, the boy she lost to Rommel, was tearing her heart.

"Hospital administration," she said, flipping files furiously. "Let's see if we can't put your medic training to work for you."

"I could do that," said T.J. picturing a commodious office where nurses would come for hirings and firings. "Why hell, ma'm, that'd be easy as sellin' watermelons on June Teenth." He reached over and patted the liver-spotted hand, watching the old woman's face brighten. "You're never goin' to regret this, ma'm. A promise from T. J. Luther is money in the bank."

T.J. was duly hired as an orderly, on probation, earning $1.15 an hour. He told Magda and Peavine he was a "floor technician" and inflated his anticipated salary to $150 a week. If Magda needed something surgically excised, like a gallbladder, he promised to get her a discount and the best blades in the house. He swiped a white lab coat and wore it in his jeep, anxious to get stopped for speeding so he could tell a policeman that it truly was a matter of life and death. When ignorant patients misaddressed him as "Doctor" he did not correct them, and he often perused their charts with the enigmatic mask of a master surgeon. He mopped floors poorly, but he had hurried and exciting sexual union with three nurses and a female pediatric resident in the Ob-Gyn nap room. And his career ended after three weeks, due specifically to an overly long lunch of four Budweiser quarts followed by the clumsy prepping of a seventy-three-year-old minister for double-hernia repair. As he unsteadily leathered the fearful patient's groin, T.J. spun fraudulent but fascinating yarns of battlefield surgery near the 38th parallel. He then nicked the old man's thin-as-parchment skin and bloodied not only the preacher but his Bible and his bed.

Next came brief tenure at the Royal Dutch Ice Cream & Frozen Dessert Co., where each morning at seven T.J. dressed like Admiral Byrd for labor. He put on three sweaters, a thick parka, two pairs of gloves, and a fur-lined aviator cap necessary to enter the storage vault where temperature was zero minus ten. For $1.20 an hour, T.J. performed chores that an orangutan could have accomplished if taught to distinguish between chocolate, rocky road, and almond toffee. Pints and quarts of freshly made, still soft ice cream bobbed into the frigid chamber on a conveyor belt. All T.J. and his co-worker, an elderly, near-deaf Negro named Abner, had to do was pluck these cartons from the belt and stack them by flavor in large steel roller racks. At first the job was unusual, weird, fattening, and delicious—until T.J. got sick, more from unlimited sampling of product than from work conditions. But he construed matters differently. Twenty minutes in the deep freeze followed by ten permitted outside to thaw seemed unbalanced. He made complaint to the foreman, a German from south-central Texas named Schmitt, suggesting that fifteen minutes in and fifteen out would be more merciful and more productive.

"You agitatin', boy?" asked Schmitt, whose behind-the-back nickname was Sauer Kraut.

"No, sir," answered T.J. "Just freezin' my ass."

"For which you are well paid." Sauer Kraut waved him away.

Later, seething from the stiff, T.J. engaged co-worker Abner in rare conversation. It was necessary to shout at the old man, who in response yelled back. Their words were enveloped by bursts of frost clouds and they resembled arctic bears in quarrel over fishing rights. "How long you worked here, Abner?" inquired T.J.

"Well, suh, 'bout foteen year."

"You like it?"

"Nah suh, ah hates it. Ah truly do."

"I was thinkin', Abner, iffen you 'n me was to get together and *demand* fifteen-fifteen, then we'd have us a bargaining position."

Abner pursed thick and blue lips. He was troubled. "Ah cain't jepper-o-dize mah pension, suh. Ah'm fixin' to be sixty-five next October."

T.J. nodded sympathetically. "And I 'spect your ole arteries are about froze. You might not even make it to sixty-five. When I went to medical school I saw a lot of fine old colored gentlemen with frozed arteries—and they didn't work at the damn North Pole!"

"Hoccum you ain't a doctor iffen you went to medical school?"

"Because I quit. Because I love people. Because I saw too many people get cut up in experimental surgery. Boy, would they love to get you in that hospital, Abner. You'd be in a jar by Friday."

"Ah do gets tahrd in here. That's the God's truth."

"Then you wouldn't object to slowin' things down a notch, now would you, Abner?" T.J. winked broadly and Abner grinned.

In the adjoining workroom, where Mexican women in hairnets methodically snapped lids on the ice-cream containers and set them on the conveyor belt, a jam-up occurred the next day at the entrance to cold storage. Pints and quarts waited and jiggled and tumbled over like weary petitioners at the gates of justice. Sauer Kraut stormed into the vault and found T.J. and Abner working like crazed automatons. "Belt's been stoppin' and startin', sir, Mr. Schmitt, sir," said T.J., puffing and subservient. "It's crazy. Nothin' comes in for five minutes, then pow! Three hunnerd at once. We're doin' our best, sir."

Complaints next arrived from merchants whose customers were returning ice cream with lids that said one thing and innards that contained another. Somebody was switching tops. The foreman questioned T.J. and Abner, but accepted their pleas of innocence. As T.J. pointed out, anybody from a disgruntled bitch on the conveyor belt to a pissed-off truck driver could have caused the mischief. Whatever, Schmitt was jumpy and rattled. It was time for the finale.

T.J. carefully gave Abner his dialogue and stage directions. Though the old man would play the starring role, he disliked the script. Abner did not want to take off his protective clothing, suffer the shock of cold for the several minutes necessary to induce genuine shivers, and then stuff icicles under his cap so as to resemble a victim of impending terminal frostbite. "Naw suh," declared Abner firmly. *"You* be the snowman."

"I can't. I'm too young and too strong and Schmitt won't buy it. He hates my ass. Lissen, Abner, I double-dog guarantee you this'll work. It's foolproof. I wouldn't be atall surprised if they give you an extra hunnerd so's you won't file a claim with the disability."

"A hunnerd? You thinks so?"

"At least. Now come on, Abner. Stand up for what's right. Would Martin Luther King let 'em freeze *his* arteries?"

Once again cartons began to jam up at the conveyor belt entrance and Schmitt rushed angrily inside the vault. He discovered T.J. leaning distraught over the body of old Abner, who was supine. Soft ice cream was pelting his spasmodic limbs. Cartons were spilling onto the floor, splitting open, forming a sweet, sticky, slippery, and soon-to-be-smelly mess.

"Abner's sick, sir," cried T.J. *"Real* sick! I was an army medic in Korea and I'd call it frostbite."

Concerned, the foreman rushed toward his stricken worker, but on the way his feet skidded in a pool of chocolate and he fell mightily on a raspberry ass. T.J. bit his lip to hide a whoop, but Abner sat up, miraculously healed and revived. "Ah'm feelin' better, suh," he announced. "Musta blacked out for a minute."

"What the fuck is this?" said Schmitt, staring at Abner and plucking an icicle that hung from his cap like a crystal earring. He snapped it in two and said, "I'm glad you're better, Abner. 'Cause your shiftless ass is fired."

Abner trembled for real. "Oh, suh, please! 'Tweren't my idea. It's *him!"*

T.J. was as calm as a heifer in clover. "He's lyin' . . . I do about ninety-five percent of the work in here, Mr. Schmitt."

"Oh, Jesus, that ain't the truth. He done caused *all* the trouble. Ah been here foteen year, boss. Never gave nobody no grief."

Schmitt was granite. "I ain't got time to play Solomon, boys. So tell you what. You're *both* fired."

Abner's eyes pleaded with T.J. for absolution. But none came. "You're bad," he said. "You're the devil's own man."

"And you're a liar, nigger. Schmitt, I can't believe you're gonna take a nigger's word over a decorated Korean War vet. The newspapers might like to get ahold of this."

Schmitt almost laughed. "Well, son, between a black liar and a white fuck-off, there ain't nothin' worth choosin'. Now get outta my ice-cream plant."

In parting shot, T.J. hurled one quart of butter pecan that landed smack on target, that being the foreman's left ear. His follow-up was pretty good, too. He pushed a rack of rainbow sherbet a-skittering across the floor, knocking Sauer Kraut flat and gasping in a bath of orange, lemon, and lime. The registered letter that T.J. received a few days later informed him that he owed $674.50 for spoiled product. T.J. responded by placing a fresh dog dropping in a Royal Dutch pint carton and mailing it with just enough ice to survive the crosstown journey to Schmitt. Then he filed a claim with the state labor commission, contending that cruel and dangerous work conditions had impaired his mental and physical health. T.J. got $1,670 in settlement and spent the windfall to purchase a used but splendidly tended '55 Mercury hardtop coupe, with Flo-Tone persimmon and white paint, a 245-hp V-8 engine, and a radio strong enough to pick up Chicago.

For three days straight he drove prideful loops of his neighborhood. He was his own parade. He looked so good in that car that he wanted to get out at intersections and applaud. On the fourth morning he rose and prepared to leave for an appointment to purchase automobile insurance. But as soon as he stepped out the front door he realized that would not be necessary. The car was gone, stolen during the night, plundered from the fortress of ethic and security that was Cloverdale.

Police did find the car after a time, in niggertown, wrecked, minus tires, radio, V-8 engine, windshield, and seats. They sent T. J. Luther a bill requesting $52.13 for towing and impound fees. He did not pay.

Brigham (Bun) Luther, youngest brother to Peavine and uncle to the Prince of Temptation materialized unexpectedly on Cloverdale with a new wife, number six or seven depending on whether one counted a cocktail waitress in Oakland who only lasted over an exciting World War II weekend. "This here's Spike," said Uncle Bun, presenting his newest, a tall, skinny ebullient woman. "She's a keeper. Too damn big to throw back." Spike laughed loudly and shook hands firmly all around. Spike had orangy hair and a diamond on her wedding finger that was knuckle-to-knuckle. Outside at the curb was a banker's-gray Cadillac with a horse trailer hitched, from which a lovely palomino mare whinnied and attracted neighborhood kids with carrots and sugar cubes. Bun was one member of the Luther family who had Dame Fortune's private phone number.

Magda was embarrassed. She had nothing but a pot of warmed-up black-eyed peas and ham hocks simmering on the stove, but Uncle Bun came prepared. He toted in ten pounds of barbecued ribs and a gunny sack of roadside produce—beefsteak tomatoes six inches across, two dozen ears of sweet corn, a yellow-meat watermelon, and a can of jalapeño peppers that he ate like popcorn. In no time at all, the family was feasting. "Magda, I swear you're gettin' better-lookin' ever' day," said Bun. "If you'd ever given me six cents' worth of encouragement,

I'd a took you away from brother Peavine. I always did like ample women." Magda giggled and warmed to the fraudulence. She weighed 270 pounds and the only exercise Peavine ever got was pulling his wife up out of overstuffed chairs. Sometimes she wore a funny hat to church with one feather sticking straight up; T.J. thought his mother resembled a unicorn packed for shipping.

Concurrently, Peavine seemed to shrivel each day, like air slowly leaking from an inner tube. He was not much past fifty, but aging poorly. Thin, stooped, coughing from an eternal cigarette burning in his turquoise-studded holder, he dyed his hair shoe-leather black and waxed his mustache religiously. The air of an old vaudevillian hung about him, waiting for a booking that would never come. Peavine continued to call himself an "independent oilman" although his business had dwindled to a stool in the Hotel Texas coffee shop and a pay telephone at the Greyhound bus depot.

The usual subjects of family reunion were covered: weather, pecan failure, what aunts had died and what uncles were stashed in rest homes since Peavine and Bun last saw one another. They were the only two brothers remaining from a sibling crop of nine. War and traffic and cerebral hemorrhage had thinned the Luther line. T.J. slipped in a few Korean War hero stories that made Audie Murphy a potato peeler. Peavine grumbled about cheap foreign oil—three dollars a barrel—flooding into America in such gully-washers that in Texas only eight producing days a month were allowed by the state's regulatory commission. It was Ike's fault, began Peavine, hinting of conspiracy between the President and the Ayrabs, but he started coughing and turned as blue as Camel smoke. Clearly Peavine would soon check out of life's hotel.

But Uncle Bun gleamed rich and mellow as a brenda saddle. He wore tight cowboy-cut gabardine britches with a German silver belt buckle that said "BUN" as loud as a neon cross on a church house. His face was lined like a creek bed but his eyes sparkled like shards of a Jack Daniel's bottle. He was lean and mean. He had a rich wife and a Cadillac. He was everything T.J. wanted to be.

While Magda and Spike, who looked like Mutt and Jeff's wives, cleared the table and washed dishes, the men sat on the front porch and smoked Bun's Cuban cigars and drank Bun's French brandy from a silver flask. T.J. sighed deeply, as if accustomed to pedigreed smoke and spirits.

"Spike seems like a nice woman," opined Peavine.

"*That* was clear as well water the day I laid eyes on her," said Bun. "Feller never knows when the wheel of fortune's gonna stop on his number. I was in Bakersfield, California, drunk as a skunk and broke as a nigger on Sunday mornin'. I mean, if Betty Grable'd been sellin' her pussy for ten dollars, I couldn't a bought a handshake. Feller says to me, 'Some ole gal's lookin' for a trustworthy gentleman to drive her horse to Texas.' I look her up, expectin' Granny Grunt, and out pops ole Spike. I always did admire red-headed women, and Spike's a *real* redhead. We established *that* right away. Turned out her old man had just run off with some masseuse from Palm Springs, leavin' Spike with a house and a horse. She sez to me, 'Doobie Dale of Dallas, Texas, wants to buy this horse for twenty-five thousand dollars, but I have to deliver it and I'm afeared to drive that far by myself. I'll give you two hunnerd fifty. I sez, 'Red, if you'll come with me, I'll do it for six bits and two beers.' "

At the curb, the palomino commenced to whine and kick her trailer. Lithe as a sixteen-year-old kid, Bun vaulted off the porch, whispered sweet things in the mare's ear, and was back to finish the tale. "So, Spike and me stopped off in Vegas, where she divorced the no-account son of a bitch, and we drove ten blocks down the Strip and got married ourselves. The Desert Inn was next door, and seein' as how it was the eighth day of the eighth month, August 8, we slapped a hunnerd-dollar bill on the roulette table. Eight and eight make sixteen and that's what we played and that's what hit. Thirty-six hunnerd dollars."

T.J. whistled and grew faint.

"Wait. Seein' as how it were Spike's third marriage and my—ahem —seventh, we let the sucker ride. Thirty-six hunnerd dollars on numero ten."

"Gawdalmighty," yelled T.J. "That comes out to . . ."

"Shit," finished Bun. "The fucker rolled in and outta ten like a cock-teaser and came to rest on double zero. Well, easy come, easy go, Spike says. On the way out the door, she spies a silver dollar on the floor and drops it in the slot machine. Wham bam, thank you ma'm, eighty-five hunnerd dollars. Time to depart. We'd a been here last week iffen we hadn't found this motel bed in Albuquerque. You put a quarter in and it vibrates. Spike claims we spent a hunnerd and ten dollars on tingles."

"So what's next, Brigham?" yawned Peavine, who did not seem very interested in the yarn of sex and fortune.

"Tomorrow we sell that horse and the day after that we're settin' up shop right here in the ole hometown."

"Horse tradin'?" wondered T.J.

"Naw. We're gonna start a dude ranch and chinchilla business. Spike has this notion she can make beauty cream outta chinchilla oil and sell the pelts as well. My job'll be encouragin' the little fuckers to make babies so we can grind up chinchilla gizzards. And if that don't work, we'll have the dude ranch as a backstop. Spike says rich women'll pay three hunnerd a week to eat beans and get their asses pinched by cowboys. Hell, if I had a dollar for ever' ass I pinched, I could buy Guatemala."

The horse was sold, money collected, and Spike sallied forth to Dallas for visiting of kin and ravaging of Neiman-Marcus. Bun asked T.J. if he wanted to drive around and look at potential dude ranch property. "Whatever happened to that old farm you used to have out near Weatherford?" T.J. blurted impulsively, remembering, for the first time in years, the night and the storm and the girl who, unbeknownst to him, continued to haunt his two friends, the bastards whose names he never spoke anymore.

"Hell, I dunno, son," answered Bun. "Land's fallow. Worthless as tits on a boar hog. Truth is, I clean forgot about it. Probably got sold for back taxes. Wanna go take a look?"

T.J. said no. Bun chomped a large chaw of Red Man and spat routinely out the Cadillac window as he sped east out of the city. He didn't arch an eyebrow at his nephew's abrupt recollection, which contented T.J. once and for all. If anybody had ever pestered Bun about whether some ole country girl had been laid at his place, surely he would have mentioned it.

The afternoon was hot and fast. Bun drove the Cadillac about 80 m.p.h. and got stopped thrice between noon and four for speeding. But he talked his way out of a ticket each time. T.J. envied his uncle's ability to make men dance without even firin' bullets at their feet. They looked at several spreads, but only one was promising—eighty acres between Fort Worth and Dallas, nice rolling land threaded by a frisky clear creek with perch and catfish, and blanketed with scrub oak and cedar. The main house was yellow brick with fairy-tale trim but the barn and tack shed, silvery with authentic age, looked like Wyatt Earp and Belle Starr might have slept there and maybe together. The price was $37,500, which Bun told the owner was "highway robbery" but which he later admitted to T.J. was "in the ball park."

They stopped for beer at a 7-Eleven store near Grand Prairie where Bun won four dollars on the punch card and eight dollars arm wrestling with a football player from SMU. Some rednecks from the Bell helicopter plant drifted in and began suggesting that Bun was a drugstore cowboy. Realizing the potential for vast quantities of spilled blood, the store manager persuaded Bun and T.J. to depart, thrusting two six-packs of Lone Star as grateful door prizes. Uncle and nephew, fuzzed and happy, found a patch of green beside the Trinity River and spoke of memorable women.

"Can I ask you somethin'?" asked T.J., shifting gears. Bun nodded.

"Well, I don't exactly know how to tell it."

"Lessen you speak in ancient Aramaic, chances are I'll understand, son," said Bun.

"I just cain't get goin'," said T.J. "I'm nearly twenty-six years old and I definitely planned on bein' at least half a millionaire by now. The truth is, I ain't got forty dollars. I ain't got a job. I still live at home. My jeep won't start. And I got a carbuncle on my ass."

"Well," remarked Bun. "Mebbe you could be Queen for a Day." He looked sternly at his nephew. "We ain't much different, boy, you and me. What we got is the slow starts. It's the legacy of Luther blood. I never in my whole life figured anything was worth doin' lessen it happened after twelve o'clock noon. I carried this attitude for forty-nine years and six months, until the day I met Spike. Now, looking back, I notice a lot of other fellers got up before the sun did. And they got to the feed trough afore me. But I finally made it. Just took a spell."

T.J. absorbed the counsel and shook his head. "But I cain't wait till I'm fifty years old, Uncle Bun." He was close to tears. The day's beer had washed his emotions to flood tide. "Did you know I was the *Most* Popular Boy in my high school? That's somethin', ain't it? I mean, that's as good as a lifetime railroad pass. A man don't just stop bein' popular overnight, does he?"

Bun mulled the paradox for two more beers. "Can you get hold of ten thousand dollars?" he asked.

"Not unless you know a bank Clyde Barrow overlooked."

"I used to," grinned Bun. He turned serious. "You locate ten thousand little ole measly pitchers of George Washington, and I'll make you a junior executive in the Spiked Bun Dude Ranch & Chinchilla Co., Inc. We'll do it legal. Enrich some goddamn lawyers. If you ain't half that millionaire before you're thirty, then roosters don't shit."

On the way home, while T.J. wondered how to grab the pot of gold, Bun got lost on the back roads, circling around like a drunk farmer on a tractor. "Goddamn, I know these parts like my dick," he said. "Just over yonder's where the Arlington Downs Race Track used to be—afore the Baptists decreed horse racin's worse than fuckin' for fun." He found a side road and roared down it, burning rubber and spraying gravel. "Yore daddy and me used to spend an occasional hour at that track," recollected Bun. "Some feller, yore daddy. Wore fine white suits, carried a silver-headed walkin' cane. Looked sorta Eyetalian-like. Little old gals saw Peevie and flat pissed their pants. Course, that was afore he met yore mama."

Bun turned right and left and cussed and stopped to look out the window. He saw something and said, "Well, I'll be a son of a bitch." T.J. glanced at whatever made Bun express himself so fervently, but he saw nothing. Nothing but a big oak tree with a thick and twisted trunk, out of which a chunk was missing from the side, as if a cannonball had passed through. Bun got out of the Cadillac and approached the tree. Something must have struck him as hilarious because he plopped down in a patch of Johnson grass and laughed his ass off.

"Well, if this ain't fate," he said. "See that tree over there? That's the very same tree where you was . . ." Abruptly Bun cut himself off and returned to the car and said he knew the way home now. Best that they hurry.

"Wait a minute," protested T.J., his curiosity aroused. "What's so funny? Whatta you mean by 'That's the very same tree where you was . . .' Where I was *what?*"

"Nothin'."

"Nothin', shit. You just about busted a gut. Had to be *somethin'!*"

"Well, 'tweren't. Nothin'. I just remembered a picnic we all had out here one day. Yore mama and yore daddy and me."

"Whoa, hoss. I ain't that gassed. Bun Luther, you said, and I

heard it very clear, you said, *'That's the very same tree where you was
. . .'* Was *I* on that picnic?"

Bun shrugged and turned on the radio. "Mebbe," he said, muttering, barely audible over Patsy Cline. "Mebbe not."

CHAPTER THIRTEEN

On a blank contract sheet he stole from the Panther City Office Supply
Co., T.J. signed a bargain with himself:

I, Thomas Jeremiah Luther, almost 26, do hereby solemnly prom-
ise myself that I am going to find $10,000 before January 1, 1959,
Year of Our Lord, so I can be a Junior Executive in Brigham
(Bun) Luther and his wife Spike's Dude Ranch & Chinchilla Oil
Beauty Business. This is the biggest opportunity of my life. I hear
it knocking at my door and I am going to answer it. So help me,
Jesus. P.S. Nothing is going to stand in my way.

He cut his finger on the paper edge and it seemed appropriate to
write his name in blood. This didn't work, so he settled for a smeared
and earnest thumbprint.

Showering until the hot water ran out and his skin gleamed pink,
shaving carefully so as not to nick himself and have to staunch with a
piece of toilet paper, combing his thick black hair with Vitalis so the
cowlick at back stayed down and the shock in front hung neat and sincerely boyish, T.J. said to himself, "You are one good-lookin' dude. I
would buy anything a sumbitch who looks as good as you is sellin'."
He put on his army dress pants and a white shirt and a navy blue tie

that said trust me. He found Peavine on the front porch, squinting at the *Star-Telegram*'s financial page.

"Hi, Pop. How's the market?"

Peavine glanced up. "You gettin' married or buried?"

"Just dressed for business, Pop. How do I look?"

"Like you got an ace up your sleeve." Peavine lit a new Camel off the one still going, giving his lungs fresh cause to complain. He coughed and spat into a geranium pot.

"You oughta rest a little, Pop," suggested T.J.

Peavine eyed his son with skepticism. Rarely was his youngest solicitous of his health. "What I got, son, is somethin' all the rest in the world won't cure."

Brief but genuine alarm crossed T.J.'s face. Peavine shooed the worry away. "Naw, it's nothin' no doctor's gonna make money on. What I got is an acute case of realizin' my life ain't worth Robert E. Lee's musterin'-out check."

"Hell's bells, Daddy, you ain't ready for plantin'. I'd say you got a good twenty-five years left."

"That'd be real nice. Now what's on your mind, son? You got some little ole girl in trouble?"

"No sir. I'm too busy with my plans."

"Watch them women, son. They are potholes on the highway of life." Peavine spat again and returned to his paper. This was about as lengthy a conversational exchange as ever passed between father and son. T.J. cleared his own throat, putting aside the nag that it was not the best moment to ask his daddy for anything. He jumped in. "Pop, I've been thinkin' that I sure would like to start payin' some rent and help you and Mama out a little."

Peavine looked startled. "Well, now that you mention it, son, most younguns are outta the house by the time they're twenty-six."

"I know. And, Daddy, maybe once in man's life comes the chance to make it big. Hit the jackpot. I just got that chance. I have the opportunity to become a junior executive in a brand-new growth company."

"I say hooray and hallelujah."

"The only thing is . . . well, Daddy, lemme be candid. I always figured when a certain day comes, a *looooong* time from now, on that day when you go to your . . . *reward* . . . I 'spect you'll be leaving me and my brothers a little somethin'. . . . So I was wondering, see, maybe I might borrow on that inheritance right now. I figure I could pay you back double in no more'n eighteen months." T.J. paused to see how he was doing. The way he heard himself, his words came out humble and earnest, calculated to appeal to a man who had drilled a dry hole or two.

"Just how much money you talkin' about, son?"

"Ten thousand dollars."

Peavine threw his paper in the air like a volcano erupting. He whooped with laughter. Clearly this was the high point of his week. He said, "Boy, if I had ten thousand dollars, I wouldn't be settin' here on this front porch. I'd be in Paris, France, with a red-headed woman wearin' red shoes and a red hat and nothin' else."

T.J. muttered something about missing the golden opportunity, and Peavine, filled with juices that had not coursed through his tracks in half a decade, said, still laughing, "I'll give you this, boy. You are definitely *my* son. You got more balls than a pool hall."

On her dresser table, Magda found a laboriously calligraphed note: "You are cordially invited to have dinner with your son at Joe T. Garcia's for no reason except he loves his mama. Love, T. J. Luther, Your Son." Suspicious, it being no day of celebration, Magda nonetheless accepted the strange bid. She adored Mexican food, and Joe T. Garcia's was to *chili con queso* what Boston was to scrod. Squeezing into a bright scarlet dress and draping a shawl around her mighty shoulders to cover the place in back where the zipper wouldn't close, Magda curtsied when her son told her she looked gorgeous. But she fell and T.J. had to help her off her knees. Away they sped to the north side of town, a region odiferous as India, uniting the aromas of the stockyard, the tan and sluggish Trinity, and a thousand little frame box houses most of which were stuffed with Mexicans but only one of which was world-famous. People in New York and Paris have been known to suffer the need of a Joe T. Garcia meal and have flown to Fort Worth for an enchilada fix.

Mother and son entered per custom through a kitchen whose temperature was that of the equator, where ancient old crones in black stirred cast-iron pots. Shimmering waves of chili pepper steam cleared sinuses and watered eyeballs. At long family tables, they attacked platters of *nachos* and bowls of *guacamole* while Magda swept into ecstatic reverie of her one-eighth Mexican ancestry. She ate about three pounds of food, drank four Carta Blancas, flirted in hesitant but flamboyant

Spanish with a toreador of a waiter (causing T.J. to realize, stunningly, that Magda was sexy to *somebody*), and closed her porcine eyes dreamily as a guitarist, pre-tipped by T.J., serenaded with "Cielito Lindo." T.J. knew he had to strike quickly, before Mama found inspiration to tell—for the nine millionth time—how her great-grandmother waltzed at Chapultepec Palace and how, if destiny had not been so callous as to send a recklessly appealing but totally good-for-nothing Texas gold speculator who stole the near-royal dame and took her to San Antonio, where a few generations later Magda popped out, then she might have been a Mexican princess or Pancho Villa's niece, or something like that.

"Mama, I'm real glad we could be together tonight," said T.J. "Another round of enchiladas?"

"It's a treat for me, too, son, but I'll have to diet till Christmas." She patted her stomach, which was not difficult because its dimensions prohibited a fit under the table.

"Mama, remember a long time ago when I was real little and you told me if I was good, I might inherit some money someday?"

Magda's eyes narrowed. "I don't remember that. No."

T.J. hesitated and handed his mother a plate of pralines, a coach sending in a fresh backfield of brown sugar, butter, and pecans. Magda ate six. She was happy again. "Well," continued T.J., "I know I haven't always been good, Mama. In fact, I reckon there were times when I tried your soul. I just want you to know I appreciate all you've done for me. And I've turned over a new leaf. Notice I didn't even drink a drop of beer?"

Magda nodded, suspecting now that in one way or another she would get the check. "I think we'd better get home," she said. "Peavine's already jealous."

"But I wanted to be with *you,* Mama. . . . Well, I better just spit it out. I've gotta chance to get rich, Mama. And I need ten thousand dollars. Will you loan it to me?"

At least Magda did not laugh. All she did was shake her head in wonder and say, "Of course not," thinking as she refused how all the women of her family either married hustlers or bred them. Uniquely, she did both. Driving home in guarded silence, T.J. abruptly asked, "Did you and Bun and Daddy ever go on a picnic out near the old Arlington Downs Race Track?"

Magda belched, for which she blessed her belly. It gave her time to sidestep. "Who could remember that?" she said. "It's been closed for twenty-five years." Magda knew her voice was shaky but she didn't think T.J. picked up on it.

Uncle Bun called with a bunch of news. Spike liked the eighty-acre spread with the yellow house and was buying it for $32,000. Twenty-one chinchillas were arriving (three families of six females and a male per unit). A dozen slowpoke horses with sway backs and tired legs had been saved from the dog-food factory and would soon be carrying rich Yankee women. A ranch cook who could make spoon bread and *huevos rancheros* was being sought. Signs were on order that promised YOU WILL LIKE BUN & SPIKE, soon to be planted on the highways of America, with a mock gunshot wound through the heart of Texas that was Fort Worth.

"Tell me the truth, Uncle Bun," said T.J. "Was you serious about making me a junior executive if I get ten grand?"

"I don't bullshit when it comes to money or blood kin," said Bun.

"Then what's my absolute final deadline?"

"Yestidy."

"Be serious, Bun. This is my big chance."

"When you got the money, I got the honey."

More avidly than Kleber ever devoured the *Star-Telegram* for news, T.J. searched it for treasure. One day he saw this:

$1000 A WEEK!

National Firm Seeks Fired-Up Men for Public Relations. Refs. Rqd. Contact Mr. Kelly. Room 633 Westbrook Hotel.

In twenty minutes flat, T.J. was pounding at the door of room 633 and that very afternoon he had become an encyclopedia salesman for the Universal Books of Total Knowledge. The district boss, Jocko Kelly, was more full of fizz than a shook-up Dr. Pepper. He hired T.J. on the spot, not bothering to ask for the references which the applicant had so laboriously forged. "I see integrity on your face!" Jocko exclaimed. Every sentence out of the man's mouth was a declaration. He drove T.J. to a subdivision near Carswell Air Force Base and dumped him on a street of tract houses. "This is hot territory, kid!" enthused Kelly. "This is a break for you! Nobody's ever plowed this field before!" Promising to fetch his new representative at 6 p.m. sharp, Kelly barreled off, leaving T.J. nervous and deflated. The street sign said he was standing on the corner of Heavenly Trail and Moonglow. If this is heaven, thought T.J., then all the angels wear toreador pants and all the cherubs ride broken tricycles. The frame and brick veneer houses were built so close together that a fat man from the gas company couldn't slip through to read the meter. The unmowed front yards, brown as pie crust, looked like the plains of Africa. A few skinny magnolia trees were giving up, like vaccinations that didn't take. T.J. summoned courage from Jocko's parting words, "Just remember, kid, these people wanna *better* themselves. They're sitting inside waiting for you—the man who's gonna change their lives—and make fifty dollars' commission every time you do it."

The woman who answered his first knock said, "Yeah?" She was young, no more than twenty, with a yelling baby locked to her legs. The kid's diaper was full and his face was red with anger. Mama was in the middle of a home permanent. Her hair was stiff and yellow. "Afternoon, ma'm. My name is Tom Luther and I'm conductin' a *public relations* campaign for the Universal Books of Total Knowledge Company." Immediately Mama's face turned into a lemon, but T.J. spooned on the sugar water. "Oh, lemme assure you, pretty lady, I'm not *sellin'* anything. Put your mind at ease. My company picked your house out of the entire neighborhood for a once-in-a-lifetime-never-to-be-repeated opportunity. It'll take just two minutes and I'll be—ha-ha —outta your hair."

Mama said no about twenty times but T.J. countered each negative with a positive. Before long he was inside, which smelled like burned barbecue sauce and baby shit. He drank ice water and bounced a slobbering kid on one knee and played peekaboo with another. He even persuaded Mama to turn off the soap opera and sit beside him on the Naugahyde couch. "You see, ma'm, we're gonna *give* you the twenty-four-volume set of the Universal Books of Total Knowledge. *Free*. Like Christmas! All we want in return is for you to give me the names of two or three neighbors who might be interested in *buying* a set." Here came the wink. "They don't need to know that you're gettin' for free what'll cost them six hundred and fifty-five dollars." Mama began to soften, just as Jocko said she would. T.J. danced merrily on, displaying the "genuine gold-leaf-embossed leatherette" sample of Volume I, "chock-full of color plates" with "every bit of information conceived by the genius of man since time began." It was enough to "get both of your younguns into Harvard."

"Well, it sounds real nice," said Mama, now looking at her savage children in a new light. Ten minutes ago both were for sale; now they might win the Nobel Prize. "But what's the catch?" Her eyes narrowed.

"Ain't no catch, ma'm. Free's *free*." T.J. paused, wishing he could quit winners right there. The fish was hooked, but the trick part was reeling it in without snagging the line on tree stumps. "Of course," he said tentatively, "you'll wanna keep this set up to date. These modern times . . . why, every day science discovers so many new things Einstein couldn't stay even. . . . He's on our advisory board, by the way. So the Universal Books of Total Knowledge, which is a nonprofit organization dedicated solely toward making your kids the smartest ones in school, brings out a new volume every year. It's called the Universal Update. And this costs only twenty-four ninety-five a volume, handling and shipping included. Hardly four bits a week. A few packs of bubble gum. Not much sacrifice for straight-A report cards."

Mama allowed as how she better wait for her husband to come home, but T.J. said there wasn't time. Now or never. Husbands were to encyclopedia salesmen what German shepherds were to burglars. Mama said she didn't have a bookcase; T.J. said that for another twenty dollars he'd throw in a "walnut veneer" shelf that would fit "any decor." Mama bit her nails and pulled her yellow hair, but T.J. kept crooning and had the contract under her nose and the pen in her hands—and damned if she didn't jump right into the old bait bucket. She signed—and obligated herself to buy ten Universal Updates, the bookcase, carrying charges, all of which came to $405.15. She didn't notice the whole sum had to be paid in forty-five days. She even gave T.J. the names of three best friends, one of whom he had to finger-fuck an hour and a half later, but he got her sixty-five-dollar deposit check, too. When Jocko Kelly picked him up at six, precisely calculated to beat husbandly homecomings, the boss slapped T.J.'s back and said, "Ain't nobody ever sold two sets the first afternoon. You're a born salesman, boy!"

T.J. worked the neighborhood another fortnight, making eleven more sales, even pulling off the equivalent of a triple somersault on the high wire—signing up an out-of-work hod carrier whose wife had just run off and left him with three-year-old twins and a new baby with a cleft palate. After Kelly deducted twenty-five dollars for his "sample case" and ten dollars for "transportation," T.J.'s first paycheck would come in right near $650. "You can collect your money tomorrow afternoon at four o'clock," said Jocko. "Don't come any earlier 'cause the funds are being transferred from Kansas City. Pretty soon we better talk about your movin' up to assistant district manager."

When T.J. knocked at room 633 at two minutes to four, nobody answered. Three other salesmen materialized and they all waited and sweated and knocked and cussed until four-fifteen. Then T.J. went downstairs and asked the desk clerk where Mr. Kelly was. "He checked out this morning," said the clerk, immediately stepping prudently back. On T.J.'s face was craze and anguish. Just then two men in crisp tan gabardine suits and sunglasses strode out from behind a potted palm. "That one, ma'm?" asked the first tan suit. A woman nodded firmly. It was his first customer, yellow-haired mama. The other tan suit flashed a badge and twisted T.J.'s arms behind his back to fasten cuffs. He was under arrest for fraud. "That's a felony, son," warned the detective.

"I hope you get the electric chair," said the mama whose children would never read the Universal Books of Total Knowledge because, well, other than the six-page sample, they didn't exist. "Einstein died in 1955, ha, ha, ha," she said.

Magda let T.J. rot in jail three full days before she posted $1,500 bail. She screamed at her son that he was a dagger in her heart. She asked him to find another place to live. As her car crossed the viaduct from downtown to the west side, she pointed at an old Mexican man on the bridge who sold tamales wrapped in newspapers. He had been there a thousand years. "That man is better than you," said Magda. "That filthy, smelly old tamale man is better than my own son."

Having seen the world from the shadows of a jail bar or two, Uncle Bun lent compassion to his nephew. "We all sell phony encyclopedias one time or t'other," observed Bun. He gave T.J. a room in the ranch bunkhouse, forty dollars a week for odd jobs, and located a lawyer to negotiate a slap on the wrist. Fortuitously, Jocko Kelly was himself collared a few days later in Tulsa for selling a woman $800 worth of driveway asphalt coating that was black paint. An investigation revealed that Jocko was actually one Ramon Corello, free-lance gypsy, seller of bogus books, nonexistent insurance policies, and Irish linen tablecloths made in Taiwan. All of this was laid before a district judge in Fort Worth who, happily, had once chased skirts with Bun. The judge lectured T.J. on the necessity to check out dogs for fleas, reduced the felony to disorderly conduct, and fined him $500, to be suspended on proof that the victims of encyclopedic fraud had been repaid their deposits. T.J.'s bill, including legal fees and court costs, was $640. "I ain't ever gonna scrape the shit off my boots," he moaned to Bun on the way home. "You will if it gets to smellin' bad enough," remarked Bun.

Very much the whipped dog, T.J. licked his wounds a few days. Bun let the boy get away with sloppy strokes of white paint on a fence and listless dandelion weeding. The kid was about nine-tenths no account, judged Bun, but the leftover was hound dog and tough sumbitch —qualities the old cowboy respected. He saw a lot of himself in T.J.— ability, guile, and the desire to take shortcuts. Furthermore, Bun had commenced to wonder if T.J.'s unusual entry into the world hadn't cross-circuited his nerve wires. He almost broke down and told his nephew the truth about the oak tree. But Bun decided it was best not to start a blood feud.

One crisp October morning, Bun rousted T.J. from a snarl of dirty blankets and the pit of liquored sleep with a task—a routine errand— unknowing that the devil god of coincidence was planning a more momentous collision. He ordered T.J. to fetch some buckets, milk cans, and two bales of hay from a feedlot on the north side. Just as the boy was driving off in the ranch pickup, Bun ran out of the yellow house a-puffin', waving an envelope, a deposit that had to reach the bank by noon. Bun was red in the face and the veins on his temples were throbbing. "Spike's on a tear this mornin'," said Bun. T.J. took the envelope and left, thinking that his uncle and aunt-in-law had been yelling quite a bit lately. Everyone was under strain to get the dude ranch finished in time for the official opening.

At the Fort Worth National Bank, the wait was interminable. T.J. was beginning to figure that life intended his place to be at the end of all lines. Somebody had discarded the morning paper on a check-writing table and T.J. picked it up to browse. Right there on page one was the first jolt of the day: FORT WORTH MAN WINS NATIONAL WRITING AWARD yelled the headline and under it beamed the smug mug of Kleber Cantrell, Prince of Power. He had cream on his whiskers, a tweed jacket, a button-down shirt, knit tie, and hair cut short and neat.

Kleber Cantrell, 26, former Fort Worth resident, yesterday won the National Headliners Award for investigative reporting. His series of articles in the Houston *Call-Bulletin* exposed scandals in the construction industry.

A graduate of Columbia University, Mr. Cantrell has won numerous local and state journalism prizes. He recently married the former Adelle Maynard, a Houston socialite, and they are expecting their first child.

He is the second graduate of Western High to achieve national recognition. His friend and fellow member of the Class of 1950, Mack Crawford, is currently starring in a Broadway play.

To which T.J. muttered, as he crushed the paper into a compact wad and scored two points in a distant spittoon, "Well, lick my dick." He tried to feel Christian over Kleber's success, but he surrendered to the truth: he hated the fucker. Over the years, from many places, from a roadhouse near Fort Hood, in a moment of unrepellable attack from demons and loneliness at Magda's, T.J. had pursued Kleber by long-distance. Only once, in a short dark hour, had they connected, T.J.'s voice blurred with whiskey and smoke and fawning apologies for the intrusion. Kleber was blurred by sleep and irritation. They had spoken *at* each other, hanging up with the vow to "stay in touch." But their paths and voices had not found junction again. Kleber never called him back, probably did not even remember the promise by the next daybreak of his meaningful morning and resumption of his prize-winning life. And the one time he had seen Mack was on Camp Bowie Boulevard, driving in one of Bear's red Fords. T.J. had pulled alongside in his jeep and honked, but Mack just glanced over and nodded and roared away.

T.J. grew emotional as he edged slowly toward the teller, glancing at the pinstripe suits all around him, hating *them,* feeling like a turd on a string of pearls. Every life in the line had form and purpose. His was defined by his clothes: jeans caked with mud from Bun's tourist corral, a tee shirt worn inside out to hide the sweat stains. His face had two days' growth of beard and his hair had not been washed or combed since a court appearance one week past.

It occurred to T.J. that he might rob this bank. He saw only one guard on duty, a doddering old coot who slept standing up and whose sidearm, a mistreated .38 Colt Detective Special, would probably shoot his nuts off the moment he tried to open the holster. But the way luck was running, reasoned T.J., he'd get knocked off by a lucky ricochet. But what he *could* do, fantasy suggested, was watch and see who cashed a big check and follow 'em outside and demand a substantial donation to the T. J. Luther Deserves Success Foundation.

Then a voice broke his concentration. "Howdja like this?" said the teller to a woman in line just ahead of T.J. The woman said, "Oh, twenties and fifties will do just fine." Practically salaaming, the teller counted out five hundred dollars in clean crisp new bills, the kind they keep in wrappers for valued customers. Then without even verifying its accuracy, the woman stuffed her wad into a real leather purse, mentioned that rain was sure needed, and spun about-face, bumping head on into the Prince of Temptation.

"Oh, sorry," she apologized. She looked at T.J. and her face lit up. "Why, T. J. Luther!" she exclaimed. "How *are* you?" The Five Hundred Dollar Woman knew his name! Trouble was, he didn't know hers. He smiled and howdied quick, hoping the freight train in his head would stop at some depot of recognition. "You don't remember me, do you," the woman rattled on. "It's Missy," she said. "Missy Craymore."

"Hell, Missy, course I remember," lied T.J. "I was just taken by how fine you look. You haven't changed a bit." Melissa Craymore was a girl from high school to whom no attention was paid. At least not by T.J. Of pretty girls and rich girls and smart girls and easy girls, Missy was a blank scrap in the quilt. All T.J. could recall was a vague image of Missy on the front line of the girls' volleyball team. She had fire-pole legs and wore horn-rimmed glasses. Maybe she drew posters for the homecoming dance. He could not remember if she even signed his yearbook. Everybody who *counted* did.

They left the bank together, Missy raving about coincidences because only that very morning had she read in the paper of Kleber's journalism prize. "That set me to thinking about you boys," she gushed. "I still remember the Three Princes. That play we made up in the ninth grade. It was so romantic."

"Romantic?" said T.J. "You mean sexy?"

"No." Missy laughed. "There's a difference. Have you guys kept up with each other?"

"Oh, sure. Kleber woke me up in the middle of the night last week. Talked my damn ear off. We're still thick as thieves." Missy seemed impressed. Celebrity once removed has value.

"Have you seen Mack's play?" she asked. T.J. shook his head. He hadn't even known Mack was in a play until he read the morning paper. Just when he was set to tell Missy about the jock's separation from Susan—he did know *that*—she one-upped him. "Well, my dear, I was in New York last month and let me tell you Mr. Crawford is the toast of the town. I had to pay a scalper fifteen dollars for a ticket. His part's not very big, he doesn't say much of anything, but he practically steals the show. The first time he comes out, he's wearing blue jeans and no shirt. The second time he's in his underwear . . ." Missy stopped. Her face was turning pink.

T.J. said he had a couple of letters at home from Mack but he hadn't had time to read them. "Well, if you write back," said Missy, "tell him I tried to get backstage, but there were a thousand squealing little girls in the way."

By the time they reached Missy's car, an Olds 98 that T.J. snap-appraised at $6,000 minimum, his interest was kindled. The lost years since high school were hopscotched. Missy had gone off to some Yankee school—Radcliffe—that T.J. had never heard tell of, had studied art, had intended to find work in a New York museum, had returned instead to Fort Worth when her mama suffered a paralyzing stroke, had stayed on after the funeral, and now lived all by herself in a house near "the club." That meant Rivercrest Country Club. How near? wondered T.J. He could certainly find out quick. In turn, T.J. recounted, with modesty befitting a reluctant hero, his army career, his period of adjustment. He was careful to deliver generalities.

He apologized for his appearance. "I'm right ashamed to run into an old friend lookin' like a shit shoveler," he said.

"I didn't even notice," said Missy. "You should have seen me yesterday. I was clearing out what is laughingly called my back yard. They could use it to film Tarzan movies."

"Next time you get ambitious, call me," said T.J. "I've swung a sickle or two." He opened the Olds door, smelled the sweet perfume of leather seats, lent an arm of support to Missy. She would never be pretty, her face too long, her jutting jaw too firm. But she was wholesome, and with five hundred dollars in her pocket and a house near "the club," T.J. reckoned she was close to Rockefeller stature.

"How do I find you?" asked Missy.

"Oh," said T.J., hastily improvising. "My uncle and me are in partnership. We're developing some ranch property out near Arlington." Missy nodded appreciatively and drove away. T.J. caught her looking back at him in the rearview mirror. Later that afternoon he asked Bun what he knew about the Craymore family. After a few calls around, Bun informed his nephew, "Big bucks."

One drive past Melissa Craymore's house gave T.J. a new encyclopedia to sell: himself. She lived in an immense emulation of a Deep South plantation house that sat in noble neighborness to the fairways of Rivercrest golf course. Dark green shutters were not only closed but seemingly nailed shut, as if the owners were abroad, and the row of pillars were no longer white but gray and peeling. The front yard was poorly mown and on the sides was an encroaching jungle. What Missy needed was a man around the house.

With zeal but enforced economy he set out to woo. Intuition told him to play cowboy since that had attracted her in the first place. For their first date he chose a Saturday-night rodeo at Hurst, where Missy agreed it was "much more fun" to squeeze under the fence than to pay the two dollars. The next night they dined "for old times' sake" at James' Coney Island, stuffing two-for-thirty-five-cents chili dogs into mouths already crowded with backed-up news of who had married, divorced, birthed, or died. They picnicked at Lake Worth and went to a drive-in movie to see *Cat on a Hot Tin Roof*. Just looking at Elizabeth Taylor in a slip gave T.J. a hard-on and he sort of slouched sideways in Bun's pickup so Missy would think it was her sex appeal. But she didn't seem to notice T.J.'s arousal and in fact got so upset with Big Daddy bullying Paul Newman that she demanded to leave. He had come to observe that Missy had these moods, sudden, like a little black cloud sliding in from out of nowhere to spoil a clear blue sky.

One other thing chewed at T.J.'s game plan. He was never asked inside Missy's house. On the first date she was on the front porch waiting for him—and ever thereafter. And she always loitered until he drove away before she went inside. He couldn't figure it out. On the telephone she welcomed his voice. And out on dates, she was game for mischief and attentive to his yarns. Of course he had not yet made a lunge, recognizing that Missy was not exactly a waitress at the Shamrock Truck Stop. But he damn well knew when and why a woman's palm sweated, and she sure didn't stop his fingers from marching around the base of her tits.

About three weeks into the campaign, T.J. let it all out. "I was wondering, maybe could I come in and say good night?" he asked. Melissa hesitated, making him feel like the yardman asking for a drink of water. Then she nodded. "Might as well," she said, pushing on a foot-thick slab with hinges that squealed like "Inner Sanctum." A warning, as it were, but T.J. didn't listen. In the blackness, the living room smelled the way a trunk discovered and opened in the attic does, the kind that sends out the sick malodor of sachet and crumbling satin and dead mice. Melissa turned on a table lamp, the base of which was a stuffed tiger's head, and yellow light swam weakly around. "Holy shit," said T.J.

The place was huge, sixty feet long at least, and so crowded with hotel lobby furniture—the kind with claws for legs and shrouded with drop cloths—that a child couldn't have found room to turn a somersault. On ceiling beams were painted Oriental dragons with giant tongues that rolled on and on in lacquer red; cobwebs trailed from them like torn lace nets. When he took a step across the Persian carpet, dust rose in little gusts like bullets pocking the sand of a firing range. But all of this was *Better Homes and Gardens* compared to the company the Craymores kept. Nailed to the walls like ancestral portraits were at least two hundred stuffed animal heads and carcasses—mournful buffalo, frightened does, snarling lynx and lions and panthers with glistening teeth, an elephant, couple of giraffes, parrots, quite a few coiled rattlers, and even a goddamn rhino that looked like it had charged angrily across the golf course, rammed Missy's wall, and got its head fatally stuck.

It was hard to breathe, as if the animals had sucked all the air—and life—from the chamber. T.J. felt dizzy and queasy. He thought about the secrets that are locked inside of rooms. "Daddy was a hunter," said Missy in an odd voice, beckoning for T.J. to follow her down a long hall. "If Daddy were here, he would tell you exactly which vital organ got which bullet." She passed by an enormous Alaskan brown bear, full figure, arms outstretched for something to squeeze. T.J. shook the beast's paw and said, "Howdy, podner." Stuffing dropping out of the snarling mouth like the drool of an old lunatic.

In the hallway, a glass case as long as Missy's Oldsmobile contained enough rifles and handguns to invade Arkansas. And on a shelf of honor all by itself was a stuffed cat, sitting on a gold harem pillow. Coal black, with a jagged bolt of white lightning on the nose, kitty had river-green eyes that seemed to follow T.J. as he passed.

"That's Delano," said Missy, "named after Franklin Delano You-Know-Who. Daddy hated Delano and Delano hated Daddy. One day Delano happened to be in the way when Daddy was loading his rifle. Mama said I threw such a fit that Daddy had Delano stuffed. He gave it to me for a Christmas present. I imagine it was a challenge to the taxidermist."

Presently they came to a sun porch, as unexpected as a fern garden in a tomb. "This is me," said Melissa. The long and narrow room was freshly painted white, with pots of small trees and devotedly attended orchids, a few pieces of white wicker furniture, and smack in the middle, an old brass bed smothered with pillows in a rainbow of cheerful colors.

T.J. glanced around approvingly. "Yep," he said. "I'd know your taste anywhere."

"Sorry you had to traipse through the Congo," said Missy. "One of the stupid things about this mausoleum is that there's no back entrance. I've been meaning to find a carpenter."

"You've got one," said T.J. "Wouldn't take me half a day." He shifted nervously, balancing bowlegged on the outer edges of his boots, not having been invited to take a seat. And Missy was looking at him strangely, with her empty-eyed expression, as if she was wondering whether to share a secret. It was uncomfortable. T.J. broke the spell by wandering about the room, sniffing the flowers, bending over a thick stack of sketches piled beside the bed. The first seemed to be a vase, but instead of posies there was a woman's head, with stringy vines like wandering Jew for hair and red poppies for eyes. Melissa skipped right over and said, "Don't look at these. They're silly." But already T.J. was eyeballing the second one in the pile. In ragged charcoal strokes was a strong and muscled man whose bottom half wore jeans but who was naked from there up. He was standing sideways with his thumbs hooked under the fly of his britches. It could have been T.J., except the face was blank.

"These are good," said T.J.

"Just doodling," said Missy, as flustered as an old woman who barged into the men's toilet by mistake. T.J. gathered she did not wish to pursue her art in conversation. He hemmed and hawed and mentioned the possibility of another picnic over the weekend. Missy nodded and walked him to the door, through the room of dead animals. Outside, in the cool and clean night air, she said, "I know I've been impolite for never asking you to come in, but now you know the reason."

"No," said T.J. "I don't know the reason."

"Because I didn't want you to see this god-awful house. I was afraid you'd think less of me."

"Hon, I don't care where you hang your hat. You could live under the Trinity River bridge for all I care." The lie brought mist to Missy's eyes.

"That's what I wanted to hear," she said. "I have this habit of making mental sketches of everybody. I see a man on the sidewalk and I make a picture out of him."

"So where's mine?"

"I picture you living on a ranch with everything fresh and alive and reborn each morning. Versus me, keeping house in the morgue of Forest Park Zoo."

At the irony of images, T.J. laughed privately. How you see the show depends on where you sit. He put his rough hands on Missy's cheeks and touched them tenderly, as if stroking a treasure. He kissed her for the first time on the lips, very softly, very quickly, but knowing as she trembled that he was in absolute control.

While Melissa washed the sun-porch windows, T.J. hacked at grapevines and calla lilies and thick clumps of cedar. It was Saturday noon and the first week in November. But it was as hot as August. T.J. stripped off his tee shirt and wrung half a pint of sweat from it. He wondered why in hell Melissa couldn't hire some niggers to clear her jungle, but he didn't ask. Obviously she appreciated both his presence and his muscles and she would soon enough pay well for both. Now and then T.J. worked in a discreet question, calculated to find out just how big this poker game was, but Missy played her cards close to her chest. "What's this old dump worth, anyway?" he asked. Missy shrugged. "Haven't the faintest idea. I'd sell it for a mule and forty dollars."

She brought lemonade in silver goblets with a big engraved C and told T.J. to rest before he suffered sunstroke. "Let me wash that shirt for you," she said. T.J. said it wasn't necessary; it could dry in the sun. They went inside through the new door he had hung and relaxed in white wicker rockers. Perspiration dripped down T.J.'s neck, rolling through the dark chest hair and collecting in his belly button. Worn and sore, he tipped his head back and closed his eyes, dozing for what seemed only a minute. But it was longer. When he awoke, Missy was sitting on a stool and drawing on a sketch pad. T.J. bounded over to see, and there he was on the pad, head tipped back, so lifelike he could hear snores. "Can I have this?" he asked.

"If you want," said Missy. "I can do better."

"So do better," said T.J. "I'll pose for you. I once sat still for five minutes so I could get a quarter from Daddy. He bet me I couldn't do it. When there were only ten seconds left, he said, 'Look at that rabbit!' and I said, 'Where?' and the son of a bitch tried to weasel out of the two bits."

"Just stand for me. Better still, lean against this stool."

"I oughta comb my hair and put on my shirt," said T.J.

"No, I work from life. Just be quiet and don't look for rabbits."

T.J. obeyed and froze for a few moments, but he soon got bored and curious. Some mischief came to mind and he deemed it worth trying. "Can I stretch for a minute?" he asked between clenched teeth. Missy nodded. T.J. yawned and flung his arms out sideways and rotated his fists so that his arm muscles bulged and corded. "It's sure hot," he said, resuming his pose. He slipped his hand inside the waist of his jeans and shifted his cock from dress right to left. Then, slowly and suspensefully, he undid the first two brass buttons of his fly. His pubic hair showed, damp with sweat, and the elongated bulge concealed by Mr. Lee's denim could not have been mistaken for a Swiss Army knife. T.J. could get it up for a napkin ring.

Melissa fussed with her charcoal box for a while but T.J. knew it was just a matter of time before she looked. She did. Her hand began to shake and her tongue tip tried to moisten very dry lips. T.J. got off the stool, separated the frustrated artist from her sketch pad, and, noting how appealing she looked and smelled, leaned in open-mouthed for a semi-major kiss. Missy beat him to it. She clamped her body against his, threw one hand around his neck and the other against his ass, kissing him with such clawing ferocity that had he been a drowning man, Missy would have sucked him back to life.

Just as abruptly she disengaged, pushed him away, smoothed her hair. Never having encountered a woman quite like this, T.J. stammered, not altogether untruthfully, "I really care about you, Melissa."

She said, "Well, Lord knows I need somebody, too." She thought on this a minute, then rather savagely ripped her sketch in half.

CHAPTER FOURTEEN

Calvin Sledge was studying the ballistics report and when his intercom buzzed, he answered with a voice that could have peeled paint. "I said *no* calls, dammit."

"Ah, yessir," said Darlene. "I know you did. I truly remember. But there's four angels out here to see you."

"Four *what?*"

"Angels."

"Christ," moaned Sledge.

"He's not with 'em," said Darlene pleasantly. "But they've got a lawyer named Leo. Otto Leo. From Dallas."

Sledge closed the button and began a count of ten. At four he quit, recognizing that neither his temper nor his mood would soften if he counted until Christmas. "Okay," he said. "Tell 'em they've got two minutes." Hurriedly Sledge covered his work papers, slamming dossiers and stuffing folders into drawers. Otto Leo could read upside down. "Otto Goddamn Leo," he grumbled to himself. "Why did it take so long?" The Dallas attorney was dishonest, unethical, and, arguably, the most cunning criminal law tactician in America. Sledge loathed Leo, had lost to him thrice, felt now his blood stir at the prospect of his bête noire prancing into the corral.

With heads bowed, four angels entered. Their lips intoned a unintelligible chant, presumably part of the repertoire for heathen territory. They wore white gowns of coarse cotton that touched the floor, plastic thorn wreaths about unstyled hair, and no makeup at all. Sledge, who suspected they slept on barbed wire, could not estimate their age. They could have been thirty or sixty, having lost the identifiers of years. He envied their serenity.

One of them, the tallest, a woman with raven hair that spilled well below her waist, seemed a sort of Mother Superior. On her breast she wore a red felt heart, bleeding crimson drops sewn in a trail that flowed to her privates. Her eyes disturbed the prosecutor. They were bluish black, but empty, like a blind beggar's, mirrors that did not reflect. She approached Sledge and stretched out her hand as if blessing him. Attended by her sisters, she commenced to sing in a sweet cello contralto. The DA permitted but a few bars of "Abide with Me" before he snapped, "Hold it, ladies. I've told you people a dozen times this is an office, not a . . ."

"Calvin, dear boy. How in the world are you?" Through a crack in the wall of angels burst forth an imp with a moist plump hand ready for shaking. On its pinky was a Masonic ring with a brace of diamonds. The owner was about five feet six, even counting the lifts in his black patent slippers that thrust his body in forward tilt.

"Hello, Leo," said Sledge coolly. "You in this thing now?" Pointedly the prosecutor did not accept the hand.

"Just helping out," answered Leo. The toupee on his head was ill-fitting this humid summer morning; the line where it fastened onto his head was a circle of sweat. He wore an expensive silk suit of burnished gold hue, probably purchased in Rome. And on his necktie was a diamond and ruby pin—the Lady of Justice. She was blindfolded so she couldn't see what Otto was doing. "The Chosen has honored me by asking if I couldn't discuss a little . . . accommodation."

"How wonderful for you, Leo. He won't give me the goddamn time of day. Maybe that's why he's still upstairs in the slammer."

One of the sisters gasped and pressed a strong hand to her breast. Otto frowned. "Ah, Calvin, dear boy, it would be an act of Christian good manners if you could contain your profanity while in the presence of these devout women." Sledge chewed back the impulse to mention something about hypocrisy. By highball repute, Otto Leo was a devotee of sexual weirdness, possibly including German shepherds and pythons. Yet he stayed married to the fourth-richest woman in Texas, a lady of strong devotion to the Baptist Church. He was also the author of a widely read book on legal ethics and a regional best seller called *Defense!* which half the buyers in Dallas probably thought was about pro football.

"You've got one minute left, Leo. Next time do me the courtesy of calling for an appointment." Sledge tapped his Timex, sat down on his desk so that his butt smothered his case.

"I see that you are out of sorts, Calvin," purred the lawyer. "Of course, I have not studied the particulars of this matter, but I don't blame you. How difficult it must be trying to fabricate murder from accidental death."

"About as accidental as the St. Valentine's Day Massacre."

"At barest minimum," continued Leo, "manslaughter. Perhaps assault. Self-defense also comes to mind."

"It's *murder,* Leo. I have nothing to discuss with you and your cheerleaders."

"Then I must tell you I'm on my way over to file a writ," rasped Leo, tough now, voice drained of honey.

"No chance," snapped the DA. "No bail."

Bleeding Heart moved to Sledge and stood a breath away. "God's will cannot be questioned by mortal man," she said. Her face was caught by a shaft of sun and Sledge noticed that a long healed but once savage scar began at the corner of her right eye and slithered to her neck. It looked like the kind of brutality inflicted on a hooker by her pimp.

"Come, sisters," said Otto. "The death of one man is a terrible thing. And how tragic that other lives will be irreparably damaged when the truth comes out." The delegation began to leave, but Bleeding Heart turned and in her dead eyes was sudden fire. "In the war with Satan," she said, "Lord God is our Commander in Chief. Judge not, lest ye be judged."

This prompted Otto Leo to rummage in his reservoir of quotations for all human behavior—his court summations were usually peppered with reference from scholars so remote that opponents suspected he invented them. "Mr. Shakespeare cautioned, 'Be certain what you do, sir, lest your justice prove violence.' Keep that in mind, dear Calvin, and in heart."

Sledge could not let these nuts exit winners. "John Ruskin said it better. 'One's heart ought to be shown in the *enforcement* of law—not in its relaxation.'"

In false tribute, Leo bowed. But he fired the morning's last shot. "John Ruskin, a worthy man. But John Ruskin challenged the moral order. He lost the love of every woman he knew, and he died from depression. Quite possibly, they say, insanity. Good day."

Of the four major cities in Texas, Fort Worth alone, like its troubled son, T. J. Luther, suffered most from lack of identity. At birth Fort Worth was an orphan, the whim of misguided ambition. In 1849, a U. S. Army colonel with the dashing name of Ripley Arnold picked a pleasant site on the banks of the Trinity River where he built a ramshackle fort from rough cedar logs. The intent was to provide white settlers with shelter from the "bloodthirsty butchery" of Comanche Indians who had owned the land before there was Texas, before there was America. In an amusing twist of history, the fort opened its doors and the very first people to seek refuge therein were Indians, a tribe of Tonkawas in flight from the Kiowas, both afraid of Comanches. Though turned away, they camped nearby. Not surprisingly, no white settlers elected to accept the fort's hospitality, and four years later, the U.S. government shuttered Ripley Arnold's thrust for glory. He had hoped that a town would spring up bearing his name.

Only then did a few pioneers drop around and, finding empty cabins, settled in and started a trading post. They named it Fort Worth for no known reason. There was no need for a store, really, Dallas being but thirty miles away. But Fort Worth clung stubbornly to the map, developing in the years that followed a culture rich as myth. She sired sons who stood at her city limits and cried at the world, like carnival barkers, "Look at us!" The sad part was, hardly anybody did.

Hollywood made shrines out of Tombstone, Arizona, and Abilene, Kansas, and a score of Texas burgs less historically colorful. Fort Worth was enjoyed by Butch Cassidy and the Sundance Kid, Sam Bass, Luke Short, and Doc Holliday, all of whom gave custom to the town's gunsmiths and poker tables and soiled doves (Fort Worth's whores were celebrated and remembered along the nearby Chisholm Trail). City fathers pinned all manner of labels on their town, "Where the West Begins," "Queen City of the Plains," and "Panther City," the last being the prank of some Dallas bastard who claimed Fort Worth was so dull and sleepy that a panther slept on Main Street. But only "Cowtown" ever stuck and after a time her people began to like it.

If they were men, the four cities of Texas, Houston was Paul Bunyan driving a solid-gold bulldozer, Dallas a bank president with a .38 under the pillow, San Antonio a lover who lost his watch. And Fort Worth might be defined as T. J. Luther attending the Assembly Ball. In deepest autumn, when the cosmic scheme has turned the face of Texas away from the scorch of summer sun, just before winter's winds shriek down from Canada across the flat waist of Uncle Sam, a rite of anachronistic beauty is held in Fort Worth, ostensibly to introduce a dozen young women to "society." The Assembly Ball is more than the supreme social event of the Cowtown year. It is Fort Worth's private pat on the back, an evening of opulence to rival Manhattan and Paris, a circling of the Cadillacs in haughtiest enclave. The city that began as an abandoned pile of logs becomes, on one late-November evening, a rarefied kingdom.

On the night that the Prince of Temptation, in rented white tie and tails and wearing gold-tipped boots borrowed from Uncle Bun, escorted Melissa Craymore to the Assembly Ball, he did not reckon himself as a poseur. He considered his presence not only rightful but overdue. He was ready for his own debut. It mattered not that two months prior he was weeping in county jail, waiting for Mama to bail him out on charges of fraud. The proof of his worth was in the cameras that raised expectantly as he opened the carriage—Bun's Cadillac—for his princess. Missy looked as fetching as a plain girl could possibly accomplish. Her hair was swept up and gathered by a diamond brooch. She wore an elegant forest-green gown with billowing panels edged in gold thread that made her resemble a treasury bond. Tomorrow morning, thought T.J., Magda would fall in her scrambled eggs when she saw the son she rejected dancing across the society pages.

It was fortunate that fantasy so gripped T.J. he failed to notice the photographers lowering their cameras unfired, nor did he hear a woman reporter's sotto voce negation. "Nobody."

T.J.'s bravado disappeared quickly. Once across the threshold of the Ridglea Country Club, he felt his white collar stiffen and his stomach jerk. He looked around and saw that he was the only rook on a chessboard of kings and queens. Missy didn't help. She saw a pack of young women en route to the powder room, joined the expedition, and left her date abandoned. When time passed and it appeared that Missy had truly fallen in, T.J. sallied forth alone. "Connections," he reminded himself. "Here is where they're at." Two double bourbons tossed down neat restored his courage. He tried to tip the bartender five dollars, but the fellow said, "No thank you, suh. This is a private party."

"I know it's private," glowered T.J. He lit the fin with his cigarette lighter and burned the money. Henceforth, Sambo would know for whom he was pouring whiskey. He toured the ballroom, which decorators had transformed into an emulation of the gardens of Versailles. At one end was a gold fountain with water obediently spurting ten feet into the air. Nearby were statues of reclining women, copies of Louis XIV's artisans, sulking in the glow of silver light from three enormous Marie Thérèse crystal prism chandeliers. Each wall of the room was smothered with silver leaves from floor to ceiling, and every few feet was a towering arch of smilax hedge, thirty arches, thirty chandeliers as crowns. Gilded urns contained cascading pyramids of white roses and orchids as tall as a two-story cottage.

Straight down the middle of the hall stretched an eighty-five-foot strip of royal red carpet, the aorta of a king, leading to the stage where the debutantes would soon give their daddies their money's worth. Missy had told T.J. it cost about $50,000 to "come out," covering the price of a gown from French couture, jewels, a private party preceding the main event, and lessons from a demanding mistress of etiquette who taught each young woman how to drift ethereally onto the stage, arms filled with blossoms, and to bow with backbreaking grace until the forehead touched the floor. T.J. grabbed another bourbon off a tray, and two glasses of champagne. He stepped onto the royal carpet, it being the only open lane on a crowded freeway. Immediately a liveried waiter with a powdered wig on his nappy head tapped the trespasser's shoulder and ordered him away. T.J. apologized meekly.

Beside a silvery tree with cherry blossoms glued on the limbs, he saw a friendly-looking woman with snow-white hair talking to three penguins. She espied T.J. out of the corner of an eye and smiled. Emboldened, he squeezed into her conversational circle. "I'm Tom Luther," he announced, pumping limp hands all around. "Luther?" said the woman, squinting at a puzzle. She had six perfect rubies around her neck. T.J. counted them intently. "Your father must be Claude Luther. Wonderful family." She introduced T.J. to the penguins, who stared at him dully. "This young man's father gave us twenty-five thousand dollars for the Metropolitan Opera tour last year."

"Well, ma'm," said T.J. "I'm not that Luther. We may be distant cousins. I'm the chinchilla Luther."

"The *what??*"

"Chinchillas. You know. Cute little buggers. Furs real soft and thick. Fit for a queen."

"Sable gives me hives," said the woman.

"But you'd look super good in chinchilla," said T.J. "If you'll just gimme your phone number, I could have a coat ready for you by spring. They screw like maniacs. Females drop a litter ever' ninety days."

Her mouth fallen open, the woman laughed mechanically. "Yes," she said, "wonderful story. How amusing." She steered her courtiers away. Another hour passed, during which T.J. searched and failed to find Melissa, drank more cocktails, and stuck out his hand to a lot of people who did not seem thrilled to meet him. He got sick in the men's room and stared at a silver plate of coins and dollar bills on the attendant's counter, wondering if he could take some home as souvenirs. He wandered outside and tried to make the carousel in his belly stop spinning. He squatted on the putting green and thought about calling Kleber in Houston so the prize-winning prick would know Who was really Who. He stretched out in a chaise beside the pool and watched silver torches float by. He had nodded off when a voice and a rough hand shook him awake. "Luther?" said a dissipated man with pocks on his cheeks. It was a classmate from high school, a boy named Joel whom nobody liked but who was now scrutinizing T.J. He asked, as if checking passports, "Who the hell are you with?"

Upon learning that T.J.'s credentials were Missy Craymore, Joel whistled and said, "No shit?"

T.J. pretended boredom. "I hate these fuckin' parties," he said. "Missy pestered my ass into bringin' her."

Joel said, "You ever meet her old man?"

"He's dead."

"Hell, I know he's dead. Ask Missy if it's true he kept all his money in a Stetson hat box."

"I will, Joel. I sure will."

Later, when he located Missy, T.J. wrapped arms around her as if she had been missing for six weeks in the Grand Canyon. She was testy. "Where have you been?" she demanded.

T.J. tried desperately to recall the question Joel had given him. "Did you . . . did . . . oh shit, honey bunch. I flat-ass forgot. Let's just dance." He attempted to guide Missy onto the floor where people were revolving to the sedate tempos of Lester Lanin's orchestra, but her battery was dead. "Listen," she said sharply. "You better sober up. Somebody said you tried to sell Sara Leonore one of your chinchillas."

T.J. found this enormously funny. "That ain't true," he said. "I didn't even bring one." A silver-haired man who looked like God's lawyer approached and whispered into Missy's ear. She nodded and gripped T.J.'s elbow, discreetly directing him toward a glittering forest. She said, "Hon, let's go home. This party is boring. I'm hot."

"Whadda'd that bastard just say to you?"

Missy pretended ignorance. "What?"

"That queer who just slobbered in your ear. He said somethin' about me, didn't he?" Squinting, T.J. focused on the old fart, who glared back at him from across the silver shrubbery. "Fuck off!" yelled T.J., raising his hand in well-known gesture.

"Sweetheart," sighed Melissa, "you just gave the finger to the governor of Texas."

The view from the depths of a bourbon bottle being golden and blurred, T.J. clung to Missy as they worked their way out of the gardens of Versailles. Near the front door, he saw what he took to be the offended governor. "Jes' a minute," gushed T.J., planning to offer contrition and apology. Breaking into a crowd of celebrants, mashing jeweled slippers and jostling champagne on ruffled bodices, T.J. lurched to where the tall man was signing autographs. He seized the man's arm and jerked him roughly around at the precise moment of an orchestral fanfare. A spotlight splashed upon both. And over the public-address system, a buttery voice confirmed the startling revelation that slowly seeped through T.J.'s eyes:

"Ladies and gentlemen, his plane was a little late, but he just walked in the door. Let's welcome a great athlete, Fort Worth's best car salesman, and Broadway's newest star—Cowtown's own Mr. Mack Crawford!"

There were probably thirty people clustered around Mack and twenty-nine stepped obediently backward, deferring to the exclusivity of a spotlight and granting celebrity its due. Only T. J. Luther remained rooted at center stage, clutching Mack's sleeve, grinning delightedly at the applause and feminine flutterings, a transfusion by osmosis for his bruised ego. As the welcome faded and women reached into their husbands' pockets for compacts to check their makeup should a confrontation with masculine magnificence occur, Mack glanced down at the pest. "Hey," he said good-naturedly, "do you mind?" When T.J. raised his bleary countenance, the star failed to recognize him.

"Well hey yorself, ole buddy," burbled T.J. "Goddamn, it's good to see you." He threw both arms in a fierce hug. "This here's my best friend in the whole fuckin' world," he wanted everybody to know.

"T.J.," said Mack, as happy as any man would be upon being squeezed by an apparition which he had tried for almost a decade to eliminate from his memory bank. He attempted to move away, but shielded from truth by the spirits of the night, T.J. was undaunted. He insisted that Mack come and meet Melissa. "Later, okay?" said Mack, sending an eye signal to a swarthy, muscled young man who was in his entourage.

"Please excuse us now," said the dark friend. He pushed a meaningful hand onto the tedious drunk's chest. But T.J. failed to get the message. "Jesus, Ma-Ma," said T.J., resurrecting another corpse from the graveyard of the past, "I musta tried a hunnerd times to call you . . ."

Politeness abandoned, the attendant seized T.J.'s right arm, twisted it into a pretzel, and pushed him into the anonymity of darkness. However appropriate the deed, it failed. T.J. came scrambling back. "Get the fuck outta my way," he cried, grabbing Mack's waist in a flying tackle and hanging on. He did not see the loathing in Mack's eyes.

The rest, the crucial twenty seconds, was like a grease fire in the kitchen—unexpected, alarming, and over as soon as somebody found the extinguisher. What happened was that Mack Crawford impulsively clutched T. J. Luther's boiled shirt, squeezed it into a crumpled magnolia blossom. Then the Prince of Charms slapped the holy shit out of the Prince of Temptation, dispatching him like an unwanted ball that rolled into a waiter. A squad of security police grabbed Missy's humiliated beau and hustled him to Bun's Cadillac. On the way, T.J. sputtered, "I'm gonna *get* that fucker . . . I'll kill that shit-ass . . ." Several people heard the threat, considered it whiskey talking, told the tale in years to come until better scandals took its place.

Missy chauffeured her disgrace to the mansion in Rivercrest and dragged him inside. She washed blood from the corner of his mouth and went to make coffee. When she returned, T.J. was sprawled in his underwear on the brass bed, sobbing. On the floor were his evening clothes, a muddied pool. His knee was bruised, his cheek striped red. Tears and confession spilled from his split lip. He was a liar. Deceitful, too. From the moment they met in the bank, he had romanced Missy, cut her weeds, used her as the key to a world for which he had neither birthright nor bank account.

"I'm sorry, hon," he wept. "I did wrong."

"It doesn't matter," she assured him.

"I don't understand why people don't like me anymore," he said. "Everything I touch turns to shit."

"Don't feel sorry for yourself," she said. "I want you to take these. They'll make the pain go away." T.J. obediently swallowed the two white pills—aspirin, he assumed—and washed them down with a new glass of whiskey. Immediately the tumbler fell from his hand and the night cracked into a broken mirror. Dimly he heard Missy babbling and singing two lovely words, *"bella donna."* But then he fell into what had to be a nightmare. Else he was going mad. Images flickered in and out like a movie screen whose projector kept breaking. He moved somehow to the living room, where candles had been lit, furniture stripped of shrouds. He lay face down on a leather couch, cushions slippery with baby oil. Melissa was spanking him and his ass hurt. He cried some more. He blacked out, cartwheeling into empty space. The room whirled and the dead animals leered from their perches. Their eyes spun like shooting gallery targets in the glow of candles. The great Alaskan brown bear advanced menacingly, stopping just short of seizing him, whereupon Missy bounded out from between the beast's legs. She was stark naked. T.J. could not remember whether she had slipped voluntarily from the billowing green-gold gown, or had he ripped it from her body by command? Whatever, it lay in shreds beside a neatly positioned row of sketches. Six sketches. They told a story of sorts. In the first, a man was fully clothed in jeans, lumberjack shirt, hat, boots. In the second, the shirt was gone and the chest was bare, though pocked as if by bullets. By gradation, the man became naked, and in the sixth and last, T.J. saw himself, standing sideways, his hands covering an enormous penis. His cock was a rifle aimed at a girl who looked like Melissa and was blindfolded. He screamed the soundless cry of a dream and Melissa climbed onto his thighs, holding a pistol from the gun cabinet in her hands. She placed it against his sex, smearing both weapons with baby oil, moaning gibberish and slowly lowering herself. She received metal and flesh and enduring blackness slew the night.

When T.J. awoke, he was in Melissa's brass bed. His clothes, neat, clean, and pressed, hung on a chair. Presently Missy brought breakfast —freshly squeezed orange juice, ham steak, and, protected by a silver dome, steaming mounds of eggs and mushrooms. Solicitous for his aching head, she was a tender nurse. T.J. struggled up and was immediately stabbed by pain in his head and in his ass. "I feel like some mule kicked me," he said.

"It's called paying the piper," she said.

"Honey, I'm sorry," began T.J., memories of the fight with Mack flooding back. "I really messed up."

Melissa shook her head in disagreement and kissed T.J. with cool lips. "I'm sorry we even went," she said. "Those people are all phony, anyway. We don't need them."

That afternoon, after he had returned to Bun's and vowed several times to God that he would never ever take another drop of strong drink, T.J. remembered the rest of the night. It seemed real. But reason insisted there was no way on earth for a girl like Melissa Craymore to shove a .38 up her twat.

A few days later, in the cabin of Bun's pickup, parked beside the duck pond in Trinity Park, T.J. proposed marriage. He said, "I think I love you, Missy, and I sure would like to marry you." She responded quickly. "I think that's a good idea." But before they kissed to seal the pact, Missy laid down one condition. Her fiancé would have to provide new living quarters. It was imperative that nobody had ever dwelled before them in the rooms where Mr. and Mrs. Thomas Jeremiah Luther would begin legal union.

"But you've got a house," said T.J.

"I hate my house," she said. "It's too big. You can't get help anymore. And the light's no good for my work."

Well, reasoned T.J. to himself, that was no big deal. He could find a little rent house somewhere, install his bride, sell her daddy's chamber of horrors for a hundred and fifty thou, then lie on his back and count the stars. Missy must have read his thoughts. She said, "And I don't want us to rent. Renting means somebody else owns us. I don't want any strings to bind our love. Hon, I'm not talking about something pretentious. Just a little place for you and me where we can shut out the rest of the world." As inspiration, Missy whipped out a watercolor she had drawn of Basic Enchanted Cottage, roses climbing by the window, thatched roof, wishing well in the garden, and—T.J. blinked twice—two shotguns leaning against the Dutch door.

He took his predicament to Bun, who had one of his own. The chinchillas were kicking the bucket. Two females died during the night and now the last male was lying on his side and quivering. "I don't understand," mourned Bun. "I done ever'thing right. I bought the little fuckers their own Fedders air conditioner. I imported the same damn seeds they eat in the damn Andes Mountains. I sang Meskin songs and I loved 'em and tickled 'em and I told 'em how happy they was gonna be snuggled next to Jane Russell's tits. But the damn things quit on me."

Bun looked not only sad but old. The little sun crinkles around his eyes were suddenly furrows. His neck was shrinking, folding like an old pumpkin. T.J. shook his head in sympathy over the chinchillan demise, but he worried more about Bun's rapid ascendance to the station of life where the end is nearer than the beginning. A fellow always sees the marks of time on somebody else's face before he recognizes them on his own.

"Can I ask you somethin'?" asked T.J. politely.

Bun nodded. "Sure. I can still listen." They walked across fresh-frozen earth and sat down on a bed of pecan leaves near the main house. All was still, eerily quiet. For several days no carpenters had been around, nor plumbers, nor electricians. Nobody. Spike was gone, too, something about "family business" in California. A chilling gust of wind whipped the tree and a few nuts fell. Bun cracked a couple; the meats were rotten, mummy-shriveled. Bun winced and T.J. noted that his uncle's eyes were the color of dried mustard. He presented his case as Bun listened attentively, whittling a stick. "So you see," said T.J. eagerly, "if you could just advance me enough money to build Melissa a little house down yonder by the creek—I can put it up myself, I know I can—then we can get married and we'll sell her daddy's house and I'll pay you back—with interest. And you'll have an extra guest cabin here on the ranch."

"Well, son," Bun finally said, resting his head against the pecan trunk, "asking me for advice on women is like asking a Baptist preacher the best way to pull your pud. Afore we get practical, we better establish one thing. Do you love this little ole gal?"

"Love?" echoed T.J. "Yessir, I think I love her. Sure do."

"You don't sound too certain. And she's rich?"

"Yessir. Believe so."

"Well, would you love her if she lived in a trailer court on the Mansfield Highway?"

"But she don't."

"It gets mighty tiresome fuckin' a checkbook, son." The old cowboy slowly stood up, straightening his back as if it were a bent nail. With nephew at his side eager for an answer, Bun shuffled across his land, melancholy in December, the grass a frayed gray blanket, the trees almost naked, looking lonely.

"Well, my answer is yes. Hell, yes," said Bun. "You can have a little piece of land. I'd be proud to have you and your little wife livin' here. But . . ."

T.J. waited. The "but" dangled like an unfinished prayer. "But *what?*"

"Spike's done gone," said Bun. He had his head down and the words were muffled. "She ain't comin' back. Don't ask why, 'cause I don't know. Maybe she didn't like the music so she quit the dance."

"She'll be back," insisted T.J. "Y'all *love* each other. Y'all act like little kids."

Bun shrugged and said he was cold. He headed for the yellow house. His eyes were wet, T.J. reckoned from the wind. Inside, Bun unlocked a rolltop desk and found the ledger. "I told you I don't bullshit my blood kin," he said. "I've got to level with you, son. The jar is fresh outta jelly beans. I couldn't loan you a dollar's worth of penny nails." T.J. stared at the accounts book. The list of overdue bills fairly yelled from the page, crying like unfed baby birds. Spike's handwriting had shifted from neat to despair. "You're kidding me, Bun," protested T.J.

Bun was older by ten years than an hour before. He looked at his nephew with the eyes of a hanging judge and he said, quietly, "No." T.J. fell apart. He banged his fist on the ledger and slapped the desk. "Well, shit," he proclaimed. "If you got a rope strong enough for two, let's just hang together out yonder on the pecan tree."

Bun poured whiskey from a crystal decanter. A lot of it. T.J. welcomed the warmth, his only dependable source of comfort. "I'm a jinx," he said. "I don't see much use in tryin' to go on. I fucked up you and Spike. I fucked up Mama and Daddy. I fucked up my whole life."

For a long time Bun stared glumly out the window. Something was needing to be said. When the whiskey was drained he cleared his throat. And when he spoke, he broke open the closet where families hide their secrets.

Upon returning from mass the next Sunday noon, Magda and Peavine discovered their youngest son sitting insolently on the couch in the living room. His fingers drummed against a small metal strongbox held between his knees. "Howdy," he said, cheerful as robins. "How y'all doin'?"

Magda's eyes zoomed in on the box and she said, "We've raised ourselves a thief, Peevie. You just hand that right over, mister."

T.J. smiled. "Sit down, Mama. Sit down, Daddy. This'll only take a minute. I bring news. Item Number One: I'm getting married. Her name's Melissa Craymore."

Magda's eyebrows rose. "A Craymore? I'll see about *that*. She may change her mind when she learns she's caught herself a liar and a crook . . ."

"Mama, *hush*. Number Two: It has finally come to my attention exactly what happened one very interesting afternoon in 1933. It was on that day, I believe, that you, Mama, got a butcher knife and went out to the Arlington Downs Race Track to kill Daddy. I also believe that you stole a car, knocked down a tree, got arrested, and dropped a bouncing baby boy—yours truly—in a cornfield. Then, I hate to use this word in the bosom of the family, but you *blackmailed* Daddy here into stayin' home and keepin' yore mouth shut."

Peavine's hand flew to his heart and he sank deep into a floral wing chair, fanning his face with the *Reader's Digest*. Magda tried smiling and purring. "T.J., honey, I've got a real nice pot roast. I'm going into the kitchen to make lunch. Why don't you lie down in your old room and rest a spell."

"Number Three." T.J. opened the strongbox, its lid twisted like a crumpled fender by his screwdriver. "I have here a notarized letter from one Victor (Peavine) Luther, dated August 27, 1933, repenting of his sins and promising to pay his lawful wife, Magdalena Carmella Alicia Gomez Luther, the sum of two hundred dollars a month until her death for 'mental anguish' suffered by her and her newborn son. Number Four: I show you a passbook from the Fort Worth National Bank in the name of Magdalena Luther, Trustee for Thomas Jeremiah Luther, which in twenty-six some odd years has accumulated to the current balance of, ah, $54,617.42."

At mention of the sum, Peavine wheezed. Magda squealed and rushed to her husband, mopping his brow. "Your daddy's having a heart attack," she accused. "Is that what you want? You come home on Holy Sabbath to kill your daddy?" T.J. glanced brusquely, diagnosing guilt and astonishment, not cardiac disturbance. "Lastly. Number Five. Pay close attention to this. I may well be semi-crazy. In fact, I always wondered why I get more'n my share of shit from the dump truck of life. But I do believe I have solved that riddle. Yessir. And as reward, I further believe it is time for my mama to give her little boy some long overdue medicine to heal his . . . uh . . ." T.J. read from the letter, ". . . *mental anguish*."

At 9 a.m. sharp Monday, the moment the bank opened its doors, T.J. rushed inside and deposited a check for $25,000 and waited for it to clear. "I'm not greedy, Mama," he had told Magda when she wrote the payoff with trembling paw. Her only proviso was that T.J. sign a letter promising that he would never speak, write, communicate, or show his felonious face to his parents. T.J. considered this the most edible dish ever prepared by Magda Luther.

On an exceptionally lovely piece of sloping land, amid a protective grove of oak and willow, beside a clear and lazy creek, far enough from Bun's yellow house to be totally private, T.J. began to build the cottage where he would temporarily install a bride. For two months, T.J. sawed and nailed and framed, learning as he went, aided by a crew of Mexican wetbacks hired for seventy-five cents an hour. Missy was around most days, drawing sketches, usually happy as a child in the sandbox. But more and more there came sudden tantrums, mood swings unexpected as cuss words in a sermon. And they always resulted in T.J. spending more money. An unplanned second bathroom was, Missy decreed, *vital*. The north side of the house, where her art studio would be contained, *had* to be moved three feet because the light was not quite perfect. She made him cut down a fine stand of cedar trees. The kitchen doubled in size. The original $8,000 he planned to spend soared past $14,500. He relished the rare days when Missy stayed away from the construction site, shopping for fabrics or meeting with the family lawyer concerning probate of the Craymore estate. It had been ensnarled in rigmarole for almost two years. Melissa was close-mouthed about her legacy, mentioning only that "it takes time" to excise the legal thorns that grow on a grave.

In late January 1960, a new decade began and the house was nearly done. T.J. concocted a celebration, a delayed Christmas. He cut down a spindly, misshapen little pine tree in a corner of his lot, festooned the spare limbs with two dollars' worth of ornaments from Woolworth's, lit logs in the new fireplace, and spread a blanket on the still splintery floor. Bun was invited, but he had left the ranch a week before, mumbling something about a trip to Houston for "refinancing." In his wake, he left a bottle of Chivas Regal for the special night.

Emotion and the pride of accomplishment filled T.J. He felt as good as a man could ever hope to feel. Mellow whiskey in his veins, a fine fire in a hearth laid with his own hands, a rich and noble girl who loved him. T.J. looked at Melissa and raised his glass. "I really love you," he said, and he thought to himself: I think I mean it. They disagreed only on the nature of their wedding, which was planned for

April. T.J.'s scheme was a rite commensurate with his new stature and the social caste of his betrothed. He envisioned a pageant attended by hundreds, a half page in the newspaper, a mountain of gold and silver gifts. Conversely, Missy wanted to slip quietly away to Mexico, marry in secret, reveal the surprise later on.

At midnight, T.J. shyly plucked from the branches of the tree a black velvet box. "It'd be bigger," he said, "if you hadn't insisted on a second toilet." Missy squealed over the engagement ring and put it on her finger. She held it in the glow of the fire. Not much was there to sparkle. "It's a quarter carat," said T.J. "But every year from here on out, it's guaranteed to double."

Missy ran outside to fetch a gift for him from the trunk of her Olds. The package she toted to the tree was large and heavy and wrapped in paper sketches of the cottage under construction. "Hurry!" urged Missy, eyes wide with anticipation.

When T.J. tore the wrappings off, he saw it was a Stetson hat box. An old unasked question from the Assembly Ball popped right out. "Hey, is it true yore daddy used to keep his money in a box like this?"

Melissa looked offended. "How come you're always putting my daddy down?" she asked. Before T.J. could defend himself—he had never said doodledee-squat about Wyman Craymore—she got hot. "My daddy was a great man," said Missy. "You want *evidence?* I'll give you evidence. You know all those stuffed animals in our living room? Well, he didn't kill them. He went to Africa and bought them already dead. He had respect for life. Somebody had to provide those animals a good home."

T.J. nodded uneasily. "That's real generous of yore daddy," he said, wondering how this unasked skeleton crashed the party. "Can I open my present now?"

"Wait," ordered Missy. Her voice was now icy cold. "Daddy spent his money on charity. He even bought me. Did you know that?"

"What does that mean, hon?"

"Well, it's all in the family archives, mister. So do your homework."

"That's interesting," said T.J.

"Why haven't you opened your present? It's Daddy's blessing for our marriage."

T.J. lifted the lid and drew back in flash shock. But Melissa commenced to laugh so heartily that he figured there had to be a joke somewhere he didn't quite get. He managed a few ha-ha's but the fact of the matter was he didn't see a goddamn shred of humor in her gift. It was a dead stuffed cat, Delano. She had gussied up the murdered puss with a red velvet ribbon around its neck and taws the color of blood stuck newly in its eye sockets.

CHAPTER FIFTEEN

"So much tragedy," said VeeJee Cantrell fifteen years later. She led Calvin Sledge once more into the room where she kept her son's papers. "When I look back at things," she said, "it seems that Luther family must have been cursed." She knelt and began opening and sniffing cardboard cartons as if they were plastic containers of food stored on the back shelf of her refrigerator. "I think you've got everything that's the least bit important," she said. "The rest of this is duplicates."

"Please, Mrs. Cantrell. I need to look at everything."

VeeJee nodded. She slumped against the wall and looked, in her pink nylon bathrobe, like a refugee from a midnight fire. "I forgot what I'm looking for," she said. "You know how old you are when you can't remember one minute to the next just why you come into a room."

"*Anything* you can find about T. J. Luther," the District Attorney reminded her. "Surprisingly, he's the one I know the least about."

"That little devil," said VeeJee, rummaging again. She stopped and thought and something came to mind. "I told you about the time T.J. came running over here in the middle of the night, didn't I?"

Sledge shook his head.

"Well, Lord, I've forgotten exactly when. Don't pin me down. Years ago. I remember he wanted Kleber's telephone number down in Houston. I wouldn't give it to him, of course. He was wild-eyed drunk, waving his arms and acting crazy. It was not long after he married that Craymore girl."

"That would be the spring of 1960."

"If you say so. His uncle, the one they called Bun, the poor man had shot himself in Houston. Terminal liver cancer. He walked out of M. D. Anderson Hospital and sat down on the front steps and put a gun to his mouth. . . . Then the bank foreclosed on that ranch property where T.J. was building a house. I think it burned down. Yes, I remember now. There was talk that T.J. set his own house on fire. . . ."

Sledge already knew that. One of the several entries on T.J.'s police record was the notation of arrest for questioning on suspicion of arson. No charges had been filed. The prosecutor also knew that Peavine Luther suffered a cerebral hemorrhage soon thereafter, lingering almost a year in a world without speech or movement. Magda had cared for him at home until, worn beyond hope, she dressed her husband in a dapper linen suit, lifted his frail body, carried him to their automobile, affixed a garden hose from the exhaust pipe into the barely cracked window. She pressed him against her massive breast until both slept forever. Their wills specifically excluded T.J., stating, "Our fourth son, Thomas Jeremiah Luther, is disinherited."

"I just can't think straight anymore," said VeeJee. "I'll go through these papers first thing tomorrow."

"Please," begged Sledge. "There's no time. Would you let me look?"

The old woman gave assent and went away to sleep. Sledge sifted and speed-read and tortured his eyes until, near dawn, he came across a letter. Scribbled hurriedly, in a wild hand on lined notebook paper, it was from T.J. He seemed whirling close to the edge.

April Fool, 1960

Dear K — Remember me? This is from T.J. your best friend. I need help, buddy. So much SHIT is going on I can't begin to tell you and they're probably reading my mail. You cud writ a *big* story on this. Conspiresy. K, believe me, I didn't do *anything*. Not one fucking thing, and they say I burned down my house. My wife, Melissa Craymore, maybe you heard of her name, she got real sick and had to go back to the sanitarium. I didn't make her sick. Her lawyers say I did and I'm supposed to pay her doctor bills. Please, K, PLEASE. Everybody's dying and they'll kill me next. Send me your phone number and I'll tell you something to win another prize or 2. Your best friend, T.J. P.S. Don't give out my address. *Promise.* I'm living out at Bun's old place near Weatherford. I'm sure you remember. Ha Ha. I'm fixing it up nice and we'll have another party. Come see me. But we won't invite shit ass Mack.

Sledge was disappointed. There was nothing in this loony tune that connected two disparate lives, no bridge from the innocence of youth to the horror of twenty-five years thereafter. The DA would not have even taken the letter with him for further study had a second piece of paper not been paper-clipped beneath. It was a yellowed clipping, neatly pasted onto a piece of white typing paper. Obviously Kleber intended to keep it. Puzzled, Sledge read it twice:

SAN ANTONIO, DEC. 4, 1960 (AP)

Bexar County deputies last night arrested a 48-year-old mechanic who confessed to a string of burglaries. They then got an unexpected bonus—a confession to a sex murder allegedly committed more than ten years ago.

The suspect, Raleigh (Butch) Sawyer, said his conscience had been troubling him. According to his statement, Sawyer said he picked up a teenage girl hitchhiker on a farm road near Weatherford, Texas, in May, 1950. A heavy storm was in progress.

"I forced the girl to have sex with me and I threw her out of my truck."

Sawyer told deputies. "She was dead. I was drunk and didn't mean to kill her." Weatherford authorities confirm that a girl named Laurel Killman disappeared in May, 1950, and presumably drowned. Her body was never recovered. Sawyer is being held on $25,000 bond.

Well, Sledge asked himself, what the hell does *that* mean? Did Kleber write the article? Probably not, the dateline being San Antonio; there was no by-line, either. Then why did he keep it? And why did he make it *special* by pasting it on a piece of paper? He had not done such a thing with any of his other clippings. And why attach it to the bizarre letter from T.J.? Maybe it got slipped under the paper clip by mistake. Then something on the margin caught the prosecutor's eye. He held the paper to the light. It appeared that once there had been handwriting alongside the news clipping. But it had been erased.

Impulsively, Sledge put T.J.'s letter and the clipping into his briefcase. Maybe the crime lab could sprinkle wizard dust and bring back the erasures. He tried to steal quietly out the front door but the old woman intercepted him. "Did you find anything?" she asked.

"Not much."

"You didn't take anything, did you?"

"No, ma'm." Sledge felt guilty but he could not risk a scene.

"Every word my son wrote is precious to me," she said.

"I know that."

Rose Webb, a technician in the Fort Worth police crime lab, took the news clipping from the district attorney and bore it with gloved hands to a worktable. It would take several hours just to test the paper and determine what chemicals she dared use in an attempt to restore the erasures. "I haven't got several hours," said Sledge. "I've got five minutes."

"I may eat a hole in it," warned Rose.

"Come on, honey, just do your thing."

Rose sprayed an aqueous solution of tannic acid on the margin. She held the paper under a sensor light, her eyes at the edge, peering from a narrow angle. "Best I can make out is something like *'Tell Mack? Yes.'* And just below, it says, *'Tell T.J.'* Question mark."

"That's it?" asked Sledge.

Rose nodded.

"What the fuck does that mean?"

"It sounds like whoever wrote this was debating whether to inform somebody named Mack about the contents of this newspaper clipping. Apparently the decision was yes. But whether T.J. got the message is for him to know and you to find out."

BOOK FIVE

🔷🔷🔷🔷🔷🔷🔷🔷🔷🔷🔷🔷🔷🔷🔷🔷🔷🔷🔷🔷🔷🔷🔷🔷🔷🔷

THE
PRINCES
REIGN

People that seem so glorious are all show;
Underneath they are like everybody else.

—EURIPIDES, 426 B.C.

CHAPTER SIXTEEN

The two punks slapped the rich woman until she fell blubbering to her knees. One of them held a knife that glinted in the final shaft of cold winter sun as it slipped behind the apartment houses along Central Park West. Pepe sliced through the woman's shoulder strap and seized her purse. His partner, Spider, yanked a gold necklace from the victim's throat and kicked her viciously in the kidneys. Like a rotten log, the woman rolled down an embankment strewn with the brilliant leaves of autumn. Her dog, a toy apricot poodle with a jeweled collar, ran to the broken body and barked heroically, alerting an elderly couple strolling into the park at the Eighty-first Street entrance.

Pepe and Spider changed direction and raced deeper into the woods, toward the Ramble, where they intended to discard the purse and wait for someone else to violate. But they made a mistake in routing. Just as the two muggers bolted across a park service road, Mack Crawford rode by on a bicycle. He braked but collided with Spider. The huge athlete flew over his handlebars and knocked the punk flat. Both sprawled onto the pavement.

In fury, Spider cursed and scrambled nimbly upright with his knife in hand. He stabbed the air but Mack caught his pale wrist and squeezed until the blade clattered to the ground. Pepe ran over to help his friend, but upon seeing that Mack Crawford was six feet four and carried 220 pounds and was mad as hell, prudently detoured toward a small lake. First flattening Spider with a savage right cross, Mack secured the thief to his bicycle with the chain lock, then loped after the accomplice. In his gray sweat suit, Mack resembled a maniacal jogger, chasing Pepe onto the stage of the amphitheater where Shakespeare is performed. With a flying tackle, Mack brought the thief down, almost cracking his shin bones. But as the mugger fell, Pepe located a .22 pistol in his jacket pocket. The two men rolled together and crashed into a surrealistic bronze metal willow, a piece of scenery for *A Midsummer Night's Dream.* The tree toppled and gave Pepe the opportunity to push his gun into Mack's face. Just as his finger touched the trigger, another gun fired. And in the center of Pepe's forehead, a small hole appeared. The third eye began to bleed as the seventeen-year-old boy trembled and died.

From the pit below the stage, a man in a business suit vaulted ungracefully onto the boards. He was a plainclothes cop, about forty, with a sweet face stunned by the tragedy that the just-fired gun in his hand had wrought. "You okay?" asked the man as he hurried over to Mack.

"Yeah. Think so," answered Mack. He struggled out of the dead boy's embrace and tried to speak a fitting epitaph. Nothing came out. Mack furrowed his brow, concentrated, bit his lower lip, began to giggle, broke into laughter, sat back down on the stage. At that, the detective broke and joined him in lunatic giggling. The dead Puerto Rican also rose and, laughing, wiped the blood from his forehead.

"All right, you clowns, *cut,*" yelled the voice of Paul Caper, director of television's high-rated series "Knights of New York." A devotee of cinéma vérité, Caper had shot the entire four-minute sequence in one fluid take—mugging, encounter, pursuit, capture, execution—with hand-held cameras. Everything played until the very end, when Mack was supposed to glance at the corpse, the stage, and the empty theater, murmuring an homage to the Bard—"All's well that ends well."

"I'm sorry, Cap," apologized Mack. "I went up. All I could think of was 'Good night, sweet Puerto Rican.'" The director said it was a wrap. The light was gone anyway. He could shoot the tag line tomorrow. An audience that averaged 22.4 million people did not tune in each Wednesday night at nine to hear Mack Crawford's elocutionary eloquence. For two years the show had succeeded on the simplest of dramatic terms, good versus evil, a weekly triumph of heroism filmed in gritty black and white, laced with action and littered with death. The chemistry of Mack and his co-star, Clifford Briton, was admired. They portrayed homicide detectives assigned to the Central Park precinct.

Their relationship was the time-tested maestro and protégé. Briton, the older man, wiser, analytical, each week spent his patience trying to rein Mack's callow and impulsive rookie exuberance. Deftly woven in was a running subplot that ensnared Mack each Wednesday night with the wrong woman.

She was sometimes a dancer with the New York City Ballet who by hour's end had pirouetted out of Mack's grasp into the clutches of art/ambition, or a divorcée who inflamed the young cop but dumped him to marry a Scarsdale broker, or a poetry major at NYU who told the detective he had the intellectual capacity of a yam. Audiences (the demographics revealed more men than women) found appeal in the plight of a superbly formed hero who always cleared the territory of rustlers but who couldn't get the time of day from the schoolmarm. Female fans were said to relish particularly the show's opening montage, featuring Mack churning bare-chested and in gym shorts around the park reservoir, leaping across a pile of rowboats in dry dock, obviously performing his own stunts. A Gallup poll of the ten most recognizable male faces in America for the year 1963 positioned Mack Crawford as number seven. As his popularity increased, Cliff Briton's seemed to wane. Rumors held that the co-star had been complaining to the show's producers about his shrinking role.

At the end of the mugging sequence, Cliff entered Mack's dressing trailer, a contraption of luxury and convenience but thin walls. Elevated voices were overheard. Mack's makeup girl skipped out quickly, her fingers stuck in her ears. Then Cliff Briton left in obvious irritation. The "Knights of New York" had conducted a verbal jousting, but the subject was not apportionment of lines and close-ups.

Mack lived in an eleven-room duplex only a few blocks down Central Park West from the shooting location, but he was unable to walk. A limousine waited, as it did twenty-four hours a day, the only method by which Mack could traverse from point A to point B. So intense had his celebrity become that fans were threats to life and limb. At the birthday party for President John F. Kennedy in Madison Square Garden that year, attended by stars the caliber of Marilyn Monroe and Frank Sinatra, Mack was spied trying to slip discreetly into a side entrance on Fiftieth Street. A mob of howling young women blocked his passage, ripped off his tuxedo jacket and clawed at his shirt trying to steal his cuff links. His only option was flight. Mack hightailed it east to Eighth Avenue, turned uptown, and like an unwilling Pied Piper threatened by the children, escaped entrapment only by diving gratefully into a passing black-and-white police car, a real one, unamused by the delight of the two rescuing officers who would have a tale to tell the little woman that night. The Law delivered Mack to his apartment house and escorted him through the fans who were always growing around the entrance, unwanted, like scraggly bushes that defied weed killers. The police deposited Mack in the elevator and waited until the doors shut safely, sending the threat to public order up to his aerie. Eighteen floors up, Mack stripped out of his shredded tuxedo and washed the lip prints off his cheeks. He ate a frozen dinner and drank a large glass of scotch whiskey. He was annoyed less by the attack of fans than by missing Kleber once again. The main reason he had accepted the Kennedy birthday party invitation was to rendezvous with his old friend. Kleber was writing a profile on the President for the New York *Times Magazine.*

The Prince of Power had moved from Houston to New York just one year ago but already was becoming an admired and valued writer on the national scene. He was rarely in the city. For several months, Mack and Kleber had been arranging quiet let's-catch-up dinners that never came to pass. It was the writer, not the actor, who had the more difficult schedule. And it irritated Mack that Kleber canceled in favor of some power broker like Clark Clifford, whose celebrity quotient was light-years less. Mack Crawford was one of the most popular men in the United States, but he spent most nights alone, wandering onto his terrace and surveying the twinkling splendor of Manhattan, a party he was unable to attend.

Arnie Beckman waited in the limousine beside Mack's trailer in Central Park. When the actor, still wearing the sweat-suit costume, entered the Cadillac, Arnie proceeded immediately to business. His lap contained a stack of scripts, memos, and legal correspondence. On this October dusk, Arnie worked hurriedly, for he could see that his client was shredded by strenuous shooting and by another flare-up with Cliff Briton. He handed Mack a sheaf of financial documents.

"What's this?" asked Mack.

"That tax shelter stuff we talked about," said Arnie. "You're buying an apartment house in Baltimore. Just sign." Mack scribbled his name obediently.

"Tomorrow during the lunch break you're going to City Hall. The Mayor is giving you some award for promoting the image of New York. Saturday you're doing that *Vogue* layout. And Sunday *Look* is going to take those pictures of you at the Giant game. Here's the schedule." He handed Mack a neatly typed agenda that covered every waking hour for the next several days. "Now, NBC went up to three thousand per show. They say it's their final offer."

Mack interrupted. "Arnie, can we wait on that? I haven't decided . . ."

"We get thirty-three guaranteed weeks, twenty-five percent of world syndication, which doesn't mean shit right now but which may later on, and fifty percent ownership of the negatives after five years. I think they'll go to five thousand."

Mack had refused thus far to sign for a third season on "Knights of New York" and the press was covering negotiations as a major news event. The *Wall Street Journal* had even asked Kleber if he would write a piece, but the reporter declined. He felt privately that it was obscene for an actor to make more money than the President of the United States. But of course he could not tell Mack that. In this afternoon's New York *Post,* Earl Wilson speculated that NBC, in order to accommodate Mack's unprecedented salary demands, might drop co-star Clifford Briton and reassemble the show around one knight.

What the press did not know was that Mack was profoundly weary of his series and his stature. He wanted to take six months off during which he intended to return to Fort Worth and visit his son Jeffie, now almost three. And after that, if he even returned to show business, he planned to accept an ensemble role in a low-budget motion picture. The part did not require him to take off his shirt or appear in his underwear. He would speak intelligent words, portray a schoolteacher counseling a homicidal student, and make $150 a week. It had all happened too fast. Mack was a star before he was an actor. Now he had an acute case of feeling unworthy. He had hinted of this to Arnie, but the agent was less inclined to permit his client a few steps backward than the owner of Citation would have been toward letting his horse run at a county fair.

The limousine pulled up in front of the apartment house canopy where several score youngsters, mainly pubescent girls, squealed and raised their cameras. Two policemen on horseback were keeping a path open for Mack to enter his building.

"I'll wait down here," said Arnie. "Your tux is laid out on the bed."

Mack groaned. He had forgotten about the Broadway play opening. His legs hurt and he wanted to turn in early. His call the next morning was 6 a.m. He asked Arnie for the night off.

"Not possible," said Arnie. "You're expected. We're picking Allison up at six-fifteen." Allison Visioni was another of Arnie's clients. She was an Italian model who had made the transition from Via Veneto to Madison Avenue and was now preparing to try movies, provided she learned English and did something about her flat chest.

"You take her," suggested Mack.

"I don't need to take her," said Arnie. "I don't need to be seen with one of the world's most beautiful and desirable women."

"I'm gonna take a Nembutal, Arnie. And I'm gonna take the phone off the hook. And I'm gonna take a long if not permanent vacation." Mack climbed out of the door and sliced like a golden knife through the adoring crowd. Arnie Beckman was irritated but he knew not to press his luck. He dared not antagonize Mack further during these critical negotiations over contract renewal. He dismissed the limousine and started walking west. At the back entrance of the apartment house, where trucks make deliveries and garbage cans are stacked, Arnie paused momentarily, long enough to catch the eye of a young Latino in a maintenance uniform. The agent nodded imperceptibly at the youth, who caught the signal, loitered briefly, made an excuse to his superior, then followed Arnie all the way over to Riverside Park. There the two men talked urgently and money changed hands.

From the night that Arnie Beckman heeded the "Bears Love You" commercial on Dallas–Fort Worth television, he knew he finally held the ace of trumps. And about time. Until that fateful moment, Arnie had begun to feel the deck was stacked against him, even though he knew how to play the game. Born in the Catskill village of Liberty, the son of a waiter at the Concord Hotel, Arnie quit school at thirteen and started hustling. By day he toted guests' luggage at Brown's, one of the resorts in the mountains above New York whose clientele was largely Jewish and whose raison d'être was to provide a hunting preserve for young men and women. At night Arnie toured the hotels, slipping into the showrooms and catching every comic, writing the best jokes on a note pad. These he used to elicit substantial tips from his hotel's guests, showing some Jewish American Princess to her chamber and, depending on his mood, playing Milton Berle or Henny Youngman or Shecky Greene. The guests usually laughed at Arnie. By the time he was eighteen, he augmented his income by providing after-hours booze stolen from the hotel's stock, marijuana for the rare guest who requested the still novel drug, dildoes, vibrators, and, on one occasion, two quarts of Crisco. Over a good summer's work, he averaged $200 a week, most of which he lost on trotters at Monticello Raceway. Then he tried performing, but he failed to amuse patrons of unfashionable mountain inns or bottom-of-the-barrel catering houses in Brooklyn. Oh, his material was good, lifted as it was from masters, but Arnie, who billed himself Eddie Best, was unable to manufacture an identity of his own.

Very well, reasoned Arnie. If he could not perform, then he would produce, deciding to learn the business by serving at an unusual apprenticeship. He worked for two years as legman for a "column planter." Hilly Trip, a press agent of sorts, was a unique Broadway shadow who created a cottage industry out of gossip. People who wanted to be in, say, Dorothy Kilgallen's column, paid Hilly Trip, who had cultivated over the years a working relationship with the purveyors of rumor and revelation, so close in fact that he offered a money-back guarantee to any name he failed to plant. The secret of his success was that Hilly usually provided a columnist with two or three items of legitimate news, tucking in his client amid them. Arnie was one of several ambitious young men to whom Hilly paid five dollars for each usable piece of gossip. At any Broadway opening in the mid-1950's, Arnie could have been seen in the pre-curtain and intermission throngs in front of the theater, mingling, listening, scribbling surreptitiously with an inch-long pencil stub inside his pants pocket what Arlene Francis said to Josh Logan about Elia Kazan. Not only did Arnie know all the mouths worth listening to, he usually managed to see the second act of every Broadway show, slipping in after intermission. Although nobody knew his name, Arnie was a festival of intimate information. He was both seller and keeper of the secrets.

One night, at the opening of *Damn Yankees,* Arnie was hovering at the elbow of producer David Merrick when the warning buzzer for the second act sounded. A young man in a thin raincoat slammed a thick manila envelope into Arnie's belly. "Please," the young man pleaded with an air of desperation, "give this to Mr. Merrick." The stranger, whose name was Chauncey Hourman and who was the garden variety species of starving playwright, mistook Arnie Beckman for an aide-de-camp of the successful producer. Well, Arnie did not give the play to David Merrick because he did not know David Merrick. But that night on the subway to the Bronx, Arnie glanced at Chauncey Hourman's labor. It was entitled *Mirror Man,* and Arnie instinctively felt it was the best American drama since *A Streetcar Named Desire.* He located Chauncey Hourman in a cold-water flat on the Lower East Side, told him that David Merrick hated the play. "Merrick is wrong," said Arnie. "I think it has slight possibilities. If you'll give me a free option for six months, maybe I could put together a workshop production." Eagerly, Chauncey Hourman agreed. He further aided the career progress of Arnie Beckman by suffering the dramatic misfortune of walking in mid-Manhattan one afternoon when a piece of construction material fell from forty-two stories up. Chauncey Hourman not only died, he died intestate. There was no need for Arnie to extend his option of *Mirror Man.* Fate gave him a free ride.

For three years, Arnie tried in vain to raise the $50,000 necessary to produce the play. He was reduced to resuming legwork for Hilly Trip and one night outside the Winter Garden Theater overheard David Rockefeller mention the "astonishing recklessness" of Texas investors. Using his last $300, Arnie thereupon flew to Houston and raised $2,500. He tried Dallas next and found no funds there. But he watched television at a motel.

When Mack Crawford arrived in New York City on a Greyhound bus, Arnie was waiting for him at the Port Authority Bus Terminal. The two men walked up Forty-second Street, turned left on Broadway, and entered the theater district. Mack read the marquees, *Sweet Bird of Youth, The Miracle Worker, A Taste of Honey.* He had never even seen a play, and now Arnie was going to make him the star of one. While Mack gawked, people stopped and looked. Deeply tanned, clad in jeans, a red plaid cowboy shirt, and carrying a duffel bag marked "UT Athletic Dept.," Mack radiated masculinity and power. He towered a full foot over Arnie Beckman. As Mack left Sardi's restaurant, where he happily signed a three-year management contract, the crowd of professional autograph seekers outside asked for the big man's signature, assuming he was a western star from Hollywood.

"When do we start rehearsals?" asked Mack during the twenty-block walk uptown to the West Side YMCA, where Arnie had booked him a room.

"Couple of days," lied Arnie. "You just rest and work out and trust me." He gave his client a twenty-dollar bill to cover "expenses."

Over the next several weeks, for it would be months before *Mirror Man* went into rehearsals, Mack discovered certain facets of his character whose value he had not fully realized. He took and passed a course in sexual economics. At first he was an unwilling matriculate. In the prison of a YMCA room six feet wide and nine feet long, sleepless on an iron cot from which his feet protruded, Mack was miserable. He felt thoroughly sorry for himself, a morose exile from the hometown where everybody knew his name and from the comforting attention of a wife.

The night he hit New York, Mack telephoned Susan and was disappointed when she answered in a strong and cheerful voice. He had imagined her to be the prisoner of tears and loneliness. He had anticipated that she would be contrite over the breaking of their marriage. Once again he apologized for the "farce" in Acapulco and blamed Catalina Bowman. Surely, repeated Mack, Susan realized that the fault was not his.

"She's not the problem," said Susan from 1,500 miles away, from the house where Mack had lived for almost twenty-six years. "When you figure out who you are, my darling, then maybe we can talk." Click.

Mack read the script of *Mirror Man*. It was the drama of a fifty-eight-year-old spinster and took place on the last night of her life. As she prepared to commit suicide, the woman remembered several men from her past. There were tedious men and empty men and lying men, all of whom she had loved for a moment and sent away. After each memoir, the woman looked into her dressing mirror and saw the man of her dreams. This man never spoke, and when the despairing woman reached out for him, he disappeared, as dreams do. When several dozen sleeping pills thickened her senses, she threw a cold-cream jar against the mirror. The glass cracked, but the mirror man remained somehow perfect, laughing, unobtainable. "Take my word for it," Arnie Beckman had said, "you were born to play this part."

Wherever he ventured in New York, people looked at him. It was not a new experience, for Mack had known since puberty and pimples that his stature and countenance commanded attention. A man figures out fairly early on what he's got and what it can get him. But by his own introspection, Mack had never used the gift of beauty as currency. Only Cat Bowman had made the crude suggestion that he was for sale. At the YMCA, Mack could not find a mirror that reflected him alone. There always seemed to be someone else lurking in the background when he combed his hair or lifted weights or dried his body after a workout. At night he could not even open his door and break the oppressive summer heat in the cubicle. If he did, a procession of uninvited men stopped at the portal and boldly waited until Mack kicked the door shut in disgust.

When he telephoned Susan long-distance again, sweating in a lobby booth for twenty unanswered rings, wondering where his wife could possibly be and with whom, an athletic youth loitered outside the glass door. He was ostensibly perusing the Yellow Pages but he was fondling his genitals provocatively. Mack raised his hand to keep the door of the telephone booth firmly closed and the gold band on his wedding finger glinted like a red traffic light. The youth shrugged and went away.

One afternoon Mack ran a hundred laps on the indoor track, pressed 200-pound weights until his muscles pumped up, pushed his physique in satisfying and painful communion. He swam a thousand yards, churning the water like a 50-hp outboard motor. He peeled off his shorts and, hurriedly wrapping a towel around his body, entered the steam room. No one was there. Mack sat down in a distant corner, welcoming the anonymity of the dense white heat and enjoying the purge. Then an old man came in. He was bald and heavy and fish-belly white, whooshing like a bellows. He went to Mack and sat pointedly beside him. "Please," he said presently, "let me touch you." Mack moved away. "I'll give you twenty dollars," said the man. Mack shook his head and wondered if twenty dollars was his price tag. The door opened again, this time presenting the athletic youth who had molested Mack's telephone call to Susan. Naked, he was a well-formed middleweight who looked alarmingly like T. J. Luther. Going to where Mack sat and standing directly in front of him, the boy began a languorous rite of self-worship, halfhearted calisthenics. His strong hands caressed his body, collecting sweat from his arms and thighs and flinging it to the tiles. Mack pretended not to watch, burying his face in his bunched-up knees, thinking he should get the hell out of this perverted chamber but fearful that the stirring in his own loins would be misinterpreted. He was aroused. "You want it?" whispered the youth, thrusting his penis like a sexual dagger. Mack hissed, "I'm not . . . what you are." The youth said mockingly, "Yeah. I'll bet." Mack secured his towel and started out, just as another man crept into the silent steam.

The newcomer saw the strutting middleweight, sank immediately to his knees, and took sex into his mouth. Dimly through the vapors Mack watched the urgent union, repelled by the sin but envious of sex that was sudden, sex that was hidden, sex that asked no name or commitment.

Later, dressing, another man at the next locker asked, "You play handball by any chance?" The man was carefully hanging up a well-cut checkered sports jacket and flannel trousers. His cordovan shoes were highly polished. He was in prosperous good shape. Mack shook his head, having vowed to punch the next fairy who waved a wand. This guy looked like he knew Whitey Ford's e.r.a. but Mack was wary.

"Too bad," complained the man. "My partner didn't show up. You oughta learn handball."

"I wouldn't mind," said Mack.

"What's that accent?" asked the man. "Georgia?"

"Nosir, Texas."

"Texas!" The man grinned and slipped into a fake drawl. "Podner, ah shoulda known. You look mighty lak one of them hosses on Darrell Royal's defense."

"Well, I played for Mr. Royal," said Mack, pleased at mention of the University of Texas' celebrated football coach. It gave him back his threatened masculinity.

"Then seeing as how I'm from Oklahoma," said the man, who stuck out a strong hand and shook Mack's paw firmly, "it would give me the greatest pleasure to not only teach you the game, but to whip your teasip ass. Name's Paul Caper." They played for two hours. Mack learned the game immediately, performing with less grace than pent-up power, an awesome force who slammed into walls and slapped the ball with such strength that it actually split in half.

That night Paul Caper tried but failed to locate a couple of girls, so they dined stag at Toots Shor's restaurant. The host himself, a potato sack of a man with cheeks broken by whiskey, welcomed Mack, examined him quizzically, went away to insult Phil Harris, returned suddenly and slammed the Texan's shoulders. Toots had finally recognized Mack from the old *Life* magazine cover. He roared at his customers, "Any of you creeps gimme trouble tonight, this here's my new bouncer." It was the best night Mack had spent in weeks. Several sports nuts asked for his autograph; Frank Sinatra signed his napkin; Toots picked up the check for T-bone steaks and half a fifth of scotch. And he had a solid new friend who seemed to like him on unconditional grounds. Paul Caper, learned Mack, was thirty-eight years old, divorced twice, father of an infant daughter who lived in Los Angeles, and a fanatic of the New York Rangers, Knicks, and Giants. He made his living directing shows, a confession that Caper made almost sheepishly. He had never heard of Arnie Beckman, but he wished Mack well on his upcoming Broadway debut.

Soon thereafter, Mack moved out of the YMCA and into a spare bedroom at Paul's apartment. It was a sparsely furnished five-room flat in an old brownstone overlooking Washington Square. The apartment had leather sofas and nautical chests that Caper called "early divorce." It was littered with scripts, unwashed clothes, and had a manly, messy ambiance. Paul found Mack a job waiting tables at a steak house near NYU and got him into acting classes conducted by an ancient Greek actress named Maya Pandokis. The old crone asked Mack to stay one night after class was over. She bade him read a speech from *Desire Under the Elms,* listening quietly as his Texas accent wrapped uncomfortably around Eugene O'Neill's New England passions. When he was finished, Maya, several inches shy of five feet, ordered Mack to lift her for visual parity.

"Please listen, child," she said. "I teach you only lesson you need for theater." Mack felt considerably foolish, holding the old rag doll in his arms. He grinned nervously. "Stop being happy," she commanded. "I did not hear what you read. I only look at you. You are the most beautiful man I have ever seen." Mack laughed. Maya slapped his face, hard, her old fingers stinging him like whips. "You are fraud," cried the teacher. "You know why I hit you? I hit you because I do not believe your modesty. You will never be good unless you believe you are ugly. People are threatened by beauty. I would give you a blessing if I scratched your face. You must play against your curse."

"I don't understand," said Mack.

"Of course not," said Maya, shaking her head in melancholy. "Neither did Narcissus."

"Ma'm?"

"A Greek boy you should know. He loved himself so much that he could not give himself to anybody. He tried to kiss his reflection in a pond. He drowned. As the gods intended."

Arnie Beckman was forced to take a major risk. He had been unable to raise the capital to produce *Mirror Man* and now his discovery was slipping away from him. Mack had grown cool on the telephone and was rehearsing for a workshop production of some avant-garde piece of crap in an off-Broadway garage. Arnie yelled at Mack that he was contractually prohibited from such dangerous exposure but the fledgling actor had hollered back that Paul Caper advised him it wasn't so. "Paul Caper doesn't know shit," warned Arnie. To which Mack said, "He got me out of the YMCA."

One night while lurking under the marquee of the Morosco Theater, Arnie overheard a bit of useful information. The next day he went to the restaurant where Mack was waiting tables and pretended to be bringing a special treat. "You ever been to Fire Island, kid?" asked Arnie.

"No."

"Then it's time you went. There's a party out there Saturday night with some very important people invited. Producers, directors, critics, above-the-title names. You gotta be seen at parties like that."

It did not tax Mack to compute the sexual arithmetic on this particular Saturday night. There were four women visible among the eighty men who congested the house set back in a wooded grove of Fire Island Pines. The walls were lacquer red padded vinyl and glistened from the humidity of so many bodies packed together. Furniture had been taken out and some of the guests were crawling about in the forest of legs. Somebody grabbed Mack and he swatted the unseen marauder like it was a pesky dog. Men wore everything from bathing suits and nothing else to navy blazers from Brooks Brothers with white silk shirts and deftly folded scarves about their necks. Elvis Presley rampaged from a phonograph turned up to the limit. Mack smelled marijuana for the first time in his life. He had to ask Arnie if somebody was burning weeds outside.

Arnie took Mack by the hand and led him through the crowd. They parted the sea. Whistles and murmurs accompanied their progress. Arnie located the host, a small but athletic man in his early forties who was wearing a shirt and a tie and a bikini. His name was Arthur Cossett and he was worth, Arnie whispered, $75 million. Arnie introduced Mack, made small talk over the din, and vanished. He took a taxi down the beach to Fair Harbor, rendezvoused with a secretary from the Shubert Theater organization, fucked her on the beach all night, and stopped now and then to pray.

Meantime, Mack was squirmingly embarrassed. He started to excuse himself. He intended to find Arnie and strangle him. Then Arthur Cossett gripped his biceps. "I suspect you are offended by the cast list at this party," he said quietly. "But you are supposed to be an actor. I would be very pleased if you would stay for the rest of the evening. Just give a performance. You don't have to *do* anything. I promise nobody will bother you. I assure you that it will be worth your while if you stay beside me and make people think . . . whatever they want to think."

Mack stayed the weekend. Arthur Cossett's reputation in his world was enhanced and he paid the bill on Monday morning by putting up the necessary funds to put *Mirror Man* into rehearsal.

Six months to the day that he arrived in New York on a Greyhound bus, McKenzie Crawford made a historic debut in *Mirror Man*. At Sardi's afterward, he received the de rigueur and in this case genuine standing ovation. A few minutes later he covered his ears in disbelief as Arnie Beckman trumpeted an early notice:

" 'When Mr. Crawford materialized in jeans and nothing else, shoulders wide as an ox yoke, a shock of blond hair lit by some inner spotlight, eyes wide and blue as the skies of Texas, a wave of audible electricity jolted the Shubert Theater.' "

Another critic commented, "Mr. Crawford melds the sensuality of Marlon Brando with the aw-shucks, all-American virility of a young Gary Cooper."

In a second but unreviewed debut of the night, Mack Crawford returned to his apartment roaring drunk, carrying a dozen copies of the New York *Times* under his arm. He fell sloppily into bed but could not sleep. He replayed his performance, remembering the curious embrace of isolation that the stage awards an actor. On the football field he was always cognizant of the spectators, they being a primal partner in the conflict. But in the theater he was divorced from the audience, the footlights a tangible barrier between him and them. He knew he was on display and he liked that. He was mothered by the hot lights, protected, sheltered from the beyond which was nothingness.

Sometime during the night he heard the bedroom door open and Paul Caper tiptoe in. He sensed his friend standing over the bed. Mack was sprawled nude on his stomach. "You okay?" whispered Caper. Mack pretended not to hear him. He did not want company. "You need anything?" asked Caper.

"About eight hours of sleep, which I ain't gonna get," murmured Mack. "Arnie wants me at the theater by eight a.m. for publicity pictures."

"You wanna drink?"

"Had too many."

"You wanna compliment?"

"You already gave me one."

"You were good, Mack. You were natural and real and you owned that fucking stage."

"You tell that to all the girls."

"You wanna sleeping pill?"

"No."

"I'll see you in the morning, then."

"Okay. Night." Mack groaned and stopped Caper from leaving.

"You sick, pal?"

"No. Is there any more of that Atomic Balm liniment you rubbed on me that time I got a charley horse playing handball?"

"I'll see."

Mack drifted off in the interim, or thought he did. The next thing that happened was Paul Caper kneeling over his body on the bed, applying salve and baby oil to his sore muscles. It felt stinging cool. He had memories of a hundred locker rooms. Caper's hands were strong. They kneaded Mack's tense shoulders, squeezing out the knots. "Just relax," said Caper. "Relax and let it feel good. So good." Both men began to breathe heavily. Mack buried his face into the pillow, which was a good hiding place. When it happened, he did not protest because he somehow knew it was going to happen. He wondered only if he had invited it.

It hurt. It hurt like hell when Paul Caper slipped his cock into the ass of Broadway's newest star. It hurt so much that Mack bit his lip to keep from screaming. But remarkably soon it felt good. One of the reasons it felt good for Mack was that he gave nothing. He only received. He was a receptacle for others.

Mack moved out a few days later, which he had intended to do anyway, the reviews of *Mirror Man* guaranteeing a substantial run and allowing a step-up in living conditions for its star. Nothing was ever said about what happened sometime between 3 a.m. and dawn on the night Mark Crawford refound celebrity. Nor did it ever happen again between them.

When Paul Caper called several months later to offer Mack the co-starring role in his new television series, "Knights of New York," the conversation was friendship and business. After he accepted the part, Mack cajoled Caper into throwing in a pair of season tickets for the Giant games.

Raoul Martinez lived well in New York City in 1962. The emigrant from Puerto Rico earned seventy-four dollars a week salary as night elevator operator in the Saint Cloud apartment building on Central Park West. On this modest sum, he maintained a three-room apartment of his own in Morningside Heights, had numerous girl friends, and a wardrobe of silk shirts and linen trousers as varied in hues as a macaw's feathers. He mailed thirty dollars a week to San Juan for his mother to buy rum for her belly and digitalis for her heart, and novenas for the soul and flowers for the grave of his father.

To be sure, Raoul Martinez had additional sources of income. Residents on his elevator bank were generous with dollar tips when Raoul toted in groceries or walked dogs in the park or ran speedily over to Columbus Avenue to fetch midnight cigarettes or whiskey. Other tenants depended on his talent for obtaining special items, marijuana being a specialty, and in the case of a world-famous actress-singer on the seventh floor, heroin from Raoul's contacts in Spanish Harlem.

When Raoul Martinez telephoned Arnie Beckman to report on the latest and loudest incident overheard by cautious eavesdropping outside the service entrance of Mack Crawford's duplex, it was in his mind to demand more than the $100-a-week retainer. The way Raoul figured it, Arnie would have to peel $1,000 minimum off his wad for revelation and silence.

CHAPTER SEVENTEEN

When men study their lives, wondering why they turned left instead of right, or, worse, made no turn at all, the momentous decisions often turn out as the children of caprice. Journalists see the evidence every day, those whims that change and shatter existences. Kleber Cantrell reported well the sad tale of a Houston bookkeeper who was estranged from his wife.

The fellow decided one afternoon to leave his office and drive to Memorial Park for a breath of air and to puzzle why his marriage soured. A whim, nothing more. Coincidentally, a male teacher of third-grade children had brought his class to the same park for an unscheduled outing, mainly because the instructor, who had fought with his own wife the night before, had not prepared a lesson and because he had a headache. Follow closely: The bookkeeper spotted his eight-year-old son playing softball, decided to surprise the child by fetching him and treating him at a refreshment stand. The child began to cry and refused to leave the ball game. His turn at bat was next. The father swatted the kid; the teacher rushed over to arbitrate; a passing police car saw an agitated man trying to drag a child from the park. One thing led to another and the tally was tragic: the teacher was shot and killed by mistake, the little boy paralyzed by a misfired bullet that severed his spine, and the father went to prison for two-to-ten.

Kleber stuck on a couple of paragraphs philosophizing about the banality of tragedy, but Casey chopped them off. "Until your collected wisdom is published by the Harvard Press," grouched the city editor, "I would dearly prefer you stuck to the simple Who-What-When-Where-and-Why." But, complained the reporter, "Why" is abstract and subjective, open for rumination. "The next time you quote Heraclitus," said Casey, reading out loud Kleber's summation line about the price of impulsive desire being the loss of a man's soul, "I will have you writing obits until 1984. The reason *why* will be neither abstract nor subjective. It will be as clear as a boot up your ass."

As Kleber ripened and grew in intellect and introspection, he became, despite his city editor's pragmatism, intrigued by men whose ethical posture got an epic squeeze. He envied Sir Thomas More's surrender of head rather than integrity, Hamlet's joust with the inequity of existence, St. Peter's denials and redemption. He wrote to a contemporary idol, the fine South African writer Alan Paton, commending the battered liberal's continuing pricks against the conscience of his country. But the awful truth, alas, was that Kleber Cantrell only fantasized over his thirst to confront a moral crossroads. He failed to recognize a pretty good one when it spilled all over his typewriter; the felony was compounded because this was the caprice that made him a national commodity.

On any given day, on the city desk of any metropolitan newspaper, a thousand telephone calls are answered. At the other end of the line are, more often than not, the nuisances and nuts, the housewife whose neighbor won't cut the grass, the club ladies who cannot see why the sale of dried flowers to finance a new school auditorium curtain is not of page one interest, the press agents, the woebegone complainers against everything and everybody. Reporters stumble through life despairing of why friends and families accuse them of being curt if not rude on the telephone. The complaint is accurate because early in a journalism career one learns to get on and off the phone fast, a practice that slops over to social commerce.

One afternoon in 1960, Kleber stared glumly at five flashing buttons on his telephone, wondering which one to stab, fantasizing that the treasure would be the voice of John F. Kennedy in need of a speech writer. Ever since the Massachusetts senator had burst into national prominence, Kleber was staggered by his elegance and potential. He was ready to abandon the expected neutrality of his profession. Already he had made a minor and unethical contribution to the cause. Casey dispatched his star reporter to some stereotypic Houston neighborhoods—one blue-collar, one middle-class—for a highly unscientific poll, asking whoever answered his knock whether Kennedy or Richard Nixon would get a vote. When he added up the numbers, Kleber gave

JFK three extra percentage points, knowing it was cheating, but reckoning that the scales would balance when the paper's management predictably endorsed Tricky Dick.

He pressed a button and the waiting voice was quite a piece away from Boston. It was hometown, female, brusque, and colored. "My name is Regina Brown," said the caller. "I want a reporter with guts and eyes wide open enough to see something wrong. Are you whom I want?" Normally Regina Brown would have gotten the old heave-ho, a kiss-off, and a promise from Kleber to get back to her. But there was something in this dame's tone, an edge sharp as a tomahawk, a challenge that was provocative. Kleber agreed to meet for coffee. But as soon as he hung up, he regretted not having answered the adjacent telephone button. Millie instead of him was grinding teeth in ecstasy over the tale on line three, the page one story dumped in her lap about a group of Houston playboys who, celebrating the eruption of a wildcat well, stripped naked and drenched each other in crude oil, along with two strippers from Dallas, all winding up in jail and resembling rejects from a minstrel show.

Regina Brown, the sixth daughter and ninth child of a Houston laundress who could not read or write, was twenty-four years old, and, in a contest very close to a dead heat, every bit as beautiful as Ceil Shannon. She was the first colored woman, excluding Lena Horne, at whom Kleber ever really looked. Her skin was burnished gold, the shade desired by white women who bake their bodies in the Galveston sun, and her hair was mahogany, neither kinky, nappy, nor musky, those textures Kleber always assumed were indigenous to the species. They rendezvoused, per Regina's suggestion, at the Rice Hotel coffee shop in downtown Houston. Regina watched the reporter's face stiffen when the hostess, confronting a white man and a tan woman, said she had no available tables. There was, in fact, a half acre of empty tables, it being four in the afternoon. Nonetheless, all were "reserved." Kleber grew argumentative, but Regina whispered that such effort would be in vain. Next they went to Foley's Department Store, where Regina routinely purchased a scarf for eight dollars and plastic earrings for four dollars on the way to the luncheonette. Foley's hostess simply shook her head silently, not bothering to fabricate an excuse.

Kleber was not going to let this happen. He improvised quickly. "My companion is a distinguished poetess from New York and she has just made several purchases in this store. Foley's is delighted to take her money for merchandise. But am I to assume that Foley's will not serve her a cup of coffee? Can that possibly be correct?" The hostess retreated hurriedly toward the kitchen. "Hey, I'm from the press, lady," called out Kleber sharply. "What's your name? I'd like to put it in my story." Regina nodded and pulled the agitated scribe away.

They found service nearby, at a barbecue stand a literal stone's throw from downtown Houston, in a ghetto wedged between the erupting skyline of America's fastest-growing city and River Oaks, the enclave of merchant princes and plantation manors. Kleber had never seen the Fourth Ward, though he worked but a mile away and used to drop his ex-wife's family maid at the edge. Many of the streets within were not even paved; the dust from passing autos shrouded sagging frame houses that looked like moonshiner cabins. Children played naked on the roads, dogs roamed mean and hungry, and nothing seemed to grow. In a city pestered by rain and humid air, in a territory where settlers had to chop through jungles of tropical vegetation, here endured a dull gray tumor.

When the couple entered Rocky's Bar-B-Q, a smallish room with pictures of the white Jesus Christ and the black Joe Louis side by side, with gospel music hot and sweet, the owner, who was a mountainous Negro of at least 300 pounds, made Kleber feel less welcome than Regina had been at the Rice Hotel. He set down two mugs of thick chicory coffee and returned wordlessly to a worktable, chopping briskets and stirring fiery red sauce as efficiently as a coroner. With each whack of blade on meat, Rocky looked malevolently at the alien customer. "I think," whispered Kleber, "the boss butcher over there would like to serve my ribs as the Thursday-night special."

"You're probably right," agreed Regina. "He's killed two men I know about. But they were justified and he's on probation right now. He also makes the best barbecue in the South." She went over and fetched two sandwiches overstuffed with tender smoked pork, wrapped in pages from the Houston *Call-Bulletin*. Kleber took one wary bite, sighed ecstatically, and sent a thumbs-up salute to the chef. Rocky glowered and chopped.

"I should tell him you work for the paper," said Regina. "He reads it every night and wraps his sandwiches in it the next day. The *Call-Bulletin*'s very popular with colored people. Did you know that?"

"We can use all the readers we can get," answered Kleber mechanically. Life is indeed a tease, he was thinking. Who could have anticipated that by answering one of five possible flashing telephone buttons, he would a few hours later be sitting—by choice—in a nigger joint, fascinated and perhaps endangered by black beauty? Thus far Regina had not revealed the purpose of the meeting and thus far Kleber had not asked. At the moment he was giving rein to fantasy, playing the plantation owner's son visiting the slave cabins, his possible *droit du seigneur* imperiled only by VeeJee Cantrell's oft-repeated warnings that colored women were repositories of social disease. Nonetheless a quickie in nearby Memorial Park was on his mind, until Regina forced his thoughts to a level less base.

"How come your paper doesn't allow colored people the simple dignity of Mr. or Mrs. or Miss?" she abruptly asked.

"I don't know," said Kleber honestly. "Style, I guess."

She read aloud from her sandwich wrapper:

"Lee William Crown, a twenty-five-year-old negro, was jailed last night on charges that he stabbed his common-law wife, Ruby Mayberry. Crown complained that the Mayberry woman refused to iron his overalls."

Kleber smiled. "Funny you should pick that out," he said. "I wrote it."

"Funny? Permit me a little analysis. Why is it necessary to refer to Lee William Crown as a negro? If Crown were white or Mexican, his race wouldn't be worth mentioning, would it? And if you insist on using the word Negro, it should be capitalized. Like Caucasian. You write that Ruby Mayberry was his common-law wife. Did you ask her?"

Kleber shook his head. The term was on the police report.

"Common-law spouses are legal in the state of Texas and carry the same moral, fiscal, and ethical responsibilities as church weddings. Your paper—and the others as well, I'm not indicting only you—make common-law sound like what niggers do in the cotton patch."

"Wait a minute," injected Kleber. "Is that why you wanted to meet? To complain about my paper's style, something over which I have no influence whatsoever?"

"Partly. Just one more thing. Why refer to Mrs. Crown as the Mayberry woman? It makes her sound like a prostitute."

"Or a Victorian heroine. Hell, I don't know, *Miss* Brown. It's the way things are done. The paper doesn't use Mr. or Miss for white criminals, by the way." Kleber wanted to withdraw that remark but it popped out.

"If I won the Nobel Prize," said Regina, "and forgive me for sounding pretentious, then I would read in Houston's newspapers that the Brown woman went to Stockholm. If, that is, the story even got in. Fifteen percent of the population of Houston is colored, but we do not die by natural causes in your newspapers or marry or win scholarships. What we do is stab, jive, fornicate without marriage certificate, and play policy numbers. That's the image we grow up with—and goddamnit, I want it changed."

Kleber ducked the fire. It was deserved. "It's wrong," he agreed. "I'll bring it up with my city editor."

"Wait," said Regina. "I'm not through. Give me one more hour. I'm not intruding on a wife or children, am I?"

Kleber shook his head. "Not anymore." He wiggled his newly naked wedding finger.

"Sorry. I know what you're thinking. You're saying, 'I've been snookered.' Right?"

Kleber nodded. Not only snookered, but threatened. Rocky's Bar-B-Q was filling with ebony faces and hearty laughs that died the moment they saw him. He wanted out. He called for the check. Regina said the meal was free. He learned why when Regina stopped by the counter and kissed the huge proprietor. "Thanks, Daddy," she said. "I'll be home directly. Don't worry about me."

In a few weeks, under the tutelage of Regina Brown, Kleber became educated in a subject that he sensed had major news value. He worked without asking Casey, listening and learning on nights and weekends. From prior reading of New York newspapers and magazines, he had casual knowledge of the civil rights movement. He knew that a colored woman named Rosa Parks had refused to move to the back of a Montgomery, Alabama, bus in 1955, sparking a boycott and giving birth to the rhetorical rise of a minister named Martin Luther King. But he did not know, until Regina told him, that in 1959 a man named Roman Duckworth, a colored army corporal and MP, refused to sit at the rear of a Trailways bus and was shot to death by a Mississippi peace officer. Duckworth was on emergency furlough, en route to his wife's sickbed. The tragedy had not made the Houston papers. Nor did Kleber know that one month prior to his eating barbecue with

Regina Brown that a group of Negroes in Greensboro, North Carolina, began "sit in" demonstrations in that city's segregated public lunch counters. They vowed not to vacate until given the same service as white customers. "It's gonna work," predicted Regina. "It's brilliant. It's gonna spread like wildfire across the South. Your paper might want to know a storm is headed this way."

Regina was a cunning woman, recognizing that pinpricks can bother a man more than distant cannons. She took him to a third-grade class where fifty-six children sat in crammed and noisy disarray. "By the time I take roll call," she said, "the hour is half gone." The textbooks were ten years out of date; worse, they were hand-me-downs from white schools. She asked Kleber to pick a child, any child, and when his finger stopped on a pretty little girl in a pink pinafore who glowed with apparent health and promise, Regina asked several questions. The child did not know the name of the President of the United States, nor who won World War II, nor the sum of seven plus four. After school, they went to the child's home, where Kleber interviewed her mother. She was preparing supper for eight. The menu was macaroni and corn bread. The night before, spaghetti and mashed potatoes. Beans, white bread with gravy, an occasional treat of fat ribs or possum stew, these were staples. "The human brain must be nourished," said Regina as Kleber made notes. He would fill up a dozen steno pads in three weeks. "If a child is fed starches and carbohydrates because these are cheap, then that child's brain cells are malnourished. That child cannot function at the same level as a Caucasian youngster who routinely eats lean red meat, green vegetables, fresh fruits. Dig?"

"I dig," said Kleber with intended insolence. "Can you back this up?" He knew she could. She did. She tossed him a document commissioned by the NAACP on nutrition and mental capacities. "Some of us niggers *are* shiftless and stupid and lazy," said Regina. "Read these and you'll know why."

Kleber wrote a ten-part series, entitled it "Fire on the Way," and dropped his labor casually on Casey's desk. "What the fuck is this?" growled the city editor. "The Yellow Pages?"

"Just a little bonus from the kid," said Kleber, enormously proud of himself. He invited Regina to his apartment to celebrate that night, and though she had to enter through the rear door prepared to tell anyone who asked she was the cleaning girl, they drank two bottles of red wine and came perilously close to a meaningful embrace. One of those awkward moments between two people who care about each other came to pass. Regina broke the heavy silence by rolling her eyes and sounding like Aunt Jemima. "Law, massa, ah cain't let mah animal instincts make trouble for you'n me. Miscegenation's a felony in this heah state." She laughed and asked to read his work. Quickly she was absorbed, amused at jive talk remembered from Rocky's Bar-B-Q, growing emotional and borrowing a Kleenex over his description of colored children and dead-end lives. He had deftly compartmentalized his series into sections on housing, education, crime, ghetto life, a recent history of desegregation tragedies and triumphs, concluding with an eyewitness report of a CORE chapter forming in Houston with intentions of staging lunchroom sit-ins and, if necessary, violence.

The conclusion was a personal admission, in rare first person, Kleber's painful confession that it had taken him twenty-eight years to discover that the line severing white and black was immoral. "There are rooms in our lives that are dark and locked, and whether out of tradition or fear we do not enter them. But I have learned that unless we throw open these doors and look at the black man and his wife and his child and his mother and his father, unless we realize that their dreams and bellies are no different from ours, unless we accept that a black life is no more alien from a white life than the night is from day, unless we understand that color is the least valuable mark of a man, then the fires of ignorance will sweep over us all."

The next sunrise, when Kleber reported for work, he noticed that his epic was not visible in Casey's box of unedited copy. The city editor was in one of his copperhead moods and it seemed inappropriate to ask for a grade on his term paper. Nor did it surface for several days. A volcanic gas fire erupted near Beaumont and Kleber was dispatched to cover. He telephoned back theatrical descriptions of the flames, hoping that Casey would discern the parallel between this heat and that which his series predicted was coming. Next he was exiled to the Big Thicket, ordered to investigate the report of a Big Foot relative rumoredly stalking through tangled groves of water oaks and sweet gum and mayhaw. Upon receiving the absurd assignment—Big Foot was a hardy perennial in Houston news gathering—Kleber blurted out, "What did you think of my series?" Casey said he had not yet read it. Too much was breaking. The news had just come that John Kennedy was coming to Houston for a campaign appearance with Lyndon John-son. Over a static-filled wall telephone in a tiny outpost grocery, Kleber pleaded, "I'd give half a year's pay to cover it." Casey was cool. He hung up muttering something about politics being the bastion of the Washington correspondent, a dry and colorless writer named Abrams whose work read like a civil service job manual. Kleber telephoned Regina to report the delay but Rocky answered, chilly, blunt, saying his daughter had left Houston and was in Georgia with Martin Luther King.

Back at the paper, in his mailbox, Kleber found his series, encased in a manila envelope and carrying a terse note: "Let's talk. C." But every time the reporter requested a conference, Casey shook him off. One night when everyone was gone, Kleber trapped his boss and said, "I think I deserve an answer." Casey nodded and took off his glasses and rubbed his eyes until they were angry red.

"I know it's long," said Kleber hurriedly. "But there are places we can cut . . . and maybe I got too emotional here and there . . ." He was fumbling for time, knowing now what he had suspected for two weeks. "It's no good, is it?" said Kleber, pronouncing his own condem-nation.

"No," said Casey. "It's not good. It's terrific. It's powerful. It's im-portant. It's got your goddamn sweat and blood all over it. And I'm not gonna run it."

"I guess I need to know why," said Kleber.

"Jesus, son, don't do this to me. Don't make me feel worse than I already do. There is no reason why. If it helps any, the downtown stores are quietly integrating their lunch counters. All your colored friends can sit down tomorrow and eat a tuna fish sandwich."

Kleber brightened. "That's great," he said. "That's a peg for the series."

Casey shook his head. "We're not gonna make note of it," he said. "To quote the editor in chief, 'We don't want Martin Luther King com-ing to town and staging a love feast.' Your fire is out, son."

"On a list of what Negro people want, eating tuna fish at Foley's is about number ninety-five," said Kleber.

"But it's a start," countered Casey. "And if there is trouble in this city, we'll report it. But we ain't gonna prophesy it."

Kleber seized the night final edition on the city editor's desk. An eight-column headline across the belly of page one shrieked: MON-

STERS IN OUR MIDST—BIG FOOT'S BROTHER SPOTTED IN BIG THICKET. The babblings of a lunatic white woman about an imagined black ape were entitled to twenty-four column inches of space. He pointed out the inequity to Casey. "There's no defense for that, son, except that you write it good," he answered. "Nor is there justice or fair play or majesty in much of anything we do. But there *is* economics, and if we ran ten straight days of news from niggertown, I'd expect circulation to drop thirty percent and what few ads we have to dwindle down to peep shows and hemorrhoid ointments."

Kleber made one last defense. A year before, in the summer lull, idling at the cop shop one afternoon, he found an FBI crime report that warned of Houston becoming, proportionately, America's most homicidal city. More for the hell of it than anything else, Kleber assembled a hurried and sloppily researched clump of articles dealing with violence in Houston, focusing on a dozen weekend slayings— mostly of the Rufus Washington-Killing-the-Smith-Woman-with-a-Saturday-Night-Special—loping around the familiar journalistic track of how easy it is to buy a handgun, and slapping on an inspired headline, MURDERTOWN: USA. To Kleber's astonishment, the series was both praised and admired. The conceit of his city was nourished by recognition; excelling in death was as major a blue ribbon as innovation in heart surgery or leadership in bank deposits. The label not only stuck for years; it was perversely valued. A song was even composed and stole Kleber's headline.

How, he demanded, how could his paper so joyously splash a blood-dribbling exploitation of murder on its front pages and now reject a serious and important study of an issue that would change the history of America? Casey was not without sensitivity. Bear that he was, he lumbered through the hours with sorrow in his eyes and pain in his gut over the terrible things people did to one another. He wanted no man to be unfed, no child unlearned, no hurt to linger if there was a balm. But he was also Texan and his answer was honest: "Because when a lot of niggers kill a lot of niggers, and J. Edgar Hoover takes note of it, then it's news." Kleber fumed and snorted and muttered, "I really ought to quit this chickenshit paper."

"You do what you have to do, son," answered Casey. "It would break my fuckin' heart to lose you." He returned to editing overnight copy. Class dismissed. Kleber just stood there glaring, heat creeping up his body like the red line on a thermometer. He was searching for a sledgehammer exit speech but Casey threw a rabbit punch. "Which pisses you off the most?" wondered the city editor. "The plight of the coloreds? Or me not runnin' your splendiferous tome?"

Kleber ducked his confrontation with principle. He did not resign because Casey—damn him to hell and back—was right. The wellspring of anger was indeed rejection of his work, not his beliefs. For several days he cast himself in the imagined role of martyr for the word—Robespierre publishing secret tracts to topple the French throne, Russian dissidents banished to Siberia for intellectual insolence. But all he actually did was show his series to Millie, who affirmed that "Fire on the Way" was somewhere on a scale of polemic excellence between *J'Accuse* and *Uncle Tom's Cabin*. Millie also said, "No paper south of Chicago would publish it."

When Regina checked in from somewhere near Birmingham, speaking in a hushed voice and hinting that the telephone was tapped, Kleber lied. He said that Casey liked his series but wanted it pruned by one third. It would probably run sometime before the presidential election. Regina said she hoped so, because it might help John Kennedy's cause. "Are you okay?" asked Kleber. "I think so," answered Regina. "It's rough, baby. But we're chippin' away. One of these days Jericho's walls are gonna come tumblin' down." Kleber passed on the news that Houston's department store lunch counters had been quietly integrated. "Save me a seat," exclaimed Regina. "In fact, save two of them. You can take Rocky and me to lunch." She hung up suddenly without saying goodbye.

On September 12, 1960, in a meeting room of the Rice Hotel which the day before had contained a convention of hardware dealers, John Fitzgerald Kennedy confronted a hostile pride of lions. His quest for the presidency was endangered by malicious tongues, those who whispered that the Pope of Rome would sit by proxy in the White House, pulling Jack Kennedy's Catholic strings. The principal reason for Kennedy's visit to Houston was a major address in Sam Houston Coliseum that night, but when a sudden press conference before Protestant ministers was announced, Kleber practically stretched out on Casey's desk and threatened to open his veins. "Shit, son, you're as crazy as Kennedy," said Casey. "I'd rather elope with Millie than face a hundred Southern Baptists. Compared to that bunch, Pontius Pilate was the Easter Bunny."

For years thereafter, Kleber carried two sharp images of that broiling suppertime hour in the Rice Hotel. The first was a troubling discount of his personal stature. In Houston the local lad was an acclaimed shark, but Kleber was a guppy at best in the national current. The press corps covering John Kennedy swept into the blue velvet chamber like bulldozers of divine right. Mr. New York Times, Mr. Washington Post, Mr. Newsweek, Mr. Teddy White, all of them carried power that danced like waves of electric shock from their strides and notepads. They pushed past Kleber as emirs would ignore a beggar of alms, occupying the choice positions, perusing the cue-ball faces of the assembled preachers, enjoying the camaraderie of belonging. The room blazed with the hot lights of television cameras, a new and enormously disliked guest at the feast of news. In recent months television developed the capacity to move out of studios, and now technology was turning headline events into bewildering metallic forests with thick cords that coiled on the floor like dens of serpents. The guys with pads and pencils cursed the electronic invasion, sometimes toppling a tripod with a secret kick like an Italian's dead hand pinching a comely ass. Kleber was accustomed to being on the front row of any momentous occurrence in the city of Houston. Today he was straining to see from a corner, co-tenanted by black and brown charwomen. He felt like a hick and a crasher.

When John Kennedy materialized, slicing through hostile territory with a substantial but not altogether believable smile on his face, Kleber was overcome with emotion. The candidate had been speaking several minutes before the reporter collected himself sufficiently to write down the words. It was a new feeling. Kleber had never been particularly dazzled by celebrity. But this was the day he found his hero. He knew he had a hero because he both exalted Jack Kennedy and envied him, envied the hand-tailored suit that Brooks Brothers no doubt sewed on his back, envied the chestnut hair that once brushed at dawn needed no further comb and even tousled looked perfect, envied the slender hands that chopped the air like a conductor's baton, envied the defiance that would tempt a Mick from Boston into the presence of hard-shells who would have stoned Mary Magdalene to death. But most of all he envied Jack Kennedy's youth. Suddenly, alarmingly, Kleber fretted that his own life was wasted. The man who would be President was only forty-three. Fifteen years his junior, Kleber was seized by angst. Jack Kennedy was almost crowned; Kleber's work wrapped sandwiches at Rocky's Bar-B-Q.

Kleber committed the candidate's words to paper and they were as good as the man. "I believe in an America where the separation of Church and State is absolute," said Kennedy. "Where no Catholic prelate should tell the President, should he be Catholic, how to act." And, almost impishly here, "Where no Protestant minister would tell his parishioners for whom to vote." He reminded the pastors that it was "Virginia's harassment of Baptist preachers that led to Jefferson's statute of religious freedom. Today I may be the victim but tomorrow it may be you." If people voted against this man because he was Catholic, then 40 million Americans lost their chance at being President on the day of baptism.

Those words, judged Sorensen and Schlesinger a thousand days yet to come, were integral in the victory of Kleber's hero. He had gentled the lions in their own den. Later, Kleber would recall his bearing witness to this moment in history. But what lingered was not so much the speech but the spectacle, the soft symbiotic haze of style and beauty and power.

The day had a burlesque postscript. Casey, who knew Lyndon Johnson well, took his reporter to another suite in the Rice Hotel where, in the living room, Lady Bird was—God's truth—ironing her husband's speechifying shirt. The adjoining bedroom contained LBJ and his writers. Kleber overheard the man who would be Vice-President flay his wordsmiths. Then Lyndon shuffled into view, filling the room. His trousers sagged beneath his belly, his undershirt awaited the covering of Lady Bird's domesticity, his hand choked a tumbler freshly filled with scotch whiskey. As he pumped hands, a thought must have come to mind, because Lyndon bellowed to his writer, "And put somethin' there at the end about God. That'll grab 'em." What concerned Kleber when he shook the hand of Lyndon Baines Johnson, fellow Texan, was that he felt no envy or awe. What he felt was just about equal.

Martin Luther King was arrested in Georgia shortly before the presidential election. Regina wrote Kleber a letter drenched in fury and fear. "Two nights ago I listened to Martin speak of Gandhi. He told us that if one little man could sit cross-legged and preach love and nonviolence, if that one little man could bring down the British Empire and change the face of Asia, then we can sing and pray away two centuries of hate. Last night a deputy sheriff picked me up for speeding (I was driving 20 mph) and said I was a Communist cocksucker. He wanted to know whether I enjoyed fucking gorillas or Khrushchev the most. Today Martin was put in jail. He sent word to us that he's going on a hunger strike. It may be unnecessary. They'll kill him. Kleber, it's going to be bad. I'm beginning to think that reason and appeal to Christian love will accomplish about as much as Jews asking Hitler to examine his conscience. I'd like to talk to you but the phones are tapped. I'm sending this letter via courier to Memphis. When your series runs, mail me a copy care of general delivery, Atlanta. It might lift some heavy hearts over this-a-way. Courage. Love. R."

From the campaign trail, John Kennedy telephoned the wife of Martin Luther King and expressed his concern over the civil rights leader's imprisonment. The simple, human gesture was construed by many as perilous if not political suicide. Kleber was of two minds, admiring his hero for taking the risk, fearful that decency would mean defeat. On the joyous night that Kennedy defeated Richard Nixon to become the thirty-fifth President of the United States, Kleber collected ten bucks from Casey, got gloriously tanked, and for reasons that he could not fathom even had he not been blurred by uncountable vodka martinis, drove to Rocky's Bar-B-Q. He anticipated a roof-raising jubilee. He found instead darkness and a locked door and a poorly scrawled note directing friends to a nearby house. It was not difficult to locate the small, sad cottage where colored people spilled onto the poor and barren yard like clothes blown from the line. They had not come to celebrate. They stared at Kleber's white face and he knew that he was not welcome. Even as he pushed politely through the Sunday-best suits and dresses, finding Rocky sitting alone on a davenport that groaned beneath his mass, seeing the old women clustering with baked macaroni and sweet potato pies in their hands and prayers on their lips, Kleber realized that Regina Brown was dead. The news had come at noon, a telegram from the Southern Christian Leadership Conference office in Atlanta. Regina had died in an automobile accident. She had been speeding at more than 85 miles per hour, they said. A highway patrol car had "given chase." Regina lost control, hit a bridge abutment, was burned beyond recognition.

Rocky saw Kleber and he struggled up, absurdly stuffed into a mourning suit that failed to cover him. His throat was choked by a black noose tie. The huge man lurched toward Kleber, was stopped by the old women, and his eyes were crazed. "Shame!" he cried. "Shame, boy. Shame on you!"

Kleber answered well. "Yes, sir, I'll take your shame. But I loved Regina in the best possible way. I loved what she did and what she believed. I loved her intelligence, her commitments, her strength. And I'm more sorry than you'll ever know." He hurried out in tears, dropping five bucks into a bucket to finance Regina's coffin.

The obituary that Kleber wrote did not run for several days, it being 2,000 words long and the paper lacking space during the festival of news that followed the election of John Kennedy. Kleber refused to permit a single word cut. He had prepared a little speech to pressure Casey, remindful of the city editor's long-ago lecture on the necessity to find at least one item of interest in the death of any human being. But when Casey read the obit he simply reached over and shook the reporter's hand. He further posted the copy on the bulletin board with a note: "This is very possibly the best piece of journalism it has ever been my pleasure to read." Not only was Regina's photograph published in the *Call-Bulletin,* that itself a historic first; death gave her modest dignity. She was "Miss Brown," the daughter of "Mr. Rockford Sampson Brown," and she had been working at the side of "the Reverend Martin Luther King." The paper received more than three hundred letters of protest, many obscene and strewn with biblical quotations.

At the end of 1960, Kleber received an unexpected Christmas present. He found a letter from *Harper's Magazine* in his box. The managing editor was writing to announce delighted acceptance of his series, "Fire on the Way." It would be published in back-to-back issues and a check for $2,000 was being drawn. They were hoping to get a foreword from President John F. Kennedy. Kleber couldn't figure out what the hell was going on; his articles reposed in the graveyard of his bottom drawer. He looked to make sure and there they were, beneath a copy of Colin Wilson's book on the alienation of modern man, *The Outsider,* and the Texas Almanac. Just when he started to write *Harper's* a letter professing bewilderment, Millie fessed up. Secretly she had mailed carbons of Kleber's series to an old friend on the magazine. "I thought they deserved a second opinion," she said. "And it didn't look like you had the gumption God gave a June bug."

Fortune has a way of multiplying. Kleber did resign from the Houston *Call-Bulletin* just after New Year's Day 1961. The break came not from conscience. Its sire was cash. A New York publishing house, having caught wind of the *Harper's Magazine* discovery, signed Kleber for a book, proposing a compendium of his segregation series, the Regina Brown obituary, a potpourri of earlier articles ranging from his exposé of the faith healer to an unpublished memoir of Daniel Titus and the rooming-house gang. They proposed calling it *Eyes on Texas* and offered an advance of $10,000. Kleber had to quit five days in a row before Casey finally believed him.

"I should do something grandiose like retiring your typewriter," said the city editor. "But Millie'd probably throw it out the window some morning. Go on. Get the fuck outta here." Kleber made a living out of words but he could find nothing to tell Casey except goodbye and thanks. His eyes were wet. But he did dedicate his first book to the best and only teacher he ever had. When it won the Pulitzer Prize, Casey put the news on page one.

Oh, it should be said that Kleber did not instantly cry out in joy and accept the opportunity to leave Houston. In fact, he spent several troubling weeks searching the old soul and dealing with fears both real and imagined. His ex-wife and infant son were considerations, but not of major import. Adelle by this time had opened her second boutique in a southwest corner of Houston. Quelle Surprise I and II were doing well—ten years later there would be eight branches. He went to see her and discovered Adelle unpacking a crate of Italian handicrafts.

He explained his offer and asked her advice. "Take it, of course," she said.

"Will it be . . . *all right?*"

"What am I, your mother? I'm your ex-wife, Kleber, and that relationship is as enduring as invisible ink. Just get an apartment big enough to put up a visitor now and then." She promised that when their son grew older he could spend summers with his father, wherever he was. Adelle seemed less concerned over the father of her child leaving town than discovering one of her Venetian goblets cracked. After their farewell kiss, Kleber drove away thinking he could not remember what Adelle felt like in bed. Some years later he actually had trouble recalling her name. He was ashamed but not substantially.

Buried in the darkest corner of his heart was the unextinguishable secret of a girl and a storm and a river. True, ten years had passed and nothing had happened, nothing save the gut-wrenching moments when Casey would be whispering confidentially into a telephone, would suddenly stop, would glance at Kleber as if he *knew,* would cause the reporter's throat to dry and his neck to burn. Then Casey would hang up and yell some hideous imprecation if his reporter did not write quicker and clearer. Nonetheless, Laurie was always around, in the shadows for months at a time, but chronic in her refusal to leave for good.

The fantasy arose that he had made an accommodation with fate, that in the Karmic scheme of behavior (a dip into Jung one ambitious but tedious weekend taught him this) Kleber had put out enough good "causes" through his work and conduct to forestall the counterpunch of exposure and disgrace. But if he pushed his luck, altered his course, Laurie's avenging blade would lodge between his eyes. He had just about decided to stay at home.

He was agonizing over his decision one night in the city room, finished with a routine story about a Houston man who kept a gorilla in a refrigerated chamber adjoining his living room. The beast's name was Hugo; Kleber had written of him thrice already. Casey kept Hugo in an update file for resurrection every six months. The damned idiot ape had become a constant, of which there were few in Kleber's life. I can stay here for the rest of my years and keep writing about Hugo, thought Kleber. I'm good at it. Hugo is safe.

He wondered where Mack was at this moment. He considered calling New York and asking counsel. He even paid mental visit to T.J. He was not ashamed over cutting the Prince of Temptation so coldly out of his life. The last he heard, T.J. was either just out of jail or just going in.

He would sleep on it. Leaving the city room, he stopped by impulse at the bank of news tickers, noting on the national UPI wire a long "think piece" that would never see print in his paper. Something about President Ngo Dinh Diem regaining power in South Vietnam, something about his vowing to stamp out a coalition of Communist dissidents recently united under the name of Vietcong. The article recalled the agony of France when the beleaguered land was called French Indochina and speculated that Vietnam was an inflamed appendix on the body of Asia.

The state wire had nothing of interest. He gazed blankly at the coils of rough paper emerging like a never-ending tongue, wasting time he was, more enamored of the steady rhythmic clacking than anything else. Then he saw *it*. He had not read the state wire for weeks. Chances were overwhelming that the copy editor would not have found this mundane slice of news from San Antonio worth publishing. Whether the gift of chance or the caprice of fate, what Kleber found on the wire this night made up his mind.

A truck driver in San Antonio had confessed to the long-ago rape and murder of one Laurel Killman near Weatherford, Texas, in 1950. Kleber did not understand it; he tried to reassemble the dimly remembered night. He finally concluded that the girl from the storm had not died from the ravage of three princes. Indeed she had *not* been seized by the Brazos River. She had risen! Someone else had found her, desired her, destroyed her. He stood over the machine and read and watched, hypnotized, waiting until Laurie fell to the floor of the wire room, coiling and shuddering. And when she had become nothing but a tiny segment of a thousand other lives and deaths, one character in the cast of unending news and buried in the banal torrent of daily history, Kleber fell against the ticker tape in uncontrollable laughter.

CHAPTER EIGHTEEN

There was and is a lovely cluster of harmonious buildings on a wooded green clump of land near Dallas. Outwardly, little betrays its purpose. The sign at the beginning of the used brick driveway, Silverlawn, could mark a great ranch or an artistic commune. Indeed, vegetables are grown and pictures are painted, but they are the labors of madmen who, in order to dwell at Silverlawn, must also be rich.

T. J. Luther discovered this on the spring morning in 1960 when he went to visit his bride. A psychiatrist name of, fittingly, Golden informed him that Melissa would require "a very long period of treatment" at Silverlawn, whose ministrations cost a basic fee of $1,000 a month. T.J. protested that such fees were beyond his capacities and should be paid by the Craymore family fortune. Whereupon Dr.

Golden tapped a silver pen against his teeth and produced a lengthy letter from the firm of Ward, Megal and Schumac, attorneys-at-law: there was no Craymore estate. The mansion in Rivercrest was mortgaged beyond its worth with unpaid back taxes totaling $12,400. Its furnishings, including all of the stuffed animals, had been willed to the Fort Worth Zoological Society, which did not wish to claim them. The Olds 98 that Melissa drove was scarcely hers, six out of thirty-six payments having been made. Her jewels were paste. On the day that T.J. first encountered Melissa at the bank, she withdrew all but $230 in her only account. She was a trespasser in the land of money. And as there were no other living relatives, the husband of Mrs. Melissa Craymore Luther was expected by law to pay for her psychiatric bed, board, electric shock, and chloral hydrates.

T.J. wondered why Melissa had come to Silverlawn, seeing as how she disappeared the night their honeymoon cottage burned. "Your wife has been with us here before. Oh my, yes," answered Dr. Golden. Several times. Beginning at the age of twelve when she spent two months of summer vacation recuperating from what the psychiatrist euphemistically called "paternal abuse." Again at fourteen when father Craymore threatened to shoot her in the breasts and mount her head on the living-room wall between the lioness and the giraffe he had purchased in Kenya. And once more following high school graduation and the simultaneous suicide of Daddy, whose will revealed that Missy was the illegitimate daughter of a New Orleans prostitute named Clothilde. It took eighteen months that time at Silverlawn for Missy to "assimilate" this cruel legacy, whereupon she was released and spent two cloistered years nursing her stroked-out mother.

Missy had not gone to Radcliffe, had not studied art, had not done much of anything except get crazy and uncrazy and entrap the Prince of Temptation as a husband.

"Would you like to see her?" asked Dr. Golden.

"I wouldn't want to trouble her," answered T.J.

"I think she would be very pleased," said the psychiatrist, who escorted the thoroughly confused bridegroom to a cozy red brick cottage (it looked very similar to the one that Missy had ordered T.J. to build for her) which contained four female patients, one of which was Missy wearing a gray smock with orange splotches of poster paint. She was on this morning completing her fourth drawing of a cat licking its penis and she did not recognize T.J.

"Missy, this is your nice husband who's come to visit you," said Dr. Golden.

Missy took her paintbrush and painted her left cheek orange.

"Don't you remember your husband, hon?" pushed the doctor. "The man you married two months ago in . . . Where was it, boy?"

T.J. cleared his throat. "Ah, Matamoros, Mexico."

Missy nodded up and down like one of those toy birds that dips its head incessantly into a bowl of water. Then she threw her pot of paint at him and shrieked, "Fuckin' liars!" On the way out, Dr. Golden said the "poor child" probably had Capgras' syndrome, a rare mental disorder characterized by claims that a sufferer's mother, father, lover—anyone ever close—is an imposter.

That very night T.J. hurried to the Craymore mansion and turned the spook house upside down searching for something worth stealing before the repossessors came. He settled for smashing the gun cabinet and scooping up a large collection of rifles and pistols. In his fury, he found a box of bullets, loaded a .38, and blasted the hulking Alaskan bear into confetti. Pity that he didn't direct his fire at Delano, the stuffed cat with the eyes of scarlet glass, his unwanted Christmas gift. Had this puss been shot, its innards would have spilled five thousand hidden $100 bills. Delano kept his wondrous surprise for many years thereafter, passing from junk dealer to attics to garage sales and finally on down to a black woman on welfare, living in Tulsa on an eighty-five-dollar-a-month disability pension. Her mongrel dog chewed up the moldy old cat on the day that Richard Nixon resigned the presidency, a human-interest paragraph of splendid fortune thus crowded onto the back columns of America's newspapers.

One bitter night in 1961, T.J. was consuming legal beer and illegal Four Roses in a saloon called the White Elephant, just outside the Fort Worth Stock Yards and fabled as the watering hole where Butch Cassidy and the Sundance Kid paused for refreshment en route to their deaths in South America. He had been there since midafternoon and had shut up only long enough to watch an installment of "Knights of New York." Several times T.J. had informed the bartender that he knew Mack Crawford intimately, hoping that the revelation would be worth a house drink. Instead the barkeep, noting complaints from other customers about the bragful bum, suggested it was time to pay the fourteen dollars and fifteen cents due for spirits consumed. T.J. grinned and said, "The truth is, ole buddy, I ain't got a red ass dime."

To the threat that police would be summoned as collection agents, T.J. laughed and laughed. He climbed onto the bar stool, waved his arms, and drew the attention of the crowd. He said, "My uncle just blew his brains out, my house burned down, my mama and daddy committed long overdue suicide, and my wife went crazy. I ask you . . . who wants to pay for my beer?" Whereupon he drooped and fell soundly asleep on the floor where real outlaws once trod, waking the next noon as guest of the city drunk tank. With Magda deceased, there was no one to bail him out and he had to cut weeds for thirty days along Tarrant County's highways.

Reckoning it was time now for seclusion, T.J. passed several months in the tumbledown shack near Weatherford where a decade before, a girl had wandered in during a storm. Her ghost did not disturb him; Laurie was scarcely worth a skipped heartbeat in the breast of a twenty-eight-year-old loser who would have gladly joined Missy at Silverlawn if he could find a spare $1,000.

What T.J. did was tack cardboard into the wall gaps, sleep on an army surplus cot, and open hundreds of cans of chili and ravioli and beer. He ventured out only to sell one of the Craymore weapons, always able to find buyers in the roadhouses that dotted the outskirts of Fort Worth like unwanted relatives. It was one such clandestine transaction that brought T.J. into the company of a bug-eyed gentleman named Ralph Emerson Machado, known more widely as Mash.

He was a fence whose reputation for ominous behavior exceeded his weight, which was more than 300 pounds. He not only purchased stolen merchandise, he had a pudgy finger or two in the placement and collection of slot machines and jukeboxes, occasionally ran prostitutes in and out of steaming beds, and played rather good golf, although he once threw a caddy into a pond at Colonial Country Club because the lad misadvised a choice of irons. Actually the caddy got off light, seeing as how Mash broke the 5 iron across his knees and shredded his putter into toothpicks. Mash was a substantial Texas gangster of the sort indigenous to Lone Star soil, with roots going back to the days when crime was an individual act of passion and need, without the ties of Sicilian structure. Organized crime never succeeded to any great extent in Texas, the Mafia giving up after modest forays into Galveston slots and Dallas horse wires. The bad guys were run across the border into Louisiana. Score one for the good book and the good boy, Jesus Christ Himself. Few were the American states so throttled by theology. The Baptist Church owned Texas. Eyetalians with dice up their sleeves and odds on their lips felt the fire of the Lord and they were sore afraid. Thus was America's largest state—nobody counted Alaska—left to its native sons, and anybody inclined toward a violent dollar did business with Mash out of Waco, not Carlo out of Palermo. The profits were, compared to the family ledgers of, say, Philadelphia, minuscule. In his best year, Mash netted $83,000, but that was enough to purchase each October a custom Coupe de Ville with the seat moved back, fortified, iridescent rust-hued sports jackets that unless double-lined tended to burst like Kleenex would if used to gift-wrap a watermelon, a pinky diamond that was usually raised directly beneath Mash's hooded eye both for worship and for watchdogging. He devoured at least one T-bone steak each lunch and dinner, twelve bottles of ale per evening, and made dependable contributions to the Boy Scouts, Future Farmers of America, Big Brothers, and the Community Chest. Mrs. Mash was a slender—some said flattened—woman named DeeDee who mothered a Cub Scout den, wrote a column for her church newspaper, and on the day in 1970 that Mash was shot to death by four Texas Rangers in a stakeout near Austin as climax to a marijuana import war, insisted to reporters that her husband had been mis-slain, that he was a kind and loving spouse who sold insurance policies to motels.

On the night in 1961 when Mash purchased a 9-mm. Luger Colt Commander and a S&W Chiefs Special .38 revolver from T. J. Luther in the parking lot of Horse Feathers Inn, he perceived immediately that beneath the haggard, unshaven countenance was true badness. A week later the Prince of Temptation hired on as Apprentice Hoodlum, Mash having learned through a police contact that T.J.'s criminal record contained little more than a few snags of garden variety hell-raisin'.

With the $4,200 cash that Mash paid him for the remaining stock of Craymore firearms (T.J. held back a couple, including one superfine Magnum, for personal reasons), the new man was transformed. Through his employer's graces, T.J. purchased a fine recently stolen and repainted Chrysler automobile, a wardrobe of shiny sports jackets in emerald green and aquamarine, matching white patent shoes and belts. The sleek hawk nested in a two-bedroom apartment on the fashionable west side of Fort Worth, about a mile from Cloverdale, choosing furnishings reflective of the resident: harem pillows on which to sleep and screw, a water bed, paintings of Polynesian maidens with magnificent tits set against midnight black velvet, a lava lamp that when illuminated gurgled amoeba-shaped globs of a Poly-Glo rainbow, a bar on which sat matching glasses and decanters that, when filled with whiskey, revealed the private parts of a dozen virgins.

Initial work assignments were offensively simple. T.J. was dispatched to a score of honky-tonks each Saturday night at curfew where, using the vernacular, he "robbed the jukeboxes." That meant ceremoniously opening the machines, cleaning and counting the coins, and splitting 50/50 with the proprietor. Mash was not worried that his new deputy would shorten the take, because he well knew what each location dependably produced. Nonetheless, T.J. became adroit at skimming the other side, staging the rite of building columns of dimes and quarters with such flair, arm waving, dirty jokes, and distractions that he managed to pocket an extra fifty bucks on every tour. He soon suggested to Mash that sixty for us and forty for them would be tolerable, seeing as how "inflation," "labor costs," and "maintenance" were rampantly rising. All of the proprietors complained and refused, but sooner than later acquiesced—due either to the gleaming gunmetal glimpsed when T.J. unbuttoned his jacket, or to the tires of automobiles slashed in his wake, or perhaps to neon roadhouse signs blasted just as the bells of Sunday church began to chime. Six months after that, the split went to 80/20 and nobody dared complain.

T.J. had wonderful ideas. Observing that revelers were forced by Baptist law to leave the halls of hedonism at twelve each night save Saturday, it seemed worthwhile to provide a place for after-hours spirit and sport. Thus for several prosperous months in 1962 did a three-bedroom ranch house hidden in a wooded dale near Lake Worth spring into vibrant life between midnight and dawn. Whiskey splashed like April rain; women danced naked and squatted to the floor and clamped half-dollars with their privates. Cards were dealt; dice were rolled. Unseen but very present was T.J., his perch above the crap table in a low-ceilinged bedroom. Because wee-hours gamblers were traditionally quite drunk and careless, no one ever knew that floating above their heads, peering intently through a mouse hole, manipulating a powerful magnet that could make dice tumble on command another infuriating —and losing—turn, there reposed the Prince of Temptation! And oh how he enjoyed himself! Enormous was his power, particularly when he trained his currents on some chickenshit bastard from the Class of '50, one of the rich ones, some prick with an inherited desk in Daddy's office and a one-eighth share of forty producing wells, some low-life asshole with receding hair and a brow that T.J. could dot with sweat. *Goddamn* it felt good to suck those bucks! After the bars closed, until the sun rose, T. J. Luther was god, dispenser of fortune fair and foul, deciding who would win and who would lose. You down there, Eddie Ray Pearson, you didn't call me back that summer after graduation. Too bad. That'll be $300 and kiss my ass. And here comes Lester Wagenvoord, *almost* as popular as me. But he didn't win then. And he never would.

Everybody on earth was either a dog or a tree. T.J. raised his hind leg.

The only downside was the anguish of anonymity. If only he could burst from the heavens, descending to the green felt plateau in a storm of sparkling plaster, revealing his presence and his power. But of course he couldn't do that; he couldn't wreck a money machine; he couldn't spoil the sweetest scam since Hadacol. Despite swindle-by-magnet being as frustrating to the ego as spending $2,000 on caps for unseen teeth at the back of a mouth, T.J. had to stay aloft. His celebrity was hidden. Unless one night he looked down and saw Kleber or Mack—or better still, both. In that event, wrath and judgment of the new god could not be denied.

Mash summoned his junior partner for a conference one morning at ten. Having slept but ninety fitful minutes, T.J. felt like a flogged mule. Following Uncle Bun's custom, he normally did not rise until near noon. The behemoth had leased new offices, decorously snuggled in a shopping center between a tennis boutique and a candle emporium operated by some damn hippies. The sign on the door said VENTURES UNLIMITED, Ralph E. Machado, Esq., President. Joyfully had DeeDee decorated her husband's workshop. The decor was cowboy chic—chairs approximating saddles, a bleached longhorn skull on Mash's desk which was the slab of an old ranch cookout table, prints of Indian ponies drinking at sunset ponds, pots of cactus. Mash presided from a county sheriff's swivel chair that moaned from the burden. T.J. entered and watched Mash eat twelve chocolate doughnuts. The boss glowered with more than standard menace and T.J. frantically searched his conscience for a poorly stolen dollar.

"Whores," Mash finally said, introducing his topic and falling silent.

T.J. waited a spell. "Whores?" he echoed.

"You know whores?"

"I have indeed seen the inside of a professional pussy or two, sir."

"Never found much money in whores," said Mash.

"Tough business."

"Should be, though. Money."

"Certainly should."

"Used to have a few ole gals," said Mash. "Ugly as witches' tits. They was lucky to get five dollars for an around-the-world with a long stop in France."

Mash licked the remaining chocolate icing from his plate. He stared glumly at his reflection. "Tell you what, son," he said without looking up. "You be my whore man. Make us some cock 'n' cunt money."

Fort Worth police did not tolerate streetwalkers, a needless posture since downtown was traditionally so deserted by nightfall that wars could be fought without worry of injuring strollers. Commercial intercourse was, of course, available at second-rate motels called "spots" by members of the profession. Every major Texas city had a few such inns, where night porters provided rooms and girls and got 40 percent of all fees. Revenues were modest and undependable. Knowing all of this, T.J. sought imaginative counsel from Large Marge, entrepreneur of the Pink Lady Club on the Jacksboro Highway. Like Mash, she was a woman whose proportions neared those of a parade float. Before suds and chili dogs swelled her frame, Marge had enjoyed a diverse career, including truck driving, decorated service in the WAC's, professional wrestling under the name of Princess Amazonia, and was now devoted wife to a circus clown named Bamboozle, an invalid, alas, since the wedding night. When Marge emerged from the bathroom of the Jack Tar Motel in Galveston where the honeymoon commenced in 1956, Bamboozle lay naked on the bed, wearing his tramp hat and floppy shoes. A circle of salt was on his belly into which he dipped celery stalks.

Marge tee-hee'd and Bamboozle accepted his bride, desiring that she cater to his long held fantasy, i.e. wrap her mighty and muscled limbs about his salted torso. Half an hour later, Bamboozle was in the emergency room of John Sealy Hospital, his pelvic bones crushed by passion and a celery stalk protruding gaily from his ass.

But the reason T.J. sought the ear of Large Marge was because her legend also contained experience as a celebrated whore, having once toured the Southwest in a flatbed truck with a bedroom-under-canvas that briefly housed and aroused many of Texas' most boisterous men.

"If you was to go into the whore business today," hypothecated T.J., "just how would you start?"

Marge roared and patted her hair, a pinkish bubble so lacquered that darts could not penetrate her skull. "Well, hon, you start with the Three D's—a dick, a dame, and a donation to John Law."

"Be serious," pleaded T.J. "Be creative." He dropped a twenty on the bar that sent Marge's gears a-swirling.

"The funny thing is, hon, I was thinkin' about this very subject just the other day. I had to throw a little ole gal outta here. She was hustlin', which Lord knows I don't object to. But she was about seventeen, had braces on her teeth, was about six months pregnant, and didn't have the brains to read a Bisquick box. I told Boozle this new generation of pussy ain't got a drop of refinement."

T.J. nodded, vaguely following Marge's dissertation.

"So there's your answer, hon," said Marge, stuffing the twenty down her bosom. "*Class*. Sell 'em ass with class and you can buy the bank."

"Class?"

"I'm talkin' Jackie Kennedy class. Lemme think a spell. Call me Sunday after church."

When T.J. reconnected with Large Marge, she had such a good idea that he engaged her as a silent partner. An imaginative wrinkle soon appeared on the sheets of sexual commerce. It seemed at first of minimal risk and major reward. Adding a fourth D to the triad of requirements, Marge and T.J. opened the Delilah Produce Co., consisting of one telephone presided over by Bamboozle, delighted to obtain a function beyond performing tricks in his wheelchair at his wife's tavern. The produce offered by Delilah was choice—a stable of fillies acquired by Marge, none previously professionals and all between eighteen and twenty-four. They included a few suburban housewives, some legal secretaries, two coeds from TCU, and one instructress of ballet and tap dance. Each was personally coiffed by Marge—her credits included training as a beautician—in hairstyles that slavishly copied Jacqueline Kennedy.

The fee was a non-negotiable seventy-five dollars an hour, plus taxi fare to the hotel room or private room of the carefully screened customer's choice. Those who sought the services of Delilah Produce Co. telephoned a frequently changed number, dropped a code phrase into the ear of Bamboozle—"grain futures" and "pork bellies" were typical—and within the hour, paradise was guaranteed to arrive. Kinky requests were not encouraged but normally satisfied. Large Marge herself filled an occasional exotic need, always speeding directly home to Bamboozle, lifting his frail and broken body from the wheelchair, and cradling her husband as she recounted intimate details of some old pervert's desire to be whipped by a 275-pound, sixty-two-year-old, Crisco-greased lady.

Within three months, Delilah Produce Co. netted $16,545, strictly cash. Mash was pleased, particularly since his after-hours lake house had mysteriously burned to the ground. He told T.J. that the chief suspect was a competitor from Dallas. The likely torch was named Chick Sader and mere mention of the words compelled Mash to throw the bleached longhorn skull against an Indian pony print. Though members of the same fraternity, Mash and Chick chaired different committees. Mash held himself well above the Dallas character in professional caste. After all, Mash only catered to a fellow's need to get laid, play cards, smoke forbidden cigarettes, or sell a hot stereo. Chick Sader made his money from sinister arson, heavy drugs, extortion, and murder. He once bragged to Mash in a moment of détente that thirty-two corpses reposing in the Forest of Graves—an unmarked but frequently tilled boneyard near Eagle Mountain Lake—slept with Sader slugs in their hearts.

The woman who would disarrange once again the life of T. J. Luther arrived in Dallas on Valentine's Day 1963. Priscilla Gallant, a New York fashion model of such beauty that she was often mistaken for Grace Kelly and whose hands were so exceptionally boned and textured that they appeared in magazines promoting gloves or creams or gems, had been engaged to present a line of French couture at a gala to benefit autistic children. When Priscilla reached the Adolphus Hotel, there was no reservation in her name. When she called the chairman there came a fumbled, awkward apology. The event had been canceled due to poor ticket sales. A message had been telegraphed to Priscilla in New York but she never got it. The phone went dead and when Priscilla re-dialed, there was no answer. Steaming, angry, tired, she elected to pass the night anyway in Dallas before returning to New York.

Three months thereafter, Priscilla was still in Dallas, overwhelmingly attracted to a craggy and dangerous man, the type for which she had long held unrealized fantasy. His name was Charles ("Chick") Sader and whatever he decreed, Priscilla would do, be it lashed with leather thongs to the four posters of his bed or licking his freshly fired sperm from the tips of his leather boots. When Sader suggested she might enjoy sniffing a dab of white crystal powder off his penis, Priscilla, believing it to be cocaine, a drug she had used routinely in Rome, inhaled readily. She enjoyed the rush, although the cumulus pillowy fog that settled over her senses was the antithesis of a cocaine high. Then Priscilla learned how to "chip" the drug, injecting the powder with a tiny stab beneath her creamy skin, hungrily graduating to plunging heroin directly into the mainline vessels of her blood. On her twenty-third birthday, June 2, Priscilla's valuable and celebrated wrists bore the scarlet trails of profound addiction. One summer night, Sader took his girl friend to a poker game in Fort Worth and when she refused to obey his demands to stop yelling for a needed injection, Chick opened the door of his silver Lincoln and pushed Priscilla Gallant onto the red cobbled bricks of Camp Bowie Boulevard.

Chance directed a taxi driver to cruise promptly by, and when the hack sized up the abandoned maiden's worth, he delivered her posthaste to the Delilah Produce Co.

Narcotics had tampered with, but not ravaged her patrician beauty. The moment T.J. beheld the splendorous Priscilla (and this, too, was a prank of coincidence because he rarely visited the spare room where Bamboozle directed the traffic of price-tag pussy) he achieved erection so monumental that the steel teeth of his zipper fly almost burst. Feeding her hastily procured morphine tablets, T.J. bore his unexpected treasure to the pad of harem pillows and Polynesian portraits, laying her down beside the lava lamp and marveling at the patterns of colored lights that bathed the slender limbs and silvery blond hair. They made love for three days and nights, she curiously unreceptive at first, he soon catching on that Priscilla liked to play rough. The instant that T.J. donned old faded jeans with patches at the crotch, a chambray work shirt, and a sweat-circled cowboy hat, she was ready to ride. The sexual tempo increased when T.J. found a towrope in the trunk of his Chrysler. Suspecting that love, enduring love, predestined love had finally come to him, T.J. knew that Priscilla had to be detoxified before any long-term commitments could be discussed.

He asked Large Marge to pose as a worried aunt in a necessary charade. Suspicious of its worth but loyal to her partner, Marge placed Priscilla in the Silverlawn sanitarium. T.J. was eager to pay the $1,500 required for a month of withdrawal treatment that would reduce if not eliminate her appetite for the poppy's nectar. That his still undivorced wife, Melissa Craymore, had been kicked out of Silverlawn for non-payment of services rendered and consigned to the state home for the insane at Rusk, Texas, did not connect with irony.

Large Marge wanted to warn T.J. about the peril of loving a junkie, no matter how classy and well placed. But she saw the passion in his eyes and did not speak. She was too gracious to tamper with a man's conception of love.

Having squeezed sufficient throats to satisfy his suspicions that Chick Sader had indeed torched a major source of revenue, Mash concocted revenge. He summoned T.J. and floated various methods of murder, and for each the deputy pointed out flaws. That old reliable bomb-beneath-the-car-hood would not work, because Sader never entered his automobile until an aide had first ignited the engine and let it idle five minutes. The Sader home, a fortress on the fashionable north side of Dallas ringed by an electric fence and guarded by a half-dozen Dobermans, was impenetrable. Sader rarely traveled anywhere unless protected fore and aft, like a South American dictator, by anonymous Fords filled with loyal lieutenants.

"You're a smart boy," said Mash. "You find somethin'."

Reluctantly, T.J. agreed to nose around Dallas, assigned to locate a way to kill a killer. He did not want the duty, believing that his love for Priscilla was so precious it was time to leave the world of illegalities and embrace responsibility. But this move would require delicate disengagement, and Mash's demeanor was clearly unreceptive. Thus did he spend several nervous days in Dallas, returning to Mash with one remote possibility. Each dawn, Chick Sader padded in pajamas down a brick path edged with petunias to fetch the Dallas *Morning News* from his mailbox. The positions of numerous pines and oaks made a sniper's line of fire uncertain, but it might be arranged for the target to discover something more than news in his box. T.J. said he didn't want the job. He needed some rest.

Silverlawn released Priscilla and she emerged with clear blue eyes and a few more pounds. She was glad to see T.J. and they proceeded immediately to the harem pillows. During the night, T.J. produced an expensive 35-mm. camera that some petty thief had fenced to Mash and requested to take a photograph of his beloved. Priscilla declined, revealing for the first time that she did that for a living. Now it was Priscilla Gallant's beauty that first arrested T. J. Luther, but when he learned that she was famous as well, his passion soared. The next day they went to the public library, where Priscilla found old magazines that contained her features in advertisements. Excising each one as carefully as a thief would slice La Gioconda from her bindings in the Louvre, T.J. had his beloved framed in swirling gilt baroque. He nailed a score of Priscilla's parts on the walls of his flat. Each noon he awoke, kissed the genuine article in his bed, murmured "I love you, I never really knew what it meant." Then he went around and kissed each picture in the house. Though the relationship was barely three months old, T.J. was searching for a way to ask Priscilla's hand in marriage. Sorely did he need advice, but the sad reality was that T.J. had no friends he could trust in this matter—none save Mash, Marge, Bamboozle, assorted whores and characters. Terrified that if the marital question was improperly asked Priscilla might reject him, T.J. decided to ensure union by a bizarre process of sexual accumulation and isolation.

He disconnected the telephone, locked the door, drew the shades, turned the air conditioner up to full, rattling strength. The pantry was heavily stocked with bourbon, cigarettes, and the new and convenient meals known as frozen TV dinners. His closet contained fresh supplies of the items Priscilla liked—leather chaps, the rope, gloves, a couple of carnival-bought toy whips. His lady would be worshipped and fucked in a castle of love. And if it took until Christmas before the princess realized how perfect was her realm, then the Prince of Temptation was prepared to wait.

T.J. had planned for every eventuality except one: silence. They ran out of words. He sensed that Priscilla would not be entertained by fraudulent tales of Korean War heroics, would not enjoy anecdotes of Magda, or the mad Melissa, or mischief in an ice-cream vault, or how to sell imaginary encyclopedias, or the art of cheating dice and ass with class. Of course he informed his prize that once the crown of Most Popular Boy had graced his brow. In fact he told her about forty times.

As urgent was his need to explore Priscilla's life—the men who had come before him, her rooms, her dreams, her cars—he dared not probe her past, worried that his clumsy tongue would trip and she would pronounce him a rube. Worse, he might remind her that outside their castle was another world. Shy by nature, Priscilla volunteered little. She dropped but a few words, T.J. seizing them like pearls fallen from an imperial gown. She was from Rhode Island (and T.J. could not even recall its capital). She was convent-bred, the daughter of an army colonel, stopped on the streets of New York at the age of seventeen by a photographer and on the cover of *Vogue* two months thereafter.

Never did she actually speak the words "I love you," but T.J. knew she did. Why else would the lady scream and yell and scratch his back, then nap ten minutes and wake up begging for more? Nevertheless, to assure her devotion, T.J. began using the dependable hour each midafternoon when Priscilla snoozed to rush out and purchase tribute. He grabbed the best-looking dress from the window of The Fair without even asking its cost, beaded bags, perfume in bottles big as a pint of gin. She loved them all, or said she did, but she never tried anything on. What she did was stack each gift neatly in a corner of the room, and when the silences fell, look at them instead of him. He noticed that she was growing more restless and scratching her arms a lot.

On the tenth day, T.J. blurted out, "If we could live anywhere, where would it be?"

"Paris," said Priscilla quickly. Except for boots, she was naked, lying on the floor and eating potato chips and watching cartoons on TV.

"How much would that cost?" asked T.J.

"To do Paris right, oh, about twenty-five thousand dollars a year."

"I've got ninety-five hundred," said T.J. rather proudly.

"Then Paris must wait."

The President of the United States broke into their early-evening intercourse. When his voice was heard, Priscilla abruptly pushed T.J. off her sweating flanks and hurried to the television set. She watched rapt as John Kennedy parried with the fourth estate. "He's beautiful," she said, and her eyes gleamed. "I met him once in Newport."

"Did you fuck him?" asked T.J. coarsely. She liked dirty talk, usually.

"He didn't ask," said Priscilla. Clearly, felt T.J., she would have. He cared little and knew less of John Kennedy but now he hated the bastard. Priscilla began to tell a promising bit of gossip concerning an actress friend who was regularly smuggled into the White House for private meeting with JFK, hidden beneath a throw rug on the floorboard of a Secret Service automobile. Then she stopped. On the front row of the journalists was a self-assured reporter asking a complex question about the nuclear test ban treaty, demanding to know how the United States could keep Russia from cheating. Priscilla listened and said, "That boy is smart." And when T.J. focused on the object of her favor, he came quite close to kicking the screen out.

It was Kleber Cantrell questioning the goddamn President of the goddamn U.S. of A. "Well, I know that sumbitch," announced T.J.

"The President?"

"No. That boy on the front row."

"Really?" Priscilla was impressed.

T.J. changed tone. "Sure. Him and me went to high school together. He's my best friend. Didn't I ever tell you that?"

Priscilla turned away from the box and searched T.J.'s face for a lie. "Then what's his name?" she asked skeptically.

"Kleber Cantrell," answered T.J. "Whatever you wanna know about him, I can tell you. Down to the size of his little-bitty pecker—which he uses damn little."

Priscilla peered again at the reporter, watched him scribble Kennedy's answer. Kleber seemed impatient and crammed with many more inquiries. "He's cute," she said. "I think I may have met him in Paris. Did he go with Jack and Jackie that time they met De Gaulle?"

T.J. snapped off the television and felt anger swirling through his limbs. "Did you fuck *him,* too?" he demanded.

"No. But I'd like to fuck his mind," she said, fleeing to the bathroom and locking the door and refusing to respond to T.J.'s cries and knocks. Priscilla was not interested in either President or press. What she wanted more than the cock of any man was a sniff or a chip or a shot of Chick Sader's heroin. The hunger had returned full force. Silverlawn had failed.

The next morning Mash broke down the castle door and ordered T.J. to zip his fly and get the fuck back to work. Rather than quarrel with the monster before the eyes and ears of an increasingly complaining Priscilla, he obeyed. The two men sat in the refrigerated gloom of Mash's Cadillac, parked in a lot beside the nearest Methodist church. Mash bore directly to the point. He could not find an assassin. Every dependable gun in North Texas had turned him down. "I'm shoppin' a twenty-five-thousand-dollar contract," said Mash. "You want it?"

"Well, hell no," said T.J. But he thought a minute and in his head materialized the Eiffel Tower and he corrected himself. "Lemme think on it."

Sometime well after midnight on a late-September morn, T.J. fell exhausted onto the harem pillows, took Priscilla into his arms, had in mind a quick rear-ender, but dropped immediately and deeply asleep. Later, Priscilla slipped cautiously from his embrace, dressed hurriedly, took T.J.'s car keys and $500 from his pants pocket, and crept out into the humid night.

Well, the newspapers never did figure it all out, but they squeezed the story like it was the last lemon in the bar. Down in Houston, Clifford Casey swore for weeks, cursing the fickle geography of fate, enraged that Dallas got what was pretty near the murder of his dreams. When the *Call-Bulletin* drowned in red ink and folded the following year, Casey insisted that the dame in Dallas might have saved his sheet.

But T.J. put most of it together. He found out that for almost a week, the very same week he was out shopping for copper wiring and timing devices and nitroglycerine and humming "April in Paris," Priscilla was telephoning Dallas, trying to connect with Chick Sader. She would have crawled on her knees thirty miles across the turnpike if he had asked her. When he would not take her calls, Priscilla slipped away, drove to Dallas, found the Tudor mansion that contained the man who had her drugs, rang the bell, got no answer, rang again, drew back at the savage rush of steel-jawed guard dogs.

She wrote a sweet but desperate note. "Please," she scribbled, "I love you, Chick. I need you. Please take me back. Whatever you want me to do, I'm ready. I want to be your slave. Oh God, please, please."

The note was never found. It and the face that had been on magazine covers were blown into a thousand shreds of paper, flesh, and bone the instant Priscilla opened the little door of Chick Sader's mailbox. T.J.'s bomb had worked well. True, it failed to harm the intended victim, Sader having left suddenly for Las Vegas the midnight before. But it slew the woman loved by the Prince of Temptation, the six-week-old male fetus growing in her womb, and three out of six Doberman pinschers.

CHAPTER NINETEEN

Calvin Sledge was looking for a pattern of consistent behavior. There were ways a clever prosecutor could slip through loopholes in the rules of criminal court procedure and present the secrets of a man's life to the jury. He reread the criminal dossier of T. J. Luther and found few items of real interest. No mention of Priscilla. No allusion to Mash. Nothing but a few pissant encounters with the law—a pair of drunk busts, another for attendance at a high-stakes poker game, some questions over a shadowy oil deal, a slew of hot checks. Pimples on the face of a hustler that flared and faded. During the tempestuous decade called the 1960's, there was one notation that mildly aroused the District Attorney. Even though he doubted it could be used, Sledge dictated it into his case file:

"Thomas Jeremiah Luther bio, continued," he read into the microphone. "On November 26, 1963, subject was stopped by Texas Highway Patrol on Dallas–Fort Worth turnpike for speeding, clocked at 74 mph. Subject was booked for possession of concealed weapon, i.e. a .44 Magnum found in glove compartment. Subject stated to arresting officers that quote I was taking my pistol to a sporting-goods store in Dallas for repair. I only use it for target practice. End quote."

Sledge studied the entry. Somehow it spoke to him. "Darlene, hold on a minute, lemme see what the hell happened next. . . . Okay, here it is: Disposition: Case continued once, twice, passed again, dismissed on October 3, 1964. Subject paid twenty-five dollars on reduced charge of speeding. Weapon? Shit, it doesn't say what happened to the .44. . . . Darlene, ask Sandy to call Wade's office in Dallas and see if they've got anything on this. . . ."

When nothing of further clarification came back from Dallas,

Sledge forgot the episode. Which was too bad. Had he been privy to the events of that cold and sorrowful November a dozen years past, it would have abetted his notion of consistent behavior. On that good-as-forgotten evening, T. J. Luther was tearing ass to reach the Dallas airport. He had learned that someone he despised was preparing to board a flight for New York. The pistol in his glove box was in splendid order. It had pierced the guts of six oil drums that very afternoon. But for too heavy a foot on the accelerator, it would have sent three-fourths of an inch of lead into the brain of . . . But it didn't, and T.J. had to wait.

The two men embraced with such delight and strength that other customers idling in the Polo Lounge of the Beverly Hills Hotel on a November morning in 1963 between breakfast and lunch stared and remarked. The maître d', haughty arbiter of who could cross his threshold into the dim and somewhat shabby bar and grill, did not recognize the shorter, slighter man. No mark of celebrity was on his forehead. Obviously the stranger was from the East, his skin being pale, his jacket thick and woolly, his demeanor that of a tourist who had come to gawk. Had not the blond and certifiably famous giant swept the infidel into his arms, the pretender would have been expelled.

But when Mack Crawford verified Kleber Cantrell, the maître d' melted obsequiously and led them to a favored booth, tolerating the film star's breach of fashion. Mack was dressed in tennis shorts, an orange polo shirt from Texas, and a golf cap. The two friends had not communed in almost two years and there was much to tell. It was agreed that both looked and felt terrific, Kleber deprecating the alarming retreat of his hairline, Mack blessing the lounge shadows that smoothed the crinkles at his eyes. Homage was paid for mutual triumphs, Kleber praising the new film in which Mack was currently billed in letters larger than the title, *Falling Sands.* Mack was equally proud of Kleber's book, *Eyes on Texas,* and the just-opened hit Broadway play on the secret life of Daniel Titus.

The truth was that Kleber had not seen Mack's film, and Mack had not read Kleber's book. No need to spoil the moment with truth.

As they spoke, Kleber's eyes darted discreetly about the room, capturing, per custom, the scene. He intercepted many opposing glances. The Polo Lounge reminded him of a magician's box, a beautiful woman imprisoned within, a dozen swords thrust at but not touching the body. "Everybody's looking at us," said Kleber. "Correction, at *you*."

Mack nodded. "But they won't bother us. Not here. They've got gorillas hidden in the potted palms trained to attack anybody who takes out an autograph book."

"How do you cope with it?" asked Kleber.

"Cope with *what?*"

"Celebrity. What's it like? I mean, can you go in the May Company and buy a pair of socks?"

Mack considered the unusual question. "Probably not. The trouble is, I'm too big. And this damn blond hair. If I was five feet eight and brown-headed, maybe. Steve McQueen says it's all a matter of attitude. If he wants to be recognized, he turns on the famous switch. If he wants to be left alone, he sort of slumps and walks around like a tire going flat."

"I don't envy you," said Kleber. "I'm proud as hell of you, but the idea of forfeiting privacy is as awful as leprosy."

"What is this country-mouse shit, anyway, K.? I read your clippings. Your name's in the columns as often as mine, and I *pay* a press agent to plant me."

"I'm thinking about hiring one to keep me out," said Kleber with a small shudder.

"What brings you to paradise?"

"Nixon. Again."

"Nixon! I went to a cocktail party at his house in Trousdale. He's got those Herblock cartoons of him crawling out of the sewer hung on the wall over his toilet. It figures Tricky Dick would buy a marble house in the one part of town that's truly *outré*."

"*Outré!* Jesus, Mack, I can't believe you said *outré*. I guess they *can* take the boy out of Texas."

"The boy's learning French. I may do a war picture in Normandy next spring. I took Jeffie to Paris last summer."

"How old is he now?"

"Almost five. He'll be in kindergarten this fall." Mack fell silent. It was obvious the subject was touchy.

"Did you get divorced? I missed the news."

Mack shook his head. "Nope. Not yet. Susan wants one. I guess I've been stalling. She's the best woman I ever met. . . . By the way, Kleber, this is off the record, right?"

Kleber was taken aback. "What do you mean?"

"I mean, I don't talk about my personal life. For print."

"Well hell, Mack, I'm not interviewing you. Gimme a break."

"I just wanted to set some ground rules."

"For a friend?" Kleber's feelings were hurt. He felt like a pretender.

Mack smiled cautiously and changed the subject. "Let me give a dinner party for you Saturday night. Who'd you like to meet? Mae West? Natalie Wood?"

"That's quite a span. I do admit to serious fantasies about Miss Wood. But, alas, next time. I'm leaving tonight. I owe the New York *Times Magazine* forty-five hundred words on whether Nixon has been truly buried by Pat Brown or if, as I suspect, he eluded the stake in his heart. I wouldn't be surprised if he ran against Jack Kennedy next year."

They talked a few minutes more like flat stones skipping across a lake, nothing going very deep. The room began to fill with its customary luncheon mélange of agents, studio executives, performers, money men, lots of wives. Delegates of varying categories stopped at Mack's table and pumped his hand. The actor tolerated the intrusions for a while, then proposed a change of scenery. "Let's get the hell outta here. My place is just up the hill. But be warned. It's a holy mess. I'm putting in a new john and I've got plumbers and pipes up the kazoo. But if you wanna see the difference between Cloverdale and Summit Drive, here's your chance."

Kleber nodded and followed Mack out the back door of the Polo Lounge. "A new toilet? I didn't know movie stars shit."

"We do," acknowledged Mack. "But they're blue chips."

They walked through the lush gardens of the hotel, a tropical overgrowth of banana trees and bougainvillea and sweet honeysuckle and exotic lilies that threatened to strangle small stucco cottages that from the exterior looked no more luxurious than a motel on the wrong side of El Paso. Mack suddenly stopped. "Heard anything from T.J.?" he asked out of left field.

Kleber shook his head. "Nothing new. Same old chamber of horrors."

"What'd he think about . . . about that guy in San Antonio? The one in that clipping?"

"I'm afraid Butch's confession has not reached the ears of Mr. Luther. I decided not to share it with him."

"You didn't tell him?"

Kleber shook his head. "No. If T.J. has any conscience at all, I would like to think it occasionally gets nibbled on by poor old Laurie."

"What happened to this Butch? Did he get convicted?"

"Fate closed the circle. Butch hung himself in San Antonio county jail. We'll never know the rest of the story."

"That was a long time ago," said Mack.

"And I seem to remember we made a pact never to mention it again."

Mack smiled and started playing tour guide. He pointed to one of the Beverly Hills Hotel bungalows. "Hundred bucks a night to sleep in one of those," he said.

"I know," said Kleber, not to be one-upped. "I camped out just behind that banana tree last year looking for Howard Hughes. He's supposed to keep at least three bungalows full time, in case he ever needs a place to sleep."

"Did you see him?"

"Nope. I personally think he's been mummified for years." On assignment from *Life* magazine, which contracted him for several articles a year, Kleber had pursued Howard Hughes, fellow Texan, for a pair of amusing weeks, fascinated by the ultimate paranoia of celebrity. He recounted for Mack a tale of enterprising journalism. A tipster, it seemed, had whispered that the actress Jean Peters, reportedly the secret wife of the recluse, would attend a concert at the Hollywood Bowl to hear Joan Sutherland. As Miss Peters had not been glimpsed publicly for almost a decade, it would be a minor coup to snare her face and comments.

"The only trouble was I couldn't find out just where she would be seated," explained Kleber. "So the photographer and I bought scalper's tickets for forty dollars each and then spent two hours slowly walking up and down the aisles. I never knew the Hollywood Bowl was as steep as Fujiyama nor that it held 20,000 people. I inspected approximately 19,995 of these faces and about ten notes before the end of Miss Sutherland's assumedly beautiful performance—Minnie Pearl could have been on stage for all the attention I paid—I found her. In a box hidden by shrubbery. The photographer took some long-lens pictures and I followed her out. She had a circle of guards. Wish you had been there to run interference. She started to step into a limousine about a half block long and I grabbed her arm. I said, now are you ready for this gem, I had Mrs. Howard Hughes in my grasp and all I could think of to ask was 'How are you, ma'm?' She said fine and got in the car. I said, 'Where's your husband tonight?' And she smiled and shook her head. I said, here's the *really* intelligent question, the one all America was waiting for, I asked, 'Are you ever going to act again?' She stuck her nice little sort of sad face out between the cracks of the palace guards and she said, 'Not unless they ask me to do Eliza Doolittle in *My Fair Lady.*' "

Mack said it was a helluva story indeed and tactfully avoided reminding Kleber that he had read the account in *Life*. He pointed to his new jet-black Jaguar, a torpedo drowsing in the sun. But Kleber had more to tell, remarking not at all on his friend's expensive chariot. He climbed in with the nonchalance of entering a taxi. The night after the Hollywood Bowl search-and-discover mission, Kleber wasted another six hours in a rose garden on the highest hill of Bel Air. Rumor had it that Hughes himself was the secret lessee of a Greek Renaissance home at the summit of Los Angeles' most exalted neighborhood and occasionally took the night air between midnight and dawn. "We hid out the whole night," remembered Kleber. "Stretched out in a neighbor's bushes, certain that Howard would step outside at three a.m., grin boyishly at being trapped by an enterprising kid from Fort Worth, and then and there appoint me biographer of his life."

"And? Did he?" Mack was less interested in the story than once again being respectful to the leader of the block. He had always deferred to Kleber. And even now, coiling up a serpentine road of celebrity on which he had earned the right of occupancy, Mack was forced to endure the monologue of a blotter man.

"Zip. We shot the house and a shadow at the window. It could have been Howard. It could have been a dracaena tree." The Jaguar's approach caused a pair of ornate iron gates to swing open and a house as big as a high school came into view. It was a palace of glass and redwood, levels dripping down a hillside like melting butter. They drove across a bridge beneath which flowed a noisy brook that meandered to a swimming pool shaped like, Kleber commented, a woman's breasts. "Okay, I'm impressed," said Kleber. "It looks like the capital of Hedonia. Where do you keep the hot and cold running starlets?"

"They come out after sundown," said Mack. He parked the Jag

between a Lincoln and a jeep. Several people materialized at once to welcome the manor lord—a secretary with a yellow legal pad filled with telephone calls, two Japanese gardeners, a gaggle of plumbers with requests for additional moneys and autographed pictures, and a startlingly handsome youth with dark hair and a swimmer's body—all shoulders, no waist, thighs like palm trunks. Mack waved everybody away except the young man. He took him aside and said something privately that caused a frown.

"Who's that?" asked Kleber when the youth left and drove off in the jeep.

"A guy I'm working on a script with," said Mack with a jump in his voice. Kleber started to say that the kid seemed scarcely out of college but another anecdote came to mind. They sat down in chaise longues beside the pool, sinking into canvas pads thick as mattresses, and waited for gin and tonics.

"I was telling you about Howard Hughes and the rose bed," picked up Kleber.

Mack nodded without encouragement.

"So I got back to the hotel, hit the sack, and the phone rang at six a.m. One of the *Life* editors in New York says, 'Marilyn Monroe just killed herself. Get the hell out to her house.' I must tell you that this particular editor is a joker, so I say, 'Very funny. Fuck off. Over and out.' I hang up. Ring. Ring. 'Cantrell, dammit, Marilyn Monroe is eighty-sixed. Meet Klein at the Bel Air Sands Hotel on Sunset and Sepulveda. He's got her address.'"

Kleber had arrived at the cottage an hour after the most desired woman on the planet was found pitifully dead, nude, tangled in dirty sheets, the same drapes that covered her body for transfer to the coroner's ambulance. The actress's press agent, a comely young woman consumed with hysteria, started screaming at all the cameras and notebooks. "Vultures!" she shrieked, to which Kleber shrugged a plea of not guilty. He had never even met Marilyn Monroe, had only watched her undulate onto the stage of Madison Square Garden and sing in breathless off-key enthusiasm a happy birthday to John Kennedy.

Later on that morbid August Sunday, 1962, Kleber and the photographer went to the Los Angeles county morgue, where they bluffed passage through a maze of "No Admittance" corridors, strewing twenty-dollar bills as passkeys, reaching finally a chamber of refrigerated chill and harsh fluorescent light, of stainless-steel counters and worktables, smelling of blood and formaldehyde so strong that it watered the eyes of the living. The wall was crowded with tiny doors, each of which when opened revealed a deep sliding platform that contained a corpse. "I'm not too proud of what we did," Kleber told Mack. "We bribed and conned our way into stealing a picture of Marilyn's body. They pulled her rack out and the photographer swiped a shot of her big toe. It was protruding out the end of the sheet. Her toenails were dirty. I don't think she had washed her feet for days. She had surrendered, somehow. She didn't want it anymore. There was a big tag on her toe. It told her name and her morgue number. It all came down to that."

"I don't like that story," said Mack.

"I said I'm not too proud of it," agreed Kleber.

"I see why that girl cried 'vultures.' "

"Hey, it's my job."

"Where's the ethic of intruding on somebody's corpse?"

"There isn't any. Privacy has no value in journalism. But I got a bonus from *Life*."

Mack jumped up. He offered to show Kleber around the house. He had an earnest desire to tell Kleber that nothing came out of his mouth but memories of *other* people. He wanted to say, "Don't tell me what you've written, K. Tell me *who* you are." There didn't seem to be a Kleber anymore. Like the Chinese proverb, there was noise on the stairs, but nobody came into the room.

Mack did not have the opportunity to chide his friend. Not this trip. Before they even reached the door, the secretary ran out with her face twisted in shock. She was carrying a portable radio that blared agitated voices. "They've just shot Kennedy," she cried. "Listen!"

The secretary was disintegrating into tears but Kleber was cold. "Where?" he demanded, shaking the girl.

"It says Dallas."

"Of course," said Kleber. He ran straightaway to the Jaguar, not bothering to ask if Mack would drive him to the airport, knowing that his celebrity was superior at this moment and had to be attended. On the San Diego Freeway, just before the turnoff to LAX, the radio said Kennedy was dead. Confirmed. It was only then that Kleber sobbed, one awful solitary break in his control. Mack welcomed it. It was the only personal sound of the tedious morning. They would not see each other for five more years.

On the twenty-second night in November 1963, Dallas was cold and empty. A norther had swept in like punishment and no one was on the streets. Kleber would write that the city resembled a surly dog that had bitten a child, was now locked in its pen, was unrepentant and capable of doing it again. He disliked Dallas. It had always struck him as a braggadocial city with a chip on its shoulder. When, ten days before this night, Kleber had heard that Kennedy intended a stop in Dallas on a fence-mending tour of Texas, he was worried. He had cornered Ted Sorensen at a cocktail party in Georgetown and presumptuously suggested that their President skip Dallas. This was, after all, the city where Adlai Stevenson had been assaulted by right-wing extremists, spat upon, cursed, bopped on the shoulder with a placard demanding that the United States get out of the United Nations. The photographs of this appalling event had been disgraceful, portraits of malcontents, people frustrated by everything from the intolerable John Kennedy proposal that oilmen pay an equitable tax to the Supreme Court's recent denial of children's "right" to begin school each morning with recitation of the Lord's Prayer. Mostly they were fearful that America was changing, that there were new claimants to the national pie besides white Protestant conservatives. They had attacked Adlai in their fury and now, believed Kleber, they had killed John Kennedy.

Kleber's flying off impulsively to Dallas had been a rash act. Now that he was in the city, there seemed very little story left to cover. The pageant of history had moved to Washington. The President's body was en route to the capital, as was the new leader, Lyndon Johnson. The only item of interest left in Dallas was the man being held in the police station as the possible assassin. Kleber entered the cop shop and on the third floor grew immediately alarmed. There were hundreds of reporters milling around, more than had buried Marilyn Monroe. The business of news was growing and the competition was extreme. Every pencil pusher and photo snapper in the corridor devoutly coveted an exclusive moment with the man whose name was Lee Harvey Oswald. Chances of brief contact were scant; something exclusive was impossible. Nothing was known of the assassin, nothing but his very Texanesque triple name, nothing but that the suspect was young, adamant in his denials, and under police interrogation somewhere on this third floor. If Kleber got anything worth writing, he would offer it to *Life*, but the hard realities of a deadline made his task challenging. If he had still been working for a daily newspaper, any scrap could be set to print in hours. But *Life* demanded a choicer cut, a full meal that would seem freshly cooked a week later when set before the appetites of 28 million readers.

"Is there going to be a press conference?" Kleber asked a policeman who was threading through the noisy crowd.

"They say he wants to make a statement," said the cop, who was not awed by the crush of correspondents. He ambled down the hall toward a soft-drink machine. Kleber followed him, putting a coat of hometown shitkicker varnish on his voice and stance (negating the recent years in the East, where he was anxious to shed his identifying birthright). He bought the officer a root beer and wondered, by the way, "What was that Oswald boy's address?"

"Some rooming house in Oak Cliff," said the cop.

"You got the number?" asked Kleber. The policeman eyed him with the same warmth southern sheriffs bestow on outside agitators. "Ah'm from Foat Wuth," drawled Kleber quite honestly.

The moment that Kleber parked in front of the rooming house at 1026 North Beckley, he felt the gift of confidence. Homecoming. He knew that when the landlady opened the screen door of her dulled red brick home that she would be not unlike Edith Saller in Houston. In fact, she might have been a sister. The men in the living room lounged in the same undershirts, sprawled on the same Naugahyde sofas, drank the same Pearl beer, watched the same blizzardy black-and-white TV that had filled the lonely hours of Howard the Bragger and Leo the Lothario and crafty old Daniel Titus. The cubicle where the mysterious roomer who called himself "O. H. Lee" had slept was exactly as Kleber expected it to be. Oswald's digs were not big enough to swing a cat in. For eight dollars a week Oswald got an iron cot with springs that cut into a man's spine, was embraced by dirty, faded walls that penned young men with dreams and old men with none. "Mr. Lee was your loner type," said the landlady. "Very polite. Prompt with the rent. He only lived here six weeks, you know. Never said boo to anybody. Didn't join the other gentlemen out yonder in the television room."

"Was there anything . . . *unusual* . . . about him?" asked Kleber.

The landlady brightened. She remembered something! "Oh, yes, he always got up early and took a bath and washed the ring out of the tub. He was the only guest I ever had who did that. And he made a lot of lunch meat sandwiches; he ate them for breakfast and dinner."

Kleber agreed that a man who washed the ring from the tub and favored bologna was indeed interesting. But was there anything else?

"No. Nothing at all. He never tried to fix up his room. He told me he had two baby daughters, but he didn't have any pictures of them. I know he loved his daughters."

"Where was his wife?"

"I don't know. He never mentioned her."

"Did any friends visit?"

She shook her head. She was trying to be helpful, caught up in a drama whose historic magnitude had not yet hit. "Well, there's one thing. He talked on the pay telephone out there in the hall. Talked in a foreign language. *German,* I think."

As the world knew nothing at this early moment of Lee Harvey Oswald, the tease of a foreign language was provocative. "Whom did he talk to?" begged Kleber.

"I don't know. Perhaps somebody in Irving."

"Irving?"

"A little town between here and Fort Worth. One night last week he talked longer than he had paid for, and the operator called back and wanted another thirty-five cents. Mr. Lee had already left the house. But I remember the operator saying his Irving call required another thirty-five cents. I may have to pay it, if he forgets. If you see him, can you remind him?"

With nothing more substantial than the name of a town called Irving, Kleber drove there, grappling with the apprehension that he was not only barking up the wrong tree, he was not even in the right forest. The bedroom community was down for the night—it was now close to 10 p.m.—and most of the houses were dark. A few of the front windows glimmered from the pale flicker of televisions within. Common sense dictated that news was in downtown Dallas, at the police station. But instinct told Kleber there were secrets on these quiet streets. Somewhere. If he could only find them. He decided to gamble, to search, acting on the command of reasons he scarcely paused to analyze. Whatever, he was in the grip of incredible adventure. He was fully alive. Nothing else mattered.

He found a sheriff's substation open for business, a one-room office with glass walls where inside a dispatcher sat at a console. The deputy's world appeared to contain nothing more grave than two-car smashes and prowlers. Kleber prayed he would have a torch to illuminate a crime beyond comprehension. This was the picture: hotshot reporter lost in the sticks, about to ask a twangy clerk if by any chance he happened to know whom Lee Harvey Oswald used to telephone in Irving and why he spoke in German. The reporter tossed a wide net: "Ah, sir, I was wondering if anything went on out here today concerning the shooting of the President." He figuratively sat down beside the campfire and warmed his hands, trying to appear like a needy stranger. As a matter of fact, allowed the dispatcher, the feds had been out looking for some woman a few streets south, just before the sun had set on this saddest day. Kleber's heart sang! Who? Where? Why? But he got nothing else. If the deputy knew anything more, he wasn't telling.

Up and down the lanes he drove, once again comforted by the embrace of familiarity. Any of these streets could have been Cloverdale, none quite as elderly and enduring, but each a belt on the robes of the middle class. Then he saw a cottage whose only point of interest was a light in the window and a yard with slender trees, crooked and twisted, as if their job was to guard and hide the lives within. Later, after he wrote the story and told the story at dinner parties, the question would always come: But *why?* Why did you knock on this particular door? And Kleber had no answer, none save the unlikely truth. "I don't know. I just did. Maybe I was supposed to."

The woman who answered his rap was tall, of stately posture, a brunette in middle years. She projected strength and dignity. Her face had no makeup but her eyes were clear. She probably read Thoreau and baked her own bread. Kleber made these snap character assessments and it pleased him how often he was right. Initial impressions are necessary in journalism, particularly to a man like Kleber whom Ceil Shannon once stung with a flippancy: "Some people live in the past. Some people live for the moment. You're the first person I've ever come across who lives for the next moment."

The woman shook Kleber's hand firmly and introduced herself as Ruth Paine. "Come in," she said graciously. "I've been expecting the press. You're the first." Her living room was crowded with people watching the events on television. Air Force One had just landed in Washington, its cargo a dead President, a bloodied First Lady, a new

President. Collectively the people in the room gazed mutely at Kleber and returned their eyes to the screen. Ruth Paine did not introduce them. Nor did Kleber ask their names. He saw none who looked like leading players in *any* worthwhile drama, only neighbors, cousins, a child or two, a man in mechanic's soiled overalls, an old woman with reddened eyes and wearing a white nylon nurse's uniform.

Ruth Paine and the reporter sat on the floor, facing one another, like chess players. Kleber wanted to say, "I haven't the faintest idea why I'm here or why you opened your door or why you were expecting the press." But instead he began, "Do you know Lee Harvey Oswald?"

"Of course," she said. "Lee is my friend. We were learning Russian together."

"*Russian?* Why?"

"Because Lee lived in Russia. He married a Russian wife." As routinely as explaining to third-graders how the world is round, Ruth Paine talked for half an hour, scarcely requiring reportorial prods, speaking with composure and clarity, weaving a bizarre tapestry. Kleber wrote furiously, trying to concentrate on his astonishing discovery, diverted nonetheless by the incongruity of the moment. He worried that another knock would soon come at the door. If he had found this treasure so easily, then surely the competition would presently find Irving. He had to work quickly. "Then, based on what you know about Lee," he asked, "do you think he killed the President of the United States?"

A woman screamed. The woman on the sofa in the white nurse's uniform leaped up and cried, "Don't you think I should answer that question? I'm Lee's *mother!*"

Kleber's mouth flew open in shock as he shook hands with Mrs. Marguerite Oswald. But before he could repeat his question, the door from an adjoining bedroom cracked and a young, pale, troubled woman appeared. She held a fretting baby in her arms, and she did not even glance at the television set. She made her way through the crowd into the kitchen to fetch a bottle of formula. But she paused on the journey back and spoke to Ruth Paine in a guttural language that sounded like German.

"Who was that?" asked Kleber when the woman left the room.

Ruth Paine smiled. "That's Marina Oswald," she said. "Lee's little wife. And his baby. Their other daughter is asleep."

"What language were you speaking?"

"Russian. Marina scarcely knows twenty words in English."

The Prince of Power thus possessed the mother, wife, and daughters of a suspected assassin. His heart immediately went out to Marina. The young woman's predicament was excruciating. She had exactly $1.65 in her purse, two crying children. And on the television set in a language she could not understand was the accusation that her husband had committed the century's most shattering murder. She looked barely eighteen, a little dumpy, hips not yet narrowed from childbirth, hair pulled back into the drab bun of a babushka, not a splash of color on her face. Lee, said Ruth Paine, always forbade his wife the enhancement of cosmetics.

Mother Oswald destroyed the moment. She yelled in counterpoint to the television commentary, "My boy didn't kill anybody! I'm his mother! And a mother knows!" For a minute Kleber felt sorry for her. Then she set up shop. Mama wanted money. Mama had information. Mama desired quid for her quo. She suggested to Kleber that he purchase in coin of the realm any interview about her boy, throwing in as bonus like the prize in a Crackerjack box pictures of Lee from the cradle to the U. S. Marines and letters he had written home from Russia.

"How much money are you talking about?" asked Kleber.

"A lot. I need money to defend my son. I haven't even got enough to take a taxi to the jail."

"How much money?"

"Twenty-five hundred dollars." In retrospect, Kleber always wished he had whipped out his checkbook then and there, purchasing a franchise whose worth would swell to incalculable sums before the month was done. But he was troubled by the notion of getting into financial bed with the mother and wife of an assassin, was nagged by the possibility that these women might somehow have been involved with the death of his President. It would not advance a career to fund the futures of potential accomplices. Instead Kleber countered with the sensible offer of chauffeuring the Oswald family immediately to downtown Dallas, of installing them in a fine suite at the Adolphus Hotel, where they could order lavishly from room service and where—of course he did not mention this—the prize would be safely hidden from competition. Mama was agreeable; Marina was not. She had by now coaxed her children into sleep with Russian lullabies. Through the helpful but inexpert translation of Ruth Paine, Marina said, *"Nyet."* Come back tomorrow morning.

Throughout the night, Kleber sat outside in a rented car parked on a nearby corner, eyes trained on the house that held the scoop of his career. He was prepared to halt, tackle, and if necessary tie up anyone who approached with a pad or a camera. He passed the cold night eating a stale peanut candy bar and drinking water from a neighbor's faucet and appreciating the absurdity of his life. Twelve hours previously he had been lolling on the patio of a summit in Beverly Hills, in pleasant fellowship with the Prince of Charms. Now he was watching the house where Lee Harvey Oswald had begun the day by strolling out with a rifle wrapped in a blanket that would alter the course of history.

He had lost his hero. Kennedy was dead. But on this night he did not mourn or weep. Where was the emotion? He wondered about this fleetingly. Maybe I don't have any, he thought as he drifted against his will into fitful sleep.

Jack Kennedy had been dead a dozen hours before the news seeped into the drugged brain of T. J. Luther, hiding on this November night in a tourist court on the outskirts of Shreveport, Louisiana. He had taken refuge, avoiding the cross fire of a minor war between the forces of Mash and Chick Sader that had been ignited by the bloody scandal of T.J.'s bomb in the mailbox. Quite a lot of shit had gone down. In retaliation, the Dallas mobster commissioned the burning of Mash's office and was furious that the ensuing ashes of Ventures Unlimited contained only the bleached skull of a longhorn. The obese human target had prudently fled to Mexico. But just before Mash crossed the border, he stopped long enough to tip off federal narcotics officers that Chick Sader was peddling heroin. This resulted in the arrest of two valuable Sader lieutenants. The next night, in Fort Worth, the Pink Lady Club blew like the patriotic finale on July 4, sending Large Marge to the hospital with third-degree burns where she would spend the next year in excruciating pain, clutching the hand of Bamboozle, who slept beside her every night, sitting in his wheelchair and making clown faces.

T.J., who from Day One of his association with Mash had used the alias of Tojo Rutledge, did not believe his name was on a murder contract. He doubted if Chick Sader even knew his real identity. And though crazed with grief over the dismemberment of Priscilla and the tragedy of Large Marge, he had enough sense to go on retreat. For a couple of months, the Prince of Temptation became a homeless, nameless mongrel, slinking about the great expanses of northeast Texas, rarely passing more than one night in Tyler or Longview or Texarkana, always sleeping sitting up with a loaded .44 in his hand, the chest of drawers pushed against the motel room door. If he needed money, he robbed a filling station or burglarized a farmhouse. He didn't require much; twenty bucks a day usually covered a bed, a quart of whiskey, a plate of fried eggs. He stopped shaving, stopped looking in the mirror because the gray streaks in his beard and the yellow dots in his eyes scared him. A whore in a trailer park near Amarillo said he smelled like shit and should take a bath but he slapped her teeth and she didn't complain again the rest of the night.

Just before the midnight of November 22, he woke suddenly, sweating and screaming from a dream that had recently come to stay— in it Priscilla was on some kind of a platform standing next to Kleber Cantrell and John F. Kennedy, and T.J. was down below, in a crowd, trying to get their attention but always being ignored. It was then he heard on television that the President had gone and gotten his brains blown out.

Later this night, on the early morning of November 23, while the Prince of Power sat on a slumbering Irving street watching the house that contained the family of an assassin, the Prince of Temptation took a bath, combed his hair, thinned the silver from his beard with a pocketknife, found a J. C. Penney's store, broke in, selected a tan checked sports jacket and a pair of forest-green slacks, a raffish porkpie hat, took $165 from a cash register, and obeyed an impulse to drive to Dallas.

The morning was scarcely born, still gray, the faintest streaks of pink edging the eastern sky, when Kleber rapped again at the door of Ruth Paine. There was first autumn frost on the grass. Incredibly, no other journalist had found the house with the prize. The purveyors of news had passed instead a frustrating night at the Dallas police station, feeding on rumor and hope. Kleber routinely collected the mother and wife and daughters of the assassin, stuffing them into his car and breathing comfortably at last. One more delay. Marina insisted on fetching a fresh laundry of diapers and baby clothes on a line in the Paine back yard. Kleber went with her, snatching the items hurriedly and feeling foolish. Then, like a suburban father finally leaving on holiday, he drove into Dallas.

En route, nobody said much, save Mama Oswald, who confided, "Lee's father died, you know. He died in New Orleans while Lee was still in my womb. There is a Creole saying that when a father dies before his son is born, then that baby will be blessed with special rewards. A fatherless baby carries the gift of God."

If the rest of the morning did not have undercurrents so bizarre and mordant, Kleber would have collapsed in wild laughter. He smuggled his ladies into the Adolphus Hotel through a freight entrance, carrying one Oswald daughter in his arms, holding the hand of the second and urging her like an impatient parent not to dawdle. Mama commenced to cry, bellowing bassoon sobs, ignoring Kleber's pleas to shut up. It occurred to the reporter that Mrs. Oswald dearly wished to be observed. Installing the brood in a suite registered in his name, Kleber ordered breakfast for everybody from room service and, while waiting, welcomed the arrival of a Russian woman pediatrician who had been unearthed during the night by *Life* to serve as translator. But what he had feared all night promptly happened; his cover was blown. Some alert pair of eyes spotted the caravan entering the hotel and now the press was in heat. The Adolphus boiled with starving news collectors, desperate to carve a slice of Kleber's golden goose. Three times that morning he switched suites, changing names each time, finally settling in at ten-thirty under the pseudonym "Sam Schwartz and family," occupation "hosiery salesman," home address "Chicago." Room service waiters trailed each change of quarters, anxious to serve chilled eggs and limp toast that had been cooked two hours before. Finally came a fragile moment of peace. Kleber began his interviews, anxious to elicit answers from the pale and confused wife of Oswald. The young Russian girl, he felt, would be the Rosetta Stone of the assassination. He put on the demeanor of sympathetic friend, speaking softly, moving gently, trying to look pleasant. But he had not reckoned with the force called Hurricane Mama.

Each time he asked a question of Marina, a query no more intrusive than, say, how and when did she meet Lee, Mother Oswald rose, bolted to the chair where her daughter-in-law sipped lukewarm tea, hovered like a thundercloud, and shrieked, "Whore! You Russian whore! You got my boy and me into this!" Then she sat down. When Kleber attempted another question, the old woman, still wearing her nylon nurse's uniform, became the most tender pacifier since Florence Nightingale. She flung her thick fleshy arms about the Russian girl's shoulders and cooed, "I love you, daughter. And I will stand by you until people learn we are all innocent."

Alternating between harridan and helpmate for the rest of the morning, Mama made the gathering of news challenging. Kleber poured continuous cups of coffee for the old nuisance, praying that her kidneys would grant him respite. His task was further tortured by frequent telephone calls from a *Life* editor now in the hotel, reminding Kleber that the magazine was "holding open" in New York awaiting his copy, making him feel that the empire of Henry Luce might topple in red ink lest he hurry.

At high noon there came a pounding at the door, in the tempo and volume of machine-gun fire. Kleber bade his guests fall silent, but the baby decided to howl. From outside in the corridor came a gruff command, "Cantrell, this is the FBI. Open the door."

"You've got the wrong room," growled Kleber in displeasure. "My name is Schwartz. I'm a hosiery salesman from Chicago."

"Cantrell, open the goddamn door. We know you've got those women in there." As punctuation, an identification card of an FBI agent glided like a serpent's tongue beneath the entrance. It was genuine.

A squad of feds swooped in and collected the women and children of Lee Harvey Oswald. One of the agents saw the pain of loss on Kleber's face and he said, "I'm sorry, son. I know you've got a helluva story here. But the U.S. government needs to talk to these people more than you do." The agent promised that when official interrogation was completed, he would reconnect the reporter to his subjects. If, that is, the women wished it. Kleber protested, quoted the First Amendment, did everything but fall to his knees and tug at the trousers of J. Edgar Hoover's finest—but it did no good. Left alone, with a shamefully naked steno pad, he had barely enough words to construct an adequate story, which *Life* eagerly accepted and ran in its remarkable coverage of the assassination.

In vain Kleber waited the rest of the afternoon beside the telephone, hoping that the FBI would call and give him back the women. In the last moments of this Saturday, he grew bored and walked outside, wanting to see the place where Kennedy had been murdered. He bluffed his way to the sixth floor of the Texas Book Depository, where a photographer for *Paris-Match* was taking pictures of the plaza below. The Frenchman was marveling at the marksmanship that Oswald must have possessed. Kleber peered through the long lens. "Yeah. The bastard was one lucky shooter," said Kleber. He appreciated the distance, the angle, the path of the bullet.

From the sixth floor of the book depository, Kleber also looked down and saw, but paid little heed to, a large number of people milling around the site where Kennedy's limousine had been intercepted by gunfire. Some were mourning, some bearing flowers, most playing detective. One of them was a slim and hardened man with a beard. He wore a checked jacket and porkpie hat. T. J. Luther looked up at the sixth floor of the Texas Book Depository and, observing the long lens of a camera poking out the now notorious window, moved hurriedly away. He did not wish to be included in any photograph. T.J. had come to the place of murder only out of curiosity. He wanted to see how a piece of shit like Lee Harvey Oswald could have knocked off a President. He envied the little bastard they had over at the crossbar hotel. Yesterday morning nobody knew his name. This afternoon he was a headline that circled the world.

On Sunday morning, Jack Ruby, a merchant of watered drinks and striptease dancing, became the next celebrity, managing to plunge through a cordon of Dallas lawmen and fire a bullet into the body of Lee Harvey Oswald. This T.J. saw on television, it being history's first live murder, and though its audacity thrilled him, a face in the crowd caused him even more excitement. He watched the replays again and again, until he was convinced that Kleber Cantrell was only ten feet away from the killing of the killer.

T.J. passed the remainder of the afternoon in restlessness. He was drunk, but not drunk enough. Being Sunday, dry day, it was necessary to pay a nigger who hung around the Sleep-Eeze Motel on the east side of Dallas an extra ten bucks to locate a quart of bourbon. He nursed the bottle, intending to shepherd its blessings all night, but by sundown it was gone. A feeling that he was in the grip of history took hold. He began to imagine what it was like to be Lee Oswald, to be Jack Ruby, to be Kleber Cantrell. All three hats slipped easily on and off his head. The trouble with me, he told himself, is that I'm always on the outer edge or in the attic with a magnet. "It ain't fair," he muttered. "I'm better-lookin' than Mack, smarter'n Kleber, meaner'n Lee Oswald. Jack Ruby couldn't wipe my ass." He told this to the mottled mirror that gave him back a swaying derelict with inflamed eyes.

Fitting his .44 neatly into the breast pocket of his stolen coat, the Prince of Temptation thus stumbled forth to search, to find, to demand validation of his worth.

Three men were buried in remarkable juxtaposition of caste and circumstance. One, a President, was returned to the earth in the witness of kings and emperors, his rite of majesty the equal of classical tragedy. The second, a Dallas police officer, was honored by a thousand citizens and colleagues in an overflowing Baptist church, thence borne with an escort of motorcycle officers to a plot of Texas soil reserved for honored dead.

The third was planted in the red gummy clay of Fort Worth; a furtive rite it was, attended by mourners totaling five—the assassin's mother, brother, wife, and baby daughters. For an embarrassing several hours, it was difficult to even find a cemetery that would accept the corpse of Oswald, the reason being that such infamous remains would taint a graveyard and make it difficult to sell the plots nearby. Who, after all, would want to sleep for eternity beside such villainy?

The city of Dallas, some of whose citizens applauded at the news of John Kennedy's execution and whose police bungling allowed the assassin to be slain, now wished to disassociate itself from all maniac deeds. The garbage was tossed to Fort Worth for disposal. A modest cemetery called Rose Hill agreed to bury Oswald—the $500 cost of his embalming and coffin being guaranteed by the U.S. government—but no minister was willing to preach the funeral. Then Fort Worth's police chief, a bulky man with the centurion name of Cato Hightower, took charge. He rang up the Reverend Louis Saunders, executive secretary of the city's council of churches, who, though not having preached a funeral in many years, agreed. "No man should be buried in Fort Worth without a minister," he said.

They tried to keep it secret. But Kleber found out from one of the FBI men, drove at ninety miles an hour across the turnpike, reached Rose Hill, hoping to take custody of the women. He and the hearse arrived together. There was a three-hour wait, the time required for hastily summoned gravediggers to scoop out a hole. The coffin, a cheap wooden box covered with burgundy cloth, was stashed meantime inside a rock-studded chapel and guarded by Fort Worth police. "They're taking better care of Oswald dead than Dallas did with Oswald alive," wrote Kleber. The women came and he tried to catch their eyes, but under their veils they did not see him. The service inside the chapel was brief and unreported.

At that moment, a riderless stallion pranced a thousand miles away toward the place where a President would rest. With muffled drums, with tears on the cheeks of Charles de Gaulle and Haile Selassie, the heart of the nation crumpled. Kleber watched instead a cheesy tableau of embarrassing poignance. The doors of Rose Hill chapel flung open and the coffin of Lee Harvey Oswald wheeled from the gloom within. It abruptly paused. No one had remembered the need for pallbearers and now there were no hands to lift the assassin's box and carry it down a steep flight of stairs, thence to the grave a hundred yards away.

For an instant, Kleber wondered if they would try and dolly the coffin down the steps like a packing crate, risking the grotesque spectacle of it tumbling out of control, splitting open, spilling the assassin into the light of the living. Wrung hands. Squirms. Whether from the grace of good manners or the deceit of currying favor, Kleber volunteered. Five other reporters and cops joined his gesture. The press and the law toted the assassin to his grave.

At the gates of Rose Hill, the harried man told police that he had come to pray at his mother's grave and in the excitement of the day they believed him, mistaking the red of his eyes for grief. T.J. lurched across the beds of the dead toward the faded green canopy where the Oswald women sat in battered folding chairs. He stopped and listened. The old woman was screaming, "Privacy at the grave! Privacy, please! Give us the respect of privacy!" He saw—as he expected—Kleber Cantrell, standing on the other side of the coffin and wriggling like an encyclopedia salesman. He watched the undertaker open the coffin and by standing on his tiptoes could glimpse, barely, the corpse. Oswald in death was dressed neatly in a brown suit and tie. He saw a younger woman, Oswald's wife, take a ring from her finger and place it on the finger of the corpse. He saw her lean forward and kiss the waxen lips. He thought it was revolting. He tried to get closer, but the police blocked his way. He wanted a drink.

They closed the lid and lowered the box. They hustled the women away. Kleber ran after the federal cars, trying to cash his due bills. But the cars sped off and he stopped, beaten, exasperated, breathing heavily, not expecting the sordid coda about to be played.

Walking dejectedly to his car, Kleber was suddenly hit from behind. He crumpled, falling to the seared grass under the weight of an assailant. He smelled the fumes of whiskey. Kleber yelled, "What the shit?" He struggled and tried to free his wrists from the clamp of some powerful force. Was this the final act, the closing of some homicidal circle? Now they're killing *me,* he believed. Then the monkey on his back laughed and it was the bray of an ass.

"Welcome home, you old son of a bitch," whooped T. J. Luther.

Kleber froze. Slowly he stood up, dusted himself, started to yell for the aid of nearby police. Then he recognized the wrinkled, sodden, paste-faced, unwanted, unexpected fool. "Jesus, T.J.," he said, "you're crazy."

"Why hell yes," agreed T.J. "Always was. Aren't we all? Damn sad day when a feller's gotta crash a goddamn funeral just to say howdy."

"T.J., listen to me," said Kleber, trying to keep control. "I *am* glad to see you. But I'm working. I'm on deadline. I've got to write about this funeral. So I'll call you. Okay?"

"Nope," disagreed T.J. "Ain't gonna let you go anywhere without us settin' down for a nice long catch-up. We're brothers and I love my long-lost brother. What we need's a little whistle-wetter. You got somethin' to drink in your car?"

Just beyond, bulldozers were hurrying to push earth onto the assassin's grave, smoothing the red clay, working with urgency as if the deed could be covered up and forgotten. The mortician tossed two bedraggled floral wreaths of dying carnations and roses onto the fresh roof of Oswald's tomb. Clouds like the clenched fists of anger were moving in, turning the day dark and sour. Kleber had mentally composed a piece while witnessing the pathetic rite and now a thief was robbing his senses. He shook his head blankly and started again toward his car.

With a howl, T.J. leaped once more, missing this time, falling alone and rolling beside the reporter's feet. The stolen sports jacket flew open and Kleber caught the glint of gunmetal. He ran. The idiot had a gun. T.J. screamed at him. "Why dontcha look at me, huh? You give your time to that Oswald chickenshit. He's checked *out*, Kleber. He's done gone. We're *here*. Talk to me."

"Later," cried Kleber over his shoulder. "Tomorrow. Some other time." He was almost at his car. He was fighting the insane fantasy that T.J. was going to shoot him in the back. The day was spinning into a grotesquerie. He had the notion that Oswald had burst out of the earth and had transmogrified into the Prince of Temptation. Gratefully he tore open the car door and threw his body inside, slamming the locks, shuddering on the razor's edge of lost control. Through the window was the face of T.J. A death mask was pounding at the glass and screaming.

At the exit gate of Rose Hill, Kleber was stopped by a policeman who, it turned out, was an old news source from Houston. They chatted routinely and briefly. The officer glanced for no reason back toward the notorious grave. T. J. Luther saw the cop, felt his stare, believed erroneously that Kleber had tattled on him. He raced to a distant fence and hid in some woods until dark. Reckoning that his best friend had betrayed him, T.J. held court and passed judgment. Kleber Judas Cantrell was sentenced to death. Later that night, after finishing his article and telephoning it to New York, Kleber checked out of the Adolphus Hotel and drove in exhaustion to Love Field.

He did not know that in the car behind him, in the grip of a hand that shook with rawest fury, was a .44 pistol trained at his head. And if T. J. Luther had not been intercepted by a highway patrolman who caught him speeding, the tale might have ended then and there.

Kleber stumbled onto a Braniff flight, hoping that it would be sparsely filled so he could take out the armrest and curl his body across two first-class seats. During the boarding process he dozed and failed to see the woman who sat down beside him. He did not wake up until the plane was in the air and was annoyed because his fellow passenger kept the overhead light on. She was reading through a stack of newspapers about the assassination.

He shifted and tried to find room for his legs. The woman turned toward him. "Does the light bother you?" she asked politely. Kleber saw her full face. It was Ceil Shannon.

"I know you," he said. "We met once in Houston."

She pretended to remember but Kleber had to help reconstruct the long-ago afternoon at the Alley Theater. "I'm sorry," she apologized. "I'm not thinking clearly."

"Nobody is." He apologized for his appearance. He could smell the dried sweat on his shirt. His hair was uncombed. He needed a shave. His breath smelled like clabber. Of all times to re-meet the woman of fantasy.

But she asked the same forbearance from him. Ceil had been in Yucatán visiting an archaeologist girl friend on a dig. She had been bathing in cold spring water for a week. She held her nose. Her hair was shoved up carelessly under a gaucho hat and she wore a cheap orange poncho from a street market in Mexico. She was as embarrassed as he.

He told her briefly why he had been in Dallas. She begged for more. She had been a hundred miles from nowhere when the President was shot. A young boy had come running into the camp on Saturday afternoon. "Kennedy, *adiós!*" he had cried, putting his finger to his brain and pulling an imaginary trigger. As she told the story her eyes filled with tears.

Kleber began to tell his adventure haltingly. His words sounded like someone dictating to the city desk for the night final. Ceil kept interrupting and asking, "But how did you *feel* when you saw Marina Oswald?" Or "How did you *feel* when you carried Oswald to his grave?" And always Kleber gave an evasive answer. He had no feelings. He was trying to feed her facts but she wanted to be nourished by emotions. Those were not his franchise.

He ran out of story somewhere over Virginia, about an hour before the plane was to land. And he fell silent. Ceil switched off her light and in the darkness reached out and took his hand. Her touch was gentle and comforting. After a while she began to cry. "Hold me," she asked. "I'm sort of scared." So was he. He wrapped her in his arms until the landing at Idlewild. Then they took a taxi to her apartment and held each other the rest of the night. By the next morning they were lovers.

CHAPTER TWENTY

In 1968, the year that Mack Crawford became thirty-five (although his official biography and listings in various Who's Who publications shaved that by two years), he appeared on the covers of 214 magazines in 47 countries. In Italy and France, in Rumania and Czechoslovakia, in Thailand and Singapore, in Argentina and Chile, in Australia and New Zealand, he was both recognized and desired. He was the American fantasy and the symbol of universal masculine myth. He was every woman's imaginary lover, every mother's son, every man's best friend. Two young girls in Cape Town committed suicide because their parents disallowed a trip to Hollywood where their most passionate desire was to lay eyes on his actual flesh. The joint suicide note was penned precisely at the bottom of a form letter, one of thousands mailed each month from a post office box in Los Angeles, the text of which read:

Dear [blank]:

Thank you for your friendship and support.
I cannot do it without you.
I am happy to send you my photograph, my love, and my kiss.

The signature at the bottom was scribbled by a machine so realistically that if a finger was wetted and rubbed against the ink, it would blur, indicating that Mack himself had penned his name.

Four middle-aged women who had never met Mack, either, were employed to handle his fan mail, not a piece of which he ever saw. He was given a monthly statistics report, rather like a postal rating of his popularity. Rare was the week when fewer than 3,000 letters arrived.

The weekly average contained a dependable hundred or so proposals of marriage, a couple of hundred requests for contributions of money or of personal articles (a pair of socks, a hairbrush with hairs intact) for auction at charity functions, a dozen threats of violence (these were turned over to the LAPD and usually dismissed as nut city), and several score snapshots of prurient nature. There are always people out there who wish celebrities to view their private parts, usually because no one else wishes to.

Though Arnie Beckman became respected and wealthy for guiding Mack's career, the actor's success was due as well to his own intuition. Of the several hundred scripts submitted to the Beckman office each year, none of which Mack would consider acting for less than $1 million salary and 5 percent of the gross receipts counted from the first dollar taken in at the box office, Mack seriously considered only those which cast him as a rigidly defined hero.

He perceived himself as the heir to a cinematic legacy passed down from Douglas Fairbanks, Sr., to Clark Gable to Gary Cooper to John Wayne. Though he envied artistic career risks taken by fellow actors such as Warren Beatty, who played—and flopped—in pictures like *Mickey One,* Mack could have prophesied that nobody would go to see the story of a broken-down cabaret performer brutalized by a fuzzy force of evil in Chicago. He respected the talents of Keir Dullea but knew that the actor would not enjoy an enduring career playing *in dementia.*

An article in a French cinema publication gave scholarly analysis of Mack Crawford's *oeuvre,* the author suggesting that Mack succeeded by playing—and playing again and again—the hero of myth: "Whether this impossibly well-formed actor is cast as a courageous sergeant in the American Army fighting fascism in World War II, or the young sheriff defending his Texas town against Comanches and the violence of vice, or the hulking farm boy who overcomes polio to achieve a World Series victory on the pitcher's mound, Mr. Crawford epitomizes heroism as defined in ancient literature. This hero is always a superior being who excels in war or great adventure, who upholds the virtues of strength and personal discipline and noble ideals and courage and loyalty. His screen lives are those against which the common man can measure a mundane existence. Crawford thrusts for a personal summit and in so doing delivers the message and challenge, 'I did, and so can you!'"

Nevertheless there was cause for concern in this year when a second Kennedy was assassinated and man prepared to walk on the moon. Mack Crawford's career was slipping. The character of America had darkened. There was a bear market for heroes.

Every other Thursday afternoon, excluding those when he was on a film location or able to invent an acceptable excuse, Mack was expected to endure a meeting at the Beverly Hills offices of his attorney, Karl Zakariah. Each session began promptly at twelve-thirty with the serving of a lavish lunch arranged by Arnie, who had become a gourmet, and paid for by his principal client. Then business was conducted until 6 p.m. Others in attendance were a certified public accountant, a financial adviser, a press agent, and, from time to time, various studio executives or prominent independent producers seeking the expensive services of Mack Crawford, more specifically, the corporation that he had become. Macra, Inc., chartered in Delaware, performed one service (beyond certain ruses conducted to confound the IRS) and that was selling the face and figure of McKenzie Crawford.

Though aware of the importance of these dry and tedious Thursdays, Mack loathed them. Never did he feel less like a human and more like an object of commerce. His name was rarely even invoked. Attorney Zakariah, Agent Beckman, CPA Nesmith, Financial Consultant Beggers, Press Agent Tellens—all possessed surnames and were so addressed. Not Mack. He was called by either the second-person "you," the third-person "he," or the corporate-person "Macra." Dialogue went like this:

"Macra should consider investing $75,000 in three units of the Tiburon Vineyards as a tax shelter." Or "He is being audited for the fiscal year 1967 and must produce a corporate diary of the formation of its pension and profit-sharing plans." Or "You have been offered a two-picture contract with Universal. The subjects of such motion pictures and all approvals—director, casts, publicity—are awarded to Macra."

One Thursday morning in the summer of 1968, Mack arose at eleven, having overslept, an unsurprising event due to the fact that he did not close his eyes until the sun cracked shortly after five. It would be a momentous day for which he was not at all prepared. The first thing he did after staggering out of a bed large enough to contain a football scrimmage was throw up the torment of the night, that being most of a quart of Polish vodka, several containers of takeout Chink food, a full package of Oreo cookies, and a mélange of macadamia nuts and Godiva chocolates. If the ingested smoke from a pipe of Nepalese hash could have been vomited, that would have come up, too.

Mack stumbled into his glass-walled shower, from which he could see a dozen miles away the Pacific Ocean and, below, a wilderness that plunged almost a thousand feet into a densely wooded canyon. Six jets of icy water hit his body like flagellators; he crumpled to the hand-painted Mexican tiles, penitent. His penis hurt. He looked down at the member, that bulge in his jeans that sold millions of movie tickets, and he was alarmed to discover an angry rose memoir. At first he feared it to be venereal in origin but closer inspection revealed a source more basic—teeth. Somebody had bit his cock during the night. Worse, he could not recall into whose mouth it had been placed. When a man encounters that riddle, the only reaction is laughter. Mack rolled around in the fragrant suds of Aramis, wishing at the same time to be outside, in a helicopter, operating a camera with a long lens that could zoom in on the lunatic sight of the most famous male star in the world and his anonymously chewed prick. Entertained by the image, he entered the toilet, both cloister and metaphor for his life and art. The walls of the *cabine* were papered by Mack himself, a collage of his image on magazine covers from all continents of the earth. As he defecated, he was able to see himself as others saw him, a pleasure of such sweet irony that it cleared his senses along with his bowels. His life was a charade before and behind the cameras; he knew that. But he was reasonably honest with himself. To the world he lied; he told himself the truth—as best as he understood it.

The mystery of the cock biter was partially solved when Mack pushed a button that caused black- and crimson-splotched draperies reminiscent of Jackson Pollock paintings to part and admit the sun to his bedchamber. Revealed therein, a pretzel knot of alien paleness, was a prominent French actor who had arrived *chez* Crawford at midnight, accompanied by a folk singer famed for her crystalline soprano and between whose young but motherly breasts was wedged a thumb-sized chunk of hashish. Sometime during the short hours when all three were abed and nude, the girl had turned morose and guilty. She had cursed the two men and left the house on foot. How or if she negotiated a several-mile twisting journey down the mountains of Beverly Hills was of no concern to Mack. All he wanted now was to expel the frog. Wordlessly, Mack hoisted his guest, collected his clothes, deposited him in the shower, and locked the bathroom door, knowing that the banishee would sooner or later locate an adjoining corridor that coiled downstairs to a guest cottage. There a trusted, discreet, and generously paid driver would take him home. Normally Mack evicted his partners during the night, bidding them to leave on a pretext of his need to rise early for work. The truth was he wanted his visitors gone before the servants arrived at 8 a.m. His delusion was that no one knew the secrets of his bedroom.

There were not many. Mack was scarcely a prisoner of sex. His carnal thermometer registered well below average. Weeks often passed with no lover on his sheets, no one but himself, the image that reflected devotedly back from the mirror on the ceiling. When he masturbated, it was like watching himself on film. And that was as close as he ever came to observing his talents. He never went to daily rushes. At premieres of his movies, he showed up in the forecourt to be photographed then slipped out before the picture began. He confessed this once at a dinner party in Malibu and across the table Richard Burton nodded in agreement. "I concur wholeheartedly," said the British actor. "I wouldn't touch the stuff."

"Why?" asked the hostess.

"I loathe meself on a screen. I have been known to get physically ill."

The lady, an elderly social lioness recently enamored of meditation, yoga, and LSD, commented that such feeling was perhaps akin to an old Japanese superstition. "Once photographed," she said, "your shadow will fade. Twice photographed, your life will shorten."

Beside her, a trendy psychiatrist disagreed. "If a man doesn't like himself," opined the shrink, "he cannot look at himself." Mack started to say bullshit but Burton beat him to it.

At this midpoint of his fourth decade, Mack considered himself a casual bisexual, an uncomfortable traveler on either side of the boulevard. On special occasions he managed to copulate with women, provided a precise mixture of alcohol and drugs was achieved, not so much that he would fall like a hewn oak, but just enough to stir his currents, to make him desirous of a human body, *any* body, a pair of arms to hold him—*if* at that moment he wanted to be held. He believed that the world held him to be a great womanizer—the pictures on his toilet walls were testimony. Arnie Beckman provided an unending rope of feminine jewels, spectacularly beautiful women who were pleased to decorate Mack Crawford's arm, realizing their pictures would thereafter appear in almost every newspaper in America save *The Wall Street Journal.* Some of these ladies wanted more, but years of practice had made Mack adroit at dodging the emboldened desires of midnight. He always retreated with grace, making the excuses of work or unattended house guests or sick animals or a hint of stomach flu sound genuine. Mack could block a pass so gallantly that the lady spurned felt no need to rise on the morrow and telephone for a plastic nip and tuck. Besides, everybody knew he was still married.

Though separated for almost ten years, Mack and Susan had never divorced. In his interviews, Mack discouraged queries on this touchy subject, sometimes muttering something like "Yeah, we're separated, but I have great affection for my wife and we are still the parents of a terrific little boy."

Mack called Arnie Beckman and begged off from the Macra meeting. He felt unwell; he had not read any of the several scripts that were to be discussed; a loose dental cap required emergency repair.

"I'm profoundly sorry about all of your afflictions," answered Arnie in a tone uncannily reminiscent of Mack's dead aunt. "But there's no question of you not coming today. Several important matters have to be dealt with . . . and I need to catch you privately."

"Private?" echoed Mack. "What for?"

"I don't discuss anything on the telephone. Just take my word for it."

"Arnie, my head hurts. There's a virus going around." Mack knew he sounded whiny and he wondered why he was afraid of his agent.

"So skip lunch. Join us by one-thirty."

"What's this *private* matter?"

"Something's come up."

"Money?"

"I don't think so. One of those pain-in-the-ass things," said Arnie, pausing pointedly, then adding, ". . . like New York." Having lit his fuse, the agent hung up. He then hurriedly telephoned Paramount and asked for Arianna Corinth, the costume designer. She was off the lot, so Arnie told a secretary to find her. Fast.

Mack made himself a bullshot and drank it while pedaling ten kilometers on his Exercycle. He was worried. All it took was the vaguest allusion from Arnie about "one of those pain-in-the-ass things . . . like New York" to weaken his stomach. A new demon had obviously presented credentials to join the club. His whole adult life had been a cover-up, beginning with Laurie. She had haunted him for a decade, threatening exposure. When Kleber telephoned in 1960 and then mailed the curious news clipping of Butch's confession in San Antonio, Mack was relieved. But not for long. There soon came another reason for chronic fear, causing him to believe that the gods had decreed he must always carry a secret.

The distant night in New York was indelible. He even had a tape recording of it. For a long time he had kept the cassette, listening to the angry voices with the objectivity of attention paid to an overacted scene. Clifford Briton, his co-star in "Knights of New York," had come to Mack's apartment on Central Park West with a bottle of Pouilly-Fumé and intentions of erasing the quarrel that had erupted at the end of the day's shooting. When Mack looked back on it, he realized it must have been an impulsive act, one reached after extended intake of gin. Not only was Briton bombed, he had stuck his hairpiece on carelessly, like a mayonnaise jar top improperly replaced.

"Hey, listen," began Cliff, "I'm sorry about that bullshit this afternoon."

Mack was good-humored. "It's okay. You didn't connect." He rubbed his jaw.

"I guess that's why we use doubles. I can't throw a punch for shit."

"I said it's forgotten. Okay? I'm really bushed. I've got four pages to shoot tomorrow."

Cliff poured himself a large glass of wine and gulped it. "You *were* just kidding, weren't you?"

"About what?"

"About quitting the show."

"No, I wasn't kidding. I'm gonna hang it up. I can't face another thirty-nine weeks of running around Central Park."

"Mack, be serious. We've got another two seasons left in the run."

"They can find somebody to replace me. I'm tellin' Arnie tomorrow. I think he already suspects."

"He'll piss his pants."

"Too bad. I'm also quittin' *him*."

"Mack, you should get better advice. Arnie's built your career. I wish he was my agent."

Mack yawned. He wanted to get Cliff out of his apartment. "Well, I'm sure he'd be happy to sign you. Just be sure you count your fingers after you shake on the deal to make sure you get all five back."

Cliff did not take the hint. He fell silent for a time, wandering aimlessly about the expansive apartment with black enameled walls and chrome furniture and Chinese red lacquered doors and cabinets. Then he turned around, so emotional that he practically stumbled into Mack's startled arms.

"You're killing me, I want you to know that."

"Cliff, hey, listen, Cliff. Let's take this up tomorrow. It's not the end of the goddamned world."

"You've got a gun at my head."

"Come on. You've got more credits than Brando."

"I can't get a movie. I've been up for five thousand and I never got a single one. I'll be lucky to get a soap."

"Well, don't dump on me tonight, Cliff. I've got enough to worry about." Mack pushed Cliff away. The older man flopped face down on a leather sofa.

"You don't know what I'm talking about, do you? You don't know what it's like," he said, his words muffled by a pillow.

"What *what's* like?" demanded Mack impatiently.

Cliff Briton's voice broke. "Oh Christ, you know. It's *you* I don't wanna lose. . . ."

Up to this point, Mack had not known or fully comprehended the source of Cliff Briton's pain. But the awkward confession resurrected a wellspring for tears and mawkish behavior. Now Mack made the connection. Right after "Knights" initially caught on, when the co-stars were both wearied by the demands of fourteen-hour workdays and publicity, they had gone together to the Catskills for a weekend. Hunting deer was the announced reason but all that was in Mack's sights was an interlude of peace. It was a Saturday afternoon in Indian summer with crystalline beauty that was visceral—a feast for all the senses. Their eyes absorbed the autumn fire of maples turning crimson and hot yellow. In the air was the smell of cider mills and moss beds fermenting under dying leaves. They hiked for miles, never firing a shot, not caring, discovering secret places of primitive beauty—rock fences built by hands in centuries past, wild thickets of plump and juicy black grapes, a bear cave, streams so pristine that it was fun to pretend that no man had ever seen them before. Cliff Briton was the best of companions. He knew this land and loved it and showed his friend from the flat heart of Texas where Indians with the enchanting tribal name of Calicoon had lived, where emigrants from Germany—Briton's own great-grandparents among them—had arrived before the Civil War with deeds to earth purchased from speculators sight unseen. The pioneers had been promised paradise, but they discovered instead plots so steep and rocky that generations of spine-knotting labor never really cleared much more than a corn patch. Cliff's forebears had tilled stones and fought winter snows that stacked twelve-foot drifts. Just before World War I their house became an inn for summer tourists. Cliff's dream was to reclaim his ancestors' homestead, now occupied by Orthodox Jews from Brooklyn who passed blistering August holidays wearing full-length black wool coats and who turned their sons into little old men with black hats and sad faces. When Cliff explained his idea, Mack liked it very much. He wished he had more to share with his friend than a demented aunt in a dark house. The man with whom he acted each week had suddenly become a real person, someone with ancestors and a comforting nature that made an afternoon warm and secure. Subconsciously he appointed Cliff Briton his surrogate father. He had never known his real one.

At the end of this fine day they made camp beside a swift fork of the Delaware, throwing down sleeping bags on a bank carpeted with ferns. They started a roaring fire and prepared to cook T-bones and baked potatoes. First they stripped off and plunged naked into a cold, clear beaver pond. Splashing around like prankish kids, the two men laughed at impossible attempts to catch the tiny darts of silver trout that swam in rocketing trails about their legs. It was a moment to remember, a slice of silence and privacy and almost dark excepting the melting apricot rays that trespassed through the forest. Then it got spoiled.

Mack saw that Cliff was looking at him, looking at him differently, looking at him too long, to the point where he felt uncomfortable. Cliff smiled strangely and waded to the bank. There he stood naked, his back toward Mack, drying his body. And when Mack followed him out of the pond, Cliff turned around. He had a towel across his stomach and he dropped it. He was starting to get sexually aroused and, obviously, he wanted Mack to see it. Later, when Mack replayed the episode in his memory, he paid the presentation no heed. A real man doesn't notice that sort of thing. Mack simply yelped over the cold and jumped into his jeans and flannel shirt and set about cooking steaks. That was what he *should* have done. But what he did in truth was stand there and look, puzzled by how he had misread the day, wondering if Cliff's hardness was accidental or maybe it was always that way, wanting to avert his glance but unable to move his eyes, feeling his own penis stir. Before Mack could break the scene, Cliff was standing in front of him and saying, "Maybe we better do something about that." But just as Cliff reached out to touch him, Mack said, quietly and firmly, "No." He laughed awkwardly and put on his clothes. They didn't talk much more that night, nor was reference made the following cold dawn when both agreed it was time to cut the weekend short and return to scripts and stunt doubles. On the drive back to New York, Cliff did say one little thing. "I don't really do *that* . . ." To which Mack simply shrugged. "No harm," he answered. But there was. For several days Mack fretted over the sordid memory. He asked himself some old questions: What did I project to make Cliff take that liberty? Do I come across as available? Can I ever find a friend worth trusting without worrying about sex as a silent partner? There were no answers and after a time he managed to forget—or so he thought.

And now, in his apartment, it was back. Nor did Mack play the sequel any better.

The exchange was recorded crystalline-clear on tape:

CLIFF: Give me this. Let me stay the night. Just one night.

MACK (another false laugh): Pal, you're gassed. I gotta study lines and hit the sack.

CLIFF: Please, don't patronize me. Don't throw me out.

MACK: Listen, Cliff, if you wanna cave in, feel free to use the couch.

CLIFF: You're some cold-blooded son of a bitch, Tex. I want you to live with that. Who do you think you're kidding? Turn around someday and catch the grips imitating you. They start out with their hands on their hips.

MACK: I can whip their ass. You know that.

CLIFF: Particularly when you're down on your knees, cuteness.

The tape recorder that Raoul Martinez held in his hands picked up only part of the scuffle that ensued. But from his hiding place just outside the kitchen service entrance where he had opened the door with a passkey, Raoul heard Mack land a solid right to Cliff's chops. And he was entertained further by the roar that broke out of Mack's throat like flesh tearing. "Get the fuck outta here, Briton!"

Cliff did not work for two days, pretending his swollen jaw had come from root canal dentistry. Which was just as well because Mack Crawford was out with laryngitis. The punch-up cost $23,440 in lost time.

On a bench in Riverside Park, chilled by the winds that gusted across the Hudson River, Arnie Beckman listened attentively to the tape. He tried to hide his concern. "It ain't much, Chico," he lied to Raoul Martinez. "Just a couple of guys horsin' around. They're actors. They were rehearsing a scene."

"I don't think so," said Raoul. "I think you want, no?" He needed to make the sale. He had already made a twenty-dollar down payment on a winter coat with a fur-lined collar. He had written to a kid brother in San Juan promising plane fare within a week.

"Oh, I guess I'll take it. Play it at the Christmas party. Maybe it's worth some laughs. How much you want?"

"Two thousand."

"Get outta here. Fifty max."

They settled on $225, payable at five forty-five the next afternoon, the rendezvous point being the subway platform at Columbus Circle. When Arnie laid his eager hands on the spools, he used them effectively. He played the endangering contents for Mack and convinced his client to pay $10,000 cash for destruction of the master.

"How do I know he didn't make a hundred others?" demanded Mack prudently.

"Because Chico's a punk and because I say he didn't," answered Arnie. "Just trust me."

"I didn't do anything, Arnie," said Mack brokenly. "Will you believe me? I'm not one of . . . those."

"Sure. But my earnest advice is don't be seen in public without a blonde on one arm, a redhead on the other, and both better have tits big enough to fill four columns."

Arnie made a little lecture about the necessity of protecting Mack's virile image and urged his client to put himself totally in the hands of Beckman. Mack renewed his contract, this time for seven years, agreed to play another season of "Knights," and then moved to Los Angeles, where he made an easy transition from the black-and-white confines of television into stereophonic sound and color. Cliff Briton was unemployed for two years, then got the lead in a soap. He remained in the role for another decade, enhancing his income with commercials for dentures and camping lanterns.

Many times Mack wanted to ask if Raoul Martinez had ever bothered Arnie again. But he never did, which spared Arnie the necessity of inventing another lie. This was something that Arnie did not like to remember. What happened between the agent and the Puerto Rican elevator attendant on the subway platform beneath Columbus Circle was a tragedy of mundaneness, indigenous to New York. Just after he received his payoff, Raoul was in a throng of passengers waiting to squeeze aboard an overdue train. Someone from behind shoved—who it was police never learned—and the slim young man fell into the path of an oncoming IND express. Raoul's body was scattered from Fifty-ninth to Times Square. Along the path of fifteen blocks, police found a swatch of fuchsia silk shirt, a strip or two of high-sheen black leather boots, and a hand severed from a body. In death, the hand grasped ten twenty-dollar bills and five fins. Fingerprints were taken from this hand but as Raoul Martinez, incredibly, had never been arrested, his unidentified remains were placed in a burlap bag, thence in a plywood box, and finally into a pauper's grave. Nobody missed him enough to file a missing persons report. Certainly not Arnie, whom nobody had seen in the platform crowd.

"Another one of those pain-in-the-ass things . . . like New York."
Mack wondered what it could be this time. He finished the Exercycle, then swallowed a handful of vitamin tablets. He plunged into the pool and churned half a hundred laps, jogged two miles around the perimeter of his estate, went into the gymnasium he had constructed over the garage and bench-pressed iron until his muscles swelled and corded. Whenever he had important thinking to do, Mack slipped it in between sweat and pain. By the time he had finished dressing for this afternoon's Macra meeting, satisfied that his frame still accommodated khaki trousers with a 32-inch waist and an X-large royal blue velour sweater almost pasted to his shoulders (but bothered somewhat by the furrows on his face that long sideburns and a rakish mustache failed to

mask), Mack reached a decision. He was tired of living a lie and done with being afraid. He would tell the Macra board within an hour.

His secretary yelled down from the office just as he stepped into his new 450 SLC Mercedes. "Do you want to talk with Mrs. Crawford? She's on long-distance. I told her you were on the way out."

"Susan?" said Mack, taking the call beside the pool. "What's up?"

"Nothing. I'm sending Jeffie out tomorrow. . . ."

"Tomorrow! I thought he was coming on Friday."

"Tomorrow *is* Friday. Unless Hollywood counts different from Fort Worth. Anyway, Mack, if you don't mind, I thought I'd fly out with him. I'll pay my own way, of course. There's a patient-care conference in Pasadena. . . . Mack, I want us to talk. Face to face."

"Sure. You can stay here. I'll pick you guys up at the airport."

"That's sweet. But I'll make other arrangements. Just save me an hour. Maybe Sunday?"

Mack saw his son twice a year, the week after Christmas, two weeks in August. He had not seen Susan for five years, although they spoke regularly if gingerly on the telephone. He read in her voice what she wanted and it cemented the revelation he would shortly announce to Arnie and company.

They rose as if a judge had entered chambers, tribute to the man who would pay for the splendid lunch now being removed from a table where—the Sotheby certificate of authenticity said—Disraeli signed documents. Arnie passed around Havana cigars with kind words for the caretakers at Dunhill's vault. "Glad you could make it," said Arnie. He was thirty pounds heavier than the day he fetched Mack Crawford at Port Authority Bus Terminal in New York. All of it was stuck now in his middle, like a snake digesting a hare. He proceeded immediately to business, opening the first of many folders in black leatherette.

"Before we start," said Mack hesitantly, despite his resolve, "I've got something to say."

Arnie bade him sit. "Just hang on to it, will you? We've got a lot to cover today."

"It's important, Arnie . . ."

"*Everything's* important." The afternoon quickly mired in litigious ooze. Zakariah the Lawyer announced that Macra was being sued by some wretched writer, his contention being that the story line of Mack's last film was stolen from a script submitted to the actor (but never read). Macra's defense posture was strong, but it would probably take $50,000 in legal fees to swat the gnat. Nesmith the Accountant was regretful over the IRS's insistence that Macra owed back taxes of $185,613.87 with the interest meter running. Beggers the Financial Consultant was optimistic that Macra's investments in Oklahoma feedlots and Oregon fruit orchards would pick up despite the 42 percent loss due to weather and labor for the fourth quarter. Tellens the Press Agent warned that *Time* magazine was preparing a cover story on the sorry character of American films and that the publication intended to fix principal blame on overpaid/undertalented actors of megalomaniacal power. He was attempting to get the boxed feature inset on Mack toned down—but doubted his chances. Of modest cheer was the box of recent magazine covers Tellens dumped before Mack, more wallpaper for the toilet. Arnie said two roles that Mack had coveted went instead to Steve McQueen and Paul Newman.

"Do I drink my hemlock now?" asked Mack.

Ha-Ha-Ha went everybody.

Arnie said there was no need for worry. The movie industry was— like the whole damn country—splintered and confounded. The Vietnam War was tearing America's soul. "Kids who oughta be sitting in the picture show are out there in the streets burning down banks. They're stoned outta their skulls. Fuckin' studios don't know what anybody wants to see."

"Clean family entertainment," suggested Zakariah the Lawyer, who was a frequent guest at the dinner tables of Walt Disney and Jack Warner. Jimmy Stewart was his favorite actor, next to Mack.

"Yeah?" said Arnie. "So howcum *Doctor Doolittle* did dogshit? Howcum they're standing in line to see *Bonnie and Clyde,* a clean family entertainment about two bank robbers, one of 'em a guy who can't get a hard-on? Howcum you can't see the screen for the goddamn marijuana smoke in the audience when *2001* plays?"

The agent flung an accusatory thumb at newly shabby merchandise. Mack. "His last picture barely broke even," reminded Arnie. Mack had portrayed a dedicated Texas sheriff chasing narcotics smugglers back across the Rio Grande. "The night I saw it," said Arnie, "there were maybe thirty paying customers. And they were cheering for the bad guys. People don't want heroes anymore. It's not the fashion. Dusty Hoffman killed heroes once and for all last year in *The Graduate.* I say we gotta change his image." Arnie dealt out copies of a script. "Everybody read this," he ordered. "It's got Fort Knox written all over it."

Mack recognized the property. Its title was *Hiding Out* and it was a messy, unfocused yarn about a college baseball coach who grows disenchanted with his structured life, abandons wife and team, discovers "a meaningful existence" in a commune just across the Canadian border, sheltering draft resisters, growing organic food, and meditating. It was written by an Arnie client, would be directed and produced by Arnie clients. If Mack agreed to star, Arnie would take 10 percent of everything but the popcorn sales.

Mack had been listlessly tuning in and out during the long afternoon. He had never taken much interest in business affairs, signing this document, that check, initialing whatever clause the paper boys told him to. From the beginning he had told Arnie, "All I want to do is act. You take care of the rest." That was tolerable in 1959, when his income was $11,100, less Arnie's tenth. Now, a decade later, he grossed close to $2 million a year, still less Arnie's tenth and salary checks for thirty-eight people on his payroll. His income tax had grown to eighty-seven pages and was employing one of the new computers for its formulation. Everyone had hooks in Mack, he had grown to feel, and he couldn't even write a check for more than fifty bucks without calling Arnie or the accountant to ask permission. Which reminded him, he needed to get $500 for Jeffie's visit. Maybe he would take his son and Susan to Le Bistro for dinner tomorrow night; at least he could sign the check there. Susan would be impressed. Le Bistro's staff would walk on their hands if Mack asked them to, and outside there was always a band of autograph seekers.

Arnie jerked his strings and pulled him back to business. "I say it's a helluva script. If Macra commits, I can put it together at Columbia by lunch tomorrow. They're looking for youth pictures."

Through the gray-blue layer of Cuban smoke, the actor saw everyone looking at him, waiting for his okay—one word or nod that would cause $6 million to be spent. But he was not going to comment on *Hiding Out*. He had something else to say. He had rehearsed his speech on the drive down the hill. Now he cleared his throat and searched for courage lost. "Well, it's academic, guys. The fact of the matter is, I'm tired. Really tired . . ."

Like a rocket fired, Arnie leaped up and began ushering Macra from its boardroom. "Yeah, we're all tired. Let's sleep on it." Before Mack could swallow twice, class was dismissed. Everybody gone. Nobody left but dunce and teacher. Arnie kicked the door shut and ceremoniously planted his larded buns on the table where Disraeli signed documents. He looked down at Mack from the choicest angle of power.

"You're really somethin'. . . . You knew I had somethin' important to say," said Mack.

"So tell *me*. I give good ear."

"Then listen carefully, Arnie. Maybe you oughta turn on that tape recorder you've got hidden in your briefcase. I don't want to be misquoted."

"It's always on. Speak to me."

"All right. I'm quitting." There. Done.

"Quitting *what?*"

"You. Macra. The business. I don't want to make movies anymore. I've done it and I'm reasonably proud of my work and I've got enough bread to last the rest of my life. So here's my blessing, Arnie. Take that script, roll it up nice and tight, and shove it—all the way to chocolate."

Arnie smiled tolerantly. "Actors! Someday they'll find out actors cause more heart attacks than cholesterol." He turned serious. "I won't waste time reminding you who found who in what cowtown where you know who was peddling cars. Nor will I bother to recollect the remarkable career I built, the arms I twisted, the paint I slapped on a chipped reputation. So if you wanna hang it up, that's your decision. You're a big boy now. You may be getting out while the getting's good. Lew Wasserman ain't exactly down on his knees begging for your services. But before you sink slowly in the west, tell me what to do with this."

The agent unlocked his briefcase like a demolition expert and carefully withdrew an envelope. Cheap, legal-sized, it had pasted on the front a circular picture of Mack Crawford's head—with angry red slashes. "You still get a lot of mail," said Arnie, indicating that his client was not totally in the back yard. "One of the girls came across this and gave it to me. She thought about turning it over to the police. I'm glad she didn't."

Mack reached for the letter but Arnie dangled it just out of reach. "It's probably cuckoo time. I'll tell you what it says."

"Gimme the goddamn letter, Arnie," cried Mack, seizing the

agent's arm and prepared to shatter bones if the envelope was not surrendered. He read it with alarm:

"July 9, 1968

Dear Devil Star:

You're not good at answering my letters. This is the third and last. I know all about you, McKenzie. I know what you did to Mable and Susan and Jeffie. I know the filth of your life.

Listen, you better get in touch with me. God wants the truth. God knows you ruin people. Answer this letter by putting an ad in the L.A. Times Personals. Say, 'Confession is good for the soul. Tex.'

Then, keep reading the personals."

There was no signature. The handwriting, in faint pencil, was neat but urgent. "So?" asked Arnie. "Want me to handle it?"

Mack shook his head. "Not unless you wrote it." He put the letter in his shirt pocket and left the room without another word. That night, after studying the threat several times, Mack wondered why Arnie had taken almost a month to reveal its existence. Rattled and confused, Mack did not remember telling his makeup man three months earlier that he was seriously considering quitting the business. The next morning, Mack called the L.A. *Times,* placed the advertisement in the Personals column, then drove to LAX to fetch his wife and son.

It is the nature of man to believe—at least in the sweet, fresh early years—that he is in charge of life's journey, that what course he plots, what winds he follows, what he says, what he does will bring safe harbor on a mirror sea at sunset. Then, usually somewhere about the middle of the voyage, when the sails rip or catch no breeze at all, when the tides swell and capsize what was thought to be an unsinkable craft, he falls back on explanations for the unexplainable. Every culture has developed lifelines, ropes grabbed to hold on a few minutes more. Delusions, excuses they are. "God's will" works for some. "Predestination" and "fate" for others. But the French, the fatalistic French, while not actually solving the secret of life, accept perverse currents by remembering the advice of an obscure countryman named Alphonse

Karr, who wrote, in 1849, "The more things change, the more they remain the same."

Three unhappy people intended on this Friday morning in August 1968 to perform corrective surgery on their lives, having reached individual decisions that were long and painful in the forming. And, a month or so later, considerable alterations in these three lives had indeed taken place. None of the changes were what the sleepless hours of countless midnights had forecast. But how often do people get what they really want?

What Mack Crawford wanted, by his reckoning, was easily obtained. He wanted out. Abdication seemed the only remedy for the malaise that tormented the Prince of Charms. Earlier this year he had tried to explain things to a psychiatrist whose services he purchased for three unpleasant hours. The therapist, a rigid Freudian favored by the entertainment industry, was an unattractive, swarthy Italianate man whose three-piece suits were as impeccably tailored as the palomino suede decor of his Beverly Hills office. When Mack sat down in an Eero Saarinen chair, the therapist asked one simple question, "How can I help you?"

To which Mack honestly answered, "I don't know." He waited for a nudge and when none came—the analyst was sitting at a desk on which nothing but a Steuben glass ashtray as clean as a scalpel rested —Mack stumbled clumsily through a monologue of fits and starts. The first thing he did was list his credits, as if auditioning for a bank loan. He itemized his assets, his automobiles, his wardrobe, the cost of his house. He told the plot of the film he was then making. He described the Macra meetings. And, finally, he said, "I believe, or so they tell me, at least I think—people say I'm one of the most famous people in the world. . . . Three women followed me off the elevator today and I played like I was going to the dentist next door. I opened the door and went in, just for a minute, and . . . I mean, I could take you down there on Wilshire Boulevard and we couldn't walk a block without a hundred people stopping and turning around and looking at me. . . . I have to get the windows of my Mercedes painted black so people can't see in. . . . The thing is, I . . . Do you know there are days when I get maybe two hundred fifty telephone calls? That many people want to speak to *me*. . . . I've got this secretary who follows me around with a list as long as my arm of calls I'm supposed to return. . . . The other thing is, at night, the phone doesn't ring very much. . . . I guess I'm mainly popular during office hours. . . . What do you think of that?"

The analyst only shrugged.

On their second seating, Mack delivered a line that had come to him in the interim, a confession that seemed at origin both bold and revealing. "I think I'm a hero to everybody except myself," he said. This got no response, either, and Mack glared, an expression of strength and purpose valued by filmgoers familiar with his work. He did not speak for a quarter of an hour, an expensive pout. When the session was almost done, Mack was trying to explain how easy it had all been, how his success had not really been sought but only handed to him as if deserved.

"I'm not really a very good actor," he confessed, hurriedly throwing in, "But people *think* I am. It's all little bits and pieces. They put it together cleverly, you know. I may do one good minute in the morning and two minutes in the afternoon—and the thing about movies is that I never know when I'm good. The director has to tell me. Isn't that a helluva way to make a living?"

Mack went one last time. He talked nonstop for the hour, as candid as he could possibly be. He spilled it all. He talked of fear and guilt, of ghosts and secrets, of sex with men and sex with women and the desire to run out of the bedroom once it was finished no matter who did what to whom or where. "The bottom line is, I'm just not happy," he said, almost crying. "I know it's a cliché, but here I am at the top of the heap and the air's too thin. I don't like my life. I don't like it any better when I'm drunk or stoned. I'm getting old—older. My hair's thin on top and they've got to comb it carefully before they shoot. A lot of days I think about running away where nobody knows me— but I don't think there's a place left where nobody knows me." Mack waited.

The psychiatrist wrote something down. Mack assumed he had finally said something worth noting. The therapist gestured for the patient to continue talking.

"So that's it, that's the story of my life," said Mack. "And I don't think I'm a bad person. I've never hurt anybody on purpose. . . . I've never stolen anything, or killed anybody, and I sure didn't ask to be born with this face and this body. . . ."

The psychiatrist, who a few years hence would become enamored of gestalt therapy, would write a best-selling pop shrink book on taking charge of one's life, would begin immediate dialogue and confrontation of problems revealed by a patient in as much obvious anguish as Mack Crawford, on this day did nothing but gesture with his sculpture-cut head toward the door. Mack asked what the doctor had written down. Oh. Nothing but a change of appointment. He handed it to the patient.

Mack wanted his term paper graded. He cried, "Jesus, man, I've just torn out my heart for you. Can't you say anything?" No. Nothing today. Come back next Tuesday. And the week and year after that.

Mack did not return. Nor would he ever read portions of his confessional—cloaked and paraphrased to be sure—in the therapist's yet-to-be-written book on narcissism. All he did was send eighteen ten-dollar bills in an envelope bearing no return address, paying for time poorly spent.

As he waited in a VIP room at the American Airlines terminal, attended by a nervous public relations girl and a photographer whose job it was to capture the star's reunion with wife and son (and make goddamn sure the American logo showed in the shot), Mack rehearsed. He felt sure what he had to say would play.

Susan French Crawford, thirty-eight years old, had a speech in mind as well. She had known her lines for many years and had intended on numerous occasions to speak them. She had chided herself for lack of courage a thousand times in the bathroom mirror. It took a while—fourteen years to be exact—but Susan was now prepared to tell Mack that "hypocrite" was perhaps too harsh a definition of her character, but "dishonest" and "deceitful" applied. She had murmured divorce for many years. Now she would demand it. This is what she intended to say:

"My darling—and you are my darling still and very dear to me—I don't know why you've stayed married to me so long. I could speculate, but there's no merit in guessing games. As for me, the reasons have finally become clear. Let me go back to the beginning. I trapped you from the start. I wanted you because you were—you are!—a great big handsome lug for whom every woman who ever laid eyes on you has lusted. You didn't have much choice. You were lying there with a couple of broken legs and I came along and helped you mend them. I heard a crude phrase the other day. Mercy fuck. I think ours was a mercy marriage. You felt indebted, so you took a wife. And about that silly night in Acapulco. Hell, honey, I knew who was the seducer but I also knew our marriage was a charade. I used Cat Bowman as an excuse to break us up. Then when Jeffie came along, I wanted him to have a father—at least for a while. And I'd be lying if I didn't say the money you sent was generous. A woman can get used to $2,500 a month plus perks.

"The years go fast. I've been busy. I've gone back to college. I've almost got my master's in psychology—though what I'll do with it is anybody's guess. I wouldn't pretend to counsel another life the way I've abused my own. Here comes the hard part, so please listen and don't interrupt because I've got to get it all out fast. Sometimes I step outside of my life and examine it and I say, 'Girl, you're healthy and normal so why the hell do you stay married to a man who hasn't touched you since Ike Eisenhower was President?' And I answer, in my own defense, 'We're very modern, Mack and me. We're liberated and avant-garde. He goes his way; I go mine.' I've had men, some men. I can still turn a head, believe it or not. But when the men try and get down to business, I close the office. Maybe I don't need a lot of sex. Maybe none of the others measures up to the fantasy of what I once had. The truth is, if I ever told anybody the truth, not until now, the truth is I've been living long-distance. I've been hanging on to an identity that doesn't belong to me. I like it when the columns talk about 'Mack Crawford's estranged wife in Fort Worth.' I like it when bank tellers and shopgirls ask for *my* autograph. I like the tribute of celebrity without having to do anything except stay ridiculously married to a real one. I like people thinking you want my body. . . .

"I've decided that's not healthy, Mack. I've been carrying your train. I'm some sort of emotional stowaway. I've been using you as excuse to mask my own laziness and fears. It's not fair to either of us. My lawyer's drawn up all the necessary papers. Just sign here and on the way back to Texas I'll stop off at El Paso, cross the bridge, and cut us both free. And I'll still love you, Mack. When I die, I hope they'll write in the paper that I was the first—and best—of your wives. Please, my darling. Please."

A woman with the lovely name of Arianna Corinth arose without sleep this very same morning in the Brentwood section of Los Angeles with what she believed was the solution to an ugly and otherwise unsolvable problem. She prepared a special breakfast—French toast with cinnamon and powdered sugar, hot chocolate with marshmallows—for her six-year-old daughter. She permitted the child, a beautiful but somber little girl named Molly, to select whatever trinket she desired from the cask of costume jewelry. Molly wanted to wear a chunky necklace of amber beads and that was fine with Arianna, despite the strand having come from St. Petersburg and being passed down the maternal line for over a century. Arianna wanted Molly to have a perfect day because she loved her so very much.

As soon as Molly left for the special summer school for gifted children, Arianna telephoned the studio and said she would not be in until late, if at all. Her day—she lied—would be spent in combing thrift shops on Melrose Avenue in search of costumes to be worn in a new Paramount "youth picture." The secretary told Arianna that Arnie Beckman had called again. His third. "He said quote tell that broad it's somewhere between urgent and life-or-death unquote." Arianna said she would return his call. Into her burgundy leather appointment book from Gucci she stroked the name of Arnie Beckman, in writing as flamboyant as every gesture of her life. She flipped through the pages. Her days were crowded for weeks yet to come, for nights never to be.

The doorbell rang. Arianna peered down cautiously from her second-floor bedroom and saw the postman. In his hand was one of the familiar envelopes, those bulky, bloated documents that Eric's lawyer kept sending by certified, registered mail. She never thought that circumstance would turn the postman into an enemy to be avoided. But he was now—and Arianna could not leave her own house until the messenger with bad news departed. He rang again, and again, and finally he stuffed a pink notice into the mail slot and went away.

She dressed hurriedly, jerking down an odd lot of clothing that few women could have assembled into fashion. The envious speculated that Arianna spent enormous time and money on her wardrobe (or else borrowed illegally from studio closets). Wrong. Today she had less than thirty bucks on her slender, tanned, and thirty-three-year-old body: plaid trousers hand-sewn from an ocean steamer blanket, a skinny-ribbed ocher jersey from the children's department at Sears, rope sandals from a sidewalk merchant on the docks at Piraeus, and enough clank and glitter about her unusually long neck to suggest a percussion section. Not wanting to do her hair—at 4 p.m. she would have a final wash and set, and so would Molly—Arianna tucked it under a beret once purchased from a circus vendor in Montmartre. A few wheat-colored strands refused entry. Arianna didn't care. She knew she looked fine. If a photographer had taken her picture at this very moment and had it appeared in some fashion magazine, a hundred women in Beverly Hills would attempt to make wisps of their hair straggle casually out from beneath a cheap beret. Such was Arianna Corinth's reputation for the *avant-vogue*.

She attended to one last chore. Each morning Arianna wrote a few paragraphs in her journal. She had begun the custom while studying costume design in New York, those first entries being reserved and discreet comments, more like the strained communications between strangers at a cocktail party. She wrote of what she did, not of what she felt. She wrote as if her mother might read it, even though the woman had been dead since an hour after Arianna's birth. But over the years, as her life and her emotions grew more complex, the journal became a best friend, a demanding force that required—on the penalty of insufferable guilt—truth, discipline, and attention. Even after Eric had found the journal, broke the lock, read the incriminating pages that fueled both uncontested divorce and bitterly disputed custody of Molly, Arianna continued to fill the pages.

Today she wrote, "I must hurry. So much to do. So little time. Perhaps, later, I can get back to you. There's nothing much new to tell, anyway. You know it all. I feel both calm and just. Let there be no mistake about my course of action: I am perfectly sane. The brook may have babbled now and then, but the river runs strong and deep. Oh yes, one thing I must decide is whether to burn you. In one ear a little bird whispers, 'Strike the set.' But in the other comes a rebuttal, 'Perhaps these pages are a legacy worth leaving.' Shall I kill my secrets?

"Old Spanish proverb: Love, pain, and money cannot be kept secret. They soon betray themselves."

At midday, Arianna rapped the brass horseshoe for admission to an imposing Georgian home in the Holmby Hills district of Los Angeles, knowing full well that the lady of the house, a friend best described as intimate, was attending a fund-raising luncheon downtown at the music center and was at this moment probably gushing over Zubin Mehta. Welcomed nonetheless by a Costa Rican maid, Arianna requested to use the bathroom. In her absent friend's medicine cabinet, she located a vial containing more than 200 Seconal tablets. Secreting half of these in a pink Kleenex, she thanked the maid for the pit stop, then drove to fetch Molly from school. The air was hot, smog thick as Dijon mustard. That her clear blue eyes were watering, Arianna attributed to pollution and not to second thoughts.

The obituaries, she reasoned, would not be in the *Times* until Sunday. The trades would spread the terrible news further on Monday. Her final notices would be substantial but not epic. The suicides of an Academy Award-winning costume designer and her six-year-old daughter would not stop the world, not lower flags, not even be remembered very long. Only a very few would weep and read the hidden message: a lesbian mother, overwhelmingly in debt to lawyers, on the verge of losing her child to an ex-husband threatening exposure and disgrace, impossibly in love with a well-married society matron from whose abundant collection of sedations were procured enough barbiturates to check out in style.

Love, pain, and money soon betray themselves.

CHAPTER TWENTY-ONE

It was six months later. It was Valentine's Day 1969. After the surprise wedding, Arnie Beckman chartered a Lear and flew from Las Vegas to L.A., where he hand-carried the film to *Life* magazine's bureau on Wilshire Boulevard. He insisted on going into the lab and standing beside the technician, waiting impatiently in the darkroom, gulping coffee and antacid tablets, feeling that until the images swam out of the acid and onto the paper, his *coup* would not be completed.

The lab chief, a temperamental German who in his day had bounced luminaries as renowned as Alfred Eisenstadt and Lord Snowdon from his chamber, tolerated Arnie Beckman only because *Life*'s entertainment editor explained the nature of the exclusive. *Life* had purchased first rights in North America for the secret wedding and would syndicate the pictures around the world. Arnie would make $100,000, a secret between him and the Time, Inc., syndication department.

"Who's the old lady?" muttered the lab chief, gesturing to the emerging features of a plump moonbeam with peppermint-pink hair.

"Can you crop her out?" asked Arnie.

"She's in more frames than the bride."

"*Oy.* Give me strength," said Arnie. "Maybe you could dump a little extra acid on Grandma's face?"

Her resolve had weakened the very moment Susan stepped off the plane that Friday morning in August. Mack was waiting at the end of the walkway, grinning like a hound dog, juggling dew-fresh yellow roses and packages for Jeffie from F. A. O. Schwartz wrapped in brilliant-colored papers. He looked larger than life, like all the magazine covers she had back home pasted in a dozen scrapbooks, but still the same boy-man who made her hide behind statues on a campus fifteen years past, trembling and wishing. Jeffie ran, as instructed by his mother, plunging like a determined tackler into Mack's great arms.

As strobes fired, father hoisted son high above his head. Susan marveled at genetic legacy. The boy—thin but tough—was the equal of his father in acting. Jeffie had pouted for weeks over displeasure at reunion with Daddy. Only Susan's discovery that Disneyland had new attractions since Jeffie's last visit to Los Angeles persuaded him. Typical spoor of broken marriages, the child neither liked nor disliked his father. Fact was he didn't know the man well enough to have much feeling at all. Susan had tried to shield her son from the glare of inherited celebrity—private schools, anonymity when possible. Until Jeffie turned ten, she had not permitted him to see one of Mack's films, finally realizing that the ban was worthless because the child's friends told him plots and a magazine counter did not exist without Daddy's features for sale.

Mack thrust out arms for her, too, but Susan only shook his hand and brushed her freshly perfumed cheek against his lips. Purposefully, she chose an angle to thwart the airline photographer. "Welcome, hon," said Mack happily. "You look terrific." Susan made some deprecatory remark, but she knew she did. A month of slavish dieting —750 calories—permitted the size 6 afternoon dress from Neiman's, frothy white raw silk with faint scatterings of pale blue cornflowers. It had hurt her conscience to dye her hair, but she was almost forty and she wanted Mack to mark—and mourn—the girl he left behind.

At the curb where an electric cart deposited the strikingly handsome family before a limousine with opaque windows, Susan found herself getting used to the clicking of cameras and the yelping of fans, "It's-Him-It's-Really-Him," found herself forming easy but false wide smiles, found herself understanding as Mack whispered, "Don't stop. Don't make eye contact. Don't sign an autograph. You can get stuck for an hour." She lowered her head, gripped her son's hand, and pushed through the tumult as if by second nature.

And when Mack insisted that she stay at least one night in the guest bedroom before attending the conference in Pasadena, Susan did not bother to conjure an excuse.

Swept by panic, Arianna did not reach Molly's school until half an hour after the children had been dismissed for the day. She had gotten snarled on the San Diego Freeway, victim, along with five lanes of vehicles three miles long, of an overturned butane truck. The radio told her that the Democratic National Convention in Chicago was preparing to nominate Hubert Horatio Humphrey for the presidency while a mob of youth revolutionaries were rioting on Michigan Avenue and enduring the clubs and tear gas of Mayor Daley's police, that 3,122 Vietnamese died or suffered serious injuries in this week's body count, that two more heart transplants had been performed in Houston, and that commuters should avoid the San Diego Freeway and use "alternate routes."

At insanity in general, at a world that would not even let a woman kill herself and her daughter as so carefully planned, Arianna beat her fist against the dashboard and laid her head on the steering wheel. She laughed and cried.

Molly, she was to belatedly learn, had left school in the care of a schoolmate's mother, their destination the Los Angeles Zoo, their purpose the viewing of a newly born pair of lion cubs. "I hope it was all right," said the assistant headmistress. "Molly waited and waited for you."

Arianna nodded.

"Mrs. Corder promised to get Molly home by six sharp in time for dinner."

Shortly after seven, Molly tottered in the front door, her jumper stained with mustard and snowcone syrup, her tired eyes wide with visions of panthers and carousels. Arianna hugged her fiercely, but the child disengaged. "I have to draw a picture for homework," she announced, rushing for paper and crayons.

Later, after she had prepared Molly's favorite food—barbecued hamburgers cooked on the grill—Arianna fixed two chocolate milk shakes with enough fudge sauce to hide the taste of fifty Seconals in each. She went into the living room and set the tray on the hearth. Her daughter was asleep, sprawled beside a rather good drawing of a roaring lioness and the beginning of what would have been two cubs. I'm going to have to wake my daughter up to put her to sleep, thought Arianna and the mordancy of the act made her break.

The telephone rang. A dozen times. The service did not answer. Wearily Arianna seized the receiver. "Hello?"

"It's *me*," said the woman's voice. She spoke clandestinely. "I just got home. Consuela said you came by around twelve. I thought I told you I was having lunch downtown."

"Maggie, I'm just sitting down to dinner with Molly."

"Is something wrong? You sound dead."

"Just tired. One of those days."

"I can't talk. We're going to the Bloomingdales' for dinner. Listen, I think he's off to Africa next week. Some mining deal in Salisbury. Heaven? I can open the house at Arrowhead. Can you steal two weeks?"

"I'll see. Maggie, forgive me. I'm really whipped."

"Aren't we all. I love you. It's right. I really need you."

"I know." Arianna hung up before she sobbed. She sat beside her daughter for a long time, crying, trying to refocus the blurred intent. She whispered once into Molly's ear that dinner was ready, that her milk shake was waiting. But she didn't say it loud and she didn't say it again and about nine-thirty she carried her child to bed and fell immediately asleep beside her.

At dawn, when the chimes rang, Arianna assumed the determined postman had returned like some bounty hunter. But when she peeped through the curtains, Arnie Beckman was the intruder on her step. He was as cheerful as a robin with a worm in his mouth—and he was looking straight at her. After she dumped the milk shakes down the garbage disposal, Arianna let him in.

At the Los Angeles *Times,* the woman who took down the odd advertisement for the next day's Personals column said to the caller on the line from the San Fernando Valley number, "Let me read this back to you."

"Tex: We rejoice in cleansing of your soul. Special letter with instructions for salvation forthcoming. Prepare to make a contribution to good deeds."

"Is that correct?" asked the ad taker.
"Yes," said the caller.
"Do you want the three-day special? $14.90?"
"No. One time will be enough."

Her first night in Los Angeles, Susan was touched by Mack's thoughtfulness. There were several bouquets of fresh flowers in her room, back copies (hastily procured) of *Psychology Today* beside her bed, dinner by the pool with torches rimming the dark velvety water. Caterers served salmon mousse, duck with green peppercorn sauce, and poured Dom Pérignon out of a magnum. When Jeffie announced he did not like any of the food, Mack sent one of the French waiters down to Sunset Boulevard to pick up hickory-smoked ribs. How could she request divorce on an evening like this?

The second night—yes, she stayed a second night—Susan so enjoyed dinner at Le Bistro and met so many famous people (Gregory and Veronique Peck, Irving and Mary Lazar, Billy and Audrey Wilder, Betty Bacall, David Niven), and all of them courteously signed Jeffie's autograph book and wished him a pleasant stay in Hollywood, that it would have been cruel and ungrateful to broach her purpose. When they returned to the mansion, Mack screened three Bugs Bunny cartoons and his latest picture.

But on the third night, when Jeffie fell asleep early after a ten-hour day at Disneyland, where a public relations guide whisked them to the front of every line, she got her bearings back from the weather. They were sitting outside on a brick patio when abruptly, from the sea, a thick wet fog sent them metaphorically into the house. Mack brought her a glass of cold white wine in a Waterford goblet and before she took a sip she said, "We've got to talk, Mack."

"So talk, hon."

She said it quickly. "I want a divorce. I really mean it."

Mack made it very difficult. He took her demand and stuffed it in his cheek like he was a squirrel and divorce was a nut, lit a fire that leaped up from a gas jet and ignited eucalyptus and avocado logs, put some clean-sounding jazz on the stereo and fiddled with the speakers so that it drifted from faraway corners. Then he sat on the marine-blue carpet, looking like a child lost at sea and colored by the flames of a sinking ship. The transition was as seamless as the segue in a well-crafted film; Susan felt ashamed if not guilty.

"Do we have to?" Mack said quietly. He was heart-stoppingly beautiful, thought Susan. Initially she had disliked his new mustache and buccaneer sideburns, surprised that he would obey at thirty-five the dictates of young men and their hirsute fashion. Now she found the raging need to kiss him, to surrender then and there and feel his shaggy face against hers. The theatricality of the moment made her feel like a player. If Mack had just stopped talking for a moment, Susan would have made a fatal digression.

But Mack was overrehearsed and unable to forget his speech. He said he did not blame her one bit. He said they should have severed years ago, by conventional rules. He said he had hung on this far because marriage was the only thing at which he had ever failed—"the only hurdle I couldn't jump" was his not quite appropriate analogy. But he also said, compelling her to stare and listen in near-paralysis of intent, "I just want you to know that I still love you. I was never much good at showing it. But that's the way I am. You've enriched my life. And I hope I haven't screwed up yours totally."

So genuine did the declaration sound, so wrenchingly believable were the tears that welled in famous eyes and spilled on fire-reddened cheeks that Susan heard the rest dimly, like cries of help kidnapped by the wind. Mack was saying something about retiring from films, saying that even if they divorced she might like to move to Los Angeles or he could just as easily return to Fort Worth, suggesting that *perhaps, maybe, why not,* they *might* even get back together on a trial basis. "I need you, hon," said Mack. "I can't promise you a conventional relationship. But I want . . ." He got no further. Susan stood up like a heckler in an audience. She shook her head to clear the fog that had somehow followed her inside.

"You really know which buttons to push," she said. "I'm sitting here with an almost master's in psychology, and you say the magic words, *'want,'* and *'need,'* and Jesus help me if I'm not fourteen years old with clammy thighs. I know that women are basically masochistic and guilty—we have been since Eve—and women get trapped in fantasies, and women make a life out of fooling themselves. I know these things because I've been one of those women since 1956. I read an article the other day that said *a bad marriage is better than no marriage.* Well, bullshit to that. I've thrown damn near half a worthy life down the toilet because I once got the guy every girl wants. To use your splendid image, I jumped the hurdle. Isn't that something?"

"Susan, wait a minute. I'm trying to get something started."

"I'm trying to get something finished, mister. I'm trying to get out of a shadow and find a piece of the sun. And I'm goddamn proud of myself."

"I need you, Susan."

"Don't get started with *need,* boy. I've got more needs than Carter has pills. I think you're scared of something—maybe yourself—and I think what you *need* is somebody to run interference. You used to be pretty good at broken-field running. You'll score, Mack. Someday. Somebody. Something."

They quarreled stormily for most of the night but Mack signed the divorce papers at breakfast. Two months later, a generous property settlement bargained, Susan passed the most satisfying hour of her life one brisk and sunny autumn morning in Juárez.

Someday Arnie Beckman intended to fill a void in his life, an ache that neither sex nor power nor money had gentled. He coveted recognition beyond the polars of his influence. He wanted the whole country, the America he liked to define as "that great sandwich—two crusts of bread called L.A. and New York with three thousand miles of baloney in between," to know his name. Even if he rose to head a motion picture studio someday, they weren't calling them Metro-Goldwyn-*Mayer* anymore. But what could transform his name into a slot on the marquee of contemporary history was a book, an autobiography, a veritable cultural responsibility. Generations now and yet to come would value the blood and sweat he had spilled—unheeded!—to pull the tangled strings of painted dolls.

The trouble with Arnie's dream, and he had not negotiated this sticky clause in his personal contract, was how to circumvent the nuisance of libel. One possible solution was to publish his memoirs posthumously, but that would be like worshipping a dead saint. Another would be to change the names, but steak tartare is still hamburger. The most legally troubling portion of the book, he realized, would necessarily deal with the miraculous salvage of Mack Crawford's disintegrating career. On the night of the surprise wedding (a surprise to everyone but him), Arnie—for his own amusement—mentally dictated two widely varying accounts of his greatest production. They were rather like the domestic and foreign versions of a choice American melodrama:

For American Consumption

You remember what it was like in the summer of '68? Mack Crawford was depressed over Bobby Kennedy's death and Martin Luther King's assassination. And on top of all that, he and his lovely wife Susan decided amicably to divorce. They had been married for fourteen years and had a fine young son. The break sent Mack into a tailspin. He came very close to stepping aside a year or two. I wouldn't have blamed him. Then one night I gave a very small dinner party at my new house in the flats of Beverly Hills. I didn't really expect Mack to show up, knowing how down in the dumps he felt. About halfway through the sorrel soup, in he comes. I squeeze a chair for him between me and one of my guests, a really beautiful girl named Arianna Corinth, the costume designer. Well, later on, after the fact, everybody accused me of playing matchmaker, seeing as how she was just divorced as well and all that. But I swear to God it never entered my mind. The table was talking Nixon and Humphrey and Gloria Steinem and Allen Ginsberg—but Mack and Arianna were talking each other. I don't think I'm betraying any secrets to tell you that those two kids fell in love at first sight. They left my party together and stayed together. Mack's spirits perked up like it was Christmas and the Fourth of July all rolled into one and he decided to star in

Hiding Out. Arianna agreed to do the costumes and the rest is history and hearts and flowers.

FOR EUROPEAN AUDIENCES

There are no secrets in Hollywood, friends. They last about as long as foam. That summer in '68, I had a real problem on my hands. Word was getting around that America's hero worked both sides of the street, *if* you know what I mean. Does that do it for you? In the old days, it wouldn't have mattered. The studios kept those things under control. Besides, the newspapers didn't sift through a man's garbage the way they do now. I was terrified. Mack's last two pictures hadn't performed like they should have, and the studio guys—they'll grab any straw to save their own necks. Before one of those wet-eared sheep dogs in blue jeans and gold chains could tell Arnie Beckman that his star client ought to stop copying John Wayne and start quoting Oscar Wilde, I had to move fast. Remember the motto of the hour, "Tell it like it is." Jeez, I started dreading the checkout line at Jurgensen's for fear that Mack's picture would be on the cover of the *National Enquirer* with him in a wedding dress.

So, when his pitiful little "wife," Susan, walked out on him—I keep a pretty good ear to what's going on with my clients when the lights go off—there went Mack's last mask of respectability. Well, it just so happened I knew a wonderful girl, a client of mine, in need of something bad. Real bad. She required a husband. Oh, not a husband in the traditional sense of the word. She didn't enjoy cocks placed in her pussy unless they were made out of rubber and strapped around an older woman's waist. What she was was a dyke and what she had to locate was a husband. Follow me carefully here. This young lady, Arianna Corinth, gorgeous she was, you'd never believe she was queer, married a genuine man once and produced a baby daughter. The guy was a lush and roughed her up all the time and turned her off of men. But she loved her little girl and nobody would ever suggest Arianna wasn't the finest of mothers. Ex-husband Eric didn't want his daughter raised in dyke city. He was starting a messy custody fight. Arianna was so desperate she was ready to walk off stage in the middle of the play.

Oh, sure, it took some talking. I never negotiated such a contract. I doubt if David Selznick had as many headaches putting *Gone With the Wind* together. But I finally wrote a deal memo, got 'em both to sign a prenuptial agreement that is today safely locked away in the bowels of Bank of America. Arianna got enough money out of Mack up front to turn up some *very* interesting dirt in ex-husband Eric's back yard, so much of it that he stopped trying to steal his daughter. I'm proud to say I was best man at Mack and Arianna's lovely wedding in Vegas.

Sort of like icing the wedding cake, I, ah, *persuaded* Mack to do *Hiding Out,* which as we all know ran twenty-seven weeks in little old New York City. Worldwide gross may reach $26 million and that makes Mackie boy so cherished on the boulevards of Beverly Hills that he can fuck German shepherds for all anybody cares, which he may, even as I write this, be doing.

P.S. I swear to God I don't know anything about that extortion letter, the one that shook Mack so much. He accused me of sending it at first, but I swear on the grave of my mother, may her soul rest in peace, Arnie Beckman would not stoop to *that.* But in retrospect, I can't deny that I'm glad it turned up the time it did. Mack found another reason to say, *"I do."*

It rained out of season that late-September afternoon, for which Mack was grateful. The windshield of his rented car, an anonymous tan Ford, was dirty. Behind the screen he sat and waited, eyes drilled on the little beauty parlor with its pretentious sign, "Belle Coiffures." He was somewhere in the bleak and dusty heart of the San Fernando Valley, that gigantic sprawl of suburban horrors, that desert nurtured by stolen water and transformed into mother church of shopping centers, fast-food emporiums, women in hair curlers loved by men in bermuda shorts. It was like the back side of a piece of scenery. Mack was not even sure what city he was in—it could have been Van Nuys or North Hollywood or Reseda, there being no more definition between these towns than cells in a prison block. But he knew he was at the right place and within the hour, once Belle Coiffures had turned out the lights, once Mack had put on his dark glasses and ski-toboggan cap and affected the stoop and limp he had practiced, he was confident that life would successfully imitate art. He had played enough cops to know how to scare the shit out of amateur blackmailers. The man he had watched since five-fifty snipping the bored blonde's hair would not presently suffer a broken neck; Mack intended no homicide. But the twinkie's greed would be stuffed down his throat.

Mack was already in ill temper when the special delivery letter had come. It had arrived a few days after Susan's return to Texas and toward the end of Jeffie's summer visitation. The boy and his father had not gotten along well. In fact, Mack had called him an "ungrateful little shit" when Jeffie argued with a talented prop man from Warners who came to assist the child in building a birdhouse for his Cub Scout project. Almost gratefully, Mack had stuffed $100 in Jeffie's new blazer from Saks and sent him back to Texas.

The letter was almost laughable. Right out of a Monogram movie. Somebody had laboriously snipped random words from magazine headlines, "fruit" and "pansy" used so many times that Mack speculated a year's supply of *Better Homes and Gardens* must have been ravaged. Strung together, they demanded $300,000 in non-sequential one-dollar bills, another tip-off that the sender was inexperienced. Such a package would not only be difficult to assemble but rather bulky. Mack would have torn the letter up had it not been for the final tease, "If You Fail, What a Surprise Waits for Jeffie. He Will Be Missed on Cloverdale." The extortionist, no matter how novice, possessed intimate and disturbing information.

Through a reporter friend at the *Times,* Mack learned the telephone number that had been used to charge the classified ad in the Personals column. And from the services of a cop who moonlighted as a security guard at film colony functions, Mack traced the number to an address. For a week he had cruised past the sad little shopping center, satisfied finally that Belle Coiffures contained but two possible blackmailers. A Mexican maid who swept the floor? Unlikely. But the owner, a frail young man named Arthur Wiggins in his early twenties, had apparently sampled hair dyes so frequently that his locks had become the color of tarnished silver. Modest deduction caused Mack to believe that a screaming Valley crimp was reaching beyond his grasp.

The last two nights, Mack had idled near the salon, thwarted by Arthur's custom of departing immediately upon closing shop and driving to a homosexual steam bath on Lankershim Boulevard, where Mack deemed it not wise to loiter on a side street past midnight. He did, however, entertain fantasies of choking the little faggot amid the vapors and was amused by what his presence would cause inside the "club."

Tonight being a Friday, Mack speculated that his quarry would first go home—if he had one—and preen for the weekend's hunt. Sure enough, Arthur came out, got into his car, drove west on Victory, turned right beside a supermarket bigger than an airplane hangar, and parked his dead gray VW bug beneath a clump of palm trees with the beards of unkempt old men. Arthur apparently resided in one of three tiny stucco bungalows hidden by shrubbery and facing onto an empty swimming pool, cracked by the most recent earthquake.

Pleased that no one seemed to be at home in the other units, Mack crept silently behind him, waited until Arthur placed key in lock, burst there and then from his hiding place, and made the greatest flying tackle of his life. The two men crashed through the front door, over a plastic sofa, shattered a glass coffee table from which exploded a nearly completed jigsaw puzzle of King Kong, rolled like a bowling ball into a corner, stopping at the foot of a rocking chair in which sat a serene old woman trying to eat a TV dinner.

Rising with difficulty and using a cane, she scrutinized the intruder whose dark glasses had flown in mid-assault from his blue eyes and whose ski cap had slipped to betray a shock of almost golden hair. "Well, Mack, for goodness' sakes!" the old woman cried, while, meantime, Arthur squealed like a mashed cat and flew out the front door. And, from the sound of it, fell into the empty pool.

Mack stared at the old woman—with good cause. Her face was greeting-card grandma, round and sweet. Her body was ample and hidden within the folds of a muumuu colored passion fruit. Her hair was the towering and silvered *belle coiffure* of Madame Pompadour. And all around the room, on every wall, on shelves and tabletops, were pictures of Mack Crawford. He was in a museum of his image. Atop the television set was his first *Life* cover in football glory at the University of Texas. The old lady had more magazine covers of Mack than his toilet.

This was the moment, thirty-five years and eighteen days after the bastard was born, when the Prince of Charms laid first eyes on his very own blood mother.

The story was uncomplicated. Lureen Hofmeyer, having long ago abandoned her unsuccessful *nom de cinéma,* Cassandra Astor, worked for a quarter century as beautician in many Valley salons. Finally accumulating enough money to open her own business in 1962, she engaged a talented but troublesome homosexual assistant, Arthur. He was the stereotypical stylist, receiver of rumor and merchant of gossip. He pretended to be a servant to the gods and goddesses. When Lureen fell painfully ill with frequent attacks of sciatica, she sold Arthur half the shop and continued to function as surrogate mother. Undisciplined with his personal finances, Arthur suffered frequent evictions from apartments and in recent months had been in residence at Lureen's modest bungalow.

Blackmail? "I simply can't believe Arthur would do that," sighed Lureen as she stirred hot Postum for Mack, routinely, as if she did it every night for her son. "But he has been acting strange lately. He has a weakness for what the boys call rough trade, excuse my French. Maybe he needed money. I shall certainly scold him."

"How long have you known me?" asked Mack. "I mean, known *who* I am?"

Lureen settled into her rocking chair and glowed. "Oh, the longest time, son. My sister—your aunt Mable, God rest her soul—never suspected it, but I kept an eye cocked on you. Texas blood runs deep. I was so ashamed. I did the most terrible thing a woman can do. I denied my own child. A thousand times I got ready to call you. I can't tell you how many Greyhound bus reservations I made for Fort Worth. But I never did call. Never did go. I'm proud of you. You can rest assured of that."

"Susan? Jeffie? You know about them?"

"Why, sure. I'm your biggest fan. Tell me, son, are you going to make *Hiding Out?* I read in the trades where you were considering it. Seems like a wise change of pace."

They drank Postum until 3 a.m., when Lureen dozed off in her rocking chair and Mack fell asleep on some floor pillows beside her, surrounded by himself. Not long after that, he invited Mama to move to the summit of Beverly Hills, where she became an excellent supervisor of staff, companion, adviser, occasional secretary, and enthusiastic conspirator in the planning of her son's secret marriage in Las Vegas to Arianna Corinth.

"A lovely girl," pronounced Mama Lureen, and thus quoted in the *Life* cover story that included her photograph. "I always wanted a daughter. And a granddaughter, too. The Lord does indeed work in mysterious ways His wonders to perform."

CHAPTER TWENTY-TWO

The profound weariness in Kleber Cantrell's face and eyes was apparent to Ceil Shannon. She watched the monitor in the green room for a while, then, her worry growing, she slipped into the wings of the little theater on West Forty-fourth in New York to see her lover banter live with David Frost on national television. From her vantage point, all she could glimpse was a sliver of Kleber's head, a fraction of flesh framed between interrogator and traveling camera. No matter how she shifted and strained, Ceil could not see any more. The metaphoric perfection—her share of Kleber—was momentarily amusing. But still she silently implored Frost—and the clock—to hurry.

Kleber was sick. He had never recovered fully from the AR-15 Colt rifle shell that tore into his shoulder sixteen months earlier near a miserable Vietnamese hamlet called An Dien. The wound was healed now and the double-S scar that snaked about his left arm socket was the faint white of medically forgotten. But he had returned to work too quickly, refusing the doctors' dictates that a year of rest would be desirable. The injury became the last chapter of his newest book, *Coonskin Capers,* an angry and funny—black-comedy funny—assault on America's disastrous fall into the quicksand called Vietnam. Its title was an allusion to Lyndon Johnson's megalomaniacal call to arms, the now dead thirty-sixth President's desire to win the war in Southeast Asia as if the Red gooks were raccoons to be nailed by American purpose to the log cabin wall of history.

Kleber's injury—and he almost bled to death beside a pigpen in a village of tar-paper shacks with roofs patched with Coca-Cola signs— was what he wanted to tell David Frost about on television. He had a witty and acidic set piece prepared, the thrust of which was that he never knew who shot him. He could not distinguish between the white hats and the black hats. The projectile that very nearly amputated his arm was American—but the unforeseen skirmish that tore An Dien involved South Vietnamese, Vietcong, and U.S. "advisers," all of whom were shooting at each other with AR-15 Colt rifles. The casualties of the day were one journalist, (Kleber), one seventy-two-year-old peasant farmer (dead), and two sisters, age four and seven (one dead, one losing both legs). Plus pigs and water buffalo. Not a drop of centurion blood was shed. That several hundred soldiers of diverse political allegiance and passion could waste incalculable time and money to kill and mutilate only peasants, scribes, children, and animals seemed to Kleber the absurd heart of the matter.

Coonskin Capers had been published in April 1971 to reviews reflective of America's mood. From the left came hosannas; *Rolling Stone* scheduled a cover on Kleber but scrapped it at the last minute in favor of a profile on Yoko Ono. From the right thundered screams of traitor and suggestions that the author unite carnally with Jane Fonda and take up residence in the Hanoi Hilton. Despite the news-engendering cross fire, the book was not selling. The publisher had printed an overly ambitious 50,000 copies and they were stacked in bookstores like undiscovered pyramids. Thus did Kleber agree to a national publicity tour, ignoring Ceil Shannon's argument that he would drop dead sometime between "Today" and "Tonight."

On the limousine ride downtown to the Frost show, Ceil told Kleber he looked pale and clammy, whereupon he directed the chauffeur to detour by his doctor for a quick "vitamin" shot. Kleber went every morning to the offices of a fashionable physician named Kriekmann who had a dozen booths curtained with red velvet. His clientele, which included a remarkable number of celebrities in media, politics, and entertainment, waited hungrily for the good physician to inject their buns with a potion of vitamins and "nutriments." Ceil noticed that every time Kleber came out of Kriekmann's booth he was newly wound up. But she never said what she thought. There was just so much criticism Ceil could lay on Kleber. He had a habit of running away.

Upon arriving at the theater, Kleber had been delighted to learn that one of the scheduled guests, a rock musician, failed to show. Kleber's allotted quarter hour would be doubled, giving him presumably enough time to sell his book and denounce the war. It would not turn out that way.

Though enthusiastic over Kleber's book, Frost introduced his guest as "one of America's most celebrated and controversial writers, the progeny of H. L. Mencken, the man who lunches with Golda Meir in Tel Aviv and dines with Nasser in Cairo, no mean trick—chronicler of the rich and famous—and infamous." Kleber strolled on to applause and a few boos, still pale despite the expertise of Frost's makeup woman, and slightly swallowed by the size 42 long sports jacket that Ceil had grabbed off the rack at Brooks that afternoon. She had told him that his clothes no longer fit a body twenty pounds lighter and he had gruffed, go buy something new. But Kleber could not tolerate a physique damaged by long illness and he had incorrectly given Ceil his old size.

Frost lingered but briefly in Vietnam. When, he asked, when would it all end?

"You must ask Mr. Nixon," replied Kleber, raising two empty palms to the great beyond. "Three years ago he told us he had a quote secret plan end quote to conclude the war. That secret plan got him elected, so one must assume that this valuable secret will not be revealed until 1972, when the second coronation comes to pass."

"Your book," said Frost, neither referring to its title nor gesturing to the copy sitting like an unwelcome guest beside the host, "is extremely critical of Lyndon Johnson, for whom you wrote speeches in 1964."

"Guilty to the crime of criticism. Not guilty for reasons of temporary insanity to the charge of putting words in LBJ's mouth. I tried to make him sound like John Kennedy, which was like entering a longhorn steer in the Kentucky Derby." Kleber drew a breath during the gasps and titters, preparing to speak kindly of LBJ's domestic ledger and brutally of his foreign follies. But Frost, not wanting his program—and ratings—to fall in a thicket of war and politics, deftly changed conversational direction. He knew that Kleber was a dependable guest, as well stocked with topics as the ice cream store of thirty-one flavors. The Prince of Power's tongue was as quick as his typewriter.

From the wings, Ceil saw Kleber's distress at being forced to abandon his book, but like an actor whose pants threaten to fall down, he remained in character. During the next commercial break, Ceil almost rushed onstage to whisper in David Frost's ear that his guest had 102 degree fever and might throw up on national television unless spared further questions about non-relevant subjects. But she knew that Kleber would have hissed back to ignore this strange woman, that she had just escaped from Bellevue.

Frost harked back to 1963, to Kleber's presence in Dallas on the night of John Kennedy's assassination. "Hardly anyone believes anymore that Lee Harvey Oswald acted alone," said Frost. "Yet I know that you scoff at conspiracies and grassy knolls. Why?"

"I've always thought Oswald was aiming at John Connally and missed," said Kleber, drawing an unintentioned laugh from the studio audience. "Seriously, the guy couldn't shoot straight, he had a cheap rifle, and he was sore at Connally, who used to be the Secretary of the Navy—his mama told me that—and was thus the core of Oswald's discontent. Oswald had been trying in vain to get in touch with Connally."

"But there are experts who claim Oswald could not have acted alone," said Frost. "There had to be a conspiracy of some kind."

Kleber sighed, exasperated. "Assassination Buffs, Inc., is indeed a major growth industry. But I can't buy a used conspiracy from Mark Lane and Mort Sahl. If you believe there was a conspiracy to kill John Kennedy and then a conspiracy to hush it all up, then you must accept an incredible—I use the word in its purest sense—an *incredible* cast of conspirators. It has to include Lyndon Johnson, J. Edgar Hoover, Earl Warren, Gerald Ford, I could go on and on—and it must also contain Bobby Kennedy, not only the Attorney General of the United States at the time of the murder but the brother of the assassinated President. Bobby Kennedy loved Jack. He *worshipped* him. Bobby was the chief legal officer in America. He had access to every file, every secret drawer. I think if Bobby Kennedy had ever whiffed the faintest aroma of cover-up, he would have torn down Washington brick by brick with his bare hands to arrest and convict the killers of his brother. Sorry. I can't conjure conspiracy, no matter how delicious the temptation. Besides, eight years have passed. Eight years! *Somebody* would have tattled by now. Somebody would have signed a contract with Doubleday. *I Killed JFK* would be the biggest book since the Bible. Secrets are scarce and valued commodities. Secrets exist only if they belong to one man."

At that, Ceil relaxed. Kleber was *on*. He was performing; if his heart stopped, he would still get through the show. That was one of the reasons Ceil loved him. He dazzled her sense of theater. Pretending to be a curmudgeon, he owned no real malice. He was opinionated but not arrogant. He talked like he wrote—assembled, provocative, well packaged, and impersonal. Language, on paper or on stage, was his hiding place. Kleber revealed nothing of himself, a magician pulling doves from his sleeve and fire from his fingertips, bidding tigers to materialize from empty boxes and jump growling through wreaths of paper roses—then all disappearing, including himself. Leaving only the remembrance of flash and color.

A stagehand grasped her shoulder and thumbed Ceil away. She could not stand in the wings. Union rules, lady. The temptation was to hiss that she damn well knew the rules, that she had once written a play that kept this theater in business—*legitimate* business. But it would waste energy to pull rank and she would lose. Obediently, Ceil wandered outside, to the tepid air of Forty-fourth Street in early evening, calculating that Kleber would be done in seven minutes. When his tour was over, she intended to ensure his needed rest by lashing him to the bed if necessary, disconnecting the telephone, and intercepting all channels of news for at least one month. She laughed privately at the casting: Nurse/Mother was one role yet unplayed in the continuing melodrama of Shannon and Cantrell. For almost a decade, Ceil had essayed Elaine May to his Mike Nichols, Katharine Hepburn to his Spencer Tracy, an occasional and usually funny stab at Circe to his Ulysses. They were the Bickersons and sometimes Laurel and Hardy. Whoever, whatever, their affair was one helluva piece of theater even though the principals were now old enough to be character actors.

Ceil leaned against a wall of theater posters on Shubert Alley and watched the district come to life. A knot of professional autograph seekers gathered in front of Sardi's restaurant, their territory as surely staked out as begging corners in Calcutta. They both fascinated and repelled Ceil, not because her signature and photograph were rarely requested anymore (she had not written a successful play in years and maintained tenuous celebrity only by appearances on game show panels and gossip-column linkage with Kleber). He almost punched one of them out the week before when his refusal to sign his name was construed as snobbery. "I only autograph my books," Kleber had said lightly, pushing aside a plastic folder in the grubby hands of a heavyset fan in a pea coat. "Your autograph ain't worth nine ninety-five," sneered the seeker. "I got two Cary Grants and fourteen Ingrid Bergmans for free. They know my *name,* too." Shoving began, and Ceil had pushed Kleber into a taxi. "Can you imagine spending a life waiting for autographs?" seethed Kleber. "It's the human equivalent to leeches and Spanish moss." Ceil had agreed the custom was idiotic, thinking later on that a play entitled *King of Signatures* might be worth writing.

A voice broke into her dusk dreaming. "Is this the 'David Frost Show'?" asked a man who stood puffing in front of her, words spilling from a red face. He was, Ceil assumed, a tourist searching for faces to enrich his Instamatic. His costume gave him away: a garish sports coat of Rorschachian green blobs and white patent-leather shoes. Under his arm was an accordion folder, the kind conventioneers stuff with pamphlets and sales brochures.

Ceil nodded and pointed. The man looked at her curiously, as if assessing her celebrity quotient. Ceil was used to the once-over. Any woman six feet tall gets it, particularly if her hair is coppery and the clothes on her back as flamboyant as this night's red trousers, white blouse, and Isadora-esque blue scarf wrapped around her throat and flapping in the wind tunnel. Kleber had commented that she looked like Aunt Sam.

"Where's the stage door?" asked the man. Ceil gestured ten feet away.

"Have they started yet?" he wondered.

"Almost finished," said Ceil.

"You're Ceil Shannon, aren't you?" said the man in happy discovery. She nodded and watched him disappear hurriedly into the theater. She was pleased to be recognized. She started to follow him, but the drama of the boulevard arrested her eye. Since 1938 when she first came to this street to see *Our Town,* the theater district had held her in fascination. In three decades plus, Broadway had changed radically. Policemen on horseback were clopping into the heart of the area just like they had the first night she had come, clutching the hands of her parents. But tonight they were ignoring the prostitutes setting up shop like cooch dancers on a midway. The working girls, who no longer loitered beneath canopies and pretended to be waiting for taxis, now paraded boldly. On their flanks were micro-minis and leather boots to the knee. They wore pounds of lipstick, yards of false eyelashes, gallons of scents. Ceil watched and began to fantasize a comedic drama—an update of *Lysistrata.* She wished for the courage to mingle with these sisters, perhaps single one out for an hour of information and revelation. Kleber would. If Kleber desired to know the ins and outs of hookerdom, he would simply introduce himself, flash a gentling Texas smile, whisk Jezebel off to the nearest saloon, oil her throat with rye, and extract her who, what, when, where, and why. He was always doing that.

One midnight in a taxi ride from Elaine's on Eighty-eighth to an artist's loft in SoHo, Kleber passed the time by quizzing the cabbie, one Isadore Rabinsky. So thoroughly did he question that within twenty fascinating minutes a life was laid bare. Characters materialized—Izzie's ancestors from Poland, his hateful wife Sonia, who wanted to move near her beloved slot machines in Nevada, his adored daughter Nadia, who had leukemia under control and who was in anguish over whether to reveal the disease to a fine young NYU law student who loved her. Passions flared. Izzie hated the mayor, drivers from Long Island, women passengers in front of Bloomingdale's with armloads of packages and hands clutching cheap tips, coloreds, PR's, welfare chiselers, and, most of all, his brother Lou, who owed him $1,150.

"You're stunning," Ceil told Kleber later. "I wouldn't have asked that old man the time of day. You made him Chekhovian."

Kleber shrugged. "Bad habit," he said. "I'm just a nosy fucker." And the next day he had forgotten it all.

That was both bond and barrier between them. Ceil was an *observateur* peering through rain-blurred windows in a violent storm, not needing to experience the force of nature to fabricate drama. She looked at strangers and set her imagination loose as collector of human experiences. She perceived character by the stoop of someone's shoulders, their unpolished shoes, scars, the way lovers parted on railroad platforms. That was enough to measure other lives against hers. She *felt*. Kleber acted. She created. Kleber reported. Both envied the other. Both never intruded. The sign said "No Trespassing" and by honoring it, Ceil and Kleber had remained lovers, or reasonable facsimiles thereof, for a decade. They each reminded the other often that their second—and most important—meeting came on board an airplane, a never-never land of neither here nor there.

Ruefully, Ceil realized as she reminded herself it was time to go back in and fetch her ailing friend, perhaps that was why Kleber the Doer was onstage, performing and posturing for 6 million viewers, and why Ceil the Watcher was out on the street, propping up a dirty brick wall festooned with obscenities and spray paint graffiti. Handbills had been slapped one atop the other like young fists working their way up a baseball bat: "America—Love It Or Leave It" was covered by "Vietnam Veterans Against the War," which in turn was smothered by "Sultan's Massage—24 Hours a Day of Turkish Delights." Handbills clogged the gutters; mothers seeking to ban the bomb swirling into sewers along with abortion clinics and topless go-go dancers. Richer theater smeared the walls and littered the streets than was on the stages of Broadway. No wonder the season was anemic and poorly attended. Derivative musicals like *The Rothschilds* and *Two by Two* were saline solutions compared to the hot and real blood found for free on the seven o'clock news. *Hair* was blatantly commercial counterculture that offered—for fifteen dollars top price—blue-shadowed glimpses of pubic hair. But every Sunday afternoon in Central Park was a pageant of youth protesting war and proclaiming love, some costumed as gypsies, some defiantly naked and splashing in fountains. Minstrels with flutes and mandolins serenaded them, making *real* theater, passionate street drama performed beneath clouds of cannabis that were far more conducive to enjoying a play than watered orange juice in wax cartons.

Ceil Shannon, almost forty, was lost. She was exhilarated by the stridency of America in 1971, yet her pen was dry. In three years she had written—and burned—fragments of a half-dozen plays. Always she had located truth from the mirror of the past. But it didn't reflect anymore. Where in the two centuries of America's adolescence could she find understanding or explanation for middle-age malaise: for disintegration of family, for the shattering of male and female identities, for priests pouring blood on draft board files and then marrying nuns in cropped hair and short skirts, for adolescent children stabbing their veins with heroin and stabbing old women to pay for it, for black power, woman power, homosexual power, brown power, gray power, for government swirling with more deceit and distrust than the court of Versailles?

Or, for that matter, where was the moral antecedent for the relationship between Ceil Shannon and Kleber Cantrell? They loved and were married—but to other people. Though she did not use his name, Ceil was by law the spouse of Saul Greene, a fifty-eight-year-old producer and professor of drama, a man whom she saw perhaps once each quarter of a given year. And though the marriage was *blanc,* she liked him very much. Kleber was now on his second legal union, having wed, in 1967, less than one month after meeting her, an off-Broad-

way actress named Noel North, an effervescent blonde with a calculated aura of Judy Holliday. Within seven months, the new Mrs.
Cantrell had given birth to a daughter, and though Kleber's calculation
did not convince him that paternity was necessarily his, he accepted,
and loved, Anna North Cantrell. Each of Kleber's wives and children
had been like a package to be opened, examined, enjoyed for a time,
and then set aside. He told Ceil as much but she knew an emotional
hummingbird when she saw one. The only reason he married Noel—or
so he said one night when drunk and angry—was because Ceil would
not divorce Saul Greene and marry him. Ceil had said why wreck a
wonderful love affair?

Ceil's husband knew about Kleber; Kleber's wife knew about Ceil.
And nobody seemed to care. The game was mixed doubles, and in
1970, no shot went out of bounds. Ceil messed around with a wildly
disguised theatrical sketch concerning this quartet, but her intent was
romantic comedy and what came out veered from burlesque on this
page to soap opera tragedy on the next. The truth was she wasn't too
happy with the way everybody's life had turned out, but it was too late
to change.

Journalism owned the franchise now. Journalism had become both
the show and the spectator. Ceil realized this on the day in 1968 when
Kleber returned from covering the Democratic convention in Chicago.
He looked like a boxer who had won the fight—but had lost his senses.
He told her of standing in the middle of Michigan Avenue on the cli-
mactic final night. Rather than attend the nomination of Hubert
Humphrey, Kleber chose to cover the confrontation between the disci-
ples of Abby Hoffman *et al.* and the storm troopers of Mayor Richard
Daley. His grasp of news suggested that here was the perfect encapsula-
tion of American grotesque—a few thousand rag-tailed kids vs. 16,000
Chicago police, 4,000 state troopers, and 4,000 National Guardsmen.
Law and *dis*order. Kleber had not anticipated how violent the night
would turn. Tear gas rolled over the city like fog from the Great Lakes.
Clubs smashed into the skulls of children who that very sunrise had
been meditating beside Lake Michigan and chanting "om" to the
cadence of poets. It was war—and Kleber by custom was dead center,
filling his pages, vision blurred and throat parched from the fumes. Beside him pranced a black demonstrator with the red band of rebellion
lashed across his glistening forehead. He wore jeans patched with peace
symbols and his shirt was shredded. He was taunting a policeman just

three feet away, pleading insolently, "Hey, baby, Mace mah face!" His tease became a chant and soon the angry cop spun around with canister in hand. A choice presented itself. One target was a black yippie. The second was a reporter, Kleber, in flannels and tweeds, his respectable chest decorated like a military hero with the badges and credentials of journalism. "Come on, baby, Mace mah fuckin' face!" cried the black.

The policeman took careful aim and squirted poison directly into the eyes of the Prince of Power. Kleber fell, his world dark, feeling rough hands yank back his head and then water flooding his eyes. Medics from the Students for a Democratic Society tossed buckets of water that saved his vision while a camera from ABC-TV recorded his agony. A woman reporter shoved a microphone into his face. "How does it feel to be Maced?" she asked, and what Kleber responded was blipped from America's living rooms.

When Kleber related the tale, Ceil kissed his eyes gently but felt a twinge of envy. She could not manufacture such a scene, even with her talent for fabricating drama. Journalism (and Ceil never used the more trendy "media" after Kleber growled at her that "media" meant watercolors) was running her out of business. She had companionship in the desert. Novelists were turning out thin-blooded accounts of squabbles over tenure in academe, or mothers warring with daughters. The last ten books she read all seemed to deal with divorce as the key plot point. And films were just as anemic. The night before the Frost show, Ceil suggested a spur-of-the-moment movie. *Love Story* was the hot ticket. Kleber made a gagging sound. They stayed in and played Scrabble and listened to Joan Sutherland singing French arias.

She hurried back into the theater. Kleber was surely finished by now, probably prowling impatiently. But on the monitor Ceil discovered that her lover was still center stage. So hot was his act that Frost canceled the rest of the bill. Ceil was upset. Though dependably glib, Kleber was looking more tired. Frost was playing a titillating game, tossing out the names of famous people whom Kleber knew, challenging him for instant analysis. Keyhole peeping. But Kleber had been in a lot of hotels.

"Elizabeth Taylor?" demanded Frost.

"Gorgeous. Earthy. Tough. Childish. The first time I saw her was in Paris; she was sitting in her dressing room beside a window through which streamed a cold winter light, holding that big rock up to her eyes. It threw off sparks like the revolving ball on the ceiling of a dance hall."

"You're talking about Richard Burton's diamond?"

Kleber nodded. "Yes. He had just given it to her. I stared at it and I said, these are my first words to this remarkable lady, I said, 'Jesus, Elizabeth, that can't be real.' And she looked up and said, 'You bet your sweet ass it's real; it's the Krupp Diamond.' Then she went into the toilet eleven times in the next hour and scrubbed the damn thing with Prell Shampoo on a toothbrush."

"Warren Beatty?"

Kleber groaned. "Unique among men. The only smart satyr I ever met. In fact, the only satyr I ever met. And about as dependable as the wind."

"Mack Crawford?"

"Was and is my best friend. I can't knock him. I always bear in mind that he is six inches taller and forty pounds heavier than me."

"You're from the same hometown?"

"The same block."

"How did it happen that one neighborhood produced two famous men?"

"I dunno. And the interesting fact is that it is all a mistake. I was supposed to be the sex symbol and he the wordsmith."

Frost observed that Kleber seemed to find fault with the celebrities he profiled. "Not true," said Kleber. "I feel sorry for them. Celebrity is by my definition a ghastly accomplishment."

"What is celebrity?" asked Frost.

"It's a peculiar American need. It grows out of insecurity and the breakdown of our institutions. We used to look up to family members. Then we decided to detonate the family and worship film stars and baseball players. And heart surgeons. Somebody, Fred Allen I believe, once said a celebrity is a person who breaks his ass to get recognized, then puts on dark glasses so he won't. My own definition is when Frank Sinatra goes to the bathroom."

"When *what?*"

"I was interviewing Frank once in Miami. We were in some nightclub. He said he had to, ah, attend the call of nature, and, feeling the same urge, I accompanied him. From the darkness of the chamber a couple of gorillas materialized—bodyguards—and while Frank did his business, they stood directly behind him to fend off autograph seekers. Celebrity means not being able to urinate without attendants."

Frost laughed mechanically and leaned in, a prosecutor ready to reveal the surprise witness. "But you're a celebrity," he accused. "How do you deal with yourself?"

"I can still pee alone, David. Can you?" answered Kleber tartly, delighted that the censors would be scrambling for the kill button. "And I don't consider myself a celebrity. I'd like for my words to be celebrated. But not me. Privacy is the only thing that makes life worth living."

"But surely you see the paradox," pushed Frost. "You've become famous by prying into the lives of the famous. That's why you fill that chair so well."

"That's hardly true." Kleber was annoyed and it showed. "I came here to talk about Vietnam, not about myself."

Frost fished out a clipping and read from it. "Your wife, the lovely actress Noel North, recently was quoted, 'What's Kleber Cantrell really like? Don't ask me. He's a man I married who calls now and then from airports.' Tell me, did you enjoy reading that?"

Kleber was not allowed an answer. In still another scene that Ceil Shannon could not have written—nor any farceur—the man in the green-blob sports jacket streaked onto the stage, thrust a thick folded document into the hands of the journalist, mumbled something barely audible about "duly served," and raced away.

David Frost called for a commercial and announced to his studio audience, "A television first, ladies and gentlemen. Before your very eyes, a man is served with a summons for divorce." Kleber bolted from his seat in rage and chased after the process server. Backstage, just as Green Sports Jacket was a foot from the exit, Kleber seized his shoulder, cranked him around, and punched him mightily in the mouth. Ceil cried out, though part of it was laughter, dragging Kleber through a gaggle of whores and fans into a waiting limousine.

On the ride uptown, in the middle of a profane tirade, Kleber, his forehead drenched, suddenly fell silent, swallowed hard, said to Ceil, "Honey, I feel bad," and passed out cold in her arms. She could not find a pulse.

It was not cardiac arrest, as Ceil initially feared. The doctor at New York Hospital called it "severe vago-vigal attack," which translated into a fainting episode. "It could be brought on by emotional stress in a warm crowded room, or by shocking news," said the young resident. Ceil said he hit it right on the head. Twice. An exceptionally foul virus, probably idiopathic, flattened Kleber for another week, stripped a dozen more pounds from his frame, and canceled the remaining publicity tour for *Coonskin Capers.* Kleber telephoned Noel North and said he shared her desire for immediate divorce, so much so that if she wished his left foot as part of property settlement, then by God send her sword to France, where he intended to sleep until deepest autumn.

Less than an hour out of Kennedy Airport, before the Air France 747 broke free of the North American continent, Ceil Shannon sensed that her carefully arranged interlude of R&R was endangered. Kleber began behaving rudely, a plateau from which he descended into boor, churl, and pain in the ass. It was obvious he had stopped off for a farewell fix from Dr. Kriekmann. He scarcely needed the plane. He pretended to be asleep, his head in her lap. Ceil had booked a night flight to Paris, obeying his desire for passage unmolested by food, films, or pilot talk.

He complained, "Do you have to read *that?*" Her copy of Kate Millett's *Sexual Politics* rested just over his head. "Does it bother you?" asked Ceil.

"It does. I feel like Damocles."

"If it's a threat to your masculinity, I will dutifully obey, my liege."

She switched to *The Greening of America,* which brought forth from Kleber a warning of impending air sickness.

"Kleber, what in the hell do you want?" snapped Ceil.

"I want you to turn off the light and . . . could you just hold me till I get to sleep?"

Touched, she embraced him until her arms began to throb, pleased to fill a rare admission of need. Such moments did not often come. In their decade, both kept their dukes up. As she held Kleber, she remembered introducing him once at a cocktail party in New York as "my sparring partner." Kleber had loved the billing and shamelessly appropriated it as his own. Sparring partners! The perfect label for a relationship that endured on punches pulled, on emotions never fully revealed, on a lot of bobbing and weaving and careful avoidance of the knockout blow that total commitment—marriage—would surely deliver.

She slept. She dreamed and was naked in the dream, running, stumbling. She was clutching the hand of a man whose face she could not identify. He seemed angry. She could not figure out whether they were running *away* from some peril, or toward it. But she fell and the earth was dry, cracked like a creek bed. The man cursed her and left her behind, alone. She struggled to her feet but they were nailed to the earth. She screamed at the man to wait for her, but nothing came out of her throat.

She awoke with the joy of reality and realized that the burden in her arms was shutting off circulation. As she shifted Kleber gently, he stirred. Ceil stroked his face in the darkness and on his brow she felt the lines of high-tension wires. She leaned down to kiss him but he moved his head away.

"Where are we?" he asked.

"Halfway," she guessed. "Past the point of no return."

Kleber flipped over in her lap, his eyes staring directly up like two eggs in a skillet watching the cook. "I always admired that phrase," he said. *"Past the point of no return."*

"Yes, quite. It has flair."

"Would you do me a favor? Would you stop judging everything that comes out of my mouth like it was dialogue?"

"I'll do better than that," said Ceil. "I'm going back to sleep."

Kleber shrugged and yawned. He opened the shade a crack and watched a thin orange line in the distant east shimmer. Europe was still there. He fell back onto Ceil's now less accommodating lap and disbelieved her closed eyes. "What I meant was," he continued, "the idea of actually going past the point of no return—in one's life, that is—fascinates me."

"Yes," said Ceil. And, after a time, "Have you?"

"Not so I've noticed, thank you very much." Later, still in her lap, he murmured, "How would you like to hear my confession?"

Ceil opened her eyes. "Your mood inhibits conversational banter."

"I'm not after banter. I just want to confess. You don't have to say anything. Play like there's a metal mesh between us." Whereupon he cleared his throat and said absolutely nothing. Ceil waited, not knowing if she was supposed to play mother, lover, friend, therapist, or wiseass. She had no script. She felt incapable and uncomfortable.

Then, cautiously, she prodded. "About that confession?"

"Oh, yes," he said. "But first let me tell you about hookers. I've always envied hookers. Think about it. They fuck all week, then go to church on Sunday and tell the priest they're sorry. Fifty Hail Marys, two dollars for the poor box, and *voilà!* Guilty conscience cleansed. Free pass for another week."

Okay. Ceil could improve this scene. "Several things come to mind about hookers," she said. "One is that their shelf life is not very long. They are a perishable commodity. Number two, I personally don't believe a prostitute has anything to confess, since fucking for money is no greater sin than fucking for a station wagon in Scarsdale. And last but not least, confession is not available solely to guilt-ridden Catholic hookers. Confession can be communication between two people."

Kleber sat up and feigned applause. "Succinct and cogent. Lacking only a snapper at the end to be worthy of a second-act curtain."

Ceil flared. "Listen, Kleber. This is supposed to be a vacation. If you intend to act like an emotional vandal for the next month, best you buy a mirror for company."

"My goodness, exposed nerves."

"*No* nerves."

"If I were a doctor, I'd advise you to swear off Millett, Friedan, and Greer. The soup of sisterhood's got you on edge."

"I wish 'male chauvinist pig' wasn't such a goddamn cliché."

"I'll bet you ten minutes of tranquillity you don't know the meaning of cliché."

"How about *hackneyed?* The prefix of which is *hack,* that usually applied to facile writing."

"Wrong. Despite your gratuitous knee to the nuts, the preferred definition of cliché is a metal die onto which have been assembled a series of identical stamps."

Now it was Ceil's turn for fake clapping. "How wonderful to possess that knowledge," she said. "I doubt if my life could have continued much past teatime without it. Now, excuse me. I'm going to ask the stewardess where the best singles bar in Paris is located."

Surprisingly, Kleber did not return fire. After a time he said, quietly, *"Hack* hurt."

"You know I didn't mean your writing. I was just shooting a scatter gun."

"Freud says you never say anything you don't mean."

"Oh, for heaven's sake, baby, you know you're good. You've got a wall full of prizes that testify to that. You know everybody in Europe and America worth knowing. You couldn't write a sympathy note with-out power."

"Power? That's a strange noun."

"All right. Make it strength."

Kleber squeezed. "Define power."

Ceil wished she had not opened the door. "I don't know what I mean by power. I don't know what you want from me." She stared at the exasperating man beside her and tried to say, without saying: I'm sorry you've been sick, and I'm anguished that you got shot in Viet-nam, and it's unfair that your book isn't selling, and it's too bad your wife is suing for divorce. But stop casting me as the virus-Vietcong-philistine-home wrecker. I'm trying very hard to love you.

Her message went unreceived. Harshly, Kleber repeated, *"Power."*

Ceil had no way out. She had to answer. *"Example:* You sent four people to federal prison after your series on those IRS auditors with sticky fingers. One man's wife killed herself over the disgrace. That's power. *Example:* You put words in the mouth of the President of the United States, the most powerful man in the world. That's power."

"Disallowed. Lyndon didn't like my speeches. He said I didn't write Texan. Continue."

"Example: Power is being able to sell whatever you choose to write. Power is sitting at the best dinner tables. Power is having people listen to whatever drivel comes out of your mouth on television. *Exam-ple:* Power is manipulating anyone who dares get close to you, be they wives, children, friends if you have any, and one very frustrated almost furious lover. Me. Who is not going to take your bullshit one moment longer. End examples. Power defined."

Kleber immediately seized one of his notebooks and began scrib-bling furiously, guarding his words with a cupped hand from Ceil, who, pretending indifference, resumed her reading of *Sexual Politics,* invent-ing enthusiastic grunts of approval. Words did not pass across the fron-tier again until the jet broke through a layer of thick clouds and rain to set down bumpily on the soil of Mother France. Hurriedly Ceil ran a comb through her hair, put lipstick on the face of the woman in her compact mirror who seemed eighty-three years old. She found dark glasses and dabbed perfume on a taut throat.

Kleber watched her every move. "You look nice," he said surpris-ingly.

"Thank you," she said with counterfeit courtesy.

He reached over and took her hands. "Do you love me?" he asked. "I mean, *really* love me?"

"At times . . . more often than not."

"Straight. *Please.*"

"Of course I love you."

"Why?"

"Because . . . because it's never boring. That's a constant in it-self."

"Then what would you think about getting married?"

Now Ceil Shannon had fielded this question many times, many ways, over many years. But at this moment she was unprepared. Eight hours of skirmishing at 38,000 feet was hardly prelude for proposal. She answered simply and bluntly. "What would you *feel* about getting married?"

"I asked you first."

"And there's my answer. Work out the difference between *think* and *feel*. Then get back to me."

"I feel," began Kleber tentatively, like a writer uncertain over a character's mood and unable to make transition, "I feel like I wasted my time to ask you. My work has power—and my life is a goddamn blackout."

Ceil had carefully planned their autumn in France. A perfectionist in everything she did, be it selecting the precise shade of sea-foam green for the walls of her Manhattan kitchen or devoting weeks to carpentering one line of dialogue, she orchestrated a sabbatical for Kleber's physical and mental restoration. First would come a week in Paris with only one necessary intrusion: a theater was presenting the first French production of Ceil's 1965 play, *No Trump,* and she had promised to attend the opening night. Afterward, they would motor leisurely—with no deadlines and no telephone calls—to an eleventh-century château in the Loire Valley where the only decision of the day would be whether to have dinner in bed. If the weather turned foul, a friend's villa near St. Tropez was available for the warming Riviera sunshine. She had even booked Christmas Day luncheon at a favorite restaurant near Cannes, and, if Kleber's health was repaired—as surely it would be—they would pass New Year's 1972 at St. Moritz. She projected, as benediction to a year of emotional and creative discontent for both, a night of wine and love.

Kleber disliked the little hotel on the Ile de la Cité that Ceil had chosen, complaining that sleep was impossible at night because of the noise and lights from the *bateaux mouches* that glided along the Seine. This carp Ceil found difficult to accept, as the tourist boats were gone by midnight and before that the accordion music drifting from their decks was charming and romantic. "There's not even a phone in the room," argued Kleber. "What if I get sick in the middle of the night?" Reluctantly, Ceil agreed to leave what seemed to her the most lovely hotel room imaginable, moving to the Hotel George V. Ceil swallowed the desire to point out that it contained more Americans than the Omaha Hilton. Very quickly she discerned the reasons for Kleber's choice. Even as they registered, he shook hands with a U.S. senator, two Hollywood producers, Shirley MacLaine, and—pretending impatience—he posed for a picture that would appear the next day in *France-Soir*.

Within twenty-four hours, Kleber's sullen mood soared, concurrent with the stack of messages and invitations that grew beside their bed. They included invitations for cocktails with the Time-Life bureau chief, lunch with the U. S. Ambassador to France, and numerous "urgent" cables from Kleber's New York publisher, attorney, accountant, and assorted magazine editors. Kleber said things like "How did they find out I was in town?" He moaned, "I'm never going to get any rest unless that phone stops ringing." But each clang of the bell and each rustle of an envelope slipped beneath the door crack enhanced the Prince of Power's sense of stature. He also partook liberally of a vial of triangle-shaped orange tablets, so many that Ceil grew alarmed.

On their third day in Paris, Kleber dragged her across the city, behaving like a stone fired from a slingshot, rushing in and out of the Louvre and the Jeu de Paume, sitting down for a glass of wine at a café on the Rue de Rivoli, then changing his mind in sudden desire to hire a limousine for an afternoon at Versailles, abandoning that notion halfway to the palace and suggesting instead a stroll along the Quay d'Orsay that became a footrace. By nightfall, exhausted, Ceil pleaded for an evening in, but Kleber, energies restored by the orange "vitamins," took his lady to Maxim's, where he ordered 800 francs' worth of elegant food and ate not a bite, pushing his fork about the plate as he spun an endless recollection of France's student-worker "revolution" in 1968—a tale he had told her many times before, the latest that very afternoon.

Ceil's play, *No Trump,* had been a flop six years prior off-Broadway and only ran two weeks. Seeking co-defendants for the crime of failure, she believed it had been miscast and misdirected. She was surprised that a French translation had been made and en route to the Théâtre Molitor for the opening-night performance remarked to Kleber, "I expect the worst. If I pinch your leg during the first act, that means get me the hell out of there." Kleber assured her that the play would be terrible. He had not liked it much in English. Besides, it was, he believed, a plagiarism.

Early in his newspaper career, Kleber had covered the tragedy of a Houston lawyer and his wife who went each summer to a beach cottage at Galveston. Beginning with their honeymoon, the couple spent the month of August at the shore. The custom continued for years, even after their four-year-old child drowned in the surf. On their tenth wedding anniversary in the summer house, they quarreled bitterly. Neighbors heard screams and threats. The husband was yelling something about their long dead child. The wife shot the lawyer dead and then tried, unsuccessfully, to drown herself in the storm-tossed Gulf of Mexico. She was indicted for manslaughter but acquitted after testimony concerning the husband's reputation for violence.

When Ceil heard the story, she mused, "But why would they have gone back year after year to that house following the death of a child?" Kleber shrugged, unknowing, uncaring, not even noticing that Ceil made notes of the conversation. In the late summer of 1965, returning from his first trip to Saigon and possessed of enough stories to dine out on for six months (and fill two goodly portions of the New York *Times Magazine*), Kleber was annoyed to discover that Ceil was in San Francisco, nursing a new drama. On long-distance she was vague, muttering about an "experimental piece." A few months later, when *No Trump* opened at a Greenwich Village theater, Kleber fretted half an act before figuring out where Ceil had found her conflict.

No Trump commenced with a couple playing bridge in a beach house, transferred from Texas to Cape Cod. Immediately the husband was revealed as a tyrant, criticizing his wife for inattention, silences, poor bidding, sloppy housekeeping, and slovenly appearance in front of guests. The wife accepted his abuse, as if well deserved. Later on, unable to sleep, listening to a storm, the wife relived in flashback a terrible tragedy. Many years before, she had taken her two small children to the beach for a swim and while there rendezvoused secretly with a lover. Sending the children off to play unwatched in the surf, she engaged in sex. During her passion, the children drowned. After hearing her confession, the husband, as punishment, brought the woman back each summer to the cottage, forcing her to live with ghosts. Deep into the play, the wife discovered her husband preparing to fondle an eight-year-old girl who had come to the house searching for a lost cat. He confessed his intent readily and braced for outrage. But at final curtain, the wife only shook her head enigmatically, indicating that though she now possessed a trump card in the game of guilt, she would not play it.

Kleber rummaged through his scrapbooks to find the old clipping from Houston about the original event. In his memory, the article seemed strong meat. But when he reread his journalism, he encountered twelve tight paragraphs of facts and facile visceral impact. Junk food. "How on earth did you see a play in that?" asked Kleber. "I don't know, really," answered Ceil. "I didn't *see* anything. I *felt* something. It just happens."

When *No Trump* was included in a published anthology of her plays, Ceil added a dedication, "To K.C.—the Unknowing Catalyst, as Usual." He was pleased.

The Théâtre Molitor was located on a street unfindable except by elderly Russian immigrant cabbies who have studied the Left Bank of Paris for decades. Around the corner was a nightclub whose transvestite revue drew large crowds. At first, seeing the throng congregating ahead, Kleber believed a horde had come for Ceil's play. Ceil was amazed. *"Pas ici,"* groused the chauffeur. He spun a skidding right turn and deposited them before a dark and sepulchral building, once a convent in which noble French women hid from Madame la Guillotine. "You wouldn't want to reconsider and catch that drag show instead?" jested Kleber.

Through an ancient courtyard and along corridors damp with sweating walls they explored, locating the playhouse just as the curtain rose. Kleber counted fifty-four people sitting uncomfortably on bleachers. The stage contained a well-painted backdrop of the sea and angry knots of clouds. When four actors entered carrying a card table and chairs, Kleber groaned. Bargain-basement time, and in Frog as well. He popped his last upper, hoping that his photographer friend at *Paris-Match* could obtain a refill tomorrow morning. He would have to hide them from Ceil. He suspected that she had thrown half of his vial away but he hadn't called her on it.

Kleber's French was adequate—he had once broken protocol and asked Charles de Gaulle a question during a press conference, this being a startling breach of journalistic etiquette due to the great man's custom of answering only preplanted queries. But he needed no competence in the language to realize that the Théâtre Molitor was performing *No Trump* with exceptional skill and insight. In New York, the actress who played Wilma, the tortured wife, had been physically the stature of Colleen Dewhurst and vocally the peer of Judith Anderson. She blew everybody off the stage and evoked little sympathy. Here, a frail, Piaf-like woman came on looking like a Gauloise butt ground beneath the sole of her husband's boot. Uncombed hair hung over her face like laundry drying from a windowsill and when she lifted strands to see her bridge cards, the eyes were sapphires frozen in ice. Wondrous stage magic came: a storm that raged like the terror in Wilma's heart, an act of love that had Wilma coiling naked and sensuously in a young man's arms and, moments later, holding instead a dead and blue-skinned child. In the last scene, Wilma became a woman pardoned from the sentence of terminal guilt, a creature of newly found strength and power, a lioness able—if she desired—to destroy her pitiful husband. The final blackout provided no certain answer. Darkness dwindled to one last dot of light encircling Wilma's lips, a mouth preparing to sneer—or to laugh—or, as Ceil intended, to endure. The French had interpreted Wilma both as the classic heroine of tragedy and—new twist—as *une femme de libération*. The tear-drenched audience rose in ovation.

For reasons he did not immediately explore, Kleber slipped quietly out of the theater during the curtain calls, telling himself he did not want to intrude on Ceil's moment of attention. But while he waited on the curb, smoking a cigarette, he understood the cause of his hasty exit. He was jealous, and dammit, with good cause. The woman he loved stole a story he found and wrote—and she made people cry. He felt like the father of a child kidnapped at birth and uninvited to the kid's inauguration.

He heard street noises, welcome reality to dispel the shattering force of Ceil's theater. Horns were honking. A *flic*'s whistle. People yelling. Brassy music swimming through the *quartier*. Then, from around the corner, flew a man and a woman racing like pursued thieves. Behind them came sudden flashes of light that looked like silent bombs exploding. Immediately Kleber discerned the arsenal of paparazzi. Somebody worth photographing had apparently been in the nearby nightclub. When the fleeing man and woman came near, she stumbled and broke the heel of her shoe. The man cursed and laughed and swept her into his massive arms. She giggled and said, "Mack, you idiot, put me down!"

Kleber grabbed the big man's sleeve and pulled him into the safe harbor of the Théâtre Molitor's gloomy courtyard. "Hey, good buddy, wanna buy some French postcards?" he asked. The Prince of Charms and the Prince of Power fell delightedly into an embrace. As Mack and Kleber had not snagged the other's kite string in years, there was much to tell. Proudly Mack introduced his new wife, Arianna, a woman who earned Kleber's instant approval because she said, "The only person Mack talks about more than himself is you. And if you're not tired of hearing it, I loved *Coonskin Capers*. It's the first thing I've read that makes sense out of a senseless war." She also looked terrific, having enriched the economy of France that very afternoon with purchases at Yves Saint Laurent, Hubert Givenchy, Pierre Cardin, and Cartier's boutique next door to their suite at the Ritz.

Kleber swept backstage, extricated Ceil from a throng of actors and patrons, insisted that she beg out of a long-planned midnight supper and dine instead (and he whispered the name so as not to arouse Gallic fever) with his best friend.

"But these people are expecting us," said Ceil.

"You can see them tomorrow," said Kleber.

"I can't just walk out. It would be rude."

"It's impossible to be rude to a Frenchman. The word isn't in their vocabulary." He pulled her away, not noticing the sense of loss on her face, nor the pain that showed as tangible as Wilma's. Ceil allowed herself to be bullied, just like her own heroine. Insensitive to his thievery, Kleber had restored the balance of power.

Mack knew a restaurant in Montparnasse that stayed open until 3 a.m., owned by an enormous black man from South Carolina. And there they dined on inedible food—barbecued ribs and tough corn on the cob, a vegetable the French feed to pigs. Ceil hated the meal but might have enjoyed talking with Arianna. She assessed Mack's wife as an intelligent woman with talent and purpose, even though she perceived a tenseness in the costume designer's eyes and an artificial warmth toward Mack. There was some sort of commitment, but its source was not love. Similarly, Arianna would have relished getting to know Ceil, a woman whose art she likewise respected—and whose sexuality was provocative. But all the women were allowed to do was attend their men like Japanese geishas, observing from a distance and risking no rebuke.

Mack was in Paris en route to the Normandy coast, where he was to begin filming still another World War II epic. "It's sort of a *Red Badge of Courage* thing," said Mack. He was to enact a veteran army sergeant from Arkansas who panicked as the D-Day invasion began, only to recover his courage and win the DSC. As he told the story he suddenly stopped, looked at Kleber, and snapped his fingers. "Are you ready to go back to work?" the actor asked. The script needed urgent repair and Mack had contract approval of any dialogue doctor. "What we've got is a good basic story and a lot of smoke and fire," explained Mack. "But the characters are empty. Nobody's home."

"Scripts aren't my cup of tea," demurred Kleber.

"You just got back from a war," encouraged Mack. "I suspect you've got some untold tales. Think on it overnight."

A few hours later, at dawn, foolish cries ripped the purple velvet cloak of light in the Place Vendôme. Beside the obelisk Napoleon brought back from Egypt, one very famous actor threw uncaught footballs at one very clumsy writer. While the boys played, their women yawned, feeling like mothers unable to yank sons in for supper. Ceil and Arianna sat glumly on the steps of the Hotel Ritz.

Ceil Shannon flew home to New York alone, passing the long flight by consuming three splits of champagne and fiddling with a macabre notion for a play: four women conducting a meeting whose purpose was to determine which of their husbands was worth killing. She gave it up when one of the characters said spontaneously, "The trouble is, all men need killing. Let's meet each week and keep hearing the evidence."

Kleber stayed in Europe several months, at first rewriting the screenplay in which Mack starred. He received $5,000 a week in cash and banked most of it every Monday morning in a Swiss account (thus concealing the income from Noel North's greedy attention). But he held back enough to assure unlimited supplies of amphetamines and cocaine, drugs easily available in the acting company. He had first started using uppers and blow in Vietnam. There they were recreational. Now they were essential.

In the summer of 1972, Kleber was queried by a newspaper syndicate that wanted him to cover the Republican National Convention in Miami. He did not respond to several telephone calls left on his answering service, nor to telegrams sent to his apartments in New York and California. Ceil Shannon said she had no idea where he was. In the summer of 1972, Kleber was in residence at the Clinique de Merriac just outside Lucerne, where leather straps lashed him to a cot, that being the only piece of furniture in a room with padded walls. Their purpose was twofold: to protect him from injury and to keep his cries from being heard outside the suite where wealthy drug addicts were separated from their habits.

The eight months he spent in kicking his need spared Kleber the embarrassment of attending the premiere of *Normandy,* a $16 million film that was devastated by critics and public. It was generally agreed that the major fault was in the script, that the characters were mechanical men with no feelings worth caring about. Happily, he used a pseudonym on the credits and very few people knew he wrote the hackneyed and stagnant piece. Mack, conversely, was praised for making the best of a poorly-designed role.

CHAPTER TWENTY-THREE

By definition, maybe it was not a miracle, such being in the strictest sense events manifesting the supernatural powers of God. The skeptic could find further cause for disbelief considering the fact that the "miracle" would have gone unremarked had not an ambitious young newspaper reporter been present in Tarrant County jail that dry, blazing

August noon in 1966. And if the day had not been a barren interlude in the business of news, one of those droughts of political scandal and interesting murders, perhaps the story would have been crowded out or left to perish in overset.

Nonetheless, the headline said "miracle" and those who thereafter believed could not be dissuaded. If the worth of art is in the eye of the beholder, then the substance of miracles is in the need to find God.

Prisoner ⚔214C53, according to the criminal identity card on file in Fort Worth, Austin, and Washington, D.C., was the sum of these parts: NAME: Thomas Jeremiah Luther, WEIGHT: 157 pounds, HEIGHT: 5 feet 9½ inches, RACE: Caucasian, COMPLEXION: Sallow, DATE OF BIRTH: April 18, 1933, IDENTIFYING MARKS: Small portion of left earlobe missing, tattoo of coiled serpent on right biceps, ALIASES: Billy Bun, Billy Mack, Mack Cantrell.

The most recent photograph of prisoner ⚔214C53, taken at the occasion of T.J.'s arrest in 1966 on a slew of petty larcenies, chiefly hot checks that bounced across central Texas like a spilled load of Mexican jumping beans, revealed the Prince of Temptation at nadir. His eyes were dead—more sad than sullen. His hair, sideburns, and mustache were the trimmings of a nineteenth-century desperado, streaked with gray that had lost the dye of gunmetal black. His tee shirt bore the sign of peace favored by those protesting America's undeclared war in Southeast Asia. The insignia carried no political connotation for its wearer, T.J. having no feelings of right or wrong in global posturings. He bought the shirt and knew the lyrics to "The Times They Are a-Changin'" and tried, rather poignantly, to pass for a thirty-three-year-old hippie just so he could peddle inferior Mexican marijuana to the genuine young and morally disenchanted.

His goal at the time was to raise $12,000 for the purchase of one-third ownership in an elderly airplane that would import large bales of cannabis, but a blizzard of illegal checks blew him into Tarrant County jail. None of the worthless drafts was over fifty dollars, the embarkation line in Texas separating misdemeanor and felony, so T.J. shrewdly negotiated a plea bargain. He accepted eighteen months' punishment. He cried "guilty" lickety-split, not wanting the District Attorney to paddle through the backwaters of a brackish life. As it turned out, the decision was wise. The two men with whom he intended partnership in the sky-high dope business crashed their plane soon thereafter. Some $60,000 worth of joints burned in a rice field and both went to Huntsville for life.

In August 1966, T.J. calculated that he would be released by Thanksgiving. His behavior had been, for a change, exemplary. Without protest, the Prince of Temptation cut familiar weeds beside county roads, obediently said "yessir!" to any fellow in a blue suit or a tan uniform, read Norman Vincent Peale and Billy Graham in his cell (making sure that any passing guard noticed the book jackets) and drew pretty pictures.

The hobby began when T.J. impulsively asked a social worker if he might purchase sketch pad and colored pencils. Although he had scant talent for art (Missy had given him a few ineffective lessons), T.J. knew that prison officials appreciated inmates who demonstrated worthwhile use of time. Down the row was a Mexican whose cell-made Christmas cards earned him favor and attention and probably a shortening of sentence.

The first thing T.J. decided to draw was what he looked at all the time: the bars of his cell. Committed to paper, they looked naked and silly, like the score of a domino game. Then he added a pool of shadow below and in the distance, followed by silhouettes of prisoners across the corridor. Dissatisfied yet intrigued, T.J. tore up his sketch and began anew. He drew the same tableau many times until his tablet contained an image sufficiently competent to cause a guard's remark, "Ain't bad." Pretty soon T.J. was good. He quick-sketched the road gang sitting and eating lunch in a thicket of Johnson grass. He got relieved from swinging his machete so as to create the portrait of a guard who wanted a novel and free wedding anniversary gift for the little woman.

One Sunday morning some strange things happened. On the radio, T.J. heard Paul Harvey, the newscaster, telling about some unknown prisoner up in Chicago who a long time ago had painted a religious picture on the wall of the drunk tank. So beautiful was the picture, Harvey said, that critics convinced the sheriff to keep the thing on the wall and turn the coop into a shrine. T.J. thought it was too bad the feller couldn't take a deserved bow.

Then, not ten minutes later, along came the Baptist preacher, a Sunday-morning regular on the eleventh floor of Tarrant County jail. Dogged he was, considering the fact that just about everybody greeted the reverend by giving him the finger when he paused outside a door to pray and counsel. On this Sabbath, T.J. listened tolerantly to the old boy's spiel. He then not only cried "Amen!" with fervor, he requested and was given—with joy—one of preacher man's Jesus books.

On the cover was the basic Sunday-school fantasy of old J.C.— true blue eyes, silk honey hair, and the same sort of mustache and scraggly beard that every daddy in Texas wanted to shave off his young-un's damn hippie face.

T.J. well knew the rules. The high sheriff sternly disallowed graffiti on the walls of his rarely painted jailhouse. But seeing as how the plaster of paris canvas beside his bunk was already marred by amateurish icons of male and female genitalia, Spanish obscenities, and chipped pits reflecting the clinched fists of despair, T.J. reckoned that no serious offense would be taken at artistic celebration of Lord God.

He quick-sketched a giant face in hard lead pencil, recessed for liver loaf sandwiches and two Pepsi-Colas at lunch, and worked until well past dark, adding layers of charcoal, Crayola, and lubricating oil. Weary then, hands cramped and sore, he fell onto his bunk dissatisfied, staring at a gloomy countenance eight feet tall and four feet at its widest point. Despite the enormity of dimensions, nobody resembling a gentle Saviour with halo and choir robe stared back. T.J.'s obsessive labor had produced only a brooding mask of shadows, a forbidding figure of authority with absolutely no compassion. Its closed eyes were darker than night as if burdened by centuries of pain and betrayal. He fell asleep intending to scrub the failure from his sight. He would remember tossing all night.

At dawn, T.J. obtained a bucket of soapy water and a jar of ammonia and lye from the maintenance closet, telling the trustee his intent was to wash out his toilet. But he knew something was afoot the moment he saw Pedecker scowling outside the lockup. T.J. had long since tamed the 250-pound redneck guard, having learned on opening day of incarceration that Pedecker was given to squeezing cantankerous heads as gleefully as a man snapped walnut shells. Every time T.J. drew Pedecker's picture, which was about seven times, he made the ugliest man in Texas look like Cary Grant.

At this moment Pedecker had a black boy under his left arm, a new detainee whose aura was that of a ball of water moccasins. The kid, about nineteen, was strung out and had foolishly tried to knee

Pedecker's nuts. That the right side of the boy's head glowed like a red Easter egg testified to what he had gotten for his misbehavior. Pedecker seized T.J. with his other paw. "I want you to babysit this coon," suggested Pedecker. "I'm short-handed this mornin' and what I don't need is a slippery-assed piece of black shit. I cain't leave him alone ten seconds 'cause he's threatenin' to commit suicide, which by me would be cause for rejoicing. Now, T.J., you watch ole soul here a spell while I get his papers done."

T.J. nodded obediently, ignoring the nigger, head still locked in Pedecker sinew and mouthing "mothahfuckah." His Afro looked like an electrocuted porcupine.

"And while you're waitin', boy, you wash that shit offa that there wall, heah?" ordered Pedecker. He meant for the troublemaker, name of Martin, to erase T.J.'s Jesus Christ. Bang went the door, click went the lock, and POW! went T.J. into the corner, shoved rudely by Martin. En route T.J. stumbled over the bucket of soapy water, which provided a skating rink for his ass. Martin said affirmatively, "Ah ain't cleanin' up no honky shit. An' *that's* mothahfuckin' *that.*" Had not T.J. been hurled onto his butt, chances are he would have undertaken the eradication of his art himself. But now he was mad. Kettles at full boil had less steam than what poured out of T.J.'s eyes and ears. Across the soaped floor he scurried, cracking Martin's knees and felling him with immediate result. But at the age of sixteen Martin had won the Golden Gloves welterweight semifinals and uncountable street fights since. Even under conditions stoned and scared attendant to Monday sunup in county jail, he had no notion of calling it square.

Snatching a bottle beside the door, Martin yelled and plunged. His left fist slammed T.J. flat against the wall, and his right flung a half gallon of ammonia and lye into the honky's eyes. Though T.J. next felt knuckles pounding his kidneys and pummeling his liver, that pain was irrelevant. He sagged to the floor and said, quite softly, afraid to scream, "I'm blind. Oh God, I'm really blind."

And above him, Jesus, similarly soaked, wept ammonia tears.

Kelly Coker, hustling cub reporter, wandered around the jail that morning in search of Pedecker, his usually dependable source of gossip penal and political. He located the enormous man standing outside a cell, huge hands gripping the bars, and looking like an ice sculpture.

"What's up, Pecker Decker?" piped Kelly, to which the guard whispered, as if on the front row of church, "Don't know, son."

Kelly glanced inside the cell—and looked again. The scene required sorting out. In one corner was a tough black dude on his knees in reverence, rocking back and forth and floating a gospel song. Crouched nearby was a young prison doctor who was shaking his head and shining a penlight into the fireball-red eye sockets of a white prisoner.

And on the wall—the wall against which Thomas Jeremiah Luther pressed his body like a child unwilling to leave a parent—radiated forth an astonishing, eerily beautiful face of Jesus Christ. Art experts who would later come to study the portrait said the work resembled that of a Renaissance master, the kind discovered on a hidden wall in a Florentine cathedral and aged by the centuries. They would marvel over the flesh tones—pale ochers and mustards that gave the cheeks of the Saviour a texture reminiscent of old parchment. But most of all, they would exclaim over the eyes of Christ. Half open, lachrymose, mirrors of sorrow and pain and hope.

Being a pretty fair reporter, Kelly Coker tried to discredit the "miracle." In his article, he pointed out that "perhaps" the Jesus picture was artistically enriched by the breaking of a water pipe during the night on the floor above T.J.'s cell. "Perhaps" an unexplainable interaction of charcoal, hard lead pencil, lubrication oil, lye, ammonia, the humid heat of an August night, "perhaps" these had embellished a stark and primitive sketch.

But one fact was indisputable, wrote Kelly Coker in an article picked up by AP and transmitted around the globe: "The injured prisoner, Thomas Jeremiah Luther, 33, suddenly and inexplicably regained his vision after three hours of blindness and excruciating pain. Dr. Cran Wydman, an ophthalmologist, said Luther suffered severe scarring of corneal tissue and retina burn from an attack of ammonia and lye hurled at him by another prisoner. 'I would have thought that this patient would have suffered permanent loss of sight,' Dr. Wydman told authorities.

"Luther said he heard a voice speaking to him during the period he was blind. The voice allegedly said, *'I will heal thee for thou hath done Me honor.'* When Luther opened his eyes, or so he said, the pain was gone and he could once again see normally. The first thing he noticed was the picture of Christ, whose eyes had also opened.

" 'The reason I know it's a miracle,' said Luther, 'is that I had not painted in the eyes on the Saviour. The night before I had gotten frustrated and I quit. I realize now that Jesus Himself finished His own portrait.' "

Eight years later, on February 3, 1975, Lisa Candleman, once falsely predicted to become the wife of Kleber Cantrell, mailed 277 envelopes from the Fort Worth post office. Each contained a sunny yellow, blue-bordered (class colors!) invitation to: GASP—SOB—YES IT'S REALLY TRUE—WE'RE NOT GETTING OLDER WE'RE GETTING BETTER—TWENTY-FIFTH REUNION OF THE CLASS OF 1950. She and her roommate, Sandra, the physical education teacher, had labored for many months to track down addresses for all but seventy-six students, a monumental task that required the persistent assistance of Simon Judger, a private detective who a quarter century prior had been solo trombonist for the school marching band.

Their sleuthing was informative and often sorrowful: at least thirty members of the class that stepped out to change the second half of the twentieth century were dead, most from traffic crashes, three by self-decision, two from cancer, five from heart attacks, and one former captain in the ROTC shot to death by his wife, a class beauty. Occasionally Simon traced amusing trails: Carralou King, daughter of a police captain and protected virgin, had married and divorced five times and was at present a middle-aged coed at UCLA studying sex therapy. There were at least twenty-four certified millionaires. But twice that number could simply not be found. Their lives had disappeared. Missy Craymore Luther, for example. She dropped out of sight fifteen years ago.

Within a month, enough responses had come to ensure success. Lisa booked a dining room at Ridglea Country Club and mailed a notice to local newspapers. The *Star-Telegram* called and asked if Kleber Cantrell or Mack Crawford would be coming. Lisa said there was every hope.

Then, from a post office box in Hollywood, she received an 8 × 10 manila envelope and found inside a glossy photo of Mack. At the bottom corner a machine had scrawled, "Love, Mack." The actor looked, in Lisa's judgment, "absolutely gorgeous." As indeed he should have. It was the first new picture of Mack taken after a six-month sabbatical from filmic endeavor. Arnie Beckman had issued a press release informing the devoted that Mack was using a long overdue vacation for "meditation" and "travel with his wife, Arianna, and children, Jeff, 17, and Molly, 15." Not exactly.

Mack was secluded at a condominium in Palm Springs, recovering from several hundred hair follicles transplanted from the back of his crown to the worrisomely thin regions at forehead, and from blepharoplasty surgery that reduced the puffiness beneath his eyes and trimmed the overhang of lids above. Everything took; everything worked. At forty-three years of age, Mack and his money and the marvels of medicine pushed back a decade.

Attached to the glossy was a computer-printed letter signed with flourish by Mack. It seemed genuine, but its message was somewhat less than intimate:

"Hi! Thanks for your friendship and support.
I cannot do it without you.
I am happy to send you my photograph, my best wishes, and my kiss."

That was all Lisa got. She read it and said, "You rude son of a bitch."

From West Fifty-seventh Street in New York came an arrestingly designed letterhead resembling a miniature newspaper. The headline, in stark black type, read: KLEBER CANTRELL. At the bottom of the page, in smaller, gray type, were two subheads:

HOT LINE	THE CANTRELL REPORT
Syndicated Television	Thrice-Weekly in
42 Major Markets	More than 300 Newspapers

"Dear Ms. Candleman [the letter began, another computer subterfuge but at least clever enough to fill in somebody's name]: Thank you for your recent letter. Alas, due to the large quantity of mail received in response to my work in journalism, I am unable to answer personally. I do value your comments, however. Feedback like yours helps shape my opinions. Please keep writing. Sincerely.

P.S. If you wish a written transcript of Hot Line, please send $2 and a self-addressed, stamped envelope to the above address, indicating the date of the desired telecast."

To which Lisa remarked about her long ago beau, "Creep."

Last to arrive was a package wrapped in silver-colored paper and as thick as a family Bible. When opened, out spilled more pamphlets, beribboned documents, and photographs than Lisa had obtained when registering once at a National Education Association convention. It had cost $7.15 just to send the bulky mailing from nearby Granbury, Texas, a testament of somebody's eagerness to lavish money.

Lisa passed a fascinated hour perusing booklets entitled:

THE CHOSEN—God's Miracle Man
THE DECLINE AND FALL OF AMERICA—The Coming Tragedy of Humanism
MIRACLE COLLEGE—The Campus of God and His Children
DOCUMENTATION OF MIRACLES—Science Has No Answer
MIRACLE CATALOGUE (Sermons, tape and video cassettes, photo albums of The Chosen in Miracle Crusades—Available at spring discount prices)

Finally, once unfolded both lengthwise and horizontally, Lisa beheld an eight-by-four-foot replica of THE MIRACLE THAT BEGAT THE MIRACLE MAN. She stared dumbly at Jesus Christ on the Tarrant County jail wall. It was big enough to cover her dining-room table. The last enclosure was another glossy photograph. Unlike the picture of Mack Crawford that delivered superstar face in tight close-up, this was full figure from the vanity of middle distance. Atop a hill in West Texas that was presumably chosen because it looked like Calvary, standing in the majesty of flowing black robes and with a pristine white Bible in clasped hands, was posed Thomas Jeremiah Luther, AKA the Prince of Temptation, AKA The Chosen.

He was wearing dark glasses that caught sun fire. On the back was scribbled: "Lisa—God love you. I will be delighted to come. How fitting for us to commune in fellowship and joy. I am praying for you, as always. The Chosen (T.J.)."

Lisa complained to Simon, the private detective, about the mechanical kiss-offs from Kleber and Mack. "Well, what do you want to do?" asked Simon.

"I'm tempted to say fuck 'em both. But the marquee would sure blaze with their names. Is there any way to get private unlisted phone numbers?"

"I think so," said Simon, nodding tentatively. "Nobody is that big a celebrity." And soon thereafter he did.

Lisa called Beverly Hills, spoke briefly, then rang New York.

BOOK SIX

WHEN PRINCES DIE

When beggars die, there are no comets seen;
The heavens themselves blaze forth the death of princes.

——William Shakespeare

CHAPTER TWENTY-FOUR

Harris Hospital was quiet on this end-of-July morning at a few minutes after 5 a.m. The two detectives who guarded the entrance to room 610 sagged against the wall, imploring the clock to speed one last hour, anxious for their shifts to end. Their legs ached from eight hours of vigilance; their throats were parched from another night of cigarettes and machine coffee. Babysitting the celebrated sick man had long since become a pain-in-the-ass duty. Grumbling among those cops ordered to stand watch was widespread. After the first month of hysteria, media attention waned. Yet Calvin Sledge continued to demand twenty-four-hour surveillance for the man whose eyes stared at the ceiling blankly and whose voice box was locked.

A black orderly appeared with a rolling bed and a slip of paper directing that the patient be transported down to X ray. Neither of the detectives questioned the trip. It happened routinely. "How long you gonna keep him?" wondered Joe Dillard, one of the guards.

The orderly shrugged. "Boss, I just fetches 'em. You welcome to ride down with us." The detectives shook their heads. Their night was almost over. They would wait until the 6 a.m. replacements.

Several minutes later, three floors below, the orderly positioned his patient in a deserted corridor outside the X-ray department and locked the wheels of the rolling bed. Promptly, a tall, handsome woman in a white physician's coat and mask opened an office door. "They want you on four south, Leroy," she said. "Some patient took a bad fall in the shower." The orderly grimaced, annoyed at the sudden flurry of duty at shift's end. "I'll watch this one for you," said the woman doctor, gesturing toward the famous patient.

As soon as the orderly loped out of sight, the tall woman cautiously pushed the rolling bed down the corridor and into a freight elevator. Mercifully, no one else was within. "This is my first kidnapping," she whispered as soon as the doors shut, "so please be patient."

Dress rehearsal.

Calvin Sledge instructed his most able and cunning assistant to hear the case he would present to the grand jury that afternoon. "You just listen carefully," said Sledge. "Play like you're a nice old lady who doesn't know a tort from a tortilla. But if you think I'm tryin' to slip into the circus without a ticket, then pin my ass against the wall."

Sanford Double, the assistant chief prosecutor who performed as a rodeo clown several weekends a year, behaved similarly in professional duty. He was famed for sitting quietly in the courtroom, just like he was hiding in a barrel, then bursting out to divert or ridicule the snorting bull of defense counsel. Most everything Sandy said was crackerbarrel funny, but behind the self-deprecation and pranks was a legal mind of scholarship and substance. Calvin Sledge knew that if Sandy Double bought what he was selling, any grand jury would.

"Before you start singin', Calvin," said Sandy, "and I sure hate to spoil this beautiful Monday mornin', but you look purt' near like a possum squashed on the turnpike. If I was a grand juror, I'd indict you for perpetrating all unsolved rapes, hijackings, and child molestations since 1965."

Sledge ran an impatient hand across three days' growth of beard and blinked angry red eyes. "Sandy, just shut the fuck up and listen. If I look nine-tenths dead, it's because the taxpayers are gettin' their goddamn money's worth." Sandy nodded obediently and folded his arms, electing not to press further the courthouse gossip, i.e. that Calvin Sledge was on the edge and people were worrying that this case was about to consume a good man. Then the intercom buzzed. Sledge fairly shrieked into the box. "No calls, Darlene. Dammit, I mean *no* interruptions. IS THAT CLEAR?"

He threw two Excedrins down his throat. He nodded pleasantly. "Good afternoon, ladies and gentlemen. The State of Texas, in the matter of Kleber Cantrell, McKenzie Crawford, Jr., and Thomas Jeremiah Luther, seeks the following criminal indictments: (1) Misdemeanor, Class A, Unlawful Carrying of Weapon, (2) Felony, First Degree, Burglary and Criminal Trespass, (3) Felony, Third Degree, Assault, and (4) Capital Murder. On the night of May . . ."

Sandy butted in. "Wait a minute, Calvin. *Capital* murder?"

"Yeah. I believe we can prove that during the course of a trespass and burglary, the homicide was committed. This qualifies as capital murder under the revised Criminal Code, for which I intend to seek the death penalty."

As he was sixty-three years old (but looked barely forty), Sandy Double had no fear of losing his job from impertinence. For a decade he had been trying to quit public service and go into private practice to make some money, but old-fashioned sense of duty and the increasingly rare challenge of a fascinating court trial kept him in harness. Sandy's juices flowed only when prosecuting, and in recent years there was precious little of that. Out of 5,000 indictments each year in Tarrant County, only 140 or thereabouts went to trial. The rest, upward of 98 percent, were, just like in all American courthouses, horse-traded in advance, the kind of paper shuffling easily handled by a law clerk. Nothing would have thrilled Sandy Double more than riding shotgun beside Calvin Sledge in a murder trial certain to make history. But he held grave concern that the DA was fixing to play high-stakes poker with forty cents in his pocket.

"Calvin," he said bluntly, "I was sending men to the penitentiary before you had hair on your balls. And I never lost a night's sleep over a single one of 'em, even those fellers I didn't have much more evidence on than the fact they pissed me off and looked like they needed a little hard time. But, son, I do believe you're overreachin' yourself."

"I ain't askin' for a lecture, Sandy. You're supposed to just sit there and be a grand juror."

"*You* listen, then I'll listen. What I know about this sucker is admittedly damn little, since you've been keepin' the thing as secret as the D-Day invasion site. But the way I figure things, you'll be lucky to convict that ole boy on criminal trespass."

"Murder, Sandy. *Capital* murder." Sledge got about halfway through his case before the interruption. He summarized for Sandy the biographies of the Three Princes. He revealed how the three men had spent the early hours together on the morning of May 9, 1975. He was just about to the point where he would explain the series of crimes. And it was then that Darlene, nervous, apologetic, twisting her fingers into pigtails, broke in. "I know you don't wanna be disturbed, Calvin, but I think you better know what just happened. That Dr. Witt just called from the hospital."

Sledge felt excitement. "He started talking!"

Darlene shook her head. "Nossir. He left the hospital."

"Who left the hospital?"

"Mr. Kleber Cantrell did, sir. He's gone. Dr. Witt says he either walked out on his own—or somebody stole him."

Then, in splendidly melodramatic underscoring, gospel music erupted outside the window. Defying the court edict, twenty-four women in white robes commenced to writhe atop the flatbed truck and speak in tongues. Bleeding Heart toted a cross on her back.

And Sandy Double whooped, "Great gawd almighty, Calvin. You done got yourself the best murder case since Cain clubbed Abel."

The house was a good place to hide, situated behind locked wrought-iron gates and embraced by thick cedar hedges like a duenna's fan. It could not be seen either from the road or from boats passing by on Eagle Mountain Lake. The woman braced to carry the frail man out of the car and into the house, but he walked by himself, listing only slightly.

"This is madness," said Ceil Shannon. "If you die on me, Kleber, I'll kill you."

She tucked him into bed, drew the curtains to make the room dark, and held his hand. Both of their hearts were pounding. The adrenaline high was gone. The enormity of her deed was in focus. Kleber turned on the bedside lamp and, with effort, wrote on a note pad: "Thanks. IOU one."

"Don't thank me," said Ceil. "Just thank your lucky stars Samantha Reiker and I went to Vassar together. I knew she was a good ear-nose-and-throat doctor. I didn't know she would turn out to be such a terrific co-conspirator."

Kleber wrote quickly, "Sam says I'm going to be fine."

"Not *fine*. Samantha says there's no reason to keep you locked up in the hospital anymore. She's coming by tomorrow to check on you. She's put her career on the line."

"I've never loved you so much as this very moment," wrote Kleber.

Ceil was touched. "I love you, too," she said. "Her last words before they hanged her: I did it because I loved him."

Kleber scribbled again. "Passport?"

Ceil nodded. "I found it. But I don't think we could cross any border in the world without getting recognized. Besides, I've finally got you where I want you. Helpless. And unable to say a damn thing about it."

"Mexico?" wrote Kleber.

"Maybe. You just rest. If you're good and eat your chicken soup and take your medicine, we'll talk about Mexico. I suppose if I was able to bust you out of a guarded hospital room, it shouldn't be all that difficult to drive across the Rio Grande. How do you feel? I'm still frozen."

"Horny," he wrote. "Get me a typewriter."

"That's some non-sequitur. Later. For both requests."

"Get me a newspaper."

"Day after tomorrow. If you don't go to sleep, I'm calling the DA, just before I get on the plane to Rio all by myself."

She held his hand until he dropped off, feeling like Mata Hari and Bonnie Parker. And very, very scared.

The news of Kleber's disappearance steamed matters up so much that when the DA raced before the grand jury and presented his case, not only hurriedly, but sloppily, he was so passionate that the panel filled every item on his grocery list. In a delectable side skirmish, Otto Leo was in the courthouse this very day thundering before a district judge that his client, "a man of God, a citizen of rigid moral principles should be released from the confines of jail on his own recognizance." Calvin Sledge rushed into the courtroom and was able to roar back that bail was not allowed for the offense of capital murder.

The grand jury indictment, ink barely dry, almost caused Otto to topple off his elevator shoes. His chorus of white-robed angels screamed and tore their hair. They beat their breasts before the bench, and then more fervently outside in the light of television cameras. Otto

Leo made a little speech for the six o'clock news urging the State Bar of Texas to investigate Sledge's "shocking abuse of power."

Newspapers trumpeted the incredible tidings:

THE CHOSEN INDICTED FOR MURDER
DA TO SEEK DEATH PENALTY
NO NEW LEADS IN KLEBER CANTRELL DISAPPEARANCE

Ceil Shannon, curled on a daybed, awoke. Something had struck her on the cheek. She sat up quickly, struggling for clarity, discovering, of all things, a paper airplane on her lap. Several others had crashlanded on the floor. Across the room, Kleber clapped his hands and pantomimed that she should open the airplane. She did so and read a primitive, barely legible scrawl, like the last-gasp note in a bottle tossed into the sea: "Help! Typewriter, dammit! Can't go on much longer." Kleber grinned and clasped his hands in prayer.

Ceil said, "Perhaps."

She stalled all day, playing nurse, taking Kleber's temperature, blood pressure, helping him bathe, shave, preparing high-protein meals liquefied in the blender. Samantha Reiker had warned that Kleber's throat would hurt for at least another month. "Will he ever be able to talk?" Ceil had asked her college friend. The doctor said only time would give that answer. What the patient needed most, said Samantha Reiker, was absolute quiet and freedom from the pressure of hospital guards, reporters, and overly zealous prosecutors. Under no circumstances was he to watch television, listen to the radio, or read print accounts of the carnival.

Days passed. Slowly. The fear was present but no longer caught in Ceil's throat. She filled the hours with absurd little "treats," permitting the patient to walk all by himself around the room (and applauding as if he had won an Olympic heat), or sit beside an open window to take the sun on his ghostly face. They played honeymoon bridge. If he won, Ceil had to pay a "penalty," that being the deliverance of some recent headline—Haldeman and Erlichman were going to prison, Saigon was now Ho Chi Minh City, some obscure Georgia governor with a wide smile and hummer's voice announced for the presidency. But she always refused the written plea to recapitulate his own headlines.

One afternoon Kleber wrote at length on his pad. He handed the words to Ceil along with a separate note, "Please mail this to my mother. You can read it." Ceil scanned the letter. It seemed innocuous, nothing but reassuring words to an old woman that her son was safe and well. The last paragraph was clearly a baited hook, but Ceil fell for it nonetheless: "I know you have a thousand questions, Mama, and so do I. I want to tell the whole story but I don't have the strength to write it by hand. Memory fades so fast. Isn't fate something! I possess my greatest story—and I probably won't be able to remember it. Love, Kleber."

After Ceil mailed the letter, careful to wipe the envelope clean of fingerprints, she found an office-supply store and bought a used Underwood portable for sixty-five dollars. She rationalized this probably unwise decision as being the servant to truth and an act of love. But she was also dying to know the inside story herself.

Ceil dictated work rules for Kleber: fifteen minutes in the morning, fifteen minutes at night after dinner. And though the first thing he typed for her was "Sadist!" Kleber soon discovered that lack of time was not his enemy. Keys pounded paper and creativity seemed in bloom. But the typed sheets that Kleber placed beneath his pillow, guarding their privacy, were empty and dull.

He imagined Casey standing over his bed, trying to seize the tale in handfuls. That didn't work. Nothing worked. All the tricks of his trade—anecdotal beginnings, drum rolls, cliff hangers, evocations of how the house looked and what the men said and how the madness flared—they all failed. Kleber wrote with his back pointedly turned to Ceil, and when one morning she saw his shoulders heave and jerk, she rushed over to examine the pain. "I'm okay," Kleber typed quickly, turning his face to hide his anguish. But Ceil saw it and she assumed the discomfort had come from recollection of some unbearable memory. Which, in a sense, it was.

The Prince of Power wept because he could no longer stand on the edge of horror and write from the safety of emotional distance. Oh, he remembered it well. Who, What, When, Where, and maybe even Why wedged in the brain. The story chattered in his head each night as he pretended to sleep. But only in the dark of memory, in the alien hell of *feeling,* did it live.

The first time Kleber had heard of T. J. Luther's bizarre new incarnation came, appropriately, in a news clipping. VeeJee Cantrell mailed the front-page article from the *Star-Telegram* relating the "miracle" in county jail. Kleber laughed and enjoyed the Prince of Temptation's scam, putting aside the notion to write T.J. a letter of congratulations. The most popular boy finally made it back to page one.

In rapid succession, VeeJee dispatched more accounts of T.J.'s ascension. They seemed classic Southern Gothic, *dementia religioso,* a drop of Flannery O'Connor, a dab of Tennessee Williams, and a large dollop of snake oil. Immediately upon release from county jail, T.J. attended a tent revival on the outskirts of Dallas, guest speaker on the white-carnation-and-lily-strewn stage of an evangelist called Jerry Job. Right away Kleber's antenna shot up; he recognized Jerry Job from two decades ago when he tried—and failed—to run the flamboyant preacher out of Houston. It was absolutely fitting that T.J. would hook up with a charlatan like Jerry Job.

Sensing a box office draw if ever there was one, Jerry Job paid "The Man of the Miracle" a crisp hundred-dollar bill to hype his flock and loose their purse strings. Damnedest thing happened. In the midst of T.J.'s act, right at the place where he was telling about being blind for three hours and regaining his vision at the same time the eyes of Jesus opened wide, an old woman in the Healing Section suddenly leaped up in electric shock and cried, "I can see! Praise God, I can see!!"

Through a metal forest of wheelchairs, orthopedic braces, and crutches plowed the lady, outstretched hands vibrating like tuning forks, hell-bent for the stage, where she climbed up unaided and seized, sobbing, the feet of T. J. Luther. Blind and in heavy pain for three years from a brain tumor—or so she testified—she had had her sight miraculously returned upon hearing the blessings of the "miracle man's voice."

"God bless you," she howled. "God love you. Thank you, God!"

T.J. backed off. "I didn't do anything," he said quite honestly.

Jerry Job then made an impulsive and—depending upon the depth of his faith—unwise decision. At seventy-two years old, he had a ministry that was a squalid sideshow compared to, say, the extravaganza of an Oral Roberts or a Billy Graham. His tent was patched, his organ wheezed, the seat of his peacock-blue trousers shined, his lilies and carnations were plastic and made in Taiwan. Every time Jerry Job saw

Kathryn Kuhlman on national television, his heart turned sour apple green with jealousy. Her gowns of glowing pastel chiffon came from I. Magnin. His suits were J. C. Penney.

Jerry Job knew his territory. He had studied the careers of more illustrious competitors. Each had caught lightning somewhere on the back road and had been smart enough to hold on for a ride to the top. A woman evangelist he knew from Louisiana was doing quite well even though she had the misfortune to get pregnant. When the news slipped out—and it should be remarked that the prim lady was unmarried—she pinned no scarlet letter to her breast. She simply told her congregation that hers was the second immaculate conception in history, a revelation so wondrous (and apparently believable) that the flock showered $6,500 on her as natal tribute.

This night, when Jerry Job saw, on his wobbly platform, a charismatic man in his mid-thirties filled with sexual magnetism, he knew he had a star attraction. He signaled to the organist, who obediently played a jubilation fanfare. Then Jerry Job seized the microphone and thundered for all to hear, "Do not deny the power of God! This is a true moment of destiny!" He raised the arm of T. J. Luther as if the bewildered petty hoodlum had just won the middleweight championship of the world. "Hear now what I say. God has chosen you to deliver the blessings of His healing power. God's miracles cannot be denied! Are you *saved,* my son?"

"Ah, yessir, I think so," answered T.J. He seemed to remember Magda dragging him to the First Methodist Church somewhere along the line where his duck-tail was sprinkled.

"Let us renew The Chosen's commitment to the Lord!"

"The *what?*" But T.J.'s query was smothered. He felt his head pushed down to the crotch of Jerry Job and he sank to his knees. He gazed at the floor in attempted reverence and saw, hidden behind a bank of plastic blossoms, a large cooler packed with dry ice and small bottles. Jerry Job hoorahed for a half hour, asking questions of faith and renunciation of sin, to which he responded, "Yessir." He was sure having to work to earn his hundred dollars. Then the old preacher reached down, plucked one of the vials out of the cooler, dumped liquid on the Prince of Temptation's sweaty head, dribbled some more on the dry ice, and—*pow!*—smoke gushed up in bursts of scarlet. It might not have played on national television, but in a sagging tent on the poor side of Dallas, Jerry Job made believable magic. He went to bed that night at a quarter past two, after signing T. J. Luther on as assistant healer for $200 weekly plus 10 percent of the offering buckets, feeling like P. T. Barnum did the day he put Tom Thumb in the center ring.

Word got around fast. Newspapers sent reporters out to mark the appearances of the sinner's redemption. And T. J. Luther, AKA The Chosen, earned his keep. Capitalizing on his deliverance from Satan's embrace, he designed a spectacular presentation. The organ—and a newly purchased kettle drum—and the majestic basso of Jerry Job announced his coming. The house lights went dark. At the rear of the stage, on an elevated platform, The Chosen suddenly materialized—bathed in red light and smoke. Washed in blood, so to speak. As he began to preach, earnestly telling of his errant life, ticking off (but not *too* specifically) the demons of strong drink, soiled women, crooked dice, and hot checks—the red light faded slowly and the dry-ice smoke subsided. By the time T.J. reached the moment of his temporary blindness in Tarrant County jail—this he told with closed eyes that opened as if pried by God—his spotlight was brilliant white. And white was his suit, white were his flowers, white was his radiance. In the planning, Jerry Job fretted that the shtick was corny. But in the doing, T.J. raised goose bumps from Austin to Amarillo, even his own.

Within six months, the banners on the tent and the advertisements on Saturday religion pages changed from JERRY JOB—SPECIAL APPEARANCE BY THE CHOSEN to JERRY JOB REVIVALS, INC., PRESENTS THE CHOSEN to JERRY JOB AND THE CHOSEN. Then, one well-remembered autumn night in 1968 on the fairgrounds of Shreveport, during a violent storm that lashed the canvas with frightening rain and winds, Jerry Job introduced The Chosen, listened to his confession, watched him change from demon red to angel white, stretched out a routine hand to assist the main attraction down the steps.

One eyewitness said it was rather like Michelangelo's scene in "The Creation," where the gnarled and bearded God dispatches life to Adam through His touch. Others, including a deputy sheriff who happened to be in attendance, said the tragedy was the fault of a stupid old fool who should have had better sense than to keep on preachin' in an electrical storm. Whatever, Jerry Job stepped on a frayed microphone cord at the precise instant of a nearby rent of lightning, touched the Prince of Temptation's outstretched fingers, shrieked, and expired in the lilies. Similarly, T. J. Luther fell unconscious amid screams and embryonic pandemonium. But within moments The Chosen rose and was whole.

That he did not seek to revive the fried Jerry Job was not ever discussed. That he assumed leadership of the fallen preacher's ministry —and possession of his tent, organ, kettle drum, and mailing list—was deemed appropriate and the will of God.

Five years thereafter, just before Christmas 1973, Kleber discovered in his mail, unsolicited, a polychrome 11 × 14 portrait of Thomas Jeremiah Luther. It resembled nothing less than those epidemic photos of a Nasser or Franco hanging on the walls of Egyptian mud huts or Spanish taverns. T.J. appeared to have located both the Fountain of Youth and the mines of King Solomon. He stood before a glass and coppery-metal building under construction that, according to an appended fact sheet, would be "twelve stories high—one for each Apostle—world headquarters for THE CHOSEN—GOD'S MAN OF MIRACLES." T.J.'s skin was clear and smooth and the gold of a beach boy. His hair was thick and wavy and dark. His suit was well-tailored white shantung silk, and the sparkle dancing from his ring finger under the Texas sun appeared a minimum five carats.

At the bottom of the picture was neatly and personally inked: "For the Prince of Power from the Prince of Salvation. With God's Bounteous Love. T.J."

A score of memories raced through Kleber's head—paramount among them the rape of a raven-haired child and a bier of leaves beside a violent river—before he tore the Miracle Man in half and deposited him in file thirteen. "Salvation?" he muttered, astounded at the currents of men's lives, turning hurriedly to homework necessary for the taping of "Hot Line," his new syndicated television series. Forty-eight Thursday nights each year he sat in a half hour of conversational pyrotechnics with the genuine nobility of celebrity. *Their* photographs lined his office walls, the inscribed icons of the famous attesting to Kleber's parity. There was no room for pretenders from his past.

The assumption reached by Calvin Sledge was not exactly correct. The twenty-fifth reunion of the Class of 1950 was not *per se* what brought the boys of Cloverdale Avenue together one last time. Each of them had subsidiary motivations. When Lisa finally got through to Mack Crawford one midnight in Beverly Hills, he answered personally in a slurry voice. It sounded as if he was buried under a mountain of pillows and coverlets. Apologizing for the intrusion, Lisa repeated three times the reason for her call, and after a long blank of awkward silence, Mack said, "Maybe." If he could arrange his schedule, it would be a last-minute flight to Texas. "The only thing is, Lisa, I can't cope with a lot of publicity. If you don't announce that I may be coming, if you keep it quiet, you know, then maybe . . ."

"Of course," answered Lisa. "I understand. It sure would be a nice surprise for everybody. We're so proud of you."

"Is Kleber coming?" asked Mack.

"Yes," lied Lisa. "He's looking forward to seeing you."

"T.J.?"

"Of course. He's going to give the invocation. The door prize is a ticket to heaven."

Mack mumbled something unintelligible and the line went dead. Lisa was afraid to call back.

Mack looked up and remembered there was a young man standing over him, straddling his body like a Colossus. The candlelight was almost gone and all Mack could see clearly were two powerfully corded legs attached to a semi-aroused penis in a patch of golden hair. Beyond that, darkness. The youth began to masturbate, quickly bringing his organ to full measure. He lowered his body, preparing to kneel on Mack's chest, but the actor shook his head. The boy understood and began to dress.

A few minutes later, freshly showered, the boy kissed Mack perfunctorily and whispered good night. Mack raised up on his elbows. "Who are you?" he asked.

"Who *am* I?" repeated the youth. "You shouldn't have done that last Lude."

"Where did we meet?"

"Are you sure you want me to go? You're really bombed."

"I forget where we met."

The boy laughed. "We met last year at the Academy Awards. I parked your 450. Remember?"

"Oh yeah. How old are you, Jeff?"

"*Jeff?* I'm Johnny. And I'm twenty. And you're thirty-eight—but it's only a number."

"I'm forty-three. You should know that."

"So? That's only a number, too."

"What do you do?"

"I go to UCLA and I make love to you once a week. Why don't you just crash, Mack."

"Yeah. Crash. You want some money?"

The youth frowned. "I told you that embarrasses me. I care for you, Mack."

"Then get a hundred dollars out of my wallet. Pants over there."

"*Ciao,* Mack. Sleep it off."

Mack dozed off and did not hear Johnny's cautious exit. He fell into a heavy sleep but awoke during the night and passed the remaining dark hours in chaos. He remembered Lisa's telephone call. The invitation was enticing, but it demanded that he attend a convocation of peers each forty-three years old. The arithmetic might be embarrassing. He would enjoy being the centerpiece on the hometown table, but he wondered if his share of adoration would be eroded by the presence of rival princes? And would Kleber and T.J. see through the gloss of image into the heart of dust?

He needed to talk to someone. He rang Arianna's extension in another part of the mansion but she did not answer. He seemed to remember that this was her night "out" with Maggie.

He stared at the telephone. He called Susan in Fort Worth. It was 6 a.m. her time but she was cheerful and already done with the paper.

"What's on your mind, Mack?" she asked.

"How's Jeffie?"

"He's . . . he's okay," she said, her voice newly cooled.

"Where is he?"

"I haven't seen him lately. He checks in. Last week he was off somewhere in West Texas meditating."

"Why won't he come out here and visit his father?"

"Mack, I don't know. He's seventeen years old and very independent. He says he doesn't like California."

"Susan, is he there? Right now, I mean? Is he standing beside the telephone telling you he doesn't want to talk to me?"

"Mack, quit being paranoid. Of course not."

"What if I came there to see him."

"If I hear from him, I'll tell him. Mack, I've got bacon frying."

"For whom? You don't like bacon."

"I do now." She hung up.

Mack stewed until daylight and then called Arnie and told him to clear the appointment book the first week of May for a long voyage home.

Lisa's sarcasm was unhidden. "Is it really you?" she asked. "I think it would be easier to get through to Brezhnev."

"I'm sorry, babe. You know I would have called back," soothed Kleber.

"I hate to go through this again, seeing as how I've already made my spiel to your press agent, your secretary, your producer, and I believe your office boy." She repeated the invitation to the class reunion.

Kleber began concocting diplomatic brush-offs when Lisa intruded. "Mack's coming," she said. "And T.J., too. It won't be a full house without you."

"Three of a kind is not a full house, Lisa," instructed Kleber. "But then, maybe it is. I'll get back to you."

The reason Kleber taped two "Hot Lines" in advance, giving him two weeks clear for a trip to Fort Worth, was that his show was sagging badly in the ratings and teetered on the edge of cancellation. He knew a way to save it. The idea had come to him weeks earlier but he had encountered a series of stone walls in attempting to arrange an interview with T. J. Luther. The irony annoyed him. If he wanted T.J. on his show, the little prick should walk on his hands to West Fifty-seventh Street. But The Chosen, having been burned by a number of magazine and television profiles early in his sudden climb to celebrity, was now surrounded by a palace guard of public relations counselors. Policy forbade interviews unless written questions were submitted in advance to which The Chosen would respond similarly. He also demanded text approval, picture approval, caption approval, and in the case of radio or television, screening in advance and right of editing or censorship. Since The Chosen was now seen twice weekly on his own television network—some 350 independent television stations in the United States and Canada alone, plus another 80 in Europe, Asia, and South America—T.J. felt no deprivation in the publicizing of his ministry and his message. It made him feel good to leave Kleber Cantrell's "urgent" phone calls unanswered.

Kleber desperately wanted to land the fish who had swum smugly past the lures of "60 Minutes," a guaranteed cover on *Time,* the infuriated importunings of Barbara Walters, Dick Cavett, William Buckley, Mike and Merv, and Dinah Shore. He had written and called and cabled and sought the help of the governor of Texas and several of the state's congressmen and senators. T.J. did not respond, because, after all, Kleber had not written to thank his childhood friend for the Christmas photograph in 1973.

When Kleber called Lisa back to say yes-he-would-attend-the-reunion, he was feeding an obsession. Not only was he going to sweet-talk The Chosen into an uncensored exclusive interview, the Prince of Power intended to nail the phony son of a bitch to the wall of truth.

May 8, 1975.

Mack flew into Fort Worth on a leased Lear jet. The ride cost $2,700, the price tag of privacy coming high—but deductible. An anonymous plain-vanilla rented Ford waited on the landing strip. With memories resurrected of laughing bears and clawing cats, he drove about his hometown like a cloaked king. He passed a theater on the north side where his last picture, *Clancy's Rebellion,* was playing. It hurt him that no one was in line to buy tickets and the cashier was drowsily reading a paperback romance. He decided to proceed immediately to Susan's house but his courage required stoking. At a 7-Eleven store, Mack bought a fifth of vodka and a gimme cap that he yanked over his brow to conceal his face. The young and pretty Mexican girl who took his money glanced briefly at the customer but she did not ignite with recognition. He teased himself with the power of celebrity. *I could take off my cap and glasses and give this girl a story to tell the rest of her life,* he thought. *I can make her important.* But he left as he had come—unknown.

When half the vodka was gone, Mack drove to Cloverdale Avenue, where Susan did not expect him until the next day. He believed she would be thrilled by surprise. It took two loops past the old house before his annoyance simmered sufficiently to turn into the red brick half-moon driveway. He felt violated. True, Susan French Crawford held legal title to the only anchor of his life, but she had no moral authority to tart up Mable Hofmeyer's respectable home into an airy-fairy mock Moroccan villa. He drank the rest of his vodka and weaved to the entrance, where he banged his fists.

A guy in a powder-blue polyester leisure suit opened the door. "Yeah?" he said in a tough voice. It did not go with his appearance. He looked to Mack like a florist.

"Where's Susan?" demanded Mack.

"Who are you?"

Rather ceremoniously, Mack removed his gimme cap, shook his hair into razor-cut order, jerked off his dark glasses, and squared shoulders that would have burst two of Powder Blue's jackets sewn together.

"Oh my Lord," said the man as if punched in the stomach. Susan swept into the living room carrying two glasses of red wine. She looked lovely, slim and solid in a lime-green hostess gown. She looked at Mack and was unable to disguise displeasure at encountering an ex-husband on the hearth.

"Hello, Mack," she said coolly. "Still having trouble with time, I gather. You were supposed to call tomorrow."

"This really is a pleasure, sir," said the man in the middle, unaware of cross fire. "I know you get tired of hearing it, Mr. Crawford, but I love your movies." He held out his moist hand for shaking but it dangled unaccepted.

"This is my friend, George Parsons," said Susan. "George, this is Mack Crawford." She almost laughed at the absurdity of introducing a face as recognizable as the quartet on Rushmore.

"Get rid of him," ordered Mack.

"Oh, I'll be happy to leave," agreed George, scooting out, not even making an excuse to Susan. He was transfixed by celebrity.

"Can I come in?" asked Mack.

"You're already in," said Susan. She handed him the unused glass of wine.

"Who was that prick? Your decorator?"

"You're really rude. George is a lawyer, Mack. A very nice, kind, dependable, well-mannered lawyer. He lives on a different planet than you."

Her rebuke hit him. Mack sat down in a leather sling chair and sipped his wine. He thought about trying to embrace Susan and wondered if she would push him away. He tried to make small talk. "I got in early," he said. "So I was driving around and I got lost and I just sort of happened to be in the neighborhood. I didn't know you'd have company. . . ."

"You look tired, Mack."

"I just finished a picture." He set his glass down on the end table and noticed a new photograph of Jeffie. The boy was encased in Plexiglas and looked remote, as if he was running away from the camera. He was thin and his hair was as long as a courtier's.

"Why did you let Jeffie leave the school in Switzerland?" he demanded.

"I didn't have any say about it. He just showed up one night."

"How'd he buy a plane ticket?"

"*You* gave him the American Express card, Mack."

"Why'd he drop out?"

"He said quote I need to get my head together end quote, whatever that means."

"I wrote him. He never wrote back."

"He's . . . busy."

Mack stood up and swept Susan into his arms. "I need to see my son, I'm entitled."

"I don't know where he is."

"Susan, don't lie to me."

"I'm not. Mack, Jeffie's . . . well, he's *changed*."

"Changed into what?"

"He's a very introspective kid. He's questioning his values. I don't see any harm in that."

"I flew all the way from California to see my boy."

"Mack, please leave. We're both tired."

Things did not seem exactly right by Mack's reckoning. To be bounced by the woman who had barged uninvited into his life some twenty years distant, who had sand-trapped him into marriage, who had rejected a serious plea for reconciliation, who now had a million dollars of his hard-earned money as divorce settlement to a marriage that scarcely existed, who owned his own house and had turned it into a travesty of its dignity, who denied him access to the only real accomplishment of his life—his son, his supreme creation—that woman deserved her due.

Mack grabbed her arm and twisted it cruelly. "I want Jeffie," he said.

"But *he* doesn't want you," said Susan. She wrenched free. Mack hit her. He felt good when he drove away.

From the rebirth of the sun each morning until its death at night, guided tours were conducted over the eighty-five-acre site where The Chosen was building the City of Miracles. Kleber chose the 4 p.m. tram ride, knowing it was the most popular and heavily attended by devotees who, this being a Thursday, would flow thereafter into the sanctuary for worship and miracles. He would be able to blend into the throng. His first stop in Fort Worth had been Monkey Ward's, where he purchased gray Dacron slacks, a wrinkle-free white shirt, and a straw fishing hat. The mustache glued on his upper lip, four days' growth of silvery blond beard, and aviator sunglasses gave him—he hoped—the appearance of a cowman from Midlothian. In the parking lot, he found a pair of country sisters with a passel of nieces and nephews in tow. One of the kids was already misbehaving and when Kleber suggested a piggyback ride, the aunts were delighted. The counterfeit Christian was, he felt, perfectly camouflaged.

He paid five dollars for the tour ("Four-fifty of which is tax deductible, so save your stubs") and passed through a security gate like those at airports. A variety of Miracle women, fresh as dew, stood around in coarse white gowns that touched the earth. None wore a drop of makeup but each face was serene and lovely. Kleber noted it would be possible to cast a score of Christmas pageants with these Virgin Marys.

"I am Sister Gentilla," announced the guide. She was in the vicinity of forty, with shining blue-black hair and morning-glory eyes that seemingly had never witnessed an unpleasant sight. A glaze was permanently across her face. "Welcome to the City of Miracles," she began. "You are about to experience two hours in the presence of God. It is not our desire to proselytize. We seek no converts. The Chosen cares not if you are Christian, Jew, Buddhist, atheist—saved or sinner. The City of Miracles is the will of God and the power of God. Our Father in Heaven commanded The Chosen to build this city. It has just begun. We are the pioneers and the pilgrims. One hundred years from today, the work will still be going on. A thousand years from today, the City of Miracles will not be completed. All we ask from you is respect for

God's place. We do not permit photographs or tape recordings because they may disturb those seeking communion with Our Lord. Twice during the tour we will pause for questions. Please do not speak except during these periods. And by the way, to put your minds at ease, no contributions will be solicited."

Almost everyone thereupon parted with cameras, leaving them at a check stand. But Kleber's Minox, secreted inside his spectacle case and tucked in his shirt pocket, stayed in its hiding place. A *Life* photographer had once taught him the trick, including running a wire inside his chest and down into his trouser pocket where a trigger could be discreetly and silently fired.

They boarded trams and were off. Sister Gentilla pointed first to the Miracle Tower, twelve stories of glass the hue of bourbon that housed "administrative offices, archives, research facilities, and living quarters for The Chosen." Kleber craned his neck up toward the penthouse and noted that T.J. was well nested. His top floor, informed Sister Gentilla, contained a 6,000-square-foot apartment, including paneling from a fourteenth-century Renaissance cathedral, and a desk "believed to have been used by an Archbishop of Canterbury."

Behind this desk sat a man in an ice-cream-colored suit staring with bemused content at a six-foot-wide television screen. By pushing a panel of buttons on his desk, the viewer was able to watch almost every corner of the City of Miracles. Some 180 strategically placed cameras permitted few secrets. From the moment the Prince of Power had stepped out of his rented pickup, the Prince of Temptation watched. Each time Kleber squeezed the Minox trigger in his pocket, The Chosen clenched his fist, the same fist that crashed into the dark craws of demons and reached out in testimony of God's wrath.

For a pleasant hour, Sister Gentilla glided her flock around the perimeters of "The Life of Christ," a fourteen-acre project barely begun. On gently rolling hills thirty miles west of Fort Worth, it would someday be possible to view Christ's nativity, the flight into Egypt, the temple infested by money changers, the Garden of Gethsemane, Pilate's court, and both Golgotha and the tomb of resurrection. "The projected cost is eleven million dollars," announced Sister Gentilla, "and at this very minute, in the Miracle Tower, more than thirty world-rank theologians, scholars, and artisans are laboring to re-create the Holy Land. Incidentally, the soil of Texas on which we stand is very similar to Galilee."

A woman near Kleber murmured, "Jesus Land," and though she intended no sarcasm, the remark rippled on with laughter. Sister Gentilla frowned. "Please remember, no talking until the rest break." After a whirl through the campus of "Miracle College," which at this time consisted only of three stucco buildings resembling cheap condominiums in Israel, the tram stopped. They were now in front of an unimpressive, roundish dome that poked its head but a few feet above the ground. It could have been a tomb or a bunker or a landed spacecraft. But the face of Sister Gentilla promised something special. In beatific pantomime, she instructed the tourists to form a single file with heads bowed in prayer. Near the end of the conga line, Kleber was struck silly and almost snickered. But he sobered quickly when a quartet of Miracle men strode by. All day he had glimpsed these stalwarts, pegging them for security guards or students majoring in Goon, First Class. In Nehru jackets, glossily polished desert boots, with hair cut to stiff bristles of Marine recruits, none was more than twenty-five, none was less than handsome. And they all wore what a layman would take for hearing aids but what Kleber recognized as the miniature radio transmitters to be found in the ears of Secret Service men. A little attack of paranoia swept over him, that he was emitting alien vibrations surely being picked up by the palace troops.

The line began to enter the dome. Ahead, he noticed people stepping into darkness, then vanishing. What the hell was going on? Kleber soon learned. He stepped across a marble threshold where stood Sister Gentilla, directing traffic to her right and left, only dimly seen now by a pair of ancient oil lamps that sent out smoky yellow light. Behind her was a velvet retaining rope, and if she stepped backward, Sister Gentilla would have tumbled into what appeared to be a bottomless shaft.

Kleber turned right and walked down three steps where he took his place on a huge circular scaffolding whose circumference was that of the chamber. He guessed the shaft was at least fifty feet across.

"Fall silent!" cried Sister Gentilla. "And do not be afraid. This is the heart of the City of Miracles. Prepare to feel the power of God! Prepare to experience the journey of The Chosen."

First came a humming noise, motors grinding. The scaffolding, to everybody's surprise, was some sort of elevator. It descended. "We are going down forty-eight feet," said Sister Gentilla. The elevator jerked. The trip was not smooth. "This chamber is fireproof, earthquake-proof, erosion-proof, and can withstand any nuclear weapon yet designed by man. Around us are walls ten feet thick, made of steel and concrete. They surpass safeguard standards for U.S. missile silos."

There came a great clap of thunder. Lightning streaked across the darkness. Winds howled and tidal waves crashed against unseen rocks. As the elevator dropped, its passengers were treated to the damnedest *son et lumière* extravaganza Kleber had ever witnessed. Crimson laser beams like cosmic weapons slashed through hideous faces of imps and demons that materialized as floating spirits. Cacophonous music—Bach, boogie, snatches of Schönberg, disco, soprano voices fearsome as Harpies and seductive as Loreleis swam from above and below. Foul odors —rotting fruit and the stench of chrysanthemum stems lifted from weeks in vase water—offended the nose. Then, silence. And absolute blackness. It was unsettling. The elevator touched bottom, shuddered, stopped. The whole trip had taken maybe three minutes, but Kleber breathed a sigh of relief. He tipped his mental hat to T.J. The Chosen must have hired half the artisans of Disneyland to cook up a thrill ride that registered somewhere between Dante's Inferno and Basic Haunted House.

Glissades of harps sounded, recorded but reassuring. Then a new female voice, warm and maternal. "And the Lord said, 'Let there be light.'" Eight stories above, ceiling panels opened and, seemingly from Heaven, rained shafts of brilliantly colored lights, spilling pools of amber and pink and yellow onto a raised circular platform that was swaddled in thick red carpet. Revealed thereon was what Kleber first believed to be a magnificent statue, a woman frozen in worship with hands outstretched to God. Regal and tall, she wore the coarse gown of the tour guides, but in this eerie light the folds of her robe seemed as finely carved as the marble of the Pietà. At her breast was a felt heart and from it dripped blood.

She began to sing.

Up to this point, Kleber was protected by the dependable shield of journalism. Other than a fleeting moment of apprehension over the mechanics of the elevator, he had cocked a bemused eye and ear at the spectacle. But this woman's voice wiped him out. She was singing some hymn vaguely familiar from his Protestant youth but the words were not important. Her vocal instrument was of astonishing range, at its lowest the velvety shimmer of cellos, soaring to notes beyond the grasp of coloraturas. And each tone was as clear and unique as crystal facets. As she sang, the platform revolved, allowing each visitor on the circular elevator to marvel at a face in the grip of rhapsody.

Never had Kleber heard a voice so ravishing. He wished he had concealed a tape recorder in his shirt. Then the woman with the bleeding heart rotated before his eyes. She looked directly at him. She lowered her right arm and stroked her hair, a gesture almost sensuous. He shivered. Had he blown his cover? Had the Nehru jackets seen through his disguise? But she revolved routinely past him and once again lifted both arms toward heaven.

The light fell and dimmed to near blackness as her song ended. An organ erupted with the opening bars of "Death and Transfiguration." From the heights boomed a rich baritone that echoed as if drifting across the centuries. "All of us must journey into a bottomless chasm. It is the curse of man that he must tumble through the darkness, tossed by winds, tormented by storms and fires and temptations, distracted by false idols and tongues that promise gold but spit poison. What you have just experienced is the symbolic voyage of The Chosen. God's Man of Miracles had to fall to the bottom before the power of Our Father saved him from the jaws of hell. All eyes please close. Open them not until the sound of God's trumpet."

The elevator shook convincingly enough to make Kleber feel grateful over Sister Gentilla's earthquake promise. More thunder. Then a clarion brass fanfare. Kleber opened his eyes obediently and beheld a large stucco slab that had moved into place during the blackout. It slowly filled with golden light. "Jesus Christ," whispered Kleber, an accurate oath. He was looking at the wall of a Tarrant County jail cell, the very one on which T. J. Luther had painted his portrait of the Saviour. Encased in bulletproof glass and framed in the rough cedar of a cross, the benevolent Son of God revolved for sixty seconds. Then lights out—and quick ascent amid excited whispering and a recorded choir singing "In the Garden."

Later, topside, at a refreshment stand built to resemble a grape arbor in Jerusalem, Kleber drank weak fruit punch. A buck a shot. Sister Gentilla entertained questions. "Who was the woman who sang?" asked an old lady in a pants suit.

Sister Gentilla smiled. "Wasn't it lovely! That was Sister Crystal. She is one of the greatest miracles. Many years ago she lost the ability to speak. Doctors never knew the reason why. She lived in an insane asylum. She had no name because she could not remember hers. One day The Chosen visited this institution, as is his custom. He often travels to places where unfortunate people cannot experience the joy of God. As The Chosen was speaking, he noticed a sad woman with tears streaming down her cheeks. He asked her name, but she could not answer. He asked the doctors why she was mute but they could not give him a medical reason. They only shrugged in despair. The Chosen went to the woman and prayed for her. He placed his hands on her throat. Her tears dried. She smiled. She opened her mouth but she did not speak. She began instead to sing. God restored her vocal cords through The Chosen's touch."

Kleber wondered impulsively if he could slip in another trip to the bottom of the pit. He had this crazy hunch—but he had built a career out of such lightning bolts—that Sister Crystal sounded suspiciously like T. J. Luther's daffy ex-wife. What was her name? Matilda? Martha? Damn! Kleber could not remember. But he almost laughed. This would be a double-whammy twisteroony. Making a demented and divorced spouse sing for her supper at the bottom of the well.

"How old is Sister Crystal?" asked Kleber guardedly.

"No one knows," answered Sister Gentilla. "Sister Crystal has no memory of her life before the moment that The Chosen touched her. Medical verification of this case is on file in the Hall of Miracles, which is our next stop."

Kleber risked another query. "How did all of this happen so quickly?" His arms swept across the mammoth building program. Everywhere one looked there were bulldozers and piles of stones and planks. He had to pitch his voice to be heard over the drone of machines. "I read where The Chosen only began his ministry a few years ago."

"Since you like to read, you should pick up The Chosen's autobiography, which can be purchased in the Hall of Miracles bookstore. God does not wear a Timex." Sister Gentilla dropped her smile and looked at Kleber a bit insolently. She raised hackles on his neck. All of these women in their coarse robes did. "Any more questions?"

He shook his head.

Sister Gentilla gestured for Kleber to walk beside her. After a few steps she stopped and said softly, "Excuse me, sir. Have we ever met before?"

Kleber recovered quickly. "I don't think so, ma'm."

"You look familiar," she said. "Like somebody I might have known long ago."

"Well, where are you from?" he asked, trying to keep his voice level.

"Lots of places. I moved around a lot when I was little. Around here mostly. Where are you from?"

"West Texas," lied Kleber carefully. "This sure is a right nice tour, ma'm."

"Thank you. We best hurry." Several times in the next half hour, Kleber caught Gentilla observing him, none too surreptitiously.

"The Hall of Miracles," informed Sister Gentilla, "will someday occupy a space larger than the floor of the pagan Colosseum in Rome." Alas, right now it was gimcrack, a couple of Quonset huts strung together and lined with glass display cases. The "miracles" were mainly "before" and "after" photographs of people supposedly cured of goiters, tumors, harelips, clogged blood vessels, and a few bizarre shots of crazies. The "testimony" beneath each set forth in first-person narrative how The Chosen mended limbs, opened eardrums, and in the instances of mental disorders, seized and exorcised actual demons. On one shelf was a row of glass jars with what Kleber recognized as horned frogs and lizards in formaldehyde. But the legend beneath disagreed: "Actual demons and monsters driven out by the Power of God through His servant, The Chosen!"

Well, Kleber could not hold back anymore a long overdue snort of derisive laughter. The "demons and monsters" reminded him of the toads dissected twenty-five years ago in biology, of Mack on his left repelled by the task and of T.J. on his right, stabbing the creatures with zest. As he recalled, T.J. flunked the course but was by far the best frog cutter of his day.

The tour drifted after Sister Gentilla. Kleber collected himself and prepared to follow, but a strong hand gripped and bit into his shoulder and a voice hissed into his ear:

"Write this down, for what I tell you is trustworthy and true. . . . Cowards who turn back from following me, those who are unfaithful to me—the corrupt, the murderers, the immoral, those who speak with demons, who worship idols, who lie—their doom will be the Lake that burns with fire . . ."

"Good Lord," gasped Kleber, whirling to confirm his ears.

Behind dark glasses, T. J. Luther winked. "In other words, good buddy, you ain't supposed to laugh. Come on. I've been expecting you." The Prince of Temptation led the Prince of Power into a glass-walled lift that climbed up and up to glory.

CHAPTER TWENTY-FIVE

"Look, old friend," said T.J. "Let me show you something." He pressed a button on a suede-covered wall. Loose-woven draperies opened to reveal a bank of windows ninety feet across. "We don't tell the folks on the tour the whole story. There isn't enough time. But I want you to know *everything*."

"How did you know I was here?" asked Kleber.

"Just save your questions for a while. Oh, by the way, I think you'd feel more comfortable without that pissant camera in your pocket." The Chosen snaked deft fingers into Kleber's shirt, extricated the Minox, and handed it without comment to one of the Nehru jackets who appeared and disappeared.

"Thou shalt not steal," said Kleber weakly.

"Nor shalt thou bear false witness," answered T.J. "Now just hold your horses, Kleber, and you're gonna see some things worth seein'. Look down yonder there to your left." Twelve stories below, toward the west, silhouetted by the late-afternoon sun, grazed herds of beef and dairy cattle. "Four hundred head of sirloin strips and sweet milk," said The Chosen proudly. "We lease a few hundred acres from an old widder woman. One of these days she's gonna listen to the Lord and give it to us. I'm prayin' hard for her. We need the room for a herd three times as big as what we got now. . . . And see that pretty patch of garden that looks like an emerald brooch? Our boys and girls raise watermelons as big as green torpedoes, and string beans and okra and tomatoes better'n any you ever bit into at '21.' Lemme tell you about that garden, Kleber. Nobody ever grew a dandelion on it before. Hard and dry it was. Godforsaken, that's what they said about that land. Well, I don't believe anyplace or anybody is Godforsaken, so one Easter sunrise we went out there and planted a couple of rows of black-eyed peas. Practically had to dynamite the holes. Sister Crystal stood beside me and sang like an angel, sang so beautiful that both she and I wept, and our tears fell on that so-called Godforsaken ground. Six weeks later we had to go out with machetes and cut back the vines because they was fixin' to take over West Texas."

He spun and pointed to a low-slung factory building where food was processed and stored. "Enough to feed everybody in our organization for five years—even if the bomb hits." On another distant plain rared up a dozen oil and natural gas wells, all flowing into the coffers of the City of Miracles. There was enough gasoline stored, winked T.J., "to keep God's trucks movin' no matter what the Ayrabs do." Bids would soon be taken for construction of a hotel-apartment project directly across from the main entrance of the city. There would be special access ramps for the handicapped, "like Lourdes." "And just wait'll you eyeball this," exclaimed The Chosen, whisking Kleber to a glass table on which rested a royal purple coverlet. He swooped away the cloth and revealed a scale model of the City of Miracles, the most perfect toy a child ever possessed. Elevated monorails glided across futuristic spires and domes and structures glinting with silver and gold. Around the perimeter of the City snaked a breathtaking wall studded with jewels and broken by twelve gates over which hovered marble and pearl-encrusted angels. Up to now, the voice Kleber heard was that of salesman and show-off. But when The Chosen spoke again, his words were messianic: *"The home of God will be among men and He will live with them and they will be His people.* Yes, God Himself will be among us. He will wipe away all tears from their eyes; and there will be no more death, nor sorrow, nor pain . . . Revelation 21."

The Chosen reached beneath his glasses and wiped away a convincing tear. "On January 1, in the year of Our Lord 2000, we will be ready for His Coming. Behold the great wall around the City! It will be just as God commanded in Revelation—built of jasper, on foundation stones encrusted with sapphire, chalcedony, emerald, sardonyx, sardius, chrysolite, beryl, topaz, chrysoprase, jacinth, and amethyst.

And the gates of the angels will be pearls. The gates will never close, for we have no fear of harm. Nothing evil will enter; no one immoral or dishonest will come; only those whose names are written in the Book of Life."

"Am I invited?" asked Kleber, staggered by the opulent nonsense.

"If your name is written in the Book of Life," answered T.J. "Alas, old friend, as of now—I suspect it is not."

"Well, what does *that* mean, T.J.?" asked Kleber. "Assuming I can still call you T.J."

"Certainly."

"I'm glad, T.J. Because it would be hard to call somebody who took me to whorehouses and taught me how to jerk off 'The Chosen.'"

T.J. sighed and sat down in a fine-tooled high-backed leather chair behind his desk. "I don't deny my past, old friend," he answered. "My soul was stained black with sin—sins you cannot even imagine—but every shame has been rinsed by the blood of the Lamb. Can you say the same?" He gestured for Kleber to sit and the journalist realized he was forced by subtle positioning to look up at the seat of power. The last time Kleber had seen this face was at the grave of Lee Harvey Oswald. For twelve years he had carried the memory of a deranged apparition stumbling across the chilled, menacing afternoon. Now he beheld a countenance ironed free of wrinkles and shadows and middle-age whiteheads, plumped like a coddled dauphin. Reportorial speculation suggested excellent nips and tucks, perhaps injections of silicone to fill the craters of debauchery. Whatever, T.J. glowed like a honey-glazed peach. He wore a creamy linen suit with gold blazer buttons and carried no more than five pounds extra from the day a quarter century distant when the Three Princes posed on Kleber's front porch for a commencement eve photograph. Only his eyes were hidden, masked by ever-present dark glasses. There was the repository of time, thought Kleber. Behind the mask had to be eyes old, dead, concealed.

"You're looking at my eyes," said T.J. "You're wondering why I keep them hidden."

"We're both forty-three," answered Kleber. "Maybe you've got astigmatism. Maybe you think you look good in shades. Maybe you work for Foster Grant."

"I'll show you my eyes," said T.J. He jerked off his glasses and Kleber flinched reflexively. The sockets were inflamed, tissue scarred by the famous bath of prison acids. There was little white in the eyeballs, only splotches of bloody red. Had a madman thrust fiery coals into his face and then filled the holes with eyes borrowed from a cadaver, this was what he would have wrought.

"My God, T.J. I had no idea. I'm sorry." Kleber stammered, regretting the condescending prejudgment that reporters all too often make.

"There is no pain," said T.J. "I only wear these glasses because it upsets others to look at me."

"Look, T.J., I don't want you to think I was sneaking around your place," said Kleber. "I'm home for the reunion. I figured I'd see you at the dinner tomorrow night. And in the back of my mind was the idea of maybe asking you to do my show. Admittedly, I didn't have much luck breaking through your wall of flacks."

"I'm sorry about that," said T.J., scribbling himself a memo. "My press people should have let me know an old friend was inquiring about me. They tend to screen too thoroughly. Boy howdy, you must be right hard up to want a country preacher on your program. I'd feel presumptuous sitting in the same chair where Jonas Salk and Jane Fonda and all them Rockefellers sat. You sure know how to take 'em apart, friend. I'd say you do the only conversational autopsy on TV."

"But you wouldn't have to sit in that chair, T.J. I'll tape the show here. Two old friends just chewin' the rag. Nod your head and I'll have a crew fly down by tomorrow morning."

The Chosen made a church house from his fingertips. "It don't matter, K. You know that, don't you? They've all tried to burn my ass. When I think about all of God's fine trees they had to cut down to make the paper to print foulest poison about the City of Miracles and my ministry, it makes me cry. They slip in here every week or two, lyin', drunk, atheistic, left-wing defilers . . ." He stabbed a button on the desk and gestured for Kleber to turn and face a huge television screen. The reporter saw himself in replay, disembarking in the parking lot, hitching up with the elderly sisters, passing through security, adjusting his hidden camera, jotting surreptitious notes inside his work pants. "Boy, you are the worst-lookin' excuse for a rube I ever did see," continued T.J. "I may just have to show a clip of this on *my* TV show. My folks might enjoy a little slice of cinéma vérité, snoop dog exposed, as it were."

Kleber squared for a fight. "If that happened, I'd sue The Chosen's butt on a bill of particulars that begins with illegal use of my face for purposes of commerce and ends with theft of property, namely my camera. The First Amendment of the U. S. Constitution doesn't seem to exist in the City of Miracles."

Instantly, a Nehru jacket entered and placed Kleber's Minox and a roll of exposed film on the desk. T.J. held the strip to the light and frowned. He tossed it and the Minox into Kleber's hands. "Nothin' came out," he said. "But don't feel bad. If you need pictures, just ask. I got ten thousand poses. Every damn one is perfect. . . . And if you wanna talk lawsuits, we best discuss criminal trespass. The back of your admission stub warns folks against coming into the City of Miracles under false pretenses."

Kleber climbed down quickly from his high horse. Diplomacy suggested a salaam and a so-long. "We go back too far for threat, counterthreat, T.J. I'll just say thanks and maybe I'll catch up with you tomorrow night. I promised Lisa I'd buy her dinner."

The Chosen smiled warmly. "Yes, the reunion will be a joyous occasion. By the way, is Mack coming?" The tone seemed to reveal eagerness to measure miracle against myth.

"Haven't seen him yet," answered Kleber. "I wouldn't depend on him showing up. Waiting for movie stars is like juggling Jell-O."

"It sure would please me for us to break bread together," said T.J. "We're way overdue."

"Yes," agreed Kleber, wondering if Mack might be used in some way to seduce T.J. before the television cameras. He remembered an oversight. "Did I say congratulations, by the by? This is the goddamnedest setup I've ever seen."

"Another commandment broken," sighed T.J. "Do you take the Lord's name in vain just to mock me?"

"Nope. It just slipped out, goddamnit." Kleber grinned pleasantly but T.J. was grimly serious.

"Answer me one thing, Kleber. Answer me with the honesty of brotherhood—and we were once bonded like brothers. Answer me from your heart—and perhaps, just perhaps—we might talk business."

"Shoot."

"Do you believe me?"

"Believe *what?*"

"Do you believe *in* me?"

"If your question is, Do I believe in God? then the answer is, with all due respect, no."

"Not necessarily or specifically God. *Me. My* work. *My* ministry."
Kleber hedged his answer. "I believe in your success. I recognize
your celebrity."

"Don't fudge. Look at me, Kleber Cantrell, and answer this: Do
you think I'm a phony?"

"Well," started Kleber, planning a careful waltz around the mul-
berry bush. Fuck it, he decided. "Yeah," he said. "I do."

"Great!" cried T.J. with what seemed enormous relief. "Now we
are nearing a meeting ground. Now we know where each other stands.
Come to the Miracle Service tonight. Sit on the front row. Sit in the
Healing Section. Sit on the stage beside me. Hang from the balcony.
Watch me through binoculars. Stick me under that see-all-know-all-
tell-all-sneer-all microscope of journalism. Then tell me tomorrow
night the definition of phony."

From nowhere materialized another Nehru jacket. He gently led
Kleber away. "Excuse me now, old friend. I must prepare for the visit
of God." He raised his Bible and pressed it to his lips.

Kleber left the City of Miracles and found a nearby pay telephone.
Wondering if it was tapped—his paranoia was running riot—he telephoned his mother. VeeJee passed on a string of messages from Mack,
who was drifting all over Fort Worth, trying to shake the press and
visit simultaneously all the watering holes of youth. The actor had
checked in and out of three motels and was finally located at the home
of a Westover Hills art collector who enjoyed putting up money for independent motion pictures. The man grilled Kleber closely before putting Mack on the line.

Kleber invited Mack to attend T.J.'s jamboree, but the Prince of
Charms, in his cups, declined. "I'm drunk, pal, but not drunk enough
for that," said Mack. "Call me after the last amen. I'll probably be at
Susan's. What the fuck am I doing in Fort Worth?"

Kleber had three hours to cram. He tore open a thick research
packet prepared by his staff in New York and began a crash course in
hard-core religious fundamentalism. It seemed a great revival had broken out in the American South immediately after World War II, a natural antidote to the upheaval of world conflict. In the late 1940's, *faith
healing* was something done on the poor edge of lonely towns, its
believers drawn largely from blacks and poor whites whose lips moved

when they read their Bibles. The practitioners were brilliant performers who, had they not found spotlights in patchwork tents, would have barked on carnival midways or tap-danced for pennies on the sidewalks of Dallas. Orthodox religion cast a dim eye on what was frequently deemed "shamans and charlatans," positioning such primitive worship on the lunatic fringe along with feet washing, snake handling, and seizures of glossolalia.

Yet Texas was the unlikely soil in which the phenomenon of faith healing flourished. The state where hard-shell Baptists rigidly shaped the postures of government and education and culture somehow made room at the altar for Brother Jack Coe, who by 1948 was operating out of a tent that accommodated 25,000 believers. On a widely remembered Saturday night that year, Brother Coe supposedly caused eighty-seven tumors to fly out of malignant bodies. By conservative estimate, he grossed $500,000 that year from collection buckets. Word does tend to get around concerning that many sheep waiting to be sheared.

Next out of the chute was Asa Alonzo Allen, whose gothic career was notorious, bizarre, and—as Kleber mordantly observed—rather funny. Rev. Allen was quoted for his advice to a brother evangelist: "Son, let me tell you something. Do you know when you can tell a revival meeting is over? Do you know when God's saying to move on to the next town? When you can turn people on their heads and shake them and no more money falls out, then you know God is saying, 'Move on, son!'" When A. A. Allen shrieked, writhed, danced like a dervish, and slammed a sweat-soaked palm onto the afflicted part of a crippled body, great Gawd almighty what wondrous blessings! Swallowed safety pins flew out of stomachs; shortened legs grew six inches before your very eyes; malodorous screeching tumors spilled out of mouths like devil tongues and were measured and displayed in bottles. For a while Allen pretended to possess the power of raising the dead, but he obviously did not have the custom down pat. Even as he lay dead of alcoholism in 1970 in a Galveston motel room, A. A. Allen continued to speak on the radio, having ghoulishly prerecorded sermons that kept the money coming in quite some time after he went to the hereafter. In his final year, Allen's corporation mailed out an astonishing 55 *million* pieces of mail.

But it was not until Oral Roberts came along that the show moved from back roads to main street. An Oklahoma farm boy and son of devout Pentecostal parents, young Oral fell to the floor of his high school basketball court at the age of seventeen. Blood was pouring out of lungs ravaged by tuberculosis. Then and there he diagnosed the source of his disease. 'Twas Satan. He prayed for health, vowing, "Lord, if you heal me, I will preach the Gospel." Immediately, young Oral "felt the presence of Jesus Christ enter my feet and my entire body began to quiver." Then, in the tent of a nearby faith healer, Oral experienced, in his own words, "a blinding flash that engulfed me—and that light was all I could see for several moments . . . I felt light as a feather, I felt the sudden impact of divine power." He leaped from his chair and cried, "I am healed!"

With a signal like that, it was unsurprising that Oral Roberts plunged into full-time faith healing. He spent the better part of a decade in ministrations not unlike the primitive posturings of A. A. Allen. He sermonized graphically on the character of demons, informing his multitudes that when Satan invades a sinner's body, the wretch gives off a foul stench and takes on the eyes of a cobra. But when confronted with the God-powered right hand of Oral Roberts (not the left, mind you, only the right), demons shrunk, breath turned sweet, eyes sparkled, and checks got written. Roberts became prosperous and influential—but it was television that made him rich and famous. And powerful. He was the first to recognize the enormous potential of the electronic pulpit, purchasing cheap time from independent stations and stitching together a private national network.

By 1965, there were an estimated 5,000 evangelists shaking tambourines in every corner of America, but only one—Oral Roberts—had 3 million people who watched him every week; only one—Oral Roberts—commenced the building of a university bearing his name whose cost would one day exceed $30 million; only one—Oral Roberts—received 20,000 letters each and every day. And Oral solemnly swore before God that he read every one and prayed for its sender. One critic calculated that if the pen-pal reverend worked fourteen hours a day on his mail (as he said he did), it would mean the devoting of less than two seconds per letter. He built up plenty of detractors, all presumably possessed of foul breath. They wondered how a simple man of God could fancy $500 hand-made suits, drive a Mercedes, practice intricate and most creative cost accounting, and hold membership in a Palm Springs golf club whose initiation fee was $20,000.

That faith healing had become mainstream was evidenced in 1972 when Oral Roberts addressed not a backwater church but the Democratic National Convention. He asked God to "heal America."

From his reading, Kleber discerned that The Chosen had borrowed liberally from the fanatic fringe of the A. A. Allens and Jack Coes and mixed it with the new respectability of an Oral Roberts. None of that concerned Kleber personally or professionally. If the Prince of Temptation was cunning enough to blend bottled horned toads with television extravaganzas, and if 6 million people a week found it more nourishing than reruns of "Gilligan's Island," then so be it—and a pox on *Americanus ignoramus.*

What did prick Kleber with unrest and the need to know was alarming evidence that The Chosen was reaching for more than fishy miracles. Whether by intelligence (possible) or intuition (unlikely) or the kiss of caprice (probable), T. J. Luther had caught the crest of a conservative wave, the backlash of the liberal 1960's. Researchers for "Hot Line" traced the pilgrim's progress. The year before, in early 1974, The Chosen told a convention of evangelists in Florida, "I cannot accept an America that forbids our blessed little children from saying the Lord's Prayer in home room—and at the same time permits pornography beyond the wildest perversities of Sodom to stain the national soul." Later that same year, in Cleveland: "Isn't it time for those of us who *don't* want abortion, who *do* want the right to teach our youngsters the facts of life at home and not hear it from the perverse lips of some pot-smoking pedagogue, isn't it time for those of us who are saddened over the collapse of America's military strength and her weak-livered give-in-to-the-Russians policies that portend a globe turned Communist red—well, if there's anybody out there who believes the way I do, it's time to stand up and be counted."

By the beginning of 1975, The Chosen often alluded to a "coalition of the righteous," teasing now and then of a master computer that could easily list 20 million Americans on the right side. *The Right Side.* No letterhead could be found that bore the name. No one admitted it even existed, yet Kleber kept picking up storm warnings of distant thunder. An Iowa congressman who supported the Equal Rights Amendment, who voted against a bloated Pentagon budget, who suggested on the floor of Congress that both the IRS and the FCC probe deeply into the finances and demeanor of the electronic church, this congressman, a moral and worthy man, was defeated for re-election. His opponent, oft seen on the platforms of conservative preachers, made frequent references in his campaign to being on "the right side" of key issues—against gun control, against "humanism," against school busing, pro-family, pro-church, pro-morality. After the election, The Chosen hoorahed on national television that "God blessed America—and He will do it again and again for candidates on the right side."

The Right Side! Kleber marveled at the simplistic genius of the cause. By implication, anyone who differed was wrong. *The Right Side!* Hardly a year had passed since the fall of Richard Nixon, since Watergate's revelations of how fearfully close the country had come to a totalitarian embrace. *The Right Side!* Ultraconservatism was one of those trick birthday candles that refused to be blown out. Perhaps, as Kleber was growing to believe, it accurately mirrored the character of America. The most liberal nation on earth was becoming—or had it always been?—mean-tempered, prim-lipped, layered with more castes than India. "Do you believe that life in America is getting better or worse in terms of happiness?" asked the Gallup poll of 1974. *"Worse,"* answered 49 percent, citing the offenders: exploding crime, inflation, narcotics, environmental pollution, disintegration of family, alienation of youth, loss of trust in government, racial injustice.

The Chosen delivered himself of comment on the poll. "How did it come to pass that the land of the free and the home of the brave turned into the land of the angry and the home of the heartsick?" he asked. "Oh, dear friends, how simple is this answer. America is tumbling into darkness because we have turned our face from God. I fell to the bottom and I can tell you that the cesspool is waiting for all of us. Not unless we find God again and beseech Him to lead our nation as our forefathers intended, not until that day when an entire nation is *born again* will Mr. Gallup find happy folks on his clipboards."

The First Amendment to the U. S. Constitution decreed separation of Church and State. Marriage of preachers and politics was thereby discouraged. But, if Kleber was right, The Chosen was planning a fearsome love affair.

It was seven-fifteen on a May night clear and silvery. Kleber drove to the City of Miracles feeling the exhilaration of his craft and a curious apprehension that he could not measure. He was dressed in the puritan navy wool of a Parson Weems. He had vowed to behave irreproachably; he would be as exemplary as a Baptist deacon. He would not scoff or groan. He was a little scared.

At the Gate of Miracles where someday a dozen layers of gems would support an angel carved from marble and pearl, two guides welcomed Kleber. One was a sweet clone of Sister Gentilla. The other was a boy whose name tag identified him as Brother Paul and who acted as if he had drawn the short straw in the Nehru jacket lottery. Paul smiled ungenuinely at the media infidel. He presented Kleber with a leatherette briefcase that contained a blizzard of Miracle information and a credential badge that would permit unmolested wandering about the auditorium. Someday, felt Kleber, the lad would make a good Intourist guide at the Kremlin or press liaison for the next Nixon.

"Can I help you in any way?" asked Paul, leading Kleber through a side door that shortcutted the 5,000 people thronged at the main entrance.

"Thanks, but I don't believe so," answered Kleber. "I'm just going to look around and find a good seat." Paul bowed and backed away, presumably to turn on the spy cameras.

The foyer of Miracle Sanctuary was a curving bazaar, constructed so that worshippers had to pass by a two-hundred-yard stretch of booths exactly like the sideshows on a midway that led to the big top. Everything except T.J.'s underwear appeared to be for sale. Vials of "Miracle Earth," two grams of pea-patch dirt, brought $5 each. Amber tubes of "Miracle Oil" required a minimum donation of $10, but each came with a blessing from The Chosen. For the affluent, aluminum-framed swatches of The Chosen's "original and historic Miracle Tent" were available, a certificate of authenticity personally signed by Himself on the back. The six-inch square cost $25, but if a wall over the family sofa required decoration, strips a yard-square could be purchased—for $100. Kleber bought the economy size to hang on the wall of his New York apartment next to a swatch of the old Metropolitan Opera gold curtain. Ceil would love it. All manner of recorded sermons, "actual sounds of miracle healings," package tours to the Holy Land, tee shirts ("I Believe in Miracles"), bumper stickers ("Honk If You Love The Chosen"), even construction bonds in denominations of $1,000 to $100,000 (promising 8 percent interest) were on sale. A long line of concerned-looking men and women waited for service at a booth whose banner said: THE STAFF OF LIFE. Here, by the transference of $814.35 in cash, money order, check ("three ID's required"), or credit card, the prudent, far-planning Christian could obtain a full year's supply of food to feed a family of four that would come delivered "in a module designed to fit under anybody's bed." A bulletin board behind the busy clerks offered photographs and headlines of African famine, Cambodian slaughter, and Depression breadlines.

At a display of books and pamphlets where more than two hundred titles covered subjects as diverse as "The Christian's Right to Bear Arms" and "Why God Chose The Chosen," Kleber found none that dealt specifically with *The Right Side*. He asked the clerk, who turned out to be Sister Gentilla with granny spectacles on to count the money, but she said there was no such tract and she had never heard of the right side.

A recorded organ fanfare shooed the crowd into their seats. Kleber took one halfway down front and immediately noted that the auditorium was several degrees warmer than the air-conditioned bazaar. "Probably calculated to inflame the crowd," he jotted on his pad. He looked around at his neighbors. "Bedrock Texicana," he wrote. "90 percent white . . . Mr. and Mrs. Poly and Ester . . . few mustaches . . . no beards . . . the patrons of bowling alleys and K-Marts . . . air of friendliness . . . boosterism, like a Rotary Club luncheon . . . Beauty parlor business must have boomed this afternoon; every lady has been teased and sprayed . . ." It was easy to brand them malcontents leading unexamined lives.

But against his sophisticated will, Kleber felt, for the moment, secure. He was in the bosom of Texas, at home, among 5,000 people less intelligent, less traveled, but not necessarily less valuable. In the early years of his fifth decade, Kleber had begun to assess the restless life he chose. There were moments when the *Flying Dutchman* envied rowboats tied fast to the dock. He made a mental note to detour by Houston and visit his son. The boy, fifteen now, wrote now and then rather plaintively asking for his father's autograph to give to friends.

Miracle Sanctuary resembled a Las Vegas showroom, though thrice the size. Tiers of red plush theater seats cascaded down to meet a massive thrust stage, on which rested circular flying saucer platforms that seemed to have landed at different levels. A warm-up man bounded ebulliently into view and dispensed hymns, jokes, and promises of "a night of miracles . . . a night of joy . . . a night that could be the most important night of our lives . . ." At once Kleber's skepticism returned, slamming the goodwill from his brain.

In his preparation, Kleber had interviewed an actor named Marjoe Gortner who had spent twenty years as an evangelist. At the age of four, in silk britches and more curls than Shirley Temple, Marjoe actually performed legal marriage ceremonies. By his fourteenth birthday, the boy had collected $3 million, all of which somehow disappeared. Even after Marjoe recanted, appearing in a documentary film that brutally exposed the racket that was his religion, the faith-healing circuit was not damaged. "They said the devil made me do it," Marjoe told Kleber. "And do you want to know something unbelievable? I could go back to preaching tomorrow. I could stand up there and *recant* my recant, and I couldn't buy a tent big enough to accommodate the crowds. Marx was right, you see. Religion *is* a narcotic. God is the supreme drug." Marjoe, whose name was a calculated marriage of Mary and Joseph, had regaled Kleber with memories of galvanized metal garbage cans used to collect money, so employed because a cheapskate coin clanged loudly and identified the giver, whereas paper money floated silently to the bottom. He recalled the scam of "special-added-attraction nights" to keep audiences coming back during a two-week gig. Favorites were "Drug Nights" in which sinners brought marijuana and placed it on the altar of forgiveness, unknowing that later that night Marjoe and his associates praised God and smoked the demon weed. "I finally quit preaching," Marjoe told Kleber, "because I could no longer accept the fact that I was a fraud. I should have done it years earlier, but there were a thousand justifications to keep going and keep counting the money. I told myself, 'Those people out there lead boring lives. They come to my tent and they dance and shout and feel good for a couple of hours.' So it costs five bucks. So what? It's entertainment, less than a drive-in movie. I gave 'em a helluva good show. By the last amen, I could pour sweat outta my shoes. . . . Oh, it's so hard to give it up. When a fellow gets on the treadmill of God power, he wants more. In his guts, he knows he's a hick. He knows he's a nobody. But for three hours every night, he's Caruso and Laurence Olivier and maybe even a god lowercase. When he starts building monuments to himself, that's the time he thinks he's God capital G. Then, watch out."

The sanctuary was plunged into darkness. The hush of drawn breath came that precedes all good theater. Clarion brass bands sounded in stereophonic power from every corner of the huge hall. Then, out of the darkness, filtered beautifully lighted tableaux. A saucer of angels—eight young women of identical colorings, their arms laden with white roses—was suspended high above the stage, frozen momentarily, then borne on the moving platform like the presentation of a master chef. They sang a capella at first, sweet pure voices, thickening into intricate harmonies and tempos that segued into hard-rock gospel. Kleber felt an emotional rush.

More saucer platforms materialized to thrust forth interesting cargo—Sister Crystal all by herself, sprung from the bottom of the pit and looking happy about it; a squad of sturdy Nehru jackets, teenage boys with pre-Beatle barbering and Clearasil-rinsed faces, Brother Paul dominant on the front row. No longer was he the suspicious, narrow-eyed host whose counterfeit welcome made Kleber feel like the Antichrist. Now his features blazed with the radiance of a warrior for the Lord.

Finally came a flying saucer of "Executives for Jesus," and among them Kleber picked out a former U.S. congressman whose American Conservative Coalition report card was 98 percent and who still maintained that the resignation of Richard Nixon was a "media-Communist lynching." He clasped hands with a Waco multimillionaire named Stanley Noah, who, if Kleber's memory served, had been indicted in 1972 for the murder of his wife, son-in-law, and a neighbor child who ran over to see why bullets were being fired. Initially public sentiment in the heavily religious town had been against Noah, but The Chosen went to visit him in his jail cell. A photograph was taken and put on the AP wire of T.J. down on his knees praying for the repentant sinner. After numerous trials, mistrials, and the expenditure of a reported $4.5 million to an attorney named Otto Leo out of Dallas, Noah was acquitted. Presently he was elected to the board of The Chosen's mother corporation and was rumoredly a massive contributor to the City of Miracles. Waco police had totally dropped the search for some other triple murderer and still insisted Noah was their man. But tonight he was beaming and bellowing hallelujahs.

The true mark of celebrity is when no introduction is needed or given. Frank Sinatra enjoys strolling onstage unannounced, the gasps and shivers of surprise more tribute than all the fanfares ever composed. T. J. Luther's appearance tonight defied drums and made language empty. Revealed in a thunderclap at the top of stairs that coiled seemingly into infinity, The Chosen slowly descended, backlit by starbursts of golden light that delivered him on apparent heavenly commission. Waiting midway was the last saucer onto which he stepped, was thence swept directly out and back and forth over the first few rows of the devoted. If Florenz Ziegfeld and Busby Berkeley were looking down, then surely they were pleased. Kleber clamped shut his dangling jaw and wrote hurriedly, "Il Duce never had such a ride." Prudently he scratched it out, mindful that reportorial indulgences were becoming all too often the objects of subpoenas.

An agenda exists for these miracle services, be they staged in wind-whipped tents or splendiferous sanctuaries: warm-up man, appearance of the star, hints of impending miracles, declarations of supernatural power in the air, a midway offering like *sorbet* to cleanse the palate in a lengthy meal, sermon, then, finally, as headliner of the bill —healing. Followed by one final round of collection buckets. The gamble is waiting until the end for solicitation, but if the preacher man has confidence in his act and if the expected frenzy is reached, then the lambs will part with their wool.

T.J. seemed to be following custom. Immediately he threw out his arms like a crucified Christ. Spotlights danced like flashing gems on his dark glasses; he proclaimed the expectance of "miracles beyond computation and comprehension." The vision had come that very afternoon while meditating in the tower. To which Kleber privately muttered, "I'll bet." Then The Chosen struck the stance of a pointer dog in the presence of exceptional pheasants. What did he see? *Angels!* "I see angels," he whispered, the microphone taped to his breast dispatching the news like windows rattling at midnight. "I see angels there—in the balcony—and here—on the stage—and over yonder—on the arms of your seats. Oh glory, what a night of miracles! The angels themselves have come to bring God's wonders!" Kleber craned his neck around and about but saw nothing but everybody else looking in vain for the same harps and halos.

Quickly, The Chosen introduced the opposing team. He threw his hand across his masked eyes as if threatened. *"Devils!"* he hissed. "Oh my, we've got devils and demons! *More* devils and demons than angels! Holy war! Tonight Satan challenges the Saviour!"

Stirrings in the crowd. Neighbors examined neighbors in search of horns and forked tails. Helpfully, The Chosen categorized the enemy forces. "Where are the diabetes demons?" he demanded. "Everybody with diabetes stand up!" About fifty people obediently rose. "High blood pressure demons?" A hundred got up. "Cancer demons? *Hidjooooous,* eeeeevil monsters?" Biggest delegation yet. "Arthritis? Nicotine? Alcohol?" Up popped scores. "Adultery demons?" Whoops, nobody present from the infidelity coven, or at least nobody willing to own up to membership. "Homosexuality?" cried T.J., making it about a sixteen-syllable condemnation. Two ushers sat *down,* not wishing mis-inclusion. "Drugs?" On Kleber's own row of seats, a weary-looking mother yanked her sleepy, stringy-haired teenager onto unsteady feet. He wore a phosphorescent green tie at half-mast and Mama straightened *that* up for him, too. Before long, just about everybody in the house was risen. Feeling conspicuous and in the minority, Kleber got up with intent to roam about the combat zone.

"Atheist demons!" screamed T.J. And Kleber stopped dead in his tracks. He felt like a streaker, but nobody seemed to pay his immoral nudity much heed, there being such exceptional demon rivalry on the tiers tonight. Amused, he walked to the back of the hall and slouched beside a hell-red exit sign. "My oh my, have we got our work cut out for us tonight," breathed T.J. heavily, building into a chant and a jig. He commenced to whirl about the stage with the grace of a danseur noble and the sexuality of a rock star. Kleber wrote on his pad, "He looks like Tyrone Power imitating Elvis Presley."

"Sit down, good people, sit down," gentled The Chosen. "But get ready. We may be here until sunrise. And here's a bit of news I'll bet you never expected to hear from this poor mouth. Ladies, close your purses. Gents, button your wallets. There's not gonna be any money talk tonight. Oh, God knows we need your support—and nobody's gonna slap your hand if you try to force a check on the usher as you go home. But the stakes on the table are devils—not dollars."

He tiptoed to the edge of the thrust stage, knelt, and beckoned attention as if about to tell a secret. T.J. spoke guardedly. "I may be in big trouble tonight. *Big* trouble. I wanna warn you good people what you and me are up against. The Lord is testing me—and Satan thinks I'm gonna flunk. What we got here tonight is the force that has threatened God since the day after creation. You know what I'm talkin' about? What we got here tonight is a power stronger than all the armies of Red Russia and an evil more horrible than all the murderers who ever sizzled on death row.

"I'm talking about . . . the forces of disbelief. Did you hear me? I said *the forces of disbelief!* Oh, we've fought these devils before. You may have thought we whipped 'em—but they're back. They slipped in here tonight to mock and laugh. Lemme ask you, have these devils ever won?"

"NO!"

"Not *yet*. That all of us sit here tonight in God's beautiful palace of miracles is testimony to the warm-up bouts. But tonight we go against a heavyweight champion. Somewhere out there I smell the foul stench of mockery. Above our heads these forces of disbelief have placed a caldron of boiling poison—and if we lose, nobody gets out alive. The City of Miracles will become the Lake of Eternal Fire."

With the threat of Armageddon settling gloomily across the chamber, The Chosen flung a throbbing arm of accusation. It moved across the room like a swaying serpent and Kleber knew the target.

"Just who is this demon? Well, I know his identity. But I dare not speak his name. Let him remain anonymous. Let him feel this challenge: *Watch* us. *Listen* to us. *Search* for one loose stone in this house of God. And if you find that flaw, then come pull down our walls. If we are false, then we deserve to perish."

While 5,000 chickens fluttered in search of one endangering wolf, Kleber considered his options. Better judgment suggested that he get the hell out now—and would that he had obeyed first instinct. Ill-prepared for a moral shoot-out, three decades of journalism nonetheless made him cocky. Believing that intelligence and well-earned, *hard*-earned celebrity were capable of standing up to hypocrisy, ignorance, and freakish fame, the Prince of Power found himself walking down the aisle. Misgivings fell like broken limbs across his path. But a dare is a dare and he stepped defiantly over them. He glimpsed Sister Gentilla piercing him with eyeball lasers from one corner of the stage and he heard Sister Crystal floating stratospheric hallelujahs from her parked flying saucer.

When Kleber reached the edge of the stage, he stuck out his hand and squeezed that of the Prince of Temptation until his flesh paled and blood stopped. "You're on, T.J.," he said. "Prove it."

He sat down in a chair soft as clouds and realized he was past the point of no return.

CHAPTER TWENTY-SIX

Somehow they got through six weeks of dangerous exile on the lake near Fort Worth. Kleber regained his physical health and Ceil Shannon no longer studied each motorboat that zipped past the cottage with the heart-stopping fear that its pilot was a disguised police officer. Even when turned upside down, life has a way of finding a routine.

It was the end of August 1975. Each day was hot and lazy. Nurse and patient even dared venture into the tepid waters of Eagle Mountain for an occasional swim at sundown, when the lake was shimmering orange. And sometimes at night, Kleber fished by lantern and typed out instructions for Ceil on how to drench catfish and crappie in corn meal and flash-fry fillets in bacon grease. When she mastered that, she moved on to popovers, then buttered squash casserole and platters of cantaloupe and beefsteak tomatoes.

Samantha Reiker came for the last time to check on her patient. Physically, she told Ceil, orthodox medicine had done all it could. Kleber's wounds were healed, the scars fading and blending under the Texas sun. His blood tests revealed no sign of infection. But psychologically? The two women walked outside and Ceil risked a few minutes of needed conversation. They embraced, both aware of the enormous risk the adventure had entailed. Ceil was grateful beyond words for what Samantha had done. After Kleber "vanished" from the hospital, every doctor, nurse, orderly, and guard who had even brushed against the door of room 610 was ruthlessly grilled by the men of an infuriated Calvin Sledge. The DA had yelled at Dr. Reiker for a full afternoon but her lies were crisp and cool. The DA obtained a bench warrant for Kleber Cantrell's arrest, an impulsive act debated by lawyers all over Texas. It seemed, well, *curious* to throw a criminal lasso around the missing neck of the witness most needed to make a murder trial.

"We'll be leaving soon," said Ceil. "We can't afford to stay here much longer."

"I think he'll travel well," said Samantha.

"The only bad times are at night, sometimes. He wakes up screaming—only there's no sound. Just these terrible, violent spasms. His eyes are wild. He holds on to me like he's drowning. Then he sort of curls up like an abandoned baby and won't let me touch him."

"I talked to a shrink friend of mine," said Samantha. "I pretended to be asking about a patient who was raped and stabbed. Apparently there are four stages a victim of violence has to go through. The first is shock and denial. Then comes what they call 'frozen fright.' They cling to those around them like frightened children."

"Then we must be in stage two," said Ceil.

"Stage three is no picnic, either. The patient falls into traumatic depression. Insomnia, jumpiness, anger. He 'replays' the event. There can be terrible nightmares and fantasies. Various shades of guilt come into play. Kleber may start asking himself why it happened—and what he could or should have done to prevent it."

"There's nothing he could have done."

"But only he knows. He has to work it all out. That's stage four. When you get to . . . *wherever* you're going . . . it would be helpful to have him see a therapist."

"Am I doing anything wrong?" asked Ceil.

Samantha embraced her old friend once more. "I'd say you're doing everything right. He's lucky as hell to have you. Listen, be sure and call if anything comes up. I'm available day or night. Ten minutes away."

When Ceil made hurried trips to buy groceries, cautious never to visit the same store twice, she caught up with news of their personal melodrama. On the car radio, speculation placed Kleber Cantrell in such diverse hiding places as the South of France, Bangkok, and Malibu. Her name was mentioned but thus far only as the subject of rumor. Early on in the hunt, NBC reported that "Mr. Cantrell's frequent companion, playwright Ceil Shannon, was believed to have been in Fort Worth. But her agent in New York today issued a statement insisting that Miss Shannon is in northern India filming a documentary."

They might as well have been. The six weeks of hiding out was, all in all, scary and delicious. No television, no newspapers, no telephone. Six weeks of closeness never even approached by two people in almost fifteen years of being intimately involved with one another. One morning early on Kleber typed a furious sentence and beckoned her to read. "I have a great new play idea for you," it said, "the title is *Silent Sex*." Ceil giggled nervously and got busy with the sudden need to wash dishes. Kleber rattled the keys again: "Classified ad in NY Review of Books: Wanted: Mute man of considerable endowment—intellectual *and* physical—seeks woman who wants all action and no talk. Must be statuesque, red-headed, and insatiably horny." When Ceil, shyly and with difficult euphemism, inquired of Samantha Reiker if her charge was, er, "up to it," the doctor burst out laughing. "You'll just have to find that out for yourself," she said. "But by me it sounds great."

Now, two weeks before the beginning of a murder trial expected to be attended by eight hundred representatives of the world press, Ceil well knew that getting out of town was overdue. But her heart was the villain of delay. Fed by the lunatic nutriments of scandal and peril, love had grown between the exiles to dimensions beyond the objectivity of Kleber and the fantasies of Ceil. After Dr. Reiker paid her last visit, Ceil went inside and a few hours later lay in the arms of a man who could not speak to her. She was exhausted by revels that could only be categorized as sexual abandonment, somewhat ashamed that she had cried out in the excitement of orgasm and had sung solo for a good five minutes. But Lord was she happy. "I'm glad right now you can't talk because I couldn't take a counterpoint," she told him. "I just want you to know that in the past dozen some odd years I have said 'I love you' perhaps seven thousand times and I was *never* lying, even when you were your jackass worst like that night in Paris. So get ready for a truly original line. I never knew what 'I love you' meant, not until now, this moment. I hope you understand what I feel."

Kleber pulled her face down so that she could see his in the candlelight. He mouthed carefully two words, "Me, too."

Entwined, they lay still and dried the sweat from their bodies in the spare evening breeze that came from the lake. An hour later they made love again, furious, back-scratching, blood-rushing love. "This is crazy," said Ceil. "The two of us together total eighty-eight years and we're going at it like I wear braces and you have pimples." Over the years, theirs had been selfish sex, routine sex, incomplete sex, drunken sex, guilty sex, accommodating sex. Weird, she thought. All it took for incomparable sex was a night with God and a dance with death.

In the morning, Ceil reluctantly addressed the realities of life. She said, "The trial begins in twelve days."

He nodded blankly.

"If you want to leave, then let's do it now. But I feel it's my duty to ask you one last time: Do you want to turn yourself in and testify?"

He did not hesitate. He shook his head.

Ceil did not want to pick at the psychological scars but there was a moral imperative involved here. "You're *sure*," she said. "On the radio it says Sledge can't possibly win without you."

He mouthed, "I don't care."

"I'll only intrude this one last time. Why?"

"Because . . ." Kleber's pen hesitated. Then he wrote quickly. "Because I feel guilty enough already. I've said too much and written too much for one man. . . . And because I don't want them poking around in my past. OK?"

Ceil drew a sharp breath. "Okay," she said. "The major part of love is acceptance. I'm going to get cracking. I'll have to leave you for a couple of hours. I'll make some phone calls, get some maps." She kissed him tenderly. "If we get busted, do we both get a phone call?"

Kleber smiled wanly. "I have influence at court," he wrote on his pad.

She had been gone more than an hour when Kleber dressed and wandered outside, breaking the house rule—no ventures into the risky light of day. And *never* alone. Circumstance had forced them to be night crawlers. But Kleber wanted to think—and he needed to walk. His unexercised body resembled a wrinkled seersucker suit. At lakeside, the tide was out, offering a hitherto unexplored boulevard of brownish ooze and glistening pebbles. He followed it around the shoulder of a nearby cove and encountered a neighbor house, seemingly shuttered at the end of summer. It intrigued him but he knew it was best to turn and hurry home. Then a work shed caught his eye. Piled high beside a cord of wood was a column of newspapers. Now the temptation was irresistible. He scrooched easily beneath a split-rail fence and with the hunger of a man breaking a four-month fast began to read. In the thick late-morning heat he stood rapt, sweat pouring off his face and splashing onto pictures of himself that decorated the front pages. The sound of an approaching motor registered in his ears but he took it to be a powerboat. Then a rough voice shouted from the driveway of the house. Kleber looked up not with fear, only annoyance over being interrupted. A black handyman beside a truck was yelling at him. "Hey, man, what the hell you doin' down there?"

Kleber seized an armload of unread newspapers and fled into the shallow waters, mindful of his foolish spectacle but hugging the staff of life to his breast. The black man hollered some more but did not rush in after the paper thief.

Ceil returned to the cottage at noon, flush with schemes and schedules. She found Kleber sitting on the floor, surrounded by furiously wadded balls of newspaper pages. He looked like the target in some nursery toss game. But his typewriter was humming like the Industrial Revolution. He scarcely looked up to nod hello.

"What happened?" she cried. "Who brought these newspapers?"

On the margin of a front page he scribbled, "Nobody. It's OK. No questions. Must get it all down. *Must!*" And for the rest of the day, nonstop, full flood, copy churned forth like steam from a foundry. At the bottom of each completed page, Kleber bobbed his head urgently, his signal for Ceil to rip this one out and insert fresh paper. So caught up did Ceil become, so absorbed by the fury and power of his narrative, so content with Kleber's apparent "working out" of his traumas, that she put aside the urgent need to pack. She decided not to intrude with her own exciting news, that a Piper Cub would be waiting for them at 5:30 p.m. on a private airstrip west of Fort Worth. Since the pilot she engaged had $1,500 of her cash in his pocket, he could damn well grease his dipstick until the prepaid fares arrived, however late they were.

Even when Ceil heard the car doors slam outside just before sundown, followed by muffled talk of stalking men, she did not make Kleber stop. Oh, her heart leaped at the bawl of the first bullhorn, when she realized police were at the door. But she waited for Kleber to finish the page on which he was working. Then she kissed him hurriedly and said, "They've got us. But I love you even more."

In Kleber's eyes were pride and tears. He scribbled one last directive: "Burn it." There was just enough time for Ceil to start a fire from the angry wads of inaccurate newspapers and dump a bottle of cognac onto her lover's *flambée*. When six police and deputies kicked out the door and burst into the smoky room, every word Kleber had written was turned to ash. The Prince of Power was mute.

In her jail cell that night, Ceil did not sleep. The mother of her torment was not really the ordeal of having faced a violent mob of cameras and questions on the courthouse steps, not the humiliation of having to smear her fingers and palms in the criminal ink of Tarrant County–The State of Texas–The United States of America, not the numbers draped on her breast for the mug shots full face and right and left profiles, not the first of what would surely be numbing interrogations from Calvin Sledge, not even the realization that she was by magisterial dictate a certified felon and accused of conspiracy to obstruct justice, conviction of which might merit two to ten years in the state penitentiary.

What denied Ceil Shannon the peace of exhausted sleep was neither shame nor regret. She was less the confinee of law than the prisoner of an uncompleted story. A hundred times this night she shifted on the squeaking metal cot and tossed and thought: *If only the bastards had waited one more hour.* The part of Kleber's tale she burned she would always remember—and keep it, as he intended, secret. But the rest, the part left untold, if those pages were never filled, then the coroner would have no need to dissect her innards for the cause of death. He could write with accuracy: Ceil Shannon succumbed to curiosity.

"Verisimilitude," Kleber had written at the top of his first page, "that being the *appearance* of truth . . ." He commenced his account at the very moment he accepted T.J.'s dare and stepped onto the stage of Miracle Sanctuary.

For a time, The Chosen had only stood shaking his head, lips formed in a silent whistle, seemingly a man in checkmate. Then he made his move. He gave Kleber lavish introduction, "my dear friend of more than forty long years." Tributes spilled so effusively from the preacher's mouth that Kleber began to feel less like a Force of Disbelief and more like the drowser at a book-and-author luncheon where the chairlady impresses—endlessly—her parlor with the stature of her catch.

The lull of flattery being, by custom, fragile, Kleber was listening inattentively to T.J.'s drone, believing him to have segued into this night's sermon on the mount. Then, midway through a convoluted laundry list of the stains on Lady America's gown, The Chosen hurled a cunning lance. He pointed at Kleber and he said, "How fitting it is that you come here tonight, my lifelong brother. It must be God's will that *you* send forth the news. Scoop-de-doodle-do, here's God's exclusive for you."

The virgin-white leather folder that sailed into his lap bore gold-embossed letters: THE RIGHT SIDE. "Read it later, friend," counseled The Chosen, who proceeded to summarize—amid football stadium roars from the partisans—"God's plan to save America." Boldly, baldly, it was the intent of Thomas Jeremiah Luther to coalesce the fundamentalist right into a frightening political power. "The polls say we got twenty million folks on the right side," whooped T.J. "I think that arithmetic is modest. I think we got a hundred million Americans. And once we get everybody together, I believe we can throw out the judges who say, 'Go-ahead-and-kill-your-unborn-baby-Mama.' I think we can evict any senator who says, 'Let's-be-sweet-to-the-Russkies-'cause-they-don't-want-to-conquer-the-world-and-there's-no-reason-to-fret-over-the-fact-that-our-defense-is-as-rusty-and-worthless-as-a-roller-skate-left-ten-years-out-in-the-rain.'" And on and on, up to and including the need for a constitutional amendment that would require every officeholder in the land—from dogcatcher to President—to swear an oath of belief in God.

"Can we do this?" he demanded.

"YES–YES–YES!" resounded the feverish amen corner.

"My dear parents—God rest their souls—gave me three names," thundered T.J. "*Thomas*—he was the doubter, remember? *Jeremiah* —he was the prophet of despair. There's even a noun named after poor old Jeremiah. And *Luther*—the feller who nailed some pretty fair country news on the old bishop's door. God said to me this afternoon —and yes, Kleber, the Lord *does* talk to me, and he'll talk to you, too, iffen you'll just listen—God says, 'Son, there must be a reason why your fine mama and daddy pinned those handles on their baby boy.' So

I figured it out. Anybody named Thomas Jeremiah Luther who *doubted* that his country could ever get out of the swamp of *despair* is heaven-meant to *reform*. That's the only thing to do. That's the *right* thing to do. And we're gonna do it—'cause we're standing on the right side. The *glory* side. And we ain't a gonna budge!"

With a little Jackie Gleason penguin shuffle, T.J. flapped before Kleber's chair and said insolently, "Any questions?"

No more than a thousand, thought the journalist. But none for now. He shook his head. If awarded but one wish, it would be to peer behind the mask of darkened glass that concealed the Prince of Temptation. Was there merriment in those eyes? Did T.J. really *believe* what he was saying? Was he a puppet whose strings were being pulled by rightist regents? On their saucer, the "Executives for Jesus" glowered at Kleber like a Supreme Court refusing to hear the final plea.

The Chosen commenced the healing portion of the program and Kleber pulled out a steno pad from his breast pocket, an act that caused murmurs in the audience, akin to the moment in movies when a street fighter clicks open the switchblade. Just for the hell of it, Kleber made overelaborate strokes, hoping they would seem as ominous as the ticks of a time bomb. But a funny thing happened. Within a quarter hour, his pen was still. The skeptic was held enthralled by the emotional theatricality of Born Again Boulevard.

To receive the "healing ministry of Our Lord," supplicants were required to assemble in a large pit that opened in front of and beneath the stage, then trudge up a coiling ramp whose apex was where The Chosen stood. Effectively, the sanctuary was plunged into near-darkness, excepting needles of brilliant white light that rained on the spot where T.J. exhorted miracles. The afflicted thus had to voyage from the grasp of fearsome dark, to the apprehensive edge of gray, finally to cleansing hot white light that bathed The Chosen. The "miracle healings" of T.J.'s weekly jamborees were never shown on television—only the aftereffects, i.e. once crippled old women pushing no longer needed wheelchairs onto scrap piles of crutches and braces. Kleber thus expected a dose of hard-core tussles with debbils. The rule book called for the preacher to scream at migraine headache demons and slap foreheads silly. Anybody feels better when the hitting stops.

Due presumably to Kleber's presence onstage this night, The Chosen worked quietly and gently. His face was encompassingly tender. He seemed not only to heal but to mind-read. "Don't tell me what demons afflict you, brothers and sisters," he dictated to the dark mass of ailing people below. "Tonight I devoutly believe that God is giving me X-ray vision. I can see demons better than you can see warts." Well, there had to be some kind of code, reasoned Kleber. Some hired hand along the ramp was giving secret signals to the boss as to whether a brain tumor or a palsy was approaching. Whatever the ruse, Kleber couldn't catch it. T.J.'s "X-ray vision" was nigh infallible. He pressed his sweaty palms on about seventy-five people in a fast fifty-two minutes, and out flew—if taken on face value—hardened artery demons, arthritis demons, cancer demons lodged all the way from "brains" to "privates." He mind-read a wife beater demon and a very pretty, very chic "whiskey" demon in the form of a young woman no more than twenty. Several small children whose mothers testified thereafter that their kiddies had been born stone deaf left The Chosen's stage in delirium, with each of the younguns mumbling sounds reasonably close to "Amen" and "Jesus."

For Kleber's notebook, T.J. cried over his shoulder, "I do believe the angels are ahead. That's six new pair of ears created for God—six new soldiers on the right side." He instructed each newly healed "miracle" to permit questioning from Kleber after the service. "Don't be afraid of him," counseled The Chosen. "Answer anything he asks. God is on your side."

Kleber noticed that one person on the stage was more caught up in the passionate goings-on than he. As she watched T.J., Sister Crystal stood on her platform and writhed, almost sexually. Her eyes glistened and she sang a low-key, unintelligible but eerily beautiful private melody.

While he worked, T.J. sermonized continuously. No dead air. "I want you to understand the difference between *cure* and *heal*," he kept repeating. "I am not capable of curing cancer," he told an ancient farmer whose ruddy face was cratered by surgical scoops. "I can expel the demons that infect your flesh—but only if you are born again. If you are not, then don't waste our time."

"I believe in Jesus," said the farmer with hand on heart.

"Jesus Christ said that man *must* be born twice—the first time of the flesh and the second, born again in the spirit of God. I ask you, old-timer, are you *born again?*"

"Yessir, sure am."

"Well, hallelujah!" cried T.J., hugging the foul old man to his breast. When released, the farmer looked radiantly happy, then promptly passed out cold. "Behold," announced T.J. "Here is proof for the disbeliever. Not only does God pull out this old man's cancer demons, he fills him with so much spirit that Grandpa just had to *fall back*—knocked flat by the power of God!" All around him, copycats in the audience began to collapse.

Kleber's common sense told him that nobody was really being healed, at least not permanently, that these people were psyched up, that they had traveled long distances to get here, that they wanted desperately to believe and cooperate with the miracle maker. But it was hard to smell snake oil when a pathetic woman crept into the light and was obviously gripped by terrifying emphysema. After a solid press-on-the-chest from The Chosen's paws, she gushed gratitude in a voice somehow cleared of rasp and smoke. Five minutes later, she could be lying dead on the far side of Born Again Boulevard. But Kleber was privy only to the rapturous moment in the spotlight.

He was trying to sort out these conflicting emotions when there a sharp scream of horror. A commotion built at the rear of the darkened sanctuary. A Nehru jacket rushed up the ramp and whispered urgently into T.J.'s ear. The Chosen nodded and looked worried. "Give us some light," he ordered. What was going on? Kleber ran to the edge of the stage and watched a wedge of Nehru jackets progressing unsteadily down the center aisle. The burden in their collective arms was a limp body. Beside them a woman was screaming near total collapse.

The body of a youth had just been found in the men's toilet, slumped over the bowl. His name was Billy Ray and he appeared to be quite dead—an overdose of heroin. When the attendants reached the stage, Kleber recognized the seemingly lifeless body in their arms as the teenage boy who had sat on the same aisle at the service's beginning. It was the youngster with the fluorescent green tie at half-mast whose mama yanked him out of his seat to answer the roll call of "narcotics demons." Somehow during the healing he had slipped out of the room for a fix.

T.J. did not hesitate. He leaped down from the stage and landed like a crouched panther. Kleber followed, determined to watch carefully. By reportorial estimation, the kid stretched out on the floor was long gone departed. Gray paste face. Blood flow ceased. Fixed, wide-open eyes. Fresh needle tracks on the arms. One of the Nehru jackets estimated that the dead boy had been undiscovered a good seven minutes. Well, Kleber was sorry for the lad, but a little buoyant over The Chosen's predicament. What could T.J. do besides pronounce last rites? Chalk one point up for the devil.

T.J. knelt and touched the dead flesh. He asked Kleber, "You reckon this un's gone?"

Kleber nodded. Mama screamed. Old women engulfed her.

"Reckon Satan's got him?" asked T.J.

"That's your department."

"Well, let's just see." T.J. motioned for aides to lift the boy. He hung between them like a banner stilled. T.J. embraced Billy Ray on both cold gray cheeks. "There was a time when I used to wrestle with these demons," he informed. "But I don't need to anymore. I have authority over demons—because I am God's agent. Well, well, you know what, Kleber? I think God can save this boy, I truly do. I think the devil's gonna turn loose. . . . Tell you what, will you believe in m—" He almost said "me" and then quickly corrected himself, "in *miracles*, if I do?"

Kleber backed away without commitment. He was uneasy. The "amens" peppering the room were like stones landing near him.

"I see you're on the fence, old friend. Maybe you'll help me. Hold this." T.J. tossed his white leather Bible. "Hold on to it tight, K. I mean *tight*. When the demon flies out of this boy, it's gonna head straight for the heart of *somebody*. It'll try and get into the first heart it can find that denies God." Well, why not? Kleber went along with the show, feeling like a magician's assistant.

The Chosen squared his shoulders and faced the dangling body. He prayed mightily: "You may not have this youngster, Satan! God will not let you possess a soul in the City of Miracles. You hear me right! I'll call you by your name, foul demon of heroin, hid-jooous demon of waste, pernicious Satan—by the authority of God *I command you to come out of that boy!*" Hard slaps on the door of death. "I said, *come out, Satan!*" Quite incredibly, the youth gasped and choked. His skin turned to mottled purple. The Chosen fell to his knees and grasped the youth's blue jeans. "Free! Free! The devil is gone! The torment is over! This is the power of the Lord and let no man think otherwise!"

The white Bible in Kleber's hands grew suddenly warm, as if radiated with energy. He stared at it, heard The Chosen purr in his ear, "Believe one thing, old friend. This ain't no setup. Ask this boy. Ask his mother." Kleber declined. He watched Billy Ray limp away in the arms of his hysterical believers. Though taken aback by the spectacle, he was not yet ready to give any devil his due.

T.J. spoke again. "Do one more thing for me, Kleber. Turn to Matthew 13:15 and read it."

Kleber found the scripture and read softly aloud: *"For this man's heart is waxed gross. And his ears are dull of hearing. And his eyes he has closed . . . Lest haply he should perceive with his eyes, and hear with his ears, and understand with his heart, and turn to Me, then I shall heal him . . ."* Kleber tried to keep a poker face. Unknowingly, T.J. had just dealt him the fourth ace.

"Okay," began Kleber. "Brother Matthew here, a pretty good journalist by the way, raises an interesting point. Namely, Mr. Chosen, if you're so adroit at driving demons out of everybody *else's* flesh—then how come your own eyes look like the devil's campfire?"

Flustered, T.J. touched his dark glasses, assuring his mask was in place, that his burned sockets were hidden. "Don't tease me," he answered. "The world knows what punishment I paid for my sins. I'm blessed just as I am. God returned my sight. I was blind—but now I can see."

"Is that so?" sniped Kleber mischievously. He was about ready to leave. "It sure seems like the Lord is parsimonious with reward, don't you think? I mean, if you make miracles so routinely, why not conjure some new retinal tissue for yourself?" He threw back the Bible into T.J.'s trembling hands. "Well?" demanded Kleber.

"I can't ask God to do more for me than He's already done," said T.J. He looked to his flock for comfort and support. Their mood was edging toward testy.

"Why the hell not?" pushed Kleber. "Maybe I can help." Peering up at the nest of ceiling spotlights, he cried, "Any miracles left, Lord? If you're not too tuckered out from tumors and goiters, could you maybe fix up The Chosen's eyes? They look like—if you'll excuse the expression—*hell.*"

"Leave this house, blasphemer," hissed The Chosen.

Delighted, thought Kleber. But not without a punctuation point.

He reached out and yanked T.J.'s dark glasses away. He heard them clatter satisfyingly on the floor. He started to push an exit path through the crowd, but the horror he anticipated on their faces did not come to pass. Instead, people were backing away in awe. Some fell to their knees. A woman cried out and fainted, smacked with the spirit. Kleber spun back.

The Prince of Temptation raised his naked face to the scrutiny of bright light. He was joyful. His eyes were whole. The pupils had become soft, glowing brown and around them the whites were clean as angel raiment. The scars were gone. T.J. began to weep and he threw his arms in gratitude about the Prince of Power. "Therefore if any man be in Christ, he is a new creation," said The Chosen. "Old things are passed away. Behold, all things are become as new." He kissed Kleber on both cheeks, tenderly. "Thank you, Jesus. And thank you, K. God has given you a personal miracle to write."

Immediately The Chosen aborted the service and sent his flock out the gates of the City of Miracles. "I must talk privately to God," he told them hoarsely, hustling Kleber through a maze of underground tunnels that led from beneath the stage to the tower elevator. Kleber's composure was shredding. He thought he knew power and understood its worth. He had stood at the edge of the presidency and drank at the cup of celebrity. But never before had he experienced the frightening power of *belief*. People had rushed toward him in Miracle Sanctuary as if he was a true healer, begging to touch him, pleading that he lay his hand on clogged hearts and withered limbs. Seared on their faces was a primitive passion burning on the far side of ideas and common sense. They perceived him as a piece of God, and Kleber could no more snuff their belief than spit down an erupting volcano.

T.J. had his dark glasses on again. As the elevator rose, he was unapproachable, in some sort of trance. Kleber looked down through the bronze glass walls of the lift and saw clumps of people below, huddled outside the gates, staring up at the tower, pointing, some on their knees in prayer. They were worshipping *him*—and he was sorely confused.

They walked into T.J.'s office and Kleber said immediately, "I want a doctor."

"Are you ill, my friend?"

"Not for me. I want a doctor to come and examine your eyes," said Kleber. "I want a qualified specialist of my own choosing to come here right now."

"There's the telephone," said T.J. wearily, gesturing toward a bank of instruments. "It's almost midnight, you know."

"I suppose it can wait till the morning," said Kleber. "And in case you have any ideas about press releases, I want it clearly understood I'm not connected with anything that happened in that hall tonight. I still don't believe you."

"What more do you want?"

"I want documentation. And if you're pulling mumbo jumbo on me, I'll crucify your ass."

T.J. sighed. "Miracles are by nature very difficult to accept. Both for the receiver and the giver."

"Let me see your eyes again," requested Kleber.

T.J. shook his head. "No."

"Why not?"

"Because God has been generous with His blessing—and it will take me a while to get used to it. I will not participate in your attempt to mock Him."

"How did you do it, T.J.? Hypnotism?"

"From what I know about hypnotism, the subject has to cooperate. A feller's got to want to be hypnotized. Somehow, I don't think that was your mood." T.J. smiled. "By the way, did you feel any warmth?"

"Warmth?"

"When you touched me."

"No," Kleber lied.

"I always feel the warmth of healing power. Some say it is simply a transfer of cellular energy from my hands to the believer. It's more than that, of course. It's divine. I'll clue you in on one secret if you promise not to print it."

"I don't promise anything. It's all *on* the record."

"It doesn't matter. God won't punish me for telling. I can pass my hand over your body and if there's a tumor or a muscle that doesn't work, I feel absolute cold. It's chilling. That's how I know what people are troubled by, without even having to ask them."

Kleber had a torrent of questions backed up but he was weary. He needed the night to sort out his confusion. Besides, he was on the verge of so alienating T.J. that he might blow whatever chance there was for a television interview. He said good night politely.

"Wait," said T.J. "Don't forget this." He handed Kleber the folder revealing formation of The Right Side. "We have labored on this a very long time. I'm real anxious to have your comments. I think you'll discover we're not dangerous."

Kleber could not resist a snorting noise. "I will indeed read it carefully," he said. "I'll be interested to discover how your lawyers and scholars circumvent that portion of the U. S. Constitution that decrees separation of Church and State."

"The Right Side does not seek to govern, my learned friend. We have but one purpose, to bring back old-fashioned morality. The Constitution does not forbid God's people from voting for candidates who are pro-family, pro-life, and against dangerous humanism."

"My, what delicious code you offer, Grandmother. All the better to fool us with. Pro-family means anti-women's rights. Correct?"

"Wrong. We exalt women."

"Pro-family means against single people living and loving together."

"It means we revere the legal family."

"Pro-family means against homosexuality, which would include at least twenty-five million Americans if Kinsey was right. Shall we execute one tenth of our population?"

"I can heal them and bring them to Christ."

"Come on, T.J. Get off it. How can you set yourself up as a one-man morality board? Something like this can tear this country apart. America was built on diversity of opinion and choice."

"Our purpose is to mend, not to rip."

"Pro-life, I assume, means anti-abortion. Pro-life means that any fourteen-year-old girl who gets raped—does that sound familiar, by the way?—any fourteen-year-old girl who gets raped and consequently pregnant must carry an unwanted fetus full term. Pro-life! Imagine what that does to this young mother's mental well-being. Not to mention the terrific kid she will give certain birth to. . . . And *humanism?* Well, I must admit you got me there. Humanism. That sounds rather desirable."

"Don't mock me, Kleber. You know good and well what humanism means. It is a secular philosophy that denies the existence and power of God. Humanism turns Adam into a monkey and puts *Playboy* magazine on coffee tables in place of the Bible."

Kleber laughed—but not as raucously as he would have wished. "I don't want to swap quotations with you, T.J.," he said. "But a rather good poet named T. S. Eliot defined humanism as the superiority of tolerance and sanity over bigotry and fanaticism."

T.J. picked up his Bible and began to flip the pages. Kleber held up his hands in surrender. "I quit," he said. "You can find justification for just about anything in the Good Book. Which, by the way, is one of the most violent and sexy manuals ever published." He winked and made for the door.

"You forgot the material I asked you to read," called out T.J. "Please do me the courtesy of studying our position before dumping on it. You may be surprised."

"Oh, I'll read it. But I doubt if I'll be surprised. Demagogues have a tendency of sounding pretty much alike."

The telephone rang, the only black instrument in a bank of cream and gray instruments. T.J. frowned. "I must answer that," he said, indicating it to be a private line. "Hello," he said curtly, but immediately his voice softened. "Well, how in the world are *you*, Mrs. Cantrell? Yes, long time no see. . . . Yes. . . . He's here. . . ."

VeeJee? How had she found her son? Kleber took the phone. His mother's voice was fraught with tension. "Kleber, thank God I found you."

"How did you find me, Mama? What's wrong?"

"I tracked you down. I'm as good a detective as you are. Listen, something's going on across the street at Susan's house."

"What?"

"Son, I don't know. Mack's over there. I heard doors slamming and voices shouting. They came out on the front porch and he was holding her arm behind her back. Then they went inside again. It just smells like trouble to me. I thought about calling the police—but the publicity would be terrible."

"Mama, stay right where you are. I'll come over." Kleber hung up quickly and gave T.J. a brief summary. He started to leave.

"I'll go with you," insisted T.J.

"That's unnecessary," said Kleber.

"Perhaps I can help," said T.J. "Sometimes it's miraculous what I can do." He winked and led Kleber to the bottom of the tower where a freshly waxed Mercedes waited. The Chosen dismissed the driver and chauffeured Kleber personally to Cloverdale Avenue. En route, T.J. hummed the class fight song and grew happy and expansive. He also glanced into the rearview mirror now and then, just to make sure Brother Paul was following at a discreet distance.

Hit the mark. All day long and now well into this night, Mack Crawford had tried to find his mark. In movies he never missed the tape on the floor, the place he had to stand in order to be in focus. But here, in the city of his roots, he could not find a definition. He had drunk enough whiskey to burn his gullet, enough vodka so that it dammed his gorge and spilled upward and out his nostrils. Sometime during the day he had heard on the car radio that Mack Crawford was in town, incognito. It seemed important that he remain undetected; he drove about Fort Worth with his cap pulled so far down over his eyes that the world was a narrow slit.

He remembered stopping at a pay telephone and calling Los Angeles. He spoke briefly and unsatisfactorily with Arianna. She said she was busy drawing costume sketches for a movie that would employ three dozen chorines. "Darling, I am trying to bring back the golden days of Hollywood," she told him. "And I simply cannot cope with a sloshed husband in Fort Worth, wherever that is."

"But I wanna talk," pleaded Mack.

"Darling, can't it wait?" She was impatient. "You know our pact. . . ." Never intrude on lives or work.

"I love you. Do you love me?"

"Well, that's a heavy question for seven-twelve on a night when I'm here and you're there."

"Tell me. I need . . . somebody."

"Then, sure. Yes. As best as I can, I love you."

"Tell me again."

"I love you, craziness. Now, let's hang up together."

"How's Molly?"

"Right this minute she's sitting beside the pool with a football player from Encino. If he makes a move, I'm calling the patrol. Now, have fun at the reunion, luv. And say hello to Kleber."

"Why am I here?"

"You tell me when you get home. Are you anywhere near Neiman-Marcus? That's the only landmark in Texas I know. Now, one-two-three." Click. She hung up.

Mack called twice again but got the answering service. It seemed unfair. He had bought and paid for a second wife—and now she would not talk to him. For six years they had endured in a widely publicized marriage, the arrangement useful for both. It no longer drew attention from even the most *au courant* gossips in Hollywood. The lasting union of two sexually unorthodox people was hardly unique in the entertainment business, particularly since Mack and Arianna were individually talented, powerful, and—whatever they did or did *not* do to one another in private—discreet. The trouble was now and then Mack got it in his head that Man and Woman by biological definition did more than banter, pose, and nod in passing; in fact they were supposed to make an occasional clutch and a demand to be held tightly. But Arianna always extricated herself gently and neatly. The line between them was defined, legally contracted, a chasm without bridge. "We're too old for that" was her standard put-down, the translation being "Don't spoil it." Nor was Mack introspective enough to understand that he was clinging to another woman because she was safe. No threat. He could pretend like he wanted love—but there was no danger in a desire unlikely to be fulfilled.

Deep into the tepid darkness of a long night, Mack forgot about Arianna. He threw the latest vodka bottle with all his might, sailing it like a beautifully tossed football across the playing field of Western High, hearing it shatter against a hidden rock in a clump of bushes. He had lost his watch somewhere, which did not matter, for he had no precise sense of time or place. Something kept nagging him; he had an appointment—but he could not remember the purpose. He ran around the cinder track thrice and was entertained briefly by his strength. Then his legs gave out and his lungs hurt and the bile in his throat would not stay swallowed. He stripped off his shirt and tucked it in his trousers because the cloth smelled foul. It seemed important that he keep running because *if* he could finish five laps—that was the bargain he made with himself, five laps—then his head would clear and he would remember what he had to do next. Another half lap was all he made. He pitched forward, sprawled onto the red dust. It hurt! He yelled and cursed his clumsy feet. Then, ahead, on a rise that glimmered in the soft half-moon light, he saw the schoolhouse. *That* was his mark. He knew where he was now and he galloped with shirttail flapping toward the front entrance. The most important task at this blurry moment was to push through the doors of his youth and visit the athletic trophy case outside the principal's office. There was his permanence. The prince desired to visit the gold he had earned and foolishly donated back to the source years ago. He had the right! But the door was locked, and though he banged on it until the glass shattered and the howl of a burglar alarm molested the night, he could not reach his treasure.

A drink. He wanted another drink. Where had he thrown the vodka bottle? As he ran in search of it, he finally remembered the most valuable item on the scavenger hunt. *His son.* Jeffie needed him and he needed Jeffie. How he loved that boy! Maybe the child did not realize the depth of his father's love. The crime of his life, he chided himself, the only genuine moral felony of forty-three years was in seeding a child and then abandoning it except for ferocious binges of extravagant love from long distance. Now he knew. It was a profound realization. Only in a son was a man's real passport to immortality. His motion pictures were ephemeral, existing only in the flickering of ninety-eight minutes required to view them. And he was simply a piece of that fragile whole. Jeffie was the accomplishment by which Mack wished now to be measured.

He ran powerfully to find his boy.

Susan let him in—although she quickly regretted it. Mack was hostile and belligerent, raging over the same ground from the night before. "Mack, honey, please listen to me," she asked. "I don't have Jeff. I don't know where he is."

"I don't believe you," he said threateningly. He found a new bottle of scotch and swigged it like cola.

Calmly, with studied caution, Susan tried to explain. Their son was coming out of a difficult adolescence. Ungifted in scholarship or athletics, Jeff had few friends and among those he was a goat. The pattern continued through several changes of schools. On his sixteenth birthday, the one Mack could not attend, Mack sent in his stead a $6,500 MG sports car in robin's-egg blue. Jeff wrecked his gift within a week. The investigating officer found marijuana in a plastic sandwich bag beneath the front seat. Several times since then Susan had been awakened by post-midnight calls from juvenile officers who requested that she fetch Jeff from the detention center, or from irate parents demanding that she persuade the boy to leave their homes. Mother and son had fought the war of generations epidemic in America. All of this she laid on Mack—finally—but she held back the psychiatrist's opinion of why Jeffie lied and stole and cheated. The shrink had told her the boy was "unable to compete with the powerful image of his father" and that he "lacked a stable masculine identity." Mack did not even know Jeffie had been in analysis; Susan had managed to pay $1,000 in therapy bills by shaving it from child support. Nor did she tell Mack what would surely wound him deeply, that Jeff had taken to using his mother's maiden name, French. He refused to write down "Crawford" on school registration forms.

No man enjoys being told that his son is a disaster, particularly when circumstances have forced that man to entrust care and upbringing to a faraway ex-wife. Besides, Mack wrote the checks—no one could accuse him of failing to meet his financial responsibilities. Not a year had passed without him shoveling a good $50,000 to Fort Worth to support Susan and the boy. That meant close to three quarters of a million dollars in seventeen years, a sum that had purchased meager portions of love and filial respect.

"But why didn't you tell me all this earlier?" demanded Mack, sobering quickly.

"I tried . . . you always seemed so busy."

"Too busy for my son?" Mack was hurt by the accusation, hurt because he knew it was true.

With that, the tenuous bond of civility and good manners broke. The night turned ugly. Mack accused Susan of being too busy chasing men to look after his son, which she found painfully ironic. George Parsons, who was evicted by celebrity the night before, had been her first date in months. Men were reluctant to ask out a woman whose ex-husband was a magazine cover fantasy. Who wanted to compete?

Susan reached for the telephone and threatened to call police. Mack slapped the receiver from her hands. She tried to run out the door but Mack grabbed her and started yelling. From across the street, VeeJee Cantrell heard the ruckus.

Finally, well past midnight, there came an urgent knock at the door. And a familiar voice. "Mack? Wanna come out and play? It's Kleber."

From within came muffled sounds. A chair was knocked over. Glass broke. Kleber worried that this was about to become journalism's cliché headline—deranged loser/lover holding hostage and defying authority. He had covered a score of these melancholy melodramas and they tended to end in a mess. Usually some wretched fool blew his head off just as police broke down the door. Kleber called out again, trying to put fellowship and humor in his voice. He got back nothing. Then he despaired of a truce and whispered to T.J. "Run over to Mama's and call the cops. Don't tell 'em it's Mack inside. Just say there's a domestic quarrel or a prowler or something. Just tell 'em to hurry."

The Chosen shook his head. "That won't be necessary," he said. He strode to the front door and almost blew it down. "McKenzie!" he cried. "We're waiting for you."

It was another miracle. Meek as a lamb, the Prince of Charms unbolted the door, turned Susan loose, and walked like a prodigal son toward T.J.'s outstretched handshake. The night changed character once again. The mean spirits were gone. Susan stood on the front steps and found herself calling out maternally, "You boys be careful, hear?"

"Yes, ma'm," smiled Kleber.

There was one thing left for her to say. "Mack, I love you. Don't ever forget it."

Mack stopped and spun around. "Sorry about tonight. All in all, we haven't had such a bad run, have we, hon?" He grinned boyishly—and touched her heart.

"Wouldn't swap a minute," said Susan. But as she watched the preacher and the writer deposit the actor into the black Mercedes, losing sight of them because the windows were darkened to protect the famous from the eyes of commoners, Susan shivered from a sudden intrusion of cold night air—and from the fingers of inexplicable fear that danced across her flesh.

CHAPTER TWENTY-SEVEN

Finally, some peace.

Comforted by the dark, leathery lap of Mercedes-Benz, Mack fell into a whiskey sleep, sagging onto Kleber's shoulder like an oversized child at the end of a long park day. Kleber scarcely felt the burden because his own head ached from the cross fire of personal events. The last few hours had been like a fast afternoon on the Houston newspaper when the city went berserk. He considered his personal headlines:

- **JOURNALIST UNMASKED AND RIDICULED AT CITY OF MIRACLES**
- **THE RIGHT SIDE REVEALED**
- **YOUTH ALLEGEDLY BROUGHT BACK FROM NARCOTIC DEATH**
- **THE CHOSEN GETS NEW EYES**
- **FAMOUS ACTOR HAS UNPLEASANT REUNION WITH EX-WIFE**
- **THE THREE OF US TOGETHER AT LAST AND WE ARE STRANGERS**

He cracked the window and welcomed the night air to bathe his face. They were on a back road somewhere, clipping along a stretch of velvety black farmland. The smell of spring was in the air, of newly turned earth, of renewal. Fort Worth had disappeared behind them, the city lights pulsating weakly.

Mack roused. "Where the hell are we?" he asked.

"You wanted coffee," answered T.J. "I know a good place."

Mack had another question. "Whatever happened to that jeep, T.J.?"

The Chosen laughed softly. "It burned. There was a time when my life was on fire."

Kleber said it was time to go home. He was tired and so was the night.

"Patience," asked T.J. "We're almost there." Presently he stopped the car on a crunchy bed of gravel and stabbed the Mercedes head-lights onto high beam. Ahead, the strong shafts picked up detritus that gleamed benign and silvery beneath the moon . . . a sway-backed tool shed choked by grapevines and buglers . . . a jumble of rusted toys . . . an overturned wagon . . . and a farmhouse that looked as if a gi-ant's fist had smashed the roof.

It was Uncle Bun's house, keeper of the secrets. Everything in our world has changed but this, realized Kleber. The darkest corner of a soul remains constant, like a poisoned piece of earth on which nothing new can ever grow. He felt wary and exhausted. Whatever mischief was portended, Kleber wanted no part of it. "Take us home," he demanded. But T.J. was already out the door, walking purposefully toward the acrid memory. Then Mack connected with the awful place and without being bidden climbed out and followed The Chosen. The reporter had no choice but to tag along. Somehow he knew a story was about to un-fold. There were still blank pages in his notebook.

It was not an impulsive stop. T.J. had prepared the chamber for guests. A fire of pungent cedar and peach wood leapt obediently at first match. Harem pillows had been tossed before the hearth, waiting sensuously for occupants. A flat straw mat was on the floor and on it was a cornucopia of fresh fruit—mirror-sheen apples, plump grapes from the pantry of Bacchus. From somewhere materialized bottles of cold frosted mineral water and a thermos of steaming coffee. Kleber glanced around for a servant. He fully expected to be asked his choice of cock-tails. But they were the only people in the room, the three middle-aged princes. The most attentive of hosts, T.J. busied himself plumping pil-lows, feeding the fire, pouring coffee, offering fruit, his face glowing but his eyes still hidden by dark glasses. The mask reminded Kleber of the odd and troubling "miracle" that broke up the sanctuary. It had rested like an unswallowable crumb in Kleber's throat but he had ignored it during the crisis at Susan's house. Now he remembered.

"Take off those glasses, T.J." he suggested. "Nobody's going to ask for your autograph."

"Later. Perhaps," answered The Chosen. He sat before the fire and leaned against a four-foot-square pillow covered with lime-and-crimson cloth from India. On the fabric were block-printed lotus blossoms which Kleber knew to be the Buddhist symbol for cause and effect. They also bloom from out of a swamp—ironies that Kleber wondered whether T.J. shared.

The glory of midnight fire was kind to all of the men, but in the becoming light Mack was impossibly handsome. A quarter of a century had thinned his hair and deposited cobwebs below his eyes. But the ancient scar from his football injury resembled only the afterthought of a sculptor whose classic warrior required one flaw to make it human. With tears not yet fully dried in his huge blue eyes, with whiskey pounding in his temple veins, with a two-day growth of silver-sand beard, even with a shirt collar flecked with vomit, the Prince of Charms, at forty-three, got Kleber's vote as the single male on earth who should be preserved for testament to the splendor of physical beauty. Kleber had looked forward to a class reunion photograph with Mack, one that he could hang on his wall, but now he knew he would not be happy posed next to a man whom time had barely nicked.

Mack seemed unaware the others were looking at him. "God, I must have thought about this shit hole a thousand times," he murmured, glancing about the shack. "I think I even tried to buy it once. Just so I could burn it down." He spoke clearly, despite the heroic intake of spirits. Kleber was reminded of their youth, of how quickly somebody sobered up when dumped on the lawn of a parent. Mack was now in focus and unimpeded.

"I always kept this house," said T.J. "For a long time it was my anchor." He stood up abruptly. "Come," he said. "Let me show you something." The preacher led them into the other room, into the voyeur's squalid nest, and by flashlight Kleber noticed immediately that the knothole was still there. T.J. gestured toward a rubble of food cans —chili con carne, beans, fruit cocktail, creamed corn—piled in a corner, tops opened and dangling like soles separated from old shoes.

Behind them was a long row of neatly placed whiskey bottles, a myriad of brands but all in the category of rotgut, stretching into darkness like forgotten toy soldiers.

"Remember that time when Kennedy died?" asked T.J. of Kleber.

"*Which* Kennedy?" asked the reporter mordantly, as he always did, having covered the murders of both brothers.

"Jack. Don't you recall me bumping into you at Oswald's funeral?"

Mack interrupted. "I never knew you wrote that up," he said.

Kleber nodded. "I must tell you sometime. It's my best set piece. Takes a good bottle of wine and an hour to get through." And as soon as he spoke he wondered why he was gilding his lily. Why was he bragging in front of them? Kleber said, "Yeah, T.J. I remember." How could anybody forget the specter of a madman stumbling across the autumn graves? At the time he had seriously considered reporting the assault to Dallas police, but, mindful of the poke he intended to take at their bungling of the Oswald matter, decided his complaint would not be regarded as worth investigating.

"I was living out here then," continued T.J. "I ate food from those cans and drank every drop in those bottles." He laughed. "After I was saved, I spent three days and nights down on my knees confessing to God just what happened to me in 1963 alone."

"You must have been a bad boy," said Mack.

"Bad is a hollow word," said T.J. He ushered his company back to the fireplace. There he filled his mouth with grapes and continued to talk, ripe red juice spilling from the corners of his lips. Good manners, noted Kleber, did not come automatically to the owner of a Mercedes and a tower of miracles. "I was evil. I did things that neither of you could imagine."

"Oh, I expect we could," said Kleber. "Considering the die was pretty well cast twenty-five years ago."

"No, my friend. Believe me. Not you, you with your eyes that have seen the atrocities of war and the cruelties of man . . ." He turned his gaze from Kleber and leveled on Mack. "Not you, my other friend, you who have spoken and acted the most violent of fantasies. Neither of you could ever know or understand what happened to me when I was in the grip of Satan . . ."

Quickly Mack rocketed a look over to Kleber that said: *Is He Serious?* And Kleber shrugged back: *I Think So.*

"I suspect you're wondering why I brought us here . . . to this place . . . tonight," continued T.J. "The answer is simple. I am obeying the will of God. He commanded me to assemble the three of us. . . . I could have told you this afternoon, Kleber, where we would all be at a quarter past one in the morning."

Kleber was not ready for a new headline. He had too many unwritten stories backed up already. "What happened at the church meeting tonight? What did you do to the boy who overdosed?"

"What boy?" asked Mack.

Kleber shushed him. "Answer me, T.J."

The Chosen only smiled.

"Dammit, T.J., you really shook me up there for a minute," said Kleber. He explained for Mack. "Foxy T.J. here planted a shill in the audience. Some kid holding his breath and playing dead."

The Chosen smiled patiently. "It *is* difficult to believe. I fought a long time before I surrendered."

"I think we should call it a night," said Kleber.

"Yeah. Me, too," echoed Mack. "I'm jet-lagged. Will somebody tell me why the hell I came home? I'm glad to see you guys . . . but I've got forty scripts to read."

"Please, dear friends," said T.J., bidding them to sit again. "Give me the moment. I've waited for it a long, long time. It's important to me. First of all, let me say how proud I am of you. The prophecies of 1950 are fulfilled. Kleber was and is the Boy Most Likely to Succeed. Your career brings honor to your name and to our generation." He reached over and pumped Kleber's hand like a general bestowing medals. And Kleber, despite himself, enjoyed the tribute.

"Mack? Mack Crawford, Most Handsome Senior, Best All-Around Athlete. I've enjoyed your work so much. That last movie of yours, the one where you leaped off the cliff and landed on the little tan horse and jumped him across that gorge. Whoee! I was on the edge of my seat."

"My double did it," said Mack. "The insurance company wouldn't let me take a pratfall."

"Whatever, old friend, you epitomize the good in American character. We need heroes who stand up for what they believe."

It occurred to Kleber suddenly that this was a fishing expedition, that maybe T.J. needed a tad of ego stroking. If a compliment would end the night, then give him one quick. "The Most Popular Boy did right well for himself, too, I'd say, judging from the delirium I saw at your church house tonight. They don't act that way for the Pope."

"Ah, but you must understand," said T.J. "They are not praising *me;* they are worshipping God."

"That's a pretty sophisticated sip of the holy water," said Kleber.

The Chosen had more to show and tell. He plucked a beautifully formed apple from the basket and held it before the firelight. It glistened like a huge ruby in his finely manicured hands. His fingers were soft and creamed, as if he had never spaded a clod of earth. Slowly the preacher rotated the apple, drawing attention like a magician preparing an illusion. "How perfect is God's creation," he said softly.

"Are you going to play serpent in the Garden of Eden?" asked Mack.

"Close," replied T.J. He slipped his thumb down from the apple's middle and revealed a muddy, mushy chunk of rot. Below that was another greenish-brown blemish. The fruit was no longer appealing. It was foul and wormy. "When we first looked at this apple, we saw only beauty and desire," intoned The Chosen. "But close examination revealed the putrid secrets."

Kleber laughed coarsely. "Please spare us the hoary old rotten-apple-in-the-barrel sermon, for God's sake."

"Grant me the metaphor—*for God's sake,*" said T.J. "I'm talking about *men.*"

"All right," agreed Kleber. "But what if you looked at the rotten part first? It'd be offensive. You'd pass right by that apple."

T.J. nodded, as pleased as a teacher whose class of dunces finally comprehended fractions. "Precisely. And journalists do tend to search for the bad part, don't they?"

"With most people, it's not too difficult to locate," said Kleber pointedly.

"Gimme that fuckin' apple," demanded Mack. He caught the underarm lateral from T.J., squeezed the Winesap silly in his massive hand, tossed the pulp into the fire. Apple, having assumed a personality by now, twitched and bled like a martyr in the flames. Tortured by blisters and blackening, soon it was a sorry corpse.

"Fire and brimstone," observed Kleber. "Simplistic, Reverend, but amusing. Have you made your point? If I agree that I'm going to hell, can we go home now?"

"But Mack destroyed the apple, not you," said T.J. "Why did you do that, Mack?"

"Haven't the foggiest idea, pardner," said Mack. "I'm not a method actor. I don't analyze the script. I just play the impulses."

With what could pass for tenderest understanding, T.J. nodded. Then he bowed his head in prayer. Awkward silence fell across the room and lingered. Kleber glanced over at Mack with the elevated eyebrows of a rational man forced to endure lunacy. But the actor was not offended by the preacher's show of faith. Indeed, Mack seemed intrigued. Kleber could not believe that Mack was falling for a carnie's pitch. The whiskey must be reborn.

"I believe," whispered T.J. from the prayer position, "that God is offering us an opportunity. I believe that the three of us—we who were children together, we who were princes as young men, we who found celebrity in our separate ways, we whom the world views as perfect apples—we have the chance tonight to cut out the rotted parts. We have not been together for twenty-five years but we have endured. Survival is not enough. God says that none of the lives in this room is worthy of paradise. Not yet. Not until we wash our souls and confess."

"Confess what?" demanded Kleber.

"Confess what needs to be confessed. Until the door to the past is closed, the door to the future cannot open." He flung out his arms and swept the four corners of the room. "I believe we are shaped and scarred by what happened here *that night*. I want you to hear the penalties I have paid." He filled the better part of an absorbing hour with a tale unimagined by Kleber or unacted by Mack. T.J. bared his hurt over rejection by the others after graduation, his swindles, the tragedies of Peavine and Magda, of Bun and Spike, of Missy and Priscilla, of Marge and Bamboozle, of Mash, of blood and money and sorrow. He re-created the miracle of Tarrant County jail, of his rapid rise to celebrity in the pulpit. And then he whipped away his glasses and showed them his eyes. In the faint flicker of firelight, they were welled with tears but the flesh that ringed them was whole and clean. Kleber's miracle was holding.

"There's a little bit more, my friends," he said. "I *must* tell it all. I want you both to know that for many years I harbored the most bitter hate. I wanted to hurt you that night at the Assembly Ball, Mack, the night when you smashed me down. And I thought about shooting you the day they buried Oswald, Kleber. I really did."

"Good Lord," said Kleber. "There must be forty movies in your life, T.J. How much of this is bullshit?"

"None of it and all of it," he answered. "But I sure feel better for finally showing you the rotten parts."

"Amen and farewell then," said Kleber, wanting to rush to the nearest typewriter and commit the Prince of Temptation's biography to paper. He made for the door.

"Why did you tell us that?" asked Mack. "I don't understand."

"I need to know if I am the only one who suffered. Do you have anything to share with us? Kleber?"

"Don't think so," the reporter said. "My life is quite boring compared to the Jacobean drama just unfolded. I've never even killed anybody."

"Never?" said T.J. "There was a girl. . . . Have we forgotten her?"

Kleber connected. He was outraged. "Fuck that," he said. "I may carry around a general load of guilt—but Laurie's not part of it." He stared down at the warped rough boards before the hearth, where all of them had fallen onto the girl that distant midnight. How clear were the images! Rain-washed hair, dog-damp pink dress, pale green cameo ring —a long-nosed queen sparking in the flares of youth. He laughed. "Here's *my* confession, Brother Luther. I never laid a cock on poor little Laurie that night. I popped off pre-penetration, as it were. Oh, I wanted to fuck her—just to impress you bastards. But I didn't know how."

"I think we tell ourselves stories," said T.J. "We become men and we tuck ourselves into bed at night with stories suited to fight our fears."

"I don't need that, T.J. I'm not making up stories. There's no need to. I deal in fact."

"Then why are you so riled, old friend? One little shove from a quarter century ago and you start smoking from every orifice."

"I'm going to walk home, Reverend. Mack? Had enough?"

The actor looked blankly at the writer and shook his head. "I wouldn't mind getting a few things off my chest," said Mack. "I used to pay a shrink sixty dollars an hour just to listen. Don't think he did me much good. Don't think he even liked me."

"God listens for free," said T.J.

Kleber had a smart-ass remark about collection plates but he left it unsaid. Obviously Mack wanted to talk. "I'm not very good at discussing myself," he began. "Remember, K., remember a long time ago when you asked me what it was like to be a celebrity? I think I know now. But first I've got to back up. The thing is, a man spends the first part of his life, the early years, building an identity. You sort out what works for you and what doesn't. You lift weights and read books and look for friends who'll tolerate you. You go to work and count money and dream of something better. In other words, you become *you*. Good parts, bad, scabs, scars, laughs, lies, you form a man . . ." He stopped and grimaced in embarrassment. "Confession's hard," he said. "I can't find the mark."

"Go on," urged T.J. "We're with you. This is the most important speech you've ever spoken."

"My point is, somewhere along the line I lost control of *me*. Other forces took over."

"No man is an island," said Kleber, "if I can borrow from John Donne."

"The point is, I never much liked what I was or *who* I was. . . . Remember my football accident? It wasn't an accident, sports fans. Mack broke his bones on purpose."

"But why?" asked T.J. "God gave you the most magnificent of bodies."

"Yeah. Suppose so. Somebody did. I guess it's mine." Mack pinched his thighs to see if anybody was home. Then he shrugged and quit talking.

"With all due respects, Mr. Crawford," said Kleber, "that's not much of a confession. You ran into the goalposts. Big deal. Hardly worth a footnote in the history of contemporary man."

Thus prodded, Mack told more. "But I did the right thing. I broke my own body—it was my choice—and it felt absolutely fitting. After that, I was accommodating just fine to being an invalid. Then Susan turns up in my bedroom one morning and one thing leads to another—and *wham!*—I became a lot of new people I never intended to be. Husband. Father. Actor. Wait, make that *star*. I was a star before I was an actor. You tell me this, how do you handle the news that they're showing 'Knights of New York' all over the world, that the most favored name for male babies in certain African countries is Mack? Are you ready for that? I've got a tribe of namesakes in the heart of Africa. Why don't they name their kids after somebody worthy like Schweitzer or Lumumba? People stare at some old cracked black-and-white television films of some not very capable actor playing a fake cop—and they brand their children with my identity."

"I saw a billboard of you once in Bangkok," said Kleber. "You were stretched out about as long as a city block. You looked like a poster for Hitler Youth."

Mack smiled. "'Tweren't me, McGee. That's the good part of the apple, the side they spray red with chemicals and make shine with lacquer. The one the merchants stack at the top of the pile as a come-on. Oh, there's certainly some schizophrenia here. I'm supposed to be a great lover. I'm in truth a fool who sells love. I haven't the least notion of what love is. . . . Okay, that's a wrap. Thanks for staying awake. I almost fell asleep talking about myself." Looking hugely embarrassed, Mack gestured at Kleber that it was time to leave.

T.J. rushed an arm about the actor's shoulders. "God loves you, Mack. And so do I. Will you pray with me?"

"Pray for *what?*"

"I was hoping that all three of us could pray for forgiveness, for the tragedy of that night . . . of what we did in this house . . ."

Mack squirmed away. "What the hell are you talking about, Luther? Forgive *what?*"

"All right. I'll confess alone. I am deeply shamed by what we did to Laurie that night in the storm."

Mack laughed nervously. "I didn't lay a hand on her. I didn't even get a hard-on, Reverend. Which is the story of my life."

"But we must *share* the guilt," insisted T.J. "We've carried poison in our covenant for twenty-five years."

Mack motioned to Kleber. "Didn't you *ever* tell T.J. about that guy in San Antonio? The one who confessed to killing her?"

"What *guy?*" asked T.J., suddenly disoriented. "What are you talking about?"

"I guess I forgot to," said Kleber impishly, "or maybe I thought you wouldn't care." He hastily improvised a fragile excuse of having intended to mail T.J. the curious AP clipping concerning Butch's admission. Alas, he could not locate T.J.'s address at the time.

The Reverend Luther was stunned. He put his hand over his heart. "That sorta made me odd man out, didn't it?" he said.

"Did it really affect your life?" asked Kleber. "Would it have changed anything?"

"I *was* entitled to know," said T.J.

Mack took the preacher's side. "He was, Kleber. You should have told him."

Even now, Kleber felt no remorse at the oversight. All he did was quote Scott Fitzgerald, "Forgotten is forgiven."

"We had a covenant. We promised to keep the secret and be like blood brothers," said T.J.

"We were kids," said Kleber.

"How much of your life is a fraud?" demanded T.J. "If you betray your friends, then where does it stop?"

"No more sermons. Please. Mack said it was a wrap." Kleber was not seriously wounded over the transfer of guilt to his shoulders. But he knew now that he would not get The Chosen in his hot seat for an interview. Not this trip. It didn't matter. What could take its place was something far more valuable. A book. The seed was beginning to germinate. He might not get another chance to probe The Chosen. Kleber pushed the preacher one more time. "All of this has been very entertaining, T.J." he began. "But somehow I think we've been sidestepping the reason you brought us here. There's been a lot of talk about truth and honesty, Reverend. I don't think you were after confessions. I think you planned this little reunion very carefully. I think you had something else in mind. What's the real heart of this matter?"

"Nothing."

"Oh, come on. The party's spoiled. Show us the light."

T.J. chewed on this a minute, his eyes narrowed and his jaw clenched. "Why not?" he muttered. Whereupon The Chosen went outside and stayed several minutes. In the interim Kleber thought he heard subdued voices, whispers, but he passed it off as the stirrings of a midnight wind. Besides, the place was as spooky tonight as it ever was. When The Chosen returned, he was wearing a trench coat, an article of clothing that seemed unnecessary. It was neither cold nor wet. He carried an expensive-looking snakeskin briefcase from which he extricated two thick folders and distributed them to the writer and the actor. Kleber scanned his quickly. It appeared to be a high-powered public relations pitch for a $2 million "Miracle Media Center." The pages were larded with wholesome youngsters operating TV cameras, sitting before computer word processors, working in photographic darkrooms. Each kid had carefully combed hair, straight teeth, and polished shoes. Captions beneath them revealed that "hundreds" of "deserving" young people were in sore need of funds for "Christian education and training in the mass-media skills."

"I don't have to tell either one of you that the real power in our world today is information," said T.J. "We're going to build a great showplace of communications. Mack, you'll be asked to star in clean, decent motion pictures about moral men. Kleber, you could hold seminars teaching our young people how to gather and write news stories."

Kleber was not paying attention. He was staggered by what was appended to his brochure by a gold-plated paper clip. It was a bank draft, made out to "The City of Miracles." It was drawn on his bank in New York. It bore his coded account number. All it lacked was his signature. It was already made out for $500,000. Kleber glanced at Mack. He got one, too.

"Holy shit," said Kleber, bursting out in laughter.

"I don't want to be presumptuous," hastily said T.J. "I'm only doing what God tells me to do. God has blessed the two of you beyond the scope of normal man. God has created your celebrity. God has given you great rewards. Now it is your responsibility to share your good fortune with God."

Kleber sat down on the floor and enjoyed laughter. The Miracle Man was selling encyclopedias again—and just as clumsily. Hustlers who tried to hawk freshly minted "antiques" at the foot of Giza Pyramid were more clever, and less dangerous, con men. Whores who aged twenty years by dawn's first light were more genuine than The Chosen.

But Mack saw the darker meaning. "I believe we're being blackmailed, K.," he said, possessed with a role he could play, Hero Imperiled. "You cheesy little bastard." He started to tear the bank draft in half, but Kleber took it from him.

"Wait, my brothers," stammered T.J. with tinny laughter. "I wasn't even going to bring this up tonight. Not until Kleber forced me. Besides, you wouldn't have to pay it all at once. You could spread your donation over five years. Ten. Whatever is most beneficial, tax-wise . . ."

"How about a dollar a year for the next five hundred millennia?" suggested Kleber. He put the two drafts in his jacket.

"Give those back to me," requested T.J.

Kleber shook his head. "I think I'll keep a couple of souvenirs," he said. "The Other Side, which is my side, might enjoy a glimpse into fundamentalist extortion."

"I wouldn't do that, brother," cautioned The Chosen. "I would have to respond from the pulpit."

"Respond? Then make sure you tell it all, T.J. Tell the flock how you raped a minor child one rainy night in 1950. Tell them how you urged your two best friends to, quoting you precisely, 'dip your bread in that gravy while it's still hot.' Tell them you waited twenty-five years to say *'I'm sorry, Laurie.'* And don't forget to point out how you tried to squeeze half a million hush-a-bye bucks each out of your two 'best' friends. Here's one final confession from the heart. I've hated your ass since God knows when. The next time you're on heavenly long-distance, ask the old boy. He'll confirm it."

Then Mack cut in sharply. "Hey." He thumped the glossy brochure and stabbed his finger against one of the happy student lineups. "Who is this?" asked Mack. It sounded like the kind of question for which he did not really want an answer.

T.J. nodded.

"What are you guys talking about?" demanded Kleber.

Mack stared at the picture soundlessly for a very long time. Then he raised his eyes at T.J. Fury was in them. "What is my son doing in this shit?" he said.

"We're so very proud of him," answered T.J.

"Answer me again, Luther," said Mack. "Answer me clear and clean. If there's one drop of bullshit in what you say next, there's a very strong likelihood I'll kick your face to hell. *What is Jeffie doing in this photograph?*"

T.J. raised his hands in half prayer. "He's one of our greatest miracles, Mack. The boy came to us half dead from narcotics. He had so much despair and hate in him that he spit in my face. He didn't tell us his name for three months. But we expelled his demons. Be proud of him, Mack. He is a mighty warrior of God. He is a tribute to his father."

"Does Susan know about this?" demanded Mack.

"I don't really know. I imagine so."

"Where is he?"

"He lives on campus. He's a remarkable young man."

Kleber was frantically scanning his own brochure. He scrooched under Mack's arm and saw where the actor's finger was frozen. Paul! The smuggest of the Nehru jackets. The little prick who tailed him all day. In the photograph, Jeffie/Paul had a lockjaw smile and an aura of brainwash so thick that all the deprogrammers extant could not break through it.

Kleber saw the fist that Mack's right hand had become and he assumed it would next smash—with good cause—into preacher man's newly healed eyes. But Mack only said, between clenched teeth, "Gimme the car keys, T.J. I'm going to get my son."

T.J. shook his head, taking a step back and blocking the waning fire. Now it was the setting for a proper Prince of Temptation. The preacher loomed in silhouette. He put his dark glasses on again. "I simply can't allow that."

"The *keys.*"

"He doesn't want you anymore," said T.J.

"How the fuck do you know what my son wants?" hissed Mack. Clearly he was ready to wreck the room and everyone in it.

"Because he knows about you, Mack. He knows *everything.*"

"Which means?"

"Don't force me, Mack. Take my word."

"Piss on your word, Luther. *What* does Jeffie know?"

"He isn't called that anymore. He denies the name you gave him."

Mack crashed clumsily across the room and tried to grab the man who stole his child. But a new voice interrupted him. It came from the doorway where a tall, slender, troubled boy was standing. "Daddy, *don't!*"

Mack whirled about gracefully and saw his son. Love flooded his face. "Jeffie!" he cried, holding out his arms. But the boy did not fill them. Kleber wanted to smack the ungrateful little bastard.

Similarly, T.J. was irritated. "Paul, I told you to leave us. Everything is all right."

"I'm sorry I disobeyed, Chosen," answered the boy. "But I just couldn't let you be threatened."

"What is this Paul shit?" demanded Mack.

"Paul is my new name," said the boy proudly. "I chose it from the Bible, in honor of another man who changed his life."

Mack tried to be pleasant and composed, although Kleber saw the hurt. "That's okay, son, a lot of people change their names. Actors do it all the time. Jeffie, come give me a kiss. I came all the way just to see you."

The boy took a step sideways, toward The Chosen. "I don't belong to you anymore," he said coldly. "A man must be born twice—the first of the flesh, for which I am grateful. But the second is in the spirit of God, and this is my new earth father." He made obeisance to The Chosen.

"That's insane," cried Mack, face white with fear and threatened loss. He grabbed his son and hugged him fiercely. Paul struggled to get loose but he could not free himself of the two powerful arms wrapped about him.

"Let him go, Mack," ordered T.J. "That's why he came to me in the first place."

"I know the perversion of your life," said the boy tauntingly. "I know the mockery of your marriage. I know what you did to Mama. If you don't let me go, The Chosen will tell the truth about you."

Mack then did what Kleber adjudged to be eminently appropriate. Still holding his son under one arm, he sprang forth and tried to grab The Chosen's smug red neck with the other. But the preacher saw it coming, ducked, slipped sideways. Mack crashed against the hearth. His head collided with a jutting brick. When he struggled up, dazed, blood was drenching his beauty, pouring from a savage gash on his forehead. He seized his son again, tucked him under his armpit, and dived once more. Missed. Smacked against the wall and shattered the peephole board. Kleber yelled, trying to stop the madness.

But Mack was fighting demons now. He made one last assault. He held his son and he limped painfully toward the man who had abducted him. "You cheap little cocksucker," he hissed. "You fucking fraud!" This time the huge, bleeding man connected with a right cross to The Chosen's cheek, a force so powerful that bits of flesh splattered from beneath T.J.'s eye.

He drew back for another punch but he didn't get to throw it. T. J. Luther calmly withdrew a .44 Magnum from his raincoat pocket, gripped it with two expert hands, crouched, and warned, "Stop it, Mack."

Mack, stunned, let go of his son and yelled, "Run, boy. Run!" Then he sprang for the weapon. He seized T.J.'s arm and the two men wrestled for control. "Shoot him!" screamed the boy. Mack cocked his fist and the gun fired. Whose finger was on the trigger did not matter. The bullet tore a great hole in the world's most desired face. A bloody, jagged crater appeared magically from just below the forehead to the cleft in the chin. His brain was sprayed out the back of his skull in a shower that rained against the wall. Part of Mack's flesh fell wet onto

Kleber's cheek. Reaching for his lost son, Mack Crawford, who had no more face, fell dead.

Kleber did not remember much of the rest, only fragments that woke him like blades in the nights thereafter. It never became a complete story, one that he could frame in the boundaries of journalism. He remembered hurting, a white-hot pain that he at first mistook for fear and panic in his heart. He was in shock, running out the farmhouse door like a coward. He saw the Mercedes ahead. He was almost at the automobile's door when, behind him, somebody, Paul maybe, yelled, "Stop!" He managed but another step or two, for his feet were heavy, as if encased in lead. Then he crumpled, too weary to cry. He waited for the next bullet, prepared to die. There was no need of a second shot. He was already hit. Part of the same slug that plowed through Mack's head had torn into the writer's neck. Blood was pouring from his throat as he accepted the total blackness.

The Chosen sent the boy away on foot, commanding him not to tell a word of this awful night. "No one will ever know you were here," said the minister. "Go to our retreat in Big Bend and stay there until I send for you." The boy nodded, too stunned to weep. He ran into the night without looking back. When the deputies came, T.J. had collected the two fallen princes, had placed them side by side, was keening and praying for their souls.

He said it was an accident. He said Mack had been drunkenly showing off with the Magnum, the kind he had used in one of his movies. He said the actor was waving it around like a wild man. The Chosen said he got worried and tried to take the pistol away from the actor. Somehow it fired—and the bullet passed through the actor's face and into the writer's throat. Two for the price of one. It was a risky alibi, but T.J. guessed—incorrectly, as it turned out—that Kleber was just as dead as Mack and could tell no more tales.

On the ride to the Tarrant County courthouse, The Chosen attended to one other pressing matter of business. Since he was not handcuffed, out of respect for his calling, T.J. managed to remove, without notice, the excellent cosmetic eye bags and contact lenses. When photographers took his picture during the booking process, The Chosen stared back at the world with eyes ravaged red, awash with grief and tears, scarred irreparably by long ago acid.

It was indeed miraculous what Sister Crystal could accomplish with her makeup kit. Thank the Lord she had studied cosmetology at the loony bin. As soon as he got out of this, The Chosen would find a way to show his thanks.

CHAPTER TWENTY-EIGHT

Sept. 18, 1975
M. D. Anderson Hospital
Houston, Texas

Dear Kleber:

Listen, you little punk, I'm pulling for you. I'd give two-thirds of the one lung I've got left to be there for the trial. Alas, I'm the prisoner of a diesel dyke nurse named Claude who gives enemas with exceptional glee.

Son, I don't rightly know what to tell you. The TV says you're deaf and dumb—but somehow I doubt it. There must be some strong currents in the river that we don't know about. What I *do* know—God damn I'd kill Claude for a cigaret—is that you're sitting on the best story of the 20th Century.

And if you don't write it for me—and quick, son—I'll be waiting with the sharpest pitchfork on both banks of River Styx.

Short takes, kid. Just tell the fuckin' story.

Love, Casey

P.S. Guess you heard Millie died. Meanness, probably. She was 84—and just as proud of you as me.

Sept. 25, 1975
In Custody of the District Attorney
Fort Worth

Dear Case:

Thanks for your letter. Sorry, but I'll have to make this reply up in my head for the time being. As soon as the world turns, if it ever does, maybe I can put real words to real paper. Case, before I go any further in this imaginary note, let me thank your black Irish ass one more time. Everything I am today I owe to you. You're the only guy who ever took the time to teach me how to write. Line by line. Paragraph A flowing into Paragraph B.

I wish you were here to write up this insane circus. Me, I feel like one of those six blind men touching the elephant for the first time and asked to describe it. From my point of view, everything's an asshole.

I've somehow wandered into that dream story you used to fantasize—and I can't write it. Not for now. Probably never. For deep and personal and profound reasons, I've chosen to present myself to the court as somebody whose senses have taken leave of him.

You told me once that the man who can communicate is the man who has power. Wrong, Case. Journalism is a body count. My life is a traffic jam of corpses. They killed Kennedy and Mack and they killed my feeling.

The Chosen is evil—and I don't think he even knows it. I guess he's a metaphor for the dark side of all of us. God is the new celebrity.

You want to know what's truly bananas? I doubt if Sledge can convict T.J. The case is meager. Even if I told everything I know, Otto Leo would pulverize me on cross-examination. He would shatter my life, my work, and those I love. Nor will I permit him to use me as a club to destroy what reputation Mack has left. Mack suffered enough. May he sleep in peace and may we remember him through his films. He was a kind man and there aren't too many of them.

No, I'm not going to tell a word. I'm just going to watch—and listen—and think. Down the line somewhere, maybe I can locate some words.

Short takes! Short takes! That's what you yelled at me. Just turn the page. That's what life is made up of, Case. Short takes and turn the page.

Your friend and disciple—K.

In 1975, the year in which Mack Crawford was shot to death and Kleber Cantrell was critically wounded, there existed in America 1,972 daily newspapers, 2,819 radio stations, and 711 television stations. The business of communication had become an empire that exerted more power on its subjects than presidents, archbishops, parents, and neighbors. On the third Sunday of September, every purveyor of news in America and in much of the civilized world devoted inordinate time and space to the trial in Fort Worth that would commence on Monday. "60 Minutes" doubled to 120 for the occasion. NBC cleared three hours of prime time. The New York *Times Magazine* devoted twelve full pages to the observations of great detectives from literature, fanciful and clever speculations as if written by Conan Doyle, Agatha Christie, and Dashiell Hammett. London oddsmakers quoted five to three on The Chosen's acquittal. Las Vegas said pick 'em.

The media covered the eve of State of Texas vs. Thomas Jeremiah Luther, AKA The Chosen, as exhaustively as mortal steps on lunar sand. In Beverly Hills, correspondents fought with one another over the right to stand in front of the ornate wrought-iron gates that electronically guarded the entrance to Mack Crawford's estate. They interviewed the sobbing delegations of fans and, after that, had little to talk about. They sounded like real estate salesmen: "The mansion has twenty-eight rooms, Olympic-size pool, lighted tennis court, six fireplaces, an indoor gymnasium where Mack worked out twice a day, four acres of lawns and spectacular gardens tended by three full-time Japanese gardeners, a screening room with overstuffed chairs in crewel for twenty-four guests, a dining room that accommodates thirty-six for sit-down dinner, a kitchen with restaurant-sized stoves, a wine cellar with more than twenty-six hundred bottles. Mr. Crawford owned his own vineyard and favored burgundies from the Mercurey region." Helicopter views captured the sprawling vista from above and, at sundown, a forest-green Corniche was snared—with great excitement—leaving the estate. Reporters swarmed about the car but failed to obtain comment from the occupants, Mrs. Arianna Crawford, the star's widow, and his stepdaughter, Molly, eighteen. Both wore dark glasses and reportedly went thereafter to Forest Lawn cemetery for a private vigil at the slain actor's crypt.

Eulogies and career appraisals were offered in abundance. ABC-TV pre-taped Arnie Beckman in the executive offices of Macra, Inc., where the agent wept bitterly through most of his ten-minute segment. He compared his slain meal ticket to the classic heroes of Hollywood: Fairbanks *père et fils,* Cooper, Gable, Wayne. "The camera doesn't lie, you see," informed Arnie. "The camera reaches into a person's soul. If there's deceit down there, it comes out—no matter how good the makeup and the lighting and the costumes. But if there's good—old-fashioned, basic American decency—then that good shines brighter than all the spotlights in the world. Whatever Mack acted, he was still Mack, you see. . . . God, I begged him not to go to Texas. . . . I feel so responsible. . . . I loved that boy. . . . The day he was killed, I fell apart. I lost my brother, my son, my best friend, my favorite actor. . . ." Here Arnie broke down uncontrollably. He recovered to say, in closing, "Oh well, maybe it's for the best. . . . He was the last leading man. . . . The way this industry's going, the filth they're putting on screens . . . Mack wouldn't play that crap, anyway. . . ." Arnie announced plans for a "major theatrical motion picture" and a "twelve-hour miniseries for television" on the life of McKenzie Crawford, Jr. He estimated the potential world audience to be "in the neighborhood of one billion people" and revealed that certain revenues from the projects would be donated to the University of Southern California's cinema department. Arnie made good. Three years later he would send USC a check for $10,000 to establish scholarships in his client's name—and one would remark on the imbalance of his generosity. *Mack!* the movie would gross $74 million in first run.

Lureen Hofmeyer, mother and most accessible member of those few near and dear to the murdered actor, gave an interview to the BBC this Sunday afternoon while posed beneath the HOLLYWOOD sign, much of which was decayed and vandalized. Hot santana winds mussed her freshly tinted coiffure as she recalled rather cheerfully highlights of her son's life, beginning with his birth "just down the Hollywood Freeway, but, of course, there wasn't a Hollywood Freeway when I was an actress," and concluding with a moving tribute to her son's thespian talents. "He used to tease me and say he inherited the love of greasepaint from his mama." Lureen reminded viewers of the martyr's devotion to Jeffie, Molly, and youth in general.

In closing, Lureen took the opportunity of publicly thanking "the thousands upon tens of thousands of friends and fans who wrote such beautiful letters." She promised to answer each and every one—but asked future correspondents to enclose stamped, self-addressed envelopes. Attending to Mack's memory became Lureen's life work. For years thereafter she made regular appearances on death anniversary memorials and continued to live in the mansion, blocking all of Arianna's attempts to extricate her. She would die of a peaceful heart attack in her son's bed.

Film clips deftly assembled reprised Mack's career, from the Ford commercial that started it all, through memorable scenes from "Knights of New York," closing with a montage of his eighteen motion pictures: Mack as Sheriff, Mack as Cop, Mack as Rancher, Mack as Private Detective, Mack as Coach, Mack as Crusading District Attorney or State Legislator. In sum, commented Charles Champlin of the Los Angeles *Times,* Mack would be remembered as an actor of exceptional *presence* as opposed to talent. "His voice nowhere approached the power of an Olivier or the cunning charades of a Brando. He rarely reached for emotions beyond two staples: shy, boyish grin and tight-lipped moral determination. What he did best was to project with that magnificent physique a male of fairest grace and carriage, of unquestioned virility, of devotion and honor to maidens. He looked at a woman the way women want to be looked at." Even in death, he was the cinema's ultimate masculine fantasy. The homage concluded with a close-up of china-blue eyes, affixed on some distant Arizona mesa, squinting in a hot desert sun. Orson Welles spoke the voice-over benediction: "Of heroes, Will Rogers remarked, 'This thing of being a hero . . . About the main thing to do is to know when to die. Prolonged life has ruined more heroes than it ever made.'"

Public television competed with a round-table discussion from New York, where celebrated criminal defense attorneys analyzed the trial. Edward Bennett Williams and F. Lee Bailey disagreed on the much discussed change of venue issue. It was widely speculated that Otto Leo would request—and probably receive—another location for the trial. But he did not. "I think he made a mistake," said lawyer

Williams. "I'd move this case to the most remote corner of Texas, wherever that is. Ideally, it should be in a county seat with no local television station, no movie house, and a weekly newspaper principally devoted to tomato blight and drum majorettes." Lee Bailey shook his head. "There's no place in these fifty states where you could find twelve men and women who haven't gorged themselves on this matter like Thanksgiving dinner. I'd keep it in Fort Worth. And I'd give five years of my life to be there right now." Richard (Racehorse) Haynes, the Houston lawyer, agreed. "I called Otto last night and said I'd swap the next fifty murders in my case file if he'd let me ride shotgun. I prejudge this to be the best trial of all time, including Joan of Arc and Sacco-Vanzetti. In fact, Jesus Christ standing before Pontius Pilate pales in comparison."

"Who do you think will win?" asked the moderator. "Prosecution? Or defense?"

"Lady Justice," said Racehorse, lifting mischievous eyes to the goddess of law. "She is, after all, the woman who carries the sword."

People magazine, noting that Kleber Cantrell had on occasion contributed articles to its pages, published its fourteenth straight story on the event, straining for one last angle. CAN HE TALK? WILL HE TALK? Interviews with eye-ear-nose-and-throat specialists from Johns Hopkins, the Mayo Clinic, and Harris Hospital in Fort Worth provided no new answer. Dr. Samantha Reiker was quoted, stalely, "I'm sorry, but I have no opinion. There is too great a barrier between physical and mental injury."

The man from Mayo speculated that Cantrell was, in lay terminology, "struck dumb by the tragedy."

Calvin Sledge clicked off "60 Minutes." His wife, Marge, complained, "We haven't seen the Man of Miracles yet. Dan Rather got a quote exclusive end quote interview quote inside the bars of the Tarrant County jailhouse end quote. CBS has been promoting it like the second coming all weekend."

"We're taping it downtown," he yawned. "Somehow I don't think Reverend Luther will make public confession." The DA stretched full out on the rented sofa in the rented condominium. It had become necessary to move his wife and daughters to secret shelter, not out of danger to their lives (the several mail and telephone threats had been mostly in the category of hell's damnation) but due to harassment by the media and the curious. Foolishly, Sledge had allowed a local TV station to film him pruning roses in the front yard of his $42,500 redwood California ranch house. The footage had run nationwide with his street address clearly visible.

During one of the pretrial hearings, Sledge had been called out of court to take a hysterical call from Marge. Two men had followed the girls home from school and tried to lure them into a station wagon. They turned out to be documentary film makers but by Marge's thinking they were child molesters nonetheless. Then neighbors began to complain of midnight tourists. Photographers hid in trees. Sledge suggested a move to her mother's house in Wichita Falls for the duration of the trial, but Marge refused.

The high drama of living with a guard outside a secret hideaway and of sleeping beside a restless, driven man whose name and fast-aging face had suddenly become celebrated was seductive. Marge fully intended to be in court from opening gavel to final verdict. The year before, Marge had sat at home and watched the Watergate wives support their husbands. She had twenty outfits newly assembled from personal closet and those of friends. She hoped the trial would not go on longer than that. Beyond twenty days, it would be mix 'n' match. Two magazines were bidding to commission her for "Diary of the Prosecutor's Wife."

From that very first telephone call, the one that broke their sleep at 3:40 a.m. four months earlier and sent Calvin rocketing out of the house to spend three days and nights at the murder scene, her husband had changed, alarmingly. The case was like a plague, some insidious disease that dropped dandruff on his shoulders, that painted his tongue red and his face gray, that short-circuited good nature and humor and turned them into impatience and anger. Now the man could barely keep his eyelids open but he was pouring another glass of scotch—he was drinking more and more—and he wrote on his eternal, endless yellow legal pad.

"Let's go to bed," said Marge gently. "I'll wake you early."

"You go on. I'll be there in a minute." He did not look at her.

"How's your stomach?"

"Okay. It stopped singing to me." Sledge rarely ate anything but a grabbed hamburger. Sometimes his left arm hurt and he worried about bursitis. He didn't tell Marge. She was bitching too much anyway.

"I still wish you'd wear your new suit," said Marge. She had bought him a $175 three-piece navy blue pinstripe from Clyde Campbell, the city's best men's store. And what did she get for her surprise? A scolding for extravagance. Calvin said he would stick with the six-year-old tan gabardine he always wore opening day. Superstition.

"You're going to be fine," she said. She kissed him and smelled whiskey and fear sweat. "I always pick winners. Besides, the *National Enquirer* psychic poll said you'll get a conviction."

"I'm tired, honey," he said. "Scared, too. Dammit, I'm scared."

"You should be. It wouldn't be normal if you weren't."

"What if I bit off more than I can chew? What if I go in there and Otto Leo pulverizes me? It could happen."

"Well, do you still think the preacher's guilty?"

"Hell, yes. But that's no guarantee of justice. You don't know what we're up against. Otto Goddamn Leo's got a small army on his payroll." Ten days ago, the defense lawyer obtained the list of 600 Tarrant County citizens on the jury panel. Each prospective juror was promptly fed into the City of Miracles computer to determine if he or she was on the right side. Many presumably were—but Sledge was not privy to the score. Next, more than 2,000 supporters and employees of The Chosen fanned out for extraordinary investigation and surveillance of the jurors. Courthouse checks were made to see if any had criminal records or were involved in lawsuits as plaintiffs or defendants. They did "drive-bys" of jurors' houses, took surreptitious photographs, noted if lawns were well tended or unkempt (the latter tending to identify a person as having little sense of responsibility, probably someone less bound to the principle of law and order). It was noticed if front windows had decals of the American flag or if car bumpers sported stickers saying "Support Your Local Police." All of this was a key to juror character. By now, Otto Leo knew every single one of 600 names, addresses, occupations, religious affiliations, educational backgrounds, political party allegiance, standing in the community, club memberships, medical records, down to and including parking tickets and rumors of philandering. The defense would prance into court on the morrow with fat and juicy early-bird worms. Sledge would have to rely on the crumbs of character elicited from old-fashioned voir dire.

"Is that fair?" asked Marge.

"Not fair. But legal."

"A poor person couldn't afford computers and spies."

"We are not dealing with poor people. We're dealing with power and money."

"Well, I think you should tell all that to the press."

"I'd sound like a whiny-ass, hon. I'd come off like Bear Bryant poor-mouthin' his chances before the Cotton Bowl. Now you go on to bed; I'll be in directly."

Two hours later, Marge wandered into the living room and discovered her husband asleep on the sofa. His face was drenched in sweat and his flesh was clammy to her touch. His breathing was harsh rattles. She prepared to lift him like a child but Calvin awoke in panic. He pulled her into a hard grateful embrace. It was the first time in four months that she felt really needed. For the rest of the night they held fiercely to one another and pretended to sleep.

If God has anything to do with shingles, then divine providence gave the State of Texas a helpful first-morning boost. On the Monday that the trial of the decade began, Judge Ferguson Cleveland Stringer awoke with an angry and painful scarlet sash of welts about his waist. He was unable even to dress. The doctor summoned to the judge's home in Grand Prairie ordered him to bed for the duration, which, from past suffering experiences, might take as long as a month to cease and desist. The other four criminal district court judges who regularly sat on the benches of Tarrant County had all, for one reason or another, previously disqualified themselves from the Luther matter. It had never happened before in the history of the county but the fact was that nobody wanted to preside over a trial expected to ravage any judge's patience and reputation. Since neither side desired to wait another month for Stringer's shingles to heal, the decision was reached to call around neighboring counties for a substitute. By wildest coincidence, a name popped up within the hour. Located on the north side of Fort Worth buying a bull was Judge Carlos P. Mustardseed, seventy-six, and three-quarters retired. Out of deep East Texas, the elderly jurist was famous for harsh penalties and severe decorum. He looked like an old bent cowman who had been thrown by many mustangs and who had encountered evil-tempered farm machinery. He scared Otto Leo to death.

Judge Mustardseed's unexpected appearance on the bench at

11:20 a.m. conversely delighted Calvin Sledge, though he took pains not to show it. The prosecutor made little worrisome noises about the surprising development but the truth was it evened things out a bit. Otto Leo had sicked his computer onto Judge Fergie Stringer and had analyzed the jurist's entire twenty-four years on the bench, giving the defense a leg-up insight into case decisions, reversible errors, and judicial propensities. Stringer was not a "prosecution-minded judge" but Carlos Mustardseed was. Boy howdy.

"Good morning from Fort Worth, Texas. Cowtown. This is Rogers Ackerby and I'm standing on the sidewalk in front of the Tarrant County criminal courthouse, where the murder trial of Thomas Jeremiah Luther, or, as he prefers to call himself, The Chosen, is in the fourth day of jury selection." As he spoke, NBC's "Today" show cameras crawled along a line of spectators that curled eight blocks. Day and night, at least 2,000 people waited for one of the sixty available seats in the small courtroom. Middle-aged women in pants suits predominated. Even though few ever got inside the courthouse, they came regularly, clutching movie magazines and scrapbooks, expecting to get their pictures taken as devotees of Mack Crawford. They feuded with The Chosen's flock, members of which daily picketed the proceedings and circled the area singing hymns.

"Judge Carlos Mustardseed yesterday scolded both the District Attorney and the defense team for what he called 'unnecessary delays and tomfoolery.' After four days, not a single juror has been seated."

A question from NBC's studios in New York hurtled down to Ackerby's ear in Texas. What was the latest speculation on whether Kleber Cantrell would testify?

"Sledge told me this morning he intends to bring Mr. Cantrell into court—either upright, in a wheelchair, or flat—on a stretcher."

"What good will it do? Can he speak?"

"Nothing new on that."

"There's been a rumor Mr. Cantrell may be allowed to *write down* his answers."

"Prosecutor Sledge says that would be acceptable. Otto Leo will certainly fight such a development. The question is, is he competent to write? Cantrell is still in custody, being held in some secret, heavily guarded location. His friend, Ceil Shannon, is out on fifty-thousand-dollar bail granted two days after her arrest. She'll be called to testify about Mr. Cantrell's activities during his absence from the hospital here. Boy, does this get confusing. Back to you."

Judge Mustardseed tolerated the opposing lawyers' juror jousting for the better part of two weeks before he threw his first tantrum. More than 150 people had been questioned and only two had been seated. Everybody was irritated, particularly the press representatives. It had become difficult for correspondents to merit a sliver of the evening news. Reporters were grumbling and interviewing one another, a sure sign of news slippage. Everybody wanted the play to begin but the stagehands were still building scenery.

It was going like this: Each side was entitled to only fifteen juror strikes, but the judge had a cancellation stamp with unlimited ink. The trick was in getting Hizzoner to excuse a juror. Both sides were abusing the technique.

Sledge was clever at discovering bored housewives shopping for a real soap opera to fill the next few months. He persuaded the judge to dismiss more than forty of them. Nor could he live with any juror who seemed enamored of personal celebrity. The dozen finally selected would be photographed, sketched, pressured, and kissed by heady spotlights. They would become famous. The State wanted people who could hold up under the glare and not vote acquittal because of sudden kinship with fame.

Otto Leo was forced to probe an area rarely covered in jury selection: motion picture attendance. Every movie that Mack Crawford ever made had been mentioned by the end of the first week. It was vital that the defense prohibit Mack's fans from sitting in the box. If some old maid once dreamt of screwing Mack Crawford, her fantasies might cause her to be overly harsh in judging a man accused of destroying them.

On the tenth morning, prospective juror number 163 survived two hours of Calvin Sledge's questionings and appeared to be a fair-minded, ideal citizen. Then Otto Leo took over and asked another hour of unnecessary questions, unnecessary because he already had a computer file as thick as his thumb on the fellow. The prospect was chairman of a neighborhood "crime watch" committee. All the lawyers in the courtroom knew what Otto was up to; he was developing some "preoccupation" outside the courtroom that might tamper with the prospect's full concentration. While Otto worked, his aides slipped in and out of the courtroom, bringing in new pieces of paper. Judge Mustardseed regarded this with lessening patience.

Otto read a new note that one of his junior boys slipped him and he brightened. He asked the juror: "Do you share equal housecleaning responsibilities with your working wife?"

"Yessir, I do."

"Well, if you sat in this courthouse maybe five or six months, are you sure your marriage could tolerate the shift of domestic responsibility?" asked Leo, drawing a few titters.

Number 163 nodded first yes, then thought about it and shook his head no—the specter of marital discord over unwashed dishes and diapers clearly on his face. Otto glanced at the bench, expecting a routine dismissal.

Judge Mustardseed jumped in quick. "Mr. Leo, I'd like to know how you knew this man does his wife's housework—and what that has to do with hearing a murder case."

"It is the defense's responsibility to develop all areas of information about a prospective juror, your honor," said Otto, a little condescendingly.

"Is that so?" said the judge, climbing out of the saddle and seeming to get interested for the first time in a thick electric cable that snaked its way from under the defense table and out the door. It had been there since Day One and surely the judge noticed it. But now he picked it up and followed it like a snoop dog out into the corridor and into an adjoining conference room where the defense had stashed a small but effective computer terminal. Every time a prospective juror took the box, the computer printed out all known facts and figures about him or her. It had even been making calculated opinions, with the fresh news being rushed inside to Leo.

Judge Mustardseed promptly did something wondrous—from Calvin Sledge's point of view. He yanked out the plug, brought the cable back into the courtroom, looped it like a lasso, and tossed it to the bailiff. "Let's get back to basics," he said. "Maybe we can pick a jury."

Otto made vigorous protest. He tossed out precedents and privileges, but Judge Mustardseed cut *him* off, too. "Until they bring a computer in here to replace me," said Hizzoner, "I don't see the need for one out in the hallway."

Otto protested some more and Judge Mustardseed responded by dismissing the entire panel of 450 computerized yet-to-be-questioned jurors, causing the defense lawyer to sizzle. The $150,000 of The Chosen's money spent on tagging pigeons had just gotten flushed.

Otto almost screamed at this and made the drastic mistake of accusing the judge of misconduct. He requested that the jurist recuse himself, a major slap in any judge's face.

"I got a better idea, young man," said Judge Mustardseed. "I'm going to recuse *you*. For the night." He directed the bailiff to book Mr. Leo a night's lodging in county jail.

Calvin Sledge burst out laughing, whereupon he, too, was directed to spend the evening as guest of the slammer. "It'll do both of you fellers good to think on how you're expected to behave in a court of law."

As the press rushed to phone in the night final headline, Judge Mustardseed dispatched bailiffs onto the sidewalks of downtown Fort Worth with orders to scoop up a hundred new prospects at random. "And don't get any of those kooks," growled the judge, needlessly reminding his posse that the hall of justice was under siege by white-robed sisters from the City of Miracles.

Autumn deepened and the plains of north-central Texas turned brown. Attorneys who had worn seersucker suits in September were coming in court in wools. At the end of Week Seven, the ninth juror—a mortician's apprentice who quit school in the tenth grade—was accepted. A postman was seated the next day. Then a retired substitute teacher of manual arts. On Halloween afternoon, a truck driver who said the last movie he saw was *The Sound of Music* passed muster.

"Here comes the good news—bad news joke," announced Judge Mustardseed to the panel. "The good news is congratulations. I'm gonna buy each and ever' one of you a T-bone steak dinner tonight at Cattleman's. The bad news is I'm gonna lock you up afterward. You are about to perform society's most important and majestic duty. You are going to hear a lot of sound and fury and arguing and strutting. I have every confidence you will be able to sort out the wheat from the chaff. Now get some sleep and be ready to start at nine a.m."

Both sides were gloomy over the character of the jury, but, then, lawyers usually are.

Before testimony, Otto threw a fast ball past Calvin Sledge. The defense presented a motion *in limine* asking the judge to forbid any questions or witnesses designed to elicit T. J. Luther's criminal past. Sledge made vigorous protest. Surely the jury was entitled to know there was mud on the defendant's robes. Leo rebutted by pointing out that no felonies or misdemeanors of moral turpitude had been committed by the defendant in ten long years (at least none that got him arrested).

"We submit that this proves 'presumption of reformation,'" said Leo.

Judge Mustardseed looked over at The Chosen with a cocked head that bespoke dubiousness. Taking this as a sign of the bench's favor, Sledge argued heatedly that Mr. Luther's numerous brushes with the law beginning with his first arrest for fraud demonstrated a pattern of consistent criminal behavior.

"You may be right, Mr. Prosecutor," allowed the judge, "but if a feller behaves himself as long as this 'un *apparently* has, we must assume he's on the right side of the road." Motion granted. The Right Side wins round one.

Thomas Jeremiah Luther would thus be judged by jurors not privy to his life of violence and danger. The nine-page record that dated from 1953 would remain hidden from the jury's eyes. He had become once again a clean sheet of paper.

By structure and tradition, criminal trials are rigged pro-state. The prosecution gets to present its case first—and fires the last shot in closing argument. The proceedings take place in the District Attorney's own ball park. The courthouse belongs, after all, to the people. Thus was it in the role of defender of this house of justice that Calvin Sledge rose to present his case. Although Sandy Double had been at his side during jury selection and would soon rejoin him to ride shotgun, Calvin Sledge chose to work alone for the opening statement. It was one man in an old, rumpled tan gabardine suit in combat against eight lawyers who followed the lead of Otto Leo and were each sartorially splendid. It was the one yellow note pad in the District Attorney's hands weighed against the four bulky filing cabinets that Otto Leo had brought into the crowded little chamber. Sledge hoped that his posture would fit the character of the courtroom, for it resembled a film set where the Declaration of Independence was signed, with blond wood paneling and colonial brass lanterns flanking the banc.

In a voice deliberately flat and drained of emotion, Sledge read the indictment, informed the jury that the State of Texas believed a capital murder had been committed by Thomas Jeremiah Luther, age forty-two, and would so prove. "Much, perhaps too much, has already been written and spoken about this matter," said Sledge. "At its heart is a simple story. Three men who were boyhood friends in this very city, three men who reached national prominence, these three men were together in a remote farmhouse on a pleasant spring night. They had a party. And during this party, Thomas Jeremiah Luther, who calls himself a man of God, decided to *play* God. He took the life of one of his friends and critically wounded the other. That's the story, ladies and gentlemen. An American tragedy." The prosecutor paused abruptly, as if he had something important left to tell. Then he shook his head sorrowfully and sat down. Six minutes flat.

Otto Leo took ten times longer to make a civics lecture. The State of Texas *demands,* he repeated endlessly, that each juror assume "the accused minister" to be innocent. How careful was Otto not to slip and refer to his client as, simply, "the accused," a mistake lawyers all too often make. Otto's task was to humanize the defendant and he gave T.J. the respect due an archbishop. "My client, an accused servant of the Lord, is one of the world's most distinguished religious leaders," said Leo, laying it on so thick that he drew a mild objection from the DA. Normally the opposition doesn't meddle with an opening statement but this was making roses out of skunk cabbage. Judge Mustardseed disagreed. Continue.

"The State of Texas has a very hard job, folks," informed Leo. "It must prove—and I'm not going to let you forget that word *prove*—guilt beyond a reasonable doubt. Let me say it again. I'd say it a hundred times if the judge would let me get away with it. The State *must*—repeat *must*—prove—repeat *prove*—guilt beyond a reasonable doubt. Please underscore *beyond a reasonable doubt*. This isn't some movie, ladies and gentlemen. It's not Hollywood, even though the characters and the trappings may remind you of Saturday night at the Bijou Theater. It's not Perry Mason, so don't expect any thunderbolt revelations. I'm sorry you must endure this. I'm sorry my client, a fine human being who reveres life so much, has to sit here and listen to the State of Texas malign him and fabricate tragic scenarios. At the end of this ordeal, if you good people have one single shred of doubt about this absurd case, then you must give The Chosen speedy acquittal and a return to his selfless labor in the house of God."

Sledge rose again. "Objection, please. Does counsel have to keep blowing the angel trumpets?"

Judge Mustardseed commented drily, "Mr. Leo, there will be ample time, I suspect, for you to introduce all the evidence you want concerning the defendant's reputation. Now get on with it." The judge neither sustained nor overruled, an idiosyncrasy that would become difficult for both sides, trying to interpret from a vague wave of liver-spotted judicial hands and a tart comment exactly what Hizzoner meant. If pushed to amplify, the judge glowered.

Otto delivered a vivid preview of coming attractions. He had to dilute the impact of the death pictures before they were introduced. "We're not quarreling with the fact that a man is dead," the defense lawyer allowed. "Just be prepared for the State to stick its thumb in your eye. They're going to be forcing gosh-awful, lurid, horrible photographs into the jury box." He made the images sound so terrible that Calvin Sledge should be considered a sadist just for bringing them to court. And Otto had to discount in advance the prosecution's charge that T.J. was illegally carrying a gun "on the night of the unfortunate death." No killing, nor murder, just "death." The little pear-shaped lawyer ducked his chin to his chest and his jowls rippled at mention of the word "gun." The unspoken message was: "Sure guns are illegal, but you and me must have one since we live in a jungle." Stop a hundred cars on the Dallas–Fort Worth turnpike and fifty of them will have guns in the glove box.

"To be sure, we do not deny that the pistol was fired that night, ladies and gentlemen," concluded Otto, whispering to the jurors as if it was a secret passed across the back fence. "What you are going to find very fascinating are the reasons *why*. Once you hear them, I have every belief that you will stop this trial and give my client back his life and excellent work."

It was past 5 p.m. and Judge Mustardseed, drowsy since lunch and barely awake, gaveled adjournment. Testimony would commence the next morning. All of a sudden, T. J. Luther jumped out of his seat and yelled in glory day gusto, "Amen!" He did it again and slammed his fist on the desk. Papers flew. He sat down and dared anybody to scold him. Nobody did. His hearty benediction was the lead-off item on that night's newly revived trial coverage. In the hallway outside, Sandy Double told Calvin, "You shoulda objected to that 'Amen!'"

"I thought about it. Then I figured it wouldn't look good for me to ask the judge to tell a murder defendant not to say 'Amen.'"

"You better watch that boy."

"I haven't closed my eyes since May 9."

The next morning, The Chosen brought a Bible to court and if that wasn't enough he was sporting a large shiny gold cross on his lapel. He sat down like a kid in church squeezed between a God-fearing clan of elders. He did not squirm, doodle, nap, or do much of anything all day except make continual steeples out of his fingertips. And read the Bible during key testimony, usually distracting juror attention.

Per custom, Calvin Sledge began with blood.

His list of witnesses, which discovery rules had forced into the hands of the defense, was embarrassingly short. The prosecutor tried to compensate by long and intricate questions. He kept the Tarrant County medical examiner on the stand three full days when two hours would have sufficed. But it was time well spent. The coroner described in graphic and far too generous detail how the .44 Magnum slug tore through Mack Crawford's mouth, angling upwards at 140 mph, shattering blood vessels, tissue, pieces of bone and cartilage that fairly flew through the air in imagined flurries. The victim bled to death in excruciating horror. Sledge got what he wanted, which was overkill. He used the coroner to get into evidence a folder of twenty-six 11 × 14 color photographs of the dead man. Otto did not object, but he raised his eyebrows for the jury as if to say, I-Told-You-So. Forewarned.

Sledge said honestly, "I apologize for subjecting you to these terrible pictures. Murder is not pretty."

"Objection, your honor," intruded the defense lawyer. "Nobody has proved a murder yet. Nor are they likely to."

Judge Mustardseed did not rule. "Just show your pictures, Mr. Prosecutor. Folks, do not react or remark. Just look at the things and pass 'em to your neighbor."

The oldest woman on the jury, a fleshy woman in her sixties who ran a beer stop, took one look and threw a wadded lace handkerchief into her mouth with knuckles for a dam. She gagged anyway. The man next to her, an insurance salesman who had drawn a laugh during voir dire by wondering how much his golf slice would worsen if away from it six weeks, trembled. The gruesome power of the pictures worked its way down the line, so much that Sledge greatly desired that the trial end here and now. The dozen peers would surely hang T. J. Luther just to avoid further perusal of the death album.

And the fillip here was that the corpse with half a head blown away and blood puddled on his breast like hell's rain was arguably the most photographed man in the world. More than murder, it was celebrity destruction. It was wrenching to look at the pictures and connect the fact of murder with the fantasy of fame. Sledge knew that an Italian news syndicate had put out a standing offer to buy any one of the pictures (full face and figure a requirement) for $30,000 cash. That was one of the reasons he had carried around positives and negatives in his briefcase since the case began, worried that somebody on his staff would succumb to the powerful temptation.

Otto Leo at first seemed uninterested in the medical examiner's testimony, a practical stance since Dr. Franco Cervone was known for chewing up pesky defense lawyers. He was a volatile Italian with the egomaniacal character that often comes with the territory of county pathologist.

"Dr. Cervone, I almost forgot to ask, in your laboratory tests did you by any chance discover anybody else's blood on the deceased?"

"Yes," answered the medical examiner.

"Oh is that so?" Otto made it sound like something important was being withheld from evidence. "Where, please?"

"On the deceased's knuckles. Right hand. And perhaps a tiny smear on the inside wrist of this same hand."

"What type blood was that?"

"Type B."

"I see. And what type blood was Mr. Crawford?"

"O positive."

"Then what does that mean? Finding two different blood types."

"It means there was a bit of blood from somebody else on his hand."

"That's interesting. And were there any flesh particles on the deceased's body that belonged to somebody else?"

"Yes. Under the victim's fingernails was a minute specimen of tissue."

"So let me get things straight. On this dead man's physical person you discovered blood from somebody else and flesh particles from somebody else. Is that right?"

"More or less."

"Let me ask again. What does this suggest to you, Doctor?"

"Objection," said Calvin Sledge. "Calls for a conclusion." Judge Mustardseed waved his hand, seeming to indicate agreement.

"Could it mean that Mack Crawford perhaps had a fight with somebody that night, Doctor?"

"Same objection, your honor," protested Sledge, and this time the judge was kind enough to sustain. He also muttered, loud enough for a few people close to the bench to overhear, "Sounds like he cold-cocked somebody."

So here it comes, worried the District Attorney. Otto Leo is going to chip away at the public statue that was Mack Crawford. Before he is done, the jury is going to beatify The Chosen for ridding society of a dangerous nuisance. He scribbled a note for Sandy Double. "Go see if you can do anything with Cantrell. We've *got* to use him." The assistant nodded and slipped out of the courtroom at the first recess. He did not expect to have any more success at putting words in a wasted mouth than his superior.

Otto was cooking now, playing like he was finally unraveling a major mystery. "Dr. Cervone, in the interest of time, can you just tell the jury this: from your examination of the deceased's blood samples, is it correct to say he was drunk?"

Sledge objected and the judge told Otto to rephrase his question.

"Had he been drinking the night of his death?"

"Yes."

"Was he intoxicated?"

"Objection. Calls for a conclusion."

"Never mind, your honor. Let's put alcohol on the back burner for the time being. Dr. Cervone, did you perform the standard postmortem examinations for narcotics?"

"Of course."

"Did these tests show that the deceased had been smoking marijuana?" Otto pronounced it with a Spanish twist that lent an air of border-town decadence.

"No."

"Was there hashish use?"

"None that we located."

Heroin? No. Mescaline? No. LSD? No. Amphetamines? No. Barbiturates? No. "How about cocaine?" wondered the defense lawyer.

Yes. There was definite laboratory evidence of cocaine ingestion.

Otto Leo seemed both startled and stricken by the news. "Would you testify that the deceased was addicted to cocaine?" inquired Otto.

Sledge had to object to that, his grounds being that the coroner was not qualified as an expert on narcotics addiction. But the trouble was, the DA came off sounding like somebody who wanted to keep a shocking secret from the jury.

"I'll sustain that," said Judge Mustardseed, looking fascinated nonetheless by the peek into Hollywood Babylon.

"Can you tell me this, Doctor. Isn't it true that cocaine users are often mean-tempered? Querulous? Prone to picking fights? Violent?"

Sledge objected four times and got four sustains from the bench. But Otto Leo sat down with a substantial victory. He had gotten the jury to start thinking that the star of color photographs was a junkie. He also muttered a getaway line, something about bringing in an expert on cocaine very soon.

On redirect, Sledge asked the coroner if "Mr. Crawford's nasal passages were inflamed," that being the traditional entry for cocaine into the body.

"I don't know," said Dr. Cervone.

"Why not?"

"Because his nose was just about blown away," said the medical examiner, ending the day with a ghastly vision.

Sandy Double spent two hours standing over Kleber Cantrell's bed. He told funny stories, praised the writer's book on Vietnam, warned him that Otto Leo was already devastating Mack Crawford's reputation. And his would be next.

"Once or twice I thought he was about to say something," Sandy told his boss. "It looked like his eyes were getting angry. But then he sank back into his zombie act."

The prosecution next called a sweet-faced lady from the Tarrant County tax collector's office. Her name was Ommalee Plenty and she was the unlikely viaduct through which Calvin Sledge hoped to send T. J. Luther to execution. She identified a yellowing, parchment-fragile deed to the land on which the body of McKenzie Crawford, Jr., was discovered. It was 10.34 acres formerly owned by two deceased brothers, Brigham and Peavine Luther.

"Formerly owned?" asked Sledge.

"That is correct. In August 1971, this property was confiscated by Tarrant County for non-payment of back taxes. The sum was . . . let me see here . . . the accumulated total with interest was $2,221.15."

"On the night of May 9, 1975, who owned this property?"

"Tarrant County, Texas."

"It did not belong to the defendant, Thomas Jeremiah Luther?"

"No sir. It belonged to the people of this county."

"Was there a sign so indicating?"

"I don't know. I believe it is policy to put one up. But sometimes vandals tear 'em down, or the wind. You know how times are."

Otto Leo passed the witness and tried to indicate that Ommalee Plenty was not worth cross-examining. But the truth was she worried him. Calvin Sledge had it on the record now that his client was criminally trespassing on county property. That was worth a $200 fine under the worst of judges. But connecting it with a murder could mean the death penalty.

A parade of sleuths from the Fort Worth Crime Search Unit both entertained and bored the jury for several days. Theirs was the tedious franchise of diagrams, room dimensions, tape measurements, chalk outlines of fallen bodies, footprints in grass, fragments of lead pried from withered old clapboards. The weight of such testimony was impressive more for size than substance. On cross-examination, Otto Leo challenged none of the offerings. But he did inquire why fifty-three detectives spent almost three round-the-clock weeks at the location, lavishing—and here Leo made elaborate pencil jottings—"more than nine thousand man-hours of time." Was that standard procedure?

"No sir," answered a detective named Weiller.

"Was this extraordinary expenditure of time and money done at the request of somebody?"

"Yes sir—the chief, and the District Attorney."

"Did the District Attorney say anything personally to you?"

The detective grinned nervously. "Yes sir. He said we should stay out there until Christmas if necessary."

"Oh? And why would he order you to stay out there until Christmas?"

"Believe he said he wouldn't tolerate screwing this one up."

"Well, I don't blame the District Attorney," said Otto, suppressing a tee-hee like everybody else. "Are we to gather that in the past certain other crime lab investigations were, to use the District Attorney's rather colorful and certainly forthright expression, 'screwed up'?"

Sledge did not have to object. Judge Mustardseed beat his palm on the desk in warning, but somehow it sounded like applause.

How a witness looks and handles himself in the box is often more integral than what he says. Such was the lamentable presentation of Arthur Capo, nineteen years old and resembling somewhat a gopher. He also came across as if he dwelled underground. He blinked his eyes continually as if unused to the light of day and ran his tongue around lips that appeared sere from anxiety.

"How were you employed on the night of May 9, 1975?" asked Calvin Sledge.

"Ambulance driver," answered Arthur.

Arthur recollected being summoned to the farm property where two men were reported "down." He threw in a rambling five-minute bonus of how difficult it was to find the place. The jury presumably wondered, as did the press, if Arthur's delay in reaching the scene was rank negligence. He testified there was no doubt in his mind that Mack Crawford was deceased and that it "looked like" Kleber Cantrell had checked out, too.

"He was lying on the ground right next to the other feller and there was blood all over his neck and chest. He was bubbling. I didn't get a pulse at all."

"But he was not dead, as it turned out, was he?"

"No sir. Still had a little life in him. I put him in the ambulance and he sorta moaned. Or sighed."

"Did he say anything?"

"He worked his lips—but I couldn't make out what if anything he was saying."

"Did you ask him anything?"

Otto Leo was poised and ready to object. Judge Mustardseed threw out a cautionary arm. He, too, was not going to permit any hearsay testimony.

"Yes sir. I asked him, 'Who did this to you?' "

"And did Mr. Cantrell answer you?"

"Objection!" Otto was beside himself with indignation.

"I think I'll overrule that," said the judge, surprising both lawyers. "I'd like to hear the answer myself."

"Well, sir, he didn't really answer me—not out loud."

Sledge wanted to throttle the little prick. That was not the response he had rehearsed the night before. "Let me rephrase it. Did Mr. Cantrell respond, in any way?"

"Respond?"

"Mr. Capo, must I define the word 'respond' for you?"

"I guess I didn't get it."

Otto leaped up with delight. "Your honor, Mr. Sledge is badgering his own witness."

"Seems that way. Mr. Prosecutor, hasn't he *responded* sufficiently to your question?"

"Your honor, I submit this is vital to the identification of the defendant. It is also similar to a deathbed statement."

"That's overdramatizing. But get on with it. Just don't be puttin' words in the witness's mouth."

"Mr. Capo, when you asked Mr. Cantrell 'Who did this to you?' did he do *anything?*"

Arthur Capo bobbed his thick head excitedly, like a grade-school actor finally remembering his dialogue. "Yes sir. He sort of raised up." Here Capo dramatized a corpse rising from the tomb. "I told him to lie back down. But he pointed over at the preacher feller there—that one in the shiny blue suit—and he got all excited. He almost convulsed. It looked like he was trying to form the word 'him.' He kept pointing and trying to say 'him' and then he passed out."

Sledge was displeased with the accusatory finger, but it was the best he could do. He passed the witness.

If there was any doubt why Otto Leo demanded such exorbitant fees for his services, he demolished it—and Arthur Capo—in quick order.

"When did you quit school, Mr. Capo?" asked the defense counsel.

"In the fifth grade."

"I see. And what was your occupation just prior to becoming an ambulance driver?"

"I repossessed cars."

Otto presented a stack of several 5 × 7 color photographs to the witness but bade him not to look for a moment. "Would you please speak the word 'him' for me?"

Obediently, Arthur Capo said, "Him."

"Thank you. Now do it again, and hold it. When you reach the 'm' part of 'him,' freeze your mouth."

"Himmmmmmmm."

"Now, please look at these photographs and tell me what these people are doing."

Arthur perused the pictures. "They all look like they're in some sort of pain. They're hurtin' bad, I would say."

"Would you be interested to know that these are pictures of fifteen people stopped at random in the line of folks outside the courthouse waiting to get in? I asked each one of them to speak the word 'him' and this is what they look like. Would you agree that when somebody says the word 'him' it looks like a grimace? Like they are in pain?"

"Yeah. Sort of."

"One last question, Mr. Capo. When a person is severely wounded, in shock, isn't it true that their arms and legs sometimes move involuntarily? By reflex?"

"What do you mean?"

"I mean, does a person's arm suddenly shoot up, like when a doctor taps the knee with a hammer?"

"Sure."

"Could Mr. Cantrell's arm motion have been a simple reflex action?"

"Yeah. Suppose it could."

Since the first day of testimony, a hatbox-sized carton sat provocatively on the District Attorney's table, an isolated centerpiece that Sledge took elaborate pains never to touch. Sometimes when Otto Leo was prancing around demolishing state witnesses, the prosecutor gazed at the box as if it was the repository of all truth. Naturally it aroused, as he intended, great curiosity.

It was time to cut the ribbons.

With the civilian chief of the police crime lab in the witness chair, Sledge sliced open the top of the box with a Swiss Army knife (making sure the jurors glimpsed his masculine blade because in Texas a real man carries a pocketknife at all times). Then he slipped both of his hands inside the container as cautiously as if a nest of scorpions guarded the contents.

He withdrew a fat and ugly pistol, risking a moment of contemplative silence. Sledge stared at the weapon in his cupped hands and bore it with care to the witness. Identification was made. The .44 Magnum was introduced as State's Exhibit H, as in "horrible." There is no romance to a .44 Magnum and Sledge was grateful that The Chosen had not employed a gun of more modest power and character. A .44 Magnum is not designed to wound or wing. Its purpose is to devastate and desecrate life. Sledge was pleased to notice several jurors playing visual Ping-Pong with the awful thing and the preacher whose lapel bore the cross of Calvary in gold.

Torrey Dale, the crime lab boss, was a dry and colorless man who looked like preachers used to before they discovered hair spray and telegenic suits. Dandruff fell to his shoulders as he talked; one of his eyeglasses was adhesive-taped to its frame. But he soon became the most powerful witness yet for the prosecution.

He handled the gun with respect, explaining that it had been "customized," making it even more lethal. The force of a customized Magnum .44 dispatches a hollow-point, semi-jacketed bullet with an exposed nose into a victim with such vicious ferocity that the exit hole is larger, much larger than the entrance.

"Why is that?" wondered the DA.

"Because the bullet drags bone fragments and tissue particles as it plows through the body. It's like a reaming machine." Dale plucked a sample bullet from his jacket pocket. "This is a lead-core bullet about three fourths of an inch long. The whole carriage is an inch and a half. The point is hollow, you see. There's also this scalloped edge. It's made that way so the bullet will expand when it hits the target. It flares. It widens. And usually it explodes into many, many jagged pieces. The purpose is to enhance destruction."

"Can you elaborate on that for us? Can you tell us just how powerful is this gun and the bullet it fires?"

Torrey Dale nodded soberly. He produced a carpet bag and from it withdrew several odd items. He held up a thick book and waved it. "This here's the Sears, Roebuck catalogue. About eleven hundred pages," he explained. There was a gaping hole in the middle, wide enough to stick four fingers through. "Using this gun, I fired at this catalogue from seven yards away. Oh, I forgot to show you this." He held up a foot-square piece of steel plate, about one quarter inch thick. "This steel plate was positioned *in front* of the catalogue. The bullet passed through the plate, as you can plainly see, and blasted the hole, which you can also plainly see, in the catalogue."

The crime lab chief bolstered his testimony by showing the jury a two-foot square of three-quarter-inch plywood which had been hit by the Magnum. On the entry side was a good-sized hole, but at the rear of the board, where the bullet exited, it was chewed, frayed, splintered, and generally destroyed.

"And this is the same kind of bullet that passed through Mack Crawford's skull?" asked Sledge.

"The very same."

Sledge led the scientist through the standard ballistics testimony, linking the gun with the recovered bullet fragments, eliciting the undisputed fact that the Magnum was smeared with the fingerprints of T. J. Luther.

"Did it bear any *other* fingerprints?"

"None that we could make out."

Then the District Attorney made a snap decision. He elected to shoot down any defense theories of "accidental" discharge. Sledge could have waited for this on rebuttal, but he anticipated that Otto Leo would call in a legion of gun experts with the hopes of proving (or at least suggesting) that the durn thing just popped off by itself.

"Mr. Dale, is there such a thing as a hair trigger?"

Torrey Dale smiled, as if overly familiar with a hoary defense tactic. "Yes sir."

"Please tell us what that means, in layman's language."

"It's a gun trigger that goes off at the slightest touch."

Sledge picked up the Magnum from the witness stand. He looked at it quizzically, his finger dancing tantalizingly on the trigger. "Does this thing have one?"

"No sir. Not by my definition." Dale explained that certain pressure from a finger was required to pull the trigger. In tests at his lab, he attached a wire to the trigger and then affixed little chunks of metal, like fishing weights, to the wire. "If the gun goes off at the addition of less than one pound of these weights, it has what we consider a hair trigger."

"How many fishing weights did you have to put on this gun to make it go off?"

"Two point four pounds," said Torrey Dale.

"That's not a hair trigger?"

"Not at all. It did look like somebody had tried to file down the hammer notch to make it fire quicker. And the gun was in excellent repair. The owner kept it in shipshape condition." Later, on cross, Otto would draw from Dale the admission that enthusiasts of fast-draw contests often filed down their notches. But it didn't make much of an impact.

"One last question, Mr. Dale," said Sledge. "Would it be possible for this gun to accidentally discharge, to 'go off by itself' as people like to say?"

"I don't think so. You could drop it fifty times and it wouldn't fire. I know that because I did it. The only way it fires is to put your finger on the trigger and pull it hard."

"A fella's got to be intent on making it fire, right?"

"Yes sir. The recoil can knock you clean into the next block. You don't do it routinely. Or accidentally."

Nodding uncomfortably, the District Attorney quit. He assessed his presentation so far. He had given the jury a corpse, a fragile but unimpeached identification, and a murder weapon. All he lacked now was an eyewitness. He had one. Maybe. With his stomach knotting, the prosecutor announced the last name on his dance card.

"We call Kleber Cantrell, your honor."

CHAPTER TWENTY-NINE

The City of Miracles needed one badly. For a time, the executive hierarchy had managed to put up a brave front, but by the eighth week of the trial, The Chosen's ministry was near collapse. What few students who showed up for the fall semester were dismissed at Thanksgiving when there was no more money to pay the faculty. Cash flow was at crisis. Mail that once flooded into the Miracle Post Office at 10,000 pieces a week was now down to a trickle of a few hundred, and not many of these contained contributions.

A skeletal managerial staff ran the businesses, juggled invoices, issued press releases that bravely but falsely bragged of the Lord's good work continuing unimpeded. After The Chosen's arrest, it was decided to carry on with television and radio schedules by using old tapes. But miracles in rerun failed to capture a sustaining audience or its largesse. Only a few of the most loyal sisters, Crystal and Gentilla among them, remained. When trucks came to haul off much of the Miracle equipment, dismantling computers and taking away typewriters and desks, the women felt fear and panic.

For a time, Sister Crystal had been able to assuage her discomfort by making daily journeys downtown to the courthouse where she participated in the services of worship and support centered on the flatbed truck. Then Otto Leo decreed that the mobile church should be moved out of public sight. He convinced The Chosen that the passionate spectacles were attracting excessive coverage from the world press and were lending a primitive character to the cause. Though he disagreed and regretted losing the cheering section, T.J. acquiesced. The sisters were commanded to stay away.

At this, Sister Crystal made a private vow to help The Chosen, for whom she held boundless devotion. She descended to her place at the bottom of the pit and began to fast. She flung her body before the celebrated portrait of Jesus Christ. "Oh Lord, tell me how I can best help my sweet master," she prayed.

Judge Mustardseed summoned both sides into his office. The potential appearance of Kleber Cantrell had already been thoroughly discussed, but the old jurist was nonetheless nervous and in unmapped territory. He demanded to know just what the District Attorney anticipated his star witness would say—or not say. He was not at all sure he would even permit the fellow into his courtroom.

"Has this witness indicated a willingness to testify?" asked the judge.

Sledge fuzzed his answer. "Well, Mr. Cantrell hasn't said he *won't.*"

"Can he talk?"

"I have reason to believe that he can," replied the DA. "I submit, your honor, that it is vital for me to at least give it a try. It may be the only way the jury can learn exactly what happened on the night of May 9."

Otto Leo jumped in emotionally. His client's right to a fair and impartial hearing would be severely if not fatally jeopardized by the appearance of a witness with a freshly healed hole in his throat, toted into the box on a stretcher. Justice would be better served by taking testimony from Cantrell "in a hospital setting," which, necessarily, would exclude jurors.

Judge Mustardseed chewed on the problem like it was sun-hardened tobacco. "Let's sleep on it, boys," he said. He looked at Calvin Sledge curiously. "You better get some shut-eye, boy," he suggested. "You look plumb tuckered out."

Waiting outside was Sandy Double, who pulled Sledge into a side corridor. "Kleber's mother is waiting for you in your office," he said. "Says it's important."

Sledge groaned. He had no time for VeeJee and her ruminations. "You talk to her, Sandy, okay? Tell her I'm busy. Tell her it doesn't look like I'll have time to call her."

"I already done that. She still wants you."

"Well, Lord. What could be on her mind?"

"She's carrying a big cardboard box of papers. Says it's stuff Kleber wrote that you haven't read yet. Some old carbons. She seems all worked up. Says her conscience would hurt her forever if you didn't have access to *everything*."

Sledge moaned again and chewed a handful of antacid tablets. His stomach was in knots. "Take care of her, Sandy. Hold her hand. Buy her a sody pop." He rushed out the courthouse door and jumped into his car before the press caught his scent. VeeJee reluctantly entrusted Sandy with her treasure but made him sign his name in triplicate on official stationery.

"Is there anything in particular you want me to read, ma'm?" asked Sandy.

VeeJee shook her head. "It's all relevant," she said. "Some words might be more relevant than others."

That night Sledge collected Ceil Shannon from the motel where she was under police guard. The first few days of house arrest were so maddening that Ceil thought she would lose her mind. But now she had accommodated to life with a television set as her principal companion and cheeseburgers from the Dairy Queen next door and guarded telephone conversations to New York that she knew were being recorded. When Sledge barged in unannounced, Ceil was wearing blue jeans and a Fort Worth Stockyards tee shirt. She was braiding her hair because it killed an hour.

"What's wrong?" she asked, worried. "Has something happened to Kleber?"

"Let's go and see," said Sledge.

Ceil jumped up excitedly to prepare her unmade face and find better clothes. Sledge grabbed her arm. "You look fine," he said. "You don't need war paint."

They drove to a small private clinic on the outskirts of Denton where a forty-three-year-old patient registered as "Chester Teton" had been under care since early September. The young doctor who led them to Kleber's room asked for Ceil Shannon's autograph on the evening edition of the *Star-Telegram*. He was eager for gossip and inside news from the trial. He assured the prosecutor that no reporters or spies from Otto Leo's camp had been around. He said the patient was doing fine, "eating like a lumberjack" and "responding" to therapy.

Sledge knew that. He had watched through a one-way mirror while nurses told Kleber to get out of bed, which he did, or roll over, which he did, or wash his face, which he did. Obviously Cantrell heard everything—and responded to commands. But every time Calvin Sledge had asked, "Will you help us out, son?" all he got back was a glassy stare cold as taxidermy.

Tonight Kleber was propped up in an elevated bed and looking without connection at a television set that hung from the ceiling. He was not allowed to watch news but was permitted unlimited rations of situation comedy. Beside his bed was an enormous pile of mail; each morning and afternoon a therapist plunged into the stack and read selections aloud. The hope was that somebody's letter might strike a spark. Thus far the only reaction was to a letter from some old newspaperman in Houston named Clifford Casey. Kleber's eyes had filled with tears.

The room was almost dark, save for the weak light of the television set. In the doorway, Ceil tensed. It took her several moments to compose herself. Then she went to Kleber and kissed his forehead. Sledge watched hawk-like for a reaction. Kleber was glad to see her, but he contained his emotions.

The prosecutor went directly to the point. "I'm going to call you in the morning, son," he said. "There's no gettin' around it. I need you.

I'm going to put you in the box and ask you simple, direct questions that can be answered 'yes' or 'no.' If you don't cooperate, then I'll ask you formally to write your answers down. And if you won't do that for me—then I'll rest my case. I imagine Otto Leo will move for an instructed verdict of acquittal—and I won't be a'tall surprised if the judge gives it to him. Then we can all go fishin' a spell, after which I expect to come back to work so renewed with vigor and purpose that it won't take two shakes to prosecute Miss Shannon here. And I will, son. I'm going to send *somebody* to jail."

Ceil felt a tremor of fear but she held it inside. She did not want Kleber to see her weakness.

"It's shitty as hell, I agree," continued the DA. "And, Kleber boy, don't think you're off the hook. Judge Mustardseed is ornery and he won't take much guff off anybody. I wouldn't be surprised if he held you in contempt of court. That's worth six months in county jail. He could—if he wanted to—bring you out six months down the line, ask you if you've changed your mind, and if you're still playing clam, he'll send you back to the slammer for further contemplation. He can do that until 1999 if he wants—and I would heartily concur."

Ceil Shannon regarded the DA with naked contempt. "That's absolutely vile," she said. "Kleber didn't do anything."

"Yeah," agreed Sledge. "Life *is* unfair. Oh, I forgot one thing. If your boy friend here decides to help us out tomorrow, I'll seriously consider dropping the charges against you."

"I can't wait to tell my lawyer this good news," she said, frankly astonished by the squeeze play. "And the press, too."

"As you like," said Sledge. "Negotiation is a necessary part of the pursuit of justice." He left them alone and promised that no one would look or listen. He said Ceil could spend the night with her lover. "You probably won't believe me," said the prosecutor, "but there are no bugs in this room tonight. I'm going to give you two some private time together. I'm not a romantic, but I'm not a total chickenshit, either."

The room was stifling but when Ceil tried to open a window, she discovered it was locked. And barred. That was what their lives had become. Two fiercely independent people were caged by lunatic tides. She poured ice water on a washrag and dabbed his brow. "I wish we could believe Sledge," she said. "I wish we could have this night together."

Kleber pantomimed the need for pad and paper. She found them in her purse. He scribbled hurriedly. "This is our first conjugal visit."

Ceil tried to laugh and whispered, "You're supposed to be sick."

"I am," wrote Kleber. "I'm sick of this whole mess. . . . Scared, too. Sorry I got you into this blind corner."

"You do what you think is right," said Ceil.

"Turn on the television set," wrote Kleber. She did so, found Johnny Carson joking. Kleber motioned for her to sit on his left side, blocking the mirror that hung on his wall. If there was a pair of spy eyes on the other side, all they could see would be a tall woman's broad back. "Now turn on the music," he wrote, gesturing at a bedside stereo cassette player. Ceil found a Vivaldi tape. "Now the air conditioner." He pointed at a large floor fan that lurked in a corner. It rattled noisily into life, sending waves of thick, humid air against the lovers.

"Is it safe now to talk?" whispered Ceil.

"It should be," wrote Kleber. "We've got comedy, music, and hot air as protection. There may be a metaphor lurking somewhere."

"How do you feel?"

"There's that word again," wrote Kleber. *"Feel."*

"Listen, love, don't worry about me. Don't let my situation affect whatever you decide to do. I'm a big girl. I've known all along what the risks entailed. I've never been so fully alive as during the last six months. I wouldn't plea-bargain one minute of it to save my neck."

"I care about two people," wrote Kleber. "You . . . and Mack. I can't let them destroy him twice."

"Add another person to your list."

"Who?"

"Numero Uno."

"I have a plan," wrote Kleber.

"I love you," said Ceil.

"Then get in bed, dammit," wrote Kleber.

She tore all of the papers into tiny pieces and burned them in his Jell-O dish. Then she slipped under the covers and held her battered lover the rest of the night. At one point Kleber curled into the curve of Ceil's warm body. She felt him tremble and she heard dry sobs burst from his throat. There was nothing she could do but hold him and caress him and whisper that she would always be there. They floated after that on the indefinite sea of semiconsciousness. Just before dawn, Ceil thought she heard Kleber say, clearly, out loud, "Dammit, why *me?*" And, a few moments after that, "I love you, babe." She bolted awake but when she looked at Kleber in the soft new morning light his eyes were firmly closed. Obviously she was dreaming.

Fights broke out in the spectator line on this morning of freezing rain and bone-chilling winds. Police closed the north end of town and tried to discipline an estimated 10,000 people who clamored to attend the trial. Monumental traffic jams. Helicopters buzzed dangerously low, bearing television cameramen; the winds imperiled their course. A photographer with a long-lens camera fell off the roof of a three-story building and broke his leg. The news posse galloped to take a new picture. A delegation of Mack Crawford fan clubs arrived in three chartered buses. Someone at the head of the line was reportedly asking—and got—$1,000 for a priority number guaranteed to gain admission to the court spectator section.

Judge Mustardseed arrived in a mood as gloomy as the December norther. Someone asked for his autograph and he threatened to have her arrested for blocking public access. On his way to the bench, he lectured the audience. If anybody felt like sneezing, best it be done right now. Any intrusion down the line would result in severest judicial displeasure. Hizzoner limped to his chair. The storm had bedeviled his bones. Everybody in the chamber past fifty sympathized with arthritic joints.

Sledge promised the bench there would be no unnecessary theatrics but it was clear the drama could not play otherwise. Kleber had been delivered to the courthouse in a borrowed Brink's truck, whisked wheelchair and all up a back flight of stairs guarded by a dozen men with drawn pistols. He waited now in an anteroom. He was wearing an ill-fitting salmon-colored leisure suit that Sledge told Darlene to buy at J. C. Penney's. He was thirty pounds underweight and looked like a poor relation come to town for a funeral. He needed a haircut and his skin was gray but he otherwise resembled a whole and rational human person. Since nobody had seen the Prince of Power in almost three months, when he had been arrested at the lake house, his anticipated appearance contained exceptional suspense.

Sledge called out the name loud and clear. Everyone strained to see the bailiff's door. Then damned if Kleber Cantrell didn't stroll casually into the courtroom all by himself. He had disdained wheelchair or stretcher. The heart of Calvin Sledge commenced to pound with happiness. Somehow he knew that the rest of the way up Pike's Peak wouldn't even make him breathe hard. Ceil Shannon must have sweet-talked him during the night. A splash of honey had worked when a bath of vinegar failed. Hooray for wimmenfolk!

Judge Mustardseed explained to the jurors that this witness had suffered a gunshot wound in the throat, but he left the who, where, and why unelaborated. The old magistrate examined Kleber like a rancher eyeing a dubious cow pony. He did everything but peer at his teeth. Then he explained what the State of Texas proposed. If Kleber chose to testify, then immunity would be granted by the District Attorney's office against any further prosecution in this matter, specifically the charge of slipping out of Harris Hospital to thwart justice.

"You understand what I'm talkin' about, young man?" asked the judge.

Kleber blinked his eyes and slowly nodded.

"Can you answer me out loud, son?"

Kleber shook his head.

Judge Mustardseed directed his court reporter to designate for the record that the witness was responding by head movements. A pad and several sharpened pencils were placed on the witness-box railing. If he wished to amplify an answer by writing, then so be it.

Otto Leo jumped up with a list of prepared objections as long as the greediest kid's Christmas wants. The judge said hold-your-horses. "Let's just see where this thing goes," he said. "You can always object down the line."

"Is your name Kleber Cantrell?" began Sledge.

Nod.

"Do you hear what I am saying to you?"

Nod.

"Are you able to answer orally? In your own voice?"

Shake.

"What is your occupation?"

Kleber raised his eyebrows and looked amused.

"Use the tablet if you like," said Sledge.

No response.

"Are you a writer?"

Nod.

"Can you write out your answers for this court?"

Kleber hesitated and made no movement of his head. Judge Mustardseed asked if that was a yes or a no. Predictably, Otto bounced to the top of his tasseled crocodile shoes. "Objection, please. Objection! I've never seen anything quite like this in thirty years at the bar. The District Attorney is putting on some dog and pony show. I must strenuously object to this inflammatory and prejudicial spectacle."

"Overruled," said the judge.

"I want an *exception* to *that,*" snapped Otto.

"You may have *that.*"

"I object to everything that comes out of his mouth," protested Otto.

"*Nothing* is coming out of his mouth," said the judge.

"This sorry charade is an insult to the American system of justice," said Otto.

"Mr. Leo, would you like a refresher course tonight in the American system of penology?" The lawyer sat down and steamed.

Sledge enjoyed the threat and counterthreat but he knew the bench was apprehensive over the unorthodox events. He had to hurry; no time remained to erect a character monument to Kleber Cantrell's distinguished standing in the community. He had to gamble that the jurors already knew of Kleber's celebrity—and that they would thus believe him.

"Do you know the defendant, Thomas Jeremiah Luther, also known as The Chosen?" asked Sledge routinely.

It would be reported that up to this point the writer had not even glanced over at the preacher, though less than first-down yardage separated them. From the moment Kleber entered the courtroom, he had occupied an impenetrable world, a man caught in the aspic of silence. He did not respond to the question.

Again. "Do you know the defendant?"

When no answer was forthcoming, Judge Mustardseed, concerned, suggested a glass of water. It was held to Kleber's lips but he did not sip. Desperation began to climb up Calvin Sledge's spine. He saw the judge reaching for his gavel. He knew that unless the damnably mute man at least bobbed his head, then it was over. *"It's time to go back down the hill, son,"* his father had said forty years ago. *"The view from here's no different from what's up-a-yonder."* Please, he implored silently. Please, Kleber. Please move your goddamn head. He asked the question one last time. "Do you know the defendant, Thomas Jeremiah Luther?" *His career was ending.* "Answer, *please!*"

Sudden murmurs in the audience built into a commotion. Behind him, at the defense table, The Chosen slowly rose, yanked away his dark glasses, knocked over his chair, raised high the Holy Bible, and cried with glorious pulpit passion, *"Answer* the man, Kleber. You cannot deny you *know* your brother!"

And Kleber did look. He found the eyes that dared him. They were scarred again. The sight smote him. He began to tremble, little ripples at first like a man suffering the damp, chill shock of a fast-rolling fog on a night beach. Then he quaked. Spasms jolted his body. His mouth worked silently, opening and closing like a creature removed from oxygen support.

The old judge yelled at the defendant to sit down. He directed bailiffs to tote the stricken witness out of the courtroom. Even though this was done hurriedly, every person in the chamber glimpsed the face of a man seized by awful, organic, unspeakable terror.

"The state rests, your honor," said Calvin, grabbing the theatrical moment, benefactor of an unforeseen blessing. Without uttering a single word, the Prince of Power had seemingly nailed the Prince of Temptation to a very strong limb.

Sister Crystal was ashamed of her weakness but the fact was she was very hungry. She tried to deny the gnawing in her stomach but the realization came that if she did not eat she would be unable to carry on with her prayers. Thus did she ring for the elevator but it did not come. She rang again. She beat on the button. Then she grew worried. Never before had the elevator failed to descend and obediently fetch her from the bottom of the pit. This being the core and soul of the City of Miracles, it was always kept in excellent repair. She whimpered and shouted, and when no one came to aid her, Sister Crystal began to climb up the scaffolding. With considerable difficulty she pulled her body upward, fearful of the plastic demons and imps and gargoyle faces affixed to the innards of the plunging circular walls. The monsters bobbed on their springs and teased her. Then her foot tripped one of the release mechanisms that set the cacophonous music into play, causing her ascent to be serenaded by shrieking atonal chords and ear-aching bursts of trumpet choirs. Twice she slipped and her hands were torn by jutting nails. She clawed her way to the surface with prayers spilling from her lips. She ran to the storehouse where food was stored, eager to partake of the abundant harvests of God. But there she discovered two of the students filling gunny sacks with vegetables and toting out cases of canned goods. They were stacking produce into a pickup truck parked outside. At Sister Crystal's unexpected appearance, the boys seemed disturbed and more than a mite guilty. "We're moving this stuff to a safe place," one of them told her, but she saw him wink at his companion.

She went in search of a piece of bread but there was not a single loaf in the bin that normally contained hundreds of freshly baked, aromatic trays. The pantries were empty. Even the supplies of salt and spices and teas were gone. One of the students threw her a fat, mushy, overripe tomato and though there were liver-brown spots on the sides she ate it eagerly.

"What is the news from the trial?" she asked.

"The Chosen says for all of us to pray hard," said one of the boys, promptly scooting out with his cohort and speeding away with their load of food. In their wake, Sister Crystal found a can of pork and beans on the floor. But she did not know how to open the can. No one had ever taught her this mundane ability. She rummaged through the kitchen drawers and found a set of honed knives. She selected a blade of six inches and commenced to stab a hole large enough to drain the beans. Then, feeling a wave of unease that bordered on indefinable fear, she slipped the knife into a deep pocket hidden in the folds of her gown.

On the ten o'clock evening news, the television commentator said, "Mr. Cantrell's bombshell appearance on the witness stand late this afternoon was considered a damaging blow to the Reverend Luther's defense. Cantrell, the former Fort Worth man who has become nationally prominent as a journalist-author-broadcaster, appeared to disintegrate emotionally at first sight of The Chosen. He had to be carried out of the courtroom in what appeared to spectators as deep shock. He was readmitted to Harris Hospital shortly after six p.m. A hospital spokesman refused comment on his condition."

Sandy Double was reading on this December night, three days before Christmas. The box of papers that VeeJee Cantrell had given to

him was neatly labeled, "KLEBER CANTRELL—EARLY YEARS—
1950–1960." It contained hundreds of articles from college newspapers, term papers, letters, laundry lists. "Lord, Lord, don't that boy
ever throw anything away?" groaned Sandy. He saw no purpose in
wading through what a man had written two decades and more ago,
but Sandy Double had a firm sense of professional responsibility. Calvin told him to read this shit and read it he would.

It was close to midnight and his eyes were squinting and folding
when Sandy came across a thick collection of carbon-copy pages fastened with a safety pin. The carbons were poor and difficult to read.
But the title page was interesting. "THE THREE PRINCES—An Exercise in Short Fiction—by K. Cantrell, New York, N.Y., 1956."

He read the first paragraph:

"It had rained for nine days straight and our mood was as foul as
the landscape. We were the Three Princes, by official decree of the
class, and our kingdom was muddy despair. The city of Makebelieve,
La., where we grew up, had no pleasures available to three hearty
young men the night before their graduation from high school. But we
wanted to make these special hours worth remembering. Maybe that's
why we listened to the siren call of C. G. Licker, the temptor prince.
Would to God that we had not. . . ."

And he kept on reading.

Otto Leo was concerned, but not overly so, by the dramatic appearance of Kleber Cantrell on the witness stand. He surprised just
about everybody by failing to ask for a mistrial that would have probably been his for the asking. The lawyers went into Judge Mustardseed's
office and Leo immediately said, "My client does not want an aborted
trial. He doesn't want to go through this ordeal again."

Judge Mustardseed offered, "I'll instruct the jury to disregard Mr.
Cantrell's behavior."

"That's like throwing a skunk into the deliberation room and telling the jurors not to smell it," said Leo, looking at the DA with professional disgust. "You should rebuke Mr. Sledge."

Calvin felt no shame. He suspected that the trial would fail to run
its course, that a verdict could not be reached. Nonetheless, every
media outlet in the country was chattering this night with reports of the
fear that came over the writer when forced to look at the man of mira-

cles. And they were saying that the District Attorney was fighting a scrappy fight.

Otto Leo had further reasons for wishing the trial to continue. One was homage to his ego, of which there were few so inflated. He existed only for his professional life. He so hated his private self that he had, in effect, banished the private man. He even undressed in darkness, taking off his toupee, his elevated shoes, and his waist-cincher and thus not having to look at the bald, sagging little fat man whom he had loathed since the pattern was set in childhood. He knew about masks and respected the cleverness with which The Chosen wore his.

Though well known in the State of Texas, Otto Leo sorely craved to be placed in the pantheon of lawyers beside Clarence Darrow and Oliver Wendell Holmes. He knew from the first night that The Chosen called him that this would be the missile that might orbit Otto Leo into history. He had prepared a *beautiful* defense! It would be written about in legal journals and become part of the curriculum for criminal law. On tap he had eighty-eight witnesses, ranging from gunsmiths who would refute State testimony about Magnum .44 "hair triggers" to medical authorities with expert testimony about the deleterious effects of too much cocaine. He had a psychiatrist from U.T. ready to attack the fallibility of "eyewitness testimony." *En bloc* he had, Otto felt, enough testimony to acquit T. J. Luther for the burning of Atlanta.

There was a secondary reason. In Otto Leo's fat briefcase were half a dozen letters of inquiry from New York publishing companies. Each passionately desired to sign him for a memoir of The Chosen's murder trial. He had written back personally to each, expressing thanks, begging forbearance, tossing in as a throwaway line that he certainly saw the value of such a book, that he would not consider writing it for less than a million-dollar advance. It was a gamble, he knew. But he had enough faith in the brilliance and posture of Otto Leo that he could afford to wait until the end of the historic trial. Then it might cost somebody *two* million.

The Chosen was not in his jail cell when Otto Leo went to visit him. The guard grinned and said, "T.J.'s around here someplace. He makes himself to home, you know." A brief search located the minister in an office talking on the telephone. He was sitting with his feet propped on the guard's desk and as he spoke he picked at a tray of food sent over from the Fort Worth Club. He hung up and embraced his lawyer expansively.

"I'm ready, Otto," said The Chosen. "I'm glad you came. We need to pray together."

"Which we will, Reverend. First, I want us to go over this list of witnesses. I've decided to lead off with Dr. Cyman from Austin. He'll knock the crap out of Cantrell."

The Chosen shook his head. "That won't be necessary," he said. "We only need one witness."

"And who might that be?"

"God will speak through me. I will testify on behalf of me—and of my God."

During jury selection, Otto Leo cautioned the panel that "the accused reverend" might or might not testify in his own behalf, stressing urgently that this must not be a factor in adjudging guilt or innocence. At that early date, the lawyer had no intent of exposing his volatile client to brutal cross from the State. The peril was that The Chosen might deviate from the rehearsed script and pop out with some careless remark, something impulsive that could open doors better left locked. But now, as he studied The Chosen's unperturbed face, Otto calculated he could take the risk. The way this trial was going, there would probably be so many reversible errors that T.J. could stand on the defense table and deliver the Sermon on the Mount.

Nevertheless, he warned The Chosen of the danger in testifying and began to rehearse him for Q. and A.

"I know the questions and I know the answers," said The Chosen.

"Careful now, Reverend," said Leo. "Don't delude yourself into thinking this is some great epic theology trial. This isn't Galileo or Martin Luther. This is Fort Worth, Texas, the Year of Our Lord 1975, and the charge is murder one."

"There was no murder, Mr. Counselor. God knows that."

"God doesn't vote here. Twelve jurors do."

"As soon as they hear the truth of God, there will be but one vote. Now go get some rest. You look tired." T.J. dismissed Otto and went to his cell to read his Bible.

"What is your name, please?" asked Otto Leo respectfully.

"I was baptized Thomas Jeremiah Luther. Nine and one half years ago I became The Chosen."

"What is your age?"

"I am forty-two by the numbers of man."

Otto furrowed his brow in signal to his client. No funny answers, dammit.

"What is your occupation?"

"Minister of God."

"Any certain denomination?"

T.J. smiled and shook his head. "No sir. Non-denominational. Our church is open to everybody, even lawyers." His face was a poem to triumph over pain. His scarred eyes were the penalties of a martyr. He sat attentively and military-straight in the chair, knowing how to use the crook-neck microphone dangling before his lips. He did not lean forward and bark, as most witnesses do. He sat back and let the amplification pick up his natural tones. He wore a baby-blue suit that had been tailor-pinned earlier this morning by two of the jailhouse trustees. They wanted T.J. to look his best. On his lapel, the gold cross glittered and, thanks to careful posture, was always visible to the jurors. Not only did T.J. kiss the Holy Bible when sworn in, he embraced it to his heart. Sledge was getting worried anew. This was one helluva convincing witness. He was coming across so benign that Kleber Cantrell's seizure-by-terror might suddenly seem contrived, a prank of the prosecution.

"Where were you born?" asked Otto.

"Right here in Fort Worth," answered T.J. "I'm a fourth-generation Texan. My great-grandparents emigrated here from Georgia after the Civil War. They came across the South in a wagon. Almost starved to death. They were bound for Louisiana, so the family story goes, but they didn't like the swamp and the mosquitoes over there so they pushed on into Texas. Started farming out near Parker County."

The jury appeared interested in the family biography. Cleverly, Otto was establishing his client as a down-home boy. Sledge had anticipated this, but now there was nothing he could do to dispute the Norman Rockwell cover sitting.

"Did you attend school in Fort Worth?"

"Yes sir. Public school education. One of my most pleasant memories was being voted class favorite at Western High in 1950."

"After that did you perform military service?"

"Sure did. Volunteered for the Korean War. You'll remember that war. It was pretty unpopular, too. I trained over at Fort Bliss before going to the Orient." Damned if T.J.'s gold cross didn't look like a medal for heroism. Calvin Sledge snorted to himself. In the case file was T. J. Luther's sorry military record, more pockmarked with disciplinary demerits than a firing range target, but he could not get it before the eyes of the jury.

"Honorably discharged?"

"Of course."

"After the war, did you become a minister?"

Sledge had real difficulty containing his anger. The defense lawyer was now jumping from 1953 to 1966, deftly omitting a decade and a half of mischief, crime, and misbehavior. It wasn't fair!

"I never actually studied for the ministry," answered T.J. At that, Otto tapped the folder in his hands, like a signal from the third-base coach. The witness was moving into potentially dangerous territory. Sledge listened carefully; perhaps preacher man might inadvertently expose a scab he could pick.

"But you did *become* a minister, is that correct?"

"Sure did. And high time. I was two thirds down the road to hell when God tapped me on the shoulder."

Whoops! The look on Leo's face showed that *that* was not the rehearsed answer. Hurriedly he moved in a new direction. "Where do you now practice your ministry?"

The Chosen was not yet ready for further query. "I want the jury to know *everything* about me," he went on. "I danced with the devil. I did things I am mightily ashamed of . . ."

With Calvin Sledge hanging on to every syllable, expecting the witness to make a serious mistake, Judge Mustardseed broke in and shattered hope. He told the witness it was unnecessary to hark back to the shaded paths of youth. "You're testifying," said the judge. "You're not in some confession booth."

"I thank you for the advice, your honor," said The Chosen. "I just don't want this court to think I'm holdin' things back. If I lied about *this,* then I might be lyin' about *that.*"

"Counselor, move your witness along. Mr. Luther, just answer what your lawyer asks you."

Otto bowed gratefully. "Ah, Reverend . . ."

Sledge decided to get a modest, cranky lick in. "Objection. The witness's religious ordination has not been established. He is not a reverend yet."

"Sustained," said the judge surprisingly.

"Very well. Are you an ordained minister?" asked Leo.

"I am."

"Where were you ordained, Reverend?"

"In God's house. God told me to create a ministry."

Amused but careful, Sledge rose again. "Objection—and I admit to not knowing exactly how to phrase this. But unless the witness can provide some substantiation for his . . . ah . . . theological diploma . . . he can't call himself reverend."

Otto Leo, having done his homework, rushed to the bench and whispered out of jury earshot, "Anybody in Texas can call himself reverend. You don't have to have a theology degree." Judge Mustardseed covered the microphone with his hand and leaned forward. "How's that again?" he requested. His hearing aid was fouled and needed new batteries. Leo repeated his answer with amplification but it was still not enough for the judge's hearing capacities. Hizzoner stretched his ear right down to Otto's mouth but in so doing removed his hand from the microphone. Everybody in the courtroom was thus permitted to hear Otto Leo hiss, in exasperation, "Any tomfool who wants to can call himself reverend!" Amid laughter, the judge granted permission for T.J.'s self-bestowed appellation.

"Sir," compromised the defense counsel, "do you know . . ." Otto was flustered; he corrected himself. ". . . *Did* you know the deceased, McKenzie Crawford, Jr.?"

"Yes," said T.J. He shook his head sadly.

"Do you know Kleber Cantrell?"

"Yes indeed."

"How do you happen to be acquainted with these men?"

"We grew up together. On Cloverdale Avenue right here. Arlington Heights. We were closer than blood brothers. We shared much of our lives."

"Over the years, I take it, you maintained this close friendship?"

T.J.'s face darkened with a sense of loss. "Well, yes. From my point of view, I thought we did. At least I sure never changed. We did go our separate ways, of course. You could say we kept up with each other."

"I see. And on the night of May 9, 1975, did you have occasion to reunite, as it were, with McKenzie Crawford, Jr., and Kleber Cantrell?"

"I did. And I want to tell about it."

From the packed house came murmurs of excitement and one hearty shout, "Amen!" Judge Mustardseed had no trouble hearing *that*. He pounded and scolded, "This is not the church house, folks." To which T. J. Luther added a faint "Amen."

"Please tell this court, Reverend, about the night of May 9. How was it that you three boyhood friends happened to get together?"

T.J. sucked in a huge breath and nodded vigorously. "First, I want to remind everybody that what I'm about to tell is the truth, the whole truth, and nothin' but the truth—so help me God." Judge Mustardseed banged. "You're already sworn to that. Any deviation from the truth is perjury. Now get on with it."

"Please continue, Reverend."

"That afternoon, Kleber came out to the City of Miracles all got up like a spy. Turned out he was a fox in sheep's clothing. He was bound and determined to expose our church and hold us up to shame and ridicule. . . ."

Sledge objected hotly. "That's hearsay, speculation, and . . ."

The judge agreed. Otto Leo tried to appear gravely wounded by the ruling. "Your honor, as we discussed in chambers, it is imperative that the relationship between these three men be established, particularly the *state of mind* of the deceased and the accused minister."

"Well, Counselor, your witness can tell what *he* did and what *he* said, but I won't let him speculate any motivation of Mr. Cantrell. Or of the dead man. You still have the right to cross-examine Mr. Cantrell. I gave it to you."

The Chosen chose an inopportune moment to remark, "The way he looked yesterday, ole Kleber's not up to tellin' anybody what he was doin' that day."

The judge scowled. He shook his gavel at T.J. "Young man, you don't say anything in this courtroom less'n you're asked. Understood?"

"I just want the jury to understand why Kleber came to my church."

"*Hush!*" And, to the fidgeting defense lawyer, the judge warned, "Counselor, if you cannot keep your witness within the boundaries of courtroom procedure, I will undertake to do it for you."

Wonderfully amused, in fact delighted, Calvin Sledge slipped into his seat, not caring a damn about objections. What he should have done was write a bread-and-butter note to preacher man, thanking him for resurrecting the ghastly face of a witness in terror.

Sister Crystal knew she was forty-one years old because they told her so. She *knew* very little else about herself. She carried no memories of girlhood, no faces in a mind's picture album that could be studied for identity and anchor. The day she left the state hospital, the authorities said it had been a pleasure having her as a patient for almost twenty years. That was the first moment she really knew where she had been for two decades. Everything was a blur before The Chosen reached into her heart and gave her the love of God. And these recent years of cloister within the City of Miracles were wondrous.

She remembered in vivid detail every moment since The Chosen smiled at her in the hospital and laid his hand on her brow. She could recall as clearly as the lyrics of anthems how happy she felt when The Chosen decreed her new name to be Sister Crystal, a tribute to the facets and purity of her voice. She much preferred her new name to Jane Doe, which was what she had answered to at the hospital. She remembered how thrilling it was when the doctors said it was all right for her to leave Rusk and accompany The Chosen to his City of Miracles. There she gladly stripped out of the navy jumper and gray sweater the hospital had dressed her in, exchanging those garments for the warm, marmoreal, loving folds of The Chosen's bridesmaids.

Part of the initiation ceremony was the traditional giving of a dowry to The Chosen. On the day she was accepted, Sister Crystal was hugely embarrassed. She watched the other women present rich tribute. Sister Gentilla laid a handful of gold Krugerrands, shares in three producing gas wells, and two lovely lithographs on the altar of miracles. The Chosen blessed her profusely. When it was her turn, Sister Crystal fidgeted and stammered that she was ashamed. Her dowry was of meager worth. But The Chosen smiled graciously and reminded everyone in the congregation that day of the poor widow's tithe in the Bible, exclaiming in joyous thanksgiving over each item in her drawstring pillowcase. The pathetic items tumbled into The Chosen's outstretched hands as if they were precious jewels. The Chosen announced that these tributes to God would go into a special locker in the vaults of the church. It comforted Sister Crystal thereafter to imagine God accepting her possessions. She fantasized Him caressing her comb with the torn teeth, the harmonica that the black janitor at the hospital had given her so she would not tell anybody he liked to wash her body all by himself, $9.45 in nickels and dimes earned from tatting lace handkerchiefs, the ring, the dried wildflowers and colored pebbles.

At dawn on Christmas Eve, she went into the dark and sad Miracle Sanctuary. She fell to her knees on the empty stage and prayed. "I wish I had something else to give to the Chosen today," she prayed. "Lord, tell me what I can do to help my master."

"Whose idea was it to go to the farmhouse?" asked Otto Leo gingerly. He had tenuous control of his witness, like the rider of a horse which ignored the reins.

"I think it was a mutual desire," answered The Chosen. "As I testified earlier, when Kleber and me picked up Mack at his ex-wife's house, he was highly intoxicated. I wanted to sober him up before we entered the City of Miracles."

Sledge scribbled the one question he had never been able to reason out: *Why did these three men go to an abandoned shack in the middle of the night?* He anticipated keeping preacher man on the stand a full week, when and if he got his turn.

"What happened there?" asked Leo.

"Well, we all went inside. I had a thermos of hot coffee. Kleber and I persuaded Mack to sit down and behave." T.J. arched his eyebrows for the jury, inviting sympathy for the difficult chore of dealing with drunks.

"Was there a quarrel?"

"Not at first. At first it was a reunion. I was so glad to have a private moment with these old friends because I knew the spotlight would hit us, the next day. It was my wish that we could let down our hair, push back the years, reclaim the happiness of twenty-five years gone by . . . I was so proud of those boys . . . and . . ." The preacher faltered here, eyes glistening with exquisitely timed fresh tears. "And, I confess, I wanted *them* to be proud of me, too. . . ."

Mawkish as it was, T.J. made a valid point concerning the pedigrees of celebrity. He was believable in his desire to measure press clippings. Celebrity is like a stock purchase that requires daily perusal of the Dow Jones index. "Now, Reverend, please tell the court about the events leading up to the accident," asked Otto.

Calvin Sledge had to object to that. "Accident?" The indictment read murder. Sustained. "Counsel protests with good cause," agreed Judge Mustardseed. Strike "accident."

"Very well, what happened before the gun . . . *went off*, Reverend?"

The Chosen clamped his eyes shut and appeared discomfited. "It's all a blur," he whispered. This was not the answer Otto Leo had sown and fertilized in long rehearsal. Early on he had considered and rejected the tempting defense posture of temporary insanity, of blackouts and blurs, diminished responsibility. The script here called for T.J. to go into graphic detail about how drunk and menacing was Mack Crawford.

"Did the deceased threaten you?" guided Leo, trying to get his witness back on track.

"I don't remember," answered T.J. "Mack was tired. He was crying. He didn't make much sense. He seemed ashamed of his life."

Calvin Sledge objected for no particular reason other than disliking the morose character of T.J.'s testimony. He knew he would be overruled and he was.

"It was one of those rare moments when people speak candidly about their lives," went on T.J. "I told those boys that hatred and anger had dwelled in me for many years. When the three of us were in high school together, I was the class favorite. Everybody liked me. It was official. They voted on it. But the day after they handed out diplomas, my phone quit ringing. Nobody paid me any attention and it hurt. I'd be a liar if I said otherwise. . . ."

Judge Mustardseed intruded patiently but The Chosen plowed ahead.

"If you've never been popular, then it don't cause much pain when you lose it. But I *suffered*. The years went on, and I tried to be proud of Kleber for the words he wrote and the power he got. And I went to Mack's movies and sat out there in the darkness, trying to applaud. My best friends cut me off. They didn't take me along on their trip to the famous place. And that night, that night at Uncle Bun's, I told them how much they hurt me. But I forgave them, for I had been admitted to a far greater fraternity, the kingdom of God!"

By now Otto Leo's luxuriant dyed-mahogany eyebrows had become semaphores in vain attempt to staunch the stream of consciousness. Nothing is as perilous as a rambling witness, particularly a defendant trying to explain away a murder. But if The Chosen recognized his lawyer's panic, he did not acknowledge it. "So when I told my friends the source of my pain, they both denied it. Kleber said no snub was ever intended. He said he had been too busy all his life; he said there was always another piece of news waiting to be found. He said don't take it personally. He said he treated everybody that way."

Judge Mustardseed had heard enough. "Counselor, direct your witness to respond more concisely. He's wanderin' all over the lot."

Otto nodded gratefully. "Reverend, the court values your candor. . . . Now I direct your attention to State's Exhibit H." He gestured toward the table on which rested the .44 Magnum that tore the life from Mack Crawford and the voice from Kleber Cantrell. A flaw in Calvin Sledge's case was his inability to trace legal ownership of the weapon. It had been manufactured in the 1950's but no further custody was introduced for the record. Sledge had tried to skid past this shortcoming, offering instead crime lab reports that irrefutably identified T.J.'s fingerprints on the gun, along with a vague admission the preacher made the night of the killing. "Yeah, it's mine," he had stated but refused to elaborate where or how he obtained the weapon.

It was Otto's urgent task to tone down the image of a supposed man of God toting around a gun powerful enough to obliterate a rhino's snout. There are four legal reasons for carrying a handgun in Texas—and on the surface it would have seemed The Chosen flunked the tests. The "special" conditions allowing a gun to be carried are: (1) taking it from place of purchase to a home, (2) taking it to a gun shop for repair, (3) going to and from a firing range, (4) protecting oneself if one habitually carries large sums of money—but the gun can be carried by law only on the most direct route from the source of money to the bank or home.

Otto worked cautiously. "Reverend, a man in your position must get a lot of threats, isn't that true?"

"Unfortunately, it is."

"You have a reputation for telling it like it is, for being outspoken in the pulpit and on television. I suspect there are a lot of people who don't like the scorching heat of revelation, aren't there, Reverend Luther?"

T.J. nodded obediently. "Even a man of God has to worry about threats. I know many preachers who must carry a means of self-protection. There's always some self-anointed avenger out yonder."

"And I suppose there are occasions when you personally carry substantial sums of money from the church house to the bank?"

At his table, Sledge scribbled gleefully: *At one o'clock in the morning?*

"That's very true," agreed T.J. "There's no need to hide the truth, Counselor. I *do* carry a gun because I am a soldier of the Lord. Soldiers must be armed. The Lord told Moses that. It is the commandment of God."

Otto Leo started to segue into threats from Mack Crawford but his client was not yet ready to depart the munitions field. The Chosen swiveled toward the jury box. "Besides," he said confidentially, "I've owned that piece at least twenty years. My ex-wife gave it to me. She was a Craymore. People like the Craymores had to protect themselves, too. It's a part of life." He paused to let the substantial Fort Worth family name soak into the atmosphere. He did not notice Calvin Sledge writing down another note to himself: *Pull the Melissa Craymore file.*

Otto glanced at his watch. Twenty past four. He should have stopped but he was discontent with his client's answers concerning Mack Crawford's behavior on the fatal night. "Reverend Luther, on the night of May 9, 1975, did the deceased threaten you? Did you fear for your life?"

"I've never been afraid of anybody," answered T.J. "Nothing but the wrath of God. Mack threatened me, sure, but it wasn't Mack, *per se*. What I faced that night was a serpent's tongue and eyes that glazed hell's fire and breath as foul as jackal dung. Mack was gone. The thing that took his place was the embodiment of evil. I had lost Mack a long time ago. Mack died years before the night of May 9, 1975."

"Reverend, please answer this question 'yes' or 'no.' Did Mr. Crawford threaten your physical person?"

"That's beside the point. I shouldn't be on trial. There are no issues. I didn't shoot him, though I wouldn't mind taking credit on Judgment Day. The Lord Himself slew a devil." Whereupon Judge Mustardseed choked and called it quits for the day.

In his office, Judge Mustardseed discovered a fine bottle of whiskey that some lawyer had sent over as a Christmas gift. He decreed it was a worthy present and opened it immediately. He poured strong drinks in Styrofoam cups for the lawyers that crowded around his desk.

"I would be inclined, Mr. Leo, to consider any defense request for a mistrial," said the judge.

"I'm grateful for your invitation, Judge. But my client refuses to ask for one."

"He ain't got much sense," mused the judge. "He needs his head examined."

"It has been," pointed out the DA quickly. Preacher man had long ago satisfied the tests of reality, Rorschach, and reason.

Of course, the judge did not have to await a lawyer's request to abort the trial. He possessed the power to end it no matter what the feelings of The Chosen. The judge was supposed to protect a defendant's rights. But he had agreed to hear the case (when no other judge wanted to go near it) because he had the reputation for being able to squeeze, pressure, even coerce a verdict out of any jury. Moreover, the old judge had one of the most enviable appellate records in the judiciary. Rarely was his work overturned or criticized by higher courts. At the sunset of a distinguished career, Judge Mustardseed did not want to be remembered as the pilot who bailed out of a malfunctioning airplane rather than fly it by the seat of his pants to a landing of some sort. Besides, there was money to consider. The newspapers had been trumpeting that so far the trial had already cost Tarrant County upward of $700,000—and, if stopped, that would be money down the sewer. Being a conservative given to peppery scoldings concerning government boondoggles, Judge Mustardseed did not want to be accused of waste. He asked Calvin Sledge what the prosecution felt about continuing the trial.

"Well, sir, now that the Lord has just entered this case as a co-defendant, I'd sure like to see it get to a jury," he allowed.

Otto was insulted. While not necessarily *defending* his client's startling testimony, the lawyer did wish to remind both bench and opposition that "an act of God" was often pertinent in civil action.

"You wanna try and prove that God pulled the trigger, boy?" demanded the judge.

"Joan of Arc's 'voices' are well known to history," said Otto.

"And," said the judge, "if memory serves, she was French-fried."

The judge gave one of his now famous vague waves. He would let the damn thing run on awhile longer, warning that he would not tolerate side trips into the realms of theology, mysticism, and general nonsense. The way he said it indicated that he was acting against wisdom and might stop the drama at any given moment. Once again he reminded the warriors that the issues were sharply defined:

Was a murder committed? By the defendant? Can the State of Texas prove this murder beyond reasonable doubt? "It's as clear as crick water less'n you fellers pee in it," opined the bench.

That night The Chosen sent word out of the jail that he did not wish to commune with his attorneys. He was giving Christmas counseling and inspirational talks to other prisoners.

That night Sandy Double finished reading "The Three Princes" for the fourth time. He was particularly struck by a much younger Kleber Cantrell's vivid description of a farmhouse where a young girl was raped by three high school friends and fed to a swollen river. There were eerie similarities between this "fictional" shack and the one where Mack Crawford was murdered. While he was pondering on this he remembered that old AP clipping over which Calvin had been briefly enamored, the one the crime lab dumped magic dust on. He spent the rest of the night wading through a blizzard of paper, searching for a connection. Just about sunrise he put two and two together. And he called Calvin with excitement in his voice.

This night Sister Crystal could not sleep. Her peace was tormented by interior winds that howled in her ears, by tears that formed without apparent cause and splashed on her face and stained it with rivulets like dusty rain. And voices were nagging at her. They were confusing and frightening and they would not go away.

Christmas Eve.

Fort Worth indulged in a lovely spectacle. The city's downtown skyscrapers edged their building lines with colored lights, turning the skyline into a tableau of giant packages. Only the courthouse remained dark, making it look like an unwrapped gift hidden on the back side of the tree. Salvation Army Santa Clauses worked the lines of people waiting to get into the trial, a mob so swelled by students home on holiday that it required forty police to control traffic.

At the opening gavel, Sandy Double rose to explain why Calvin Sledge was not in his seat. "He has a minor medical emergency," said the assistant DA, a lame excuse which Judge Mustardseed accepted in the spirit of the season. When Sledge flew into the chamber at 10:25 a.m., it was remarked how spiffy the prosecutor looked in a new navy pinstripe suit, an ensemble befitting a bank president.

Immediately there came a surprise. Sledge declined to cross-examine T. J. Luther for the time being, reserving the right to recall him at a later time if necessary. The Chosen appeared disappointed. He had enjoyed his day on the stand and reveled in his triumph over the prosecutor, if there was one.

With that, the defense rested. Otto Leo rushed up to file a motion for an instructed verdict of acquittal. But Judge Mustardseed refused, as was expected.

"Mr. Prosecutor, do you have rebuttal testimony?" inquired Judge Mustardseed.

"I sure do," said Sledge with the eagerness of a student who had prepared an exceptionally fine paper. He announced a name that nobody knew. "Mrs. Maurice Alonzo." And into the courtroom limped a crippled old apple-dumpling woman with a tender face and a jutting jaw and eyes that sparked as if fresh painted with sky-blue lacquer. She nodded pleasantly at all concerned, as amiable as the cookie lady. Otto Leo bent agitatedly into the ear of his client. Who was she? What did she have to do with the blood of celebrity? The Chosen searched her face for a landmark but found none. Calvin Sledge was perversely thrilled by the mystery. He wanted all the bastards to squirm.

"What is your name, ma'm?" asked the District Attorney.

"Mrs. Maurice Alonzo." The voice was clear and warm and southern.

"What is your age?"

"I'm forty-three." The answer evoked murmurs. The woman did not come across as vain, but she looked at least two decades older than her count.

"Do you know the defendant, Thomas Jeremiah Luther?"

"I do. I did."

"How do you come to know the accused?"

"He was my first husband," answered Melissa Craymore Luther Colefax Alonzo, thrice wed, thrice divorced, and much worse for wear. After four exasperating months of trying to unearth this woman, lo and behold she telephoned Sledge the night before from the Dallas–Fort Worth airport. Fate could not have delivered a more valuable gift.

"And where do you live?"

"In another state." That was Sledge's bargain. Missy agreed to testify only with the guarantee that her home address would not be revealed. She liked her life on the back side of Mobile, where she quietly owned an antique store and was recognized locally for the excellent golden retrievers she bred and showed. She also took lithium every day of her life and was medicated with three hundred milligrams while on the stand.

Sledge showed Missy the sinister-looking .44 Magnum, from which she immediately recoiled. Did she recognize this gun? Indeed she did. "This .44 belonged to my father, Wyman Craymore," she testified carefully. "I remember it well. It was his favorite. He bought it in London from some duchess he met on an elephant hunt in Kenya."

"Are you certain?"

"Absolutely positive." She turned the gun upside down and pointed to two tiny initials carved under the barrel. W.C. "Daddy had that done in London and the carver cracked up at somebody wanting W.C. scratched on a gun."

Missy rummaged in her purse and located an old, wrinkled bill of sale, written in flourishy, elegant script. The gun that killed Mack Crawford was more than two decades old.

Sledge continued. "The accused, Thomas Jeremiah Luther, has testified that he received this gun as a gift from you or from your late father's estate. To the best of your recollection, is that a true statement?"

Missy laughed indulgently. "No sir. He stole it. Without permission."

The commotion at the defense table was Otto Leo struggling to his feet, while The Chosen rose in concert, furiously shaking his head. It was the first time in four months that T.J. showed any anger. Sledge noticed two of the jurors looking at the preacher with new insight.

"Are you sure about that?" asked Sledge.

"I'd go to my grave on it. T.J. stole everything I had that wasn't nailed down."

Otto objected and was sustained but Missy was believable.

"When did you last see the defendant?" asked Sledge.

Missy did not hesitate. She nailed down her revenge. "Sometime in the spring of 1960," she recalled. "It was right after he abandoned me and burned down our honeymoon cottage."

"At any time in your marriage, did you ever hear T. J. Luther threaten to harm Mack Crawford?"

"Yes. At the Assembly Ball, in 1958. He said he wanted to kill Mack. He said he would never forget his vow."

"Thank you." Sledge sat down in a new field of clover.

On cross, Otto Leo mercilessly bared how many years in sum Missy had spent under the care of psychiatrists and in mental institutions—about one third of her entire life. But she was the tar baby of witnesses; the more Otto and his legions punched at her, the deeper their hands got stuck.

"Susan French, your honor," announced Sledge, setting off a stampede in the corridors. A cordon of deputies and bailiffs squeezed her through the media gauntlet, television's hot lights warming the cold gray afternoon. Beneath her eyes were smudges of sleepless exhaustion, clues to the torment that had shaped her decision to testify. She was a woman who did not relish the glare—not anymore—but the way she took the box indicated she had sufficient strength to endure it. She wore a charcoal wool pants suit with a vivid red scarf lashed about her throat, symbolic reminder that blood had been spilled.

Until the previous midnight, Susan French had continued to rebuff the District Attorney, warning that even if she was forced into court she would not be a helpful or responsive witness. Nonetheless Sledge had kept badgering her, needing her, recognizing that her lean, tart beauty would be welcome. Moreover, Susan was hometown, a link between Fort Worth and the heady cosmos of murdered celebrity. She was vital to shore up a maligned dead man's reputation. If she did not help the prosecution, the jury might buy T.J.'s story that Mack deserved killing.

What finally persuaded Susan was Sledge's clever needle that jabbed the woman's own sense of worth. "They're fixing to dump so much shit on Mack's grave that people will wonder how you could have ever stayed married to such a public nuisance," warned Sledge.

"Please, leave me alone," she had pleaded. "I have nothing to do with any of this. I'm like one of those innocent bystanders shot in a police stakeout."

"You were one of the last people to see Mack alive," reminded Sledge. "If you ever loved that man, and I know he loved you, then now's the time to demonstrate it. If you don't, you negate every moment of happiness you ever had with him."

Susan begged for one final hour to think it over, during which she tried to locate her son. The City of Miracles switchboard said Jeffie/Paul was "not answering." She left word. At 3:15 a.m. the boy called back, listened to his mother's decision, offered neither approval nor disapproval. "You do what you think's best, Mama," he said. "God love you."

Delicately, Sledge guided Susan through her marriage, separation, divorce, all peppered with objections from Leo. And rightly so. A long-broken union was of scant import to murder. But Sledge dallied nonetheless, gambling that the judge was as interested as the jury. He wanted everyone to appreciate what a terrific woman Mack was once married to.

Susan had steeled herself to edit the truth, but she was unprepared for how easy it was to lie. When Sledge asked if Mack was drunk and menacing toward her on the night he was shot, Susan shook her head solemnly and lied firmly, "No."

Did he appear intoxicated?

"Oh, he may have taken a drink that day. I don't know. He was just out with the boys. He seemed in good spirits."

"Ms. French," finished Sledge, "in the twenty some odd years that you knew McKenzie Crawford, Jr., as husband, lover, and friend, had you ever seen him commit a violent act?"

"Only in the movies," she answered, drawing poignant laughter. "The Mack Crawford I knew was sweet . . . and generous . . . and kind . . . and caring . . ." She began to falter. "And very very gentle . . ." She broke into tears of loss. "Mack was a *gentle*-man . . . and throughout his life, a lot of people *used* him badly . . ." Calvin Sledge said he had no more questions, and Otto Leo passed, wisely. A strong woman dissolved by grief was not to be squeezed further. Judge Mustardseed dabbed his eyes and thanked the witness and praised her courage in testifying.

The old jurist glanced at the wall clock. Ten to two. It was his intention to end the session early, mindful that the jurors were having a Christmas party in the hotel where they were sequestered. He had purchased each of them a gift—cologne for the ladies and shaving lotion for the gents—and looked forward toward sharing a glass of executive clemency eggnog. "I think it's about time for Christmas," said the judge. Then Calvin Sledge approached the bench and delivered one final surprise package. An unexpected witness.

"Can't he wait until after the Christmas recess?" whispered the judge.

"Maybe. Maybe not," answered the DA. "He's ready now. I spent an hour with him this morning. I can't guarantee he'll be ready next week. I think you'll agree his testimony is crucial for both sides."

The judge nodded, checked with Otto Leo, leaned toward the jury. "Folks, I'm sorry to keep you here a few minutes longer. But it's important. The District Attorney informs me that he wishes to recall Mr. Kleber Cantrell. It seems Mr. Cantrell has recovered not only his composure—but his voice."

"Well praise God!" cried the Prince of Temptation, AKA The Chosen, sounding as if his prayers had brought forth still another miracle.

CHAPTER THIRTY

The morning was etched in bleakest gloom. Heavy storm clouds swept in from the north, blown by swirling winds. Bitter sadness rooted in Sister Crystal's heart. Defying the weather, she ran to the little hill that would have been her traditional place on this normally festive day. If The Chosen had not been away, the City of Miracles would be on this morning ablaze with joy and festive color. The crowds would have started assembling before noon to obtain choice seats for the great Nativity pageant, in which Sister Crystal had played First Angel for many years.

Chilled by the winds, she closed her eyes and tried to remember, imagining the soft white celestial robes enfolding her body and the papier-mâché wings that sprouted from her shoulders. Always she had opened the spectacle by raising a golden horn to her lips. And always she had the honor of concluding the evening by singing the exquisite melody of "O Holy Night." But now all she could do was shiver on the forlorn mound—which during the Easter pageant doubled as Calvary. She looked out and saw no radiant faces, no avenue of blazing poinsettias, no tree groaning with gifts for the poor—only brown grass and naked, forlorn trees.

It commenced to rain, stinging ice drops. As Sister Crystal ran for shelter, she saw a procession of expensive cars prowling into the compound, parking just outside Miracle Tower. She hurried over to see what was happening. She recognized certain members of the City of Miracles executive board. Sister Gentilla stood under the portico with a large black umbrella, darting out to protect the important men from the rain. They looked somber, filing into the glass elevator and rising to the penthouse.

"What is happening?" asked Sister Crystal.

"A private meeting," answered Sister Gentilla, who always knew what was going on and teased the other women by refusing to tell.

"Is it bad?" demanded Sister Crystal.

"We must wait. They are discussing the future of The Chosen's ministry."

At the foot of the bronze tower, rumors crackled among those few of the devoted who remained. They pressed their bodies against the wall and watched the blinding sheets of rain and gossiped. Someone said that a new minister was being interviewed. Someone else whispered that the City of Miracles might even close for good. The executive board was gravely concerned over the health of The Right Side, particularly since the 1976 presidential election was beginning with primaries in the next few months. The fundamentalist voice was intended to be heard in all of its newfound power at the voting booths. Now a messy scandal had endangered the will of God and the health of America.

Shortly after noon the board members filed out, their faces crumpled and worn as pallbearers. Sister Crystal timidly approached a principal elder, the Waco rancher named Noah who himself had been acquitted of multiple murder. She asked what had happened.

Elder Noah had no time for Sister Crystal. Too much else was on his mind. He said brusquely, "Excuse me, Sister." And he reached into a throng of men to pluck out a thin, crew-cut fellow about thirty who wore a parson-black suit and a bright red holiday tie. The two men began to whisper but Sister Crystal overheard.

Elder Noah said, "Now listen, son, you go on back to the Hilton and talk to your sweet little wife and then you call me no later than six o'clock."

The young man nodded and said, "I sure will, sir. This is a big decision, you understand. It's come up so fast."

"Well," said Elder Noah. "We think you can handle it. We got to move!"

Some other men bundled the confused-looking newcomer into a Cadillac and they sped off in a big hurry.

Sister Crystal had waited patiently during all of this and now she repeated her question. "Can you tell me what's going on?"

"Nothin' much," said Noah. "We're all just waitin' for the trial to be over."

"Who was that young man?" asked Sister Crystal.

"Jimmy Lee Witherspoon. Fine young preacher from Galveston. He may help us out a little."

"The Chosen will return," insisted Sister Crystal. "This is but a test of faith. God will provide."

"Unfortunately, Sister," said Noah, getting into his Cadillac and revving the motor, "the Lord ain't paid many bills lately."

Sister Crystal positioned her body so that the car door could not close. Rain fell heavily on her face but she did not care. "What can we do, Brother?" she pleaded.

"Pray," answered Noah. "And stay strong in spirit. Remember what God told Moses, *'Thy enemies shall fall before you by the sword.'* "

"I will. Oh, I will."

Then, watching Noah drive out the gates, it came to Sister Crystal. The revelation. She knew what she had to do. She hurried, even though her head had begun to ache again and was torn by fragments, by scenes that would not focus, by voices that confused her with disparate commands. She would go to *him*. She would renew her commitment. She would drench him with love and devotion. She would tell The Chosen that the City of Miracles was imperiled. She would inform him that a new man was being groomed to take his place, as if anyone could take the place of The Chosen. And after she spoke to her master, she would go to the Hilton Hotel and warn this upstart Jimmy Lee Witherspoon of the futility of his course.

In the sub-basement of the tower was located a room where personal belongings were kept. Here reposed the previous lives of all the sisters and brothers who had abandoned their empty pasts to embrace The Chosen and his love. Fortunately, the guard had skipped after two payless Fridays and there was no one around to forbid Sister Crystal from breaking into her locker. Hurriedly, worried that someone would see her, she slipped out of her coarse linen robe and back again into the asylum-issue navy jumper and gray sweater. She brushed her hair until it dried and gleamed. She found the manila envelope that bore her names: JANE DOE — SISTER CRYSTAL. She broke the red wax seal and shook out the contents. A meager life spilled into her hands. It was tempting to stop and enjoy the dried flowers and the broken comb and the colored pebbles. But she had no time. She put the ring on her finger and eight dollars into her pocket, hoping that would be enough for the bus ride to downtown Fort Worth.

Just before she slipped out the front gates of the City of Miracles, Sister Crystal obeyed a new impulse. She secreted the purloined steak knife beneath her blouse. She was not quite sure why this was necessary, but the voices told her to be armed. While she waited for the bus, she did not feel the storm's assault. With one hand she grasped her money and with the other touched the comforting edge of sharpened steel.

"Are you the same Kleber Cantrell who testified earlier in this matter?" asked Calvin Sledge.

Kleber nodded. Then he looked directly out at The Chosen and this second time in the box there was no discernible fear in his eyes. "Yes," he added strongly. "I am." The sound of his voice set off a commotion in the courtroom. It was the first public sound uttered by the celebrated writer in eight months. Everyone strained to hear and Judge Mustardseed slammed his gavel so hard it actually broke.

"When did you regain your voice?" asked the District Attorney.

Kleber shrugged. "I don't know for sure."

"Was it this morning?"

Kleber shook his head. "I spoke to you this morning—for the first time—but . . ."

"Please go on. But *what?*"

"But I haven't been completely honest about this thing. At first—after I was shot—I had no voice. True tale. Nothing came out. Then, on down the line, I don't know exactly when, I discovered it was possible to whisper. But it hurt. Physically and emotionally. So I just elected to play it mute. I decided I'd used enough words for one lifetime anyway."

"Why are you making this statement now before the court?"

"Because there's been so much untruth and distortion tossed around in this matter—and because I'm ashamed of myself."

"Why are you ashamed of yourself?" asked the prosecutor, an unplanned and injudicious question, but one for which he wanted personally to know the answer.

Otto Leo, indignant, interrupted. "Objection, please. Extraneous. I don't wonder that this witness is ashamed of himself. He has lived a lie for all these months. He has deceived the pursuit of justice. And now he throws himself on the mercy of the court. Which Kleber Cantrell do we believe?"

The Chosen reached out and grabbed Otto's sleeve. "Hush," ordered the preacher. "Let him talk."

"Answer the question," instructed Judge Mustardseed.

Kleber took his time. "Because," he said softly, almost inaudibly, "because by remaining silent, I was negating my life. I started out here in this town twenty-five years ago looking for truths, and on the day when it came time to tell what happened to me—and to Mack—I hid. I regret it. I behaved like a coward. I apologize to the court."

Judge Mustardseed slapped his palm gently on the bench. "Let's get along with pertinent testimony," he ordered. "Let it be on the record that the court appreciates this witness's candor."

The bus fare was $1.25 and Sister Crystal paid in pennies and nickels, enjoying their melody as she dropped them into the box. They sounded like Christmas bells. The bus was almost empty, holding but a handful of country people going downtown to buy gifts. The driver told his new passenger to sit down in the front-row seat opposite him so that the blast of hot air from the heater could dry her. "A person could catch double pneumonia on a day like this," he said. He was a nice man. He asked if Sister Crystal had read the morning *Star-Telegram,* and when she said no, he tossed her the paper.

"You from the church?" asked the driver.

"Yes sir, I am," answered Sister Crystal politely.

"You going to visit the preacher?"

Sister Crystal shook her head. She slipped her hand into her pocket and felt the knife. Was this man a spy? Would he try and stop her urgent mission?

"That's some trial," opined the driver as he guided the bus onto the slick highway. "And I don't mind tellin' you I'm on The Chosen's side."

Sister Crystal relaxed. She began to read the newspaper. On the front page was a huge picture that arrested her attention. It was of three fresh-faced youths, an old photograph, from twenty-five years ago, the picture that Clara Eggleston had stolen from the *Star-Telegram* morgue and framed under silver and glass. Now retired from journalism and ill, she sold her icon for gold. Sister Crystal silently mouthed the headline: RARE PICTURE OF CRAWFORD MURDER PRINCIPALS. And beneath it the same banner from the original publication in 1950: PRINCES OF WESTERN HIGH FACE TOMORROW.

She stared at the picture for the rest of the trip. And when the driver let her out two blocks down from the courthouse, Sister Crystal asked if she might keep the newspaper.

"Of course," said the driver cheerfully. "Give the preacher my support. And stay dry. And have a Merry Christmas, heah?"

Sister Crystal slipped her knife between the folds of the morning paper and clutched the Three Princes to her breast. And she ran toward the courthouse.

Sledge doggedly ticked off his questions. He and Kleber had stayed up all night rehearsing. "On the afternoon of May 8, 1975, did you go to the so-called City of Miracles?"

"I did."

"How were you dressed?"

"Slacks, shirt, fishing hat, sunglasses."

"Would you consider this to be the attire of a spy?"

Kleber laughed. "It wasn't CIA issue, if that's what you mean. I do confess to trying to blend in with the tourists. Like it or not, and I don't anymore, I have a recognition factor. I went to the City of Miracles as a working journalist."

"Please tell the court *why* you went there."

"Just a look-around. It was newsworthy."

"Were you planning to write or broadcast about the City of Miracles or The Chosen?"

"Maybe. I might have done a column, or a television show, if . . . if *it* hadn't happened."

"*It?*"

"If Mack hadn't been murdered."

Otto Leo was beside himself. He protested hotly. "I've never heard anything quite like this, your honor," he cried. "Obviously the District Attorney and this . . . this *star witness* . . . have cooked up an odorous melodrama to prejudice the jury against the accused. . . ."

"I don't see it that way a'tall," remarked the judge. "Hush. Sit down. Overruled."

Whereupon Otto demanded and got a running objection to every word that came out of Kleber Cantrell's newly functioning mouth.

Quickly Sledge worked his way through the night in question, drawing from Kleber eyewitness testimony that impeached The Chosen. He did not find Mack to be threatening or dangerous at Susan's house. Kleber then moved to the farmhouse. "Did the defendant Luther tell you and Mr. Crawford that he was the legal owner of this property?" asked the prosecutor.

"He did indeed. He said it had been his anchor for years."

"You're sure?"

"Perfectly sure. He said the house had been in his family for years."

"Did the accused mention to you that this house had, in fact, been confiscated by Tarrant County for unpaid taxes?"

"He did not."

"Did you know that by entering county property without permission, you were indulging in burglary, a felony?"

"No, sir. I did not. You don't ask to see the title papers to somebody's house. Besides, I didn't ask to go there. T.J. took us, sort of without our permission." Kleber glanced down at The Chosen, whose face was wounded, a man betrayed.

"Was there a quarrel in this farmhouse on the night of May 9, 1975?" inquired Calvin Sledge.

"Not at first. We just sort of played catch-up. We hadn't seen each other for many years. Then T.J. started preaching at Mack and me. He was coming on like a revivalist—and it didn't seem the appropriate time or place."

"Please tell the jury what happened next."

"Both of us grew uncomfortable. Mack wanted to leave. So did I. But we were stuck. We had come in T.J.'s Mercedes and we were out in the middle of nowhere. Mack got mad and demanded the car keys. But instead of taking us home, T.J. opened his briefcase and pitched two thick folders at us. It seemed The Chosen had chosen *us* to make enormous contributions to the City of Miracles. He tried to hit us up for half a million dollars each. I believe both of us, Mack and I, laughed rudely. Then . . ."

"Then?"

Kleber worked his mouth but nothing came out. He gasped for air. Judge Mustardseed directed the bailiff to bring water. Kleber drank, coughed, and tried to finish the story. His voice was now the wheeze of an old pump organ. "Then . . . T.J. pulled out the gun. . . . I thought it was a joke, at first. . . . Mack recognized it as a threat. . . . He jumped toward T.J. and . . . and T.J. shot him. I'm told the bullet . . . or part of it . . . passed directly through Mack's body and into my throat. . . . I'm sorry . . . I'm having trouble breathing . . ."

At this critical juncture, the District Attorney of Tarrant County decided to quit for Christmas. Everything went just as he planned. He passed the witness to Otto Leo, hoping and praying that the defense lawyer would fall into a carefully laid trap. He held his breath and tried to appear occupied with another folder.

It was 4:25 p.m. Outside, winds howled at the windows and thunder rumbled in echoing waves. Time to go home. But Otto Leo could not let a jury go away and open their gifts with this powerful testimony left unchallenged over a four-day recess. The defense lawyer hastened to the bench and begged for a half hour of cross. Judge Mustardseed was disinclined, personally worried over his own intended drive to the suburban ranch of his second son. He was due for Christmas dinner at seven and the roads were sheets of ice. Besides, the witness was worn out, his voice fragile. It would be cruel and medically unwise to pry further answers.

"With all due respect, Judge," begged Leo. "This cannot wait. It's a Sixth Amendment issue. A man has the right to cross-examine his accuser. We don't know if Mr. Cantrell's throat will be working or not working four days from now. It seems to come and go whenever he wants to harm my client. He may lapse back into his rather convenient hysterical aphonia."

The jurist asked for the DA's position. Sledge tried to pretend that he wanted to go home, that he would make sure Kleber was available after Christmas. But, putting on a fake mask of charity, he allowed that another thirty minutes wouldn't spoil the holiday.

"Please continue," agreed Judge Mustardseed. "You may cross-examine the witness until five p.m., Mr. Leo."

Her shoulders crusted with beads of sleet and her body trembling, Sister Crystal was turned away at the front door of the courthouse. The guard inside shook his head behind the glass and stabbed his watch in pantomime. He locked the door. The storm intensified. Lightning crackled over the city like short-circuited strobe banks. The voices came again. The voices directed her to run. The voices gave her courage. The voices told her the way. She ran down the block, grew confused, found herself in a blind-alley parking lot where the flatbed truck from the City of Miracles had been towed and abandoned. It was in disarray. The winds had shredded the blood-red draperies and the cross had fallen. The only word left on the great banner, "VENGEANCE IS MINE, SAITH THE LORD," was the first.

There would be an investigation of how Sister Crystal gained entrance to the courtroom, and though a few minor functionaries would lose their jobs, no one was really to blame. As human things are wont, the security mechanism at the courthouse broke down, the fault of the late hour and of weather and of circumstance. At the rear door of the building, the guard normally there to scrutinize entrants had slipped away to call his wife and say he would be late for Christmas Eve dinner. And at the checkpoint where spectators were frisked and forced to pass through X-ray devices to detect guns or other weapons, no one was around to stop a sodden woman from slipping into the throng of standees and pressing her body against the back wall. Hugging the newspaper and its secret against her jumper, Sister Crystal listened and waited.

Otto Leo permitted a clap of thunder to die, glancing at the ceiling in deference to a higher client. Then he slammed into the Prince of Power. "From March 16, 1972, until November 5, 1972, where were you living, Mr. Cantrell?"

"I haven't the slightest idea," answered the writer.

"Don't remember at all?" wondered Leo insolently.

"I travel a lot."

The lawyer snatched up a thick folder and turned pages furiously, teasing everybody. "Isn't it true that from March 16, 1972, until November 5, 1972, you were a patient at the Clinique de Merriac at Lucerne, Switzerland?"

Calvin Sledge objected. The material had not been properly introduced. Otto backpedaled. "I have no intention of introducing it," blustered the lawyer. "I am simply referring to my notes."

Judge Mustardseed directed the witness to answer.

"I might have been." Kleber seemed reluctant. "I'm not good at dates."

"I imagine not," murmured Leo, flipping more pages. "Isn't it true that the Clinique de Merriac is an institution for wealthy alcoholics and drug addicts?"

"Objection!" cried Sledge as the judge warned Otto against further rabbit punches. Nonetheless, damage was done. "Mr. Leo," scolded the judge, "my Christmas charity is scraped quite thin. I suggest you get to the heart of the matter. You have eleven minutes left."

Otto seemed happy to quit with a modest, below-the-belt triumph but once again The Chosen jerked his sleeve. T.J. pulled his lawyer into an urgent mouth-to-ear conversation. At the back of the chamber, Sister Crystal's heart leaped and pounded as she saw her master for the first time in full view. She wanted to call out to him and reveal her presence. But the voices told her to wait.

Freshly fueled, Otto Leo sauntered up to the box.

"Have you ever been sued for libel?" he asked.

Kleber wanted to cry foul. The proper answer was yes; the suit had been a harassment and a nuisance from a minor character in his Vietnam book. Some Marine captain felt he had been improperly portrayed. Although Kleber had more than enough substantiation, his lawyer recommended an out-of-court settlement for $5,000. He stammered a weak "Yes, but . . ."

"And I believe you *settled* this libel suit, rather than go to trial, is that correct?"

"Now that you've asked, I'd be happy to tell the whole . . ."

"*Yes* or *no*. Did you settle?"

"Yes." Kleber's eyes were ablaze with indignation. All lawyers were bastards. By denying him a fleshed-out answer, Leo dressed the writer in the robes of a collared liar.

"Now then, just a final few questions and we can all go home. Do you remember a previous occasion when you went to the farmhouse owned by the accused minister's family?"

At his place, Calvin Sledge almost whooped. Pennies from heaven. Otto Leo was about to open a door behind which stood the ghost of a raped girl.

Kleber stalled, as Sledge had coached him. He was not to appear eager to answer. "Can you be more specific, Counselor?" he asked.

"Nope. Can't be any clearer than that. I remind you, Mr. Cantrell, that you are testifying under the penalty of perjury—although your character suggests you are immune to that warning. Just answer yes or no. Were you ever at this farmhouse prior to the night of May 9, 1975?"

Nor would the investigation unearth how the woman got into the position she did. Throughout the trial, no one had dared leave the courtroom during testimony, out of either desire not to miss a key piece of dialogue or fear of incurring the old judge's wrath. But in these final moments of Christmas Eve session, despite the alluring nature of Kleber's appearance, spectators were tiptoeing away, mindful of the horrendous ice storm and attendant road hazards. For the first time since Day One, seats were available without waiting or bribing. Sister Crystal was thus able to slip gratefully into an empty place on the back row; then, as time went on, following the lead of other folks, she moved cautiously closer. Finally she nested on the very front row, beside a sketch artist with flying hands. Sitting there, she was almost close enough to reach across and touch The Chosen. An arm's length away, she dispatched him her strongest love. She prepared for the act of adoration.

Kleber answered warily. "Yes."

"Good!" cried Leo in theatrical scorn. "When were you at this farmhouse before?"

Kleber located the mocking answer that Calvin Sledge had placed in his throat. "Are you sure you want to know, Counselor?"

"We will be *very* grateful for a truthful answer out of you, sir," parried the lawyer, nobody's patsy at dirt fights.

"All right. Twenty-five years ago last May, T.J. took us—Mack and me—to this very same farmhouse . . ." His answer petered out.

"You seem reluctant to remember what happened that night," suggested Otto. "Did anything occur that long-ago hour to make you so abusive?"

"Objection," said Sledge, for the record. The judge waved vaguely without decision.

"Go ahead, Mr. Cantrell. Tell the jury about that May night in 1950."

Kleber drew a deep breath and nodded. "We were eighteen years old, more or less. We were inseparable. . . ."

Otto Leo interrupted. "Isn't it true you called yourselves the Three Princes?"

"Yes."

"Was that some sort of secret society?"

Kleber laughed. He would not let the lawyer make a cabal out of callow snobbery. "No. Just three best friends."

"Please continue."

"It was the night before we graduated from high school. The rains were hard that May. They just wouldn't quit. We had a party planned out at the lake and it was a washout, so T.J. drove us to his Uncle Bun's farmhouse near Weatherford. We drank some beer and told some tall stories and waited for the storm to stop. We were just three kids trying to make the best of a rotten turn of fate. I remember the winds throwing branches against the old house. I remember lightning and thunder. I remember being scared. It was the classic *Walpurgisnacht* . . ."

"The *what?*" asked the court reporter.

"A night for ghosts to dance. . . . Then, suddenly, from outside somewhere in the storm, we heard a girl's voice. Some young girl was screaming. Mack . . ." And here Kleber paused at the memory, smiling. "Mack was always the hero, even back then. Mack ran out into the storm and found the girl and carried her inside to dry. She had been through a terrible ordeal. She had gotten lost. . . . I remember her coat had been blown clear off her shoulders and sucked up into the sky. . . . And her dress—a pink dress—she told us it was her mama's dress—was torn. . . . She was a sad little drowned rat. . . . We talked for a while and drank and the next thing I knew, T.J. was having sexual intercourse with this girl—against her will. . . . Mack and I went into the other room to wait. . . . Then, when T.J. was *finished* . . . he

suggested that we also have sex with the girl. . . . Neither of us did."
Kleber's voice closed like a finished book and he stopped. The tale—it
was obvious to everybody—had been difficult to tell.

Sister Crystal watched the sketch artist create a drenched and dripping girl, in the arms of a huge youth. He flipped to a clean page and
drew the same girl, surrounded by three young men, advancing on her.
She wanted to tell the artist that he had it wrong but she was diverted
by the voices. They had come again. The voices swarmed over her like
exploring hands. They seemed to strip her nude. They fluttered across
her breasts and made them harden. They slithered about her body.
"You're beautiful," whispered one of the voices. *"So beautiful . . .
You'n me are gonna love each other. . . ."*

"And?" demanded Otto Leo harshly.
"That's about it," answered Kleber, his eyes in his lap.
"How do you know Mr. Luther had sex?"
"Because I saw him."
"You *watched?*"
"Yes."
"Then you are a Peeping Tom? A voyeur?"
"Objection!" Sledge disliked the sleazy turn of the tale.
"Sustained. Mr. Leo, you are on very thin ice."
"Come on, Mr. Cantrell. You've always given your fans better sto-
ries than that. This one doesn't even have an ending."
"Until now."
"This isn't over yet," snapped Leo. "Not by a long shot. You've
left quite a bit out—and edited the rest. Isn't it true that you and Mack
Crawford in fact choked this young woman to death?"
"No," said Kleber, slowly becoming aware of how his story was
about to be twisted. He felt panic. Mack was dead. Now it was his
word against a man of God. It was the testimony of a writer—a foolish
writer who had settled a libel suit rather than defend himself, a professional carp who belittled the down-home values of probably everybody
in the jury box, a tarnished brass celebrity in battle against a preacher
who breathed life into the dead and who sat in shocked silence with the
cross of Calvary glittering from his breast. The odds were ominous.
"Isn't it also true that *you*—the leader of the Three Princes—that

you suggested throwing this young woman's ravaged, lifeless body into the Brazos River?"

"That's absurd," fumbled Kleber, shooting a Get-Me-Out-of-This signal over to Calvin Sledge, who was on his feet, trying to form a sputtering objection while Sandy Double frantically dumped folders out of the case file, searching for the yellowed AP clipping that told the truth of the storming midnight.

In the tumult, Otto Leo squeezed one final question. "And what was this unfortunate young woman's name?"

It was at this moment that a great fork of lightning split the Texas heavens and screamed to earth, striking a power transmitter on the north side of the city and causing the lights in the courtroom to fade into a yellowish deathly gray. Judge Mustardseed banged an end to the day. The Chosen rose to prophesy damnation for sinners in general and Kleber Cantrell in particular. And it was during this fateful coalescence that Sister Crystal stood on the front row to answer Otto Leo's final inquiry.

"Laurie," she said, clearly and sweetly. "Laurie is my name." Then, withdrawing the blade hidden in the folds of the morning news, Laurel Jo Killman, eyes fully open to the perception of truth for the first moment in a quarter of a century, rushed into the arena of justice and plunged cheap steel into the heart of the man who had stolen her life.

The last thing The Chosen presumably saw, the image that danced in the dying light, the final vision for Thomas Jeremiah Luther, was the ring on the finger of the madwoman. It took three bailiffs to tackle the assassin, pin her down, extricate the knife from a hand on whose wedding finger rested a pale green cameo, an old crone smiling, with a very long nose.

BOOK SEVEN

SHORT TAKES

CHAPTER THIRTY-ONE

APXXXCCC112370 BREAK BULLETIN BULLETIN BREAK
BREAK
Fort Worth, TX—Dec. 24, 1975—The Chosen stabbed . . .

BREAK BREAK APXXL 1333334480 FWTX—Dec. 24,
4:59 p.m.
   A woman reportedly rushed out of the spectator section in the
murder trial of The Chosen and stabbed him in the heart. . . .

   BULLETIN
   URGENT
   FORT WORTH, TX. Dec. 24, 1975 5:17 p.m.
BREAK BREAK
   Controversial religious leader The Chosen was stabbed late
this afternoon by a woman, believed to be a fanatic spectator at
his murder trial. The 42-year-old defendant, born Thomas Jere-
miah Luther, has been on trial since September for the murder of
actor Mack Crawford. . . .
BREAK BREAK BREAK

FORT WORTH, TX. Dec. 24, 1975 7:01 p.m. CST
The Chosen dead. Petersmith Hospital admitting clerk reporting
him DOA . . . 6:50 p.m. CST . . .

BREAK   BREAK   SUPERSEDE ALL BULLETINS
URGENT
The Chosen not dead. Repeat *not* dead. Petersmith Hospital emergency room spokesman reports 42-year-old religious leader in "grave condition." Rushed into surgery . . .

AP, Mar. 16, 1976, Fort Worth, TX: Laurel Jo Killman, 42, was transferred by court order today to the Texas State Hospital division for the criminally insane at Rusk. During a brief hearing, Miss Killman sang hymns and testified that she plunged a kitchen knife into the heart of religious leader Thomas Jeremiah Luther, The Chosen, "on orders of Jehovah."

Miss Killman had been for the last five years an employee at the City of Miracles. Prior to that, she had spent her entire adult life as a patient at the Rusk mental institution having first entered the hospital's custody as an amnesia victim at the age of 17. An official of the hospital, Dr. Morgan Stein, told the court today that it was a "bad judgment call" to have released her in the first place. Dr. Stein testified Miss Killman suffered and still suffers from dementia and acute schizophrenia. It is considered unlikely that she will ever be found fit for trial in the stabbing of Rev. Luther.

From the Fort Worth *Star-Telegram,* Oct. 3, 1977, page 32:

FORMER PROSECUTOR DIES

Calvin Sledge, 43, died today of heart failure at his mobile home outside Decatur. Well known as the prosecutor of The Chosen in the celebrated murder trial of 1975, Mr. Sledge resigned from office and ran for the U. S. Senate. He was 20th in a field of 36 in the primary. His memoir on the murder trial, *Justice Denied,* was published last year to sharply critical reviews. He is survived by his wife, Marge, and three daughters.

From *TV Guide,* April 3, 1978:

BEST BET: *Verdict of Time* (CBS, 3 hours). World Premiere Movie: Based on defense attorney Otto Leo's best-selling memoir of The Chosen's murder trial, this is an innovative docu-drama that speculates on what would have happened if the aborted case had reached a jury verdict. As Leo tells it, the jury was split eight–four for acquittal at the time The Chosen was stabbed.

April 4, 1980
P.O. Box 61
Brandon, Vermont

Mrs. Clifford Casey
3221 Braeslane
Houston, TX

Dear Judy:

Word of Case's death just reached me and I am devastated. I possess no words to tell you how much I respected and loved that man.

Now I am guilty because I didn't write Case all of our news. Maybe by telling you, he will get a drop copy—wherever he is.

Ceil Shannon and I got married six months ago. We finally made it legal. And in the nick of time. Our son was born in February, a splendid, fat, demanding, rusty-haired man-child named McKenzie Casey Cantrell. Already we're calling him Case. Maybe he'll be a writer. He loves to chew on pencils.

We live on an old farm at the end of a road that is on no known map. Compared to us, J. D. Salinger is a gadabout and Greta Garbo is a public spectacle.

Some days I try to write—but it goes very slow. I seem to have lost the touch. What the hell, nothing I wrote ever did anybody much good anyway.

But there are times when I would give one half my royalties just to have Clifford Casey stand over my typewriter and yank out the copy and yell, "Short takes, kid!"

I'll miss him. And try to carry on.

Love for all seasons—

Kleber.

Five Christmas Eves after the events in the Fort Worth courtroom, a stranger stood in deep snow atop a small hill bunched with pine thickets and naked tangles of wild grapevines. He wiped the frost off his high-powered binoculars and fixed them on the eighteenth-century carriage house, its white Vermont marble façade melting into the mantle of winter. The house was well hidden, shielded by a forest of silvery birch. It was the last enclave at the end of a lonely private road. No vehicle could approach without being seen or heard.

From previous surveillance, the stranger had observed the embrace of sophisticated security systems. This was the new factor in the condition of celebrity: famous people bought hideaways in the backcountry and then violated the rural landscape with elaborate fortifications of burglar alarms and electronic geegaws. Kleber Cantrell had fenced in every exterior inch of his twenty-seven-acre homestead with a nine-foot-high chain link fence that was electrified at random surprise intervals. Within that was a thick, pioneer-built rock fence. The grounds adjacent to the main house were patrolled by a pair of lean and always agitated German shepherds, Scripps and Howard. Across the front porch stretched vertical white bars that made the residents inside prisoners in a cage. Talk in the village had it that Cantrell was installing laser beams to sweep the immediate one hundred feet in all directions. The Prince of Power had barricaded himself, *en famille,* in a melancholy electronic fortress. This was his new shield, necessary to shut out the world from which he was in emotional and physical retreat.

The violator, who wore a gray and yellow ski mask that covered his face and protected it against the blasting Vermont winds, affixed a 300-mm. lens onto his Nikon and, bringing the fine old house into focus, snapped half a roll of pictures. He worked hurriedly because the thick, heavy snow was starting again. For this he was grateful. Perhaps the storm would make his scheme more plausible. He was apprehensive, in fact scared over what he was about to do. But he had waited a long time and planned and now, on Christmas Eve 1980, he would give it a try.

Ceil Shannon Cantrell brewed a cup of herb tea and carried it into the leathery, book-lined study where her husband was, by custom, dozing in his recliner. His glasses had slid down his nose, giving him the air of a lazy scholar. Ceil tapped his shoulder and passed the aromatic, steaming mug beneath his mustache.

"Wake up, Scrooge," she said. "It's Christmas Eve."

"I am awake," he lied, yawning, startled, the way people do when needled out of the depths of an embarrassing nap. "Where's Case?"

"Asleep beside the tree. He tuckered himself out playing with the wrapping paper. Come on. Pull yourself together. I'm going to give you a present."

"Not till tomorrow morning."

"Well, this is a special one." Ceil hesitated. "It requires some work." She glided her hands under Kleber's armpits, pulled him up from his chair, and pushed him toward the living room. The house was a triumph; it looked and smelled like an Early American picture-book Christmas. It cried out for magazine photography. Bayberry and spice candles were lit, nestled in bunches of pungent, fresh-cut pine and fir. From the kitchen seeped aromas of gingerbread men with red-hots for buttons, mincemeat pies, butter cookies in the shapes of stars and crescents, a noble goose roasting and browning with oyster and truffle stuffing, freshly mashed cranberry relish. Beside the bay window, the ten-foot fir that Kleber had hewn—it took him a whole day to make the chain saw work—was listing portside and malnourished in the middle. But Ceil's lavishly made ornaments made it festive. All in all, an extraordinary amount of work had gone into preparing a Christmas that would be celebrated by two people and their one-year-old baby boy. But, then, her "projects" were what kept Ceil reasonably sane. Else long ago she would have abandoned her vintage lover and recent husband and hurried back to Manhattan, where, more often than not, she dearly wished to be.

Ever since the siege of Cowtown, Ceil had been concocting schemes to fill the lonely hours. She accepted Kleber's desire for total seclusion and, at first, was enthusiastic over finding just the right safe house in New England. That filled a year of cloak-and-dagger shopping, sending out trusted emissaries as scouts, then using assumed names and legal artifices to purchase the hideaway. Another year was occupied in "fixing it up," no modest task because Kleber was wary of local craftsmen and laborers coming onto his property. His paranoia was full fever. Ceil purchased a shelf of "How To" books and the pair became reasonably accomplished in simple plumbing and storm window installation. After that they lived as eccentric hermits, munching their own produce although Ceil sardonically pointed out that the first season of gentleperson farming cost thirty-four dollars for each hard, green tomato and seventy-two dollars per cantaloupe. They fed legions of moles, hare, and deer.

Occasionally an old, trusted friend from publishing or show business was permitted into the sanctuary, and each summer Kleber's two children from previous marriages visited. His son, an aspiring news photographer attending the University of Texas, enjoyed journalism shop talk and Kleber warmed to tale telling and encouragement. The lad, however, regarded his father as a public monument. When their reunions faded into uncomfortable silences, Ceil hurriedly cooked up picnics and outings. Kleber's daughter, ten, was enamored of the theater and found rapport with her stepmother. But both children were clearly nervous at having to visit their father inside walls.

There were entire months when no other human being pierced their isolation. This was some tedious play. Two months' dress rehearsal while hidden on a lake in Fort Worth had been exciting and stimulating. But a repeat performance that was promising to drag out a lifetime at a dead end in Vermont was shredding Ceil's patience and resourcefulness.

Perhaps if Kleber had been writing, she would have been content to act as handmaiden to creativity. But mostly what he did was thicken his ass in his easy chair, fret about security, read history books (as if he felt more at home in the distant past), and make notes about a proposed biography of some goddamned Indian chief named Quanah Parker. He threw away unopened whatever smacked of fan mail or missiles from the curious, rarely glanced at the local paper, permitted no television, and listened to radio only for weather reports and classical music. When Ceil tuned in the news, she did it so surreptitiously she felt like Anne Frank hiding from the Nazis.

Her pregnancy had been unexpected and, considering her age, alarming. Past forty-five, Ceil assumed her reproductive capacities were eroded, even though the mirror reflected back the same willowy body with no extra pounds added since college and coppery hair that required no chemicals to hide the few intruding strands of silver. But when she missed two menstrual periods, she figured it was change-of-life time. Furious with the realities of the clock, Ceil flew into New York on a concocted errand and there learned the startling truth. Immediately she decided on an abortion—she would not even trouble Kleber with the gynecological necessities. But while in the waiting room, she became overwhelmed by back copies of *Parents' Magazine,* by several radiant mothers-to-be sitting around in big-bellied sisterhood and joyous communion, by the enticement of a role the actress in her had given up on ever playing. Bolting out without canceling, Ceil hurried home to Kleber. That night, over dinner, she asked if he wanted more raspberry *tarte,* to which he said no, asked if he wanted more *café filtre,* to which he said no, asked if he wanted a pony of warmed brandy, to which he said no, asked if he wanted a baby, to which he did not respond. Ten minutes later, Kleber burst out of his study, where he was supposedly reading the Encyclopaedia Britannica's section on American Indians.

"Hey," he demanded. "What was all that about?"

"What do you mean?"

"You were just fooling around, huh?"

"About what?"

"About a baby."

"Not really."

"You're *serious?*"

Ceil nodded, perversely happy.

"We're too old to start a family."

"It's already started. I'm looking forward to having somebody to talk to."

"We talk all the time."

"We talk very little. And we talk about everything except us."

"That's not true."

"Well, here's the evening news bulletin. Ceil Shannon Cantrell announced today that she is pregnant, that she is very happy about it, that she is also quite scared, that her doctor says she is strong and healthy, and that she is going to carry this child full term."

Which she did, without difficulty. Kleber got interested in the new "project," prepared himself to be present in the delivery room but grew uneasy at the last minute and was feeling faint outside when McKenzie Casey Cantrell arrived. The baby's appearance in the house provided Ceil a busy year of infatuated love but gave Kleber cause to suffer from deeper concern. Convinced that his son was a target for kidnappers and cuckoos, Kleber strengthened the security systems of his home. Ceil protested this was being overly sensitive. She was having trouble remembering all of the combinations, digits, and abort codes necessary to go in and out the front door. In almost four years of residence, nothing untoward had happened, nothing more than an occasional tourist or journalism student who found the isolated country lane and pushed the buzzer at the front gate. The horrendous alarms shooed them away. The villagers were only too glad to leave the celebrated couple alone. In this corner of Vermont, privacy is the most cultivated crop.

Ceil had hoped that the baby would mark a new beginning for its father. But she erred. Kleber still awoke in the middle of a given night, his body torn by dry sobs and shudders. In the darkness, he often curled against his wife like a child worried over being abandoned. Obviously, Ceil knew, he had never taken the fourth step that Samantha Reiker had mentioned, i.e. "working out" his participation in the night of violence. A thousand times she had tried to persuade him to talk about the events, better still *write out* all the pain and horror. But his dictum was that he would never speak of Mack and T.J., not ever again. He was the prisoner of guilt. He felt that he was somehow responsible for Mack's murder. Thus did he turn down a blank-check advance from his book publisher, magazine offers that arrived as regularly as new moons, a tour of the lecture circuit at $15,000 per appearance, choosing instead to craft a book on a long dead Comanche chief from 1,800 miles away. Hardly eyewitness reportage. The few pages he had shared with Ceil were not impressive, even though she awarded him luxurious praise. He was writing dry and cold; his words reflected his life. One night Ceil endured one of Kleber's 3 a.m. emotional assaults, coaxed him back to sleep, and then dealt with her own anxieties until sunrise. Long ago she had fallen in love with a vivacious man of power and purpose. Their love had been nourished by partings. Now he was still and moored. On certain days she even wished for a nice little war that would catch his fancy. When the Russians invaded Afghanistan, Ceil tried to make it sound as journalistically alluring as the sack of Carthage.

She had no complaint about the burden of domesticity. Household responsibilities were shared equally, allowing Ceil several hours a day in which to do her own word-crafting. Each morning after Case was fed and down for a nap, Ceil eagerly bounded out to the shed that once housed farm tools. She had turned the spidery, gloomy room into a whitewashed playwright's lair where Kleber never intruded. In the tranquil, sometimes maddening silence of Vermont mornings, she began fooling around with sketches and dialogue. What commenced in late 1977 as random conversation between an imaginary man and woman forced to go into hiding grew slowly into a rich-blooded full-length play. It was not specifically autobiographical, although Ceil did draw heavily on her feelings and emotions from the fugitive hours. Rarely did Kleber inquire as to his wife's progress. When and if he did, she had to conjure lies. Writer's block. Dry wells. Cul-de-sacs. She could not tell him the truth. She could not reveal that *Lying Low* was her finest work, a play that made her weep and tingle even when she laid it aside for several weeks and then picked it up with the attitude of total objectivity. She was quite worried that her success at the typewriter would not only discourage her husband, it might further darken his neurotic core and perhaps destroy the marriage.

"Okay, I give up. What is it?" he asked cheerfully, upon being presented with a large present wrapped in flaming scarlet. It was a heavy box almost four feet square.

"A new invention," said Ceil. "No squire should be without it."

"A milking machine? Who needs one?"

"Don't be rude!" Ceil had only just stopped nursing Case and her breasts were heavy. "Just open the goddamn thing."

When Kleber tore the paper away and discovered the small color television set, he glanced up in the grip of betrayal. "I've told you how I feel about having a TV set in the house," he said.

"Well, I don't intend for us to start watching 'Happy Days' at the dinner table," she shot back, dancing away from the obvious reason for his concern. "There *are* worthwhile things on TV. PBS did one of my plays last spring and I never even got to watch it." She had her sales pitch well prepared. "Besides, it's not just a TV set. It's a video tape recorder and a camera. We can shoot instant-replay movies of Case . . ." The baby had awakened and was crawling delightedly about the wrapping paper, stuffing ribbons into his mouth. Ceil scooped up her festooned offspring and counseled patience. His first Christmas dinner would soon be ready. "We might even try a little home erotica now and then . . . some of our urges merit filming." Her jest received only a low, unenthusiastic moan.

"Look, I don't care if *you* want to waste your time on the tube," said Kleber. "But I won't permit this child to be brought up spellbound by the evil eye. He's going to be a reader." Then, as afterthought, "What good is it going to do us, anyway? You know we can't get reception this far out."

"Oh yes we can. I've already cleared it with the neighbors. We can hook up to Garth and Maggie's antenna until the cable comes through. And it's just down the road."

Kleber had never even met the neighbors, a sculptor and his weaver wife. He was surprised that Ceil had made their acquaintance. "And to complete my Christmas offering," she said, "the dirty deed is done. The wire's waiting outside by the gate. All you have to do is make a simple connection."

Kleber regarded his wife for a long time and was on the edge of anger. But he reckoned she had schemed hard to bring off the dubious surprise. In the spirit of holiday goodwill, he finally nodded and put on a parka and went outside. Presently Ceil and the baby, both bundled in greatcoats, joined him and watched Daddy struggle with the uncoiling of several hundred feet of cable and the need to affix it to the supportive crooks of a maple tree. The German shepherds yelped and romped in concert. The snow was falling and visibility was near zero. The late afternoon was slate gray.

On a ridge, the stranger got into his rented car, muttered prayer to a God in whom he no longer held belief, and disengaged the brake. Slowly at first, then greedily picking up speed, the automobile rolled down the steep grade. It was approximately two thousand yards and the descent was rapid. Just before the car crashed into the decorative granite rock pile that formed the first barrier to the enclave of Kleber Cantrell, the young man inside opened the door and leaped out. At point of impact he was well clear—but it looked as if he had been hurled into a snowbank. He began crawling as if dazed. Then he heard the people shouting and he fell back, pretending to be groggy. Having been rudely violated, the electronic alarms emitted shattering shrieks and electrical sparks.

Kleber commanded that his wife and child take cover while he ran, body flat as if under low-level bullet fire, to the house. There he seized the rifle that rested ever-ready in a grandfather-clock case just inside the front door. He raced back outside with it cocked—and trained on the stranger. The dogs, salivating and thrilled by it all, anticipated tearing the intruder apart. Ceil Shannon watched all of this in mounting concern and ran herself, child bobbing on her back, toward her husband. "Kleber, for God's sake. The man's been hurt!" she cried.

Ceil pushed past her husband, slipped through the gate without permitting the dogs to follow her, knelt over the young man, and engaged him in urgent questions. Believing no bones to be broken, Ceil helped the intruder in the ski mask up the front steps and into her warm house. There he reached up, peeled off his disguise, and revealed himself.

It was Jeffrey Crawford. He knew he had to spit it out fast.

"Five minutes, Mr. Cantrell. That's all I ask. Just hear me out and I'll leave." The child of Mack was almost twenty-four, taller now, fuller, and no longer possessed of his God glaze. His face was turbulent.

"What the hell are you doing here?" demanded Kleber, fury building.

"I'm sorry about your front gate. I'll pay for the damages. I lost control of the car."

Kleber whirled toward Ceil. "Call the police," he ordered.

"Kleber, don't be silly," she replied. "They're not going to come out here on Christmas Eve in this storm. Besides, it'd get in the paper. Do you want that? He's not exactly a burglar. We'd have to say that we know him."

"Are you with anybody?" asked Kleber. He ran to the window and peered through the frosted leaded windows into the darkening landscape.

"No sir. I'm alone," said the young man. "I confess I planned this whole thing. I had to do something to get in and talk to you."

"You could have written," said Kleber.

"I did. Several times. I never got an answer."

"Mr. Politeness here rarely looks at his mail," put in Ceil. She brought Jeffrey a cup of coffee, which he took gratefully. He was shivering from the cold and the aftershock of the impact.

"Why didn't you call?"

"Sir, I tried to get your number. It's unlisted. Mr. Cantrell, before you throw me out, I want you to know that I'm not what I used to be. Not anymore."

Kleber was still angry. His rifle was at arm's reach. "There's no reason for me to be civil, you little prick. I think you should be in prison. Now I'll thank you to get the hell out of my house. We're about to celebrate Christmas."

"Sir, I *have* been in prison. The worst kind. I locked up my own good sense for several years. After . . . that night . . . after *it* happened, I ran away. I lived in the desert all by myself. I was afraid Sledge was going to indict me or something. I'll never know why he didn't call me as a witness. Whatever, I never went back to the City of Miracles. I wish I had never gone there in the first place. . . . I told Mother everything and she forgave me. She and I went to Europe for a couple of years to get away from the publicity."

"How is Susan?" asked Kleber, becalmed suddenly.

"She's all right. She married a lawyer named George Parsons. He adores her. They seem to be very happy."

"I'm glad. For her. Give her my love."

"She put me up to this. Mother says you're the only one who can help me . . ."

"Help you with *what?*"

Jeffrey Crawford cleared his throat. His courage was disintegrating. He began a sentence but it fell away. Pain filled his face but it was from an old source. "I'm not asking you to feel sorry for me," he began. "I . . . I . . ."

"Go on. We're listening," said Ceil gently. She smiled at him.

"I have these nightmares," he said. "Sometimes they cause me to wake up screaming. I get these dry, racking heaves. I've heard that gun go off ten thousand times. I picture my own head splattering. Mother took me to doctors. I've been in every kind of therapy. . . . I can't get rid of the guilt. I can't stop replaying that night. . . . I'd give my own life gladly if I could bring back my father . . ." He cracked. He wept. The moment was poignant. The boy was baring his soul and Ceil's heart crumpled. She invited him to lie down and then to stay for Christmas dinner.

"Thanks. But I only asked for five minutes. . . . I even tried to kill myself—but I wasn't any good at it. . . . Mr. Cantrell, let me say it quick. I've been trying to write a book. I've been at it for two or three years. The fact of the matter is, I never really told my father I loved him. The last thing I did before he died was reject him for a surrogate. I think maybe if I tell it all, if I get it all out, if I tell how I got suckered by The Chosen . . ." Now he began to grow excited. "I've got tons of research . . ."

"Research?" Kleber's ears perked up. "What kind of research?"

"Well, The Chosen had this foundation, you see. That was the way they hid the money. They skimmed it like a Las Vegas casino. I've got dupes of Swiss bank transactions. I've got fake medical certificates authenticating the so-called healings. I've got records of people dying because they believed *him.* . . ."

"I'll look forward to reading it," said Kleber. "Sounds worthy."

The youth smiled ruefully. "Trouble is, there won't be one. Not if I keep trying. Hell, I can't write. I can't put together a simple declarative English sentence."

"Oh, I'm sure you can. You've got the passion. Just keep at it."

"Mr. Cantrell, believe me. I can't write. But *you* can. You've got the craft. Passion's no good without talent. That's why I barged in on you. I want to give all my material to you."

Kleber shook his head but not as quickly as Ceil had anticipated. "I couldn't possibly take your work," he said.

"With all due respect, Mr. Cantrell, it's *your* life we're talking about. And Dad's. And T.J.'s. You three fellows lived it. And you're the only one left who can write it. It's your responsibility. It's your moral imperative."

"But I've retired, son."

"You're not hiding from the world up here," said Jeffrey with calculated insolence. "You're hiding from yourself. All the security systems in the world aren't going to buy you a good night's sleep. . . . I'll leave now."

Kleber was stung by the well-aimed barb. Ceil saw temptation in his eyes. But he shook his head. No. Thanks but no thanks.

"One last thing. If you want to rough me up in the book, then so be it. I deserve it. By the way, I'm not interested in a single penny of royalties. Dad left me enough, more than enough. Which is another source of guilt. The man whose death I helped bring about made me a multimillionaire."

Jeffrey went to the door, shaking his body as if relieved of a burden. "Are you sure you won't stay for Christmas dinner?" asked Ceil.

"No, ma'm. You're kind to ask me. Your house is beautiful. It looks like the Christmas that everybody dreams about. I wouldn't want to intrude on your family." He pulled out a piece of paper and scribbled something on it. "I'm staying at the Val d'Isere Lodge over near the slopes," he said. "If you change your mind, call."

And he was gone, holiday bells on the door chiming his exit. He disappeared in the swirling snows.

After dinner, at which Kleber only picked listlessly, Ceil tried out the new television system. While flipping the channels she came across by chance—is anything really by chance?—a five-year-anniversary segment on the late evening news remembering the murder trial in Fort Worth. Kleber was pretending to be busy in his study but Ceil heard him padding softly back and forth, in earshot. She turned up the sound, just in case. The commentator was calling the roll of the principals and what became of them: "Kleber Cantrell and his wife, playwright Ceil Shannon, whom he married last year, live in total seclusion in Vermont." Here came a piece of film showing a shadowed, murky house hidden in the limbo of a birch forest. "They are mystery figures even to their closest neighbors." A brief, tense, door-slamming attempt to interview the people down the road, for which Ceil blessed Garth and Maggie. She had been right to cultivate their friendship.

And in conclusion, the cameras shifted to Fort Worth—"where it all began—and where it has not yet ended."

"He has been in a coma for five years," intoned the commentator, "and he has been pronounced clinically 'dead' on at least three occasions. Last month, by directive of his brothers, the life-support systems were turned off. Yet forty-seven-year-old Thomas Jeremiah Luther, The Chosen, remains stubbornly alive at his reborn City of Miracles.

"Tonight, Christmas Eve, the fifth anniversary of his being stabbed in the district courtroom where the Reverend Luther was on trial for the murder of actor Mack Crawford, several score thousand of the faithful are assembled. They have been lined up since pre-dawn, patiently waiting for a quick descent to the bottom of a pit where the comatose minister is on display behind glass bulletproof walls. He lies on a crimson platform next to the celebrated jailhouse painting of Jesus Christ that first elevated him to worldwide celebrity.

"Ironically, the City of Miracles has grown far more powerful since its leader was stabbed by a psychiatric patient he has been accused of raping. Miracle membership is estimated today at upward of ten million people on five continents. Its political arm, The Right Side, is gathering petitions for a convention to rewrite the Constitution of the United States.

"A Christmas message from the interim director, the Reverend   M4

Jimmy Lee Witherspoon, was released tonight. It says, 'If we can turn this country back to God, then our martyred leader's suffering will not have been in vain. The Chosen lives for us. And the glory of the Lord will wash and heal us every one. Merry Christmas to all.' "

Ceil watched a sea of flickering candle stubs and listened to the closing bars of "Adeste Fideles." Then she snapped off the set and went to find Kleber. "Did you hear *that?*" she asked.

Kleber shrugged. "A little of it drifted this way," he said. On his lap was a pile of newspaper clippings from the murder trial. She had not seen him even glance at the acrid memories in five years. His hands were dusty from handling them.

"I think I'll go to bed, honey," she said, kissing him gently on the forehead.

"I'll be there soon," he said.

Ceil noticed that Jeffrey Crawford's phone number was prominent on the telephone table beside Kleber's chair. And on her way out of the study, she glimpsed him fingering the dial.

At half past three on this winter night, Ceil awoke. Alone. She wanted somebody to snuggle against. Kleber's side of the bed was unwrinkled. Alarmed, she called his name. Getting no response, she crept to the stair landing. From below she heard him laughing, laughing in dam-busting purge, laughing with the power of his typewriter in full voice.

She went back to bed and, making mental note to write Jeffrey a discreet note thanking him for speaking her dialogue so eloquently— and effectively—fell happily, deeply asleep.

Thomas Thompson, a native Texan, has enjoyed a career that began in newspapering, went on to a dozen years on the staff of *Life,* and now positions him as one of America's best-known and most-admired authors. He lives in Los Angeles where he teaches book writing at the University of Southern California. He has won awards from the Texas Institute of Letters, Sigma Delta Chi, and the National Headliners Association. His landmark bestselling book, *Blood and Money,* won the Edgar Allan Poe Award. His five previous nonfiction books have been published in fourteen languages.